（汉英对照）

敬畏群山
吉狄马加文学文化演讲

Mountains That Humble And Hold Us In Awe
Selected Literary And Cultural Speeches Of Jidi Majia

吉狄马加/著
黄少政/译

Text by Jidi Majia
Translated by Huang Shaozheng

时代出版传媒股份有限公司
安徽文艺出版社

Mountains That Humble And Hold Us In Awe
Selected Literary And Cultural Speeches Of Jidi Majia

Text by Jidi Majia
Translated by Huang Shaozheng

吉狄马加，彝族，1961年6月生于中国西南部最大的彝族聚居区凉山彝族自治州，是中国当代最具代表性的诗人之一，同时也是一位具有广泛影响的国际性诗人，其诗歌已被翻译成近三十种文字，在世界几十个国家出版了六十余种版本的翻译诗集。曾获中国第三届新诗（诗集）奖、郭沫若文学奖荣誉奖、庄重文文学奖、肖洛霍夫文学纪念奖、柔刚诗歌荣誉奖、国际华人诗人笔会中国诗魂奖、南非姆基瓦人道主义奖、欧洲诗歌与艺术荷马奖、罗马尼亚《当代人》杂志卓越诗歌奖、布加勒斯特城市诗歌奖、波兰雅尼茨基文学奖、英国剑桥大学国王学院银柳叶诗歌终身成就奖、波兰塔德乌什·米钦斯基表现主义凤凰奖。创办青海湖国际诗歌节、青海国际诗人帐篷圆桌会议、凉山西昌邛海国际诗歌周以及成都国际诗歌周。现任中国作家协会副主席、书记处书记。

Jidi Majia, a native of Yi ethnic minority, was born in June 1961 in the Liangshan Yi Autonomous Prefecture, in the southwest of China. One of the most representative poets in China attaining an international reputation, his poems have been translated into over 30 languages, and published in dozens of countries and regions. He has been awarded the Third China Poetry Prize, Guo Moruo Literature Prize, Zhuang Zhongwen Literary Prize, Sholokhov Memorial Prize, Rou Gang Literary Prize, the "China Poetic Spirit Award" of International Chinese P. E. N., the Mkiva International Humanitarian Award of South Africa, the 2016 European Poetry and Art Homer Award, the Poetry Prize awarded by the Romanian magazine Contemporary People, the 2017 Bucharest Poetry Prize, the 2017 Ianicius Prize of Poland, Lifetime Achievement Award of Xu Zhimo Poetry Prize of Cambridge and Tadeusz Miciński "PHONENIX" International Expressionistic Award of Poland. Since 2007, he has founded a series of poetry events including Qinghai Lake International Poetry Festival, Qinghai Intl Poets Tent Forum, Xichang Qionghai Poets Week and Chengdu International Poetry Week. He currently serves as Vice President China Writers Association.

（汉英对照）

Mountains That Humble And Hold Us In Awe
Selected Literary And Cultural Speeches Of Jidi Majia

敬畏群山

吉狄马加文学文化演讲

吉狄马加/著

黄少政/译

Text by Jidi Majia

Translated by Huang Shaozheng

时代出版传媒股份有限公司
安徽文艺出版社

图书在版编目（ＣＩＰ）数据

敬畏群山：吉狄马加文学文化演讲：汉英对照/吉狄马加著；黄少政译．—合肥：安徽文艺出版社,2018.11
ISBN 978-7-5396-6518-4

Ⅰ．①敬… Ⅱ．①吉… ②黄… Ⅲ．①演讲－中国－当代－选集－汉、英 Ⅳ．①I267

中国版本图书馆CIP数据核字(2018)第249518号

出 版 人：朱寒冬
责任编辑：朱寒冬　张妍妍　　　装帧设计：张诚鑫

....
出版发行：时代出版传媒股份有限公司　www.press-mart.com
　　　　　安徽文艺出版社　www.awpub.com
地　　址：合肥市翡翠路1118号　邮政编码：230071
营 销 部：(0551)63533889
印　　制：安徽联众印刷有限公司　(0551)65661327
....
开本：700×1000　1/16　印张：29.75　字数：450千字
版次：2018年11月第1版　2018年11月第1次印刷
定价：88.00元
....

(如发现印装质量问题，影响阅读，请与出版社联系调换)
版权所有，侵权必究

序
[加拿大] 弗朗索瓦·罗伊

Avant-Propos
[Canada] Francois Roy

"……边疆人、外地人,啊,在这些地区的记忆中无足轻重的人;来自谷地、高原和远离我们河岸的世界屋脊的人;嗅出征兆和缘由的人,西风的倾听者;足迹和季节的追踪者;黎明微风中的拔营者;啊,在地壳上寻找水眼的人;啊,探寻者;啊,找到理由远走高飞的人,你们可别去贩卖更咸的盐……"

圣-琼·佩斯《阿纳巴斯》

18世纪的一个古老隐喻,一个关于忧伤的隐喻,它宣称人们会"像石头一样不幸"。阅读吉狄马加的这些随笔和演讲——他是中国的彝族诗人,也是一位高官——读者倒真该怀疑这些石头的不幸。因为吉狄马加思想的主线之一,正是人类与自然必须建立那种健康关系。然而,这种关系,尤其在西方,需要得到修复,因为它已经被几个世纪以来的单侧面发展严重损坏,人类自诩为居住其上的土地的主人和救世主,却像个疯子,无视土地的美,无视诸多生命之间的必要平衡。

法国哲学家、文学批评家加斯东·巴什拉熟稔彝人世界,它围绕四大元素运行,而这四大元素是被川西(吉狄马加长大的地方)的部落巫师、炼金术士和祖先们描述过的。巴什拉写道:梦有四个领域、四个极点,凭借它们,梦跃入无限空间。为了揭示一个真正的诗人的秘密……只需问一句:"告诉我你的幽灵是什么?是侏儒、蝾螈、水神还是空气中的女精灵?"吉狄马加就是这四种元素的诗人。他在

    Gens des confins et gens d'ailleurs, ô gens de peu de poids dans la mémoire de ces lieux; gens des vallées et des plateaux et des plus hautes pentes de ce monde à l'échéance de nos rives; flaireurs de signes, de semences, et confesseurs de souffles en Ouest; suiveurs de pistes, de saisons, leveurs de campements dans le petit vent de l'aube; ô chercheurs de points d'eau sur l'écorce du monde; ô chercheurs, ô trouveurs de raisons pour s'en aller ailleurs, vous ne trafiquez pas d'un sel plus fort.

Saint-John Perse, Anabase

    Une locution datant du XVIIIe siècle, qui en fait est une métaphore sur la tristesse, prétend qu'on peut être "malheureux comme les pierres". En lisant les essais et discours de Jidi Majia, poète et haut fonctionnaire chinois d'origine yie, le lecteur doutera vraiment du malheur des pierres, et ce, parce qu'un des axes de son œuvre est justement la saine relation que l'homme devrait entretenir avec la nature. Toutefois, ce rapport, surtout en Occident, a besoin d'être restauré, car il a été gravement endommagé par des siècles de développement unilatéral où les humains se sont érigés en maîtres et seigneurs de la terre qu'ils habitent: aliénés, ils sont devenus aveugles à sa beauté et à l'équilibre nécessaire entre toutes ses créatures.

    On eût dit que le philosophe et critique littéraire Gaston Bachelard connaissait intimement le monde des Yis, qui tourne autour des quatre éléments décrits tantôt par les Anciens, tantôt par les alchimistes, tantôt par les sorciers tribaux du Sichuan occidental, lorsqu'il écrivit: La rêverie a quatre domaines, quatre pointes par lesquelles elle s'élance dans l'espace infini. Pour forcer le secret d'un vrai poète... un mot suffit: "Dis-moi quel est ton fantôme? Est-ce le gnome, la salamandre, l'ondine ou la sylphide?" Jidi Majia est le poète des quatre éléments. Il a grandi dans les montagnes du Daliangshan, au sud-ouest du Sichuan, parmi les Nosus, une branche de la minorité ethnique des Yis. Il connaît intimement

大凉山的崇山峻岭中长大,那里是彝族的一支(黑彝)的栖息之地。他深知本地文化,中国一个少数民族的文化,它对大自然是敬畏的。尤其是如果同西方人相比,西方思想是被启蒙时代铸就的,它颂扬理性的胜利和所谓魔力的消失。而且,这个名叫理性的世俗女神时代的构想是,人类不仅是栖居于自然世界的朴素居民、众多生物中的一分子,而且更是胜利者,有权驱使牲畜,蔑视岩石,摧毁森林。而吉狄马加在他的诗歌和文章中,却谈起他对故乡、对儿时的壮美风景、对充满不可见自然力的荒蛮旷野的爱,这让人想起作为旅行者、漫游客、边缘人的法国诗人安托南·阿尔托,为墨西哥西部的孤绝大山写下的这段文字:

    从大山还是从我自己,我说不清那鬼神出没的东西,却是一个类似的视觉奇迹,我看见它,在穿越大山的这次长途旅行中,每天至少出现一次。
    我这个备受折磨的身体可能与生俱来,像大山一样被篡改过;却是顽念的一个容身之所:在大山中我察觉到,它可以用来计数顽念。我没有数漏一个影子,当我感到它围着什么东西旋转时;经常,我一边数着山峦投在大地上的影子,一边把数到的影子加点,我才能回溯到那些虚焦点。

  吉狄马加的作品同样表达了一种大关切。他担忧在一个全球化的世界中少数民族的身份会丧失,全球化着迷于削平差异,只提供一种仅有的有效模式,这就是新自由主义的现代化模式。他担忧各种形态下的多元丰富的磨损,无论是生物的、语言的、文化的、种族的、宗教的还是哲学的。中国目前所面临的挑战,因此是巨大的。作者多次强调这一点。因为在对外开放的过程中,中国承受了很大的压力(内部和外部),所以这个诞生过老子的国度必须战胜几乎无从逾越的困难。她必须关注诸如环境恶化、身份困境这样的棘手难题。尤其贫穷的省份青海,以前的安多地区,她同西藏自治区分享中国西部地区的高原,吉狄马加是那里的文化推动者。为什么僻远地区就不能享有舒适?正如作者指出的,21世纪的中国必

cette culture autochtone où les gens entretiennent avec la nature des rapports presque révérencieux. Surtout si on les compare aux Occidentaux, dont la pensée a été modelée par les Lumières. Les Yis ne partagent pas l'opinion des encyclopédistes, qui célébraient le triomphe de la rationalité et la soi-disant disparition de la magie. Car la déesse profane dénommée Raison se trompe lorsqu'elle considère l'être humain non pas comme un simple habitant du monde naturel, une créature parmi tant d'autres, mais comme un conquérant qui a le droit de soumettre les bêtes, mépriser les roches, détruire la forêt. Lorsque Jidi Majia–dans sa poésie et ses discours–parle de son amour pour le terroir, les paysages grandioses de son enfance, la souveraineté des étendues sauvages habitées par des forces invisibles, on ne peut que penser au voyageur, au nomade, au marginal que fut Antonin Artaud, qui au sujet des montagnes isolées du nord-ouest du Mexique a écrit ceci:

De la montagne ou de moi-même, je ne peux dire ce qui était hanté, mais un miracle optique analogue, je l'ai vu, dans ce périple à travers la montagne, se présenter au moins une fois par journée.

Je suis peut-être né avec un corps tourmenté, truqué comme l'immense montagne; mais un corps dont les obsessions servent: et je me suis aperçu dans la montagne que cela sert d'avoir l'obsession de compter. Pas une ombre que je n'aie comptée, quand je la sentais tourner autour de quelque chose; et c'est souvent en additionnant des ombres que je suis remonté jusqu'à d'étranges foyers.

L'œuvre de Jidi Majia témoigne également d'une grande préoccupation pour les causes sociales. Il s'inquiète de la perte d'identité des minorités ethniques dans la foulée d'une mondialisation qui s'entête à vouloir effacer les différences en ne proposant qu'un seul modèle valide, celui de la modernité néolibérale. Il dénonce l'érosion de toutes les formes de diversité, qu'elles soient biologiques, linguistiques, culturelles, raciales, religieuses ou philosophiques. Le défi que doit relever la Chine actuelle, à cet égard, est énorme. L'auteur le souligne maintes et maintes fois. Car dans son processus d'ouverture subite (intérieure et extérieure), dans son intégration au reste du globe, le pays de Lao-Tseu est appelé à vaincre des obstacles presque insurmontables. Ce qui jadis fut l'Empire du Milieu doit maintenant faire face à des questions épineuses comme la dégradation environnementale et la problématique identitaire. Surtout dans cette région appauvrie–le Qinghai, ancienne province de l'Amdo, qui partage avec le Tibet le haut plateau occupant la partie occidentale du pays–où Jidi Majia travaille en tant que promoteur culturel. Pourquoi les régions éloignées ne rêveraient-elles pas, elles aussi, et à juste titre, de confort? Comme le souligne l'auteur, la

须面对这一重大挑战:在绷紧的现代化这根绳索上,力求保持同传统之间的微妙平衡。

在对中国文化的新变化、对诗歌、对地理、对生态、对自然资源的使用以及对政治的一系列思考中,吉狄马加询问自己:在现代世界的混乱中,文学的位置何在?神话和传统的重要性又何在?他质疑目前这种疯狂发展的动机,指出人类已经陷入某种危险的旋涡。他把读者引入他个人的宇宙起源说、他的阅读历程、他对所偏爱的作品的激情。怀着感激和怀恋之情,他谈起他的诗歌初衷,他与俄罗斯大诗人和散文名家的相遇。他激赏莱奥帕尔迪和用光芒照亮汉语的那些文学大家。他用亲切的口吻写到他对黑非洲文学和拉丁美洲魔幻现实主义的发现。他赞赏这些文学流派的代表性作家,讲到他的风格和他们之间的缘分。无疑,他赞同那些"介入作家"关于艺术的文明角色和身份角色、关于诗歌和仪式以及传说在美学教育中的重要性的见解。

作为和平主义的信奉者,尽管在这个被敌意、战争和争端所撕裂的世界上,和平已变得如此困难,吉狄马加仍不遗余力地揭露暴力、剥削、不公、压迫、种族主义、贪婪、成功的诱惑和不讲人道。他指出,思考、灵性和感恩的缺乏,威胁着今天的人类。他以自己的方式重申了阿尔托的宣言:"我们觉得,属于无限比属于自我更让我们感到幸福。"

通过他的这些演讲,吉狄马加让我们认识了生活在地理边缘的彝族人民。我们能够读到他对故乡的爱。神圣事物这个理念,在他那里,就像一把小纺锤(它让我们想到彝族纺织女工的纺锤),丝线一缕一缕地展开。故乡因此变成了一个神圣的地方,因为命运就是在那里选择了诞生一个孩子;青海对吉狄马加来说,也是一个崇敬之地,因为她浸透着万物有灵和藏传佛教的丰富文化。诗人歌唱旷野的神灵,旷野的一部分被荒凉保存。

阅读吉狄马加的这些文章,我们不由得又想起阿尔托的一句话:在一个地下沸腾着活生生蛮力的地方,群鸟搅动的空气发出比别处更高亢的声音。这是

Chine du XXIe siècle devra relever un défi de taille: veiller à l'équilibre délicat qu'est tenue de garder la tradition tout en dansant sur la corde raide de la modernité.

Dans ce pot-pourri de réflexions sur les changements récents qu'a subis la scène culturelle chinoise-la poétique, les vices de l'excès, la géographie, l'écologie, l'usage des ressources et la politique-Jidi Majia s'interroge sur la place de la littérature et l'importance des mythes dans le chaos du monde moderne. Il remet en question la marche du développement actuel, frénétique, engagé dans un vortex dont il souligne les dangers. Il entraîne le lecteur dans sa cosmogonie personnelle, le tourbillon de ses lectures, la passion de ses préférences littéraires. Il parle avec reconnaissance et nostalgie de son initiation poétique, de ses premiers contacts avec les grands maîtres russes du vers et de la prose. Il admire Leopardi et les gens de lettres qui, en Chine, ont fait briller le mandarin de tout son éclat. Il décrit, toujours sur un ton intime, sa découverte de la dite littérature noire et du réalisme magique latino-américain. Il fait l'éloge des chefs de file de ces écoles littéraires et souligne les affinités entre leurs styles et le sien. Il partage certainement l'opinion des écrivains engagés sur le rôle civilisateur et identitaire de l'art, l'importance de la poésie, des rituels et des récits dans l'éducation esthétique.

Disciple de cette doctrine si difficile qu'est le pacifisme dans un monde déchiré par les inimitiés, les guerres et les conflits, Jidi Majia dénonce la violence, l'exploitation, l'injustice, l'oppression, le racisme, la cupidité, l'appât démesuré du gain et la déshumanisation croissante. Il déplore le manque de réflexion, de spiritualité et de recueillement qui menace l'homme d'aujourd'hui. Il reprend à sa manière la déclaration d'Artaud: "On se sent beaucoup plus heureux d'appartenir à l'illimité qu'à soi-même".

Par ses discours, Jidi Majia nous fait également connaître un peuple qui vit à l'orée d'une tradition dominante. Ses écrits sont des déclarations d'amour: ils glorifient l'endroit qui mérite le nom de terre natale. L'idée du sacré, chez lui, ressemble à un petit fuseau (qu'on pourrait apparenter à ceux des tisserandes yies) dont le fil se déroule peu à peu à travers ses poèmes et ses discours. Le terroir imprégné de l'animisme des Yis devient alors un lieu sacralisé parce que c'est là que le destin a choisi de le faire naître. La terre d'adoption qu'est pour Jidi Majia le Qinghai fait elle aussi l'objet d'une grande vénération en raison de sa richesse culturelle et des merveilles du bouddhisme tibétain. L'essayiste chante la majesté de ses étendues sauvages, que l'isolement a en partie préservées.

En lisant ces textes, on imagine volontiers, pour reprendre une phrase d'Artaud, "un pays où bouent à nu les forces vives du sous-sol, où l'air crevant d'oiseaux vibre sur un timbre plus haut qu'ailleurs". C'est "le lieu privilégié du rêve du paradis perdu" dont parle Le Clézio quand il évoque la mémoire d'Artaud, qui disait, suite à son voyage dans la sierra

"失去的天堂之梦的首选之地",勒克莱齐奥这样谈到阿尔托。在一次从墨西哥齐瓦瓦山脉的旅行归来之后,阿尔托说他在一个错生之地因为某种东西而醒悟。然而,吉狄马加从未让人觉得,他错生在哺育他的祖先文化之中。他清醒地讲到,作为一个既传统又现代的人,就像勒克莱齐奥谈到本地幻象时所描述的,"梦想一切皆成可能的一片新土地;那里,一切都古老而又崭新。梦想一个失去的天堂,星象学和诸神的魔力混合在一起。梦想重新返回知识和文明的源头"。

我们谈论吉狄马加的人文关怀,他的敏感,他对大地母亲的爱,他对文学事业的信念,就不能不提到把这些文章从汉语译入英文的译者的劳动,译者是黄少政。他生于中国湖北,初中毕业后,被下放到农村,同他那一代成千上万的年轻人一样,接受贫下中农再教育。他就从那时开始学英语,在几个右派的帮助下。英语学习开启了他对文学、哲学、历史和文学翻译的巨大热情。"文化大革命"结束后,他考入上海外国语学院学习,它是中国最好的两所外国语学院之一。2008年,他成为青海师范大学主讲翻译的教授,青海师大位于青海的省会城市西宁。他的译文语言多姿多彩,文笔古雅,读者不禁会赞赏译者丰富的词汇量,他向我们转达了吉狄马加对博学和灵性事物的迷恋和热情,正如阿尔托所说,灵性事物"让我们狂喜,因为它们在我们身上唤醒了一系列返祖性的闪光形象,而这些形象来自人类的原初时代"。

（弗朗索瓦丝·罗伊,加拿大当代著名诗人、作家、翻译家。1959年出生在加拿大魁北克省,1983年获美国佛罗里达大学地理学硕士学位,2000年在墨西哥获得英语—西班牙语翻译资格证书。其诗歌和诗歌翻译作品多次获得重要奖项。诗作被翻译成法语、西班牙语、罗马尼亚语等多种文字发表或出版。已有诗集十一部、长篇小说两部、诗歌翻译集近六十部出版。曾应邀出席在墨西哥、加拿大、法国、西班牙、罗马尼亚、中国等国家举办的国际性诗歌节或文学会议。自1992年以来,弗朗索瓦丝·罗伊一直住在墨西哥西部城市瓜达拉哈拉。）

注：本序为汉语、法语对照。

isolée du Chihuahua, "se réveiller à quelque chose à quoi jusqu'ici [il était] mal né." Pourtant, Jidi Majia ne donne jamais l'impression d'être mal né dans la culture ancestrale qui l'a nourri. Il évoque plutôt, très lucidement, en tant qu'homme à la fois traditionnel et moderne, comme le décrit Le Clézio en parlant des visions autochtones, le "rêve d'une terre nouvelle où tout est possible; où tout est, à la fois, très ancien et très nouveau. Rêve d'un paradis perdu où la science des astres et la magie des dieux étaient confondues. Rêves d'un retour aux origines mêmes de la civilisation et du savoir." C'est aussi le souhait d'un Yi qui voue à Dame Nature un amour inconditionnel.

Certes, on ne peut parler de l'humanisme de Jidi Majia, de sa sensibilité, et de sa dévotion à la cause littéraire, sans mentionner le travail du traducteur de ses discours du mandarin à l'anglais, Huang Shao Zheng. Né au Hubei, en Chine centrale, il a été envoyé dans les campagnes, après ses études collégiales, comme des milliers de jeunes chômeurs de sa génération, afin d'être rééduqué par des paysans révolutionnaires. C'est à cette époque qu'il a commencé à apprendre l'anglais auprès de certains détenus. Cet apprentissage a marqué le début d'une grande passion pour la littérature, la philosophie, l'histoire et la traduction. Après la Révolution culturelle, il a étudié à l'Institut des langues étrangères de Shanghai, une des deux meilleures écoles de langues du pays. Depuis 2008, il est professeur de traduction à l'École normale du Qinghai située à Xining, capitale provinciale. Dans une langue colorée, un style classique où le lecteur avisé ne manquera pas d'admirer une grande richesse de vocabulaire, il nous transmet l'engouement et l'enthousiasme de Jidi Majia pour l'érudition et les choses de l'esprit, qui, comme disait Artaud, "nous enchantent parce qu' elles éveillent en nous tout un lot brillant d'images ataviques qui nous viennent des premiers âges de l'humanité".

(Francoise Roy, a translator, poet and prose writer, was born and raised in Quebec, Canada, in 1959. She has a Master's degree in Geography with a Certificate in Latin American Studies [University of Florida, 1983], as well as a Certificate in Translation from English to Spanish [O.M.T, Guadalajara, Mexico, 2000], and a Certificate in Photography at the Instituto Fotografico de Occidente [Guadalajara, Mexico, 2013]. She is recipient of many literary awards and has published two novels, and eleven books of poems, and translated more than sixty books in poetry. She has participated in poetry fests and literary meetings in Mexico, Canada, France, Spain, Rumania, China, etc. She has been living in Guadalajara, Mexico, since 1992.)

This preface is in French.

目　录

序　[加拿大]弗朗索瓦·罗伊　　　　　　　　　　　001
Avant-Propos　[Canada]Francois roy

诗歌的责任并非仅仅是自我的发现　　　　　　　　008
Narcissistic Self-Seeking Is Not the Sole Responsibility of a Decent Poet

词语的盐·光所构筑的另一个人类的殿堂　　　　　014
Word as Salt · An Alternative Human Paradise Made of Light

另一种创造：从胡安·鲁尔福到奥克塔维奥·帕斯　022
To Create Differently: From Juan Rulfo to Octavi Paz

光明与鹰翅的天石　　　　　　　　　　　　　　　036
Heavenly Stones Made of Eagles Wings and Light

诗歌与光明涌现的城池　　　　　　　　　　　　042
A City Hemmed in with Radiant Beams of Poetry

诗影光芒中的茅屋　　　　　　　　　　　　　050
Du Fu's Thatched Cottage-Both A Reality and A Legend

我相信诗歌将会打破所有的壁垒和障碍　　　　054
I Believe Poetry Will Break Loose all the barriers and Obstacles

何为诗人？何为诗？　　　　　　　　　　　　058
Who Is a Poet? What Is Poetry?

高贵的文学依然存在人间　　　　　　　　　　064
Noble Literature Is Still of Interest and Moment

诗歌是人类迈向明天最乐观的理由　　　　　　070
Why Good Poetry Still Matters?

一个中国诗人的非洲情结　　　　　　　　　　076
The African Complex of a Chinese Poet

我们时代的诗歌传奇　　　　　　　　　　　　086
A Legend of Our Time

向诗歌致敬　　　　　　　　　　　　　　　　090
A Tribute to Poetry

诗歌的本土写作和边缘的声音　　　　　　　094
Localized Poetic Writing and marginalized Voice

山地族群的生存记忆与被拯救中的边缘影像　　102
Existential Memory of Mountain Inhabitants and Marginalized Images
　　Coming to the Rescue

诗歌通往神话与乌托邦的途径　　　　　　　108
Poetry as Access into Myth and Utopia

诗歌见证历史和创造的工具　　　　　　　　114
Poetry Can Anticipate a Bigger Influence in Human Society

我们的继续存在是人类对自身的救赎　　　　118
We Are Still Here-An Act Of Self-redemption For Mankind

格萨尔与世界史诗　　　　　　　　　　　　124
Gesar and World Epics

造梦空间的幻象　　　　　　　　　　　　　136
Fantasizing in a Dreamland

诗歌与朝圣的远游　　　　　　　　　　　　140
Poetry and Pilgrimage

神话永远闪烁着远古文明的诗性光辉　　　　146
Mythology As the "Song of the Universe and the Music of the Spheres"

003

诗人的个体写作与人类今天所面临的共同责任　　　158
The Individual Writing of a Poet and the Common Responsibilities
　　Facing Mankind

群山的记忆流淌成河　　　162
Memories of Our Earliest Beginnings Trickle All the Way down
　　the Mountains

多元民族特质文化与文学的人类意识　　　174
The Contemporary Culture of Plurality and a Writer's Sense of Humanity

大美青海：梦想世界与现实世界的影像　　　206
Qinghai Travel-A Movable Feast of Sights and Sensations Guranteed

青海最后净土的入口与现实中的文化创意及其品牌　　　220
Qinghai the Entrance into the Last Pure Land

当代世界文学语境下的中国诗人写作　　　274
Chinese Poetic Writing in the Context of World Literature

我们向大山呼唤，并倾听它的回声　　　286
Mountains Are Beckoning Us To Lend Them an Ear

太阳的使者，大地的祭司——诗人艾青　　　298
Herald of Apollo and the Shaman of the Earth

青海湖国际诗歌节：通向世界的门扉　　　　　　　　　　306
Qinghai Lake International Poetry Festival-A Door Opened to the World

青海湖国际诗歌节宣言　　　　　　　　　　　　　　　314
Manifesto of Qinghai Lake International Poetry Festival

一个彝人的梦想　　　　　　　　　　　　　　　　　　318
A Yi Poet's Dream

为消除人类所面临的精神困境而共同努力　　　　　　　354
Striving to Reverse the Global Trend of Spiritual Decline

鲁迅与我们这个时代　　　　　　　　　　　　　　　　358
Lu Xun and Our Age

在全球化语境下超越国界的各民族文学的共同性　　　　364
Commonality in the Literature of Various Nationalities in
　　the Context of Globalization

永远的普希金——献给普希金二百周年诞辰　　　　　　372
The Eternal Alexander Sergeyevich Pushkin

莱奥帕尔迪和他的诗将属于不朽　　　　　　　　　　　378
The Fatal Charm of Giacomo Leopardi as a Poet

我的诗歌，来自我所熟悉的那个文化　　　　　　　　　386
My Poetic Inspiration Rooted in the Daliangshan , My Quantock Hills

总有人因为诗歌而幸福　　　　　　　　　　　　　394
Some Are Numbered among the Blessed, Because of Poetry

个人身份·群体声音·人类意识　　　　　　　　398
PersonalIdentity · Group Voice · Human Awareness

向河流致敬,就是向诗歌致敬　　　　　　　　　408
A Salute to Rivers Is a Salute to Poetry

附录1
Appendix 1

重读《献给土著民族的颂歌》　　海南大学　李鸿然　412
Jidi Majia's An Eulogy of World Indigenous People Revisited
　　Li Hongran, University of Hainan

全球化语境下土著民族诗人的语言策略　首都师范大学　吴思敬　428
The Linguistic Strategy of Adopted by an Indigenous Poet in the Context
　　of Globalization
　　Wu Sijing, Capital Normal University

附录 2
Appendix 2

拥抱一切的诗歌　［俄罗斯］叶夫图申科　　　　　　　　　　436
The All-Embracing Poesy　［Russia］Yevgeny Yevtushenko

吉狄马加——"黑色河流"上的传奇诗人　［美国］杰克·赫希曼　446
Jidi Majia-Nuosu Bard of the "Black River"　［USA］Jack Hirschman

《敬畏群山》翻译后记　　　　　　　　　　　　　　　　　　454
Translator's Notes

诗歌的责任并非仅仅是自我的发现

在 2018 年"塔德乌什·米钦斯基表现主义凤凰奖"颁奖仪式上的致答辞

2018 年 9 月 18 日

尊敬的"塔德乌什·米钦斯基表现主义凤凰奖"评委会、在座的各位朋友：

非常高兴能获得本年度的"塔德乌什·米钦斯基表现主义凤凰奖"，毫无疑问，这是我又一次获得来自一个我在精神上最为亲近的国度的褒奖。我必须在这里说，对这份褒奖，我的感激之情是难以用语言来表达的。我这样说并不是怀疑语言的功能和作用，而是有的感情用语言无法在更短的时间内极为准确地表达出来，如果真的要去表达它必须用更长的篇幅，但我相信在此时此刻，我的这种对波兰的亲近之情和感激，在座的诸位是完全能理解的。

我现在还清楚地记得在一篇文章中看到，20 世纪波兰极伟大的诗人之一切斯瓦夫·米沃什在雅盖隆大学做过一篇题为"以波兰诗歌对抗世界"的演讲，他在这次演讲中集中表达了这样一种思想，就是波兰作家永远不可能逃避对他人以及"对前人和后代的责任感"。这或许就是多少年以来，我对波兰文学极敬重的原因之一。

如果我们放眼 20 世纪以来的世界文学，东中欧作家和诗人给我们带来的精神冲击和震撼，从某种意义而言，要完全超过其他区域的文学，当然，俄罗斯白银时代的文学是另外一个特例。从道德和精神的角度来看，近一百年来，一批天才的波兰作

Narcissistic Self-Seeking Is Not the Sole Responsibility of a Decent Poet

Acceptance Speech at the Awarding Ceremony of "Tadeusza Miciń skiego Prize"

18th, September, 2018

Respected judges, friends:

  I am ,indeed, overwhelmed with the award given to me today ,veritably a true literary distinction which leaves a good excuse for revisiting the realm of belle lettre mostly akin to my personal slant in the affairs of both the world and the heart. Forget any mistrust on my part of the normal function of language when I fumble for words of gratitude as a proper act of response at this moment. I surmise a narrative of a certain length might do the job. All said, all the audience today should be fully acquainted with my special affection for Polish letters.

  My mind returns to an oration delivered by one of the greatest Polish poets 20th century can offer, ie, Czeslaw Milosz, the moralist, at Jagiellonian University entitled Counter the World with Polish Poetry, a speech of enormous ethical and artistic importance, both as an incentive to his counterparts and as fair warning to world poets, wherein he set forth his unequivocal position to the effect that "Polish writers shall never extenuate themselves to their predecessors and posterity in matters of the mind, the cross of their trade". With this self-inflicted obligation and shout of call to responsibility emitted, he demystifies any claim of a literature free of commitment and he speaks for us all that poetry must always serve a cause and for this alone I bow to no one in my admiration for his poetry and his personality ,and indeed, the Polish poetry in general.

  A cursory glance at the 20th century world literature onward confirms both the popular and critical perception, that Poland, together with East Europe and Middle Europe, has startled and fascinated the world by the quality of imagination and language it was called upon and brought to bear upon both national and human experience as well as by the wealth of exemplary Polish men and women of letters, arising out of their sufferings and bringing about what was sort of provincial and barren literature to world status. Equally or more deserving of credit, it could be argued, is the exceptional accomplishments of Russian geniuses of Silver Age , as ever, standing on the high ground of artistic integrity and moral duty. For in the past 100 years or so, the great panoply of Polish poets ,in particular, taking up the yoke upon them unflinchingly, trapped in circumstances

家和诗人始终置身于一个足以让我们仰望的高度，他们背负着沉重而隐形的十字架，一直站在风暴和雷电交汇的最高处，其精神和肉体都经受了难以想象的磨难。熟悉波兰历史的人都不难理解，为什么波兰诗歌中那些含着眼泪微笑的反讽，能让那些纯粹为修辞而修辞的诗歌汗颜。

不用怀疑，如果诗歌仅仅是一种对自我的发现，那诗歌就不可能真正承担起对"他人"和更广义的人类命运的关注。诚然，在这里我并没有否认诗歌发现自我的重要。这个奖是用波兰表现主义的领军人物之一，也是超现实主义的先驱塔德乌什·米钦斯基的名字命名的，作为一位富有创新精神的思想者，塔德乌什·米钦斯基也十分强调创作者必须在精神和道德领域为我们树立光辉的榜样。

当下的世界和人类在精神方面所出现的问题，已经让许多关注人类前景的人充满着忧虑，精神的堕落和以物质以及技术逻辑为支配原则的现实状况，无论在东方还是在西方都成为被追捧的时尚和标准，看样子这种状况还会持续下去。

以往社会发展史的经验已告诉我们，并不是人类在物质上的每一次进步，都会带来精神和思想上的上升。这一个多世纪以来，人类又拥有了原子能、计算机、纳米、超材料、机器人、基因工程、克隆技术、云计算、互联网、数字货币，但是，同样就在今天，在此时此刻，叙利亚儿童在炮火和废墟上的哭声，并没有让屠杀者放下手中的武器。今天的人类手中，仍然掌握着足以毁灭所有的生物几千遍的武器。

which would easily crush and destroy any other human group, have emerged from the morass of "moronic apathy, drunken torpor and morbid, wounded nationalism" as a result of national misfortunes, to come out with works of art, of refined taste, tender irony and mingled pathos, sometimes marked by apocalyptic or humorously macabre visions. Anybody familiar with the terrible fate of Polska, again and again, partitioned by both strong and even weaker neighbors ,the Teutons, Turkey, Muscovy, Prussia, erased from the map of the world for over 120 years, will knowingly reckon with, arguably the more or less permanent trait of Polish letters, ie, "a strong emotional moralism" fed obviously by Christian ethic. What is offered is nothing short of a consummate distillation of crushing experiences of Poles in particular or of the existential depths visited practically by all of us nowadays. In comparison, any- rhetoric- for- rhetoric-sake poetry, stripped of such human caring would look outright pale and absent weight and substance.

Beyond dispute, the universal recognition of Polish poetry lends itself, in the flux of literary history, to the cardinal thesis that poetry has no meaning if contained within the bounds of narcissistic indulgences and exaggerations and this is to not deny the importance of a poet to legitimately wrestle with falsifying emotions by "concern with form" and due effort at "unsentimental purity of things." But Milosz's treatment of the basic theme of Polish poetry remains valid: "the tension between a poetic dedication to form and compassion for human suffering." This award, named after Tadeusza Miciń skiego, who earns our respect for his expressionist fascination with originality and innovation, has never disavowed, indeed, he has fulfilled preeminently the wishes of all Polish poets for a balance between an all-out social protest and faith in man as well as pursuit of artistic excellence.

We confront a world still chaotic and full of incongruities. Complaints of its spiritual poverty as well as paucity of good poetry are as old as the art itself. This heart-rending state of affairs , buttressed by a logic of material and technology holding sway the spirit, the fad of the 21st century, constitutes the biggest reason to call forth our most vigorous efforts to keep pace with the age as poets.

Carried away, as we are, by waves of technological breakthroughs, past experience sometimes surprises the pessimists who foresee the durable effects of modernization. With an awesome array of new gadgets at our disposal, robots, Genes engineering, cloning, cloud computing, internet, superconductivity material, digital currency, there seems to be a place for euphoria ,triumphant mankind and exuberant poets enveloped within the intricacy of syntax and deconstructed lexicon, who could "perform a spontaneous dance without recourse to compulsive justifications."Yet the images of Syrian imps screaming audibly over the loss of their mothers on the debris of their former cozy homes inundate our TV screens, which compels our unkempt attention, a timely reminder we are still situated between the holocaust of the last war and the atomic devastation, a danger not exactly imminent, but still lurking ominously somewhere ahead of us, for the existing arsenal of atomic bombs, we are told, can still decimate humans and all the

在这样一个时代,作为有责任感和良知的诗人,如果我们不把捍卫人类创造美好生活的权利当成义务和责任,那对美好的诗歌而言将是一种可耻的行为。谢谢大家。

sentient beings thousands of times.

Milosz rightly admonishes us that the act of writing poetry is an act of faith. Our activity is certainly tantamount to an offense if we juggle with poetry and fail to produce poems that rival the immortal pieces of the old in defense of human civilization and exemplify the attempt to resist the growing disparity in the cultural and economic life in the world.

词语的盐·光所构筑的另一个人类的殿堂
——诗歌语言的透明与微暗
在 2018 中国自贡"一带一路"诗歌之灯点亮世界国际诗歌周开幕式上的演讲
2018 年 9 月 17 日

与日常的语言相比较,毫无疑问,诗歌的语言属于另一个语言的范畴,当然需要声明的是,我并不是说日常的语言与诗歌的语言存在着泾渭分明的不同,而是指诗歌的语言具有某种抽象性、象征性、暗示性以及模糊性。诗歌的语言是通过一个一个的词构成的,从某种意义而言,诗歌语言所构成的多维度的语言世界,就如同那些古老的石头建筑,它们是用一块一块的石头构建而成的,这些石头每一块似乎都有着特殊的记忆,哪怕就是有一天这个建筑倒塌了,那些散落在地上的石头,当你用手抚摸它们的时候,你也会发现它们会给你一种强烈的暗示,那就是它们仍然在用一种特殊的密码和方式告诉你它们生命中的一切。很多时候如果把一首诗拆散,其实它的每一个词就像一块石头。

在我们古老的彝族典籍和史诗中,诗歌的语言就如同一条隐秘的河流,当然,这条河流从一开始就有着一个伟大的源头,它是所有民族哺育精神的最纯洁的乳汁,也可以说它是这个世界上一切具有创造力的生物的肚脐,无一例外,诗歌都是这个世界上生活在不同地域、族群的最古老的艺术形式之一。

在古代史诗的吟唱过程中,吟唱者往往具有双重的身份,他们既是现实生活中

Word as Salt·An Alternative Human Paradise Made of Light
——Transparence and Dimness of Poetic Diction
Address at the Opening Ceremony of 2018 Zigong "Belt and Road" International Poetry Week
17th, September, 2018

  Compared to natural language, poetic diction belongs to a distinct category, discernibly removed to a considerable degree from daily usage in the real world. However, it is not to be inferred, in this connection, there is a clear cut and ingrained borderline between both. Rather I mean poetic language ,of necessity, is at times abstract, suggestive, symbolic and cryptic. To be sure, the edifice of poetry is erected of words, one by one, one atop another, as Roman aqueducts and Egyptian pyramids ,one piece laid upon or across another adroitly and seamlessly. The similitude of this poet-as-verbal-mason analogy ends where words seem to be culturally loaded to the extent, once such a poetic monument falls to pieces, the stones scattered about will respond lovingly to the human touch. Here is an occasion called forth to reflect on the primary ,and indeed, primal origin and function of poetic language. A poet is, by definition, a word-conscious person committed to, even obsessed with words, so as to be empowered to give expressive, suggestive and precise shape to what he wishes to say, a shape that could do the trick of suggestion, evocation, while the poet needs avoid as much as possible rhetoric and moralizing and hardly ever move into explicit generalization.

  In the ultimate pooling of the Yi canonical works passed down, the pride of place goes to epics , composed without exception in parallelism or stanzas which bring with it the coming-of-age of Yi language on par with the respectable Chinese , mores, idiosyncrasies which would in good time affect every aspect of Yi culture characterized by diversity, instability and strife. Indeed, epics ,not necessarily a jewel in the literal sense, but each one, verbal emerald and verbal opal, of intrinsic quality and character, collectively mark and forge a cultural heritage which nourishes Yi spirituality and give vent to local bards who vocalize and tap the rhythmical sources of their culture. It is not coincidence that linguists all surmise in some hypothetical beginning of things poetry was the only way of using language. And anthropologists basically sign up to the same notion of poetry operating both as opener of language and preserver of identity for ethnic people inhabiting the remotest corners of our globe.

的智者，又是人类社会与天地界联系的通灵人。也可以说人类有语言以来，诗歌就成为我们赞颂祖先、歌唱自然、哭诉亡灵、抚慰生命、倾诉爱情的一种特殊的方式。如果从世界诗歌史的角度来看，口头的诗歌一定要比人类有文字以来的诗歌历史久远得多，在今天一些非常边远的地方，那些没有原生文字的民族，他们口头诗歌的传统仍然还在延续，最为可贵的是他们的诗歌语言也是对日常生活用语的精炼和提升，在我们彝族古老的谚语中就把诗歌称为"语言中的盐巴"，直到今天在婚丧嫁娶集会的场所，能即兴吟诵诗歌的人们还会进行一问一答的博弈对唱。

而从有文字以来留存下来的人类诗歌文本来看，在任何一个民族文字书写的诗歌中，语言都是构建诗歌最重要的要素和神奇的材料，也可以说在任何一个民族的文字创作中，诗歌都是最精华的那个部分，难怪在许多民族和国度都有这样的比喻："诗歌是人类艺术皇冠上最亮的明珠"，而诗歌语言所富有的创造力和神秘性就越发显得珍贵和重要。诗歌通过语言创造了一个属于自己的世界，而这个世界的丰富性、象征性、抽象性、多义性、复杂性都是语言带来的，也就是说语言通过诗人，或者说诗人通过语言给我们所有的倾听者、阅读者提供了无限的可能。

正因为语言在诗歌中的特殊作用，它就像魔术师手中的一个道具，它可能在一个瞬间变成一只会飞的鸽子，同样，它还会在另一个不同的时空里变成了鱼缸中一条红色的鱼。在任何一个语言世界中，我以为只有诗人通过诗的语言才能给我们创造一个完全不同的世界，甚至在不同的诗人之间，他们各自通过语言所创造的世界也将是完全不同的，这就像伟大的作曲家勋伯格的无调音乐，它是即兴的、感性的、

As epics anchor the riddles of life amid the mundane realities of chores and toils, traditionally, epic bards within a typical Yi community perform a dual function, ie, singers who entertain and delight by "boiling elsewhere with such a lyric yeast" as well as sages making sensible statements about the immediate world while negotiating between the secular and the divine. Thus language and poetry are believed to be linked with ritual in most of the agricultural, gathering and herding societies. Poetry, so they claim, arose at the outset in the form of magic spells invoked to fend off a famine or ensure a good harvest before being later expanded to honor forebears, explain the alteration of the seasons, life and death, and register the pathos of love forlorn lass and lad, pray away evil, comfort those who submit to bereavement. Historically, writing is subsequent to speech in that man poeticizes orally long before he writes it down. In places still inaccessible, extremely remote ,where no writing system, either character or alphabet, has been evolved. oral tradition still survives for tribesmen and tribeswomen who persist in concentrating, compressing and intensifying their speech in order to render a particular experience, crystallizing it into a channel of "the spontaneous overflow of powerful feelings", centering around subjects from nature and rustic life to show their dignity and artistic validity. One of our Yi proverbs likens poems to linguistic salt. Even into today, on important occasions such as weddings and funerals, village wits still sing songs or recite poems that have call and response patterns as Negro spirituals, with lead singers setting out a line or phrase and his rival or the group responding by repeating or playing variations on it.

From the extant poetic fragments left by people of classic antiquity, we take our cues that language accounts for the making of all exemplars for poetry, of sufficient import and weight, and we must add timely such linguistic resources that go into the production of a national treasure should be deemed the cream of a national language. No wonder many a country prides itself on possessing such blessings divinely bestowed in line with the grain of their life. Indeed, the exalted views about a poet's proper place in society have been a consensus among nations "with veins full of poetic stuff" that "most needs poets and will doubtless have the greatest and use them the greatest". For the simple reason the imposing works of language by poets, executed expressively, suggestively, opaquely or evocatively, employ language as a window on experience , so varied, complex and heterogeneous, and supply an infinity of aesthetic possibilities for audience and readership.

Poets are sometimes called magicians of words, and words to poets are like wands to magicians. Flying carpets at a time and a pigeon to take wings in a wink of eye or a red fish in a tank at a spatial and temporary nodal point. For all their variety, whimsicality and creativity, poets fashion a world of their own, in its own right , which might be a far cry from what we all know and light-years removed from what we inhabit. Just like Schoenberg's innovations in atonality, sensual, spontaneous ,instinctive, "sonic orgies"(as someone calls it who detests it) sound they might, they form an integral and indivisible whole, a multum in parvo, and his approach, both in

直觉的、毫无规律的,但它又是整体的和不可分割的。

很多时候诗歌也是这样,特别是当诗人把不同的词置放在不同的地方,这个词就将会在不同的语境中呈现出新的无法预知的意义。为什么说有一部分诗歌在阅读时会产生障碍,有的作品甚至是世界诗歌史上具有经典意义的作品,比如伟大的德语诗人策兰,比如说伟大的西班牙语诗人塞萨尔·巴列霍,比如说伟大的俄语诗人赫列勃尼科夫等等,他们的诗歌通过语言都构建了一个需要破译的密码系统,他们很多时候还在自己的写作中即兴创造一些只有他们才知道的词,许多诗人都认为从本质意义上来讲,诗歌的确是无法翻译的,而我们翻译的仅仅是一首诗所要告诉我们的最基本的需要传达的内容。

诗歌的语言或者说诗歌中的词语,它们就像黑色的夜空中闪烁的星光,就像大海的深处漂浮不定的鲸的影子,当然它们很多时候更像光滑坚硬的卵石,更像雨后晶莹透明的水珠,这就是我们阅读诗歌时,每一首诗歌都会用不同的声音和节奏告诉我们的原因。对于每一位真正的诗人来讲,一生都将与语言和词语捉迷藏,这样的游戏当然有赢家,也会有输家,当胜利属于诗人的时候,也就是一首好诗诞生的时候。

语言和词语在诗歌中有时候是清晰的,同样很多时候它们又是模糊的。语言和词语的神秘性,不是今天在我们的文本中才有,在原始人类的童年期,我们的祭司面对永恒的群山和太阳,吟诵赞词的时候,那些通过火焰和光明抵达天地间的声音,就释放着一种足以让人肃穆的力量,毫无疑问,这种力量包含的神秘性就是今天也很难让我们破译。

在我的故乡四川大凉山彝族腹心地带,现在我们的原始宗教掌握者毕摩,他们诵读的任何一段经文,可以说都是百分之百的最好的诗歌,这些诗歌由大量的排比

terms of harmony and development, has been one of the most pioneering and influential of 20th-century musical thought.

Allow me here to cite a wise passage, to the credit of a certain American poet: "A poet must be drenched in words, literally soaked in them, to have the right ones form themselves into the proper patterns at the right moment." I totally agree with him that we poets, on top of three desiderata, ie, the conventional concern with formal properties (rhythmical or riming schemes, inner cadence),typographical arrangement(the balance and shift of the line, couplet, stanza) and ultra-modern propensity to view poetry as a linguistic construct in these toppling times, we must never toy with the ultimate problem of the diction of poetry in the whole process. It is a diction, as it were, as always, "very conscious of its power of choosing terms with an affect of precision and of combining the terms into phrases with the same affect of peculiar precision." This time-honored Homeric sensitivity and striving for lexical precision is the ultimate test of good poetry vs bad which partially accounts for the emotive obscurity and riddling intellectual opacity exemplified in the poetry of German Paul Celan, Hispanic Cesar Vallejo. Russian Boris Khlebnikov. Veritably the poetic artifice they have labored at and constructed is forbidding for many, a poetic Morse code, hermetically closed , to be attacked and deciphered even by professional critics, notoriously inhospitable to translators. Imaginative creations in this vein serve to indicate the complexity of the modernist temper, for a poem is in essence, is not so much a sentiment ,volition, passion as it is a mind, a mode of thought, perception, in short, a way of both seeing and saying. All said, they have infused their artistic complexity with a profound sense of human worth, offering occasional but important lessons, moments of illumination, however dim and obscure, brimming with the quality of affirmation that we expect from great poets.

Poetic language, or rather, verbal strands woven into a poetic fabric, to the initiated, conjures up a majestic view of a starry sky, elusive sharks in the unfathomable depths, shiny pebbles on a dry riverbed and rain drops on a flower pedal after a downpour. All of these instances provide clues as to why we delight in poetry, the sounds of words, their rhythms and rimes, as it appeals to our intellects and stimulates our imaginations by demanding we visualize and conceptualize events, places and characters outside the realm of everyday experience. For a poet of any worth, the whole span of his life is too short for wrestling with language, a hide and seek game. Sometimes he tumbles along upon it-a token of genuine blessing. Sometimes he loses any track of it. When at last he comes around to the right word, his trophy: a good poem is born. The perennial squabble remains: the limits to perception, the accessibility of truth, the nature and scope of knowing and naming.

Word are both opaque and crystal, ambiguous and mysterious. This is nothing new as our Bimos would stand testimony, dating from the infancy of mankind: chanting grandiloquently a hymn, gazing and gasping at the sprawling ranges of mountains, the sun arising and setting ,and his voice being carried through fire and light to the Celestial Vaults, reverberating high and low,

句构成，而每一句都具有神灵附体的力量，作为诗歌的语言此刻已经成为现实与虚无的媒介，而语言和词语在它的吟诵中也成为这个世界不可分割的部分。我以为这个世界最伟大的诗篇都是清晰的、模糊的、透明的、复杂的、具象的、形而上的、一目了然的、不可解的、先念的、超现实的、伸手可及的、飘忽不定的等等一切的总和。

thither and hither. What a way of contemplating the mystery and power of the divinities and releasing cosmic energy in syn with motions of heavenly bodies! Here is another case of untranslatability, equally notoriously baffling and inscrutable as the most arcane poetic texts.

In my native place, in the Daliangshan heartland of Yi culture, our priest figures-Bimos, still revered to ply their trade and do their business upon the human spirit, habitually say a prayer in form of poems, the best poems the Yi people can boast, happily, "by the coincidence of forms that locks in the poem", the bulk of Yi poetry comprise parallelism, each divinely charged with a haunting ethos, energy, mythical might that escalates upward further and further, the ideal medium negotiating between reality and nothingness, an integral and indivisible part of our world. Our bimos, like all great poets, enrapture us by raising their voices always, at the end, of transcendence, because they have both seen clearly and tasted poignantly the glory and misery of the miserables. The sum total of our poetic legacy, tradition and experiment, an amazing and dazzling garnering of the transparent, the cryptic, the ambiguous, the concrete, the abstract, the metaphysical, the symbolic, the surreal, the elusive, the accessible, the pat, discloses to us this vital truth intimately and distinctly.

另一种创造：从胡安·鲁尔福到奥克塔维奥·帕斯

在北大中墨建交45周年文学研讨会上的演讲

2017年10月30日

当我在这里说到胡安·鲁尔福、奥克塔维奥·帕斯的时候，我便想到一个关键的词：创造，或者用一句更妥帖的话来说那就是：另一种创造。我想无论是在墨西哥文学史上，还是在拉丁美洲文学史上，甚至扩大到整个20世纪的世界文学史，胡安·鲁尔福和奥克塔维奥·帕斯都是两个极具传奇色彩并充满了神秘的人物。

最有意思的是，与这样充满了传奇又极为神秘的人物在精神上相遇，不能不说从一开始就具有某种宿命的味道，首先，让我先说说我是如何认识胡安·鲁尔福这个人和他的作品的。我没有亲眼见过胡安·鲁尔福，这似乎是一个遗憾，这个世界有这么多神奇的人，当然不乏你十分心仪的对象，但都要见面或要认识，的确是一件十分困难的事。

但对胡安·鲁尔福这个人和他的作品，从我第一次与之相遇，我就充满了好奇和疑问，好奇是因为我读了他的短篇小说集《平原烈火》和中篇小说《佩德罗·帕拉莫》之后，我对他作为一个异域作家所具有的神奇想象力惊叹不已，记得那是在20世纪80年代初，这样的阅读给我带来的愉悦和精神上的冲击毫无疑问是巨大的。

可以说就在短短几个月的时间内，我把一本不足二十万字的《胡安·鲁尔福中短篇小说集》反复阅读了若干遍，可以说有一年多时间这本书都被我随身携带着，以便随时翻阅抽看。因为阅读胡安·鲁尔福的作品，我开始明白一个道理，此前在世界许多地方的"地域主义"写作，虽然在语言和形式上都进行了新的开拓和探索，不少作品具有深刻的土著思想意识，对人物的刻画和描写充满着真实的力量，尤其是对地

To Create Differently: From Juan Rulfo to Octavi Paz
A speech given in a seminar held in Beijing University marking the 45th anniversary of Sino-Mexico diplomatic relations
30th, October, 2017

At the mere mention of the two Mexican names, Juan Rulfo and Octavi Paz, one overworked buzzword, not necessarily drained of its clear meaning, comes up instantly in my mind: creativity, or to be more precise in the present context, alternative creativity, as I trust these two Mexicans remain a legend and even something of a mystery for contemporary Mexican literature, for the Hispanic world and even beyond.

Therefore ,it is utter coincidence why I chanced upon getting to know and grow eventually intimate familiarity with their work and personality, cast in such unconventional tone and artistically innovative mould. To begin with, I might say a few words about Juan Rulfo. Sure enough, I never met with him in person, a seemingly pitiable thing ,although I wish that. Yet on second thoughts, one will be much consoled given this is a world populated by over 1.4 billion souls. We are not meant to meet with each of them in the average short lifespan of ours.

Yet an accidental acquaintance with Juan Rulfo turns out to be a lifelong obsession, well rewarded by a quick understanding of the various subtleties in his writing before reinforced into an informed appreciation of his greatness fed upon initial thirst and curiosity for the exotic and foreign. His two literary works, *El Llano en llamas*, a collection of short stories, and *Pedro Páramo*. a 1955 tale of a man discovering a ghost town have never ceased teasing my imagination. For a literary novice of ethnic origin from China just opening up to the world in the early 1980s, Juan Rulfo was absolutely a knock-out and eye-opener experience.

Thus the first reading of his *Burning Plain* made me his perennial fan. In the months that followed, that slim collection of stories less than 200,000 Chinese characters became my compulsory reading and for over one year I kept the book in my pocket or in my baggage for repeated perusal .It dawned upon me there were different varieties of regionalist writings the world over and much remained to be explored and aped in the way of fellow regionalists' experimentation with technique and language. Rulfo, for one, gives his work an air of historical authenticity in his employment of a unique prose style and his seemingly bizarre characterization,

域文化和自然环境的呈现更是淋漓尽致。

在这些作品中厄瓜多尔作家霍尔赫·伊卡萨的《瓦西蓬戈》、委内瑞拉作家罗慕洛·加列戈斯的《堂娜芭芭拉》、秘鲁作家阿格达斯的《深沉的河流》、秘鲁作家西罗·阿莱格里亚的《广漠的世界》等等，如果把它的范围扩大得更远，在非洲地区还包括尼日利亚作家阿契贝小说四部曲《瓦解》《动荡》《神箭》《人民公仆》，肯尼亚作家恩吉古的《一粒麦种》《孩子，你别哭》和《大河两岸》等等。

当然还有许多置身于这个世界不同地域的众多"地域主义"写作的作家，这对于20世纪而言已经是一个令人瞩目的文学现象，对他们的创作背景和作品进行解读，不管从政治层面，还是从社会和现实的层面，都会让我们对不同族群的人类生活有一个更全面更独到的认识。因为这些作家的作品都是对自己所属族群生活的独立书写，而不是用他者的眼光所进行的记录。这些作品的一次次书写过程，其实就是对自身文化身份的一次次确认。这些杰出的作家在后现代和后殖民的语境中，从追寻自身的文化传统和精神源头开始，对重新认识自己确立了自信并获得了无可辩驳的理由。

可以说对于第三世界作家来说，这一切都是伴随着民族解放、国家独立而蓬勃展开的。但是，对于胡安·鲁尔福来说，虽然他的作品和生活毫无争议地属于那个充满了混乱、贫困、战争、动荡而又急剧变革的时代，但他用近似于灌注了魔力的笔为我们构建了一个人鬼共处的真实世界，这种真实的穿透力更能复现时间和生命的本质。胡安·鲁尔福最大的本领是他给我们提供了新的时间观念，他让生和死的意识渗透在他所营造的空间和氛围里，他用文字所构筑的世界，就如同阿兹特克人对宇宙、对生命、对时间、对存在，所进行的神秘而奇妙的描述，这种描述既是过去，又是现在，更是未来。

在20世纪众多的"地域主义"写作中，请允许我武断地这样说，是胡安·鲁尔福

and above all, in his ability to present a thoroughly Hispanic world in thoroughly Hispanic terms forerunning the Boom of the Latin American Novel that was to sweep the literary world, east and west soon.

Although critics and writers debate which authors or works fall within the regionalist genre, the following authors represent without dispute the narrative mode. Within the Latin American world, the most iconic of magical realist writers are the Ecuadorian novelist Jorge Icaza (*Huasipungo*), the Venezuelan Romulo Gallegos (*Dona Barbana*),the Peruvian indigenous writers Jose Maria Arguedas (*Deep Rivers*)and Ciro Alegrí a (*Broad and Alien is the World*).This literary trend also includes in the African tradition eminent writers such as Chinua Achebe (*Things Fall Apart, A Man of the People, The Arrow of God*) Ngugi wa Thiong'o (*Weep Not, Child, A Grain of Wheat, The River between*).

The popularity of regionalist literature is enduring and great and the production and proliferation throughout the developing countries is extensive in the 20th century,not at all restricted to names given above who supply some of the most prototypical specimen .One thing in common is that these writers not only chronicle the contemporary social and political histories of each's country but also reflect the dominant economic plight and intellectual concerns of their own people, attaining a high artistic dimension that make it possible for them to comment on the natural and human landscape as well as the welter of forces and causes that lead to such situations in the third world.

Regionalist writing, by its logic, will yield a group of writers who have at heart an anthropological mission: to probe into the culture of each's people by studying their folklore, linguistic peculiarities, beliefs ,mores and customs and provide an insider's synthesis and interpretation other than the version supplied by outsiders. It is, in essence, an exercise at rediscovering and reaffirming one's cultural identity in a post-colonial and even post-modernist context under the implication that one can only renew one's confidence indisputably by identifying the uniqueness of individual nation's spirituality owing to their peculiar natural features.

For the third world writers, the novels were the fictional counterpart of discovering and affirming the cultural identity of individual countries in the wake of de-colonialisation waves engulfing former colonial powers in the 1950s.Yet , for Juan Rulfo, there is a stark mingling of aestheticism and social protest. Of course, he reacted in horror to the times he was living in characterized by political chaos, deprivation, incessant internecine wars, turbulence and senseless violence, but he is also one of the first to break with the lingering traces of realism-naturalism to adapt avant-garde, post-Joycean tricks to his subject matter with amazing results. His Pedro Páramo, a tale of a man named Juan Preciado who travels to his recently deceased mother's hometown, Comala, to find his father, only to come across a literal ghost town-populated, that is, by spectral figures. Rulfo , the subjective and anguished artist, by destroying the line of demarcation that separates what seems real from what seems fantastic ,what is today, tomorrow

第一个也是第一次真正打开了时间的入口，正是那种神秘的、非理性的、拥有多种时间、跨越生死、打破逻辑的观念，才让他着魔似的将"地域主义"的写作推到了一个梦幻般的神性的极致。

难怪加西亚·马尔克斯在回忆录中深情地回忆，他很早就能将《佩德罗·帕拉莫》从最后一个字进行倒背，这显然不是一句玩笑话，我们今天可以并非毫无根据地下这样一个结论，是胡安·鲁尔福最早开始了魔幻现实主义写作的实验，而其经典作品《佩德罗·帕拉莫》是一个奇迹，是一座再也无法被撼动的真正的里程碑。

一个兴起于拉丁美洲的伟大的文学时代，其序幕被真正打开，胡安·鲁尔福就是其中最重要的人物之一。《佩德罗·帕拉莫》开创了现代小说的另一种形式，它将时空和循环、生命和死亡天衣无缝地融合在了一起，它是梦和神话穿越真实现实的魔幻写照，在此之后，不仅仅在拉丁美洲，就是在世界范围内，许多后来者都继承遵循了这样的理念，成长于中国20世纪80年代的许多先锋作家，他们都把胡安·鲁尔福视为自己的导师和光辉的典范。

胡安·鲁尔福之所以能得到不同地域、不同民族的作家高度评价，并成为一个永远的话题，那是因为他从印第安原住民的宇宙观以及哲学观出发，将象征、隐喻、虚拟融入了一个人与鬼、生与死的想象的世界，并给这个世界赋予了新的意义。据我们所知，在古代墨西哥人的原始思维中，空间与时间是相互交融的，时间与空间在不同方向的联系，构成了他们宇宙观中最让我们着迷的那个部分。

最让人称道的是，胡安·鲁尔福的写作并不是简单地将原始神话和土著民族的认知观念植入他所构建的文学世界中，他的高明之处是将环形的不断变化着的时间与空间联系在了一起，这种生命、死亡与生命的再生所形成的永恒循环，最终构成了他所颠倒与重建的三个不同的世界，这三个世界既包括了天堂，也包括了地狱，当然也还有胡安·鲁尔福所说的地下世界。

and future, fuses both realistic and surrealistic approaches into one that is more universal in outlook and more sophisticated in style, language and temporal -spatial development. There are obvious mythical overtones in the story reminiscent of non-European views ,drawn from Aztec lore, of the earth, life, individual existence, all being consonant with the ambience of the fictional town and the starkness of the narrative.

Up to this point I make bold to say, among the principal and powerful regionalist trends, Juan Rulfo might count the veritable pioneer who pushes the native theme genre to its logical extreme by breaking loose the floodgate of time, logic and concretizing the magic realism to magical heights.

No wonder Gabriel Garcia Márquez has said that it was only his life-changing discovery that opened the way to the composition of his masterpiece, *One Hundred Years of Solitude*. He even boasted he could recite every word of the short novel by heart, Arguably mentor of the magical realism genre, Rulfo has written two books , of a high quality as good as most of those of his disciples, if not better, truly fictional milestones, winning him a place among the most prestigious practitioners of the new Latin American novel .

Pedro Paramo signals the coming-of-age of South American literature. Juan Rulfo enchants us by blazing trails in modern novel writing as he marries myth with narrative modeled on and further expanding Joycean formulas (dislocation of linear time, shifts in the narrator and his viewpoint, the probing of the psyche). He does not try to recapture the actual world with realist conventions but creates a new one endowed with magical coherence projecting onto the chaos of reality. There are scenes and situations that blur the line of life and death. There are beams of light that shoot through the unfathomable veils of the fantastic and unreal. As revolutionary as the technique, Pedro Paramo is not only remarkable for pacesetting the exposition through a non-linear structure, but also for its insights into the essence of what a modern novel is, affording both example for much older and more sophisticated western writers and the bulk of non-Western literary practitioners, the emerging avant garde Chinese writers in the late 1980s in particular, to follow and emulate.

How Juan Rulfo came by his magic art, of unquestioned literary merits and of universally critical appraisal remains an inexhaustible topic. Some suggest he has drawn heavily from the indigenous Indian cosmology and philosophy in depth and great value and that he has created a fictional world so much embedded in the Aztecan symbolism, metaphor and allegory inhabited by spectral beings. To the best of my knowledge, ancient Aztecs see a unity of temporal and spatial relationship in all directions, an idea both enigmatic and revelatory.

What makes Juan Rulfo truly impressive is this: apart from being one of the first to have adopted the latest literary theories in vogue in the west, he has blended the native belief systems and cognitive models in his fictional Comala town. He envisages an eternal loop into which time and space being linked in parallel ,life, death and rebirth are cast in a process of circular motion

胡安·鲁尔福的伟大之处还在于他把他所了解的现实世界，出神入化地与这些神奇的、荒诞的、超自然的因素形成了一个完美的整体，也让他的书写永远具有一种当代性和现场感，他笔下的芸芸众生毫无疑问就是墨西哥现实世界中的不同人物，他们真实地生活在被边缘化的社会的最底层，但他们发出的呐喊和其他声音通过胡安·鲁尔福已经传到了世界不同的角落。

我对胡安·鲁尔福充满了好奇，那是因为我在阅读他的作品的时候，他给我带来从未有过的启示以及对自身的思考。从比较文化的角度来看，墨西哥原住民和我们彝族人民有许多相同的地方。

墨西哥人不畏惧死神，诞生和死亡是一个节日的两个部分，他们相信人死后会前往一个名叫"米特兰"的地方，那里既不是天堂也不是地狱，我们彝族人把死亡看成是另一种生命的开始，人死后会前往一个名叫"石姆姆哈"的地方，这个地方在天空和大地之间，那里是一片白色的世界。彝族人认为人死后会留下三魂，一魂会留在火葬地，一魂会跟随祖先回到最后的长眠地，还有一魂会留给后人供奉。

是因为胡安·鲁尔福，我才开始了一次漫长的追寻和回归，那就是让自己的写作与我们民族的精神源头真正续接在一起，也就是从那个时候开始直到今天，我都把自身的写作依托于一个民族广阔深厚的精神背景成为一种自觉。记得我访问墨西哥城的时候，就专门去墨西哥人类学博物馆进行参观，我把这种近似于膜拜的参观从内心看成是对胡安·鲁尔福的敬意，因为我知道从1962年开始他就在土著研究院工作，他的行为和沉默低调的作风，完全是墨西哥山地人的化身。

那次我从墨西哥带回的礼物中最让我珍爱的就是一本胡安·鲁尔福对墨西哥山地和原住民的摄影集，这部充满了悲悯和忧伤的摄影集可以说是他的另一种述说，当我一遍遍凝视墨西哥山地和天空的颜色时，心中不免会涌动着一种隐隐的不可名状的伤感。

which ushers in three different worlds, ie, the hell, the paradise and of course the subterranean realm in Rulfo's mind.

Juan Rulfo's mythical and fantastical perspectives , as commentators aptly put it, project a sense of the complex realities by portraying "fantastical events in an otherwise realistic tone." He brings fables, folk tales, and myths into contemporary social relevance in favor of the socially and economically marginalized strata in the then Mexico, even though he seldom preaches against social abuses.

Juan Rulfe has been an obsession with me, a perennial source of inspiration and enlightenment. From comparative anthropological perspectives, both Yi in southwestern China and aborigines in Mexico share enough traits in common to permit a few generalizations. All display a profound faith in supernatural forces which they believe shape, influence and guide their lives.

Death is not to be feared as birth and death are actually celebrated as two integral parts of a local festivity. The communal stability and sanctity of living rest on a firm conception of an afterworld called Mitran, neither hell nor paradise. Similarly, we Yi people regard death as the beginning of another life. When a Yi ceases to breathe, he sets off to a certain destination called "Symmuha", situated between the sky and the earth, an imaginary white world. To the Yi who cling to ancient mores and values, they have three souls to leave behind upon dying. One soul will remain in the cremation ground. The second will follow a special soul trail to return to the final ancestral resting place, and the last one ,to be worshipped by posterity.

I owe Juan Rulfe a word of gratitude as he prompted me to embark on a long, arduous quest for identity, one to seek my tribal root and reconnect myself with my own cultural beginnings out of which I have come into my own ,a truly Yi poet ,aspiring to identify with and to translate faithfully the realities of Yi life. I still remember during a visit to Mexico City, I went to the Museum of Anthropology as a token of homage to Juan Rulfo ,my own cult of personality as he was known to be on the staff of the institution since 1962, or more specifically, he was in charge of the editorial department of the National Institute for Indigenous Studies, a government agency devoted to the protection and economic improvement of the primitive Indian communities. The meek, un-obtrusive and low-key manner in which he conducts himself is widely deemed as epitomizing the distinctive character and temperament of the Mexican mountain people.

Among the souvenirs brought back home is a photo album, much treasured and valued, by Juan Rulfo who shot the rare photos of native Mexicans by himself. To me he is simply composing a book of fiction in the visual mode. At times lost in the reveries of the melancholic Mexican mountains and sky over and over again, my heart contracts for condolence. Sadness overwhelms me unrestrainedly.

The man and his entire oeuvre are for me an image, clear and erratic , like a black-and-white movies embedded in time in constant motion as he possesses the extraordinary skills and

胡安·鲁尔福这个人以及他的全部写作对于我来说，都是一部记忆中清晰而又飘忽不定的影像，就像一部植入了流动时间的黑白电影，因为胡安·鲁尔福所具有的这种超常的对事物和历史的抽象能力，他恐怕是世界文学史上用如此少的文字，写出了一个国家或者说一个民族隐秘精神史最伟大的人物之一，也许是因为我的孤陋寡闻，在我的阅读经历和范围中，还没有发现有哪一位作家在抽象力、想象力以及能与之相适应的语言能力方面能与其比肩。

而奥克塔维奥·帕斯对于我来说就是一个现实存在，这个存在不会因为他肉体的消失而离开我，他教会我的不是一首诗的写法，而是对所有生命和这个世界的态度，他说过这样一段话："我不认为诗歌可以改变世界。诗歌可以给我们启示，向我们揭示关于我们人的秘密，可以为我们带来愉悦。特别是，它可以展示另一个世界，展示现实的另一副面孔。我不能生活在没有诗的世界里，因为诗歌拯救了时间、拯救了瞬间；时间没有把诗歌杀死，没剥夺它的活力。"

作为诗人，奥克塔维奥·帕斯虽然不是第一个，但确实是最好的将拉美古老史前文化、西班牙征服者的文化和现代政治社会文化融为一体写出经典作品的划时代的诗人，他的不朽长诗《太阳石》，既是对美洲原住民阿兹特克太阳历的礼赞，同时也是对生命、自我、非我、死亡、虚无、存在、意义、异化以及性爱的诗性呈现，他同样是20世纪为数不多的能将政治、革命、批判性融为一体，对现实的干预、对自己诗的写作把握得最为适度的大师之一，难怪他曾说过近似于这样的话，政治是同另一些人共处的艺术，而我的一切作品都与另一种东西有关。

我们知道20世纪是一个社会革命和艺术革命都风起云涌的时代，在很长一个阶段不同的意识形态所形成的两大阵营，无论是在社会理想方面，还是在价值观念方面，以及对重大历史事件的判断看法，都是水火不相容的，而在那样一个时期，大多数拉美重要诗人和作家都是不容置疑的左翼人士，当然这也包括奥克塔维奥·帕斯。

intellectual equipment much needed to symbolize and objectify his people's dilemmas, thoughts and actions whose deeper meanings remain hitherto hidden even to themselves . The combination of historiographical rigor, stylistic precision, verbal economy, and psychological insight into the generalized human misery, the plight of his country per se, has been rarely ,if ever, surpassed in Latin American fiction. Apology for my possible ignorance, due to a limited reading purview on my part, I have yet to find a single writer who can match him in intellect, imagination, and succinct mode of expression in world literature.

And Octavio Paz is a ubiquitous presence, a master of modern narrative techniques in an era that sees a general boom of poetic art. He is held high in my esteem not only because he has taught me much as a poet but also because he reaffirms powerfully his faith in sanctity of life and poetry as ultimately redemptive .In fact, as he himself pointed out in an interview, he was basically a optimist: "I don't think poetry can change the world. Poetry gives us inspiration, reveals to us the secrets of heart, fragility of life, the dilemmas of intimacy. It both entertains and educates. In particular, it creates another supra-sensible world. Show us the other face of reality. I can't live in a world without poetry because poetry salvages time and the moment: it doesn't kill it, it doesn't deprive it of its vitality."

As a poet, Octavio Paz is not the first, but he is certainly the best writer who ,by presenting an epoch-making, all embracing picture of the social ,economic and political reality, achieves heightened insights and providing important perspective on the fatal collision of the experiences of Pre-historic Latin America, Spanish colonialism and modern Hispanic world at the mercy of recurrent violence ,civil strife, economic stagnation, moral and intellectual backwardness. Epic in scope, his immortal poem, Sun Stone, is a hymn of praise to the Aztec Solar Calendar of Native Americans ,including sophisticated discussions of philosophical and theological as well as cultural and sociological subjects on life, self, non-self, death, nothingness, existence, meaning, alienation, and sexual love. He is also one of the few masters in the twentieth century who can offer sad yet affirmative views of life in all its complexity, to be admired for neither sacrificing political engagement nor compromising his artistic integrity. No wonder he once commented on politics as an art of co-existing with others and he further adds that his work points to the side of others.

We know that the 20th century is an age swollen with social revolutions and artistic fashions at one swoop. At a time, nay, for an extended span of time, the monstrous absurdity and division of our world was such that even half of the peopling was pitted against the other half based upon a set of artifices and man-made ideologies. It was a global situation that destroyed man's spirit, his spontaneous impulses towards life admitting no doubt, hesitation ,even half measures. The name of the game was unquestioning political commitment to either one cause or another without even blinking one's eyes to the extent that most of the important poets and writers in Latin America were standing up to be counted in the leftist camping. Of course, Octavio Paz was no exception.

但是，也是从那个时候开始，奥克塔维奥·帕斯就表现出了思想家、哲人、知识分子的道德风骨和独立思考的智慧能力，他对任何一个重大政治事件的看法和判断，都不是从所谓的集体政治文化的概念出发，而是从人道和真实出发去揭示出真相和本质。1968年10月20日在特拉特洛尔科广场发生的屠杀学生的事件，就遭到了他的强烈谴责，他也因为这个众所周知的原因辞去了驻印度大使的职务。

可以说，是奥克塔维奥·帕斯在墨西哥开创并确立了一种独立思想的批评文化，打破了"不左即右"二元对立的局面，他的这种表达政治异见的鲜明态度，甚至延伸到了他对许多国际重大事件的判断，比如引起整个西方和拉美左派阵营分裂的托洛茨基被暗杀事件，就是他首先提出了对另一种极权以及反对精神自由的质疑，也因此他与巴勃罗·聂鲁达等朋友分道扬镳，他们的友谊直到晚年才得以恢复。

他创办的杂志《多元》《转折》，是拉丁美洲西班牙语世界不同思想进行对话和交锋的窗口，他一直高举着自由表达思想和反对一切强权的人道主义旗帜，他主办过一个又一个有关这个世界未来发展，并且带有某种预言性的主题讨论，这些被聚集在一起的闪耀着思想光芒的精神遗产，对今天不同国度的知识分子同样有着宝贵的参照和借鉴作用。

奥克塔维奥·帕斯是最早发现并醒悟到美洲左翼革命以及这一革命开始将矛头对准自己的人之一，他的此类言论甚至涉及古巴革命后的政治现实、南美军人政权的独裁统治、各种形式游击组织的活动、东欧社会主义在全球范围内的境况，以及对美国所倡导的极端物质主义和实用主义外交政策精准批判。他发表于1985年的《国家制度党，其临终时分》一文，对该党在奇瓦瓦州操纵选举的舞弊行为进行了揭露，这一勇敢的举动使墨西哥大众的民主意识被进一步唤醒。

在这里我必须说到他的不朽之作，当然也是人类的不朽之作《孤独的迷宫》，是因为它的存在我们才能在任何一个时候，瞬间进入墨西哥的灵魂。《孤独的迷宫》是

But our Octavio Paz ,the philosopher, moralist and thinker in him, affords a detachment that makes it possible to control his passionate reactions to the brutality of events in contrast to most other engaged Latin American writers. He obviously avoids taking his stand upon the insecure foundations of political or cultural collectivism .He does not easily quarrel with those who cause his anguished antagonism for antagonism's sake .With him, things and events are humanized and individualized. In a world submerged by madness, he still deems truth a greater friend above any ideological fidelity. And for truth's sake, he was strongly equivocal in condemning the massacre of students at the Tlatelolco Square on October 20, 1968 and for which He resigned his post as ambassador to India ,a price paid for a noble gesture of civil disobedience.

The shift to a more rational and objective plane of vision becomes increasingly evident as Octavio Paz has been credited with singlehandedly initiating a non-partisan cultural status quo in which polemically leftist or rightist arguments were frowned upon in favor of measured, critical thinking and independent dissent in major international events .Take one example, the assassination of Trotsky that polarized the entire Western and Latin American leftists, he was the first to voice his query about the questionable character of the triumphant marches of totalitarianism at the expense of freedom of conscience even that meant being alienated from friends like Pablo Neruda and we are told that their intimate affinity was not restored until his later years.

The two journals "Taller" and "El Hijo Projigo" he founded ,by hoisting the haughty standard of freedom of expression and humanitarianism to defy any brand of authoritarianism, have proven to be an ideal venue where different and even hostile opinions were subjected to the rational Socratic inquiry among intellectuals in the Latin American world. Add to these vital discursive attempts are a series of seminars he hosted as to the possible scenarios of our world in a quarry and disarray ,and the opinions he put forth , the prophetic accuracy and all the virtues of intellectual honesty typical of him, a knowledgeable reader will discern and detect, forms part of his more endurable legacy , radiating with metaphysical light, leaving a rich burning, enlightening flavor behind.

Octavio Paz was one of the earliest clairvoyants who realized the stupidity of unabashedly romancing with leftist approaches to all the social and political ills plaguing Latin America. Deliberate misunderstanding, if not outright ignorance, characterized the leftist perceptions of the fatal continent. To do the job, he bothered himself to pull back the veils of myth to glimpse reality and even pointed fingers at himself. His harsh remarks did not spare the then supposedly salutary Cuban revolution and the popular military dictatorship because of their physical strength, of larger, more intricate political maneuvering, the various forms of guerrilla organizations who have had their opportunities to effect change, the reformers, theirs, yet all failing to institute development, to solve the major continental problems. He also called into question of the so called progressiveness of the Eastern European socialist bloc. His indictment of the cynicism of

墨西哥民族的心灵史、精神史和社会史，它不是一般意义上的墨西哥民族心理和文化现象的罗列展示，而是打开了一个古老民族的孤独面具，将这一复杂精神现象的内在结构和本质呈现给了我们。

在一次演讲中帕斯这样告诉听众："作家就是要说那些说不出的话，没说过的话，没人愿意或者没人能说的话。因此所有伟大的文学作品并非电力高压线而是道德、审美和批评的高压线。它的作用在于破坏和创造。文学作品与可怖的人类现实和解的强大能力并不低于文学的颠覆力。伟大的文学是仁慈的，使一切伤口愈合，疗治所有精神上的苦痛，在情绪最低落的时刻照样对生活说是。"

我要说，伟大的奥克塔维奥·帕斯是这样说的，同样他也是这样做的，他用波澜壮阔的一生和无所畏惧的独立精神，为人类做出了巨大的贡献，并为我们所有的后来者树立了光辉的典范。

从胡安·鲁尔福到奥克塔维奥·帕斯，这是属于墨西哥，同样也属于全人类的必须被共同敬畏和记忆的精神遗产，它们是一种现实，是一种象征，更重要的是它们还是一种创造，也正因为这种充满了梦幻的创造，在太阳之国的墨西哥谷地，每天升起的太阳才照亮了生命和死亡的面具，而胡安·鲁尔福和奥克塔维奥·帕斯灵魂的影子，也将在那里年复一年地飘浮，永远不会从人类的视线中消失。

the materialistic and pragmatic foreign policy advocated by the United States prove unanswerable and convincing, and perhaps, because of abundant examples of USA misbehaviors lingering longer in the public mind than its acts of benevolence. His article entitled: "The State Institution Party in 1985, at the end of its life," was a debilitating exposé of the party's fraud at manipulating election in Chihuahua, a courageous move which further purified the Mexican public's awareness of democracy.

Here I must reserve my greatest laudation to his monumental work, not only in my estimation, of course, the immortal work of mankind, "The Labyrinth of Loneliness," personally the open sesame to enter into the Mexican soul in an instant. "Lonely Maize" presents a vast synthesis of social, economic and political evils bedeviling his home country, remarkable for its insights into the workings of the Mexican mind. We understand Mexico better for having read this book as he imparts not only the grisly stark reality, the tormented mentality of a strife-torn nation whose intense wrestling with a hostile natural and social milieu leave them frustrated and alienated, but also unmasks an ancient people condemned to solitude through the humanistic elements of aesthetic perception and empathy, the essence of Mexican culture graphically conveyed.

In a speech, Paz reiterates the tenet fundamental to his work: "A writer is supposed to say something nobody has said before, or cares to say, or unable or even dare not say it. Therefore all great literary works are not electric power lines literally but so literarily in terms of their moral and aesthetic values, designed both to destroy and create. The power of a work of art to resolve and reconcile human feuds and hostility equals that of subverting reality. Great literature is merciful, healing all wounds and embalming all spiritual agonies ,affirming life at its lowest ebb and flow."

I make bold to declare our great Octavio Paz means every word of what he says. His avid interest in improving human affairs, his strength of character and devotion, his daunting and incorruptible judgment are of a kind rarely joined in an ordinary being of blood and flesh, a leading and towering personality vital and significant for the course of history, greater than his purely artistic achievements.

Juan Rolfo and Octavio Paz belong to Mexico ,to all the world, looked up to in universal awe and cherished in popular memory. Both iconic figures, they tell us more of humanity, credited justifiably as an alternative source of artistic creativity , dedicated to reflecting the dominant intellectual concerns and explaining to his people how and why their world came to be the way it is today. We also know more of Mexico which has little to do with change of the seasons or the return of the stars, Because of the grandness of their literary achievements and the seminal and revolutionary influence upon contemporary poetry and fiction the world over, the sun rising every day in the solar valley of the country called Mexico illuminates the mask of life and death, while the souls of Juan Rulfo and Octavio Paz will hover over the human scene without fail, forever looming large on the horizon of our earth.

光明与鹰翅的天石

在 2017 中国凉山西昌邛海丝绸之路国际诗歌周开幕式上的致辞

2017 年 10 月 10 日

各位女士、各位先生，各位同胞，来自世界各地的诗人朋友们：

在这个美好而充满诗意的季节，我们如期迎来了第二届中国凉山西昌邛海"丝绸之路"国际诗歌周的召开，在这里请允许我代表中国作家协会并以本届诗歌周组委会主席的名义，热忱地欢迎来自不同国家和地区的诗人光临这一诗歌的盛会，并预祝本届诗歌周获得圆满的成功。同时，还要借此机会向为本届诗歌周的筹备安排付出了辛勤努力的各相关机构和个人表示最衷心的感谢。

朋友们，今天的世界仍然是一个动荡而充满了不确定的世界，人类如何选择自己的未来同样是生活在这个地球上不同地域的人们共同面临的问题，为了构建一个更加合理更有利于和平与发展的国际新秩序，需要今天的人类在国际政治的层面之外，还应该从更多的方面贡献出智慧以及更富有建设性的意见，只有这样我们才可能在面对重重危机来临的时候，有效做到求同存异、共谋发展。

中国国家主席习近平所提出的"一带一路"宏伟构想，正是站在人类社会发展全局的高度，为真正构建起人类命运共同体而绘制的一幅面向未来的蓝图。也正因为此，由不同的文化作为深厚基础所进行的对话和互动才更显示出强大的力量，而诗歌作为不同民族精神文化的精髓，并没有远离我们的现实和生活，毫无疑问，在今天它已经再一次成为不同国家、不同民族、不同文化背景、不同价值取向的人们进行沟通和交流的最有效的方式之一，诗歌依然在发挥着介入生活和现实的作用。

朋友们，就在此时此刻，我想到了"光明与鹰翅的天石"这样一句充满了象征和

Heavenly Stones Made of Eagles Wings and Light
Remarks at the Opening Ceremony of the 2nd Liangshan, Xichang Silk Road Intl Poetry Week
10th, October, 2017

Ladies, gentlemen, my Yi compatriots, fellow poets home and abroad:

It is my pleasure to welcome you, hic et nunc, On behalf of the organizing committee, in my capacity As both deputy chairman of All China Writers Association and chairman of the organizing committee, to the 2nd Liangshan, Xichang Silk Road Intl Poetry Week on the occasion of this grand opening ceremony. I, for one, wish for a most successful operation of the week. My heartfelt gratitude must be also registered here for the wonderful myriad preparatory work put in by all individuals, institutions and the organizing staff to make this event a reality.

Friends, ours is a world characterized by turmoil and uncertainty. How we humans, inhabiting different quarters of this world, choose the life we lead in the forthcoming future is the common challenge before us all. Other than on the political planes whereupon politicians wrack their brains to come out with schemes and programs as how to construct a new world order amenable to justice ,peace and sustainable development, we need also draw in the wisdom and insight from other sectors of the society to better cope with the crisis lurking ahead and co-develop while seeking common ground on major issues and reserving differences on minor ones.

The One Belt ,One Road Initiative , proposed by Chinese President Xi Jinping is a most visionary blueprint to maneuver , hitch and move our world towards the direction with a shared future, woe or joy, rain or sunshine. Because of this, dialogues and interactions involving various cultures, races and religions have the potential to iron out the differences and oil the wheels of history. Poetry, as the best flower of each culture, more than any other social or political parameters, stands to create a status quo out of a plethora of problems, either racial or religious or cultural in origin. Poetry has the unique power to alleviate mistrust and generate a feeling of brotherhood and fraternity where only hate and injustice existed before.

Friends, the above lapse conjures up a sophisticated metaphor of "heavenly stones upon eagles wings and light" in my mind. Look, the ageless sun has never failed , on its chariot across the immense vaults of the sky to perform its daily patrol over this Yi region of ranged mountains,

隐喻的诗句，因为在这片天空与群山静默如初的疆域里，亘古不变的太阳依然在巡视着大地上的万物和生命，时间的光影同样在周而复始地行走过黑暗与光明所构筑的世界，如果你相信所有的存在都不是孤立的个体，而同时你还相信所有的存在都有其隐秘的来源，那么你的心灵和思想才可能与你眼前的这个并非虚拟的现实融为一体。

从这个意义而言，我在根本上是肯定和坚信，哪怕一粒微尘，它的运行毫无疑问也是宏大宇宙的一个部分，而一粒微尘本身其实就是一个宇宙，无论它多么微小，但它所承载的信息和能量，都是我们无法用简单的数据去衡定的。

当我们伫立在苍茫的大地心无旁骛地去聆听，我们就能从时间的深处听见风的呓语和光的赞词，由此我们也才有可能在瞬间目睹并接近真理的化身，难怪伟大的德语诗人荷尔德林在自己的诗歌中，始终把形而上的力量和具有灵性的语言紧密地融为一体，从而使他的每一句诗都如同神授的箴言。

在浩如烟海的彝族历史典籍中，探索生命和宇宙的形成一直是最为核心的主题，其中既包含了事物之间的相互关系，同时也揭示了生命的无常以及死亡作为规律的存在。作为诗人我想告诉大家，当我们今天承接下来的是如此丰富、厚重的伟大传统时，我们除了感到无比的幸福和骄傲之外，更重要的是，我们还必须树立在当下创造新的壮丽史诗的雄心，否则我们将有愧于这片土地上世代英雄谱系中的勇士们所创造的业绩。

我无法想象但这一切都是现实，当然这也给我们这个崇拜祖先和英雄的民族，找到了继续坚守自己的信仰和传统最直接的理由，不用在这里去一一陈述，我们的先人给我们留下了这个世界上最多的创世史诗，它们的名字已经深深地镌刻在了我们民族的集体记忆中，《查姆》《勒俄特依》《宇宙人文论》《彝族源流》《洪水泛滥》《阿细的先基》《阿黑西尼摩》《倮罗巫经》《梅葛》，也已经成为当今人类共同的精神财富。尤其是当我们面对这些伟大的传统和遗产时，任何溢美之词都会显得苍白无力，我以为我们只能勇敢地承担起我们这一代人的责任和使命，才可能创造出无愧于这一伟大诗歌传统的经典作品。

当然，生活在这个世界不同地域的诗人们，也同样肩负着传承和弘扬各自民族

silent and speechless from the primordial times ,flora and fauna, life forms bustling and hustling making their homely rounds. Likewise, light and shadow of time have never ceased flickering upon the sublunary world of light and darkness. Only if you are convinced of the ultimate fact of all living things being not isolated atomic substances and issuing from one common hidden source, can your heart and soul merge with the reality before your eyes that is in no way virtual and fairy.

What do we make of this occultist revelation? Well, personally I am unswervingly of the opinion that even a grain of dust acts and is acted upon as part of the overarching cosmos. The idea is, tiny and infinitesimal a grain of dust might be, it is nevertheless, self-sufficient, a cosmos carrying its own share of energy and information,   defying any reductionist attempt in the positivistic vein .

Left alone to a quiet corner of this vast domain of ours, I sometimes pause and take stock, my eyes shut and my ears open, to hear a distinct, though somewhat obliterated, soliloquy of wind in praise of light coming from the depths of time, the incarnation of truth we are on the threshold of witnessing. No wonder the great German poet Holderlin, in his poems, always identifies the supernatural as heralding the creation of a sacred spiritual language worthy of poetry. He is best read as a poet divinely inspired.

Yi is such a nation of history, culture and tradition that as one of the 9 million descendants, I am rightly proud of the oceanic repository of historic texts ,mostly epics,   left to us by our ancestors and I fully embrace our forefathers recalcitrant and relentless cosmological penchant, among other things, our deeply felt interrelatedness of humans with all creatures as well as our due respect for the law of impermanence of life and death as a precondition of mortal existence. As a poet inheriting such grand intangible matrimony, a sense of pride and being fully blessed swells up that I feel entitled to enhance my Yi heritage by initiating a process of renaissance, revitalization and regeneration worthy of the Yi spirituality.

Legacies do not just happen and persist. To be meaningful, we must keep negotiating between them and our contemporary life and carry on with the great task our ancestors have so nobly pioneered and advanced. For a people famed for hero worship , we draw inexhaustible inspiration from our animistic faith and tradition made up of an unrivalled wealth of creation epics such as: Hnewo teyy, Asei-po seiji, Amo xinimo, Chamu, Meige, Shamanic Scripture of the Lolos, On the Cosmos and Human Learning, Origins of the Yi People, The All-Engulfing Flood, all being now common assets of mankind,   commending themselves despite adulators or debunkers. Yet, this is no time for wistful thinking or nostalgic retreat. Culture changes, shifts and perishes if it does not adapt with time .This is the moment to recharge ourselves and set off on a new mission to be undertaken by our generation, that is, to actually quarry new sky stones, worthy of Yi legend, fit for the vaults of heaven.

Of course, poets from across the world are all born with the mandate to create their own heavenly stones upon eagle wings and light. Under our pens should flow poems that reach into the

诗歌传统的使命和责任，是否能真正写出划时代的具有人类整体高度的诗歌精品，都是我们作为诗人共同追求的目标。

　　诗人朋友们，我们只能把诗歌的火炬烧得更亮，当正义战胜邪恶成为不可抗拒的法则，而每一个人真的都拥有神圣的自由和尊严，那么，请相信光明与鹰翅的天石就会在我们的前方，也正因为此，我们迈向明天和未来的脚步才不会停止，永远不会停止！谢谢大家！

hearts of our people and make them laugh, cry, feel and think. Our voices should be raised anew in celebration of human glory and toil, our passionate search for justice, our tender loves and profoundest longings.

    Dear friends, let's ignite our torches to light our way, convinced of the invincible justice prevailing upon a globe "with limping sway disabled" eventually, loyal perennially to the dual principles of sanctity and freedom of each individual simply because the heavenly stones so much treasured are out there for us to be hit upon and quarried. Let this be realized among men that our footsteps forward will not be halted and reversed on our way towards a promising tomorrow. Thank you.

诗歌与光明涌现的城池

在 2017 年成都国际诗歌周开幕式上的演讲

2017 年 9 月 13 日

我在这里说的成都，既是现实世界中的成都，同时也是幻想世界中的成都，尤其是当我们把一座城市与诗歌联系在一起的时候，这座城市便在瞬间成为一种精神和感性的集合体，也可以说当我们从诗歌的纬度去观照成都时，这座古老的城市便像梦一样浮动起来。我去过这个世界上许多的国家，也有幸地到过不少富有魅力的城市，如果你要问我在这个世界上，有哪些城市与诗歌的关系最为紧密，或者说这些城市其本身就是诗歌的一部分，那么我会毫不犹豫地告诉你，那就是法国的巴黎和中国的成都，当然对我的这种看法和观点，一定会有人不同意，甚至持相反的意见。

需要说明的是，我说巴黎和成都的内在精神更具有神秘的诗性，并不仅仅是说在历史上有许多重要的诗人曾经生活在这里，有许多无论是在中国诗歌史上，还是在世界诗歌史上的重要事件在此发生，毋庸讳言，这些当然是这两个城市所拥有的诗歌记忆的重要组成部分。

巴黎不用我在这里赘述，最让人捉摸不透的是，在漫长的中国历史上，成都都是一个在诗的繁荣上从未有过长时间衰竭的城市，当然我说的这种衰竭是在更大的时间段落内进行比较的，就唐朝而言，可以说它是中国诗歌的黄金时代，如果我们做粗略统计，那个时期的伟大诗人李白、杜甫、白居易、岑参、刘禹锡、高适、元稹、贾岛、李商隐、温庭筠、"初唐四杰"等都来到过蜀地，许多人还长期在成都滞留居住，诗圣杜甫就两次逗留成都，时间长达三年零九个月，留下了两百多首描写成都的诗歌。

A City Hemmed in with Radiant Beams of Poetry
Address at the Opening Ceremony of 2017 Chengdu Intl Poetry Week
13th, September, 2017

    This ancient city of Cheng Du under discussion, with no aesthetic appeal in its modern contours notwithstanding, is very special in the sense of being both sublunary and fairy, locus of sensibility and spirit, taking wings to the skies instantly by alchemies of imagination, when we attempt to associate things urban with the poetic side of human beings, especially to probe into the fortuitous converging of its physical topography and metaphoric coordinates. A widely travelled man, I have roamed among the many charming cities of many countries on the planet, if I am approached with similar questions like "which city do you believe is mostly akin in ethos, in aura of enchantment to poetry?"My answer out of hand would be Chengdu in China and Paris of France. Some, I am aware, might not agree to my pride and prejudice, as there is no accounting for taste, so the saying goes.

    It is greatly to be debated on my part that both Cheng Du and Paris seem to be possessed with some inner ethos or mystery of sensibility qualified to be called capitals of poetry, not only because Chengdu has, over centuries, produced , and been home to a dozen of great poets and a few major artistic movements, that have impinged substantially upon literary histories of both China and the world. The near-cult status accorded to poetry has justifiably lulled Chinese into believing Chengdu is a city famed for the depth and sophistication of its poetic heritage.

    Paris, of course ,has its own share of laureates. What has perennially intrigued me is that Chengdu has continually and continuously radiated a nationwide image of inexhaustible poetic creativity, flaunting an envious continuity of tradition even since the city was born 4th century BC. While Tang, the golden of the most golden ages for Chinese poetry ,saw an extraordinary efflorescence of poetic blossoms, Chengdu has unbelievably never been short of good poets who have chronicled the China experience ,the mutations of the human condition, joie de vivre or the human idiocies of this world. Indeed Chengdu has beckoned to an awesome array of genius, Li Bai , Du Fu, Bai Juyi, Cen Shen, Liu Yuxi, Gao Shi, Yuan Zhen, Jia Dao, Li Shangyin, Wen Tingyun, not to mention the four talents of the early Tang, many of whom have sojourned here and Du Fu, our

从某种意义来讲，蜀地成了不同历史时期许多诗人，在诗歌和精神上的栖居地以及停止流亡避难的另一个故乡。难怪诗仙李白在《上皇西巡南京歌(其二)》中写出了如此经典的诗句："九天开出一成都，万户千门入画图。草树云山如锦绣，秦川得及此间无。"李白本身就出生于蜀地，我以为他对成都的赞叹和热爱，并不仅仅完全来源于对这片山水之地的乡情，而是作为一个诗人对这座汇聚着深厚人文历史的城市的理解和洞悉。

同样我们还知道，中国历史上最早的一部词总集《花间集》就出现在成都，时间是后蜀广政三年(940年)，由赵崇祚编集，其时间跨度大约有一个世纪，作品的数量达到五百首。虽然这些作者并不限于后蜀一地，但这一影响后来中国诗词形成更大繁荣的前奏，就发生在公元10世纪30年代到11世纪40年代的一百多年中，最为重要的是中国抒情诗词伟大传统的形成，也正是在那个时期达到了从未有过的高度。

在历史上蜀地也曾经遭遇过多次的战乱和政权的无端更替，正如古人常说的那样一句话"天下未乱蜀先乱，天下已治蜀未治"，但与整个中国别的地域相比，蜀地更多的时候还是丰衣足食，自然灾害也少有发生，政治权力和平民百姓的生活都趋于稳定，特别是千里沃野以成都为中心的平原地带，可以说是中国农耕文明最精细、发达，同时也是持续得最长的地方。

正因为此，古代的许多中国诗人都以游历寻访蜀地作为自己的一个夙愿和向往，其中还有一个重要的原因，就是千百年来蜀地似乎孕育了一种诗性的气场，它特殊的地理环境和能把时间放慢的市井与乡村生活，毫无疑问是无数诗人颠沛流离之后，灵魂和肉体所能获得庇护的最佳选择。我不是在这里想象和美化蜀地不同历史阶段的生活，而是想告诉大家四川的确是一个神奇的地方，尤其是在漫长的封建农耕文明的时代，中国没有一个地区能像四川那样完全能做到自给自足，粮食、棉帛、铜铁、石材、食盐、毛皮、茶叶、美酒等等，可以说应有尽有。

当然任何事物都有它的两面性，我们也可以看到许多出生于蜀地的文化巨人，他们最终成为巨人也大都是走出了夔门才被世人所知晓的，但不能不说这方土地的

Poet Saint, loyal repeat visitor, made Cheng Du home and lingered in retreat for three years and nine months, leaving a legacy of 200 poems extolling the virtues of common folks here and around.

In a sense, Chengdu has been the spiritual home of poets wandering or in exile. Hark to the Poet Immortal when Li Bai sings up: "From nine celestial vaunts emerges Chengdu, Where towns and villages loom like scrolls. Grass, trees, clouds and mountains all as chic as brocade, Whose beauty beyond compare anything China proper offers." What Li Bai so evocatively sums up does not strike only a personal note, as he is among others , more appreciative of the subtleties and richness of culture and nature of Cheng Du both as resident and poet.

Equally worth of note is the first anthology of Ci Poems ever to be published in Cheng Du which dates from 940, compiled by scholar official Zhao Chongzhen, inclusive of five hundred Ci poems ,authored by poets , many being non-natives, spanning over one century long, foretelling the dawn of a larger renaissance in days to come We are talking about another peak performance of Chinese lyrical poets in the Song dynasty in the brewing. The anthology turns out to be a major cataclysm in triggering the greatest outpourings of lyricism sweeping 270 years Song times.

In a way, Cheng Du has been historically turbulent, surviving devastations of many a renegade independent state and runaway kingdom skirmishing with one another or defying central authority. "Order and peace breaks down first in Shu and restores the last in the country." So the ancients aptly put it.Yet, in all fairness, for much of its eventful history, Cheng Du reveled in its prosperity, grateful for the strategic geography and cultural splendor which had elevated it to one of the commercial and cultural centers in medieval and contemporary China alike. Agricultural innovations, the installation of the Dujiang Yan Irrigation System, in particular, opened up Cheng Du Plain to intensive farming, which quickly transformed the area into an economic base, a cornerstone of Chinese society .Thanks to this and others, Cheng Du leapt to periodic prominence at several major national crisis's.

Where nowadays tourists predominate, Cheng Du has always been rendevousing with artists and poets as it has been celebrated in so many poems, stories, anecdotes, paintings for one important reason: remoteness from the whirlwinds of Chinese politics in Central Plains and the famed nonchalance of local population who are nicely laid back, reclining on bamboos armchairs, idling away all day long ,indulgent in their staid teahouse culture and gentle pace of living. Such perfect location and slowing down of life provide the best sanctuary for many wondering and troubled souls looking for a temporary relief. I am not idealizing the lives of struggling poor artists and nobility of peasantry. I am merely reminding you at certain historical moments, Sichuan was the place to be for some poets fleeing wars and other disasters , and indeed, for centuries past , feudal, agrarian, Sichuan has been much sustained and contained within a considerable measure of self sufficiency in terms of produce and supply of food ,cotton, cloth, copper, iron, salt, fur, tea and wine-all being prerequisites for bare subsistence of lower caste and the elite in their attempt to

确是人杰地灵,唐代的李白、宋代的苏轼三父子是其中最有代表性的,就是到了近现代,在中国文学、文化史上产生过重要影响的作家、诗人和画家就有郭沫若、巴金、李劼人、张大千、沙汀、艾芜等等,如果要排下去这个名单还会很长,而在中国近现代历史上蜀地出生的政治家和军事家更是比比皆是,他们其中的一些人深刻地改变了中国和人类历史的进程,中国改革开放的总设计师邓小平就是最重要的代表人物。最有意味的是,这些伟大的人物大都在成都读过书,有的就出生在成都,有的在成都度过了人生中一段或长或短的美好岁月。

中国新诗的开拓者和旗手郭沫若,1910年2月就来到了成都,后来入读于四川高等学堂,当时也在成都就读的、后来名闻遐迩的小说大师李劼人,也因为这片地域所给予他的丰厚滋养,其一生的创作都把蜀地作为自己永恒的主题。伟大的人道主义者巴金,这位出生于成都正通顺街李公馆里的作家,他的名作《家》《春》《秋》,所记录的是成都一段令人悲伤而又对明天充满向往的梦一样的生活。

画家张大千1938年为躲避战乱生活在成都,他创作的《蜀山图》《蜀江图》等佳作,其作品所透出的品质和韵味,完全是一个蜀中画家才可能具有的通灵和大气象,他的大写意和汪洋肆意的泼墨,直接催生了中国画的又一次巨大变革。

我说成都和巴黎是东方和西方两个在气质上最为接近的城市,还因为这两座城市在延续传统的同时,还对异质文化有着强大的包容和吸收能力,他们都有一种让诗人和艺术家能完全融入其中的特殊氛围以及状态,有不少文化学者和社会学家并非固执地认为,有些城市从一开始就是为诗人、艺术家以及思想者而构筑的。

不用再去回顾历史,就发生在20世纪70年代末80年代初的中国现代诗歌运动来讲,蜀地诗群就是唯一一个能与北京现代诗群难分伯仲的诗人群体。当然,这一影响深远的现代诗歌运动,其中心就在成都,对外面的人而言这一切就如同一个诗歌所铸造的神话,当时诗人数量极多,出现的诗歌流派更是令人目不暇接,毫不夸张地说,现在在中国诗坛最活跃、最具有影响力的诗人中,起码有数十位就是从蜀地走出来的,从他们的一些回忆文章,以及中国现代诗歌运动研究专家的论述中,我们都

create the good life.

Of course, such self sufficiency bred naturally a bias of outlook and petty-minded Philistinism. For one thing, local budding talents, as a rule, don't get scouted and recognized unless they move on beyond the secluded territory. This is, of course, not to deny Sichuan is a source of great men. Li Bai in the Tang dynasty, three father and sons of the Sus of the Song dynasty, are but four of the most illustrious poets on hand. In contemporary China, a few giants, such as poet Guo Moruo, novelists Ba Jin and Li Jieren, master painter Zhang daqian, short story writers Sha Din and Ai Wu have illuminated the night of Chinese culture and the list of lesser artists and poets can go on without end. Reaffirming the global weight of Sichuan, one must mention the name of Deng Xiaoping who, having initiated the late 1979s' reform and opening up to the world, the classic way to guarantee distinction and eminence if followed assiduously, has once for all put China on the map of one of the foremost places among the relatively well to do, advanced civilizations of the world, say, in a brief space of three decades. The rise of these great minds and the vital roles they have played all take us back to the beginnings of greatness, that is, they were all born here, got educated or spent a certain portion of their memorable adolescence or youth in this beloved city of ours.

We are rightly proud of Chengdu as our native Guo Moruo's launching pad to blaze the path of New Poetry a hundred years ago. In 1910, Guo first landed In Chengdu, enlisted as acolyte of Sichuan Higher Learning Institute and self groomed himself as the future standard bearer of New Poetry. Novelist Li Jieren's lifelong passions and theme are this land that has endowed him with a pathos and lyricism that earns him the renown of master of regionalism, on a par with Lao She. Great humanitarian writer Ba Jin came from a family of officials and scholars, residing in the grand Li Mansion in Zhengtongshun Street and rose to fame by his trilogy of Family, Spring and Autumn, half autobiography, half revelation, all being classic tales of social oppression despairing of a past beyond redemption and dreaming of a tantalizing future out of reach. For a blistering look at the decadent society, Ba Jin offers the remedy of compassion, love and magnanimity.

Master Painter Zhang daqian, fleeing war torn interior China, settled down in Chengdu in 1938 to complete his masterpieces Mountains in Shu and Rivers of Shu. In reaffirmation of traditional landscape techniques, Zhang expanded and finally exploded into dynamic fury, ink, movement, color, line-that are ingeniously patterned but in such cluttered abundance as to appear unprecedented-almost, by hindsight, tantamount to a revolution in spearheading Chinese painting in sync with post impressionist trends in France. Zhang's artistic activity in Chengdu attests ultimately to his genius in pacesetting Chinese expression of artistic styles in modern times..

When I speak of Chengdu and Paris In the same breath, they both to me demonstrate a continuity of tradition while evincing an ability to learn and absorb things foreign and new to a preeminent degree, an aura enticing and luring poets and artists with rank alien cultural background to make Chengdu their conform zone. Some cultural critics and sociologists postulate,

能发现一个有趣的现象,这些诗人毫无例外地几乎都在成都居住生活过,事实上这一切都变成了一种现实,就是成都毫无争议地被公认为中国现代诗歌运动最重要的两个城市之一,成都又一次穿越了历史和时间,成为中国诗歌史上始终保持了诗歌地标的重镇。

你说这一切难道都是偶然的吗?我的回答,那当然不是。如果说一个人的身上会携带有某种独特气质的传承,一个族群的集体意识中有无法被抹去的符号记忆,那一座古老的城市难道就没有一种隐秘的精神文化密码被传递到今天?我们的回答同样是肯定的,否则我们就不会也不可能去解析一个并非谜一般的问题,那就是为什么从古代到今天,成都这座光辉的城池与中国诗人结下的生命之源是如此深厚。尤其是本届成都国际诗歌周的如期成功举办,再一次证明了我对这座光荣的诗的城市的认识和判断是正确的,我相信来自世界不同国家的诗人们,最终也会得出这样一个同样的结论。朋友们,在我们的眼前你们所看见的这座诗歌与光明涌现的城池,就是成都!

not without good reasons, that no city was conceived and built for poets, thinkers and artists. The title of the capital of poetry is up for the grabbing.

For those familiar with Chinese poetry, an overview of what happened culturally in the late 1970s and the early 1980s when Chinese poetry, deriving inspiration from French or Anglophone or Spanish models, began to free from the orthodox rigidity of Soviet realism, whose far-reaching and profound repercussions are still felt today, will lead one to one bold claim Chengdu has staked out: as an alternate center of stylistic innovation together with Beijing perhaps in complementary pairs, like Li Bai and Du Fu, a phenomenon deserving pondering as it must represent some historic need to keep human faculties in balance. Hence the legend due to two essential facts, ie, Chengdu's poets population growing ever beyond count and the poetic schools mushrooming to such unfettered scale, as to concretize and corroborate this city's power and status ,if not greater than that of Beijing. It is not boastful at all to say over two dozen of established contemporary Chinese poets ,still clinging to the honored career with gusto and vitality, are Chengdunese, former residents or still natives. Claim is here equal to boast: Chengdu, beside Beijing, defines Chinese poetry and possesses an ingrained lineage, without peer by any other city in China. It is the country's artistic bank together with Beijing.

So to speak, the city of Chengdu retains pockets of Tang and Song's elegant spiritual past, an inheritance of certain traits atypical, some marks very stubborn to be erased in the inner layers of the collective psyche of a race, a group, carried over from generation to generation. And in the last analysis, is there any city under the sun that does not have cultural genes of its own to be inherited in a linear progression? My answers are of course, in the affirmative definitely. Although Chengdu is a city in flux culturally and socially, it still lures poets from all directions for the same compelling reason: the visiting of so many haunts of so many native great poets and artists who have lived, worked and played here. The idea alone will send a vicarious thrill down your literary spine as you will discover the city's genuine splendor and firm link with budding and maturing years of so many wonderful artists and poets, especially the presence of mementos of Li Bai and Du Fu, two minds conterminous in their depth and scope with the poetic limits of man. The fact that 2017 Chengdu international poetry week is inaugurated today in honor of Chengdu's glorious past, as reflected in its rich legacy of art and poetry, evidenced by the attendance of so many distinguished poets home and abroad, has proved the fullness of the truth value of my point.

Fellow Poets and friends, don't you see, right in front of you, under your very noses, a city hemmed in with radiant beams of poetry?

诗影光芒中的茅屋

在 2017 年第一届草堂诗酒大会开幕式上的演讲

2017 年 7 月 27 日

国内外诗人朋友们：

无论是在中国还是在外国，总有一些伟大诗人生活过的地方，被后人视为尊崇的圣地，但像杜甫草堂这样的地方，在中国民众，尤其是文人的心里更具有特殊的地位。

所谓草堂，其实就是一间茅屋，但在这一千多年被时光所雕刻的中国精神史上，这间曾经的现实中的茅屋，却毫无悬念地成为有关中国诗歌黄金时代重要的符号之一，这一符号既承载着中国诗歌传统中的一条重要脉流，同时它还寄托了此后无数诗家对先贤的致敬和怀念。

毫无疑问，伟大的杜甫代表了一种传统，因其崇高的儒家仁爱思想和强烈的忧患意识，他的诗见证了他所置身的那个非凡而动荡的社会的现实，其诗作内容的深刻性和技艺的精湛，都是那个时代无人能与之比肩的。

这位被誉为"诗圣"的诗歌巨人，不仅在当时的中国诗歌史上，就是把他放在那个时期的世界诗歌史上，他同样也是一座巍峨的高峰。

杜甫一生都在游历中，历时长达几十年，他的重要作品都是在客居他乡时写下的，尤其他在蜀地的生活在他的诗歌中留下了许多经典，其中《春夜喜雨》《茅屋为秋风所破歌》《蜀相》等都已成为千古传诵的名篇。而作为一个一生都伴随着苦难和不幸的现实主义诗人，其创造力的丰沛也是他的同代人不可企及的。尽管一直处在颠沛流离的境遇中，他还是为我们留下了一千五百多首光辉的诗章。

Du Fu's Thatched Cottage-Both A Reality and A Legend
Address at the Opening Ceremony of 2017 Intl Festival of Poetry&Liquor
27th, July, 2017

Be it in China or any other country in the world, there are certain haunts of the great writers and poets who have worked and lived being immortalized and sanctified to posterity. No other place like the present hamlet (expanded now into a huge park)holds such a special place in the hearts of the Chinese nation and Chinese poets.

This cottage has been so extensively commemorated and celebrated by posterity, in so many novels, poems, anecdotes, legends in the past millennium that it has become an abstraction instead of a reality, an arch icon of the golden age of the Chinese Tang poetry, the apogee of one of the most important poetic schools of the Classic Chinese poetry in general.

It should be emphasized that our Poet Saint, after whose name this cottage has been named, represents a great tradition, the tradition of Confucianism, state religion and state ideology for the Chinese mind since the Han dynasty, one of the three greatest spiritual pillars of the medieval and contemporary civilized world. As Jesus speaks of love, Buddha, of compassion, Confucius makes the core mental paraphernalia of the elite, the scholar, mandarin, poet, the twin preoccupation with the wellbeing of the common people who struggle and crave for happiness and the political fate of the nation. Because of this, his poems have been epic-class testament to the turbulence and violence of the Mid Tang and immensity of the sufferings sustained by the civil society in depth and artistry unrivalled by any of his contemporaries.

Du Fu is not only Poet Saint for China, but also compares supremely with any other great poet in his time and of all time. Eminent Kenneth Rexroth says he has saturated himself with Du Fu's poetry for forty five years and confesses Du Fu has made him "a better man, as a moral agent and a perceiving organism".

Du Fu's prime years overlapped with the worst ones of the Tang. Yet the personal misfortune proved to be the fortune of the Chinese poetry in its classic phase. Due to the collapse of central authority and the subsequent famine, devastations, Du Fu spent his mature years in wandering, retreat or exile. As the most famous tenant of Chengdu and Shu of all time, he wrote a

这间茅屋既是现实又是想象,它在一代又一代中国诗人的追寻中,成为被共同视为珍宝的集体记忆,杜甫曾写下过这样的名句"江山有巴蜀,栋宇自齐梁",这难道是偶然的吗？回答是否定的,当然不是。巴蜀之地的自然灵气,对人及万物的孕育滋养,曾创造过无数的奇迹,以及足以让后人赞叹的辉煌,而诗歌在这片广袤的土地上,就如同千里沃野种植的粮食,它似乎以并不引人注意的谦恭姿态,为我们这个朴实敦厚的民族提供了如此丰富的精神营养。这在世界民族发展史上也是不可多见的。

如果我们去翻阅一下中国文学史,就会发现在中国历史上许多伟大的诗人都与巴蜀之地有不解之缘,而这片土地从某种意义而言,也成了这些诗人精神上的又一个摇篮。说我们是一个诗歌浸润的民族,那是因为诗歌在很多时候代表了这个民族精神的高度,而对此没有人表示过任何怀疑。

今天的草堂国际诗歌大会就是一个最好的证明,来自四面八方的诗人将会聚到这里,共同来捍卫和守护人类诗歌的理想。而在此时此刻,我以为那间现实和想象中的茅屋,就是由我们的诗歌和精神所构建而成的神圣殿堂。我想任何狂风和暴雨都不可能将它撼动,没有别的原因,就是因为这间茅屋的根基已经深深地扎入了人类自由、正义而永不向任何邪恶势力低头的灵魂。

也正因为这个原因,我们才将诗歌的火炬一次又一次高高地举起,并始终对就要来临的明天抱有信心,人类美好的未来必将时刻会有诗歌伴随。精神不灭,诗歌不朽！

number of poems now being masterpieces chanted by primary school goers and established poets alike. For depth of observation of the political chaos of his time, and craftsmanship, for praise of love, magnanimity ,calm and compassion, his recipe to redeem the nightbound world, Du Fu is unsurpassed and unprecedented.

Both a legend and a reality, this cottage has been the Mecca of Chinese poets over centuries. Du Fu sings up unabashedly Shu land's landscape and natural bounty, not without a reason. The agricultural potential and the strategic position elevated it to a major Chinese granary, commercial and cultural center since the Han and Tang which spawned an aura, locale ,enery, imperceptibly and unobtrusively , to nurture the growth of Chinese poetry rarely seen anywhere in China or in the world.

An overview of Chinese history of literature will lead us to a discovery that Shu land (contemporary Sichuan) has always been associated with many a great poet and artist in ancient China. It has been argued that the finest flower of Chinese culture is poetry and poetry has certainly embodied the spiritual dimension of the Chinese people supposedly without a religion as center of spirit.

The successful inauguration of this poetry festival affords us solace and assurance that so many great poets from all corners of the globe are gathered in this cottage, consecrated and dedicated to Du Fu, in defense of the sanctity of poetry and the hallowing of one of the greatest poet saints China has to offer to the world . Momentarily we all revert to another time ,another place and we are all Du Fu's contemporaries. This cottage ,unfazed by any storm, unshaken by any wind, has been deeply enshrined in the inner recesses of the human psyche In their quest for justice and freedom in defiance of all the evil and dark forces, as malicious and sinister in Du Fu's time as in ours.

Because of this, I am fully convinced, hoisting the torch of poetry in our hands, as long as human eyes can see, men can breathe, poetry will outlast and human songs will forever prevail upon the face of our troubled planet.

我相信诗歌将会打破所有的壁垒和障碍

在布加勒斯特城市诗歌奖颁奖仪式上的致答词

2017年5月18号

尊敬的加布里埃拉·优伦切亚努市长,尊敬的布加勒斯特城市诗歌奖的各位评委,尊敬的诗人朋友们:

从某种角度而言,我是一个相信生命万物的存在都有着其内在规律的人,或许说大多数时候,我还是一个唯物主义者,不过尽管这样,我依然认为这个世界上,每一个个体生命之间发生任何一种联系,都是需要"缘分"的。我不知道在古老的拉丁语言中,是如何表达"缘分"这个词的,但在已经使用了数千年的中国文字的语境里,"缘分"这个词却充分表达了人与人之间的相遇,是命运中早就注定了的机缘,其中既包含了人与人,或人与事物之间发生联系的可能性,也让置身于其中的人,更坚定地相信这就是所谓命运的安排。

朋友们,尤其是在今天,在这样一个对我来说十分难忘的时刻,因为你们的慷慨、理解和厚爱,决定将以这一古老城市命名的诗歌奖颁发给我,毫无疑问这是我的最大荣幸,在此时,除了让我被深深地感动之外,就是让我再一次确信了"缘分"这个词所隐含的全部真实,的确都是现实中实实的存在。

今天的人类已经有七十多亿人口,在这个地球上不同人的相遇,其概率仍然十分低,甚至低得不可想象。在中国佛教思想中有一种观点,认为人的相遇和相识是通过艰难的修炼而来的,我不是一个佛教徒,但我对我们的相遇有着另外一番解释,那就是人类从古代传诵至今的不朽诗歌,让我们相聚在了古老、神奇而又年轻的布加勒斯特,今天我们在座的每一位,都将是自己生命中被约定或不期而遇注定要见面

I Believe Poetry Will Break Loose all the barriers and Obstacles
Reply Speech at the Awarding Ceremony of Bucharest City Poetry Prize
18th, May, 2017

Respected mayor Gabriela Vranceanu, respected judges of Bucharest City Poetry Prize, respected fellow poets:

Being born into a Nuosu tribe, I have naturally taken it for granted, ie, the co-existence with us humans as equals, of varied life forms, sentient or insentient, fauna or flora, operating dependent on laws unique in their own scheme of things. This animistic upbringing has contrasted oddly with my realistic education in adolescence and youth to the extent there is at times an occultist strain in my character that leads me to trust, for anyone to be connected with anyone on earth ,karma, allow me to use a Buddhist term, must be at work. Again excuse my lapse of doubt as to the most probable lexical slot in Latin for 缘分 ,a highly Chinese culture specific term in currency for perhaps millennium. The Buddhist karma comes close to 缘分 which means roughly any human encounter is not an accident, but predetermined in our previous lives in an endless cycle of incarnation. I have battled linguistically all this way to simply to want to say this: all of you in the audience, all the judges on the podium, we are gathered here today because we are meant to be gathered here today.

Fellow poets and friends, what a worthy moment in my life to be invited to meet with each of you today. Your largeness of mind, your compassion and even mercy combined ,from whence emerges the decision to honor me with the superb prize named after your great city of Bucharest, a decision that overwhelms me to such an extent that corroborates with my Buddhist belief in karma, human act arranged by destiny.

Our present world throngs with humans, say, 7 billion strong. How is it possible that any of us to be able to interact with any of us ,each being a drop in the ocean ,a needle in the haystack? In Chinese branch of Mahayana Buddhism, laymen and clergy alike, all impute seemingly random human meeting to the outcome of self-imposed harsh and protracted ascetic practices. Me not a Buddhist, yet I argue in the similar vein it is poetry, passed down to us by oral traditions or print from our ancestors to us all in the audience that makes all this happen. We are friends because we

的朋友。难道你认为这一切都是偶然的吗？当然不是。

作为一个出生在中国西南部山地民族的彝族人的儿子，在这里我想到了一句话，它就出自我们民族伟大的历史典籍《玛牧特依》(《先师哲人书》)，这句话是这样说的："让我们牵着幸运之神的手，骑上那匹传说中的骏马，就一定能寻找到自己的好运。"是的，在今天我就是一个找到好运的人。正是因为布加勒斯特的召唤和邀约，正是因为诗歌经久不衰的力量和魅力，我们才能从四面八方跨越千山万水来到了这里，如果说生命中真的有那种特殊的"缘分"，现在就可以肯定地说，我们今天的相遇就来自这座或许我们曾经想象过的梦与现实所构筑的伟大城市，为此我们都要由衷地感谢她的好客和盛情。

朋友们，最后我还想说的是，诗歌的对话和交流，仍然是人类不同民族和国度，真正能进入彼此心灵和精神世界最有效的方式之一，特别是在全球化与逆全球化正在发生激烈冲突和博弈的今天，我相信诗歌将会打破所有的壁垒和障碍，站在人类精神高地的最顶处，用早已点燃并高举起的熊熊火炬，去再一次照亮人类通向明天的道路！

aer meant to be friends. Can't you still believe this human congregation now in the old ,wondrous but new city of Bucharest is accidental? Definitely not.

The son of the mountainous people called Yi in the west of China's Sichuan province, I will , for your benefit, refer to one of the classics of the proud Yi nationality, Matemuyi (Sayings of Prophets and Masters),to quote:"Bound and sure we are to find our good fortune guided by the hand of God of Fortune, riding on the legendary horse". I for one, certainly should be deemed the lucky fellow who has hit the jackpot. Bucharest ,nay, the irresistible power and endurable charm of poetry has summoned us to journey, over high mountains and deep valleys and rough seas to be gathered here in the city of Bucharest, one built on lofty dreams and high ideals. I must humble myself first to bow to your hospitality and generosity.

Dear friends ,I conclude this reply by imparting to you my deepest held conviction that poetry, or dialogues with fellow poets remains to be the most effective way for us to enter into the hearts of each other. In particular in the present world swept by globalization , a world riven by geopolitical rivalries and sociological crises, I have never lost an obstinate sense of resistance vs all the barriers and obstacles on the human road to civility and progress. Poetry ,the perennial torch of mankind , will never fail us in lighting our way towards a bright future of tomorrow.

何为诗人？何为诗？

在 2016 西昌邛海丝绸之路国际诗歌周开幕式上的演讲

2016 年 7 月 26 日

什么是诗歌的地域性、民族性和世界性？这本身就是一个宏阔而抽象的命题。从一般意义而言，世界上任何一个诗人，他的出生地都在这个地球的某一域，在经度和纬度的某一个点上，从更深处来讲，作为人的出生地，抑或是诗人的出生地都是他本人无法选择的。

诗人的民族性与诗人出生时所属的民族有关系，也可以说没有关系，那是因为从最基本的民族性来讲，任何一个诗人从他出生的那一天开始，特别是他后天成长的经历，毫无疑问，在他的身上都会深深地打下他所属的族群和文化的痕迹，但也可以说某种狭义的民族性和地域性与他没有太直接的关系，那是因为任何一个伟大的诗人，他都必须在精神上和思想上超越这种地域和民族的限制，因为卓越的诗人既是他的民族优秀的儿子，同时也还是人类文明滋养的世界性的公民，因为在他的成长过程中当他面对这个世界的时候，他都会去向所有伟大的诗歌经典学习，这里既包括他所属民族的诗歌经典，当然也包括其他民族的诗歌经典。

诗人的世界性与诗歌的世界性往往是一致的，只有当诗人的作品在深刻地表达自己内心独一无二的感受，同时他的这种表达无论被翻译成世界上哪一种语言，都能找到热爱他的读者和知音的话，他的诗歌也才具有世界性的价值。

诗人的，或者诗歌作品的地域性、民族性以及世界性，是我们今天应该更加关注的一个话题，特别是在全球化的背景下，诗人的民族性、地域性与世界性似乎形成了一种并不对称的关系。有一点可以肯定，没有一个诗人不在用一种语言写作，难怪有

Who Is a Poet? What Is Poetry?
Address at the Opening Ceremony of Xichang.Qionghai 2016 Silk Road Intl Poetry Week
26th, July, 2016

In what way do we claim a poet that he is, thrice in senses ethnic, national and universal? On a more general plane, the birth of any poet is a happy confluence or a fortuitous coordinate of longitude and latitude. That is ,a poet must be connate with a locale on this blue planet ,either as a poet or a human being , he is here or there in spite of himself.

Yet, although it can be argued the ethnicity of a poet is purely accidental, he still carries , wherever he happens to be ,from the day of his birth, indelible marks and traces of physical breeding and spiritual growth peculiar to his own ethnic community and his own folks. Such connections, however ethnically embedded and tenacious, forbids not his mental development and his artistic expansion. To be really great, he must outgrow and overreach himself beyond such genetic and regional confines to emerge eventually and ultimately, both good son of his own people and model citizen of the world, nurtured and fed upon the best spiritual fruit and blossom of various races collectively called humanity. For a good poet necessarily means a good learner on a rich diet of the "selectest treasuries of the selectest forms of manners and of nature" not only of his own race but also of poetic creations of the highest order authored by people inhabiting remote and different quarters of the same earth.

This is bound to give rise to the approximation of the universality of poethood and the universality of his prosody. For only when a poet renders his unique mindset and imaginations luminous and accessible, for whatever of beautiful, true, and majestic his poems contain about the immortal pageantry of life, to which both his people and indeed all peoples are spectators , especially surviving all the travails of translations into varied languages, he will be deemed a great poet, and his work, true poetry deserving of the epithet of universality.

By implication, my reasoning leads to a tentative conclusion that against the large backdrop of contemporary globalization, the ancient trinity of ethnicity, nationality and universality all combined and embodied in a poet, an attribute taken for granted for ages ,now has been dissolved and disjoined. There is a powerful logic of homogeneity, sinister and evil you might call, at work so

许多诗人把他所使用的语言称为自己的祖国，尤其是那些离开了自己母语的本土，流落在世界各地的诗人，他所坚守的语言就已经成为他与这个世界发生关系的最后一种方式，甚至是他作为诗人能活下去的最充足的理由。

诗歌的地域性和民族性，很多时候呈现出的是一种表象，但是毋庸讳言，诗歌从它产生的那一天开始，就无法避免其地域性和民族性，然而地域性和民族性的表达却是千差万别的，历史上无数经典的诗人都给我们树立光辉的榜样，我们不能把所谓的地域性和民族性，与这个世界的普遍性对立起来，那样的地域性和民族性无疑是狭隘的、极端的。真正的诗人可以说都是这种所谓地域性、民族性的敌人，就是那些饱含爱国主义情愫的诗人，他们的作品不仅仅能唤起本国人民的爱国热情，同样也能让别的国家和民族的读者，被他的真挚情感所感动，波兰伟大的诗人密茨凯维奇的诗篇就产生了这样的作用。

地域性和民族性的写作，特别是在那些伟大的诗人写作中，都会以极其卓越的艺术方式呈现在诗歌中，这是一种高品质的地域性和民族性的呈现，或者说是一种更具有独特性的价值和诗性的表达，我们可以从这些诗中，发现它所描述的山脉、河流、岩石、树木、花草以及亘古不变的太阳，都会带有一种别样的色彩，我理解这就是一个诗人不同于另一个诗人的价值所在。我在阅读英国诗人狄兰·托马斯的时候，他的诗就给我留下了强烈的印象，他诗歌中的英国威尔士就是他带给我们的，一个不同于这个地球上任何一个地方的属于他的文学世界。

在美国20世纪的诗人中，如果就其本土代表性而言，无可争议弗罗斯特要比艾略特更具有代表性，他是一个真正意义上的代表美国移民的民族诗人，他所构筑的诗歌世界更像是一个把自然、道德观念、风土人情、对生死的态度等等融合在一起的现实，他的诗大都是从生活中的细节出发，对自然和心理的描写尤其细腻精微，如果反复阅读，甚至可以从他的诗句中感受到美国乡土家园泥土新鲜的气息。

今天我们所强调的所谓边缘的、地域的、民族的、弱势的、少数的、女性的等等领域的写作，其实更多的是关注这些作品所表达出来的不能被替代的声音，因为有它们的存在，我们才能真正地感觉到这个世界是完整的，哪怕它们的声音还很弱小，但任何强大的力量都不应该也不能忽视它们存在的价值，这不管是从社会层面还是从

that what is good poetry by a great ethnic poet might not be deemed so in an increasingly flattening world. Hence the outcome of such corruption: disintegration of traditional sensibility to pleasure and human impulse to uplifting. One last resort: Poetry begins with the imagination but is executed with the incorrigible and incorruptible means of language. No wonder poets all associate mother tongues or languages with the conception of homeland. Especially those poets, banished from their countries, scattered here and there, for whatever reason, will stick to their mother tongues as the last resort to maintain a sort of lukewarm symbolic relation with the world, even the sole raison d'ê tre to continue to breathe till their last breath.

In sum, the trinity of poethood presents itself today in a more confusing countenance than meets the eye. Rather we might say there are myriad of manifestations of ethnicity and nationality in poetry. Countless outstanding poets in preceding generations before us have demonstrated admirably the needlessness and narrowlessness of positing a dichotomy between ethnicity/nationality and universality. A great poet is necessarily a natural foe to such Procrustean conceptions. We might readily quote the 19th century Polish poet Adam Mickiewicz (1798-1855) whose intensely patriotic lyrics, justly ranked among the highest achievements in Polish poetry, has also endeared himself to millions of readers outside the borders of his motherland.

The superiority of writing in this vein consists in the visibility of those peculiar sensibilities and thoughts, which belong to the inner faculties of a certain race or a nation, their incomparable perfection expressed in a harmony of the union of all. To put it in another way, it is not inasmuch as they are ethnic /national poets, but inasmuch as they have availed to such an extent that they reveal an oddly welcome sensibility to pleasure, passion, natural scenery and eternal elements such as mountains, rivers, rocks, trees, flowers and grass and changeless sun, which is imputed to them as a rare faculty, the ultimate triumph of genius blossomed and achieved. Dylan Thomas strikes me as such a poet who belongs to the Wales as he does to the literary world recognized as such elsewhere.

The poetry of Robert Frost, combining pastoral imagery with solitary philosophical themes typifies 20th century America more than T.S. Eliot, the official Nobel prize winner pitted against the former, ie, the country's unofficial poet laureate. A real immigrant poet, highly lauded for his realistic depictions of rural life and his successful employment of rural settings in New England in the early twentieth century, Frost examines with facility complex social and moral issues, attitude towards death. Frost always tries to remain down to earth, yet behind the genial, homespun New England rustic, while "allowing both fact and intuition a bright kingdom, he speaks for many of us, he speaks better than most of us. That is to say, as a poet must." (Radcliffe Squires)

I do confess an inveterate penchant in me to always ferret out and discern the real treasures beneath the veneer of the so called marginal, local, national, weak, minority, female and give them their dues. There are truly some voices lurking somewhere ,nameless, unspoken, even unspeakable. Yet their absence or presence has enriched our inner being and has made our world intact and full.

文化层面都应该对他们的存在和价值予以尊重,我以为持这样一种态度才是一个文明社会不可被逾越的底线。

　　诗歌的民族性、地域性与世界性的关系,在很多时候它们在内在逻辑关系的联系上都是极为紧密的,特别是进入新世纪之后,人类在诗歌方面的翻译又进入了一个黄金时期,历史上从来还没有过这样一个诗歌被大量翻译的时代,许多诗人的作品被翻译成世界上不同的文字,最让人兴奋和感动的是不少用小语种写作的诗人,他们的作品也获得了被翻译的机会,这种现象是在以前的任何一个世纪都不曾出现过的。

　　一个世界性的诗歌运动,正在全世界不同的地方悄然兴起,诗歌正在回到人们的视野并进入公众生活,诗歌已经再一次成为人类和社会精神生活建设中的一部分。在物质主义和拜金主义甚嚣尘上的现实面前,诗歌又一次成为保卫人类精神家园的武器,虽然它显示的力量并没有马上被大多数人所认同,但诗歌不可被替代的作用,在人类的心灵中筑起了一道良心的高墙,当它一旦进入了人的心灵,它就能成为人类反抗一切暴力和异化的工具。

　　本届西昌邛海·丝绸之路国际诗歌周的举办,就是基于这样一个宗旨和理念,我相信来自世界各地的诗人朋友,都会带着你们的智慧和信心来到这里,为构建一个更为和谐的、美满的、善意的、幸福的人类关系做出我们的贡献。不是今天才有这样的定义,只有诗人才是人类之间进行交流的至高无上的使者!

Faint as they may, powers bigger than them ignore at their own perils. Due respect must be accorded them, either institutionally or culturally, a stance any civilized community shall maintain to its advantage.

In essence, the trinity of poethood is closely interconnected. In this new and young age of the 21st century, poetic translation has seen a surge of renaissance and revival in that more and more poems have been turned into various foreign languages around the world. What is most consoling is that some poets who compose in minority languages invite the welcome attention of translators, a phenomenon truly unprecedented in the annals of human history.

A world wide poetry movement is in the brewing, looming on the horizon, though imperceptibly and unobtrusively. Poetry has made a comeback to our civil life.The actions of poets have contributed to the reconstruction of a new social fabric of real option of life, justice, dignity and beauty, amply represented by poetry, as antidote against infatuation with crass capitalism and the vulgarity of commercialism and materialist fetish, making way for man to find an integral way of development. Although its powers ,its cohesive forces to drive changes still await better comprehension, poetry has nevertheless erected a forbidding wall in men's hearts to fend off violence, alienation and various forms of insidious social corruptions.

Once poetry descends through poets upon thousands upon thousands of civilians minds, "whence as from a magnet the invisible effluence is sent forth", it will bring into full play the potentials of humans, animates, and sustains the life of all. It is with this faith we host and inaugurate Xichang.Qionghai 2016 Silk Road Intl Poetry week today. We trust this sovereign gathering of poet friends, home and abroad does have the faculty to be conducive to the forging of human relationship based upon harmony, plenty, civility and happiness thanks to the liberating and unifying capacity of poetry.

高贵的文学依然存在人间

在"2016 欧洲诗歌与艺术荷马奖"颁奖仪式上的致辞

2016 年 6 月 27 日

尊敬的欧洲诗歌与艺术荷马奖评委会，尊敬的各位朋友、我亲爱的同胞们：

今天对于我来说，是一个喜出望外的日子，我相信对于我们这个数千年来就生活在这片高原上的民族而言，也将会是一个喜讯，它会被传播得比风还快。感谢欧洲诗歌与艺术荷马奖评委会，你们的慷慨和大度不仅体现在对获奖者全部创作和思想的深刻把握上，更重要的是你们从不拘泥于创作者的某一个局部，而是把他放在了一个民族文化和精神的坐标高度，由此不难理解，你们今天对我的选择，其实就是对我们彝民族古老、悠久、灿烂而伟大的文化传统的褒奖，是馈赠给我们这片土地上耸立的群山、奔腾的河流、翠绿的森林、无边的天空以及所有生灵的一份最美好的礼物。

尤其让人不知所措、心怀不安的是，你们不远万里，竟然已经把这一如此宝贵的赠予送到了我的家门，可以说，此时此刻我就是这个世界上一个幸运的人。按照我们彝族人的习惯，在这样的时候，我本不应该站在这里，应该做的是在我的院落里为你们宰杀牲口，递上一杯杯美酒，而不是站在这里浪费诸位的时间。

朋友们，这个奖项是以伟大的古希腊诗人荷马的名字命名的，《伊利亚特》和《奥德赛》两部伟大的史诗，为我们所有的后来者都树立了光辉的榜样。当然，这位盲歌手留下的全部遗产，都早已成为人类精神文化最重要的源头之一，在这里，我不想简单地把这位智者和语言世界的祭司比喻成真理的化身，而是想在这里把我对他的热爱用更朴素的语言讲出。在《伊利亚特》中，阿喀琉斯曾预言他的诗歌将会一直延续下去，永不凋零，对这样一个预言我不认为是一种宿命式的判断，其实直到今天，荷

Noble Literature Is Still of Interest and Moment
Acceptance Speech at the Awarding Ceremony of "The European Medal of Poetry and Art Homer 2016"
27th, June, 2016

Respected judges of the Chamber of The European Medal of Poetry and Art Homer 2016,
Respected friends, my own Yi compatriots:

Fortune has dealt with me rather too well and I should be grateful for the breaking of another dawn as it comes in such an aupicious manner, that is, today begins with such extraordinary honours like The European Medal of Poetry and Art Homer 2016 confered upon me.You might rest assured good tidings in this remote location of my beloved land travel like wildfire among my own tribesmen and tribeswomen.The award has been altogether popular with both me and my people because it indicates an European perspective that noble literature is still of interest and moment as well as a recognition that my poetry ,deeply rooted in the natioanl traits of the Yi people ,contains the whole of ethnic Nuosu, and as such, bears the social and aesthetic significance to a preeminent degree despite critical doubts of my tenacious harping on the arch theme of the Yi identity vs modernity as well as grudges as to the thematic insularity of my writings from some quarters.No wonder your option of me ,for me ,constitutes a timely solute to the Yi spirituality, so ancient, so marvellous, so glorious rivalling any other counterpart.Your prize also comes as a most suitable gift to this land , all the sentient beings full of song and virtue, its towering peaks, its wild torrents,its perpetually forested woods, its perpetually crystal clear skies ,its grassy slopes scented with nameless wild flowers.

At this moment I must sound very Unnuosu and perhaps cumbersome as to present my gratitude with a plain thank you considering you have travelled around the world to my doorstep to deliver this distinction. Why me? Well, the Yi protocols of friendship dictate, to bearers of good tidings like you,my absence amisdt you in this moment, or rather ,the Yi cult of generosity commands me not stand here to mouth some platitudes of courtesy, but to hurry and scurry as a helper in the courtyard to butcher a goat, a bull and a swine or as the blessed host to encourage the guests drink one more toast as befits authentic Nuosus at the feast.

Dear Friends, this medal to me is named after Homer, the supreme poet of the ancient

马点燃的精神火焰就从未有过熄灭。

然而最让我吃惊和感动的是,如果没有荷马神一般的说唱,那个曾经出现过的英雄时代,就不会穿越时间,哪怕它就是青铜和巨石也会被磨灭,正是因为这位神授一般的盲人,让古希腊的英雄谱系,直到现在还活在世上熠熠生辉。

讲到这里,朋友们,你们认为这个世界所发生的一切,都是由偶然的因素构成的吗?显然不是,正如我今天接受这样一个奖项,在这里说到伟大的荷马,似乎都在从空气和阳光中接受一个来自远方的讯息和暗示,那就是通过荷马的神谕和感召,让我再一次重新注视和回望我们彝民族伟大的史诗《勒俄》《梅葛》以及《阿细的先基》,再一次屹立在自然和精神的高地,去接受太阳神的洗礼,再一次回到我们出发时的地方,作为一个在这片广袤的群山之上有着英雄谱系的诗人,原谅我在这里断言:因为我的民族,我的诗不会死亡!谢谢诸位!卡沙沙!

附件

"2016年欧洲艺术诗歌荷马奖"颁奖词

大流士 波兰文学协会主席 "欧洲艺术诗歌荷马奖"评奖委员会主任委员

吉狄马加是当代中国最伟大的诗人之一。他的诗歌富于民族文化根性,深植于诺苏民族的传统之中。他的诗歌彰显彝族人传承已久的魔幻意识,毕摩和祖宗的神灵居于这一传统及意识的中枢。他的诗歌开创了这一精神的一个隐蔽的空间,诺苏这个山地民族和古老的传统不离不弃,相伴相惜,传递着人类对纯洁和完满伟大的向往。在如此广袤、风景极为美丽的土地上,吉狄马加的诗歌体现了命运的深不可测,那些诺苏人栖居的山坡把他们同更为伟大的宇宙和大自然的生生不息连接在一起。天地万物在他的作品中被视为亘古不变,白日和黑夜的更替,人的肉身,疾病与痛苦,这一切以人形的方式加以提醒:人类暴露在严酷的自然环境里,臣服于时间威力的种种摧残。这一切,在吉狄马加的诗歌中,罕见地得以呈现。如此清晰的人类意识,晶莹透亮,像一道强光,穿透了各种形态变幻莫测的时空。

吉狄马加的诗歌风格潇洒飘逸,时而细致入微地描摹蜻蜓翅膀的颤动,时而创

Occidental world.And with Homer, the two great epics of Illiad and Odyssey,the oldest extant works of the West, have now been an essential part of literatures ,West and East,a veritable legacy left to posterity by this blind poet deemed the twin fountainheads of Western cultural tradition.At this point I hesitate to comapre Homer, the prophet and the Brahmin of poetry to the incarnation of truth.He certainly is.And much more. I really would like to tell, in unguarded frankness, unabashed sincerity, my growing admiration for his meirts over time.Simplicity, unadorned language and being true to life are some of Homer's reputed qualities.There is a nobility and dignity to his simple and direct lines.In Illiad, Archilles fortells his poems will endure and will never burn to a cinder.To such prophecy,my assent is total and until this day,can't you see the literary sky is still ablaze with Homerian epics and hymns?

What perreinially holds me in awe is the fact, without a blind trabadour in the 8th century BC,our literary history would have been much deprived and depopulated.The calling of the roll of heroes like Achilles and Agamemnon, though boisterous and frivolous, has always dignified and enlivened even as bronze will rust and boulders will decompose.

Mind you, my friends,I speak of this award with pride, one associated with the great Homer. It seems like a stroke of telepathy, a mysterious message or oracle from Homer, and affected by the powers of such an oracle,I turn my gaze,to all intents and purposes,again at the Yi epics,Leer , Meige as well as Aji's Xianji.all being splendid glorification of everything in the Daliangshan Highland. Entranced,I seem to have ascended again the majestic heights of Nature and Spirituality of this beloved Yi land ready for the sacred baptism of the Sun God.Literally and literarily, I am back to where I embarked upon my virgin journey into the outside world 30 odd years ago.Allow my egoism, a poet inheriting such an illustrious geneaology of heroes as Homer sings hymns to, I rejoice at this moment, with my own folks ,by virtue of being the Nuosu bard associated with the right of prophecy that my poems will last and continue to shine before the world thanks to my people ,because of them and for the sake of them.Thank you for your attention.Kasasa!

THE EUROPEAN MEDAL OF POETRY AND ART Homer 2016
Dariusz Thomas Lebioda PH. D

Jidi Majia is one of the greatest contemporary Chinese poets. His poetry is culturally bounded, which is in fact deeply rooted to the tradition of the nation, Nuosu. He also wrote poetry to enhance the ancient magical consciousness that is moderated by priests Bimo unholding the spirits of his ancestors. Form of his art is an invisible space of spirituality, from which mountain people remain in constant interaction, that clarifies to bestow the age of great human longing for purity and fullfilment. Living in the face of vastness and natural beauty, his work constantly strives to reflect the depth of human fate, over which it slopes, and connects to the large

制广阔全景,借以反映整个时代的精神,渲染山地湖泊之间的众生——人类与各种动物鸟类和谐生存的自由气氛。天地间一幕一幕的抒情场景美轮美奂,代表着诺苏部落岁岁不息的演替,每一出这样的场景都在宣示着部族的光荣。诗人意识到他自己已经由整个部族推举出来,做自己民族的诗人。使命所系,他就必须走出凉山,与族人们告别,他不能再带上一支猎枪去狩猎,和自己的族人厮守,平平静静终老于斯。他再也不能围着篝火跳舞,或是从山巅眺望远方。命运把他播撒在更广大的舞台,厕身世界诗人之列,他要向一切同行宣示远在遥遥东方西南一隅诺苏部族的光荣与梦想。他仍然可以憧憬回到部落的小茅屋里歌唱,哪怕那里寒彻入骨,远离尘嚣;他时而仿佛又听到了族中长老和毕摩娓娓道来古老的故事,然而他的诗歌必须昭告部族身份的基本生存真相:我就是一个彝人!这就是吉狄马加的命运所系,毕摩们世世代代念诵的经文,从不间断地提醒、升华,仿佛来自古老历史的一个回响,显示了厚重华彩的过往,昭示未来光明的前景。

cosmogonic systems and the elementary mechanisms of duration. It has sensed eternity through completion of day and night; sticking to the human body, with its illness and pain, it vigils in the shape of a human, exposes to weather conditions, that is subjected to be the destructive power of time. It is rare and appears to be so clear to human consciousness, shimmering to ever shape a bright beam, penetrating to the large time intervals, and scanning space in all its shapes and metamorphoses.

Majia can write a poem similar to the gentle movement of the wings of dragonflies, and create wide panoramas, which reflects the spirit of a whole epoch, the ethos of free existence in the midst of mountains and lakes, in harmony with animals, birds and all living beings. Every scene of his poem becomes the continuation of the story of the tribe, as if it is specially appointed to proclaim its glory. The poet is aware that his work has been selected from the many in order to fulfill his desired destiny. He understood that he could not live permanently in the mountains of Liangshan, where he could go out with a shotgun for hunting and lead a peaceful life only with his family clan. He could dance around campfires and look into the distance from the top of the mountain, but his virtue is set to be among the poets of the world, and proclaim the glory of his land and people in the farthest corners of the globe. He could sing in small huts, separated from the cold, cosmic distance, he could listen to the stories of elders and shamans, but his work interpretes the elementary truth of existence: I am a Nuosu! This is his great task, and at the same time a kind of prayer that is repeated for generations, in a series of reminders and sublimations, a distant echo of history that reflects the past and the glorious future.

诗歌是人类迈向明天最乐观的理由

在第五届青海湖国际诗歌节开幕式上的演讲

2015年8月7日

  尊敬的郝鹏省长，尊敬的各位诗人，女士们、先生们，朋友们：

  在这里，我首先要说的是，因为在座诸位热情地参与和努力，今天我们才能如期相聚在这个地球上最令人向往的高地——青藏高原。毫无疑问，这是一件值得我们庆贺并将永远珍藏在记忆中的事。朋友们，在此时此刻，我们为什么不能用热烈的掌声来为我们这样一次伟大的聚会而喝彩呢？当然，作为东道主，请允许我代表中国作家协会和本届国际诗歌节组委会，向来自世界各地的诗人朋友们表示最热忱的欢迎，同时还要向为本届诗歌节的主办付出了辛勤劳动并贡献了聪明和智慧的各相关机构表示最衷心的感谢！

  是的，朋友们，我们是因为诗歌，才从这个世界的四面八方来到了这里，同样是因为诗歌，我们才能把人类用不同语言和文字创造的奇迹，再一次会聚在了这里，完全可以肯定，这是诗歌的又一次胜利！当然，诸位，在这里我不能简单地把我们的相聚，归结为诗歌之神对我们的一次眷顾，如果真的是那样的话，作为一个有着责任感和人类情怀的诗人，那将是我们对诗歌所具有的崇高价值和重要作用的极大不敬。

  朋友们，事实证明，这个世界直到今天还需要诗歌，因为物质和技术，永远不可能在人类精神的疆域里，真正盛开出馨香扑鼻的花朵，更不可能用它冰冷的抽象数据和异化逻辑，给我们干渴的心灵带来安抚和慰藉。这个世界还需要诗歌，是因为在这个充满着希望与危机、战争与和平、幸福与灾难的现实面前，诗歌就是善和美的化身，正如捷克伟大诗人雅罗斯拉夫·塞弗尔特在诗中写的那样"要知道摇篮的吱嘎声

Why Good Poetry Still Matters?
A Speech at the 2015 Qinghai Lake Intl Poetry Festival
7th, August, 2015

Respected Governor, Mr Hao Peng, respected fellow poets, ladies, gentlemen, friends:

Thanks to the wonderful organizing work on the part of the Organizing Committee, today, the very fact that this choicest group of poets travelling from all quarters of the earth, summoned to be a part of one of the most spectacular poetic pageantries-Qinghai Lake Intl Poetry Festival, will make us all proudly cherish the five days to come which will celebrate the magical gifts of poets and powers of poetry. Dear Fellow poets, let us hesitate not the least to give thunderous applauses to this unusual gathering radiant in our collective pride in being poets we are. Doubly as deputy chairman of All China Writers Union and chairman of QLIPF, I must offer my warmest greetings to all the poets home and abroad as well as my hearty gratitude to all the organizing staff.

A victorious experience I must call this pageantry, my friends, with the wondrous essence of rallying around poetic vision, when 120 special men and women, regardless of color or race or language or religion, congregate to witness poetry as a tool to push reform in society and to awaken conscience by opposing war to peace ,evil to justice. Do not for a second fancy the Muses care a whit about this cheap vanity who certainly demand us in return for her favor our collective sensitivity and our spiritual height as agents to influence society and effect changes favorable to the promising future of mankind.

Friends, it has been testified and corroborated in world history that this world of ours, this beautiful blue planet humans inhabit, cannot do and go around without poets. By this I simply mean all our technological gadgetry and our internet, marvelous providers of creature comforts and super sustenance albeit, are not enough. Robots don't bloom .Life cannot be governed mechanically or solely by reference to the audited accounts of a nation. Cold balance sheets and logic of alienation is no balm for our parched souls. While there is so little optimistic in the way our age is shaping, one of hope mitigated by crisis, peace so fragile as to seem war, happiness at times blighted by catastrophe, we mustn't be deemed preening ourselves too much upon being

和朴素的催眠曲，还有蜜蜂和蜂房，要远远胜过刺刀和枪弹"，他这两句朴实得近似于真理的诗句，实际上说出了这个世界上所有诗人的心声。

我这样说，绝非是痴人说梦，因为就在今天的现实世界，那些正在发生着冲突和杀戮的区域，无辜的平民正流离失所成为离开故土的难民。当然，同样是在那样一些地方，诗歌却与他们如影相随、不离不弃，他们的诗歌就是怀念故土的谣曲和至死不忘的母语，毫无疑问，他们在内心和灵魂中吟诵的箴言，就是他们最终能存活下去的依靠和勇气。诗歌和语言在这样的特定环境中，也已经成为反对一切暴力和压迫的最后的武器。

这个世界还需要诗歌，是因为诗歌它既是属于更多的"极少数"，同时它又从未丧失过大众对它的认知和喜爱，或许诗歌的奇妙之处就在这里，因为我们不知道还有哪一种艺术形式，能像诗歌那样既能飞越形而上的天空，伸手去触摸万象的星群，又能匍匐在现实的大地上，去亲吻千千万万劳动者的脚跟。难怪，尼加拉瓜伟大诗人卡德莱尔，在二十年前，就把群众性的诗歌运动与被压迫民族的解放事业联系在了一起。

这个世界还需要诗歌，是因为跨国的金融资本，完全控制了全球并成为一种隐形的权力体系，从而让人类的心灵更进一步远离我们曾经亲近过的自然和生命本源，当面对这一被极度的消费主义主导的时代，诗歌精神的复苏已成为必然，诗歌仍然以其作为人类精神殿堂不可动摇的根基之一，发挥着谁也无法替代的作用。

这个世界还需要诗歌，是因为诗歌所包含的全部诗歌精神，实际上是人类区别于别的动物最重要的标志，诗歌实际上成了人类所有心灵生活中最必不可少的要素。我们不能想象，一切缺少诗意精神的人类创造，还会真的有什么重要的价值。人类一直在梦想和追求诗意的栖居，实际上就是在为自身定制、以诗意精神为最高准

poets or touting poetry as a substance which transforms awareness and social life. Yes, we do stand for the Kindness and Beauty. Jaroslav Seifert, the eminent Chech poet, writes with such eloquence even when he concentrates on small and intimate gestures :

Aren't the creaking a cradle and the humming of a lullaby,

As well as bees swarming around a beehive,

More congenial a sight than bayonets and canon balls?

Invoking such homely forces as bees and nursery songs as symbols of human needs, Seifert speaks on the behalf of us all.

Don't think I am an obtrusive doomsayer. In this very world of ours, several wars of fratricide have raged on with disheartening tolls of human losses day in and day out. Displaced civilians fall a prey to the wickedness and stupidity of war lords and politicians. Yet in the makeshift huts and functionary refuge camps, their chests heave and resonate with the familiar tunes of their childhood lullaby and the most memorable lines of their best loved national poets in the mother tongues they stick to even in the direst hours and in the harshest alien milieu.No doubt,poems chanted from the bottom of their hearts prove the last buttress against hardship and tyranny.

High poetry is always in demand badly on earth. Although an element of eccentricity or anti-socialness might be present in all poets, good poets, who have achieved heroic statue since the Romantic Movement in the 18th century, have never lost their pull on the civilized populace. It is such a paradox that poetry, unlike any other form of art, is capable of soaring through the celestial vaults of metaphysics to reach out for the starry heavens, while at the same time, crawling on the tough terrain of reality, kisses the feet of myriad of working men and toiling women. No wonder, Ernesto Cardenal , the marvelous Nicaraguan poet, associated poetic movements with the liberation of all oppressed nations even 20 years ago.

Poetry still matters because in this super age wherein capital barons and financial lords, masquerading as transnational businesses ,move to globalize the world by rapidly dissolving the social and economic barriers between nations and transforming the world's diverse populations into a blandly uniform market at the expense of workers, the environment, the traditional values. Such an invisible monster increasingly tears apart our society instead of guiding it and keeping it from going off the rails as consumerist mania alienates us further from origin of nature or source of life fundamental to the sanity of human condition. To counter such disempowering dangers , we poets must rise ,with the magnetism of poetic expression, the presence and the representative voice of each poet here in the audience, to the majestic heights of opposing material forces with "soul force" by reawakening the solar spirit of poetry in the crowd and initiating a new socio-cultural renewal across our globe. The magical potential of poetry that fosters such transformation and the vilifying spirit of poets shall not be called into question.

Good poetry still matters because the solar spirit of poetry has always illuminated man's

则的一种生活方式,或者从更高的角度讲,是一种生命的存在方式。这个世界还需要诗歌,是因为作为人,也可以说作为人类,我们要重返到那个我们最初出发时的地方,也只有诗歌——那古老通灵的语言的火炬,才能让我们辨别出正确的方向,找到通往人类精神故乡的回归之路。

朋友们,尽管我们仍然面临着许多困难,但我们从未丧失过对明天的希望。让我们为生活在今天的人类庆幸吧,因为诗歌直到现在还和我们在一起,因此我有理由坚定地相信,诗歌只要存在一天,人类对美好的未来就充满着期待。谢谢大家!

pathway strewn with odds and hazards. Poetry is actually the vital dimension of man as man, the spiritual primacy by which man is set apart from other species. I cannot imagine, what little dosage of value is left in all human-made artifacts, unless inspired by the poetic spirit. While philosophers exhort us to inhabit the earth poetically, they are proposing a recipe for happiness tailored for mankind, the secret of the sweetness of living from a higher vantage point, so to speak. Good poetry is still in demand, because, at last, it has become an affirmation of the deeply held human longing to return to where we came. Only by upholding the torch of poetry, can we divine the right direction, struggle from darkness to some measure of light and walk the right road back home, back to our spiritual home. At long last, the poem "grows into a praise of what is and what could be on this lump in the skies."

Dear Fellow poets, although we face the difficulties of today, we have never lost our faith in tomorrow. Let us jump for joy of living contemporaneous with such fabulously rich veins of poetry left to us by all great poets, living and dead in the firm belief that poetry is the ultimate justification for mankind that eagerly after a tomorrow stares. Thanks for your attention.

一个中国诗人的非洲情结

在 2014"南非姆基瓦人道主义大奖"颁奖仪式上的书面致答辞

2014 年 10 月 10 日

尊敬的姆基瓦人道主义基金会的各位成员,尊敬的各位朋友:

首先,我要愧疚地向各位致歉,在这样一个伟大的时刻,我不能亲自来到现场见证你们如此真诚而慷慨地颁发给我的这份崇高的荣誉。我想,纵然有一千个理由,我今天没有如期站在你们中间,这无疑都是我一生中无法弥补的一个遗憾。在此,再一次请各位原谅我的冒昧和缺席。

诸位,作为一个生活在遥远东方的中国人,还在我的少年时代,我就知道非洲,就知道非洲在那个特殊的岁月里,正在开展着一场如火如荼的反殖民主义斗争,整个非洲大陆一个又一个国家开始获得民族的自由解放和国家的最后独立。这样的情景,直到今天我还记忆犹新。在我们的领袖毛泽东的号召下,我们曾经走上街头和广场,一次又一次地去声援非洲人民为争取人民解放和国家独立的正义斗争。

如果不是因为宿命的话,我的文学写作生涯从一开始,就和黑人文学以及非洲的历史文化有着深厚的渊源。20 世纪 60 年代相继获得独立的非洲法语国家,其法语文学早已取得了令世人瞩目的国际性声誉,尤其是 20 世纪 30 年代创办的《黑人大

The African Complex of a Chinese Poet
Written Speech at 2014 Mkiva Humanitarian Award Ceremony
10th, October, 2014

Respected Jury from both Mkiva Humanitarian Foundation and Imbongi Yesizwe Trust, dear friends present at this grand ceremony:

First and foremost, with greatest humility I must excuse my absence in your midst today, one of the blessed recipients from afar onto this podium, to partake of a moment which speaks so eloquently of your magnanimity and generosity to confer such an honor on me. I must count this absence amongst you, which may be excused by a thousand and one reasons though, the crowning regret in my life to date and presumably I will live with the perennial sense of remorse gnawing at my heart ever since after. Again I beg you to accept my apology for not being able to come to speak to you in person.

Dear friends, a Chinese of Yi ethnic origin in the remote Orient, together with my generation of teenagers in the 1960's, thanks to Mao's firm diplomatic identification with third world, either ideological or cultural, I grew up taking all people of color to be my siblings. La ceur est tourjours a la gauche, so goes a French saying. Mao's high commendation of African aspirations and mounting barrage of criticism of arrogant and thoughtless Whites in the press stoked the feeling in an adolescent mind that the black continent that you inhabit was seething with an epic fight against rapacious colonists and bloody imperialists to put their scramble to rest. This passion of onslaught of us Chinese on colonialism was easily justified and magnified by almost one century of humiliations and defeats suffered at the hands of both Western and Oriental imperialists. Inspiring stories circulated that one after another African country broke loose from their former suzerainty and won independence. We now, of course, know better. The Chinese race tend to, as Prof. Vernon Mackay puts it aptly, find a vicarious joy in empathizing with African people being ascendant as a means of giving vent to the pent-up grievances against "Ocean Devils". A vivid mental picture arises before me of how many times we youngsters, politically well attuned to the calls of our leader, took to the streets in waves of protest and demonstration of our moral support and solidarity with African brothers in their struggle for liberation and justice. It is amazing these

学生》杂志以及"黑人性"的提出，可以说从整体上影响了世界不同地域的弱势民族在精神和文化上的觉醒，作为一个来自中国西南部山地的彝民族诗人，我就曾经把莱奥波尔德·塞达·桑戈尔和戴维·迪奥普等人视为自己在诗歌创作上的精神导师和兄长。

同样，在20世纪获得独立的原英国殖民地非洲国家，那里蓬勃新生的具有鲜明特质的作家文学，也深刻地影响了我的文学观和对价值的判断。尼日利亚杰出的小说家钦·阿契贝、剧作家诗人沃·索因卡，坦桑尼亚著名的斯瓦希里语作家夏巴尼·罗伯特，肯尼亚杰出的作家恩吉古，安哥拉杰出诗人维里亚托·达·克鲁兹，当然这里我还要特别提到的是，南非杰出的诗人维拉卡泽、彼得·亚伯拉罕姆斯、丹尼斯·布鲁特斯以及著名的小说家纳丁·戈迪默等等，他们富有人性并发出了正义之声的作品，让我既感受到了非洲的苦难和不幸，同时，也真切地体会到了这些划时代的作品，把忍耐中的希望以及对未来的憧憬呈现在了世界的面前。我可以毫不夸张并自信地说，在中国众多的作家和诗人中，我是在精神上与遥远的非洲联系得最紧密的一位。对此，我充满着自豪。因为我对非洲的热爱，来自于我灵魂不可分割的一个部分。

朋友们，我从未来到过美丽的南非，但我对南非有着持久不衰的向往和热情，我曾经无数次地梦见过她。多少年来，我一直把南非视为人类在20世纪后半叶以来，反对种族隔离、追求自由和公正的中心。

我想并非偶然，我还在二十多岁的时候，就在诗歌《古老的土地》里，深情地赞颂过非洲古老的文明和在这片广袤的土地上生活着的勤劳善良的人民。当20世纪就

youthful memories of idealism and agitation spring to mind all the more sweeter today than yesterday, this year than last year.

As luck would have it, or I guess karma plays a role, I embarked upon my literary career with what I would call African complex , in my unconscious, that is, an instinctive aping of African writing techniques and styles fed upon a deep love of African cultures and peoples .We know parallel to the rise of de-colonized Africa in the late 1960s there was a gratifying development of African literature, because of its admittedly great intrinsic value, it is now widely known enough to be considered one of the major bodies of world literature. I must make mention of a few French speaking giants' names, whom I have taken as mentor and model in my poetic writing, ie, Leopold Sedar Senghor(Senegal) Aime Cesaire(Martinique) who co-founded the review L'etudiants Noir in 1935 and of course, David Diop who was such an unbelievable bard. The magazine formulated the revolutionary concept of Negritude which emphasized the cultural values of the Negro, black folklore and the basic dignity of the Negro race. I use the word revolutionary deliberately because it has served a prise de conscience not only for the entire Negro, but by hindsight, for all the disadvantaged groups scattered across each corner of the globe like me.

I am in the debt not only of writers and poets from Francophonie countries but also to literary geniuses from British Commonwealth, as the latter has evolved a spiritual tradition equally worthy of the name which has exerted a profound influence upon my worldview and my scale of values, although they appear somewhat reticent about the concept of Negritude, an attitude perhaps born of the particular cultural and political realities that confronted them still seeking independence. This is an illustrious galaxy, say, of the wonderful novels by Chinua Achebe (Nigeria),the brilliant plays of Wole Soyinka(Nigeria),the accomplished contes of Swahili speaking writer Shaaban Robert who spins his yarns so deftly (Tanzania).They have taught me, as how to retain my footing in my Yi heritage and with what fidelity to preserve a genuinely lyrical style. I must also salute Ngugi wa Thiong'o from Kenya, Viriato Clemente da Cruz from Angola, in particular, your great poet Benedict Wallet Vilakazi, Peter Abrahams , Denis Brutus, and last but not least, the Nobel prize winner Nadine Gordimer. Their work derives from Nero's suffering and woes the compelling pathos and distinguishable hope for a better world and gives insight into the social and political evolution of the whole continent, the trajectory per se of South Africa from an apartheid state toward a democracy .They certainly suggest a recipe of success for all indigenous writers and poets like me in our strenuous search for a vigorous and prospective writing. I might safely vaunt, among all the established and emerging Chinese writers and poets, my spiritual bond with African traditions has been unmistakably unassailable. I say this with the fullest extent of assurance and pride for the simple but ample reason that Africa has been thrice the object of my keenest attachment, emotional, intellectual and poetic.

Friends, I have never set afoot upon the soil of your beautiful land, yet this country called by the name of South Africa has been the Mecca that has titillated my imagination for all my life. Yes,

要结束的最后一个月,我写下了献给纳尔逊·曼德拉的长诗《回望二十世纪》,同样,当改变了20世纪历史进程的世界性伟人,纳尔逊·曼德拉离开我们的时候,我又写下了长诗《我们的父亲》来纪念这位人类的骄子,因为他是我们在精神上永远不会死去的父亲。是的,朋友们,从伟大的纳尔逊·曼德拉的身上,我们看到了伟大的人格和巨大的精神所产生的力量,这种力量,它会超越国界、种族以及不同的信仰,这种伟大的人格和精神,也将会在这个世界的每一个角落,深刻地影响着人类对自由、民主、平等、公正的价值体系的重构,从而为人类不同种族、族群的和平共处开辟出更广阔的道路。伟大的南非,在此,请接受我对你的敬意!

朋友们,我知道,姆基瓦人道主义大奖是为纪念南非著名的人权领袖、反对种族隔离和殖民统治的斗士理查德·姆基瓦而设立的。这个奖曾颁发给我们十分崇敬的纳尔逊·曼德拉、肯·甘普、菲德尔·卡斯特罗等政要和文化名人。我为获得这样一个奖项而感到万分荣幸。基金会把我作为一个在中国以及世界各地推动艺术和文化发展的领导人物,并授予我"世界性人民文化的卓越捍卫者"的称号,这无疑是对我的一种莫大的鼓励。

同样在此时此刻,我的内心也充满着一种惶恐和不安,因为我为这个世界人类多元文化的传承和保护所做出的创造性工作和贡献还非常有限。作为中国少数民族作家学会的现任会长,作为中国在地方省区工作的一位高级官员,同时也作为一个行动的诗人,我一直在致力于多民族文化的保护和传承,并把这种传承和保护,作为一项神圣的职责。在我的努力下,青海湖国际诗歌节、青海国际诗人帐篷圆桌会议、

remote and distant, I have nevertheless chanced upon your country for innumerable times in dream, between midnight and dawn when sleep comes in snatches. Since the latter part of the 20th century, South Africa has been my Stalingrad to thwart and crack the segregationist walls of Apartheid, an apocalyptical war wherein human destiny hangs on a single thread of confrontation between justice and injustice, tyranny and freedom, equality and oppression. Not without a good reason.

Back in the 1980s, when a youth aspirant of the laurel crown of the Muses, I wrote a poem hailing the antiquity of African civilizations and extolling the numerous virtues of Black people. Your industry, your innocence and courage has been one of my favored themes. As the last month of the 20th century plodded its way towards eventuality, I dedicated a long poem Looking Back to the 20th Century to Nelson Mandela, the man who has acquired an iconic epoch-making standing in the minds of peoples across all the five known continents. Again when the most saddening news of his departure from the human scene reached me, my heart contracted with grief and pain, I penned a long poem entitled Our Father to elegize and mourn over the untimely decaying of this "icon of the times" who has had such enormous impact on the domestic and global politics of our time and remains immortal to my memory and posterity. To quote Clinton, Mandela "simply soldiered on, raging against injustice and leading us towards the light." The former American president makes a point worth emphasizing. Nelson Mandela, a born leader, afire with the faith in the indomitable character of human hope, lives an epic life of hardship, resilience, eventual triumph and ultimate forgiveness of his Afrikaner opponents, revealing a towering personality and a luminous spirit that transcend racial, religious and national barriers and helping shape the trend of things to come. He awakens an echo dormant in men's hearts. He drives us all to noble deeds. He senses the absolute necessity of our time in the reevaluation and restructuring of our scales of norms and values, such as freedom, justice, fairness and equality to pave way for a more humanistic and peacefully co-existent future. Dear and great South Africa, please accept our sincerest and warmest congratulations, owing to one vital fact of your best son of Nelson Mandela, you have earned my eternal admiration and I am returning to the fold, South Africa, my second spiritual home.

Friends, I am wide awake to the fact that Mkiva Humanitarian Awards were established in 1999 in honor of another Mandela like hero, Richard Mkiva, from a obscure Bolotwa village of Dutywa, a community activist and a fighter for the rights of the rural communities, now also enshrined as a symbol of resistance against the apartheid policies and laws. I am really flattered to enter this Hall of Fame with resounding celebrities like Nelson Mandela, Fidel Castro, President Rawlings and Dr Salim Ahmed Salim as gigantic predecessors. I count myself, both humbled and blessed as you, all the distinguished jury, judge me as taking initiatives and orchestrating a number of cultural events that have somewhat global repercussions and conferring upon me the glorious title of "Champion of Peoples Freedom." What a boon to my ego! What a boost for my

达基沙洛国际诗人之家写作计划、诺苏艺术馆暨国际诗人写作中心对话会议、三江源国际摄影节、世界山地纪录片节、青海国际水与生命音乐之旅以及青海国际唐卡艺术与文化遗产博览会已经成为中国进行国际文化交流和对话的重要途径和平台。

尽管如此,我深知在这样一个全球化的时代,由于跨国资本和理性技术的挤压,人类文化多样性的生存空间,已经变得越来越狭小,从这个意义而言,我们所有的开创性工作,也才算有了一个初步的开头。为此,我将把这一崇高的来自非洲的奖励,看成是你们对伟大的中国和对勤劳、智慧、善良的中国人民的一种友好的方式和致敬,因为中国政府和中国人民,在南非人民对抗殖民主义的侵略和强权的每一个时期,都坚定地站在南非人民所从事的正义事业的一边,直至黑暗的种族隔离制度最终从这个地球上消失。

今年是南非民主化二十周年,我们知道,新南非在1994年的首次民主选举,让南非成功地避免了一场流血冲突和内战,开启了一条寻求和平协商的道路,制定了高举平等原则的南非新宪法。二十年过去了,我们今天看到的新南非,仍然是一个稳定繁荣与民主的国度。我们清楚地知道,中国和南非同属金砖国家,我们有着许多共同的利益,两国元首在互访中所确定的经济、贸易和文化上的交流任务,为我们未来的发展指明了方向,我相信,未来的中国和未来的南非都将会更加美好。

最后,请允许我表达这样一种心意,那就是再一次向姆基瓦人道主义基金会,致以我最深切的感激之情,因为你们的大胆而无私的选择,我的名字将永远与伟大的南非,与伟大的理查德·姆基瓦的名字联系在一起。同样,我将会把你们给我带来的

tenuous endeavor to enhance cultural diversity and conservation of cultural heritage in a remote economic backwater province of China!

Words fail me at this moment. Uneasiness and irritation seep in. The difficulty is that I have rendered this troubled and tormented world a very small, albeit useful, service. True, for years in my office as vice governor, I deem it incumbent upon me to protect our physical and spiritual country and my efforts have borne some fruits as I have pioneered ,as initiator and architect ,the successful staging of several cultural events, either yearly or biannual, such as Qinghai Lake International Poetry Festival, Qinghai Tent Roundtable Forum for World Poets, Sanjiangyuan International Photographing Festival, World Mountain Documentary Festival, Musical Tour of Qinghai International Water & Life Concert as well as Qinghai International Thangka and Cultural Heritage Exhibition Fair. I have also raised money for two other cultural enterprises, ie, a modern Yi Art Museum and a Dajishaluo International Poets House now under hot construction. Essential to my initiative is Qinghai's extreme alpine topography and remote mountainous terrain as famed Roof of the World, which supports a diversity of bio-species of irreplaceable value. No less important is the region as potpourri of multi-religions, multi-races and multi-cultures. I do dream of using art to bring to the world's attention the elemental processes of human cultures attached to the mountainous terrain, to enact dialogues between various cultures, to enhance the harmonious relationship between man and nature and assist the public to understand the implications of the environmental cataclysms that might jeopardize the alpine eco-system in the wake of the sweeping reckless modernization.

Infinitesimal as my contribution, your award comes as the highest token of recognition not only for my relentless bid of cultural import, but also as a gentle reminder of warm friendship that is evolving between Chinese people and South African people, simply because at each critical juncture for the last 70 years, our government and our people have chosen unswervingly to align with you in your heroic struggle to trample under feet the shameful Apartheid and other forms of insidious repression until the bright day of justice and equality emerges.

2014 marks the 20th anniversary of a new democratized South Africa, the first general election being successfully held after the most ignoble chapter in your history was turned. A bloody internecine war was evaded. Instead, a path of peaceful reconciliation and constitutional republic embracing for the first time citizens of color was blazed, pacesetting for still some to follow, awe-inspiring for many to watch breathless. The euphoria that accompanied the release of Nelson Mandela from Rueben Island has been well exploited and founded, as the past 20 years has seen the growth of a new South Africa, a land of political stability, economic prosperity and cultural brilliance. Belonging to the same bloc of the Bricks, Sino-South African relations have run smoothly due to a plethora of interests common to both sides. Presidents of both countries have exchanged visits and outlined agendas of cooperation touching the sectors of economics, cultures and trade, pointing to a promising tomorrow for both countries.

这样一种自豪,传递给我千千万万的同胞,我相信,他们也将会为此而感到由衷的自豪。谢谢大家!

To conclude, let me reiterate: I must convey my deepest gratitude to Mkiva Humanitarian Foundation and Imbongi Yesizwe Trust. Your daring and selfless decision to make me the recipient of your award has once and for all, welded my name with the worthier name of Richard Mkiva, with great South Africa. What is left on my part is to impart the sense of pride and elation such an accolade has sparkled in me to millions upon millions of my country folks. I assure you, this honor to me is also theirs. Thanks for your attention.

我们时代的诗歌传奇

给费尔南多·伦东·梅里诺颁发青海湖国际诗歌节国际诗歌交流贡献奖的颁奖词

2014年8月7日

各位女士、各位先生,诗人朋友们:

今天在这里,我非常荣幸地为费尔南多·伦东·梅里诺颁发青海湖国际诗歌节国际诗歌交流贡献奖,我以为这既是对他为当代国际诗歌交流贡献的一种肯定,同时也是为了更好地来进一步促进不同民族、不同国家、不同地域诗歌的交流。

关于费尔南多·伦东·梅里诺,不光我们在座的许多朋友熟悉他,其实,早在二十年前,他就已经成为国际诗坛国际诗歌交流领域里一位十分活跃的组织者。前不久,他的一本诗集在中国出版,我在序言中曾这样写道,"费尔南多·伦东·梅里诺在当今世界诗坛,无疑是一个带有标识性和符号性的人物。坦率地说,说他是一个带有标识性和符号性的人物,并不是讲他的诗歌作品在当今世界诗坛占有特殊位置,而是因为,他作为一个行动的诗人,在全球化背景下的世界诗歌运动中,所体现出来的无与伦比的显赫作用,以及他对当今进行的跨国界诗歌交流所做出的巨大贡献。

据我所知,他无疑是这样一个始终把行动看得更为重要,同时一直在把自己全部的力量和智慧,奉献给人类诗歌建设的人。毫无疑问,他是这个世界上我所了解和认识的、为推动当代诗歌发展和繁荣、众多的诗歌活动组织者中最为杰出的几个人

A Legend of Our Time
At the Ceremony of Presenting an Award in Honor of Fernando Rendon's Outstanding Contribution to Promote World Poetry Movement
7th, August, 2014

Ladies and Gentlemen, Fellow Poets:

I am privileged today to present an award to Mr Fernando Rendon in recognition of his excellent leadership in promoting poetic expansion across our planet as a powerful tool for change, a token of our gratitude not only for him as such a charismatic leader in initiating two of the greatest contemporary cultural movements, ie, International Poetry Festival of Medelin and WPM(World Poetry Movement) ,but also as a call for action to all our fellow poets, inspired by his example and wishing to emulate Fernando Rendon in furthering the grand cause of which the great Columbian has been such a rallying-point and a standard.

Regarding the Columbian whom we honor on this special occasion, I trust many of our friends in the audience know him quite intimately. In fact, back in the 1900s, F.R emerged to become a household name as promoter and central figure in organizing poetic events and boosting communications among world poets. Very recently, the first book of his verse has been published in China which I have prefaced thus:"The unmistakable towering personality of contemporary world poetry, the figure of Fernando Rendon has however, an even greater importance than lyrical talent warrants, that is, in the capacity of a poet in action, destiny has hoisted on his shoulders of leadership of world poetic movements in the present age of globalization, a function , as we all see so vividly , he has performed and officiated so admirably that earns him worldwide admiration and reverence.

To the best of my knowledge, Fernando Rendon's emergence has come at a difficult time of Columbian history when his home country has been bled by an almost half-century-long fratricidal wars. To the woes and burning issues of his country and the world, he has brought the resources of his powerful intellect. Poetry to him has naturally become a weapon in bringing an end to internal conflicts and social injustice, in the firm belief in a fair Colombian reconciliation, but also world peace made possible through protracted poetic actions in the ardent construction of a globe for poetry and for life. We feel compelled to honor him because he has contributed, like no

物之一。

"费尔南多·伦东·梅里诺就像一团火,他无论走到哪里,都在为诗歌而奔走呼号,因为他的努力,在哥伦比亚麦德林启动的'国际诗歌运动',才成为一个全球范围内的旨在为了促进和平、社会公正、人权和自然保护的跨文化行动。可以说,自诗歌诞生以来,还从未有过这样广泛的世界性的诗歌对话和交流,这一行动让诗歌在改变人类生命、重构更人道的人类价值体系方面发挥了不可估量的作用。

"面对今天这样一个被资本和技术操控的时代,把诗歌作为武器,并试图通过诗歌的传播和启蒙来改变人类的生存方式,并为所有的生命找到通向明天的光明路径,在有些人看来,完全是痴人妄想,但费尔南多·伦东·梅里诺从未放弃这一追求和梦想,正因为在他身上所具有的这种永远不向任何邪恶势力妥协的高尚品质,他才取得了在常人看来,完全不可能取得的成功,也正是因为这一巨大的成功,他才成为我们从事诗歌运动的榜样。"

鉴于费尔南多·伦东·梅里诺在国际诗歌交流中所做出的贡献,特别是他始终将诗歌作为人类建设未来美好生活的武器,并从未放弃过对这一理想的执着追求,青海湖国际诗歌节组委会,特别决定为他颁发青海湖国际诗歌节"国际诗歌交流贡献奖"。

one else, through inciting and organizing poetic activities in various forms, to a flourishing world poetry movement as we all are an active part of.

"Afire with passion for spreading poetic joy, Fernando Rendon is a man born with a mission, which is poetry, with a divine message to carry across frontiers between nations, races and religions ,which is poetry for peace and justice. In the wake of phenomenal success of the exemplary International Poetry Festival of Medelin, he has added luster and glory to the Muses by starting WPM in a more vigorous and multitudinous celebration of life and earth involving a truly global participation of poets worldwide enhancing the rise of 'a new planetary awareness that shall promote urgent changes in the attitude of contemporary society' in the face of all the world crises to promote peace, social justice and ecological conservation. We might safely assume, no other lay person under the sun has achieved as much as our brilliant Fernando Rendon, the superb strategist of cultural movements, since the birth of poetry, in the way and momentum of spreading poetic joy and boosting communications among peer poets on such a massive scale. Increasingly WPM has been seen as a cataclysm in rebuilding human value systems and reorienting our lives towards a more humanistic tomorrow.

"We are living in a world of manufac tured needs, mass consumption and mass infotainment, driven by the aggregate preferences of capital lords and money chasers. To all this glitter of crass capitalism, Fernando Rendon turns his back by striking his bold blow and his method is nothing short of Herculean bravery as he trusts poets can work wonders and lead people onto a royal road of liberation and freedom. No wonder to some, Fernando Rendon is a modern Don Quixote, the idealistic dreamer who 'assumes the power of poetry for change and urgent transformations' unabashedly , and Fernando Rendon's attempt at awakening people from their materialistic fetish through poetic readings resemble the exaggerated deeds of the 16th century's chivalric hero. But with what fortitude ,strategic planning, and tact our modern Don Quixote has rallied allies and defied evil forces to emerge phenomenally successful to become a model we follow, an example we emulate."

Dear Fernando Rendon, on behalf of the Organizing Committee of Qinghai Lake International Poetry, I ask you to receive this Outstanding Contribution Award in honor of your decades of persistent and heroic striving for a better world through the medium of poetry.

向诗歌致敬

在 2014 年国际诗人帐篷圆桌会议上的致辞

2014 年 8 月 7 日

我亲爱的各位诗人同行，各位尊敬的朋友：

本届国际诗人帐篷圆桌会议，在大家的共同努力下，已经顺利地完成了各项议程，今晚就要圆满闭幕了。我想此时此刻，大家都有一个共同的感受，那就是每一次诗人的聚会，就如同一种庄严、古老、崇高的仪式，为此，我敢肯定在人类所有的艺术形式中，唯有诗歌并与之相伴随生发出来的音乐和舞蹈，才会产生这样一种不同凡响、更为彰显生命本质的行为和力量。

在这里，我不由得想到了伟大的西班牙诗人加西亚·洛尔加，他始终认为，通过有生命的媒介和联系传达诗的信息，最能发挥诗歌中"杜恩德"（duende）的作用，如果直接翻译成中文就是"灵魔的力量"。是的，我坚信每一位真正的诗人，都具有这样一种上天赋予他的神奇力量。恐怕这也是数千年来，诗歌充满灵性和魅力而又经久不衰的重要理由，同样这也是人类热爱诗歌，并把诗歌视为自己精神生活中，最为美好、最为温暖、最为动人那样一个部分的真正原因。

永恒的时间和人类的心灵渴望，已经无数次地证明过，诗歌的存在，无疑是人类不断延续个体生命和集体生命的实证，因为它从生命存在更为本质的角度，强调了诗歌在精神世界中的作用，也正是这种对精神的需求和向往，才让人类与别的动物产生了更大的区别。从这个意义而言，只要人类的生命存在并把这种对精神的需求不断延续下去，那么诗歌就永远不会离开我们！

朋友们，诗歌就像一束熊熊燃烧的火把，直到今天它仍然站在人类前行的最前

A Tribute to Poetry

A Speech Given at the Poetic Evening Dedicated to Humanity
On the Closing of the 2014 Tent Roundtable Forum of World Poets
7th, August, 2014

Dear Fellow Poets, respectable friends:

At last, this latest edition of our poetry festival associated with the most beautiful lake of China, this biennial signal event attended by such a prestigious bevy of key figures of contemporary poetic writing, home and abroad, has realized, under the theme of "Poetic Writing in the Poet and the Poet in Society", all the set agendas as we are now led to the point at which to call it a day. This moment and over here, I trust a sacred, ancient and sublime sense of ritual must overwhelm this crowd of us that daily live in celebration of life. The wondrous work achieved by poetry reminds me of an ultimate fact that only poetry, among all forms of human art, with all its attendant dance and music, can reinstate the wholeness of life in a way nothing else can.

This calls my remembrance to the admirable buzz word "duende" invented by Garcia Lorca, the great Andalucian bard who trusts "duende", the magical power, can only be detonated, like nuclear fission, by good poetry which involves delving into the subconscious to mine some substance that will transform this world. Yes, I firmly trust each poet in the company of this evening is endowed by the Creator with the Lorcan duende, thanks to which we have been, since time immemorial, avid of Truth, not lies, of the Good, not of evil, of the Beauty, not of the Ugly. The secret of poetry's lasting popularity, ie, people have kept returning to poetry and reserving an important place in their spiritual life, lies precisely in this poets' almost self-indulgent infatuation with their calling.

The infinitude of time and the profundity of human cravings are eternal testament to the essentiality of poetry for the preservation and proliferation of humanity, individual or collective, at the level of either physical or spiritual. It has been our most recalcitrant act of faith that man cannot live by bread alone. The spiritual primacy, nay, indeed, the poetic primacy of man has been touchstone by which man is distinguished from all other species on earth.

Friends, poetry, the beacon light of mankind, forever in the vanguard of human progress, has radiated its warmth and inspiration upon the pathway of world peoples ahead. In the first

列,它照亮了不同种族和人类迈向明天的道路。当曙光开始出现在地平线的时候,诗歌不仅仅是黎明时的号角,它还会给我们一个又一个未卜先知的启示,并随时谦恭地为前行者擦亮眼睛。诗歌既是反抗一切异化的工具,更重要的是它会让人类重新从摇篮中苏醒,再一次认清生命的意义,并辨明人类正确、光明的前进方向!

在这个圆桌会议即将拉上帷幕的时候,请允许我代表在座的各位并以我所居住和生活的这个高原的名义,向我们尊敬的诗人法伊夫·博纳富瓦、尼卡诺尔·帕拉、塔杜施·鲁热维奇、加里·斯奈德、特朗斯特罗姆、郑玲、埃内斯托·卡德纳尔致敬!由于他们年龄和身体的原因,我们不能如愿地邀请他们来到这里,但他们的存在,却时时刻刻给我们坚守诗的梦想提供了无穷的勇气和力量。我们会从他们的诗歌中,再一次感受到对生命的热爱、对自由的向往、对弱者的同情、对暴力的反抗、对悲伤的抚慰以及对现实永不妥协的追问!

在这里,我还要借此机会,向生活在这个地球上,不同地域、不同民族、不同国家的所有诗人致敬!同样,因为你们的存在,这个充满和并存着进步与危机、幸福与灾难、创造与毁灭的世界,才会让上苍的天平朝着更加和平、正义和美好的方面倾斜!

朋友们,我不得不说"再见"这个词了,我热切地期待着与大家的下一次再见!谢谢你们!谢谢!

glimmer of dawn, it serves a clarion call to begin the day's toiling, the oracle to be divined into the mystery of the future, the tool to combat alienation as well as the balm for our agonized hearts. To crown it all, it will awaken the souls that slumber into the significance of life afresh and puts us onto the right track again.

Now, at the time of the most symbolic curtain fall, please allow me, on behalf of each of us present and of the Plateau I have made home, to pay tribute to Yves Bonnefoy, Nicanor Parra、Tadeusz Rozewicz,Gary Snyder,Tomas Transtromer,zheng Ling,Ernesto Cardenal.These veterans' marked absence from this festival due to failing health or seniority is sorely regretted, but their lifelong clinging to the poetic dreams has been a perennial source of zeal and strengthen. For their exemplary passion for poetry has brought to light the enormous potential of us younger generation to demonstrate love for life, longing for freedom, sympathy for the weak and downtrodden, to oppose barbarity, to console those in affliction and adversity, and last but not in the least, to enact a dialogue with reality unflinchingly, because ultimately "the options of life, justice, dignity and beauty, amply represented by poetry, are the only alternative left to us humans", an enterprise worthy of our lasting human name.

Once more, cap in hand, let me rise and salute all our fellow poets across the globe. Emphatically due to your presence and involvement in a world full of promise and crisis, bliss and woe, creation and destruction, the pendulum of the Providence swings in human favor of peace, justice and beauty.

Friends, though mostly reluctant to say the word, I must face the music and utter adieu to you all. And this certainly makes the best excuse for your next visit. Thank you for your attention.

诗歌的本土写作和边缘的声音

在 2014 青海国际诗人帐篷圆桌会议上的演讲

2014 年 8 月 3 日

当我用这样一个题目开始演讲的时候,我首先想到的是,在今天这样一个让新自由主义思潮和资本逻辑横行的时代,我们不同民族的文化,确实已经遭到了从未有过的威胁。所谓新自由主义的思想和主张,之所以能大行其道,那是因为不断加速的全球化进程给他们提供了自认为最实在的佐证,同样也因为这样一个全球化的过程,新自由主义思想和主张,才找到了似乎谁也无法阻挡的传播空间。

其实,所谓"全球化",就是资本的主要操控者,让资本按照其意愿自由地流动,或者说让经济和金融打破原有的国家和区域的经济界限,整合为一。这种被称为世界经济场的状态,实际上是这个世界经济竞争游戏规则的制定者们,他们强行而巧妙地带着大家玩的一场,永远只有利于他们的游戏。

我们知道的国际货币基金组织和世界贸易组织,当然也包括像世界银行这样的面向全球的机构,不言而喻,就是他们在背后用一双看不见的手,操控着的一系列跨国组织。在当下,让我们感到这种威胁越来越严重的是,这种资本的自由入侵,以及它所带来的只为疯狂营利的唯一市场逻辑,已经给我们的文化传承和发展,造成了极为不利的影响。

需要声明的是,我并不反对市场对经济的主要调节作用,而是反对新自由主义的荒谬主张,这种主张有时并不是明目张胆的,它们还常常穿着虚假的外衣,以经济的高速增长为诱饵,强势美化资本的自由流动带来的所谓种种好处。它们只强调经济增长在人类生活中的唯一性,而只把单一的经济指标的提高,作为社会发展的整

Localized Poetic Writing and marginalized Voice

Key-note Speech Delivered at the Opening Ceremony of 2014 Tent Roundtable Forum of World Poets

3rd, August, 2014

The topic for today brings me instantly to the nexus of events set off by the ascendancy of neo-laissez-faire ism and the spread of crass capitalism and attendant threats caused to cultural, ecological and ethnic diversity. The pulverizing effects in the wake of the rapid integration of neo-laissez-faire philosophy and the swift globalization, to the market fundamentalists, are a hard case of self-fulfilling prophecy. No wonder they herald a newly emerging flattening world in which their iron hearted advocacy takes a firm hold on popular imagination.

By globalization, as a provocative turn of phrase, in fact, is taken a general trend that capital barons masquerading as transnational businesses move to globalize the world by rapidly dissolving the social and economic barriers between nations and transforming the world's diverse populations into a blandly uniform market. This is a game played adroitly by the market fundamentalists who define the rules to enrich the rich at the expense of workers, the environment, the traditional values.

The so called flattening of the world, more or less, is a virtual reality created by invisible but omnipotent forces, of which, inadvertently, super world bodies like WTO, IMF, who claim to be amoral transnational guardian of public good, are major players as an invisible hand in tearing apart our world instead of guiding it and keeping it from going off the rails. Increasingly, our former warm, cozy, thriving local communities, industries, and cultures are crowded out. Such disempowering dangers must not be underestimated.

It should be cautioned from the very outset I am not mindless of the legitimate regulating function of the market in economy. Our job is certainly not to trash the market but to give its defenders on the far Right their due: market fundamentalists invariably hold the social good is best served by allowing people to pursue their self interest without any thought of the Good, the True and Beauty. Such advocacy in favor of uninhibited flow of fund, often assuming the disarmingly deceptive and beguilingly innocent mantle , is at best a perversion of human nature, no matter how much tangible and quick benefits in form of rapid GDP ratio it can deliver. The

体的终极目标。

由于这种主张,在社会生活中人的全面发展的理念,被资本形成的权力统治曲解,一些本应该由国家和政府去服务的公共领域,也开始大面积地倒退,一些新的社会问题的形成,包括失业和贫困人口的增加,社会福利的减少,可以说从根本上讲,这种所谓全球化的资本主义,给人类带来的恶果已经显而易见,它让许多国家和政府的社会功能大大减弱,甚至让一些政府在社会保障、教育、卫生、文化等方面的服务变成了缺席者。

这种可怕的利益逻辑,既抹杀了文化的特性,同时又让我们生产的文化产品,开始同质化和趋同化。在这方面我们有许多例证,比如对好莱坞电影生产模式的追捧,就使不少国家的民族电影业遭到了毁灭性的打击,这种情况在第三世界国家中尤为严重,一味要求票房的价值,已经成为衡量其作品价值的一个可怕的标准,这种商业化泛滥的情形,对真正有价值的文化发展所造成的损害,超过了历史上的任何一个时期。

在许多国家和地区,对传统的非物质文化的保护和发展,原有的许多补贴也被降到了最低。许多国家和地区,毫无秩序地过度地开发旅游,对本应该保护的原生态文化也进行了破坏性的商业利用。最让人不可接受的是,这种与灾难完全可以画等号的经济文化模式,却在必须尊重市场规律的幌子下,被许多新自由主义的宣教者,拿到无数国家去兜售,并在这些国家建立起了自己的"商业"文化王国,其结果只能是,那些被传承了数千年的地域文化,不同民族的语言、文字以及独特的生活方式,都无不面临着死亡和消失的考验。

除了这些,新干涉主义带来的诸多问题,也在这个地球的四面八方开始显现。在中东,特别是在伊拉克、埃及等地,战火不断,在原有的政治社会秩序被破坏之后,新的政治社会秩序并没有被真正地建立起来。

由此,我们不会不去深层地思考,不同文明、不同价值体系、不同宗教信仰、不同文化背景的国家和民族,如何由自己去选择和建立更合乎自己的社会制度以及发展道路,如何更好地为建立一个更加和平的世界而开展积极的建设性的对话。

面对这样一个世界,为什么我要如此坚持和强调诗歌的本土写作呢?其实,我上

overall goal of mankind must be reconciled with purely mercantile necessities.

Such logic of globalization, to say the least, is lopsided. Perversion of human nature leads to intentional mis-defining of the obligations of the government to the extent many public goods, which traditionally fall into the administrative scope, is nobody's business. Many nation states have withdrawn en masse from sectors of public goods. Many people, particularly in less developed countries, have been hurt absent being bailed out by a social security net. New social problems crop up. Unemployment is rife. Fringe benefits and welfare become scarce. This is not progress, but regress. If globalization is only about the spread of crass capitalism, indeed it has become increasingly clear the dangers inherent in the philosophy of neo laissez faire has materialized to the detriment of the fulfillment of administrative functions of many an absenteeing nation states and governments .

This naturally triggers a backlash and complaint against globalization. We are living in a world of manufactured needs, mass consumption and mass infotainment, motivated by profits and driven by the aggregate preferences of billions of consumers. Belonging by default to this global village, people emulate and toady to the Hollywood model and churn out MacDonaldized movies and soap series to the extent cultural products outside USA all have an American look and take an American outlook. Movies industry particularly falls a prey to the Mammon of "box value" in many third world countries wherein what counts boils down to blatant profiteering motives. Therefore harms done to cultural diversity is unmatched and unprecedented in the annals of mankind due to such heedless pursuit of profit, let alone the environment and other social values being either compromised or marginalized.

The development of our political arrangements has not kept pace with the development of cultural production. There is the uneven misallocation of resources between private goods and public goods obvious for anyone with the naked eye to see. In many developing countries, enthusiasm and subsidies for the production and protection of the intangible assets wane and dwindle to a record low. Over exploitation of hot scenic spots and enchanting sights, many being of un-spoilt and aboriginal character, deserving maximum degree of conservation, has been taken for granted. What abhors me most is such calamitous modes of development are everywhere exalted to the sky by neo laissez faire preachers in collaboration with various imposters and money chasers to forge their kingdoms of profit ostensibly in the name of incubating culture. Indeed, unless serious steps are taken to readdress the flagrant wrong to conserve the environment and strengthen cultures-this "juggernaut of globalization as Americanization", in just a few decades, will eradicate the cultural, ecological and even zoological diversity that took millions of years of human, plant and animal evolution to produce.

On top of these hazards, neo laissez faire advocates have created more problems than solved. Especially in the Middle East, the triumphant collapse of strongmen like Sad am Hussein and Mubarak has brought neither economic stability nor social democracy to former Iraq and

面的发言已经说明了很多问题，这也是我为什么要反对新自由主义的一个根本原因。当然，无可讳言，我是站在全球范围这样一个角度来讲的。作为生活在地球村里的一个诗人，我想无论我们生活在这个世界的哪一个区域，我们捍卫人类伟大文明成果的神圣职责，是永远不可放弃的。从人类道德的高度而言，尤其在今天，当这种珍贵文明的基础，在被"全球化"动摇的时候，我们只能选择挺身而出，而不能袖手旁观。不过需要进一步阐释的是，我所主张的本土写作，是相对于这个世界更大范围而言的，是对新自由主义"全球化"思潮的在理论上的反动。

因为"全球化"在文化上的一个最大特征，就是抹杀个性，就是让多样性变成单一性，让差异性变成同一性，使这个世界多声部的合唱，最终变成一个声音。更为恐怖的是，这种由跨国资本控制和自由市场所形成的力量，毫无疑问对文化多样性的危害，是最为致命的，这绝不是我危言耸听，在亚洲，在非洲，在拉丁美洲，这样的例子层出不穷，乌拉圭著名作家爱德华多·加莱亚诺的《拥抱之书》，就深刻地揭示了这一问题的本质。

在这里，需要说明的是，我不是在探讨一般意义上的人类在发展中存在的问题，更不是要否定人类在工业文明和科技进步方面所取得的巨大成就。我想要表述的是，这个世界上的任何一种文化，哪怕是最弱势的文化，它也有无可辩驳的独立存在的价值。但是，令我们感到不安的是，今天的市场逻辑只要求文化产品的商业价值，而把许多具有精神价值的文化产品弃之一旁。诗歌的本土写作，说到底就是要求诗人在任何时候，都应该成为自己所代表的文化符号，都应该义无反顾地代表这个文化发出自己必须发出的声音。诗人之所以被称为诗人，据我所知，其从来就不是一个职业的称谓，而这一称号却是一个人所共知的社会角色，从某种角度来讲，就如同但丁对于意大利，普希金对于俄罗斯，密茨凯维奇对于波兰，叶芝对于爱尔兰，诗人在更长的历史时空中，其承担的社会角色，毫无疑问就是他的祖国文化的第一代言人，同样也是他的民族的无可争议的良心。

在这个消费至上和物质主义的时代，或许已经有不少人，开始怀疑诗人在今天存在的价值，对此不用担心，因为只要有人类存在，人类伟大的文明的延续就不会停止，而作为人类文明最重要的精神支柱之一的诗歌，就不会丧失其崇高的地位和作用。

Egypt, or for that matter, to the rest of the world.

Such disheartening massive geopolitical disorder inclines us to rethink this global crisis has to be overcome if humanity is to assert command over its destiny. The point of departure for such self assertion must be revelation that human history is too complex to be predesigned according to a banal reductionist hypothesis of humans, regardless of religion, ethnicity, origin of civilization, value system, all factors to be taken into consideration before engaging in a constructive dialogue for a more humane and peaceful world.

Living in a "gilded age" and a globe out of control, why should I cling so hard to the stance of a poetry steeped in the native soil? The above vehement tirade against the excessive reliance on the market mechanism and the shortcomings of neo liberalism provides clues into my way of thinking. I am, of course, generalizing on the global level as a poet. There is no shirking the moral responsibility, wherever we happen to be, of protecting and defending the sanctity of all the spiritual fruits and enriching the cultural cornucopia of mankind. From a moral vantage when the forces of globalization begin to erode the very basis of civilization and sap its vitality, we poets must rise to the occasion to magnify the capacity of individuals and inscribe them on the world with the means we excel, which is, poetic writing per se. Here a word must be in place to qualify my position that localized poetic writing be used as an anti-homogenizing force, an antidote against the potential threats posed by the variant of globalization promoted by neo liberalism or market fundamentalists.

In cultural terms, globalization tends towards homogenization and erasing of personality and particularity into sameness and identity, solo into chorus, as the most salient feature. In every way this should be taken as both prognosis and diagnosis: the forces of globalization, a coalition of transnational businesses and jungle market, are sworn foes to cultural diversity. This urgent warning about the state of global cultures should not fall on deaf ears of world poets, the truth of which is poignantly illuminated in the El libro de los abrazos by Uruguayan Eduardo Galeano, one of our age's sages.

While worries about the negative outcome of globalization are legitimate, and indeed very important, it must be conceded, ignoring the ability of the industrial and technological advances to empower humans misses their historically positive role-playing on human freedom and happiness. My point here is that any culture, however small and weak, deserves a place to be sustained. What I argue against is the logic of ultra right market which demands cultural products, no matter how much spiritual value they embody and contain, unless they sell hot, will be thrust forth to scorn and scattered to the four winds. When I am talking of localized poetic writing, I mean a poet should make himself a civic voice, a mouthpiece of popular content and discontent, an icon of his own people, speak unabashedly and unflinchingly to the world and for the world. To the best of my knowledge, poetry is never a vocation, a line of business like carpentry and a poet is never a careerist a blacksmith is. Yet each ancient and great civilization accords a poet an

在当今这个让人类处于极端困惑，并正在遭遇深度异化的现实世界里，诗歌除了其固有的审美作用，以及用词语所创造的无与伦比的人类精神高度外，其实已经勇敢地承担起了捍卫人类伟大文明的重任，已经成为反抗一切异化和强权的工具。我们一定要清醒地看到，今天的诗歌写作，已经不仅仅是诗人的个体活动，当面对强大的经济世界主义和国际经济强权的压迫时，一个世界性的诗歌运动，正在这个地球的许多地方开展起来，而这一诗歌运动本身，正以其自己独特的方式，去抚慰生活在不同地域的人们的心灵，并用诗歌点燃的火炬去引领人类走向一个更符合人的全面发展的新的理想目标。这个目标不是别的，它会让人类再一次相信，这个由诗歌构建的精神高地，就是通往明天的真正的乌托邦！

esteemed status, one commonly agreed upon and respected. Their place and importance in the spiritual life of mankind shall not be challenged. In a sense, in the firmament of world poetry, Dante to Italy, Pushkin to Russia, Mickiewicz to Poland, Yeats to Ireland,(what a cluster of lyrical talent!) are all meant to be the spokesmen of their culture ,the conscience of his their folks beyond dispute.

Consumerist capitalism, which reigns supreme across the globe, does not tend towards cultural harvest and spiritual plenty. Rumors and doubts are rampant about the sweet uses of poetry .I for one, stand firm in the belief no decent society can function properly without some role reserved for poets, simply because poetry is one of the most important pillars to buttress the spirituality of its people.

We are living in a world fraught with spiritual doldrums and fragmented mentality that bring matters to a head. It is not enough to roll in wealth and bask in creature comfort all kinds of technical gadgetry supplies. People also need an aesthetic vision of a better future. Poets have in the past crystallized admirably what common people widely sensed but vaguely vocalized ideas about the justification of civilization and the dignity of man as antidote against alienation and hegemony. Let us be clear about our mission today: a world poetry movement on the rise meets head-on the supremacy of globalization that threatens to homogenize everything and engulf the civic society. Poets, attentive to the aftermath of history per se, afire with passion for justice and freedom, follow the suit of their worthy predecessors, come to the rescue and solace of people in spiritualized torment and disarray and hoist the torches of poetry ascending the heights of light and sweetness, built upon the solid rock of enlightened human Intellect which leads into the palaces of Utopia of tomorrow.

山地族群的生存记忆与被拯救中的边缘影像
在 2014 中国(青海)世界山地纪录片节圆桌会议上的发言
2014 年 7 月 24 日

我一直有这样一个看法,或许这个看法在有的人看来并不成立,但我至今仍然坚持我的这种看法,那就是人类的文明有两大系统,简单地说就是海洋文明和山地文明,当然,在这里我说的是两大最主要的文明系统,不可否认,在人类的文明传承中,经过数以千年历史的变化,我们人类在今天,还能看见这样一个现象并未改变。海洋文明的传承,最终伴随着人类的探险、贸易、迁徙、掠夺、殖民等活动,影响日益扩大。特别是在近五百年来,由于人类航海技术的不断提升,海洋文明的传播,就其速度和覆盖面而言,毫无疑问大大地超过了其他的文明。

我要告诉大家的是,我在这里说的海洋文明,完全是相对于山地文明而言的,我没有用诸如西方文明、印度文明、阿拉伯文明、中国文明等等这样一些概念。同样在此,我无意去研究和探讨,在海洋文明的传播过程中,甚至不止一次出现过的,这两种文明之间所形成的冲突,更为严重的是,这一冲突曾导致一些古老的文明开始衰落和消亡。无可讳言,拉丁美洲和非洲等地域古老文明所遭遇过的危险,并最终酿成悲剧形成的原因,就来自这种冲突。难怪在纪念哥伦布发现美洲大陆五百年的时候,美洲土著人民(包括美洲后来形成的混血人种),他们的态度就与纪念活动的主办者们截然不同,他们发出的是几百年来被压抑了的抗议的声音。

在此,我需要声明,我不是在这里赘述这一冲突产生的背景和过程,而是想要说明,海洋文明作为一个庞大的文明体系,无论你对它进行何种评价,它都是一个我们必须面对的现实存在。需要再声明的是,我在这里所指的海洋文明,是从更广义的角

Existential Memory of Mountain Inhabitants and Marginalized Images Coming to the Rescue

Key-note Address at the 2014 Roundtable Forum of Qinghai World Mountain Documentary Festival

24th, July, 2014

A supposition I have been increasingly coming under the spell of, which to many frankly personal bias, totally untenable, is this: human civilizations to date fall into two typologies, ie, maritime and mountainous. My dissenting views, of course, could be set forth or elaborated in more logical terms to avoid the blurs and distortions which ensue necessarily in such flagrant reductionist generalities. Wherever the truth may lie, the fact looks to me crystal clear: the so called human civilization is the sum total of the increased productivity and opulence by and for the evolving man and the spiritual fruits achieved which offers both an interpretation of the natural world around him as well as a consecration of his daily work and his relationship with fellow beings and higher beings. Given the inherent dynamism materialized in expansionist adventures, trading, colonies, massive exodus and immigration, gunboats pillage and plunder, the contributions and historical significance of the maritime civilization, pioneered by the Greco-Roman people and succeeded by the Germanic-Slavic races, stand out clearly and overwhelmingly. A hard and stern look at the world history since 1500, due to the superior technology, especially in armaments and naval shipbuilding/ navigation, which facilitated the diffusion of the Greco-Roman model to outperform and dwarf almost the majority on the face of the earth, confirms the maritime supremacy beyond doubt.

Here I deliberately oppose maritime civilization to mountainous civilization without positing the dichotomy between western civilization and non-western variants such as Arabic/ Indus or Chinese, not unmindful of the unfortunate rivalries between the domination of the former and the subjugation of the latter as well as their deleterious effects. The result was, due to the emergence of the maritime races enjoying the mobility and superiority on the oceans of the world, a major alteration in the configuration of world affairs at the expense of many old centers of civilization in Africa and Latin America. What is truly significant in the perspective of Stavrianosian world history is the Iberian crusading impulse, initiated by a handful of Spanish swashbuckling conquistadors and mercenaries, turns out to be an operation of global import-the ultimate tragic

度来看的,是指这一文明的产生和传播,都与海洋密切相关,更确切地说,这是自始至终相对于山地文明来谈的。否则,会发生传统意义上对世界现存几大文明的误读。只有这样,我们才会从另一极来为古老而伟大的山地文明定位。我讲以上这些,只有一个目的,那就是要为我阐释清楚山地文明的重要性,做一个必不可少的铺垫,仅此而已。

可能大家都已经注意到了,我今天发言用的题目,就是此次论坛的主题,"山地族群的生存记忆与被拯救中的边缘影像",其实这并非我的冒昧自大,我更不愿意给大家造成这样的印象,我在给这样一个论坛主题作结论性的总结,其实我的这一席话与在座各位的发言一样,仅仅是一家之言。因为我知道,围绕着这样一个主题,每一个人的发言都会从不同的角度表达出自己独有的观点,而这些鲜明的思想,都将成为我们这次论坛,最具有建设性的贡献,也正因为大家的共同参与,这样一个各抒己见的对话,才富有更加积极的意义。

现在我必须把谈话的内容,拉回到"山地文明"这样一个中心。不知道大家注意到这样一个现象没有?近一两百年来,在全世界范围内,经济和社会发育程度最高的地方,似乎都在不同国家的沿海地带,或者说许多国家经济最繁荣的区域,大都在海岸线的附近。而恰恰相反,许多国家较为封闭、落后和贫困的区域,大多集中在高原和山地,这些地方往往交通不便,有的甚至置身于大陆腹地的最深处。无论从今天社会学和人类学的角度来观察,"山地文明"所保持着的原生态性,以及这种古老文明所具有的文化特质,其珍贵程度,对于当下人类来说都是无法估量的,它的价值将随着人类对自身的深度认识,必将越发显现出来。

任何事物,永远有着它的两面性,由于"山地文明"这样一种特殊的处境,千百年来生活在高原和山地的不同族群,他们才有幸和不幸地延续着自己古老的历史,他们独特的宇宙观、价值观、生活方式才在历史的选择中得以幸存。说他们有幸,那是因为这种文化延续,一直没有被外来的力量完全中断,他们已经成为这个世界多元文化的重要组成部分;说他们不幸,那是因为,他们那不可被替代的哲学思想、思维习惯、文化传统等等,正在被力量完全不对称的,外来的强势文化所包围和消解。

但始终令人欣慰的是,直到今天,虽然面临种种的威胁和危险,许多族群仍顽强

demise of Mayan and Aztec cultures. No wonder on the 500th anniversary in celebration of Columbus's discovery of the New World, the Spaniards and the Hispanic world were sharply divided, a voice of dissent suppressed for centuries on behalf of the aborigines by he natives and Creoles included.

Here I must omit, due to the limited time at my disposal, a survey of the nature of such fateful encounters before presenting my core thesis today, that is, given its size and weight, maritime civilization constitutes the overriding status quo we are living with, despite its failings and weaknesses. It should be cautioned again I am making some generalities and that my point is although maritime civilization prevails, mountainous civilization must not be dismissed as out of date or fossilized or retarded.

Each in the audience today must have wondered what today's topic, ie, "Existential Memory of Mountain Inhabitants and Marginalized Images Coming to the Rescue" really implies. A topic as such bespeaks of something like political correctness undeniably. But still, I ascend the podium, humbled and honored by the attendance of such a team of esteemed experts and professionals and I do anticipate and appeal to you to air your views and speak your minds heedless of what the topic might frown upon. Cross fertilization of minds, as befits the occasion, is meaningful only when arguments are offered and countered, given and taken.

I must curb the impulse of digression to focus on the corollary concept of maritime civilization, which is , mountain civilization. As we all know, the material culture of mankind has changed more in the past hundred years than it did in the previous five thousand years. The name of the game for this epochal transformation is the Industrial Revolution during the 1780s when a breakthrough, of prime importance for modern world, did occur in economic productivity as it provided the economic and military basis for the hegemony of maritime civilization, a goal aspired to by most of the underdeveloped countries. A phenomenon, for everyone with the naked eye to see, is that the world's most favored regions, in terms of economic prosperity and social opulence, are either coastal or interior close to the coast. In stark contrast, mountains and upland areas remain invariably economic backwater due to physical isolation and inaccessibility to the economic sustenance and intellectual stimulation from outside. This sounds paradoxical, but it is commonly assumed, that isolated and backward mountains , from the latest thinking of contemporary anthropology and ethnography, contains qualities in the residues of aboriginal and pristine cultures, valuable and priceless for a better understanding of our past and as studies of human nature.

In this sense, mountains and uplands shorn of economic take off are a blessing in disguise. Mountain inhabitants are fortunate as physical isolation makes it possible to retain intact their old ways, value systems and worldviews ,surviving the iron law of postal-Neolithic mutation and natural selection, becoming incorporated into the overall splendid cultural legacy and to which all races and peoples claim. On the other hand, mountain people, in face of the growing complexity of

地坚守着自己的文化传统,保留着自己的语言和文字,毫无疑问,这些濒临灭亡的语言和文字,在当今仍然是记录这些族群生存记忆的工具。正因为这些古老的文化还被传承着,它就像一种声音,虽然依稀弱小,它却在人类进入21世纪的时候,再一次唤醒了人类已经沉睡的良知。特别是在今天还在不断加速的全球化时代,理性权力的滥用肆无忌惮,尤其是新自由主义重商文化,对全球弱势族群的冲击,已经到了最严重的地步,其造成的灾难性后果,已经摆在了我们面前。

据说,今天一些弱势族群的语言和文字的消亡,其速度之快令人震惊。当然,就是在这样一个危机四伏的时候,我们才越发感觉到,要保护好不同民族的文化传统,这个世界留给我们的时间已经不多。"山地文明"中留存的"基因"和"密码",或许现在已经成了我们人类必须进行抢救的最后的"记忆库",这绝不是我在危言耸听。

我不能在这里推断,如果今天的人类,失去了对过去的记忆,人类还能真正地认识自己?这种集体的失忆,是我无论如何不敢去想象的。今天,用影像记录的方式——当然这仅仅是一种方式,来拯救和记录我们的"山地文明",已经被大家所共识,这一共识在不同的国家和组织,其实已经变成了广泛的行动。最为可贵的是,有不少形形色色、数以十万计的纪录片机构,当然也包括那些纪录片独立制作人,在这一领域做出的贡献是极为非凡的。我们应该向他们表示敬意。他们的不凡之举和敬业精神,是人类能够相信自己,并能够把自己的昨天、今天和明天联系在一起的关键所在。

尽管这样,但今天我们还是要继续呼吁和倡导,对山地族群的生存状况,再进行全方位的、准确的、真实的记录。我想这些被拯救一般记录下来的影像,除了其具有重要的史料意义外,它还会让人类在认识自己昨天的同时,真正理性地找到通往明天的道路。这条道路将更合乎人的全面发展,更具有人道的精神,更兼顾公平和正义。如果没有人类的历史,就一定不会有人类的未来,我以为,这就是我们要举办山地纪录片节的,最重要的也是最直接的原因,这也是影像记录"山地文明"的价值所在。

modern society, are in jeopardy, threatening to be overun and engulfed by mainstream cultures, lost inexorably to the sway of hegemonic philosophic patterns and cultural traditions.

One thing assuring is that many traditional societies still cling hard to their old ways of life, time-honored mores and customs, ancient scripts and characters amidst menaces and encroachments approaching thick and fast. Their scripts and characters, although on the brink of extinction, are still used as tool to perpetuate the existential memory, a road sign to a living culture of antiquity, a voice, however muffled, serving its due but dignified role of awakening human conscience that slumbers for too long. In a world where globalization proceeds apace like wild fire, the rule of reason is usurped and the impact of neo mercantilism falls mainly on the weak cultures and impoverished populace with devastating consequences.

At present, we are aware on a daily basis of the alarming loss, throughout the world, one or two languages which abodes absolutely ill for mankind. An old language dies out, so does an old race, because the culture encoded in that language disappears. As such, it entails in essence a human loss and the knell of mankind. The cultural "genes" encoded in mountain civilizations might be the last pool of existential memory of not only mountain residents but also of us urban dwellers to be salvaged and conserved before it is too late.

In this world of dazzling movement, thronged as never before with so many cars and pedestrians bustling and hustling on the sidewalks and city streets, blocking each other's passage, I dare not brood over the macabre prospects of us humans in fidgeting seclusion of high apartment buildings, unable to take stock of ourselves owing to a loss of reminiscence and remembrance of our past. That is why each of you in the audience is bestirred to the rescue of mountain civilizations stranded with the means you excel-the superb tool of imaging .So in the name of camera, we are summoned and gathered under the glorious standard of saving the mountains, and you, under various covers, auspices, individual documentary artists , independent producers, professional agencies, all have a vital role to play deserving our regards and salutations of the highest order. Note your professionalism and devoted industry will prove the key linking us with our past, present and future.

I, for one, will continue to clamor for the widest attention on the deplorable state of mountain civilizations and to urge for a fuller, more comprehensive and more authentic recording of what happens under our very noses in the mountains and uplands .These footages and images, aside their historical function , will supply rich food for a better awareness of our past as well as rational clues to point to a more enlightened future , a future wherein humans will evolve in a more humanistic ,harmonious and all rounded way, a future wherein justice and equality will prevail simply because man deprived of his past is without tomorrow. Hence our forum here today as a ritual to renew our sense of mission and arouse each other to the level of intellectual and emotional intensity necessary to venture into the wilderness and mountains.

诗歌通往神话与乌托邦的途径

写给第 23 届麦德林国际诗歌节的书面演讲

2013 年 2 月 24 日

  诗歌从它诞生之日起,就从未离开过它所置身的那个时代,这就如同诗人,尽管他能通过他所构筑的那个语言的世界,最终超越它与当下现实的关系,但是无论如何,任何一个时代的诗歌,其本身所呈现出来的整体态势,都会让我们清晰地看到,那个时代诗歌主流精神的具体指向。其实这已经是一个毫无争议的事实,古希腊荷马时期的诗歌是这样,中国古代唐朝时期的诗歌是这样,西班牙黄金时期的诗歌是这样,在源远流长的世界诗歌史上,这样的事例不胜枚举。

  但在这里,我需要说明的是,一个时代诗歌本身主流精神的指向,那一定是对一个更为广阔的时代生活而言的,它绝不是狭隘的。因为阅读诗歌史和不同时代诗歌的经验告诉我们,诗歌所呈现出来的整体面貌是不一样的,这不仅仅是指诗歌表现形式上的差别,而更重要的是,不同时代的诗歌在其更宏大的诗歌精神层面上,也必然具有独特的、极为鲜明的、区别于其他时代的诗歌风貌。

  或许,这就是我说的,不同时代,尽管不同的诗人和他们的作品会发出不同的声音,但可以肯定这些声音中必然隐含着那个时代的回声。当然,任何时代,诗人作为独立的写作个体,不论从生命意义上来讲,还是从诗歌的创造力来讲,诗人以及诗人的作品,都有着自身独立的、永远不可被替代的特殊价值,因为一代又一代诗人以及他们浩如烟海的作品的存在,才使我们人类的诗歌精神源流,充满着极为鲜活的生命。

  直到今天,诗歌依然和我们的心灵及现实生活紧密相连,作为生活在 21 世纪的

Poetry as Access into Myth and Utopia
A Written Speech for the 23th Edition of International Poetry Festival of Medellin
24th, February, 2013

Poetry has always been, since its earliest beginnings, contemporaneous with the transformations of the most resilient and productive forces that shape the society precisely as a poet has always been riding on the crest of the tidal waves of the realities due to a transcendent realm fashioned of poetic diction. Yet, whatever the argument, poetry of an age has discernibly a spiritual reference point to which it strives for based on the multitude of versified literatures, a fact beyond dispute and enumeration in the long span of poetic history, attested to by the confluence of several distinguished poetic traditions such as Homeric, Spanish in its Golden Age and Tang's in medieval China.

Of course, it must be added that the spiritual reference point of poetry of a certain age is a case in point when one generalizes about the larger spiritual picture of mankind. Any study of the histories of poetry and poetry of various ages is compounded by the varied purposes for which poetry is used and the varied prosodic forms it has taken. Yet, there is to be perceived a Geist, peculiar in form, distinctive and poignant on a higher plane, that animates the rich and varied body of poetic writing of each historical period.

I have driven home my point that poets and their poetic works are bound to be mouthpieces of the civic society of the age in which they live, despite the fact that each generation produces its unique, distinctive poets. Such a spiritual reference point is the connective skein that runs through the totality of the human aesthetic experience. Of course, either in terms of the existential dimension of the poet as humans or of the poetic inventiveness, poets compose as individuals and it is this individuality and even a set of idiosyncratic traits that bestows and bequeaths a value that sets them apart from their peers and predecessors in the prolific literature of poetry, investing dismal and deplorable historical experiences with vibrant dignity and timeless beauty from the fountainhead of mankind's aesthetic endowment.

Good poetry has always been contemporarily linked to human hearts and our daily life. Good poets cannot get around the ultimate share of responsibility in shaping the era in which we

当下诗人，我们不能不想到诗歌应该承担的责任，以及它所应当发挥的作用。那诗歌在今天究竟能发挥一种什么样的作用呢？我不想从社会学的角度来讨论诗歌的社会作用，我也不愿意用现代语言学的方法去解析诗歌本体的无限可能。其实，我们要真正明确诗人的责任，和诗歌在当下的作用，并且能作为这个时代有良知的诗人开始行动起来，有一个重要的前提，就是我们必须对我们生活的这个时代有一个清醒的认识。

20世纪意大利隐逸派伟大诗人，埃乌杰尼奥·蒙塔莱曾在他的一本著名论著《在我们的时代》中这样说："我目睹了人类伟大思想成就的实现，那是神奇的成就，但也许是愚笨的……我从中发现的唯一普遍规律是，人类的每一成就和进步必然伴随着其他方面的损失。这样一来，人类任何可能的幸福的总量就依然不变。"蒙塔莱还说："这我知道，我们会一下跳进乌托邦的空想王国。但是，如果没有空想，人恐怕还是一种比好多动物还要更不聪明，还要更不合时宜的动物。"

然而，我们生活的今天，已经远远要比蒙塔莱生活的那个时代更为让人忧虑和不安，虽然没有世界性的战争全面爆发，但区域性的战争不断出现，核武器的阴影仍然笼罩在人类的头顶。人类生态环境的持续恶化，似乎已经到了不可逆转的地步。人类对自然资源的耗竭，其速度之快、数量之大，也超过了人类诞生以来的任何一个时期。

人口数量的剧增，加上资本主义生产至上的发展模式，许多国家的政府将经济增长视为施政的唯一目的，这种用无度生产、疯狂消费和所谓GDP总量来衡量价值的思维方式，已经让我们看到了，如果再让这种造成社会不公平和全球生态灾难频发的发展方式持续下去，对人的异化不受到来自道德的谴责，人类的未来必然将走向最终的毁灭。诚然，作为诗人和我们这个时代的见证者，我们从未否认过发展健康、生态、绿色、可持续经济对推动人类文明进步的巨大作用，对每一次人类重大的科技创新和技术革命，我们都同所有的群体一样欢欣鼓舞。人类只有时刻警惕自身的贪婪和遏制人性的缺陷，才能克服由于膨胀的欲望所带来的恶果和灾难。

诗歌，在今天毫无疑问，已经又一次成为我们反抗异化的工具，诗歌已经超越了一般性阅读和审美的范围，已经超越了语言和修辞学方面固有的意义。诗歌作为一

live. What role, then, is poetry playing in our age and society? It is my last wish to attempt an answer sociological in character. Nor do I intend to elucidate the infinite possibilities of poetics within the confines of modern linguistics. The responsibility of a poet today, as ever, is to be available for action in the light of his awakened conscience predicated upon a vigilant knowledge of the decisive transformations of our age and society.

Eugenio Montale, the great Italian recluse poet of the 20th century, in one of his poetic criticism, feeling detached from contemporary life, mused on man's "meeting of contraries" to the effect: "I have borne witness to the outstanding achievement of human thought, which is truly spectacular and clumsy in the meanwhile, out of which the sole law of universal validity emerges, i. e. for every human gain and progress, there is bound to be some attrition or loss elsewhere to the extent the sum total of human happiness remains constant as ever." Montale further concluded, "This much I rest fully assured that man tends to jump into a utopia one way or another. For shorn of his fantasizing tendency, man might end up being one species less intelligent and fit for the earth."

Yet the age we are living now is assaulted by a spate of hazards more disquieting and intimidating. Although a world war situation does not repeat itself so far, regional hostilities flare up everywhere and the Damocles' Sword of the thermonuclear holocaust still hangs lurking over our heads. The runaway climatic countdown seems unstoppably upon us and human depletion of natural resource is accelerating unrivalled in scope, and escalating at a pace faster than any previous historical periods known to man.

The result is an inexorable catastrophe brought by demographic spurts, reckless modernization, the primacy of economic growth prized by almost all the governments, the prevalent mentality characterized by unbridled production, maniac consumption and GDP overriding all other considerations and last but not the least, human alienation not curtailed or punctured by any moral neurosis. As poets, of course, bearing testimony to the great march of human progress, we are not purveyors of gloom. Rather, we are cheerleaders of economic growth that features being low carbon effusive, eco-friendly, green and sustainable. Like every segment of human community, we jump for jubilee at every hurdle to be surpassed in the way of major technical breakthroughs. Yet, we must ruminate on all the blunders of the past and unless we learn to practice ethical humility derived from a moral commitment in a quest for a more humanistic world, we stand destined to risk our own survival.

In this way, poetry has without doubt, become our tool against alienation, attempting to make things happen not only by delighting and entertaining but also to "bring the whole soul of man into activity". While its influence is apt to be more indirect, ambivalent, unforeseen, and vatic, poetry will, nevertheless, help people in a task on the necessity of which philosophers and saints and prophets all agree, that of prodding and cajoling mankind towards ascending the promised height of sweetness and light. Poets are proven to have the resources to lead, because

种精神和象征,它将引领人类从物欲横流的世界,走向一个更为光明的高地。人类不仅仅是依赖物质存在的动物,它同样还是不能离开精神而存在的动物,某种时候,不,应该是所有的时候,精神的至上将永远是人类区别于其他动物的鸿沟。

人类的文明史早已证明,我们的先贤们从未停止过创造自己的精神和神话,并力图去构建理想中的乌托邦。在当下,诗歌无疑已经包含着某种信仰的力量,它既是我们与自然进行沟通的桥梁,又是我们追求人的解放和自主,让生命拥有意义的途径。在全球化和资讯化的时代,由诗歌构建起来的神话和乌托邦,将促使人类建立一种更为人性的生产和生活方式,它将把推动人类精神文明的建设和精神生活质量的全面提高,作为不折不扣的价值追求。

诗歌的神话和乌托邦,将把物质生产的最后目的与人的全面解放联系在一起,物质生产的劳动,不再是对地球资源无节制的消耗,更不是对人的积极的生命意义的消减。诗歌不会死亡,特别是在一个物质主义盛行的时代,诗歌必然会闪现出更为灿烂的精神光芒。只要诗歌存在一天,它就会鼓舞人类为不断创造不朽的精神和神话,为我们致力于建设一个更加尊重生命、尊重自然、尊重平等、尊重人权、尊重信仰的明天而共同奋斗!

man does not live by bread alone. He, too, needs poetry. Sometimes, nay, empathetically at all times, man is distinguished from the rest of all species on earth by his spiritual primacy.

History books are studded with the accounts of our worthy ancestors in their inventing a body of myths and in their quest for a utopia tantalizing but perennially out of their reach. Contemporary poetic writing, more or less a surrogate for meaning-giving faith, bridges the gulf between man and nature and leads him onto a road to liberation and freedom. In an age that calls itself by grand narrative of digitalization, poetry fashions and erects its own body of myths and utopia, charged with the office of speaking intimately of those things that concern human beings most—the activity of love, of justice and of soul.

Myth of poetry and utopia of poetry will bring the end of material production in unison with the ultimate emancipation of man. Material accumulation will not ensue at the expense of the diminished natural resources and the attrition of human spirituality. Poetry is here to stay in the hard times of gross commercialism. It will shine with greater brilliance. So long as poetry stays, poets will harness words, which stand for things and thought, which rant and rhapsodize, so as to inspire people to strive for a promising future wherein life, nature, equality, human rights, and faith are valued above anything else.

诗歌见证历史和创造的工具

在青海湖国际诗歌广场完全落成仪式上的致辞

2012年8月12日

尊敬的各位诗人、各位朋友：

今天我们选择了诗歌，没有别的目的，这不仅仅是因为诗歌至今仍然是人类精神殿堂最重要的基石之一，今天我们与诗歌同在，那是因为将共同见证一个事实，在我们居住的这个星球的东方，在中国的青海，将有一个呈现人类伟大诗歌记忆的雕塑群落出现在这里，在此时此地我想说的是，它曾经似乎就是一个梦，但这个梦在今天变成了现实。

各位同行，朋友们，我想把这一切说成是一个奇迹，或许你们能理解并宽容我的大胆。首先，我认为这个最初的梦想能变成现实，并成为奇迹，完全是缘于诗歌给我们带来的相像。从这个意义上而言，这个世界上一切伟大的创造，都是充满着诗性和相像的，如果失去了想象力，人类的创造力也将会变得苍白而毫无生气。

为此，我们要感谢诗歌，是它给了我们这种无穷的想象力，同样也给了我们把这种想象变成真正现实的勇气和智慧。因为诗歌永远只代表着人类一切进步的力量，它是正义和自由永恒的化身。从人类浩如烟海的文化遗产中，选择出二十四部不同国度、不同地域的伟大的民族史诗铸成青铜，最终耸立在这个举世无双的诗歌广场上，这个足以令人称奇的结果，难道不能说成是一个想象的奇迹吗？回答当然是肯定的。

因为在这个地球上，还没有第二处集中了这么多有关人类伟大史诗青铜雕像的广场。这个广场上的国际诗歌墙，也因为其采用了嘛呢石经墙的独特形式，而成为被

Poetry Can Anticipate a Bigger Influence in Human Society

Address at the Inauguration Ceremony of Qinghai Lake International Poetry Festival Square
12nd, August, 2012

Distinguished Poets and dear friends:

It is inevitable today that we choose poetry again. Or rather poetry still sides with us as major pillar of human spiritualized passion for Truth, Kindness and Beauty, bearing a vital testimony to the inauguration of the Qinghai Lake International Poetry Square, which, as it stands now, on the tertiary pole of the globe, turns out to be a miraculous location to celebrate poetry the best outcrop of human life and sensibility in form of a roster of world's famous poets in bronze. A fancy dream, by whatever measure, I must say, but it has come true under our very eyes.

Fellow poets and friends, I am audacious enough to call what's happened today a miracle in anticipation of your understanding and sympathy. First ,a fancy dream coming true and becoming a miracle ,is to the credit of poetry when it turns its gaze towards the luminous summits of human imaginative power without bounds. In this sense, it can be argued that all the great human exploits and feats have been occasioned and detonated by flashes of poetic impulse. And bare of poetic imagination, human creativity loses its zest and voracity.

We must cheer poetry-the fountain of our infinite spiritual vision that has contributed to the nurturing of courage and wisdom to make real the promises of our fond dream. Thanks to the spreading and reading of poetry, the existence of the spiritual legacy of a living sensibility, mankind is inspired and uplifted, in constant movement towards justice and freedom, with a critical attitude in deference of human dignity evidenced by the selecting of 24 world epics engraved into bronze before erected on this poetry square, one of the rarest of its kind. Truly this must be deemed a miracle.

It so happens that in this location is concentrated such an awesome array of significant poetic artifacts, for side by side with the fantastic poetry square, another monument conveniently comes into sight, no less a potent sign of poetic glory, the poetry wall, constructed in the style of local Tibetan mani stone wall, widely acclaimed as the paragon of human import and alpine situation. It is the way for poets and sculptors to counter the constant spiritual deterioration of our

人们广泛称道的人文建筑和自然结合的光辉典范。

　　各位同行，朋友们，特别是在这样一个特殊的时刻，请允许我代表你们，代表所有热爱诗歌的人，向为建成这个伟大的诗歌广场而付出了天才般的智慧的雕塑家们致敬！是他们让我们再一次相信并亲眼看到了，真正伟大的雕塑就是一首首凝固的诗歌这样一个事实。最后，让我们共同祝愿这个诗歌广场连同这一座座精湛的史诗雕像，永远成为人类精神遗产中的一个组成部分。诗歌之神万岁！谢谢大家！

world and the reigning menaces of globalization.

Friends, fellow poets, this inauguration ceremony must count one of the events that make possible the establishment of a new symbol in honor of the poetic brilliance. I, for one, must rise and salute our sculptors who have identified themselves so deeply with poetry in executing their sculptures. Their wondrous work has convinced us that a piece of genuine sculpture can be a powerful hymn to all the earthy pleasures of living in this time. Last but not the least, may my sincere gratitude be expressed in the realization of the transcendence of this ceremony, which, from now till ever after, becomes part of our spiritual and cultural life. Thank you for your attention.

我们的继续存在是人类对自身的救赎

在青海国际土著民族诗人圆桌会议上的致辞

2012年8月10日

在我们这个地球村，人类的生命基因已经延续了若干万年，为此我们要深深地感激养育了我们生命的家园——地球。我以为无论从物质的角度，还是从精神的角度，地球都给我们提供了丰富的滋养，难怪在这个地球上不同的地域，许多民族都把地球和土地比喻成自己的母亲。在不少民族的创世神话中，地球和土地就是一个特殊的隐喻和象征，它是早期人类原始思维中的一种符号，当我们追溯人类的生命源头和精神源头时，地球或者说土地，无疑都是我们最根性的母体。

作为一个诗人，或者说在更多的时候，我是一个怀疑论者，对人类的未来充满着极度的忧虑，但是尽管这样，我仍然从未丧失过人类在面对各种困难和挑战时的勇气以及坚定的信心。特别是在今天，当我们从世界的四面八方来到这里，并将以诗歌的名义，来进行一次富有建设性的对话的时候，我相信，同大家一样，我们都怀着一种共同的期待，那就是我们作为这个地球村不同地域和民族的代言人，我们将义无反顾地承担起保护我们共同的生命母体——地球的责任。从更广阔的意义而言，我们是代表这个地球上所有的生命来发言，我想无论它是动物还是植物。

由此，我想告诉大家的是，我们这一次具有特殊意义的交流和对话，或许它最初发出的声音还不太大，但它最终所汇聚成的道德力量将是无穷的。在全球化的今天，尽管反全球化的观点很有道理，他们认为传统、差异和当地性让位给了新自由主义经济范式所主导的全球资本主义，但是尽管如此，人类今天所面临的危机，诸如资源的过度开发、生态灾难、繁荣下的极端贫困等等，都需要我们这些作为社会动物和生

We Are Still Here-An Act Of Self-redemption For Mankind

An Address at the Indigenous Poets Roundtable Forum
10th, August, 2012

In our global village, human genes have seen us through countless adversities since days of yore and for this reason, we owe a huge debt to the Earth, the Garden of Eden for us human beings which has nurtured and nourished our inner and outer beings in a spirit of generosity and magnanimity that so many races and nations, in surprisingly justifiable unanimity ,style the Earth in allegorical and mythical terms, "Motherhood". The land and the earth, in many world myths, is both a metaphor and symbol, dating from primary mentality of the aboriginal peoples. In an unflinching quest of the origin of life or spirit, we are led invariably to the motherhood of the Earth, the critical basis from which we strike out into the world.

A poet myself, frequently a synonym for skeptic, I take leave to doubt when it comes to the topic of the future of mankind. Yet in face of the many knotty issues, I have never lost an obstinate sense of courage or self-assurance, the need for taking charge and rising above our environment.

Today, we are gathered here from all corners of the globe to engage in a most fruitful and meaningful dialogue, fully justified in the consensus and anticipation that, we, representatives of a wide spectrums of marginalized nationalities and cultures, should shoulder up the ultimate responsibility to protect and conserve our Mother Earth. In a larger sense, we are here to give voice to our message, not only on behalf of humans, but also of all the sentient beings on earth, animal or plant, human or superhuman.

I want to tell our colleagues that the message we want to convey through the medium of this roundtable forum may not be so high-sounding to be heard by many, but nevertheless, it will resound with such moral potency that it will surely gather momentum in an exemplary way.

The immediate world is now fraught with anti-globalization rhetoric, not without a reason. Opponents base their major argument on the fact tradition, difference and cultural specificities have given way to globalized capitalism dominated by neo laissez -faire economy. In its wake, the olden woes of over-exploitation of natural resources, ecological crisis, the disparity of wealth between poor and rich, have further worsened, almost to the point of no cure. Yet, we must not

物动物的人去加以解决。毫无疑问，我们是这个地球村真正的主人之一，我们将承担起并肩负着保卫我们赖以生存的这个蔚蓝色星球的光荣职责。

列维·施特劳斯曾这样感叹："今天人类没有分别……人与他者直接接触，他们的感觉、抱负、欲望和恐惧对安全和兴旺毫无影响，那些曾经认为物质进步代表着优势的人……那些所谓初民和古老民族……他们的存在消失了，他们以或快或慢的速度，融入了他们周遭的文明。"在这位杰出的人类学家眼里，全球化瓦解了原有的世界，模糊了自我和他者之间、"现代"与"原始"之间的差异，全球化已经真实地颠覆了固有的国际政治、经济以及文化秩序，全球化让我们这个时代处于一个断裂的景象。

作为土著民族的诗人和文化代言人，当我们身处这样一个混淆了传统和现代、资本和技术日益异化着我们的无序的现实世界，我们别无选择，只能把我们每一个民族伟大的文化传统更完整地呈现给这个文化多元的世界，呈现给已经延续了数千年的人类文明共同体，从而让我们的文化创造成为人类共有的精神财富，也只有这样，我们才能在全球各民族都在经历的现代化过程中重塑自我，并且进一步高扬我们原始根性的文化意识，真正重构我们的身份认同，让我们的作品成为人类历史记忆中永远不可分割，同样也不可被替代的组成部分。2007年的联合国宣言，是对土著民族集体权利更大范围的承认，文化多样性是一种历史的进步，它使过去长时间处于社会的边缘的土著民族被转移到一个更为平等的位置。正是因为这样一个原因，在今天我们才更强调一个诗人和作家的文化个性，或者说文化贡献。

我们的阅读经验告诉我们，任何一个民族的伟大作家和诗人，首先是属于他的民族的，当然同时他也是属于这个世界和全人类的。伟大的诗人但丁、普希金、密茨凯维支、屈原、李白、杜甫等等，都是这方面最光辉的典范和代表。如果从当下全球四处都在大肆宣扬的直接性、压缩、新奇、速度和技术这样一些观念和行为的影响来看，人类不同民族的古老传统和文化价值体系，都将在所谓全球化的加速度状态下步入衰落，甚至可能会无可挽回地走向消亡。历史的规律已经证明，我们的这个世界是因包含了文化、集体和历史的差异而丰富多彩。从生物多样性和文化多样性而言，我们这个地球家园中的任何民族的文化传统，包含了语言、文字、古老的哲学价值体系和文化少数族群的一切权利，一旦消失，无疑都将是全人类共同的不幸和灾难。

wallow in the valley of despair and we are here today to remind the world of the urgency of the moment now, for a forum such as we have has the potential to raise awareness of what's happening to our planet and to aid the shift to a bright, ecologically sustainable, socially just and spiritually fulfilling human presence in the world.

Levy Strauss lamented: "Today people tend to look and act alike. In their direct contact with fellow humans, their feelings, aspirations, and fears have no impact on each other's security and prosperity. Those who used to prioritize on material progress, together with the few aboriginal tribes and the old nationalities scattered across the globe, cease to be such altogether. At a rate more or less, they have been incorporated into the mainstream civilization." Levy Strauss bore a brilliant testimony to the world, driven by globalization, that collapsed around him and around us into one in which the distinction between I and He ,between modern and ancient ,has been blurred, even erased. Former world order on the political, cultural and economic planes is effectively usurped or teeters in the balance.

Poets and spokesmen of the all the aborigines, we are here to stand witness to an earth in chaos and in distress. As at this time in history it is obvious we poets must constantly raise our voices in protest against her destruction by ignorant individuals or greedy institutions, we have no choice but this: to demonstrate our traditions in their entirety to a world of cultural diversity in a reaffirmation of our cultural and spiritual heritage passed down to us by our ancestors in a bid that our heritage will be patrimony shared by all and will be building blocks out of which and with which a new ego ,forged by all peoples fresh out of the narrow jail cells of modernity. Within this context of renewal and coexistence on the basis of the poetic experience, we issue our call that our poetic expression must not be ignored in celebration of the historical consciousness of mankind in general. In the 2007 UN Manifesto regarding the rights of the aborigines ,the recognition and reaffirmation of our presence and cultural diversity has been accorded legitimacy both in scope and content, a major step forward we must admit given the fact that the indigenous races have long been victimized in the hands of some motor forces, human or industrial in character. Thanks to the more equal status we now enjoy, we speak of cultural personality or individuality of a poet or a writer, let alone his or her unique contribution.

Our readings incline us in the belief that any major writer or poet or artist, first and foremost, belongs to his or her nationality before the whole world claims his or her name. We now relish the radiant lines of Pushkin, Dante, Shakespeare, Li Bai, Du Fu, the pride of all nations and races, as they personify this paradoxical truth. It has been proposed that olden value systems and cultural traditions inevitably decline and even perish facing the encroaching menaces of globalization characterized by directness, speed and technology. There is certainly a element of truth in this assumption. but the other side of the picture contains more kennels of wisdom in that, human history ,as we find ,has been much enriched due to a wide variety of cultural, historical and collective divergences, a law attested to by what has happened since antiquity. Our accumulated

我想在目前全球化的语境内，规训和消解原生文化的目的就是同质化，就是整齐划一。伟大的马提尼克诗人和政治活动家埃梅·塞泽尔呼吁以"历史权利"，来进一步关注土著民族的文化传承，他所提出的"黑人性"，无疑是非洲以及世界黑人文化复兴运动的最为重要的理论基石。埃梅·塞泽尔给了我们一个宝贵的启示，那就是我们必须找回属于自己的"历史的权利"，为真正实现和保护我们地球家园文化多样性而付诸行动。从 21 世纪开始以来，将多样性当作一种现代性的象征来用已经成了人类的普遍共识，或者说成了绝大多数人所认同的一种具有道德精神的基本原则。可以说，今天生活在世界不同地域的各个古老民族的存在和文化延续，将是人类对自身的救赎，因为我们曾长时间缺乏对不同文化和传统的理解和尊重。

在这里，我还要最后强调，任何一个土著民族的诗人，其实都具备着一个更为强大的精神和文化背景，我们的作品更能表现和反映出全球"文明"和"社会"严重错位带来的地缘政治和文化冲突。正是由于我们既是全球化过程中一个日渐被所谓全球新秩序反复考验和挤压的角色，同时又可能成为自由市场之外，被全球利益遗忘的另一种新的"边缘"，成为新的精神的放逐者、物质的贫困群体。总之，在这个新的世纪，我们唯一的体验是，思想和肉体都时刻置身于一个碰撞、交叉、重构、加速的境况之中，由此，我们没有理由不相信，在这样一个充满着激荡、变化、失落、回忆、割舍、放逐的时代，作为人类永远的良心，我们身处世界各地的土著民族诗人必将给人类奉献出最伟大的、最富有人类情怀的诗篇。

knowledge of cultural diversity and bio-diversity lead us inexorably to a conclusion that the loss of any single set of values, no matter how marginalized, in which are embedded specific language, writing system, philosophical musings, as well as all the rights enjoyed by that special human grouping, abodes ill for the rest of mankind as a whole.

I believe in the globalized context, the primary function of discipline and erosion of aboriginal cultures is uniformity and homogeneity. Aime Cessaire (1913—2008), great poet and politician in Martinique ,invents a new term" historical rights" to claim world focus on the rights of the indigenous peoples. The idea of "negrotitude" he coins, the core theoretical concept on which African and indeed, world Africans' campaign for justice and status centers, has taught us admirably we must rehabilitate ourselves by regaining our" historical rights", we must take action in defense of cultural diversity. Indeed the new century begins with a consensus ,a moral principle shared by all civic societies, that cultural continuity of each nationality, nation, race, religion is the very act of self-redemption for mankind, all the more so because a proper respect for, or understanding of different value systems and cultural traditions has been deplorably found lacking.

Here I must point out that each aboriginal poet implies a spiritual and cultural background which informs our poetic expression with a potency much more poignant than meets the eye or the ear, which highlights the fatal mal-synchronization between "civilization" and "society" as well as the worst outcrop, ie, the attendant geo-political crisis and cultural contradiction. A dismal prospect lies ahead of us: a role brought to incessant trials, being jostled about, by a "new world order or a spiritual outcast ignored and marginalized by the global interests, out of the pales of world market, languished in a corner of poverty. To conclude, our sole experience in this young age is that our bodies and our souls are thrown into the crucible of quickened squeezing, restructuring, bumping. Because of this, I trust we all have an immense responsibility with humanity at the present time, a time fraught with change, loss, memory, exile, impact, giving up. All this spiritual legacy we inherit and bring to bear upon today's topic, ensures us on time to initiate a surge of poetic blossoming for the defense of life.

格萨尔与世界史诗

在格萨尔与世界史诗国际学术论坛上的演讲

2012年7月17日

尊敬的武寅副院长，来自世界各地的同行们、同志们、朋友们：

大家好！相信诸位已经感受到，高原的盛夏带给我们的热情与惬意，正如"夏都"这个亲切的名称一样，我们总能在7月的西宁分享到她名副其实的清爽。今天，在《格萨尔》与世界史诗的神秘召唤下，我们怀着对史诗和民族文化的敬仰、热爱之情，带着如何在现代社会更好地挖掘、研究、保护和传承人类文明的深切思考，从世界各地走来欢聚一堂，切磋交流、缔结友谊。在此，我谨代表省委、省政府和省委宣传部，向论坛的如期举行表示热烈的祝贺；对各位"格萨尔"专家学者的到来表示诚挚的欢迎！是你们带来了丰硕的成果，让我们再次领略到分享智慧的愉悦。

众所周知，史诗是一种古老的民间韵文作品，和神话有着同样久远的历史。它内容丰富、结构宏大、格调庄重，在漫长的传承过程中，融进了大量的神话、传说、故事、歌谣和谚语，是一座民间文学的知识宝库，也是认识一个民族的百科全书，对民族文化传统的形成与发展有着巨大而深远的影响。作为藏族英雄史诗的《格萨尔》，同希腊《荷马史诗》、印度《摩诃婆罗多》和《罗摩衍那》等优秀史诗一样，是世界文化宝库中的一颗璀璨明珠，也是中华民族为人类文明做出的重要贡献。

随着各民族和地区间的交流不断加深，在国内，《格萨尔》从中国西部的广大藏区逐渐流传到蒙古族、土族、裕固族、纳西族、普米族等民族当中；在国外，《格萨尔》还流传至蒙古国、俄罗斯以及喜马拉雅山南麓的尼泊尔、印度、巴基斯坦、不丹等国。其跨地域、跨文化传播的影响力极其罕见。

Gesar and World Epics
Address at the international Forum on World Epics and Gesar
17th, July, 2012

Reverend Professor Wu, Distinguished academicians, comrades, friends:

I trust myself safely assume each participating this event must have already experienced the paradoxical mix of warmth and coolness an alpine venue is bound to bring about. As the nomenclature "Summer Capital" implies, the share of coolness Xining necessarily confers on us is in deed, not in name. Today, summoned by the magical call of world epics, we have gathered in Xining from various parts of the world, to exchange notes, swap experiences, renew old friendship and forge new ones. This much we will and do in deference to the perennial appeal of epics and ethnic genres, as how to better rescue, research, conserve and pass on our cultural heritage. This accords me, among other things, a privilege to extend the warmest welcome to each Gesar expert and researcher, for you have brought a wealth of academic expertise and wisdom to bear upon a subject of world significance, a subject enriched and enlivened by the rich knowledge and wisdom of an army of assiduous students of Gesar with passing years.

As is well known, an epic is a lengthy narrative poem, normally concerning a serious subject as it contains details of heroic deeds and events significant to a culture or nation., believed to date from the dawn of civilization. It draws heavily on myths, legends, stories, proverbs and ballads. By virtue of this character, an epic frequently constitutes a rich and splendid treasure house of folk literature as well as an encyclopedia of a certain race or nationality, The Heroic Epic of King Gesar, collectively created and passed down orally, is prized as one of the few epics still performed by traditional storytellers today on par with all other world cultural masterpieces such as the Ramayana, Mahabharata, Iliad and the Odyssey.King Gesar is a brilliant pearl in the world's cultural treasure and is an important contribution made to human civilization.

King Gesar has evolved widely throughout Central Asia but its classic version is to be found in central Tibet, some 100 bards of this epic being still active today in the Gesar belt of China, but sub genres and variations are conserved by other Chinese minorities such as the Mongolians, the Tu, the Yugu, the Naxi, the Pumi, etc. Sub-versions of the epic are also recorded among the

作为一部不朽的英雄史诗,《格萨尔》在广阔的背景下,以恢宏的气势、高度的艺术技巧,反映了古代藏族发展的重大历史阶段及其社会基本结构形态,表达了民众的美好愿望和崇高理想,描述了纷繁复杂的民族关系及其逐步走向统一的过程,揭示出社会历史发展的必然趋势,也反映了古代藏族民众的宗教信仰、风俗习惯和道德观念,具有鲜明的民族风格和地方特色。它既是族群文化多样性的熔炉,又是多民族民间文化可持续发展的见证。这一为多民族共享的口头史诗是草原游牧文化的结晶,代表着古代藏族、蒙古族、土族等多个民族民间文化与口头叙事艺术的最高成就。无数游吟歌手世代承袭着有关它的吟唱和表演。

截至目前,较为准确的统计数字显示,我们共收集到《格萨尔》手抄本和木刻本总数为289部,除去各种异文本,仍有200多部,若按每部平均20万字计算,总字数也在4000万字以上。仅从字数来看,《格萨尔》已远远超过了世界几大著名史诗的总和。由此可见,这部史诗传承时间之久远、流布地区之广阔、篇幅之浩繁、结构之宏伟,堪称世界史诗之最。

正因如此,长期以来,国内外学者对《格萨尔》研究给予了广泛关注和极大的热情,不少国家成立了专门研究机构,组织学者从事史诗的挖掘和研究工作。他们把《格萨尔》视为研究南亚腹地人类文明史不可多得的历史教科书。2001年10月17日,在巴黎召开的联合国教科文组织第31届大会上,《格萨尔》被列入2002—2003年联合国教科文组织参与项目;2006年5月20日,经国务院批准,《格萨尔》被列入第一批国家级非物质文化遗产名录;2009年9月30日,《格萨尔》被联合国教科文组织列入"人类非物质文化遗产代表作"名录。

新世纪以来,学术界越来越重视口头诗学、民族志理论、表演理论等新的研究方法论。我想,这并非只是一种理论和手段的花样翻新,它更代表了一种思维方式和研究视角的转变,它的应用所带来的是对整个民俗学、人类学研究规则的重新理解。

我们可以简单追溯一下帕里和洛德对荷马史诗的研究,就可以从中获取灵感。起初,帕里以语文学为方法论,对荷马史诗进行语言学分析,发现了它的程式化倾向,于是得出"荷马史诗演唱风格是高度程式化"的结论,而这种程式化就是来自其悠久的文化传统,并且只能是口头的理论预设。随后,帕里与他的学生洛德前往南斯

peoples in Bhutan, Nepal, India and Pakistan on the southern slopes of the Himalayan and among various Turkish and Tunghus tribes in present day Russia's Siberia, reputed by some to be the most influential in the world.

King Gesar is a story told on a grand scale. The epic, with deft craftsmanship, not only narrates the life of Gesar, but also describes the complicated relations among various ancient ethnic groups .It conveys the good wishes and lofty ideals of the masses and depicts the complicated relationships between China's ethnic groups and the process of final unification. King Gesar,as all epic heroes do, illustrates traits, performs deeds, and exemplifies certain morals that are valued by the society the epic originates. It is a song in praise of truth and justice on a triumphant note of brightness over darkness, of right over evil. Incidentally, one senses a rough historical picture of the important evolutionary stages of national development and basic social structure in Tibet, Placed in perspective, the epic of King Gesar can be taken as historical annals useful for students of ancient Tibetan social history, class relations, cultural exchanges between ethnic groups, moral concepts, folk customs, traditions, and culture, the crystallization of oral traditions of ancient Tibetans, Mongolians ,Tus and other indigenous highland races.

Distinctly Tibetan in style, the epic is composed of a very large body of versions, each with many variants, Although there is no one definitive text, the Chinese compilation so far of just its Tibetan versions has filled some 289 books or volumes, totaling more than 40 million words. By one count of words alone, Gesar surpasses all the world epics combined. No wonder western calculations speak of Gesar as top legend in terms of physical distribution, duration of currency, scale of thematic structure, variation in plot and motif.

Back in the 1930s, a small number of scholars home and abroad noticed this oral tradition and began researching it. Many countries have devoted personnel and resources to studying and rescuing the art, deeming it a goldmine of annals of anthropological and . historical importance for research work on central Asia. On 17th,October,2001,at the 31th session of UNESCO held in Paris, the epic of King Geasr became a candidate for the list of entries 2002—2003.On 20th,May, 2006, approved by the State Council, the epic was cataloged into the first part of the national Intangible Cultural Heritage archive. Ultimately, in 2009,the epic was billed into the UN's Representative List of the Intangible Cultural Heritage of Humanity. This epic has been granted high academic value in addition to its great worth in the research of Tibetan social history, relationships between classes, communication among different nationalities, moral concepts, folk customs, cultures

The advent of the 21st century has ushered in a shift in perspective and paradigm in epic research, with emphasis more and more placed upon methodologies of oral poetry, ethnographic theorizing, performing aspect. This academic evolution, I conjecture, is not simply jumping on the trendy wagon, but a reflection of a deepening understanding of the whole inventory of the epic study available on the paradigmatic patterns governing research on anthropology and

拉夫的六个地区开展调查,从口头传统的现场来验证自己的理论假设并形成了自己的学说,同时也让人们从荷马史诗的文本看到了荷马史诗的传统。借助这样的理论,口头诗学很好地解释了那些杰出的口头诗人何以能够表演成千上万行的诗句,何以具有流畅的现场创作能力的问题?有了这样的理论,《格萨尔》史诗研究中许多疑难问题,诸如神授艺人、故事情节的母题类型、唱词结构的程式化等问题,我想也应该可以得到合理的解释。

毋庸置疑,《格萨尔》史诗的研究由来已久,已搜集、整理、出版的相关资料和论著也不在少数,但是,如何在大文化语境中去考察我们的民族文化,如何在交叉学科的研究中凸显我们的文化传统,这是值得我们深思的问题。基于这样的思考,我想我们的研究应该完成几个转向:从对过去的史诗的关注转向对当下的史诗的关注,从对史诗文本的关注转向对史诗语境的关注,从对普遍性的寻求转向民族志研究,从对集体性的关注转向对个人(特别是有创造性的艺人)的关注,从对静态的事项的关注转向对动态的实际表演和交流过程的关注。如此,我们才有可能较为完整地关注到《格萨尔》的历史传统与现实语境,关注到为史诗的不断挖掘、传承做出巨大贡献的艺人和研究者本身。

自古以来,青藏高原是一个神秘、神奇而又神圣的地方,巍巍昆仑屹立于此,滔滔江河发源于斯。伴随着人类早期文明的诞生,《格萨尔》史诗同昆仑神话一起向世人传递着华夏民族智慧的光芒。在漫长的历史长河中,质朴的高原人始终将神话叙事和史诗表演作为自己的文化之根,代代相传。正因如此,青海——这个人杰地灵的地方,被学界誉为《格萨尔》的故乡。

在这里,我想用几个"多"来概括青海与《格萨尔》史诗的密切关系:《格萨尔》的各种版本多,格萨尔的遗迹遗物多,格萨尔的传说故事多,《格萨尔》的说唱艺人多,《格萨尔》的藏戏表演多。尤其是我们发现了说不完《格萨尔》的艺人才让旺堆,写不完《格萨尔》的艺人格日尖参,唱不完《格萨尔》的艺人达哇扎巴,画不完《格萨尔》的艺人尕日洛、东智,抄不完《格萨尔》的艺人布特尕。他们是史诗的民间创作者和传承人,为我们讲述着《格萨尔》——这首唱不完、写不完的伟大诗歌。

我们知道,早期的青海非常封闭,大部分地区没有公路,人们生活条件极其艰

ethnography.

One feels, at this moment, inspired and enlightened by a brief survey of epic studies dating from the pioneering work on Homeric sagas undertaken by Albert Lord and Milman Parry . Initially ,they approached their object of research from a philological vantage , arguing on the premise that classical epics were fundamentally an oral poetic form before concluding the performing style of Homeric exploits were highly formalized, which was furthered predicated on the established cultural tradition of the then Greek societies. To testify the validity of his hypothesis, Professor Parry led a team on a inspection tour of six locales in former Yugoslavia and the outcome of such field investigation in the Balkans by Milman Parry and Albert Lord demonstrated the paratactic model used for composing these poems. By paratactic Parry and Lord mean that oral epics tend to be constructed in short episodes, each of equal status, interest and importance. This facilitates memorization, as the poet is recalling each episode in turn and using the completed episodes to recreate the entire epic as he performs it. Parry and Lord also showed that the most likely source for written texts of the epics of Homer was dictation from an oral performance. I believe, the Parrian hypothesis still holds water in explaining how in Gesar tradition, migrant bards are heavenly inspired, in which way heroic deeds are transmitted to the audience and from performer to performer by purely oral means and why there is such a proliferation of plot and motif.

No doubt, Gesar research has become a deeply entrenched and respected topic for researchers and experts. There is no dearth of academic output in forms of papers , monographs, etc. My question is: based upon such rich literature, how we can approach Gesar and even affect a cultural turn in a supra cultural context and within the cross-disciplinary framework. I, for one, suggest several scenarios in deepening Gesar studies by shifting our former focus on epic texts to the historical context in which epics were written down, on universalist concern to ethnographic probing particularistic in character, on the collectivity of epic composition to the creativity of the individual bards, and finally, on the static contemplation to the lively aspect of communications between performing bards and audience on the spot. Only so can we expect a fuller comprehension of the fruitful interplay of historical traditions and realistic context as well as expansion of the research work and the outstanding artists.

Qinghai ,due to its alpine location ,historically home to lofty mountain ranges topped by Kunlun and China's three mega waterways, ie, the Yangtse, the Yellow and the Lancang, has exerted a special appeal upon many people down the "Roof of the World". Incidentally, Qinghai is also associated with the origins of several myth and epic traditions essential for the Hans and many ethnic groups as a whole ,but the vitality and immortality of these legends and myths are, first and foremost, testimony to the wisdom and creativity of all the local populace that inhabit this glorious and exotic place called Qinghai.

In this connection, I want to add a few more words to corroborate on the pertinence of this

苦。尽管如此,《格萨尔》史诗却像一股清澈的山涧溪水,汩汩流淌,经久不息。许多国外学者早就注意到流传于此的《格萨尔》及其独特的文化内涵和文学价值,他们纷纷背起行囊不远万里来到青海,徒步进入果洛、玉树等广大牧区,搜集和挖掘出不少《格萨尔》史诗的原始版本,从而使青海成为国内外最早发现《格萨尔》史诗的地区。与之相呼应的是,在果洛州甘德县,人们把鲁姆德果山顶的一个山洞形象地称为"岭国觉如的口袋";在热贡地区的隆务峡口处,有一四四方方的棋石,每当路过此地,人们总要在棋石旁做一下赛棋的动作;而在同仁县麻巴乡,人们都知道有个格萨尔赛马场……美丽的传说加上现存的遗迹,不免令人遐思万千、心驰神往。故此,一直以来,青海被《格萨尔》史诗爱好者和研究者所钟爱,现在已经成为《格萨尔》工作乃至整个藏学工作的重要科研基地。在发掘、整理、翻译、出版和研究《格萨尔》史诗方面,青海当属全国范围内起步最早、成果最多的省区。

今天,我们在青海——《格萨尔》的故乡举办这样的论坛,我想这应该是广大学人们共同的心愿。在这个论坛上,来自世界各地的专家学者将集中展示他们最新的研究成果,而对于常年坚守在雪域高原、为《格萨尔》史诗的挖掘和传承默默奉献的基层工作者而言,这将是一种无言的激励和肯定。我想,这里面定然有一种鼓舞人心的精神,这种精神源自史诗的主人公格萨尔。

史诗中的格萨尔幼年时即遭驱逐,同母亲流落至玛域。母子俩克服各种艰难险阻,励精图治,终于开发和治理了玛域,从而使原本荒无人烟的地方变得水草丰茂。在一次赛马大会上,年轻的格萨尔战胜群雄,登上王位并迎娶了美丽的珠牡姑娘。接下来的故事里,他降服入侵的敌人,使百姓摆脱战乱之苦,过上了安居乐业的生活,最终让青藏高原走向统一……

这是民间文学对于正义力量颇具诗性的讲述,也是老百姓对民族英雄的热情颂扬,更是长期以来,高原民众所秉承的单纯而又朴素的价值判断和审美追求。在全民构建和谐社会的今天,我想我们更需要这样纯洁而执着的坚守。用一颗敬畏之心善待自然,用一颗包容之心面对世界,用一颗热爱之心拥抱身边的每个人。《格萨尔》不仅仅是一座史诗的高峰、文学的丰碑,也不仅仅是一首历史的诗歌,直到今天,它依旧被不停地讲述,我想更重要的是,它具有某种超越时空、国家和民族界限的精神力

highland province to the proliferation of Gesar saga: While a satisfactory conclusion about the epic's origins ,variants of plot and motif cannot be drawn based on the existent evidence ,Qinghai boasts the availability of the largest corpus of variations and the largest population of the top bards and performers still active in the grassland, for example, Cairang Wandui, Geri Jiansheng, Dawa Zhaba who keep reciting episodes from memory or books, while others chant the legendary tales in a state of trance. And in this mode, the epic of Gesar has been, for centuries, improvised on, and despite the lack of canonical version, as one finds in, for example, Greek epic.

We all know, through most of the regional history, Qinghai has remained out of the pales of modern civilization. Even into the 1950s,roads and modern amenities were few and most people, either farmer or pastoralist, eked out a difficult existence. Yet, in this lonely island of poverty inaccessible to the outside world of material progress, people kept chanting the heroic accounts of king of Gesar which trickled like clear fountain water into the consciousness of modern audience. This phenomenon compelled the willing attention of many oversea scholars. They journeyed here across both the kham present day western Sichuan and Amdo (present day Qinghai)regions as centers of diffusion, and specifically the Gulok and Yushu areas upon discovering many a genuine version, thus making Qinghai the land where some of the most valuable versions were located for example, a cave in the Gulok (Gande county) at the top of the Lumudeguo Mountain is likened to the pocket, an entrance into the Lin Kingdom. At another entrance of the Longwu Gorge into the present day Regong district of Huangnan Prefecture, there stands a square boulder in form of a chessboard. Tibetans are used to tarrying here for a while posing chess players in a game. Whereas in the Maba Township of tongren county, a Gesar horse racing ground is known to local people like a household name. Experts ,epic lovers and tourists, in facing all these legends and cultural relics, are strongly drawn on a field tour. Much headway, indeed, has been made and even pioneered in the way of rescuing, conserving and researching the Gesar tradition in Qinghai.

Hence, it is altogether fitting and proper we congregate here, to lay our heads together for a push towards better understanding of Gesar stories. I do look forward to all those present to produce their solid and latest theorizing about the honored subject under discussion, a spur, I believe, on all the local research workers who stand at the alpine cradle of Gesar myth for their silent but brilliant work to diffuse the mythical king's heroic exploits to combat evil for the benefit of his own people, a spirit which Gesar himself embodies and personifies to encourage generations that come after him.

Oral heroic ballads, at their origin, usually deal with outstanding deeds of kings and warriors who live in the heroic age of the nation. Such epic cycles conform, as a rule ,to certain mythological patterns, called archetypes found all over the world. King Ge-sar ,without exception, has a miraculous birth, a despised and neglected childhood in a rustic milieu, in exile with his mother in the area of Mayu. later he fights for the possession of the Mayu, becomes ruler and, aided by his mother, he governs the kingdom wisely, turning it into a rich grassland where plenty

量,这种力量让每个人都能找到乐观和自信,也会让每个家园一如既往地幸福和安宁。

世界上,许多民族都在讲述自己的史诗,有探求宇宙诞生、万物生成和讴歌创造精神的创世史诗;也有描述部落迁徙、民族形成和颂扬民族精神的英雄史诗。从理论上讲,史诗是一种特定的文学现象,它产生于人类童年时期。随着时代发展,史诗产生的社会基础已经消失,正如雨果所说的:"史诗在最后的分娩中消亡了,世界和诗的另一个纪元即将开始。"诚然,走过漫漫历史长河,许多史诗已然成为人类文化史上的一个标本,大多以固定文本的形式被陈列在图书馆和资料室里,再无生机可言。然而,令人惊叹的是,在藏族人民中流传了千年之久的英雄史诗《格萨尔》,至今依然存活于民间且焕发着青春活力。

不可否认,《格萨尔》强大的生命力源自民间艺人。自史诗产生以来,他们的说唱活动就没有终止过,至今仍有百余位《格萨尔》说唱艺人活跃在民间,我们在特定的时日仍可以目睹并聆听其艺术生命的最原始状态。当然,由于艺人所处地域不同,各自的说唱能力及风格也各不相同。这些艺人在天赋、才华、知识阅历、内在气质和特长等方面也各有差异,因而大家口中的史诗也各具特色。就同一个艺人而言,因每次说唱的时间、环境和个人心态不同,每次说唱的内容也就长短不一,不尽相同,从而形成了"每个艺人口中都有一部《格萨尔》"的局面。如此来看,这部史诗至今仍然没有固定的文本,在说唱的过程中,众艺人不断丰富和完善着它的内容。与此同时,《格萨尔》伴随着众多说唱艺人的足迹不断传向四方。史诗的部数也在不断增加,各种不同的刻本、手抄本、说唱整理本仍然在不断增加。从这个角度来讲,《格萨尔》的确是当今世界为数不多的"活形态"史诗之一,是中华民族也是整个人类文化的宝贵财富。我们珍视它,就是珍视我们的民族历史和文化,我们保护它就是在保护我们人类曾经拥有过的美好童年。今天,它仍以顽强的生命力不断发展着、丰富着,给我们最大的启示是——人类需要更加关注自己的现在,健康、快乐地走向未来。

诚然,作为人类共同享有的一种叙事方式,史诗或阐述世界本原问题,或叙述某一民族形成的历史,里面凝聚了人们对宇宙的探求精神和对祖先的追恋、敬仰之情。在叙述过程中,它包容了一个民族全部的生活信息和文化信息,汇聚着大量的民族

and happiness prevail. He then wins his beautiful wife through a series of marvelous feats. In subsequent episodes he defends his people against various external aggressors, human and superhuman ,before reaching his goal of a unified highland politically.

These episodes are designed to stir and edify the spirit of the tribal people to heroic actions by praising the exploits of their illustrious ancestors, as the primary function of epic is to educate rather than to chronicle and to transmit basic values and sense of beauty. In today's China, while we strive to build a more harmonious society, Gesar and his lineage's fidelity to basic virtues like honesty, courage and honor are still exemplary. Gesar stories are told today for their entertainment value as much as to edify us to hold nature in reverence, to be tolerant of and nice to people we don't like, and love our neighbors as we do our immediate family. The dynamism of the mythical cycle, it must be added, is unmistakably due to the built-in ,transcendental spiritual potency it contains and their roots in the national soil, a power that accords each citizen optimism and self assurance to face life cheerfully, and each family security of justice and riches of happiness.

An epic may treat such various subjects as myths, heroic deeds, histories, or philosophical or moral theories. One motif of all oral traditions, east and west, is to try to explain how a certain race came into being and how the world was formed out of chaos. Theoretically speaking, epics are necessarily a product of a certain pre-historical , say, heroic , age, or childhood of mankind. However, even when the heroic age that gave rise to the creation of epics passed, epics survive as an integral part of the national culture. Given the fact many oral traditions in other parts of the world now survive only in the glass cases in the museums and libraries, our Gesar cycle is exempt from the common fate as it still amazes us by retaining the youthfulness and vigor in the broad grassland of the Kham, Amdo and Central Tibet.

The spread of literacy, which does have a disastrous effect on the oral means of transmission, brings about a quick corruption of the tradition elsewhere. The miraculous power of Gesar songs lies in the availability of an impressive army of over 100 living bards still active across the highland. The wide variety of cultures in which the Gesar epic is encountered means a large number of variants have always existed, and no canonical text can be written. Basically these versions differ very greatly in details, in plot and motifs,. Depending upon talent, personality , locale, time of recital and even the various moods in which Many performers chant Gesar episodes from memory or books, (some do the legendary tales in a state of trance) ,it is bound to be true that each performer acts a different Gesar.

A given Gesar singer would know only his local version, which centers around the core motifs nonetheless ,taking into account of the physical size of the highland as each bard is responsive to local characteristics, improvising the core leitmotifs as befits his mood and personality. All in all, the lack of a canonical text should not be deemed a technical deficiency, but rather symptomatic of the "living epic" rarely found elsewhere, a legacy which deserves to be

社会生活的真实图景,诸如议事、祀典、仪式等,从中我们可以寻找到古代地理、历史、医学、文学、音乐等许多珍贵资料。

它把人类早期的生活经验转化为生动的叙述语言,把最丰富的生活世界化成了一个个经典符号,人类物质的、精神的、历史的、现在的……所有的一切都在史诗中得到歌唱。这种歌唱是一个充满了神圣感和崇高感的过程,而歌唱的意义就在于表达文化群体之间的自我认同。可以说,史诗是人类对自己栖居于这个世界的一种认知方式,也是从混沌中建立起来的最初的社会秩序。

时代步入新千年以后,我们越来越清晰地认识到史诗、神话等这些古老思想文化遗产对人类自身的意义,这些财富都是先祖留给我们的思想精髓,也是他们智慧的结晶。每一部史诗的讲述都展现着文明的光芒。我们知道,在全球经济文化渐趋一体化的大背景中,东西方文明在不断的碰撞和对话中,创造着一个不断文明、和谐的新世界。在此过程中,世界各大史诗依旧闪耀着它们智性的光焰和独特的魅力。

而分别代表不同文化地域和专业背景的专家学者,就在今天欢聚中国青海,对话史诗、交流思想,把最前沿的理论和思想传递给大家,我想这不仅仅是一项学术交流活动,而且是一种价值体系的交流过程,更重要的是它承载着我们人类最终的理想,那就是各民族和睦共处,全世界和平安宁。

最后预祝研讨会圆满成功!祝各位专家学者和朋友在青期间安康如意,扎西德勒!谢谢大家!

cherished and preserved with utmost care and attention. One ultimate revelation: with oral traditions increasingly enriched and improvised associated with our childhood, it pays for mankind to attend to its immediate present, its mental sanity, its state of lightheartedness on its path to a promising future.

At a more profound and general level, epics as a genre of narrative exist to address the fundamental subject of origin or the creation of a certain nation. Endemic to human nature, an epic cycle symbolizes our deference to our ancestors as well as mythical imagination beyond the existential to identify ourselves with beings of heroic proportions. Such narratives, frequently a repository of the genuine cultural values ,the rituals ,the ceremonies, are used to sift out precious clues to ancient geography, literature, medicine and music.

An epic turns the early life experiences of our forefathers into vivid storytelling event. In a typical saga is found "the commonality of themes in all world myths, pointing to a constant requirement in the human psyche for a centering in terms of deep principles". That is, a search for the meaning of life or a reaffirmation of the sanctity of life. An epic is a metaphor for what lies behind the visible world. However the divergent oral traditions differ, they all call us to a deeper awareness of the very act of living itself. The very process of singing out an epic story is a stirring of fresh life as it ignites one's own imagination so that one's own life is charged with a sense of the sacred and the sublime .Epic sagas are thus a unique way of a certain human grouping to confirm their cultural identity. In essence, we might surmise an epic is actually one mode of knowledge to bring about order out of chaos for all the sentient and creative human beings.

In this young age, we are increasingly aware of the rich ancient legacy encoded in time-honored epic sagas, the crystallized knowledge left by our ancestors. This does not mean we are retreating from reason. It simply means our technology, our tools, our computers are not enough. In an age of economic globalization, one in which east and west ultimately meets to forge a new world where harmony and higher order of wisdom prevail, world epics will reveal their greater radiance of beauty and truth.

I am pleased to note that this forum has attracted a wide spectrum of delegates and experts and academics. Your insight, expertise and knowledge will be hugely valuable in providing a variety of brainstorming experiences that reflect the latest hypothesizing effort in the field .This is not only a process of give and take in the usual sense, but one of communication between divergent value systems wherein we pin our big hope of peaceful co-existence and co-prosperity among all nations and over the whole world.

Last but not the least, I wish the forum full success. May all present have a pleasant stay, in perfect health, and a mostly rewarding meeting in Xining. Zha xi de le! Thank you.

造梦空间的幻象

在 2012 年三江源国际摄影节开幕式的演讲

2012 年 6 月 25 日

如果能够像神鹰一样俯瞰大地，俯瞰山河与莽原……这绝不只是我一个人的梦想，不只是诗人的梦想，也不只是我们的祖先和神话创造者的梦想。

可是，远古神话的创造者和创世史诗最初的讲述者，一定曾经通过某种方式俯瞰过这个世界，他们承蒙神助，或腾云，或驾雾，或者化作神鹰君临大地。从此便有了诡奇飞扬的神话、恢宏高耸的史诗传承于世。

作为创世的杰作，青藏高原已经以其升腾的海拔凌驾于白云之上；或者说，这高原本身就是一只无与伦比的巨枭，我们站在这里，其实已经翱翔于地球之巅。

那么，我们是否还能够再次腾飞，像雄鹰一样俯瞰这片高傲伟大的疆域，俯瞰黄河、长江、澜沧江的秘密诞生地……这是对生命自信和生存想象力的巨大挑战。

走进青藏高原生活的八年间，尤其每当置身于可可西里的旷野之上，昆仑山的雪峰之下，长江、黄河的源流之中，我谦卑的生命匍匐在地，而桀骜的灵魂却如生羽翼，一次又一次地跃跃欲试，御风而起。

神鹰俯瞰的疆域啊！——我的目光无限景仰地追随着翱翔的雄鹰，心中一再回响着这句诵祷般的话语。

梦想是用来实现的。经过多年的艰苦孕育，《神鹰俯瞰的疆域》终于问世了。一批勇敢而充满才华的摄影家不仅完成了一项史无前例的壮举，而且也代表我们所有人、带领我们所有人，向这片神灵的疆域献上了心中的礼赞。

这是一个幻象丛生的造梦空间。千种姿态，万般变化。水的华丽与柔软，山的逶

Fantasizing in a Dreamland
Address at the Sanjiangyuan Intl Photographing Festival
25th, June, 2012

If I were equipped with a pair of wings of a fairy eagle, gliding far above in the celestial vaults, overlooking the earth, crisscrossed by rivers and dominated by mountains... By no means this is a dream solely to myself, a poet both by faith and profession. Neither is the dream only harbored by our ancestors and our worthy myth creators.

Yet ,those superior and celestial race of beings, such as myth creators in a primordial time in a primal society, those narrators of creation epics must have ,by divine grace or aid, rided across the vastness of space even in the incarnate of a divine eagle. Without such Herculean feat, without such wonders and prodigies of elder days, how is it possible us mortals in the 21st century, an age which has no engrossing superstitions and traditions of its own, are still subscribing to the eternal pull and charm of ancient myth and epic stories?

Marvels done by nature's hand , Qinghai-Tibet plateau dominates the whole world. Or rather, we might as well imagine this "roof of the world" to be a celestial bird gliding between towering and pristine peaks.

It follows we might as well fancy ourselves to be such gigantic fowls guiding the chariot of Phoebus hunting down the secret source of the Yellow River, the Yangtze and the Lancang. What a challenge! One against our life force as well as our imagination.

Now with 8 years of life and work behind this plateau province, each time amidst the wasteland of Kol Hil, at the base of the mighty snow-capped Kunlun or the gushing headwaters of China's three major rivers, While my body bows down unrestrainedly my soul haughtily rises into the heavens like winged creatures. Time is still and meaningless here ,for you cannot feel but your stretching soul, embracing the sky and the ground.

Ah,Sangjiangyuan, the shadowy limits of a typical fairyland admitted only to the purview of a divine eagle!

A dream is meant to come true. Years of heroic and painstaking work in the hands of a good bevy of genius photographers has paid off rich dividends. This pictorial entitled A Divine Eagle's

迤和静默,冰雪的孤傲和圣洁,精灵的自由和美丽,生活的温馨和欢乐……一切都在神话的背景中呈现,从史诗的韵律中流淌而来。

走进《神鹰俯瞰的疆域》,仿佛这宏伟的高大陆、这神奇的三江源、这万物祥和的世界,都重新经历了一次诞生、一次洗礼、一次命名。

三江源,仅仅这个称谓,就足以传达她对于一个有机的自然秩序,对于我们的现实生活和精神生活,对于人类文明的历史和未来,所具有的不可替代、不可失去的地位和意义。那么除了一种畅游于大美梦境中的欣赏与感悟,《神鹰俯瞰的疆域》也为我们更加直观地了解和认识三江源,打开了一扇前所未有的门扉。

这是祖先的河山,祖国的河山;这是一个正在受其呵护的民族和必将继续受其呵护的万代子孙的河山。

我们热爱她,我们因她的养育而高贵。愿我们也永远珍惜她、敬仰她。愿神鹰俯瞰的疆域与我们同在!

View of Sanjiangyuan has seen the day at last. A feat unprecedented in tribute to this fairyland on behalf of us all, mortals awe-struck and inspired by this Marvel done by Nature's mighty hand.

Are the things in these photos a mirage or something? The breathtaking scenes of sanjiangyuan unfold before my eyes and under the changing shadows of clouds ,the rocks, the creeks fed by frigid melting ice, the glassy glaciers, the antelopes, appear in different color and tone and show stunning beauty as if they are fresh trickled down out of epics and myth.

Thumbing through this pictorial, one simply feels going through a majestic and solemn ritual of confirmation and name giving, a baptism of aesthetics.

Ah,Sanjiangyuan! What a nomenclature that instills in us a confidence in the harmony of a pure biotic community free of any human trace as well as in the rosy future of mankind. Aside the immense reading pleasure, it has opened a window on the shadowy limits of a spectacular fairy land.

This grace is bequeathed by Mother Nature, in our care and for our well being. And for the benefit of our children and our children's children.

We Love Sanjiangyuan. We worship her. We cherish her. May Sanjiangyuan within the purview of a divine eagle last forever.

诗歌与朝圣的远游

在"柔刚诗歌奖"颁奖会上的致答辞

2012 年 4 月 13 日

尊敬的柔刚先生、尊敬的各位评委,朋友们:

感谢第二十届"柔刚诗歌奖"评委会把这个尊贵的奖项颁发给我,为此我充满了由衷的感激之情。我想大家也许能理解我这种感激的真正缘由,那就是这个诗歌奖项的设立者,包括它的评委会,无一例外都来自民间,他们都是真正意义上的公共知识分子。我不知道今天在中国还有哪一项诗歌奖已经延续评选了二十届,并且一直还保持着它最初创立时所坚守的公正立场,而从不被诗歌之外的一切因素干扰和影响,这不能不说是个奇迹。我们可以想象,这个来自民间的诗歌奖能如此顽强地坚守到今天,其中必定会有许多鲜为人知的动人故事,但对于那些真正献身于诗歌的人,这些他们所经历过的一切,似乎早已被深深埋藏在了记忆的深处,而这种经历本身,毫无疑问已经赋予了他们的人生一种更为特殊的意义。作为同行,在这里我们没有理由不对他们肃然起敬。

我要对他们表达诗歌的敬意,但我需要声明的是,我的这种敬意,完全来自我们共同的对诗歌纯粹的忠诚,而并不仅仅因为我是一个获奖者,如果真的是那样的话,那将是彻头彻尾地对人类诗歌精神的亵渎和不敬。我向他们表达敬意,那是因为在这个诗歌被极度边缘化的时代,对诗歌的热爱和坚持,仍然是需要勇气和奉献的。

当然,对于那些诗神的真正信徒来说,这并非就是一个事实,因为真理早已经告诉过我们,精神上伟大的孤独者和引领者,从来就是这个世界的极少数,或许正是因为有这样一群人的精神守望,我们才从未怀疑过诗歌是人类存在下去的最有说服力

Poetry and Pilgrimage
Reply at 20th Rougang Poetry Awarding Ceremony
13th, April, 2012

Respected Mr Rougang, respected jury, friends:

Gratitude overwhelms me when the notification came that the Rougang Award Jury decided to make me the recipient of the 20th Rougang Award. For a very solid reason in that the initiators of distinction,ie, Mr Rougang, including its jury, have nothing to do with the establishment. They are truly of the civic society, the intellectuals in Zola's tradition, that is, with a heart for the downtrodden as well as an eye for knowledge genuinely worthy in the crowd. Who can tell me, in present day China, other than Rougang Award, there is any civic honor of poetry continuously running into its 20th occasions without compromising its original principles of non-discrimination and justice, undeterred by any non-poetic circumstances or factors from either political or commercial interests, a record nothing short of a miracle.One easily senses there should be heroes unsung and stories barely told in heeding such indomitable code of heroism. Everything unspeakable they have weathered being now conveniently hid deep in the recesses of their staunch psyche, such happenings are bound to imbue their lives with a special significance. As peers, I must rise ,with cap in hand, to look them in the eyes with reverence and amazement.

I must show them due respects, in the likeminded companionship ,but this I must add, as my respects emanate totally from a common devotion to the art of poetry, by no means a gesture of the vested interests, ie, being glorified by this award. And if this being true, I stand justified of profanity and disloyalty to the human spirit in the highest degree. To openly acknowledge my gratitude is tantamount to claiming my firm bond with true lovers of Pushkin and Shakespeare as well as my unshakable faith in poetry in an wholesale prosaic age given to unscrupulous pursuit of trite objects of life, such as luxury and outward ostentation, lampooned one century ago by giants like Einstein as the ethical basis of pigsty.

Yet, this plague spot of civilization ought to be neutralized and checked with all possible speed and means, although I am deeply aware of the fact for human civilization to achieve any level of decency, there must be some great loners and leaders, poets among them, categorically in

的理由。因为诗歌包含了人性中最美最善的全部因素，它本身就是想象的化身，它是语言所能表达的最为精微的秘密通道。

诗歌从诞生之日起，它就和我们的灵魂以及生命本体中，最不可捉摸的那一部分厮守在一起，从某种意义上说，诗歌是我们通过闪着泪光的心灵，在永远不可知晓的神秘力量的感召下，被一次次唤醒的隐藏在浩瀚宇宙和人类精神空间里的折射和倒影。我们彝族人中最伟大的精神和文化传承者毕摩，就是用这种最古老的诗歌方式，完成了他们与宇宙万物以及神灵世界的沟通和对话。他们是诗人中的祭司，他们无可争辩是人类诗歌的先行者。

当然，我还想要告诉大家的是，诗歌语言所构建的世界，一直被认为是诗人的另一个更为隐秘的领域，它是所有伟大诗人必须经历的，有时甚至是无法预知的文字探险，从这个角度上来看，这个世界上所有的文字掌握者，他们在文字的最为精妙、最为复杂、最为不可思议的创造方面，都将永远无法与天才的诗人们比肩。诗人毫无争议地是语言王国中当之无愧的国王。有人曾经说过这样的话，诗歌的语言就是稀有的金属和珍奇的宝石，在文字和声音中最完美的呈现。

朋友们，在此时我还想与大家分享的是，最近我有机会刚刚完成了一次诗歌与朝圣的远游。我有幸应邀到南美秘鲁参加20世纪最伟大的诗人之一，塞萨尔·巴列霍一百二十周年诞辰的纪念活动，最令我感动的是，当我们深入安第斯山区的腹部，来到这位有着印第安血统的诗人的故乡时，我惊奇地发现就是在这样一个极为偏僻、遥远和封闭的世界里，诗歌的力量和影响也从未消失。塞萨尔·巴列霍，这位写出了迄今为止人类有关心灵苦难最为深刻的诗歌的诗人，用他忧伤的诗句，再一次为我们印证了古罗马诗人贺拉斯的名言，诗歌的生命要比青铜的寿命更为久长。

在诗人的故乡圣地亚哥·德·丘科这个古老的区域，当我们目睹了他的一个又一个土著族人背诵他的诗篇时，眼睛里面流露出的尊严和自信，无疑深深地震撼了我们。尽管作为一位彻底颠覆了一般诗歌语言的大师，读者要真正进入他所设置的语言迷宫并非易事，但他的诗歌所透示出来的人道主义情怀、对弱者和被剥削者的同情，以及他对生命、死亡的永不停歇的追问，都会触动这个世界上任何一个还保留着良知和道德认同的人的心弦。塞萨尔·巴列霍曾写下过这样的诗句，"白色的石头上，

the minority, who stand on vigil for the sanity of human cultures and whose presence speaks volumes about the fittest of the survival of human race across the globe simply because poetry contains the unique essence of man as man, ie ,the true and the good, the simulation of human dignity and imagination, the most sophisticated channels of verbal beauty and sophistry.

Ever at the dawn of humanity, poetry was with us , an integral part of our inner being. In a sense, poetry is ,with religion, the most beautiful and mysterious experience we possess, activated time and again by a force whose power and origin is totally inaccessible to our minds, a refraction or a reflection of the Almighty cosmic Gesit.We in our Yi communities still retain our age-old awe for our shamans figures, that is ,Bimos who always poetize and communion with all the sentient beings on earth and the deities. You call them priests, but to us Yi, they are also poets, the undisputed forerunners of human songs and epics.

Of course, I must impart this occultist knowledge to my fellow poets that Utopia made of poetic diction is an invisible realm from and across whose bourn very few poets have the luck to tour and sightsee around. It is frankly an adventure or venture into the unknown, the supremely aesthetic. I console myself, even of all the most remarkable and dainty human creations, all the craftsmen specialized and good at words, poets emerge supreme and divine. Poets are beyond argument the kings of all letters of men and women. Somebody asserts, with full assurance, poetry is diamond among the richest stones and the most precious metals of human spirituality, the perfect synchronization of sound and word in the best order.

Friends, I shall open my heart to you with a pilgrimage of poetry I have conducted not long ago. As luck would have it, I was invited to Mexico to attend the celebrations of the 120th anniversary of the birth of Cé sar Vallejo, one of the greatest bards Latin America has ever seen. What impressed me most, when taken to Cé sar Vallejo's hometown in the heartland of the Andes, so unbelievably distant ,isolated and backwater, poetry still has a tenacious hold upon local inhabitants. Cesar Vallejo, from whose mouth such movingly plaintive songs issue, of the human sorrows and joys in superlatives, has been one of the most recent showcases in evidence to the forcible truthfulness of Horace's adage, the Roman laureate poet: poetry endures longer than bronze.

In Santiago de Chuco, a remote village in the Peruvian Andes. I saw with my own eyes, one by one, his tribesmen, recited his poems, there was a note of dignity in their voices, an expression of solemn ecstasy on their faces. It was a scene that shocked and captivated. Considered one of the great poetic innovators of the 20th century in any language, very few readers find it an easy task to extricate themselves from his labyrinth. yet, his profound sympathy for the incarcerated and the insulted , his born humanitarianism and his relentless probing into the most stubborn issues of life and death have left the whole world awed and inspired, poets and ordinary readers who still are vulnerable to questioning of conscience mingled with good sense and good feeling. Cé sar Vallejo once wrote:" A black stone laid upon a white stone." He was penning his own epigraph in

压着一块黑色的石头",我知道这是他在用诗歌,对永恒的死亡在哲学层面上的最后祭奠和定格。

塞萨尔·巴列霍已经离开我们七十四年了,但是我们从没有过这样的感觉,他的生命已经真的死亡。作为一个精神上和肉体上的双重流放者,他至死都没有再回到自己的故乡。但让我们略感欣慰的是,时间作出了最为公正的判决,他不朽的诗歌正延续着他短暂的足以让人悲泣的肉体生命。塞萨尔·巴列霍是安第斯山里的一块巨石,但在今天他也是一位享誉世界的杰出公民。他的一生和光辉的诗篇给了我们一个启示,那就是真正伟大的诗歌和诗人,是任何邪恶势力都永远无法战胜的。因为诗人和诗歌永远只面临一种考验,那就是无情的时间和一代又一代的读者。再次感谢各位评委的慷慨之举,我无以回报,但请相信我,在诗神面前,我将永远是一位谦卑忠实的仆人。谢谢大家!

poetic diction, nay, he was philosophizing ultimately on the meaning of death.

74 years have elapsed since Cé sar Vallejo ,the most radically avant-garde poet in the 20th century, left us. Yet strangely, I never feel like he is gone. To me, he lives among us every minute of it. An exile physically and spiritually, perennially in dire poverty In Europe , he never returned to the fold of his home country. Yet his memory has been now vindicated that his fame has circled the earth, much to the consolation of all those who love his poems, as a gigantic rock in the Peruvian Andes ,as a distinguished citizen of the world. His poetic legacy is a testament to his monumental greatness that great poets and lasting poetry must prevail upon all those dark and evil forces. Ultimately his story affords us the ultimate enlightenment that weak and facile poetry will not survive its weakling maker. Time will test which is which. With this at the tip of my tongue, I must stand guard on any from of self pity and self complacency and I must keep forging ahead with the greatest measure of humility and audacity in carrying on with my artistic endeavor. Thanks for your attentions.

神话永远闪烁着远古文明的诗性光辉

在昆仑神话与世界创世神话国际学术论坛上的演讲

2011年7月17日

女士们、先生们:大家好!

我们今天聚在一起,是为了探讨一个生动而多元的话题。这个话题属于幻想的孩子,属于慈爱的母亲,属于通灵的祭司,也属于宇宙万物,因为它是神话。

这个话题属于在座的各位,因为你们是人类古老文明领域的探索者,是人类神圣精神祭坛的现代守护者。所以在这里,我首先要向各位专家学者致以崇高的敬意!对大家来到青藏高原,来到东方神殿昆仑山的故乡青海,表示热忱的欢迎!

在地球最为浩大的造山运动中,诞生了青藏高原和她的骄子昆仑山;在人类最为光辉的造神运动中,诞生了叱咤风云的昆仑诸神,他们引领东方世界走出混沌,走向文明。所以我相信,今天,各位文明的使者从世界各地来到这里,不仅仅是接受了一个学术论坛的邀请,更是响应了一种悠远神秘的召唤;你们带来的不仅仅是理性智慧的学术思想,也带来了世界各地伟大的远古创造力和各民族不朽的热情。

那么,也许我可以说,这是一个众神的聚会。

从自然神话中诞生的青藏高原,就必然成为一片诞生人类神话的土地。这就是中国的昆仑神话,一个以西王母为主人公的昆仑神话体系。它像江河一般,从大山源

Mythology As the "Song of the Universe and the Music of the Spheres"

Key note Speech at the International Conference on Mount Kunlun Mythology vs the Creation in World Myths
17th, July, 2011

Ladies, Gentlemen, Friends: Good morning!

We are gathered here today to dwell upon a subject, at once of utmost importance and charm, a topic, perhaps, more congenial to children brimming over with innocence and imagination than us adults and more kin to the loving spirit of motherhood in general. Although the subject is traditionally the preserve of shaman who alone communion with the deities, myths first and foremost belong to all creatures on earth simply because myths have both a superhuman and anthropological dimension to them.

This subject is ultimately, of course, accredited to each of you in the audience as meaning seekers of ancient civilizations and modern guardian angels at the altars of humanity today, which affords me a super reason to extend to you all the most heartfelt regards.You are welcome to the Qinghai Tibet Plateau, the original home to the fabled Mount Kunlun ,the most sacred repository of Chinese racial memories.

In the awe inspiring mountain building movements which the geological history of the earth consists of, the Himalayan ranges and the Kunlun ranges began rising some 40 million years ago during the Tertiary Period when the great Indian subcontinent ,adrift on its crusty plate collided with the Asian landmass. In an almost parallel development of myth making dated rather recently, emerged a pantheon of Kunlun deities destined to lead the Oriental people ,traversing vast distances of barbarism ,into the palace of civility and urbanity. Allow me some musings of very personal nature as I believe you have come all the way to attend this meeting not only in response to an invitation but also to the call from the distant and mysterious realm, for you have brought us not only rationalizing thoughts and rich mental food, but also the unaging enthusiasms and ever replenishing creativity of all the major races inhabiting various parts of this old planet we call the earth.

Up to this point, shall I ,under certain poetic license, call this meeting a rendezvous of a special breed of the Immortals?

起,滥觞于辽阔的东方大地。重要的是,在这片土地上,神话从未成为过去,诸神从未消失。这些神话和传说,不仅作为一种远古的精神象征和文明记忆而存在,并且作为人们仪式化生存的一部分而延续。世界的创造和文明的肇始,都是一种仪式。

无论在科学的论证还是在诗意的想象中,创世都是我们这个地球以及我们已知宇宙的最初仪式,创世神话和由它所衍生的神话传说,也因此无不具有相似的仪式结构,正是这种仪式化,决定了人类文明的神圣性。所以我觉得,在这样一片神灵无处不在的土地上,我们今天这个活动,本身就具有某种仪式感。

我要继续说的是,在昆仑山下,在黄河上游,就在我们的身边,昆仑神话绝不是想象和虚构的事物。这里有大量的遗址、遗迹,大量的自然地貌,甚至大量的考古发现,都与最为久远的口头传说和文献记载相吻合或者相互佐证。昆仑神话和昆仑诸神在浩瀚的文化中徜徉,也在人们的节日和生死仪式上、在人们的日常生活中现身。青海民间对诸神的信仰和祭拜从古至今,一如既往。它让我们相信,我们仍然处在一个令人感激也令人敬畏的神话时代。这就让我们今天的活动具有了某种现场感。

纵观历史,在世界不同民族、不同文化的交流中,神话也许是我们最容易沟通、最容易相互理解的文化语言,因为人类童年的语言如此相似,这种相似甚至超乎我们的想象。我们也许不曾共同经历过文艺复兴或者工业革命,但是我们一定共同经历了万物的诞生以及洪水滔天。那么我们这个国际论坛,目的就是为了在远古文明的交流和对话中,寻找并且确定我们今天在这个世界上共同生存、共同繁荣的理由。一个更为和平、欢乐、共享的开放与和谐的世界,是我们的远古神灵和祖先曾经在时空源头达成的默契。

我们的确迎来了神话复兴的时代。20世纪以来,自然科学的发展惊心动魄,人类战争与和平的浪潮惊心动魄,人与自然的冲突和分裂惊心动魄。

Naturally, the Qinghai Tibet Plateau serves the ideal breeding ground for mythical stories of epic proportions, and of the various creation stories that evolve in China, the Kunlun mythology , native to the Chinese people, holds a special position, conjuring up visions of an exotic realm in the west of China, featuring Xiwangmu, the Queen of the Western land and her entourage of supernatural beings, demons ,heroes and villains. What is most pertinent to us is that these Kunlun myths never cease to titillate the Chinese imagination and the Kunlun divinities have taken such a permanent hold on the local dwellers ,irrespective of religion or race. In spite of a positivistic opposition of science and myth that prevails, the tendency among the enlightened is to see myths as dramatic embodiments of a people's perception of the deepest truths, the expression of the general beliefs of a race ,social class or a nation. The legends and myths do derive partially their raison d'etre as serious scholars see in them vestiges of primordial ritual and ceremony.

Wasn't the genesis of the cosmos in every major religion a ritual and a ceremony? Either in rationalistic inquiry or in poetic imagination, creation is undisputedly the earliest known "passage of rite" from birth to maturity on the part of humans inhabiting the planet we call the earth. All the creation stories and its derivative forms share certain startlingly similar rituals central to the sanctity of human beings. For this reason, this event today ,which takes place in a land perennially haunted by legions of supernatural beings ,is in itself ritualized and hallowed.

Permit me, dear sirs, to linger a bit while in my brooding indulgences. Here at the foot of the mighty Mount Kunlun, upstream of the Yellow River, under our very noses, mythical deities and heroes, by no means abstractions, are constantly brought to life in the earliest literary or non literary literature and cross corroborated by archeological findings unearthed on massive scale in widely dispersed sites. One encounters them at every turn, in stylized narratives as much as in ritualized festivals and on dramatic occasions marking either birth of new life or the passing of the departed in the throes of death. In sum, the cultic beliefs and practices of the Kunlun deities remain firm an solid up to this day among the citizenry within the whole territory of Qinghai. Local folks approach myths ,ie, the religious formulation of the cosmic view of a people, not as a representation of truth but as truth itself. They live still in awe of the Kunlun deities which strikes resonant points in the minds of us all involved in this event to the extent we are living in full awareness of living here and now.

Looking back, myths have invariably proved to be the most accessible tool for communication when different races and cultures collide .This is mainly due to the linguistic similarity various human groupings share in their adolescence much to the bewilderment of ancient people and us alike. For one thing, historical happenings like the Renaissance or the Industrial Revolution may have eluded this highland landscape, but we are not exempt from a beginning in which the heavens and earth were still one and all was chaos. That is why we converge today on this platform as if reenacting an ever lasting dialogue with the ancients because we are in our search through the ages for truth ,for meaning and significance. We need for life to

也正是在这样的背景下,神话研究方兴未艾。学者们从众多的角度和途径走向神话,用充满魔力的话语,为我们打开了一重又一重时空的大门,而我们曾经以为这些大门早已关闭或者我们已经迷失。这不是一种偶然,也不是一种时代的悖论,它是值得深思的启示。因为自然科学在揭开一层自然之谜的同时,它又触及了另一层秘密的皮肤。换句话说,自然科学在对这个世界"祛魅"的同时,却在不断地迎接着更加深层的、更加光怪陆离的世界,并且为人类神秘文化提供崭新的支持和宽广的视野。而战争和愈演愈烈的自然失衡,让我们重新思考生存与死亡的意义,呐喊、哭泣与抗争,唤醒了祖先的灵魂;在人性复归的血泊里,在刻骨铭心的灾难中,我们比以往任何时候都更加清晰地听到神灵的话语。

神话正在重新放射光芒,正在重新照耀我们的身心、照耀我们生存的世界。这当是神话和神话研究之于今天世界的根本意义。

我们仍然需要神话,我们需要维护一个充满神奇和寓意的神话世界,用以维护我们现实世界的多彩与和谐。世界所有的民族都是热爱神话的民族。过去是,今天依然如此。

如同昆仑神话活在青海一样,作为彝族人,我也深知彝族创世神话之于彝族人民现实生活的重要意义。居住在不同地区的彝族先民,以史诗的形式创造并且传承了一系创世神话,包括《勒俄特依》《梅葛》等等。据学者不完全统计,今天活在彝族人民口头的神话史诗有二十四部之多,它们以诗歌的语言形式,记叙了天地形成、人类起源、事物来源、洪水的劫难与人类再生。在民间的婚礼、葬礼、成年礼和传统节日中,这些史诗依然被庄严地讲述和歌唱。

人们为什么不能失去神话呢?因为神话讲述的世界,是一个自由广阔的、充满活力和梦想的世界。在那个世界里,人性与神性共生共存并且可以相互沟通和影响。因

signify and we have inner problems to cope with other than achieving purposes of outer values. In such groping we somehow feel there was some kind of tacit understanding reached upon by our ancestors, ie, one of the inner values concerns the bringing about of a more open peaceful, prosperous and harmonious world.

Paradoxically ,while what we have today is a demythologized world, we moderns have also ushered in an epoch of revival of mythology. The mind-boggling advances in science, the violent swaths of death and destruction modern total wars have occasioned, man's despoiling of Nature have combined to unsettle societies, primitive or industrial alike. Old civilizing patterns go to pieces. They disintegrate. Life has become a fragile thing that exists in the crucible of terror and possible extinction. In this "tumult of anarchy", sophisticated men have reexamined mythology in light of our troubled contemporary experiences, seeking clues to the spiritual potentialities of the human life as encoded and revealed in mythological traditions.

The genesis of modern understanding of Greek mythology is evidently a reaction against the excesses of modernity. Already dating back to the 19th century ,there was a growing interest in Homer and Greek mythology. The development of comparative philology in the 19th century, together with ethnological discoveries in the 20th century, were brought to bear upon the validity of and laid the foundation of the science of myth. Thanks to a succession of first rate scholars, the study of myth has become a respectable discipline and one of the revelatory influences of modern mythological research is the unfolding of the greatest ironies of our times ,ie, while natural sciences have disenchanted the planet which is our home, by peeling off, one layer upon another of the inner recesses of mankind, they have unwittingly impinged our attention to various occultist and cultic exercises at worst and at best to the magnificent human heritage we have in our great traditions concerning the eternal values that have to do with the centering of our lives. We turn to the inner life. We need to identify who we are, where we are heading and where we came from. We want to find out what all this mess, death, crying and grabbing about so that our life on the physical plane will have resonance within our innermost beings. In harking back to the spirits of our ancestors, in full awakening to the catastrophes and their deadly aftermath, the words of the deities in the remote antiquity ring in our ears more distinctly than ever out of the dense darkness.

Yes, myths are still alive, freshening upon our faces and upon our world with their beams of the divine wisdom. That is what myths are all about to us.

Yes. Myths are still a necessity of which we must make a virtue. We need maintain a world still full of color, harmony and ethoes, still peopled by mythical creatures and nymphs. Every country has its mythology. As Greek ,Roman and the Norse mythologies are as familiar to the Western world down through the ages, so are the myths of origin clustered around the Mount Kunlun "Forefather of Moutains", alongside the Pangu(creating the sky and the earth) and Nuwa (mending the sky)to local people and the Chinese race at large.

Being a Yi poet descended from a minority group who make home China's southwest, I feel

为自然的事物丰富而多变，所以生活的颜色是五彩的；因为神灵的护佑古老而庄严，所以生存的意义是崇高的；因为天空和大地充满想象力与创造力，所以万物的存在和谐而富有情趣。在神话世界，时间的悠远和空间的广大产生于自然的道理之中，时空相互开放而交融，人与神灵、人与自然是一个整体。而失去神话，就意味着失去了万物和我们自身存在的理由。

显然，并不是只有民间才需要神话。在城市、在当代的文化主流中，神话的意义仍然根深蒂固，神话的价值仍然不可取代。人类社会的秩序是由理性创造的，而人类社会的价值属于诗，属于激情和想象力，也可以说，属于神话。德国的诗人哲学家尼采，在《悲剧的诞生》一书中这样说："每一种文化只要它失去了神话，则同时它也将失去其自然而健康的创造力。只有一种环抱神话的眼界才能统一其文化。……一种文化没有任何固定且被奉献的发源地，它注定了要丧失其所有可能性，苟延残喘地寄生于任何阳光底下的文化。"

当今世界经济的一体化，正在推动各种经济体制、经济模式、经济生产方式的解体与统一，因而它也正在对众多的民族性、地域性文化提出考验，对神话提出挑战。曾经有人问我，我们为什么要如此迫切地、执着地维护文化的多样性和差异性呢？那么在这里，我想用一种神话的思维方式作一个设问：如果这个世界只有平原或者只有山脉，如果我们身边只开一种花、只有一种鸟儿的鸣叫，如果我们每个人都长得一模一样，或者我们只吃一种食物，那么我们的生存还有什么意义呢？当然，从学术的角度讲，神话是人类最为古老文明果实之一，它是诗的源泉、歌的源泉，神话文本对于民族学、民俗学、人类学以及宗教研究等等，都是取之不尽的资源宝库，也是现代文化发展和文化建构不可或缺的有力支撑。

对于生存和生活，神话是我们精神寄托的母体。我们今天看上去显得神秘或者

as strongly as Qinghai people about what significance a creation myth story might contain. Over centuries, My ancestors have also evolved an intricate mythological system and the best known being Leerteyi and Mege in forms of oral tradition and epics. The Yi mythology without exception takes shape and substance around some common themes and they all attempt to explain the creation, divinity, and guess at the meaning of existence and death, to account for natural phenomena and to chronicle the adventures of racial heroes. These epics are still chanted and kept alive on occasions like weddings, funerals and passages of rites.

Then why humans cannot do without myths? Because what we call humanity ,the design features and the defining attributes of human beings, what human beings have in common, are actually encoded and revealed through myths. Myths are nothing but the stories of our ancestral adventures co existing with the supernatural beings in a primordial age long vanished. Deities are holy because they are addressed and prayed for their gifts of luck and escaping the evil forces. Myths are important because by reenacting them, people partake of the sanctity and the supernatural powers mythical characters possess. Thanks to the creativity and imagination of the open sky and the vast earth, all creatures, animate and inanimate alike, live in peace and harmony. In a typical myth world, time forever recedes into the distance of space where man, all forms of divinities and nature are essentially one. Devoid of myths, the paradise ceases to be what it is as myths serve among other things, a sanctifying process of our corporeal entities, and indeed, for all creatures on earth.

Obviously, while highlighting the importance of myths in the daily life of country folks, it must be added that myths are also deeply embedded in the traditions of the high brow mainstream culture of the city. Rationality brings order to the world whereas poetry renders the universe sensible in human terms and poetry in essence is a form of myth. Nietzsche German philosopher, riven by deep and ultimately irresolvable cultural, historical, and psychological conflicts, explores the possibilities that might contribute to the revival of culture. Nietzsche's own revival of the mythical dimension as essential to creative human activity is at once lyrical and intensely probing, richly complex yet thematically coherent. The following Excerpt from *Birth of Tragedy* should help to illuminate his predilection toward Homeric epic characters and his reasoning for the creation of the Ancient Greek mythos: " But without myth every culture forfeits its healthy creative natural power: only a horizon surrounded with myth completes the unity of an entire cultural movement. Only through myth are all the powers of the imagination and of Apollonian dream rescued from their random wandering around."

In an age of internet and economical globalization, welters of invisible forces are at work gravitating towards a synchronical process of disintegration and reintegration of economic systems and modes of production of various persuasion. Such a trend poses challenge to the diversity and nationality of regional cultures in existence, and incidentally, to the validity and legitimacy of myths as a constant life vivifying force. The urgency of the moment which has

奇异的那个神话世界，与我们有着最古老、最深刻的内在联系，它曾经长久主宰着我们的生存意识和生存方式。许多民族的神话都讲述了人类作为天神的后裔或者与天神联姻的故事，它让我们自豪，使我们充满生活的信心和勇气。许多神话也同时讲述了自然万物所具有的神性，告诉我们这些神性与我们同根同源，并且与我们的生存息息相关。我们没有任何理由不感激这种恩宠和厚爱，我们没有理由不为万物保持一个美丽、纯洁、多姿多彩并且井然有序的世界。这是一个大和谐，而这种和谐的精神，就来自苍茫的远古文明。

各位朋友，各位同人，其实神话从未离开过我们。瑞士心理学家荣格，曾给我们完整地论述过，在人类的生命和历史记忆中，集体无意识的存在。同样，无论是东方的神话，还是西方的神话，作为人类最古老的原生记忆，毫无疑问它至今依然存活在我们不同民族的文化基因中。

说到这里，我想告诉大家的是，在东方神话里，特别是在古老的中国各民族神话价值体系中，一直倡导着一种朴素的哲学思想，那就是对自然的尊崇，对神灵和英雄的敬畏以及对不同个体生命的热爱。而当我们今天再一次阅读或者倾听这些来自久远的神奇故事时，我们会惊奇地发现，似乎这些神话早就预言着什么。人类作为这个地球上的物种之一，他从来就不是孤立存在的，所有的生物的生命延续都是相互依存的，这一点已经是不争的事实。

许多古老的神话都给了我们一个启示，那就是要善待别的生命和物种，而只有这样，人类和地球的未来才充满着希望。天人合一的思想，在中国古代神话中随处可见，这对于21世纪的今天，无疑具有特殊的意义。这说明，古代神话所蕴含的与自然和平共处的价值取向，在这个人类正在经历的后工业化时代，同样对人类面向明天的发展，也有着更为宝贵的积极作用。东方神话的价值基础仍然坚实，虽然它和当今

informed my crusading effort, and the tenacity with which I have proceeded to protect the diversifying character of regional cultures has drawn skeptic eyes. This prompts me to counter argue thus: what if we don't act the way we do, what kind of sense we make out of a world whose landmass consists of only plains or mountains, a world wherein we only see one flower bloom, hear one bird chirp, or if we humans all look alike in appearance and stick to the same food? The importance of mythology in the intellectual, artistic, and emotional history of mankind can hardly be overestimated. Despite the relative obscurity of the origin of myths, most serious scholars would agree, East or West, mythology has formed the staple of much poetry as well as of dramatic works, influenced the thoughts of philosophers and historians to a marked degree, and major classic motifs have been continually reinterpreted and appropriated by .novelists, dramatists, composers, anthropologists, ethnologists and religious researchers to stir us as "something at once familiar and strange" and to give concrete expression to something deep and primitive in us all

Friends and lovers, I sincerely and distinctly feel myths are actually the host upon which our spirit its intimate parasite. The murky world of myths, long lost to us moderns, might look a bit alien and bizarre when reenacted, but still retains the profoundest and oldest connection to our innermost beings in that for a considerable span of time myths were at the heart of human life. There are so many oral poetic traditions harping upon the same themes of man being descended from certain supernatural creatures or a conjugal union of humans and gods, instilling us with pride, courage and confidence. There are countless mythical narrations pointing to the divine roots of all creatures with the supernatural community as well as their relevance to our daily life. To deny such holy grace and favor would be tantamount to denying the greatest raison d'etre of humanity. We certainly stand justified if we fail in our bid to keep intact a world in which beauty, justice and harmony reign supreme. Such grand harmony befitting and deserving of all creatures, is a legacy we inherit from antiquity.

Friends and lovers, myths have, as a matter of fact, never lose their power over us. Carl Gustav Jung was never more insightful and intriguing than when he held behind each individual's "unconscious" lies the "collective unconscious" of the human race, the blocked off memory of our racial past, even of our prehuman existence .Myths, as Jungian archetypal imagination, is encoded in the cultural genes of each nation and race.

Allow me here another piece of personal observation. This much I can tell you with full assurance of its truthfulness. Oriental myths, including mythical and cultural variations of different nationalities in China, distinguish themselves from their western counterpart, the Greek, the Roman, the Norse in that our foremothers (major deities in China are mostly female) have upheld a simple ideology or ethic, ie, an irrevocable reverence for nature, divine power, heroic exploits and each individual life, be it insignificant or unwanted. At moments when we come back to these mythical narratives out of a vanished past, we feel like we have sensed something, something foretold by ancient troubadours and vagabonding bards. Man, as one species out of

现实的联系已经并不紧密,但它用最浅显的道理和方式,教会了我们许多东西,那就是让我们人类真正成为这个星球和谐生活的建设者,而不是破坏者。

在信仰缺失的物质主义世界,神话是我们可以信赖的拯救手段之一。神话能够帮助我们适应并且合理改造生存环境,能够帮助我们缩小同自然界的心理距离和情感对立;生命中的神性是我们肉体得以升腾的翅膀,人以其神性而获得了不可剥夺的自由、欢乐和尊严。这就是神话能够成为诗人、艺术家、浪漫主义者和孩子们心灵营养的真正原因。神话也必然成为人类社会和自然世界健康延续的文化营养。

于是,我们仿佛已经开始期待世界各路神灵的生动对话了。那么现在,作为一个诗人,请允许我以我的诗歌《时间》中的诗句作为结束:

  所有的生命,都栖居在时间的圣殿

  哦,时间!

  是它在最后的时刻,改变了一切精神和物质存在形式

  它永远在死亡中诞生,又永远在诞生中死亡

  它包含了一切,它又在一切之外

  如果说在这个世界上

  有什么东西真正地不朽

  我最肯定地说:那就是时间!

正因为我们坚信"神话"是已经成了时间的"创造者",所以我们才从四面八方相聚在这里,为了一个古老而弥新的话题,不吝奉献着各自的聪明和智慧。最后我要提议,让我们共同祝愿昆仑神话与世界创世神话国际学术论坛圆满成功!祝愿大家在神灵的土地上平安愉快!谢谢大家!

countless species in the history of evolution, has never been alone and aloof as he sometimes imagined. The interdependence of all life forms are a point beyond dispute. Many mythical revelations advise us to be nice to all creatures and species not necessarily taking anthroporphic shapes.

Live and let live is a message meriting universal response. The idea of man's harmonizing with his environment recurs as a ubiquitous theme in all Chinese mythical literature. Therein lies a fact that oriental myths as a whole contain some of the most badly needed wisdom and mental food for mankind stranded in some of the most acute cultural crises in a post industrialized era. They teach us to get back into accord with the wisdom of nature and realize again our brotherhood with the animals and the water and the sea. We humans should be positive builders, not despoilers.

Ours is one of the worst histories due to the long held beliefs being stripped away and myths come to our rescue as spiritual prop to support our inner world. Myths also fulfill some pragmatic functions as they instruct us to be eco-friendly in using our resources providing for survival, to adapt to our environment without much unnecessary disturbance ,to minimize the emotional disentanglement between us humans and our mechanized surroundings. If divinity informs mankind ,it also invests each transient individual journey with significance ,freedom, joy and dignity otherwise not possibly gained by other means. Therein lies the perennial appeal of myths primarily to poets ,artists, and children. For this reason, I for one, categorically insist on the necessity of myths to buttress the eternal values that make human civilization a reality.

Friends and lovers, at this moment of epiphany, am I entitled to announce the kick-off of this conference drawing a new pantheon of the Olympians from distant lands? As poet, I might appropriately bring my remarks to a close by quoting a few lines from my poem entitled Time:

All life, thought and heritage

Choose Time as their dwelling abode .Oh, Time!Always at its last moment

Transforms all existential modes of mind and matter.Time revives while dying

And dies again in resurrection.That is the way it is meant to be.

Containing everything, it looms outside of everything.

If in this world, we speak of anything immortal

This much I can tell with immunity:It is Time!

Just because we are all convinced of one truth ,ie, Time is the ultimate creator, we have journeyed all the way to this forum, to pay our tribute and contribute our learning to the topic of the Kunlun myth making and the creation story and their relevance to our modern world, at once an old but ever fresh one. May this meeting participated by a group of most intelligent and enlightened scholars a genuine success. May all those present here and today be happy and blessed by our Kunlun divinities. Thanks for your attentions.

诗人的个体写作与人类今天所面临的共同责任
寄往第 21 届麦德林诗歌节暨首届全球国际诗歌节主席会议的书面演讲
2011 年 3 月 19 日

  诗歌作为一种最古老的艺术形式，它已经伴随着人类走过了漫长的生命岁月。诚然这种古老的艺术形式，已经成为我们生命中不可分割的一个部分，但诗歌作为一种真正意义上的精神存在，它却从未停止过给人类饥渴的心灵输出长久弥新的甘泉和营养。当然诗歌本身作为一门写作艺术，它的艺术形式在不同民族诗歌传统中的创新，已经是人类的诗歌史上证明了的一个毋庸置疑的真理，否则诗歌的生命就不会延续到今天。

  回望人类的历史，我们不敢想象，如果没有诗歌这一人类古老的艺术，世界各民族的心灵史将会怎样去抒写，而人类的精神生活又将是何等贫乏和残缺。在这里，我想强调的是，诗歌无论对于人类而言，还是对于写作诗歌的诗人个体，它都是存活在人类精神领域里的一种生命形式，它是光明的引领者，它代表着正义和良知，在许多古老的民族中间，诗人所承担的角色，就是这个民族的祭司和精神上的真正首领。伟大的意大利诗人但丁，就是到了 21 世纪的今天，他同样还是意大利精神领域里最伟大的象征和支柱。

  我想也正因为如此，诗人的写作才不是一种所谓的职业，把写诗说成是一种职业，我认为这是可笑的行为。从人类伟大的诗歌史中我们可以看到，诗人更像是一个角色，他是精神的代言人，通过自己充满灵性的写作，力求与自己的灵魂、现实乃至世间的万物进行深度对话。难怪在我生活的高原和民族之中，诗人被认为是那些被神所选择的具有灵性的人，他们神奇的天赋以及语言和思想，也被认为是神传授给

The Individual Writing of a Poet and the Common Responsibilities Facing Mankind

A Speech Written for the 21 Session of Medellin International Poetry Festival& the World Meeting of International Poetry Festival Directors
19th, March, 2011

The oldest form of art, poetry has been in the companionship of mankind for eons without number in life's journey strewn with odds and hazards, so much so that it has almost emerged as an invisible second self, charged with the office of administering the much thirsted vitamin and dewdrops to nourish the parched and hungry souls. Poetry unexpectedly grows in us, "body and soul," yet, being an art of writing itself, poetic sensibility would have waned and perished, "shocked by cliché s, and mired in the stagnation of life," without receiving constant nourishment from folk elements, a law that has been testified by the development of human poetic movement.

We can assert with full assurance that, the facts of life, since for much of the human history, have been so brutal, gloomy, monotonous, poets have rendered mankind a valuable service by intervening and refreshing us by turning our gaze away from this sad spectacle, at least, from time to time and plunged us into a beautiful imaginary world of ideal emotions. Moreover, the carriers of this symbolical message, i.e. the poets, have been identified in the spiritual world as herald of light, the spokesmen of society for conscience and justice, and indeed, in many of the ancient tribes and races, poets have veritably acted in the capacity of shamans and prophets. For example, Dante still stands unrivalled as a symbol of high culture to Italian poets and writers in a world that is a symbolically wasteland and that must be reborn.

Due to their power to engage in an in-depth dialogue between their own souls with reality and all the sentient beings on earth, as well as their capacity to conjure up a land of "peach blossom mountains" and to spread a new joy of living in spite of the evil and scarcity, poets are not simply careerists. It is ridiculous to deem poets as a carpenter or silversmith. In my tribe poets are believed to be endowed with magical poetic sensitivity with which they can go into the trance of words and awaken the conscience of the world.

This is hardly new. Among many primitive societies the exalted status accorded to poets has been taken for granted. Do not for a second fancy poets emerge from such sugary sentimental mode. On many occasions, poets are supposed to be morally exemplary, heroes of human

他们的。

其实这不难理解，在许多古老的原始民族的思维里，这已经是一个被普遍认同的对诗人的判断和认知。诗人在许多时候，不仅仅是精神和良心的化身，他甚至还是道德的化身。当代诗人布罗茨基在评论他的前辈曼德尔斯塔姆以及俄罗斯白银时代的诗人们时曾这样说，因为他们，聋哑的宇宙、沉默的历史发出了诗的声音——而这，就是"我们的神话"，是诗和诗人存在的意义。

我一直认为，诗歌的写作，就是诗人在不断发现我是谁，就是在不断揭示内心的隐秘，同时他又在通过一个又一个瞬间的感受来呈现现实的真相。总之，诗人只要活着，他都在生与死、存在和虚无以及个体生命所要经历的一系列冲突中，去回答似乎是宿命里已经安排好的所有命题，诗人理解这个世界的最好方式，就是他的那些来自灵魂的诗歌。

可是各位同行，今天在这里，我想倡导并提醒大家关注一个事实，那就是在全球化背景下，在这个被资本、技术和网络统治的时代，人类面临着许多共同的生存危机，如何控制核威胁、消除饥饿与疾病、遏制生态破坏、保护生物多样性和文化多样性等等，已经到了一个刻不容缓的时候。今天的人类所面临的共同威胁，其严重程度是过去历史上从未有过的。我们这个时代的许多智者，当然也包括我们的诗人，都在思考和忧虑人类的命运，人类将走向何处？特别是在后工业化时代，人类今天的发展方式是一种进步，还是倒退？显然这些无法回避的问题，都需要我们的诗人做出回答。

在我们这个危机和希望并存的时代，诗人不应该只沉湎在自己的内心中，他应该成为，或者必须成为这个时代的良心和所有生命的代言人。需要说明的是，我们对诗人作为个体生命的独立写作，必须给予充分的尊重，而诗人如何去表达其内心的感受并克服其自身的危机，都将是诗人个人的自由。但是无论如何，特别是在当下这个物质主义盛行的世界，诗歌依旧是人类心灵的庇护所这一基本事实并未改变，而诗歌应该在提高和增进人类精神重构方面有所作为。诗人是人类伟大文明最忠实的儿子，我相信，今天仍然生活在这个地球上不同地域的诗人，为了促进世界的和平、加强不同文化之间的沟通与对话，都将发挥出永远不可被替代的重要作用。

resistance in grisly circumstances, a test of genuine poetic genius. When Joseph Brodsky reflected upon his eminent predecessors Osip Mandelstam and other established poets in the Silver Age, he remarked in due deference to their moral qualities as heroes of some human resistance, because of their presence, the silent cosmos and history speak out in the idiom of poetry wherein lies the essence of poetry.

I have always held a poet's mission to keep unveiling the secrets of his identity and his inner soul and in doing so, disclosing the truth about our world. In sum, as long as a poet lives, he is inexorably thrown into the vortex of all the anguishes besetting individual lives, tormented by all the paradoxes of life and death, being and nothingness. All the naughty questions are out there to be answered, sticking out their sauce tongues at him. There is no escape by dodging or fidgeting. Indeed, the best way a poet comprehends this world is by composing poems from his troubled soul.

Here I must raise an alarm about our age fraught with crisis. In this age of globalization, with our world being rendered waste literarily, by disasters unleashed by rapacious capital and unbridled technology, the human condition is in a dismal quandary that compels us to contemplate the possibility of amendment for the mechanization of modern life and emotion. Today there exists a growing sense of global responsibility to jointly act and address the massive package disorders impending upon us—nuclear holocaust, disparities of wealth between the poor and rich, ecological disturbance, cultural diversity and biodiversity threatened with disappearance, unprecedented in magnitude. Poets as sages are society's antennas, "the fringe voices and harbingers of things to come." They pick up the first symptoms of the social malaise. They take these challenges to heart, which beats so wild, so deep to know "whence our lives come and where they go."

A poet should not turn his look away from the ugly face of this "brave new world." He should rise to the occasion and fulfill the public expectation as to his exemplary role to be both mouthpiece of civic society and conscience of the people. Of course, full respect of individuality and autonomy of expression must be allowed of the poets since poets work best when thrown upon his own resources and his own conscience. All said, in this world submerged by commercialism, by its very nature, poetry remains an antidote to greed and a sanctuary for human spirituality, a vision raised by poets, the most faithful sons of human civilization, one that renews and uplifts the spirit of a deeply disoriented community. Indeed, the stance of countering social as well as spiritual decline with the language of poetry is still the prime raison d'etre of a modern poet. I trust, all the poets living in different quarters of the globe, with their vision, poems and striving for a bright future, would continue to exert an irreplaceable influence on furthering world peace and understanding between various cultures called for by our modern status quo.

群山的记忆流淌成河

在 2010 中国(青海)世界山地纪录片节高峰论坛上的演讲

2010 年 8 月 10 日

女士们、先生们：上午好！

两年前，在与今天完全相同的场合，我曾经这样说：至少有三个原因把我们聚集这里：一、对纪录片的热爱；二、对山地自然和山地文明的关注与思考；三、对青藏高原神秘召唤的响应。所以这个节日就是一次志同道合的朋友之间的聚会，我们每个人都是这个聚会的主人。同时我还相信，无论我们说哪一种语言或者在何地生活，当那个短暂的聚会结束之后，你一定会在某个不眠的夜晚，乘着思绪的翅膀穿越时空，突然看到你在世界最高的一片土地上留下的身影，那时候，你一定会带着你的朋友再来！

我所期待的就是今天这个时刻。我看到了老朋友熟悉又愉快的面孔，也看到许多新朋友陌生却亲切的目光。这是我的幸运，更是中国(青海)世界山地纪录片节的荣耀。我们这次相聚的地方，不仅是青藏高原的腹地，而且是东方的奥林匹斯昆仑山下，神圣的昆仑山给这个节日赋予了新的象征和意义。

在这里，我将把今天想说的话分为几层意思。

我们创立了一个有价值的文化品牌

2008 年，我们胜利而成功地举办了首届中国(青海)世界山地纪录片节。我们把这一届纪录片节的主题确定为："山地世界，人与自然，多元文化的共享与传承。"围绕这个主题，我们举办了高峰论坛、纪录片采风创作、纪录片展播交流和"玉昆仑"奖国际纪录片评选等多项活动。征集到专题论文 100 多篇，高峰论坛邀请 12 个国家的

Memories of Our Earliest Beginnings Trickle All the Way down the Mountains

A Speech Given at the Third Edition of China (Qinghai) World Mountains Documentary Festival

10th, August, 2010

Ladies and gentlemen: Good morning!

Two years ago, precisely at the same venue, I tried to lay bare three reasons behind our congregation here. First is our infatuation with documentary filming. Secondly, our joint concern about the fate of the civilizations in the wilderness and mountains encroached by the modernization frenzy. Thirdly, our response to the call from the Realm of the Tibet-Qinghai Plateau-the symbol of the pristine soul and the icon of eternal life. So I deem this gathering again one of the like-minded wherein the distinction between host and guest is rather blurred. Meanwhile, I surmise this encounter, brief as it may be, whatever tongue you might speak, wherever you might make home, together with all the footages and possibly your own films on the air, will ignite your perennial sense of wonder for the hidden natures and over one of the sleepless nights, you might decide to take wings and drift back amongst these forgotten uplands with your friends!

This is the big moment I have anticipated -to see a line-up of familiar and pleasant faces back and to get to know a band of new acquaintances, strange but friendly. The privilege is singularly mine. The glory belongs to this edition of China (Qinghai) World Mountains Documentary Festival. What makes this 2nd edition so extraordinary is we are not meeting in the metropolis of the Plateau as usual. Rather we have driven all the way westward to the foot of the Kunlun Mount, the counterpart of the Orient to the Olympus of ancient Greece and obviously the chosen locale has added some deeper symbolical meanings to the event.

The Prime Consideration for Hosting an Event Like This_ Forge a New Cultural Brand

2008 marked the kick-off of the first edition of China (Qinghai) World Mountains Documentary Festival. In the memory of the successful debut, we set the tone and motto for this second edition:"The Realm of the Mountains-Man and Nature-Co-sharing and inheriting of Multi-cultures."Around the key-note theme, we decide on a number of programs including a summit forum, field tour of local mountains for filming, exhibition display and showing of

40位嘉宾发言。征集到来自美国、德国、日本、俄罗斯和意大利等22个国家和地区的343部纪录片参评，内容涵盖人文、自然和社会三大类。

国内外有30多家电视机构赴青海参加了纪录片节的采风创作活动。纪录片节设立了"玉昆仑奖"，经过来自美国、澳大利亚、印度、俄罗斯和国内纪录片界著名专家组成的评委会评审，分别授予参加展播评选的优秀纪录片和创作人员。在国内外影视机构和专家、艺术家的共同努力下，中国（青海）世界山地纪录片节的专业化和艺术性都达到了很高的水平。当然，这个纪录片节还有一个重大的收获，就是开辟了一个让青海和中国了解世界的窗口，搭建了一个让全国和世界认识青海的平台。

中国（青海）世界山地纪录片节，作为青海省人民政府和国家有关部门共同主办、国际与国内众多影视机构和艺术家共同参与打造的个性化文化品牌，每隔一年举办一届。我们相信，它将为世界不同地理环境和文化背景的艺术家们提供一个创作、研讨和交流的最好平台。

我们为什么创办山地纪录片节

我认为，有必要想重申几句山地纪录片节的创意理由和举办这一节会的目的。

我们注意到，随着自然科学的目光向浩瀚太空和微小粒子的延伸，思想和人文的视角却越来越多地投向了人类生存的原初阶段。这些年来，在众多学者和艺术家对人与自然的关注和行动中，世界上诞生了大量以山地为讲述背景、以山地生活为讲述对象，体现不同风格、不同内容的纪录片。然而据我们了解，目前世界上还没有一个较大规模的针对这一主题而搭建的国际性展示交流平台。

在青海举办山地纪录片节，有着得天独厚的条件。一是青海独特的地形地貌。青藏高原作为世界第三极的高地，联合国认定的四大超洁净地区之一，其物种具有不可复制的原生态价值；二是青海具有多民族共生、多宗教共存、多元文化相融合的特性，从而为本节的举办提供了坚实的基础。青海的山水环境创造了这片土地上特有的生命现象、生存秩序和生活方式，人类创造了与自然融合的历史、宗教、艺术、理念和故事。对这些与人类历史和世界格局紧密相连的事物，我们的认识、记录和讲述远远不足。那么，地处世界屋脊、群山之巅的中国青海，有责任，有义务，也有自信的理由，承担起这一时代的需求和历史的重托。青藏高原以山的故乡、水的摇篮而享誉，

documentary films and finally, the "Jade Kunlun" awards given to winners. As of now, over 100 papers are solicited and forty distinguished experts from 12 countries are invited to address the summit forum. The assessing and awarding panel has already received 343 entries, classified into three categories, the Humanities, Nature and Society.

Moreover, over 30 TV institutions overseas are invited to make the shooting field tour of local mountains. A panel, composed of judges, mostly world famous documentary filming experts and researchers, will sift the received entries for awarding "Jade Kunlun" trophy to winners. The combined wisdom and professionalism of all the artists and experts has contributed to making the festival a great success. Incidentally, the festival has turned out to be a window on Qinghai for the rest of China and the world, a stage that reveals much about China's unique and dynamic west.

Thanks to the co-organizing work of both the Provincial Government of Qinghai and the relevant agencies of the Central Government, and thanks to the kindness and professionalism of artists and experts in the field of documentary filming, we have been able to host this festival twice a year in the hope it will continually provide a platform on which top documentary makers showcase their talent and mirror the hidden beauty and undiscovered splendor of various mountain regions and uplands across the world.

Why We in Qinghai Step in to Host Such a High–Profile Documentary Filming Festival?

Thus one might wonder "Why is this significant? Why would it matter? How do you explain this fervor?" Let me reiterate the ultimate rationale behind this extravaganza. As we have noted, in the advanced world, while the frontiers of natural science have been pushed to the outer limits of space and particles smaller than atoms, scholars operating within the traditional bounds of the humanities stretch their tentacles into the earliest beginnings of mankind. That explains the up-coming trend in recent years why there has been such a boom in documentary filming either with mountains and uplands as the backdrops or uncovering the little known but significant stories that reveal so much about the soul and mind of mountain inhabitants. These films vary from style to style but a common thread in the vibrant tapestry of these artistic works is the focus on life in the wilderness. This being the case, to the best of our knowledge, the lack of world class shopping window for documentary films in this tradition is widely deplored

We in Qinghai deem this absence both a mission and an opportunity. Preeminent is of course Qinghai's extreme alpine topography and remote mountain terrain as famed Roof of the World, touted one of the four super-clean regions by UN, which supports a diversity of bio-specifies of irreplaceable value. No less important is the region as potpourri of multi-religions, multi-races and multi-cultures. The Tibetans and Muslims predominate, with a smattering of Tu, Sala, and Mongol. Most of Qinghai is indeed a wilderness paradise, an unpolished gem. And a huge treasure chest, when opened, its natural beauty and ethnographic/ religious /and historic riches will dazzle. Much lies in store for enterprising artists to explore, examine and document. Qinghai possesses the world's greatest chains of mountain ranges and the greatest combination of

以独特的自然、文化和人类生活而著称,于是我们决定以万山之宗、江河之源的名义举办世界山地纪录片节。这就是我们创意并致力打造这个国际文化品牌的立足点。

中国(青海)世界山地纪录片节,目的就是要借助并且发挥青藏高原得天独厚的资源优势,树起一面具有号召意义的旗帜,进一步增进当今世界对山地自然和山地文明的关注,促进人与自然的和谐共荣和多样性文化之间的对话沟通;以影视的形式、艺术的视角、人文的思考,致力于探索在一种特殊的地域环境和文化背景下人类历史的发展、人与自然的关系,讲述万物生存的故事,并以此反省人类的共同命运和人类社会发展的得失。通过创立这个国际品牌,拓展不同文明、不同文化、不同地域间的沟通渠道,建立一个平等的对话机制,这非常有利于缔造和谐、创造文明,从而推动人类的和平、进步与发展。同时通过交流艺术、传播文化,充分展示大美青海的无限魅力,推动青海走向世界。

山地存在必然与纪录片相遇

山地是和海洋、平原相对应的地理概念。山地是万物的乐园,是人类的摇篮,是我们灵魂的故土。除海洋之外,全世界山地面积占陆地总面积的一半以上,广义的山地则面积更大,在中国就占全国总面积的74.8%。山地国家众多的民族及其各自独有的山地文化、历史和社会形态、宗教模式,形成各民族独特的人类记忆。然而,在全世界正在经历的现代化过程中,人类的历史记忆正在消失,对于山地国家和山地民族更是如此。每个国家和民族都有区别于其他民族的神化记忆、历史记忆、人文记忆及宗教记忆,山地的自然构成,山地民族的文化、艺术、思维、宗教、历史和生存方式都有其独特的价值,我们不能用别的价值体系将其取代。因此对人类历史记忆和生存故事的关注、保护和纪录已经刻不容缓。于是纪录片出现了。在文字、图片和话语之外,纪录片的手段和方式,充分显示了它真实、生动、立体和传播广泛而迅速的优越性。

super river systems and comes naturally under obligation to shoulder up the mission in the name of the home of the mountains.

Qinghai does dream of placing itself at the forefront of both Chinese tourism and China's campaign for eco-system balance and conservation of cultural diversity, while constantly improving its facilities to pamper and delight outdoor adventurers and artists.

The Festival is the testimony of us mountain inhabitants that have voted with our presence and organization for love and beauty. With this avalanche of documentary artists summoned, art becomes a banner fluttering high calling global attention to the wilderness and cultural diversity in the mountains and uplands. This means we desire to enact dialogues between various cultures and help the world community gain awareness of the ultimate importance of man and nature in harmony. We must listen to the authentic stories told by artists about mountain people because of their visionary perception. We must watch in deference the valuable footages that take us to some of the least visualized alpine scenes that capture the essence of the mutely eloquent mountain aborigines in this special age of globalization, because they represent "the final link in a hitherto unbroken chain of memory which stretches to the roots of the human tribe." The employment of such natural solidarity and the poetics of origins is intended to readdress the subjugation and pillage of nature and highlight the primitive wisdom and the time-honored alternative ways of life to the edge of civilization other than those lived by their urban counterparts.

The Inevitable Meeting of Mountains and Documentary Films

Mountains are a tract of land rising considerably above the surrounding surface, a geographical concept in opposition to sea and plain. Mountains and uplands are metaphorically the paradise of all creatures, the cradle of mankind as well as the dwelling abode of our souls. The reason: apart from seas and oceans, alpine terrain covers almost half of the earth's surface. Most of China is rugged and remote, dominated by nearly 74.8% uninhabitable mountains. Over time, mountain inhabitants have evolved their own cultures, history, mode of religion and pattern of society and archetypes of racial memory. Yet, a global homogenization process in the wake of the sweeping events of modernization tends to erode and eradicate the stock of historic memory of each race, testified by all historic data that changes in technology have deeply affected man's culture-his ways of living and thinking and doing things. Homogeneity is taking place everywhere though with some residual local variations of reflecting the heterogeneity of cultural backgrounds. Yet there has arisen in the contemporary world a sense of responsibility to conserve both the bio diversity and cultural diversity. Fortunately the emergence and maturing of the documentary filming to tackle the issue of human and natural solidarity comes in time, for among other things, word processing, photographing, tape-recording, documentary films have the obvious virtues of three dimension displaying, instant duplication and swift screening to a mass audience. It has actually become the most important means through which the present holds and interprets the past.

纪录片的繁荣标志着人类文明走向新的成熟,标志着人类的目光开始从迷恋物质的表象向关注生存的价值取向转变,纪录片已经成为当今世界衡量一个国家、地区和民族的文明程度、文化品位、人口素质的新型标准之一。纪录片对人类文明的贡献,首先在于它以目前人类最为先进的手段,生动直观地记录了这个瞬息万变的世界上不可复制、不可再生、不可忽视的瞬间;然而它的价值远不仅限于此,纪录片讲述的是历史和现实,思考的是未来,纪录片作为历史、艺术和人类的记忆留下来,它疏忽并拓展我们思考与生存的空间,也必然承担着人类记忆的延续与传播的责任。

山地在它沉默而博大的胸怀孕育文明,就如同它汇集雨水、涌泉和小溪孕育江河,群山的记忆流淌成河,而纪录片,就是源远流长的水。

众神之山为我们见证

今年的中国(青海)世界山地纪录片节,我们确定的主题是:"山地民族,原生影像,人类记忆的延续与传播。"并且把举办地点选择在东方众神之山昆仑山下举办。在未来的几天里,这座圣殿般的雪山,将见证我们为人类记忆的延续与传播所表现的热情和智慧,也将向我们讲述它美丽动人的故事。

同所有古老文明一样,中国远古神话是古代文明的土壤和源泉。在中国古代神话的大观园,昆仑山毋庸置疑地立于统领地位。昆仑神话是我国保存最完整、结构最宏伟的一个体系,磅礴大气、雄浑诡奇的昆仑神话是中华民族文化的源头之一,是中国作为文明古国的象征,也是中国早期文明的曙光。昆仑神话源远流长、博大精深,有着极其深厚的影响力,代表着中国远古文化的最高峰。中国上古我们众多的神、人神和神人,大多出自昆仑,因此,昆仑山在中华民族文化史上有万山之祖、众神之都的显赫地位,不仅是中华大地的主脉,还是中华神话的摇篮。可以说,昆仑山就是中国的奥林匹斯山,是众神所居之地。

实际上,每个民族都不是为了消遣而创造神话,不是为了打发日子而讲述那些传说。神话讲述的并非仅仅是关于神的故事,它讲述的是人与神的关系,讲述的是人与自然在精神上的不可分离性。这些故事至今依然是高原民族精神生活和日常生活的一部分,它们是鲜活的、真实美丽的,它们千年不朽地一代代流传下来,成为人类灵魂和血脉的一部分。伴随几千年的演绎,昆仑神话已经由一个神灵谱系扩展为一个根脉发达、包罗万象、遍及神州的民族文化系统。在面向未来、回望过去、探讨传统文化的历史意义和现实价值的人文观照中,作为山地文明的代表,昆仑文化就必然要进入我们的视野。昆仑山让我们领悟山地的永恒和山地文化的不朽。

The vogue of documentary films constitutes a major human leap from fixation upon the surface of things to probing into the values of existence as well as one of the current standards by which the quality of demographics, cultural taste and national/regional/ethnic civilization are measured and graded. The essential point is that where words struggle to convey reality, and paintings could not catch the fleeting moment, documentary films come to achieve both, presenting in a flow of dramatic images instant history to be stored for immediate projection or future retrieval. Beyond technical flair, they are not just more than that as good film makers always believe in the dual functions of the documentary films to interpret history and to promote human understanding. A documentary is the repository of historic memory. Mountains are the nursery of human cultures. Mountains gather and collect rain water, fountain and streamlet into powerful rivers to be emptied into seas. Memories of our earliest beginnings trickle all the way down the mountains into the documentary films at last.

The Mount of All Mounts Bears Witness to Instant History

The theme set for this second edition of the festival is "Mountain inhabitants-Authentic Imaging as the Continuation and diffusion of Human Reminiscences." The switching of the venue to the foot of the mighty Mt. Kunlun has a deeper symbolic meaning as we believe this Mount of the Mounts in China will bear witness to the splendid stories we are going to tell in the few intoxicating days to come as well as to the power and dynamism of the tool for realizing the motto set for this pageantry.

Like all the ancient cultures, Chinese civilization budded from the soil of ancient myth and legend. Kunlun Mountain, China's No.1 sacred mountain, nicknamed respectively "Asia's Backbone" or "The Ancestor of The Dragon's Lineage" is a veritable cradle of cultural myths and Taoist/Tibetan Buddhist folklores .It could be safely assumed that no other place in China like Qinghai boasts such an array of awesome mesmerizing mountain ranges that occupy so lofty a place in the hearts of the Chinese race as a whole. Kunlun mythology stands supreme among the fountainheads of all known Chinese culture, due to its unrivalled antiquity. Hence, Mt. Kunlun enjoys a special renown in the collective consciousness of the Chinese, a sacred abode of the Immortals, a cultural emblem analogous to Mt. Olympus of ancient Greece.

In actuality, a myth is created not solely to entertain or to kill time. Every myth has a moral pointing both to the sanctity of the deities and man's access to them. On a more general level, it talks about the spiritual inseparableness of man and nature. Kunlun myths are still told on ritualistic occasions-tangible expression of the spiritual side of the indigenous inhabitants, still poignant and alive, passed down to the successive generations until today, crystallized into the richest veins of the lineage of all the deities of national importance. If documentary film makers heed to the established professional code of interpreting the past in the light of the present for the benefit of the future, Mt. Kunlun culture must gaze into our eyes as it is ready to unveil its mystery for welcoming ears.

人类记忆的延续与传播

很久以前,我们祖先中一些不安分的人群走出丛林和洞穴,沿着江河流淌的方向走出崇山峻岭,他们告别渔猎和采集的生活,在宽谷和平原上建立起村落。从此,人类的历史开始用稻麦和节令书写。

然而,群山没有走,森林没有走,高原没有走,江河的源头没有走,留守家园的羚羊、猎豹和传承祖先创世诗篇的人群也没有走。

多年之后,我们中间一些被梦境困扰的人开始感叹都市的狭窄与喧嚣、平原的拥挤和单调,我们应着一种源自生命深处的呼唤回望山地和高原,一如惊奇而深情地注视我们出生的摇篮,一如胆怯而感恩地投向我们成长的怀抱。我们突然发现,尽管我们已经离开了很久,我们并没有真正走得很远。

但是,尽管这个世界依然广阔而多彩,那留在我们记忆中的群山和高原却正在改变,森林与江河的面貌正在改变,生命的形态、生活的方式和故事的情节正在改变。

我们被再次诱惑并且强烈地震撼了。艺术家和诗人、思想家和智者,胶片、油彩、音符或者文字,以其对自然与文明的敬仰和热爱,以其对生存意义的终极关怀,重新踏上对这个丰富世界的探索、发现和讲述之旅。

山地,我们回来了。

我们来自东非高原的森林,身上披着浓密的毛发;我们来自云岭深处的原谋,脚底沾着湿润的红土;我们来自威严的奥林匹斯,手中握着黄金的权杖;我们来自高耸入云的昆仑,座下驾着云霞的车辇;我们来自神秘的马丘·比丘和须弥圣山之巅,口中唱着光辉的颂歌。我们从文明的记忆中来,我们从人类的记忆中来,我们向充满生命欢乐的群山致敬。

Continuation and Diffusion of Human Reminiscences

Long, long ago, it was in the hills and uplands that man had learned to domesticate plants and animals and thereby to achieve the agricultural revolution. Some of our ancestors, of more recalcitrant and maverick cast of mind, broke out of their caves and forests, and moved down to the lowlands along the rivers downstream either by necessity or by instinct, and eventually found themselves in large tracts of open land, not as constricting as the mountainous terrain. Bidding adieu to old ways of life as hunters and gatherers, they fanned out in all directions and built The sedentary Inkajijik (maasai word for a house) in wide river valleys and open plains which ushered in the persisting society and the epochal change to agriculture as a sedentary soil tiller-thus bringing an end to his former extreme subservience to nature. He could now feed himself by growing rice in the paddies. In doing so a new world with limitless horizons opened before him.

Yet the mountains could not move. Forests could not move. So did uplands, the fountainheads of great rivers. So did his siblings who remained, as custodians of the ancestral hearth, looking after their common ancestors and inheriting the creation myth .So did the leopards and gazelles guarding and roaming the same turf.

For eons and eons, some of us, finding the urban hustle and bustle unbearable and suffocating, wide awake in a sleepless night, beyond a certain threshold of desperation, follow the irresistible siren song of life and look back with special affection to the mountains and uplands, as if we gaze in wonder at the cradle of our birth. There is the sudden revelation though we are long in departing, we are not really far in departing.

This is a certainly a wide, brave new world, full of motion and excitement, as the shape of the mountains and uplands, of forests and rivers, of former forms of life, ways of life ,and plots of the story, are experiencing a major metamorphosis.

Our ancestral mountains and uplands have always eluded us. But this time, we are deeply shocked and moved. We finally embark upon this pilgrimage with our baggage of films, cameras, viewfinders, paints, musical notes, and words .This is a seeking-roots journey as it ignites our passion and respect for Mother nature, reawakens our dormant ultimate concern and kindles the fire in our hearts to document alive the instant history that unfolds at our feet.

Mountains are now beckoning us.

We're back to your fold, our dear mountains.

We come from the East African Savannah, with Shú kà (the Maa word for sheets traditionally worn ,such as animal-skin, calf hides and sheep skin) wrapped around the body.

We are the Yuanmou Branch in the heart land of the Yunling Mountain of China's Yunnan, red clay still on our bare feet;

We are descended from Mt. Kunlun, steering our chariot across the vastness of space.

We have set off from Machu Picchu nestled in the Urubamba Vall, singing a paean of our deities.

山地，一个朴实得如同史诗般的大地符号，一个响亮得有如呼唤我们乳名的声音，怎能不让我们由衷地关注和亲近？现在，我真诚地邀请：山地的使者，山地的守望者，山地记忆的记录者和传播者，来讲述你的故事吧！因为在那绵延的群山里，总有这样的时候：一个人低头坐在屋中，不知不觉会想起许多事情。

Ultimately, summoned from the deep recesses of historical memory, we have journeyed all the way to pay our tribute to the mountains.

Mountains, the most imposing emblem of the earth, reverberate deep in my souls as if someone is teasing me by my pet name, the abettor of my enlightened curiosity. Now, I sincerely invite you, the heralds and custodians of mountains, the recorders and disseminators of the alpine memory, to tell a tale in your own terms. What begins for us as the effort to capture and delve into ways of being and mind unimaginably different from our own dissolves into a quest, an odyssey of self-discovery which takes place on the Last Pure Land. Qinghai is beguiling. Qinghai's ubiquitous presence of mountains has much to offer to the really stubborn minded in the way of irresistible marvels and wonders.

多元民族特质文化与文学的人类意识

在鲁迅文学院少数民族作家创作班上的演讲

2009年11月23日

  非常高兴今天能到鲁迅文学院和大家见面,有的是过去见过面的老朋友,有的是刚刚初识的新朋友,尤其是能和这么多少数民族作家在一起,我感到非常欣慰。我非常愿意利用这个机会和大家沟通有关发展繁荣少数民族文学的问题。

  前不久,听鲁院的领导说这里正在办一个有55个少数民族作家的创作班,并邀请我来做一个讲座,我当即回答他们一定来,因为这对我来说是一个机会,是一个和大家交流思想的难得的契机。我们是同行,都是少数民族的作家,有许多共同的语言,并且我相信我们彼此能进行更为坦诚的交流。今天我演讲的题目是《多元民族特质文化与文学的人类意识》。

  大家都知道,人类正置身于一个全球化的背景,关于全球化这个话题,可以说全世界到处都在讨论,人类正在经历一个从未有过的现代化的过程,今天的人类面临着许多需要共同解决的问题。

  由于全球资讯的发达,可以说世界已经真正进入了一个网络和数字化的时代。今天在我们这个世界上任何一个角落发生的重要事件,全世界的大部分人我想都能在第一时间知道,无论这个事件发生在北京,还是发生在某个离北京更遥远的地方,我想大家都会知道,这就是网络和电视的作用,难怪有一位美国的社会学家把现在的地球称为"平面的地球"。

  今天的全球化是一个大趋势,是好是歹各国的学者也众说纷纭,但是有一点可以肯定,就是有许多关注人类命运的作家、诗人和学者,要比过去任何时候更关注不同民族的生存状况。有的学者甚至质疑现代化给人类带来的好处,要比给人类带来

The Contemporary Culture of Plurality and a Writer's Sense of Humanity

A lecture Given to a Team of Ethnic Writers at the Lu Xun Academy of Literature

23rd, November, 2009

I feel immensely flattered to come into the presence of this team of prospective writers, some of which are old friends, and some, only nodding acquaintances. I take great solace in the thought that sitting in front of me ,are ethnic poets and writers representing the fullest spectrum of China' minority nationalities, 55 of them being amazingly represented!

So when the dean of your Institute prompted me for a talk here, I accepted without any hesitation. We are all of ethnic origin and we speak the same literary idiom which will, as I believe, facilitate the exchange of views and, occasion possibly a brainstorming session rewarding to each one of us present. My topic for today is The Contemporary Culture of Plurality and a Writer's Sense of Humanity

As is known to all, we are now living in a period of great socio-political transformation, dubbed often one of globalization; a topic, which has widely been discussed and researched in all parts of the earth when various factors are playing off each other and radically altering the world out of recognition .Humanity is confronted with a spate of problems crying for joint solutions.

The flourishing information industry has ushered in a new era of internet and digitalization in a manner human distance is only a matter of hours and an instant perception of global events , wherever they it might happen, either in Beijing or anywhere far away from Beijing. The change is indeed exponential because we interconnect ourselves through internet and TV to the extent the catchword "the flattening of our earth" used by American writer Freeman to describe our world has gained immediate currency.

For better or worse, we are living beyond all possible doubt, in a world in flux. There is one trend, highly discernible, that writers and poets, throughout the globe, traditionally preoccupied with the destiny of mankind, have now shifted their perspective more and more to the quality and possibility of human existence. Some scholars are more alarmist about the advent of globalization as well as the potential hazards in its wake.

I am not supposed, today, to mete out my value judgment. Yet, either from the angle of

的潜在危机更多。

在这里，我不想对它们做价值判断。今天，无论从西方哲学的观点来看，还是从东方哲学的观点来看，我们都要就全世界都在经历的一个现代化过程做出我们的回答，因为人类将走向何处，或者说选择一个更美好的明天，是今天人类应该知晓并且应该勇于担当的重要职责。

回顾历史，远的不用说，就在刚刚过去的20世纪，人类就经历了两次非常惨烈的世界大战，今天当我们回望历史的时候，不难发现有许许多多问题需要我们去总结，比如民族的问题，比如宗教的问题，比如世界政治秩序的问题，比如资源的问题，比如环境的问题，比如生物多样性的问题，比如文化多样性的问题，比如生态的问题，比如可持续发展的问题等等，都需要我们在这个新的世纪开始对人类的过去进行反思，对人类的未来进行预测。人类社会是一个很奇怪的社会，人类一边在总结已经走过的历史，在总结我们所犯下的错误，同时人类又在新的时间、新的地点开始犯本质上相同的错误。

进入21世纪以来，据一些政治学家统计，人类的战争特别是区域性的战争没有减少，反而大大地增加了，冲突和战争有的是为了资源，有的是为了宗教和文化，有的是为了不同的价值观。从某种意义而言，刚刚开头的21世纪，并不比我们看到的20世纪要更好。对我们今天来说，人类正处在一个更为特殊背景下，经济高速发展，物质极大丰富，但同时人类的精神又在失落。大家知道从上一个世纪到现在我们正置身的这个新世纪，人类在科技上有很多重大发现，这些重大发现，已经极大地改变了人类的生活方式，甚至也改变了人类的一些思维方式，一切过去都是不可想象的。

人类在20世纪登上了月球，基因工程取得重大突破，航空事业快速发展，电脑计算机进入人类日常生活，医学上的贡献更是比比皆是，应该公正地说，人类跟过去几百年或者几千年的发展速度来比，可以说今天是创造了奇迹。但是尽管这样，人类事实上又在进行新的思考，那就是我们这种大量损耗资源、破坏环境，与自然对抗的无序发展，是不是一种真正意义上的进步？这个严肃的问题，其实已经摆在了我们所有人的面前。我的回答，肯定不是进步！

我们似乎刚发现，人类发展到今天，人口的压力、资源的过度消耗以及对环境的破坏已经变成了一个全球关注的大问题，其实这些问题的形成，也有一个时间过程。

今天有很多原生民族的生存环境遭到了破坏，强势文化和弱势文化的博弈，使

Occidental philosophy or that of the Oriental philosophy ,it behooves us, this generation undergoing all the travails and agonies of the drastic upheaval brought about by globalization, to rise to the challenge and come out with both diagnosis and prognosis, helping people see what has our world become and where it is going.

When historians look back on the past century, they do not have to be very retrospective to draw both moral and political lessons from it, a century of monstrous killings in the two world wars. Indeed, decades of bloody conflicts, overstimulation of material desire, sensual gratification and other atrocities and stupidities have generated a dynamics of uncontrolled problems, such as intensified religious enmity, massive geopolitical disorder, depletion of natural resources, eco-systems in disequilibrium, cultural and bio diversity threatened with disappearance and the sustainability of development being greatly compromised. That means we are living in an age of "global change out of control."I know nothing else that does a more daunting job of summarizing the human toll taken by almost one century of human greed and stupidity, which is to project into a foreseeable future. But we should be up to the formidable task of s historical synthesis. One tentative observation is that human beings seem to be a very queer breed of species as they have never learned from history and they have kept replicating the tragic errors previously made, only at a new locale or a different date.

The onset of the present century, for example, has not seen a decisive turn for better. It is ironical with the end of cold war that hostilities, particularly regional ones, are on the rise and wars are fought under various time-honored covers, for the sake of resources, doctrine, religion, culture, values. In a sense, the 21th century does begin badly, if not more ominously than did the previous one as it features a drastic disproportion between the material abundance and the spiritual emptiness. The great scientific strides have revolutionized the internal and external dimensions of life to a degree that is almost tantamount to a fundamental reshaping of human character and thought.

In any case, the frontiers of science have been pushed to the extremes as exemplified in a list of staggering technological breakthroughs in various fields: we have seen manned landing on the moon, genetic engineering , aerospace industry and digitalization accessible to the ordinary household. In all fairness, in terms of the velocity of economic growth, what man has achieved in a century far surpasses the sum total of what was achieved in a span of ,say, the several hundred years or even several millennia prior to ours. In reaction to the challenges of science, there is a serious critical trend skeptical of the progress made possible by overexploiting natural resources to the detriment of the organic balance between man and nature. Out of such concern there arises naturally a great intellectual consensus that we need to redefine progress.

It seems the human community has just been awakened to the truly divisive cleavage opened up in the human condition occasioned by the massive onslaught of environmental crisis, demographic dynamics and over depletion of natural resources. This is understandable since a

很多民族的文化历史和文化符号的生存空间不断萎缩。今天,我们探讨这些问题,我认为具有一种更现实的意义,因为我们承担着传承和保护不同民族文化的责任。

当然需要声明的是,文化的延续和发展,是一个极为复杂的问题,随着人类社会的不断发展和科技的进步,不同民族的文化中当然也存在着一些糟粕,随着历史的发展,它会不断地消亡和被淘汰,我想这也是一种必然。

但是从另外一个角度来说,我们又必须在这个特殊的时刻,更加关注和保护这些民族的文化和历史,要防止在现代化的过程中,我们不同民族的文化链条会中断,我们不同民族的历史和文明会毁于一旦。我提出这个问题,其实是在考问我们所有的人,考问我们生活在今天的所有现代人,不管你现在生活在什么样的文化和宗教背景,生活在哪一个国度,属于哪一个种族,我们都必须回答这样一个严肃的问题,保护地球上每一种文化是我们最崇高的使命。

我们知道,全人类现在都置身于一个整体的现代化过程中,在这个现代化过程中,我们每一个民族,都站在一个现代和传统,历史和未来的十字路口上,每一个民族都想获得自己的通行证,通过这个十字路口。

毫无疑问,它的民族历史和文化就是最好的通行证。我们要延续我们每一个民族的历史,我们就必须学会在整个现代化的过程中,继承好我们伟大的文化传统,以一种开放的眼光去学习人类所有的伟大文明,从而来丰富和壮大我们的民族文化,使之获得不断延续的生机和活力。全人类的文明和历史,都是上天给我们的恩赐,这是最为宝贵的文化财富。

当然需要指出的是,在全球化的背景下,强势文化的扩张,无疑给一些弱小文化带来了生存威胁,不同文化的同质化现象变得格外严重,许多民族的文化失去个性,表象的、共性的东西越来越多。我们经过分析可以看出,不同文明之间的沟通和对话非常重要,不同民族文化之间的交流与相互学习同样必不可少,但是,我们也要警惕不同民族文化的同质现象变得越来越严重,不同民族文化的存在,是这个世界文化多样性和丰富性必不可少的一个重要前提。

大家知道,生物多样性是联合国保护生物多样性相关决议所确定的,我们人类生活的地球就是一个庞大的生物链,无论是我们人类的集体生命,还是我们的个体生命,可以说都生活在这个庞大的生物链中,如果这个生物链一旦被打破,某一种生物消亡了,可能会连带另外生物的生命也要随之消亡,这就是我们为什么要保护生

crisis situation takes time to escalate into alarming proportions. Besides, it has been neglected for too long.

As ethnic writers, we are keenly aware of the inadvertent consequences of reckless industrialization caused to many of the natural surroundings of the aboriginal groupings .We also bear witness to the odds against the weak cultures lost inexorably to the strong cultures, with their living space of cultural heritage and racial identity steadily squeezed and dwindled .For each of us present here, to open up a debate to address these vital issues will lead to an enhanced consciousness of moral responsibility of the civil community for the cultural continuity of the indigenous people.

It must be added, of course, that cultural continuity is a very complex philosophical proposition. What part of ethnic heritage deserves preserving, what part, dismissing, is not a matter of single-sided advocacy. An enlightened attitude to engage in meaningful dialogue, with an eye to all the pros and antis of scientific development must precede any engagement and commitment we might take.

On the other hand, we must not hesitate to plunge ourselves into such intellectual inquiry to address the vital issue of our ethnicity to prevent the cultural discontinuity which will lead to the ultimate extinction of our cultural traditions. The reality of diversity and ethnicity is of paramount importance to every citizen of the world community, irrespective of race, origin, religion. We are all obliged to protect and preserve every culture on earth.

Obvious for everyone to see, our world is in a vortex of globalization which, to all intents and purposes, brings us, of every race and nation, to a crossroad, forking out into history behind and future that lies in store ahead.

The best passport into future is actually the tradition and cultural heritage of each pedestrian. Cultural continuity necessarily presupposes an open mindedness to embrace every great civilization so as to enrich and revitalize our own. All the cultural heritages evolved by races other than ours are God sent treasures, valuable in their own right.

This is not to deny, if not properly handled, we should be prepared to risk calamity. Against the large backdrop of a globalized world, the attainment of cultural preeminence of strong cultures will sometimes lead to undesirable outcome of weak cultures being further weakened and furthermore cultural homogeneity which means the loss of cultural specificity for weak cultures. The cross cultural exchange being prerequisite for the citizenship in the global village, we must guard against homogeneity, the bane of globalization, for the presence of ethnicity and the cumulative effect of diversity is essential for human civilization.

The Convention on Biological Diversity (CBD) is an international legally-binding treaty with three main goals: conservation of biodiversity; sustainable use of biodiversity; fair and equitable sharing of the benefits arising from the use of genetic resources. Its overall objective is to encourage actions which will lead to a sustainable future. Mankind is, among all creatures on

物多样性的原因。每一个生物都很重要,我们很难说谁重要谁不重要,在非洲的原野上,你可以看见许多狮子,同样你也可以看见许多斑马和羚羊。斑马和羚羊繁殖很快,如果不控制其数量,就会让草原负载过量,也不能给食草动物提供足够的食物,不少斑马和羚羊都是被非洲狮和猎豹捕杀的,这是动物间所形成的一个生物平衡。我们不能人为地打破这个平衡。

我们这里有不少来自草原并熟悉牧区生活的人,你们一定会知道,如果天空中没有鹰了,草原上的地鼠就会泛滥成灾,鹰和鼠是一对天敌,所以我们如果破坏了生物链中任何一个环节,其后果都会不堪设想,有的后果甚至是灾难性的。

反过来讲,文化多样性也是一样,据说现在全世界每天都有一两种语言在消亡,这对于人类来说是一件很不幸、很可怕的事情。有的民族可能人口很少,但是他们有着自己的民族语言,人类是靠语言进行思维的,不同民族的语言都承载着很多文化信息,承载着不同民族的思维习惯和文化价值观念,许多民族的生存智慧和哲学思想也与其语言和思维方式息息相关。任何一种古老的语言消失,都是全人类不可弥补的损失,都是人类共同的悲哀和不幸。

今天我们在这里共同探讨这个让我们感到窒息和沉重的话题,我们一定要站在一个道德的制高点上,来面对我们今天必须面对的困境;作为一个民族的精神文化代表,我们必须客观同时要充满敬畏地看待我们人类所有的文化,任何一个有良知的作家和诗人都要尊重这个世界上任何一个民族的历史和文化,不管这个民族的人口是多么少,甚至是一个极其弱小的民族,我们对他的文化也应该充满应有的敬意,文化的多样性与这个世界的文化整体性是相互联系的。我们知道每一个民族的文化存在,是使这个世界文化变得色彩斑斓的前提。

全世界的文化之所以这么丰富,是因为有不同的宗教、不同的民族、不同的历史、不同的文明,正因为这种差异性,让人对这个世界的不同民族文化充满着好奇,这个世界才可能变得如此让人着迷。我认为,现在最重要的是,我们要认识我们所处的这个时代,文化仍然在发挥着重要的作用,我们一定要在不断发展经济的同时,更加重视文化的发展,更加重视不同民族的文化传承和保护,尊重每一个民族所选择的发展道路,让每一个民族找到适合自己的发展方式。

有人说,今天的世界是一个人类走向共性的时代,因为经济和社会的发展,让今天的人类和不同地域的族群,都更加紧密地联系在了一起,这是一个基本事实,有不

earth, also a link of which the bio-chain consists, whether as individual or as community. Scientific findings have long proved certain links missing will trigger the dysfunction of the whole bio-chain which means one species dead tolls the bell for all. Hence, each creature and species matters, or as the CBD clarifies, "components of biodiversity are all the various forms of life on Earth including ecosystems, animals, plants, fungi, microorganisms, and genetic diversity". The Serengeti savanna is renowned for its largest lion population. But as gazelles and blue wildebeests reproduce too quickly, the lions are out there doing the butchery to keep the eco balance. What God thinks of this is hard to divine, but it looks like it is part of the Providence.

Some of the audience come from the grasslands. They know the maintenance of the eco-system depends upon wise anthropogenic activities such as low-intensity farming and hunting. These grasslands contain many species of wild plants and wild animals. Again there is a pyramid there dominated by the largest predator the hawks. If you shoot them all, mice will take advantage and cover the whole grassland which means the total disappearance of grass and that also means all the cattle and sheep and herdsmen starve to extinction. How do we make of this piece of ecological common sense?

I am told with each passing day, one or two languages die out. Nothing is more ominous than this, isn't it? Some ethnic groups are small, even tiny to be worth of note, but they speak a language encoding DNA of their cultural heritage, their lifestyle and value systems in it. One of American's most respected anthropologists calls us to the intrinsic connection between thought and language and us humans all stand to be losers when any of the existing tongues are heard no more on the human scene.

Inherent in the foregoing is a call for modern society to reorient ourselves jointly to the significance of the spiritual facets of life and the redemption of our civilization. These gripping and even suffocating issues must be coped with on a vantage point, or with an intellectually relevant and ethically meaningful framework. As ethnic writers, each representing a type of cultural heritage, we must develop an outlook, cosmopolitan and catholic in character, one reverential of all the human cultures available, large or small, as all the writers and poets with a conscience do, and seek to galvanize some kind of renewed humility for man's spiritual well being and to utter some pronouncements of morally infused management of the trajectory of historic change.

It must be urged upon all the people the cultural plurality-exemplified in terms of diverse religions, races, histories, cultures- is what sustains us all on earth, what makes the world so enthralling and enchanting. Moreover, the prevalent lop-sided criteria, stressing the primacy of economics to the neglect of the role of culture and the protection of cultural continuity (this is particularly true for ethnic people), for defining a good society must be revised. The cultural sovereignty of each ethnic race must be respected so that they may decide for themselves in matters pertaining to the supreme spiritual sanity, ie, which mode of development best suits them.

All this is bound to push, as someone might maintain, to the forefront a key question, that

少作家在自己的政论文字中,提出来要更多地关注人类的整体发展和命运,要去解决今天人类共同面临的、急需解决的棘手问题,也有一些作家认为我们更多地要关注人的个体命运,关注自身民族所面临的生存危机和历史命运。

我认为这两者并不矛盾,作为一个民族的作家和诗人,我们有责任去延续这个民族的文化和历史,但是作为一个世界公民,我们同样有责任和义务去关注全人类的命运。我们每一个人,都生活在一定的族群和社会里,民族的历史和民族的文化是我们生命中最重要的文化基因,每一个民族的作家和诗人都有责任去保护和纯洁自己民族的语言和民族的文字。

因为我们生活在这个世界任何一个地域的作家,都不可能说我是一个抽象的作家,而我们都是具体的存在,不管我们属于哪一个民族,来自哪一个地域,用哪一种文字进行写作,我们的文化和宗教背景有何差异,我想我们永远离不开的是对养育我们的土地的热爱,对人的命运的关注,对我们民族伟大文学传统的继承和弘扬,对我们民族语言和文字的创新和丰富。

中国是一个多民族的国家,56个民族共同创造了灿烂悠久的中华文化,中国政府历来重视发展和繁荣中国56个民族的文化。今天有55个少数民族作家在鲁迅文学院深造学习,这个事实进一步说明了国家对发展少数民族文化的真正关切,少数民族作家的培养是一项重要的文化工程。

我觉得大家在这里学习机会尤其难得,在人生的生命历程中,作为一个作家有一年能来到鲁迅文学院深造,这个机会不是所有人都有的,希望大家一定要珍惜。在这里学习,我希望大家是一种真正意义上的学习,我们要通过学习,站在一个更高的思想制高点上,从而来认识今天这个纷纭复杂的世界,让我们与我们的民族一道在经历全球化的过程中,一方面延续好我们民族的历史和文化;另一方面要通过我们的笔触,真实地记录下我们每一个民族创造新生活和新历史的壮丽画卷。

我认为,传承和延续每一个民族的文化都不是一般意义上的传承,任何一个伟大的作家和诗人,如果你离开了你的民族的心灵和灵魂,你就不可能具有深刻的洞察力,从而真正表现出你的民族的伟大精神世界。我们阅读历史上这些大师的作品,每一部作品都具有自身的民族的色彩,同时又具有超越时空和单一民族的人类意识,他们的作品是个性和人类普世价值高度统一的光辉典范。

《百年孤独》是马尔克斯的代表作,也是20世纪最伟大的长篇小说之一,它写的

is, the inner logic of globalization is increased commonality instead of diversity. We owe this to the fact that all important socio-economic decisions, whereby basic economic performance is derived from and predicated upon close international cooperation. This line of reasoning certainly holds water. Some writers have penned essays in vehement advocacy of intensified and joint actions to address the pressing issues confronting all. Of course, some writers counter-argue for a focus on the fate of individual in society as well as concern with the existential crisis and historic destiny of a particular race.

I, for one, don't see any fundamental difference in both views. As ethnic writers, we are held accountable to preserve the continuity of our cultural heritage. As citizens of the world, we come equally under obligation to care for the way the age is shaping. Each of us is born to a special group of human race, raised and nurtured on its tradition and history, in which is encoded the DNA of our people and I deem it a sacred duty to protect and maintain the sanity and purity of our mother tongue.

On the other hand, each of us writers, of whatever ethnic origin, is not an abstraction. We are living on the same earth with over six billion people who might not share the same language, religion or cultural heritage with us, but nevertheless human beings like us. In sum, our mission as ethnic writers necessitates a fruitful harmonizing of two set of seemly contradictory obligations.

There are over 56 officially recognized minority groups living in China today, and each contributing to a certain degree, in its own way, to the sum total of china's civilization. The central government has always attached due importance to the maintenance of cultural values and lifestyles of each Indigenous race. A special project involving would-be writers and poets composed of 55 ethnic groups, hosted by Lu Xun Institute of Literature, the country's famed nursery of prospective men and women of letters is indicative of the resolve and goodwill of the central government to preserve the cultural diversity.

In the lap of such luxury, we are supposed to make this rare learning session truly rewarding, and when this program is closing, we will leave this room wiser souls and better men. Every one of us wants to succeed in life. Luck, of course, plays a role. But, in the long run, success is about learning and the way we perceive learning and the way we get down to learning in this extremely complicated world. Globalization proceeds apace and in spite of us. What is at stake is our willingness and ability to identify with and to translate faithfully the realities of both Chinese life and the life of our own tribes.

Personally I believe in the digitalized age the talk of preserving cultural heritage for the benefit of the ethnic groups is no matter of old wine in new bottle."The dogmatic certitudes of the modern age must yield to the recognition of the inherent uncertainty of the human condition." Any outburst of literary greatness occurs as the combination of two things: fidelity in the chronicling of the specific mind and soul of one's people and grand assertions of ethnicity deeply steeped in the native soil. Masterpieces are invariably ingenious performances addressing some of

是拉丁美洲的精神史,写的是印第安人的心灵史,写的是整个拉丁美洲一百年的苦难史和命运史,马尔克斯用魔幻现实主义的手法,把土著神话和传说,把印第安人的原始思维,以及他们对生命、对灵魂、对死亡的观念和表述方式,都浓缩在了一部寓言般的史诗作品中。

这部作品是用西班牙语写的,它打破了一般意义上的时间和空间的关系,打破了现实世界和神灵世界的关系,它在人鬼之间构筑了一个迷宫一样的世界,在小说的叙述手法上,他运用的是拉丁美洲人固有的讲故事的语气,当然在艺术手法上,马尔克斯也大胆地借鉴了包括卡夫卡、海明威、福克纳这样重要作家的作品。

《百年孤独》对我们是一个启示,我们只有把我们的笔深深地植根于养育了我们民族的大地的子宫中,我们才可能写出震撼人心的史诗般的作品。我们的作品才可能超越国界、超越民族,成为人类共有的精神财富。

我想这才是我们每一个人应该追寻的目标。当然,作为一个少数民族作家,可以说都是他所属的民族的精神代言人,我们要更加关注人类的生存问题,当代的民族和宗教问题以及人类面对死亡、面对危机的问题,我们不仅要关注我们民族自身的历史进程,同时我们还要关注整个世界的历史进程。我们要把我们民族所经历的欢乐、痛苦、苦难等等都呈现在自己的作品中。

我们应该充分地认识到,作为一个民族的作家,我们所处的时代是一个正在发生剧烈变革的时代,我们不能作为这个时代的旁观者,我们必须是参与者和行动者。我们只能洞察我们民族的历史、我们民族的文化,洞察这个时代发生的一切,我们才有可能描述和呈现这个时代。

我们每一个作家都是人类文明的儿子,吸收所有人类文明的伟大的成果来武装自己,来丰富和强大自己,是我们的必然选择,我们真正站在了世界文化的高地上,才可能具备高远的眼光,才可能书写出我们民族的新的壮丽史诗,才可能用文字描述出我们波澜壮阔的历史画卷。如果没有这样的思想和文化准备,我们就不会真正抓住我们民族历史和现实的本质,也不可能真正找到我们民族现处的历史方位,当然也不可能写出划时代的作品。

讲到这里,我想简单地介绍一下,当前世界文坛的一些情况。在当今世界文坛,总有一些消息会让大家感到异常吃惊,可能大家已经注意到了,今年的10月8日诺贝尔文学奖评奖委员会宣布得奖的是一个罗马尼亚裔德国作家,名字叫米勒,当这

the most pressing ,albeit universal themes allegorically and metaphorically-a prime task of poets and writers under whatever circumstances.

One Hundred Years of Solitude , considered by many to be its author's masterpiece , hailed as one of the greatest novels of the 20th century, describes thematically the rise and fall, birth and death of the mythical but intensely real Macondo. As it depicts the glories and disasters of the wonderful Buendí a family, it constitutes a brilliant spiritual record of the Indians as well as an epic picture of the Hispanic life after five centuries of Spanish colonialism (the continual violence, repression, and exploitation). *One Hundred Years of Solitude* is often cited as exemplary of magical realism, a style of writing in which the supernatural is presented as mundane, and the mundane as supernatural or extraordinary. Garcí a Márquez achieves a perfect blend of the real with the magical through the masterful use of myth, legend, Indian conception of life, soul and death. There are three main mythical elements of the novel: classical stories alluding to foundations and origins, characters resembling mythical heroes, and supernatural elements.

Written in Spanish, Marquez introduces Indian idea of time other than the western linear progression (for example, the metaphor of history as a circular phenomenon ,the issue of timelessness or eternity even within the framework of mortal existence).All this combined makes his fantastic story an expression of reality, albeit outsized and deformed. This brand new school strikes at traditional novels, based upon trappings such as straightforward narrative, well rounded characters and interesting plots in the approved 19th century ways. There is also a marked degree of influence from Kafka, Hemingway and Faulkner in his tour de force.

One Hundred Years of Solitude has received universal recognition. The critical vogue holds a moral for us, ethnic writers ,who write out of the pale of the main stream literary traditions. For that quest for innovation and originality is not merely wishful thinking and should should become a Western aspiration as a whole. A Marquez ,steeped in the native soil and culture , associated with disorder, backwardness, and danger in superlatives, emerges a master figure. He helped Hispanic American literature to reach the quality of the Indo-European literature and become the common heritage of all nations.

We, ethnic writers should be the willing vehicle of literary expression of our own people, the quality of which is predicated upon an enhanced and widened preoccupation with larger issues such as human survival, current religious and racial controversies, intellectual questioning of human response towards life and death. The social and political orientation of our times and our own people are two facets of our intellectual curiosity.

Fully cognizant of the global crisis of the human spirit as well as the complexity of the human condition, instead of sitting idle as mere lookers-on, we must impact on and speak to the world. Only by getting ourselves acquainted with the finest literature of our time and of all times, not restricted to the literary, that crystallize with such clarifying power and deeply felt conviction, the perception of the scope of our own cultural heritage and the nature of the contemporary

个作家得奖的消息传到全世界的时候，不要说在中国，就是在世界上别的国家，很多重要的通讯社和文学机构，都不知道这个人，更不知道她写过什么作品。德国有一个评论家说，当他知道这个女作家得诺贝尔文学奖的消息时，惊讶得差点从椅子上掉下来，感到非常意外。

中国许多新闻机构为了报道这一消息，纷纷打电话给中国社科院外文所咨询这一情况。好在《世界文学》过去还曾经翻译过她的几个短篇小说，并且对她的一些简单背景情况还略有了解。据介绍，她的作品中国大陆推介得非常少，中国台湾地区曾翻译出版过她的一本书。

据资料介绍，在现在的德国她也不是一个所谓的畅销书作家，大众读者对她的了解也非常有限，在德国纯文学圈子里面的作家对她还是比较推崇的，她的作品写的大多是在罗马尼亚一个少数民族族群的境遇。她很长时间生活在罗马尼亚，她的家族是罗马尼亚的少数民族，齐奥赛斯库政权消失后，她和她的丈夫移民到了德国，她长期用德语写作，她的许多作品大都是在德国出版的。

我给大家介绍这样一个作家的获奖情况，是想说明什么呢？就是想要告诉大家一个信息，现在世界上许多重要的文学奖项，它们现在更关注哪一类的作家，像诺贝尔文学奖这样重要的文学奖项，在今天它们更青睐哪一种作品，有的作家虽然在世界范围内并不知名，但他们的作品引起了一些重要文学机构的关注，往往是每年的10月8日诺贝尔文学奖公布获奖者的名字时，有不少获奖者在一夜成名，全世界都知道了这个人。

我们注意到一个现象，瑞典的诺贝尔文学奖、法国的龚古尔文学奖，近二十年来非常关注作家的文化背景，对其地域性的文化贡献格外看重，对获奖作家和诗人的文化身份给予了更多的关切。当然，需要说明的是，这些作家和作品绝不是简单地代表了一个民族或者说一种文化，他们的作品表现了人类的生存状况，具有极高的普遍价值，这些作品往往深刻地描述了人类复杂的精神世界以及人类面对苦难所表现出的高尚行为。

许多得奖作家和诗人获奖前大多是区域性的作家，在全世界并不知名，其中有不少就是少数民族作家。我告诉大家这些重要文学奖项的评奖情况，并不是想说因为强调作家的文化代表性，这些奖项降低了评奖的标准，其实恰恰相反，因为世界多元文化的共存，这些获奖作家的作品，除了在艺术创新上有重要贡献外，他们的作品

historic trends, can we identify with and to adequately reflect on the contemporary life.

We are the sons and daughters of human civilization, increasingly and ultimately nourished and enriched by drawing on the most successful writing, in our possession, for our benefit, an option in spite of us. How can we practice our art unless it is derived from a moral commitment in the quest for an epic picture, metaphorically and symbolically, of our genuine ethnicity as well as historical upheavals that rock, shake and condition our world? Without such intellectual preparedness and cultural comprehension, we are hopelessly lost in the whirlwind of history to the essence of our cultural heritage, the character of reality and to the point of the slightest idea of where humanity is heading.

I will now pause for some news of lighter nature concerning what has happened recently to the contemporary literary scene, a place full of Cinderella-type surprises indeed. Some of you might be already advised of the decision announced in 10th, August by the Nobel Committee for the laureate of this year. A Romanian by the name of Herda Muller, absolutely a black horse by whatever measure to such an extent the moment the cat was let out of the bag, not only in China, but also in many major world powers, so many news agencies and professional institutions dedicated to literary studies, were all caught off guard. Nobody knew who this lady was and what kind of works credited her. One German critic acknowledged he was taken aback off the chair, literarily!

Reporters in China fared a little better than their peers elsewhere. The Institute of Literary Studies, attached to the Academy of Social Sciences, were inundated with incoming phone calls for feedback and background information. It so happened that a few short stories of the new recipient were featured in a previous issue In the Journal of World Literature, together with a rather perfunctory resume of the author appended. Mme Muller, I was told, is almost a fresh woman and a certain Taiwan guy bothers to have her stories stringed together, translated and printed in a book length form.

I keep hearing nowadays she is by no means a household name to the public readership, yet she is admired among the high brow writers and critics. Her works mainly deal with the lot of an ethnic group in Romania. A Romanian of German descent, she spent most of her life there until the collapse of the Nicolae Ceaucescu's regime when she emigrated to Germany. She now publishes in German, her second language and most of her works get printed in her guest country.

What do we make of this case? Here is my divination. I want to call your attention to a new trend that in recent years major world bodies are out there scouting and ferreting out black horses-writers who not well known to the mundane readers, but whose works, already well researched by professional institutes of literary studies composed of literary professors and critics. The 8th,October remains a big day for nobody rising to fame over night.

We have also noticed for almost 20 years consecutively, the Nobel Prize Committee or the Prix Goncourt have devoted much to identify talents who belong to specific ethnic groups,

还是这些民族的文化符号，对人类来说是弥足珍贵的，这些作品记录了人类某一部分人的历史，从社会学、人类学的角度来看，这些作家和作品都要比那些所谓时尚型的畅销书作更有价值，虽然他们并不为大多数人所知晓。

刚才我说有的作家因为突然获奖让大家感到很吃惊，并不是说这个作家的作品写得不好。还有一些知名作家，听说一直在诺贝尔文学奖的候选名单上，法裔捷克作家米兰昆德拉、美国著名的小说家奥茨、罗斯，他们虽然在全世界都很有名，但在这几年的诺贝尔文学奖最后角逐中都名落孙山。老实说，我更喜欢那些地域性很强的作家获奖，因为他们代表了一种不可替代的文化。

前几年得奖的是一位法国小说家，他还来过中国，在法国文学圈里面属于边缘作家，他大多写的都是非洲、南美印第安人的生活，基本上都是亚文化的东西；英国女作家多丽丝·莱辛写的基本上是有关非洲生活的东西，其代表作《小草为什么歌唱》，写的就是她青年时代所经历的非洲生活，很好，大家可以找来看看。总之，这是一个现象，在多元文化的背景下，许多重要奖项都授给了这样一些文化特性和民族特性很强的作家，而这些作家的作品，在艺术上也达到了相当高的水准，无论是诗歌和小说的技巧都非常精湛。把这些作品放在人类的文学史上，其价值也不会被淹没，也一定会从浩如烟海的文学宝库中凸现出来。

这不奇怪，近二十年的诺贝尔文学奖所评出来的作家，好多人在获奖前并不被大多数人所知，我刚才说到的德国作家米勒，就是这样一个人，前两天德国正在举办图书节，有记者采访参加图书节的德国观众，问他你知不知道这个作家，读没读过她的作品，大多数人都不知道，当然我并不是说她的作品写得不好，其实她的作品无论是思想性还是艺术性都很好，文学价值也非常高，我是想说在今天这样一个消费主义时代，严肃的文学已经被彻底地边缘化了，更何况她作品所写的内容都是东欧罗马尼亚一个少数民族的生活。

非洲肯尼亚有一个作家叫詹姆斯·恩古吉，写过一部小说叫《孩子，你别哭》，据说这个作家作为诺贝尔文学奖获选人已经排在了前几名；尼日利亚世界级的小说巨匠，黑人作家钦努阿·阿契贝现在也是诺贝尔文学奖的热门人选，他的同胞、诺贝尔文学奖获得者索因卡，称他为"非洲文学之父"，这是一位了不起的大作家，我建议大家可以找他的小说看看，他的小说已有好几个中文版本。

阿尔及利亚有一个作家叫穆罕默德·狄布，其三部曲小说《大房子》在法语世界

focusing on his or her contribution to a specific region. Of course, the primacy of ethnic element must overlap with universal themes embodied. One dimensional depicting of one race and one culture is out of the question. A conscious effort at chronicling of the complex spiritual world and the heroism in which protagonists in torment and agony rise to the occasion is hotly sought after and prized.

Many of the latest prize winners, as I have stated before, have attained at most a regional status, not well known in the rest of the world. This new trend tells us what is really in the air now. The truth must not be obscured that emphasizing on the cultural identity or ethnicity does not represent a laxity in the rigor of selecting criteria. Instead, the new recipient does not leap onto the stage without a serious reason. Apart from technical innovations, linguistic quality, rich themes. Such work has to be iconic. It has to be approved for its intrinsic value and rise as a spiritual record of a special group of people, operating on several levels of meaning which can be construed as even sociologically and anthropologically relevant and revelatory, standing by a class by itself higher than bestsellers, though relatively inaccessible to the wide reading public.

Let me reiterate black horse writers are now coming into fashion, winning the favor of literary judges, aside the solidity of their work, there is another interesting phenomenon to be pondered. A few names, big names indeed, recur year in year out, on the list of hot contenders but are always out at the last minute, for example, French emigrant writer Kundera from Czech, American writers Roth and Oates. To be frank with you, I take delight in hearing ethnic names exalted for their representation of a culture in jeopardy.

One of the French writers, a laureate a few years ago, who visited China and operated on the margin of French literature, wrote mainly of the scenes or life set in Africa or the Hispanic world, sort of sub-culture stuff in actuality. Doris Lessing, British writer, Nobel prize winner In 2007, is acclaimed for her masterpiece *The Grass Is Singing* (1950) in which African theme is dominant. In sum, in a context of cultural diversity, important accolades go to ethnic writers or writers of ethnic themes, concerned with bringing the authentic experience of a specific ethnic life to a wider world.

This new trend among the elite literary judges must be deemed extraordinary and applicable to a roaster of Nobel literary laureates in the past decade. The German writer mentioned above is a case in point. Two days ago, I read from the newspaper that at a book fair held in Germany, a few participants were approached by reporters and most of them in the dark as of either her works or of her life. She is no celebrity but that does not mean her novels are not well crafted. In fact they are superb, either in terms of artistic value or of her technical skills. My point is that in an age of mass commercialism, high culture is swamped, let alone the fact Muller deals with a theme so marginalized, ie, the life of a tiny ethnic group in Romania.

Another case concerns Kenyan author Ngugi wa Thiong'o whose *Weep Not, Child*, was the first novel in English to be published by an East African. Rumour has it that she is on the list of

具有广泛影响,这些都是非常优秀的作家。阿尔巴尼亚是一个非常小的国家,但出了一个大作家名字叫卡莱达,作家出版社过去翻译出版过他的一部长篇小说,书名叫《亡军的将领》,这个作家在西方具有很大的影响。2005年英国布克文学奖大奖首次开评,获奖人都是过去获得过布克奖的世界级小说家,评委会经过激烈争论,最终将这个奖颁发给了阿尔巴尼亚的卡莱达,你们可以找他的小说看,写得也是非常好。卡莱达是一个世界一流作家,他生活在阿尔巴尼亚这样一个小国,但是就是因为其作品的特殊价值,他让世界又开始关注巴尔干,关注阿尔巴尼亚这样一个山鹰之国。

同样,中亚的吉尔吉斯斯坦也是一个小国,也出现了一个大作家,名字叫艾特玛托夫,这个作家大家比较熟悉,他所有的作品基本上都被翻译成了中文。如果按人口比例,吉尔吉斯斯坦绝对是一个小国,在20世纪后半叶出现这样一个伟大作家,无疑是吉尔吉斯斯坦最重要的国际荣誉。哈萨克斯坦,在上一个世纪同样产生了一位伟大的作家,他叫穆合塔尔·阿乌埃佐夫,可以说他和艾特玛托夫也是同时代的人,据说后者还深受其作品的影响,阿乌埃佐夫写的《阿拜之路》,在苏联时期该作品就与俄罗斯杰出作家肖洛霍夫的名著《静静的顿河》齐名,成为苏联文学中经典作品之一。

这些作家的作品大多有一个特点,就是在你阅读时都能深入你的内心,深入你的灵魂深处。我曾经说过,作为作家和诗人,我们能不能用我们的手抚摸到人类灵魂最柔软的部分,是不是能真正写出这个最柔软部分给我们的感动。

这就需要我们除了具有特殊的勇气之外,还应具有崇高的人文主义理想和人道主义思想,必须深入历史本质的底部,深入人类思想情感的最深处,只有这样才有可能写出真正的大作品。在今天写作,首先我们一定要树立信心,千万不要被这样那样的说法所迷惑,一个优秀的少数民族作家,首先在思想上我们要树立文化上的信心,要用一种开放的眼光和意识来进行学习和思考,我们要不断提高作为一个作家所应具备的综合性素质,同时我们要不断地提高我们的写作技巧和驾驭文字的能力,那些前辈作家的经验告诉我们,许多伟大的作家和诗人都是语言大师。总之,今天这个世界对多元文化的认同,已经超过了历史上的任何一个时候,这无疑是历史的进步,可以说,这对于我们常常处于所谓文化中心边缘的每一个少数民族作家,的确是一个优势而不是劣势。

下面,我想说一说关于民族的心理结构问题。这固然不是一个简单的问题,我们

rather front running contenders for Nobel prize. Also on the contending list is Nigerian Achebe, distinguished for his world famous Africa trilogy. His friend Soyinka, himself winner in 2001, ranks the former above himself, dubbing him "Father of African Black writing." Achebe is well translated into Chinese with several translations available.

Mohamed Dib is probably Algeria's most prolific and well-known writer in the French speaking world. His debut novel *La Grande Maison* was the first part of the Algerian trilogy about a large Algerian family. It covers the breadth of 20th century Algerian history, focusing on Algeria's fight for independence. Even a tiny country like Albania boasts a writer of global reputation like Ismail Kadare known for his *The General of the Dead Army*, for which he won the British Man Booker award. He has been a leading literary figure in his own country since the 1960s and he brings the world's attention to the plight of his own country.

Similarly, Chingiz Aitmatov, from Kirghizia in Central Asia, is another literary giant from a mini country. Aitmatov represents a minority writer who hits the top by world standard, and his works are almost translated into Chinese without exception. Mukhtar Auezov from Kazakhstan, has produced *The Path of Abai*, a book some critics even rank next to Sholokho's *Silently Flows the Don*, considered one of the most beautiful achievements of former Soviet Union literature.

All these writers have one thing in common: their works are capable of reaching into the deepest recesses of human souls. I have stated somewhere writers and poets will fail to the point of no cure unless their hands feel all the way where their hearts beat ,because this is the most tender human place, the source of genuine lyrical sentiment.

A poet ,unless he asserts command both of a humanist tradition and a humanitarian vision , he is not in a position to penetrate into the bottom of history and spirituality. Only then will he come out with works that assure him the tangible expression of the nation's genius .Ethnic writers and poets must cheer up to an environment of cultural diversity, in the belief that success is really about the zest of learning and the ability to learn from all the best that has been written by previous and contemporary peers. We ought to keep an eye to constantly improve and polish our skills, as experience shows us all literary giants are ultimately linguists. There is increasingly a build-up of literature in favor of cultural diversity, unprecedented in magnitude, a status quo rather benign and conducive to the literary outpouring of ethnic writers.

Now let me shift my focus to the second facet of today's lecture, composed of actually two topics. In the foregoing I have dwelled upon its first facet, ie, a Writer's Sense of Humanity. Now is time for the Contemporary Culture of Plurality, which means specifically the mental processes of ethnic writers. To excel as ethnic writers, we have to be of a different stamp to endure the atmosphere of this complex period and our works must exhibit a historical depth and sociological breadth of our own way of life, capable of being read as spiritual record of our people. A firm gripping with the specificity of the feelings and emotions instead of parading the exotic, the bizarre and the primitive is the touchstone prerequisite.

的作品能不能准确地把握不同民族的历史和文化，能不能写出这个民族的心灵史，这就要求我们必须准确地把握这个民族的思想和情感，而不是简单地通过文字去展览我们的民族风俗，这一点对于我们来说是尤其重要。

普希金是一位世界性的诗人，他离开我们已经很长时间了，但是今天我们阅读他的作品，仍然能感到其作品的鲜活，仍然能被他的作品深深地打动，普希金的作品就是俄罗斯民族的心灵之歌，他天才般地描述了俄罗斯民族的历史、苦难和希望，他诗歌中那种向往自由，追求平等，赞美爱情，同情弱者的思想，已经成为全人类共同的财富，作为一个诗人，普希金首先属于俄罗斯民族，但他同时又属于全世界。

就是现在我也经常阅读普希金的作品，这是放在我床头经常阅读的经典作品之一。苏联著名的诗人后来流亡美国的并获得诺贝尔文学奖的约瑟夫·布罗茨基，在被驱逐出苏联的时候，他曾给当时苏共中央总书记戈尔巴乔夫写过一封信，他在信中表明，虽然他离开了他的祖国，但是因为有俄语，有这种伟大的语言，他就永远不可能和伟大的俄罗斯民族和历史分隔开，因为俄罗斯美丽的语言养育诞生了普希金、列夫·托尔斯泰、屠格涅夫、叶赛宁、帕斯捷尔纳克、阿赫玛托娃、茨维塔耶娃这些伟大的作家和诗人，所以他认为俄语永远是他的故乡，而俄罗斯的文化和历史也永远是他的故乡。

可以看出，这些杰出的作家和诗人都是他所代表的那个民族的良心，他们就像热爱生命一样来热爱民族的文化和历史，他们都倾其一生在任何时候都捍卫自己民族的文化权利。他们是我们永远学习的榜样。

但是有的作家，不去研究自己民族的历史和文化，作品大多是无根之木、无源之水，写的作品缺少根性，更没有他那个民族的文化特性。从世界文学和艺术的更广泛领域去看，像卡夫卡这样的作家，像艾略特这样的诗人，像毕加索这样的画家，他们都是某种艺术形式创新变革而改变其发展进程的巨人，说实在的，这样的大师级人物一个时代或许可能就出一两位，这是时代的选择。但是我们不难发现，人类漫长的文学史和艺术史告诉我们，还有不少同样伟大的作家和诗人，他们的作品无论就其提供的文化价值和民族的历史价值来说都非常大，同样他们的作品在艺术上也有很高的审美价值。

我认为，爱尔兰的叶芝就是这样的诗人，法国新小说派的代表人物尤瑟拉尔就是这样的作家，他们的诗文都具备经典作品的品质。在文学史上，一个作家的重要性

Take the example of Pushkin again. At home or abroad, his work is acclaimed as the quintessence of the Russian genius endowed with freshness, sensuality and rich inventiveness and Russians turn to him with special affection. His refined, robust and lyrical language expresses the poetic impact of quotidian things as well as evocative meditation on the spiritual and political havoc that plague his homeland and his people, providing a liberating image of the indomitable spirit and versatility of man, He is not only adored by Russians but also held in awe by the people of the world.

He's really a voice of his own people. I place a copy of Pushkin beside my pillow for he is a poet to be both read and browsed in. We have all heard of the moving letter of Brodsky to Gorbachev, the then Party boss of former Soviet Union, before his forced departure to USA in which he bewailed of the pending exile but took solace in the thought the haunting lines of Pushkin written in Russian would resonate in his breast. He prided himself in speaking and writing in the same language spoken and written by the most illustrious constellation of Russian geniuses, because that language has been their spiritual home and literary nursery.

We can see clearly great writers always leave a lasting legacy to posterity and depart as an icon and the conscience of their people. The cultural heritage has been their lifelong passion, as sacred as life itself, and their work, invariably absorbed into their own cultural heritage, becomes a mirror we should look up to, an example we emulate.

We do have some writers who do not care about their own culture, history and tradition and their work palliates, impinged with no trace of their culture and their people, into paraphasia, a tree without root, a river without origin. A rough survey on contemporary world literature and world art suffices to convince us that towering personalities occur, but rarely. Once they do-say figures like Kafka, T.S. Eliot, Picasso- their moral qualities, their innovation and their patriotic fervor will be of equal significance for a generation and the course of history as their literary and artistic fruits they bore. Similar truths are revealed in investigation into the world history and the world history of fine arts that we have but a close-knit coterie of master figures to thank for the intrinsic values displayed in their works, culturally ,historically as well as aesthetically.

Irish poet Yeats and Yourcenar Marguerite who dominated the New Novel belong to the above elite. One of the greatest difficulties for literary historians to grapple with is the just estimate of the importance of writers and poets contemporaneous with them. Sometimes it takes decades, maybe a century before the puddle is fathomed.

We know some of Chinese writers are already enshrined in literary history and I dare to bet that Dong Xuiying, based in outlying Yunnan, southwest of China, as anonymous as nobody, will emerge a great novelist. Her trilogy saga of the survival of three generations of a Wa family can be read on the levels of anthropology, sociology and ethnic studies aside its intrinsic qualities as a set of novels. The fact that she is a Wa writer, an ethnic group living in the Yunnan highlands- and she is no recipient of major awards is revealing of what still goes on the modern literary scene. But as

怎么衡量,可能要有一个较长的时间。有的作家现在的文学史给的评价很高,但是再过几十年或者说上百年我看就会有另外的评价。

中国有很多作家都进入了文学史,但是大家或许并不知道云南有个作家叫董秀英,她写了一个佤族部落三代女人的故事,在我看来,她的小说在人类学、社会学、民族学领域内所提供给我们的研究价值,要比现在好多所谓获得许多重要奖项的作品的价值大得多。作为一个作家,我肯定愿意把董秀英的书放在我的书架上,我对她充满着一种敬意和尊重。对我来说,董秀英就是她民族的托尔斯泰,就是她民族的巴尔扎克,诚然,她的长篇小说还可以提高其文学技巧,还可以加大这本书的思想和艺术容量,但是即便如此,我认为她给我们提供的佤族的史诗般的画卷,也足以让我们向她表达一个同行最崇高的敬意。

说到这里,我们还可以举世界级的小说家为例,前面我已经讲到过马尔克斯,他把美洲印第安人的独特价值体系在小说中进行了呈现,神话传说、离奇的故事、神鬼之间,都被巧妙地融进了这部复调般的小说中。

《百年孤独》是拉丁美洲民族的一部心灵史,是一部真正意义上的史诗,难怪有人把马尔克斯的《百年孤独》看成是拉丁美洲的《圣经》,我想这是有道理的。我们要了解一个民族和一个国家,最好的办法就是去读它优秀的作家和诗人的作品,因为阅读这些作品我们就能深入这个民族的灵魂中去,从而真正地认识这个民族。我就是从读马尔克斯的《百年孤独》、读乌拉圭作家爱德华多·加莱亚诺的《拉丁美洲被切开的血管》认识了拉丁美洲,并开始理解和同情拉丁美洲,最后全身心地爱上了拉丁美洲。作家要思考这些重要的问题,作家首先应该是思想家。今天大家在鲁迅文学院学习,就要对一些深层次的问题进行思考,我相信通过这种思考,你们会有长足的进步。

大家或许已经注意到,许多国际性的文学会议都在谈论文化中心与边缘的问题。欧洲文化中心形成已久,如何打破欧洲文化中心的垄断,其实是许多亚文化国家、第三世界国家的一个基本共识。由于欧洲文化中心论的影响,很长时间西方学术界,基本上是以欧洲的文化价值观来衡量世界的文学,这其中不乏存在着偏见和误读。在上一个世纪的中叶,世界上最有影响的作家和诗人也主要集中在欧洲和美国,比如说美国的菲茨杰拉德、海明威、福克纳,法国的萨特,意大利的莫拉维,德国的伯尔,爱尔兰的乔伊斯等等,但是随着20世纪后半叶民族独立运动的蓬勃兴起,第三世界国家除了获得了国家独立外,在文化上也开展了一系列的民族文化复兴运动,

writer myself, I take pride in placing her works on the shelf in my library. Personally I believe Mme Dong is Balzac to her Wa people, despite some shortcomings technically. Even so, I want to pay my tribute to a worthy peer and colleague for the epic picture of the Wa ways of life captured in gripping, moving and uplifting details.

Let me, again return to the eternal Marquez. The magical realist style and thematic substance of One Hundred Years of Solitude has established it as an important, representative novel of the literary Latin American Boom of the 1960s and 1970s, stylistically colored and inspired by Modernism . We are offered a new style, thoroughly of this world that celebrates the mundane. The book succeeds in the constant intertwining of the ordinary with the extraordinary, blending myth, legend, bizarre stories about ghosts to deliver a true history of contemporary Columbia and Latin America in general.

There is something clearly magical about the world of Macondo. It is a state of mind as much as, or more than, a geographical place. Truly it is a modern epic, a spiritual chronicle of Indians, credited by some as the literary Bible of the Hispanic world. It has been widely agreed we only understand a people best through their novels and poetry, the finest flavor of their culture. I, for one, develop my lifelong love and understanding of the Indians and their cultural heritage , occasioned by breathless thumbing through *One Hundred Years of Solitude* and Uruguay's best-known contemporary writer Eduardo Galeano's *Las venas abiertas de América Latina* (Open Veins of Latin America).These essential intellectual issues confront any serious literary aspirants.

Some of the audience might have noticed the recurring theme, I mention, of resistance to cultural dominance by Europe and United States at the international literary seminars and conferences, a reflection of the consensus widely reached among writers from the developing countries in particular. Euro-American cultural hegemony has been an established fact .This is understandable since for almost 200 years most Asian, African and Latin American communities were either under British dominion or under the tutelage of other European colonial powers. European law and commerce and other forms of culture were adopted. So impoverished and backward had the third world become in centuries of material backwardness that it hardly the strength to resist the political and cultural domination of the West. For a long period of time, non-western culture and literature are subjected to the scrutiny of Euro-centered values and criteria and necessarily prejudice and misreading ensue. For example, in the popular consciousness, the first half of the 29th century has been dominated by exclusively men of European stock, Fitzgerald , Hemingway and Faulkner in the USA, Sartre in France, Moravia in Italy, Boll in Germany and Joyce from Ireland. The de-colonialisation movement that swept the world in the second half of the last century had culminated in the national independence of most of the third world countries which triggered a surge of literary activity in its wake hand in hand with an awakening of cultural identity. The influx of successive generations of talented writers and poets of world status has once and for all reshaped the map of world literature.

一些国家在这时也随机涌现出了许多世界级的诗人和作家,从而开始改变这个世界的文学版图。

就是美国这样的国家,在文学领域也发生了很大的变化,原来美国的所谓的主流文学一般不包括黑人作家和犹太人作家,但是随着犹太作家艾茨巴·辛格、索尔贝娄获得诺贝尔文学奖,黑人作家埃里森写出《看不见的人》、黑人诗人兰斯顿·休斯一系列重要抒情诗歌的出版,从此开始颠覆美国文坛所谓主流文学和非主流文学的关系。半个世纪以来,美国文坛已经真正形成了一个多元共存的格局。

其实,美国文坛的这一现象,在当代中国文学中也有相近的情况,中华人民共和国成立之初的中国当代文坛上,重量级的少数民族作家和诗人为数很少,但是今天再来看中国当代文学,如果列出一百位重要而还健在的作家的话,我想其中有二十位一定是少数民族作家。

在这里,我要顺便说说母语写作,在我国的少数民族作家群体中,有不少作家是坚持用母语写作的,这当然应该得到充分的尊重,用母语写作能更好地表达那个民族的生活,特别是能表现独特的思维习惯,母语具有一种独特的魅力,但是这里又有一个翻译的问题,许多少数民族母语的使用人数和范围都非常有限,为了扩大作品的影响,就必须进行翻译。近十几年,中国许多少数民族母语作家的作品,都被陆续翻译成了汉语,但尽管这样,还有许多作品不为更多的人所熟知。前面我讲到的美国犹太作家艾茨巴·辛格的作品都是用意绪第语写的,后来是经过他的同胞索尔贝娄翻译成英文才使他的作品享誉世界,许多国家都出版了他的小说,绝大部分都是从英文转译的,可见翻译的重要。

现在大概有十二个国家出版过我的诗集,包括法语、德语、捷克语、波兰语、意大利语、韩文、西班牙语等等,我感到最难的是诗歌语言的翻译,从严格意义上讲诗歌是不可译的,它永远要留下遗憾。

用一个形象的比喻,诗歌翻译就像一条小船,它正在从此岸驶向彼岸,而彼岸永远是可望而不可即的目标,而翻译家就像一位舵手,他要力争离岸边越近越好。诗歌的翻译最好由诗人来完成,我有一本保加利亚文的诗集,据说翻译得很好,它就是由一位保加利亚诗人和一位汉学家共同合作完成的。

读外国诗人的翻译诗,我还是喜欢读穆旦、戴望舒、戈宝权的翻译作品,因为他们都是诗人。当然,也有许多天才的作家,他们掌握和使用语言的能力都很强,比如

Mention should be made of the USA where extreme diversity is apparent and no single tendency typifies the age. For one thing, the emergence of the former sub-culture writing, ie, the Yiddish and Black varieties, has proved to be subversive of the traditional literary history. Jewish writers I.J. Singer and Saul Bellow were awarded the vital distinction of Nobel Prize. Ellison came out with his masterpiece, *The Invisible Man.* Langston Hughs published his lyrical poems. They have all become respectable names appropriated into the textbooks, made required readings for captive and compulsory readers to the extent the contemporary American literary scene is a choice locale where de-centering cultural diversity reaps its most spectacular harvest.

I believe what has happened on the other shores of the Pacific Ocean supplies a fresh perspective on the burgeoning upsurge and importance of the ethnic writing, either writers being of ethnic origin or their works addressing ethnic themes In China. If, say, an attempt at ranking 100 top living Chinese writers in the Hall of Literary Fame is to be made, I rest fully assured 20 ethnic contenders will come off victorious. The same cannot be said of the early years of PRC when heavy weight ethnic writers and poets are both a rarity and oddity.

A word here must be in place of writers persisting in the writing in their mother tongue, a decision that deserves respect and applause. The unique virtue of the folk tongue consists in enabling the writer to give it the scope and dignity of a literary medium ,capable of expressing the subtlest thoughts and deepest emotions specific to their native people. The only problem is the size of the readership. Translation has a role to play, a very difficult one again. Despite the increasing inventory of ethnic writers being translated into Chinese, the language "enjoying the widest national currency", much more remains out of the perception of the larger reading public. I made the mention of I.J.Singer, the most esteemed writer of the Yiddish literature. Yet the world had to wait till his friend Saul Bellow translated his works of literary permanence to hail what a haunting treatment he had made of the superstitious pieties of Hasidic life. Translations of other languages were based upon Bellow's.

Roughly speaking, my poetic works have been translated into 12 foreign languages, including French, German, Czech, Polish, Italian, Korean and Spanish etc. Translation has been a nightmare in allcases .Even the best translation leaves the original stripped of most of its color and flavor, its weight, irony and poetry, without any intention to disparage the service translators have rendered us. In a strict sense, poetic translation is impossible, as aptly jibed by Frost "Poetry is what gets lost in translation."

I intend to compare it to a small boat adrift in the river. The translator almost rows himself out as he attempts to get as close to the opposite bank as possible. Poetic translation is best executed by poets-translators. I am told my poems come out brilliantly in Bulgarian, a feat co-achieved by a Bulgarian poet and a Bulgarian sinologist.

When it comes to poetic translations, I prefer those done by Mu Dan, Dai Wangshu and Ge Baoquan to others, because these three are poets translators in one. Of course, there is a special

说俄裔美国作家纳博科夫、苏联少数民族作家艾特玛托夫,他们大都使用母语之外的第二种语言写作,并且都取得了骄人的成就。

从20世纪70年代以后,世界文学的格局发生了很大的变化,就美国而言,许多少数民族裔的作家诗人开始纷纷进入文坛的主流。美国黑人女作家托尼·莫里森,她的小说《所罗门之歌》《柏油孩子》在英语世界产生了广泛影响,她的大部分作品也被翻译成了中文,你现在到任何一个城市稍大一点的书店去找她的书,能找到六七种。

20世纪50年代兴起的拉丁美洲爆炸文学、魔幻现实主义文学可以说影响了全世界。长篇小说《玉米人》《总统先生》的作者阿斯图里亚斯,早在20世纪60年代就获得了诺贝尔文学奖,大家所熟悉的智利诗人巴勃鲁·聂鲁达,也获得了诺贝尔文学奖,其实在此之前,他的同胞女诗人米斯特拉尔早已获得了这一荣誉,马尔克斯在20世纪80年代初又将诺贝尔文学奖揽入怀中,将拉丁美洲文学推到了世界文学的最前沿。

因为这些作家和诗人,拉丁美洲文学不再被边缘化,在这个时期还有一些作家和诗人,无疑是拉丁美洲文学中永远不可被遗忘的名字,他们的文学成就或许一点都不低于前面所提到的那些获奖者,这里面有西班牙诗人洛尔迦、秘鲁诗人塞萨尔·巴列霍、阿根廷作家诗人博尔赫斯等等。

东欧文学很长时间也不为人所关注,其实在今天世界文学的版图中,东欧的作家扮演着重要的角色。捷克诗人赛弗尔特、作家米兰·昆德拉、波兰的女诗人申博尔斯卡、诗人米沃什、诗人鲁热维奇等等,都具备广泛的国际影响,其中有三位还获得诺贝尔文学奖。有趣的是,这些作家都是文化特性非常鲜明的作家,像捷克的诗人赛佛尔特,就被捷克人尊崇为他们的民族诗人,这些作家和诗人甚至终其一生都在歌颂他的民族、祖国和生养他的土地。

有的作家一生都在写他生活的"小地方",这种情况在中外文学史上并不鲜见。美国作家福克纳的小说,写的是美国南方的一个小地方的生活;中国作家沈从文一生都在写他童年的生活,写他永远的湘西。现在看来,这些作品的价值都非常高,他们的作品都是地域特色和人类意识相统一的杰作。

以上我向大家随性介绍了这么多杰出的作家和诗人,他们无疑都代表着他们的民族,是他们民族精神和文化的代言人,这些世界级的作家其中不少在他们所生活的国度也是少数民族,他们已经为我们树立了光辉的榜样,增强了我们的文学信心。

group of writers proficient both in their mother tongue and foreign languages. Nabokov and Aitmatov are two bilingual users who have left us brilliant, immortal creations.

Back in the 1970s of the 20th century, world literature had witnessed a fundamental metamorphosis as evidenced by the rise of the sub-culture writers and poets being critically acknowledged by main stream critics. Toni Morrison is an American women novelist, winner of Nobel Prize in 1993, known to the English speaking world for masterpieces like *Song of Solomon*, *Tar Boy*, for their epic themes, vivid dialogue, and richly detailed characters. Most of her works are well translated into Chinese, some appearing in 6 or seven versions.

Again as is known to all, Magical realism has burst forth as one of the most influential literary schools in the 20th century and in vogue across the whole globe. Guatemalan, Miguel Angel Asturias has best showcased his talent and influence in two major novels, ie, *Hombres de maíz* and ,*El Senor Presidente*.Previously Neruda ,enjoying worldwide fame as a poet, and his books were being translated into virtually all the major languages of the world .In 1971 Neruda won the Nobel Prize for Literature.Together with a Guatemala women poet Menchú Tum Rigoberta, winner of the Nobel Peace Prize (1992), Garcia Marquez, Latin American literature has been pushed to the forefront of the highest order of the human imagination.

Thanks to the above galaxy of distinguished writers and poets, far from being marginalized, Latin American literature has grown into one of the most prestigious literary traditions in the world. Apart from these lionized in the west, the Hispanic world has also produced a host of talents of note, though not recipients of major literary distinction, but nevertheless, of equal merits and their names deserve our remembrance, such as Spanish poet Lorca, Peru poet Vallejo, Argentina writer-scholar Borges.

A traditional enclave much neglected, eastern Europe buds with a string of resounding names such as Czech poet Serfeit, Czech writer Kundera and Polish poetess Borka, poet Czesaw Milosz, poetTadeusz Rozewicz and three of them being winners of Nobel Prize.Eastern European tradition has matured and flourished, giving us these men of letters of exceptional literary brilliance whose works all take roots in the native soil and they seek to sanctify again the cultural grandeur of their home country.

In neutralizing Euro-centered "power discourse", regionalist writing wins universal respect as exemplified in the novels of Faulkner's stamp-sized "Yorknapatawpha country", "pictured in a condition of stasis, feeding on old memories and atrophied by old hurts". Chinese regionalist Shen Congwen's works, exclusively devoted to his idealized small town west of Hunan, celebrate the virtues of medieval pieties in jeopardy to affirm the primacy of the mythical imagination under the menace of modern civilization. In retrospective, this strain of fictional primitivism commands the regard of posterity because it is on a very high moral plane in advocacy of reinstating the wholeness of life in modern society, a perfect fusing of the sense of ethnicity and the vision of humanity.

这些作家的作品,大多深刻而全景式地反映了他所处的那个时代和民族的真实生活。

难怪有人把马尔克斯的小说称为拉丁美洲的百科全书,把阿契贝的小说称为非洲的百科全书。我觉得树立文学的信心和文学的理想都同样重要,我们只有真正置身于我们民族伟大的文化传统,深入我们民族的心灵世界里面去,我们才可能准确地呈现出我们的民族在这个新的时代进行的创造,这里包括物质的创造和精神的创造。

讲到这里,我给大家介绍一个有趣的事,在20世纪70年代末,中国已经翻译出版了马尔克斯的中短篇小说集,说实在的,当时的阅读者并不多,马尔克斯1982年获得诺贝尔文学奖之后,他的作品才开始畅销。特别是《百年孤独》在中国出版后,才掀起了一股拉丁美洲爆炸文学热,有意思的是,在此之前所谓处于中国文学中心的北京、上海许多作家对马尔克斯是何许人根本不了解,而相反我们处在西部的少数民族作家却早已开始阅读他的作品。我记得我和藏族作家扎西达娃、色波等人,那时候就在一起相互热议马尔克斯的小说,这是因为我们对马尔克斯有一种天然的亲近感,我们从他的作品中能找到许多对应的东西,他的作品给我们很大的启示,就是处于弱势的边缘文学,在某种时候也能创造文学的奇迹。马尔克斯的道路,从某种意义而言就是我们的道路,他给我们提出了一个又一个疑问,而这些疑问最终以他的作品所获得的世界级的成功而得以解答。

由于马尔克斯的影响,扎西达娃的作品《西藏系在牛皮结上的魂》无疑是那个时期最优秀的小说之一。在这方面西班牙诗人洛尔迦的诗歌、古巴黑人诗人尼古拉斯·纪廉的诗歌,在当时的文学环境下都对我们产生了重要影响。我现在已经去过全世界四五十个国家,经历了许多重要的文化事件,也结识了许多不同国家的重要作家诗人,我认为,一个作家一定要具备高远的文化眼光,要善于向别的作家和文化学习,当然我们一方面不能妄自菲薄,同时也不能狂妄自大。文学是需要借鉴的,我们一定要向那些世界级的大师借鉴,要把我们追求的目标定得更高一些。许多少数民族作家,在成长的过程中都有一个文化觉醒的过程,作为作家,我们应该是这个民族中最早苏醒的人,我们是黎明的号手,同时又是未来的预言家。所以说一个作家的学习和借鉴是非常重要,就是一个成熟的作家,一生中也不能放松对经典作品的学习,在这方面俄罗斯文学巨人列夫托尔斯泰就是我们的楷模。

尽管我现在行政工作非常繁忙,但是对经典的阅读,对当代一些世界性作家的

In the forgoing survey, I have introduced a roaster of exemplary writers and poets, most of whom being of ethnic origin, who have earned the distinction of world standing by identifying with and faithfully depicting the way of life specific to the nationality to which they belong by birth. Their artistic ardor enables them to author novels, poems, short stories that both entertain and delight their contemporaries, reveal the spiritual depths of their cultural heritage with technical mastery and profound human insight and provide the foundation and impulse for an increasingly enriched body of world culture.

No wonder Marquez's novels and Achebe's are credited to be encyclopedias of two continents, economically, politically and culturally marginalized in the scheme of things. For literary pursuits, confidence matters as much as zest. We must be steeped in our own traditions before we attempt to take our own language and give it the scope, fluidity and grandeur of a literary medium capable of translating our subtlest thought and deepest emotions into works of immortal worth and lasting glory in this brave new world.

I shall pause here to tell you an anecdote. Back in the latter part of the 1970s when Marquez's translated Selected Stories was made available, the reading public gave it a cold shoulder. Only after he was awarded the icon prize in 1982, his works appeared on the list of bestsellers. Following the publication of his masterpiece One Hundred Years of Solitude, Latin American Literature became a buzz word on the tip of every body's mouth. Interesting to note, in what is known as the centers of high culture, Beijing and Shanghai, Marquez was absolutely nobody. Yet prior to the onset of his vogue in China, we ethnic writers operating on the margin in the west of China, including Tibetans Zhaxi Dawa and Sebo, were fascinated with him, approaching him with special affection. There is a natural affinity at work that we read much of him that is absent from other sources. The moral: that is how the steel is tempered and the marginalized might one day come off triumphant. He poses both quarries and solutions typified in his phenomenal success in beating a path to the podium of the Nobel Prize awarding ceremony.

Inspired by the magical realism, Zhaxi Dawa came out with *The Tibetan Soul Fastened to the Ox Hide Knot*, one of the finest short stories at the time. The seminal influences of Spanish poet Lorca and Cuban Nicolá s Guillé n (1902—1989) must also be acknowledged in the then literary environment. As luck would have it, I am a widely travelled man, setting my foot on the soil of over 50 countries, participating many cultural events, befriending a host of major poets and writers in various countries and these personal contacts, occasions and others, I have made of learning experiences a good learner will miss at his own peril. We ethnic writers ,trumpeters of dawn and prognosticators of future, must be the first to awaken to the importance of learning from all that is the best of being written and having being written by classical and great writers, because what has been preserved of their work counts among the most precious possessions of mankind. As Einstein points out, what a person thinks on his own without being stimulated by the thoughts and experiences of other people is even in the best case rather paltry and monotonous.

作品的阅读从未停止过,我始终保持着对阅读的兴趣,最近我正在阅读刚才提到过的阿尔巴尼亚作家卡莱达的作品,这是重庆出版社刚刚出版的他的一本小说,名字叫《破碎的四月》。我建议大家一定要有更为广泛的阅读面,哲学、人类学、民族学、社会学的领域我想都应该涉猎,这是一个作家必备的文学素养。就我的经验看,一个作家的文学修养好,他的文学气质也会很好,而他的作品都会达到一定的高度,不会太参差不齐。但是我又要提醒大家,面对浩如烟海的文化遗产,我们的阅读也要有所选择,要选择一些和你的文学气质很相近的作家的作品来阅读,有的作品要精读,要进行反复研究。契诃夫、莫泊桑是短篇小说大师,写短篇小说的人就应该很好地去研究小说的结构、对人物的细节描写。

意大利作家布扎蒂、卡尔维洛都是具有幻想主义色彩的作家,他们的小说技巧都非常高,读他们的长篇小说就像读一部寓言。当然还有不少作家,可以说他们的小说都充满着诗意,比如像古巴的卡彭铁尔、法国的玛格丽特·杜拉斯。说到这里,我想起一件事,前不久在北师大参加一个国际性的文化活动,有一位中国作家在演讲时说到,马尔克斯的《百年孤独》他只读到一半就再读不下去了,我不知道他是想说明自己对《百年孤独》不屑一顾,还是因为这本小说不忍卒读,但是我想不管是什么原因,我们对这样一本20世纪的经典小说应该给予充分的尊重,当然作家读什么书是个人的选择和自由。

在我即将结束今天演讲的时候,我想朗诵最近写的两首诗给大家,算是赠送给大家的礼物。前不久我刚刚访问了南美的智利,去朝拜了巴勃罗·聂鲁达的故乡。聂鲁达是艾青先生的朋友,艾青先生更是我的老师。聂鲁达是20世纪最伟大的诗人之一,他一生去过世界许多地方,最后离开这个世界的时候选择的长眠之地就在智利海峡上,这次我专门去了他的故居,祭拜了他的墓地。在聂鲁达的故乡——智利北部,我们去了一个叫巴塔哥尼亚的地区,这个地方有一个叫卡尔斯卡尔的印第安人族群,由于历史的原因这个族群只剩下最后一个人,这个人被誉为"玫瑰祖母",她活到九十八岁,她的死让这支印第安人族群在地球上永远地消失了,这首诗也是我献给"玫瑰祖母"的挽歌。现在我念给大家听。

  你是风中
    凋零的最后一朵玫瑰

Tolstoy sets us an example by keeping on learning to the end of his days.

Despite a busy agenda incurred by my administrative office, I have never loosened a constant browsing in the works firmly established in world literature. My zest for reading seldom wanes. Moments ago I made the mention of Albanian Kadare's Broken April, a Chinese translation recently released by Chongqing Publishing House, a book in my recent companion. I make a point here urging all to browse in, at least, books of philosophy, anthropology, ethnography, sociology, etc, as I believe a kaleidoscopic knowledge is a prerequisite for fostering a literary temperament for a modern writer. My experience shows good literary accomplishment necessarily presupposes good literary temperament. But of course, there are whole libraries of learning to be pursued and we must make a choice. Some books, say Chekov's, Maupassant's, both masters of short stories, must be intensively read and studied with an eye to structure and characterization to be absorbed and adapted.

Italian writers Baraldi and Calvino are sometimes classified as magical realists. To read them is like reading an allegory with technical mastery and peculiar human insight to be perceived. Still others, such as Carpentier and Duras, lyrically reflect the pains and pathos of life. This topic reminds me of a small incident. Not long ago, I was invited to attend an international cultural event held in Beijing Normal University. One Chinese writer confessed to a very sorry reading experience of *One Hundred Years of Solitude* during his lecture, saying he was barely half way before he dropped the book totally disappointed. I construed this as a gesture of his disdain for Marquez. I feel sorry for him because we are talking of an established canon. Due respect is due respect, as a writer to a peer writer of world renown, no matter how our reading penchant.

Before I conclude my lecture, I am in the mood to recite to you two of my recent poems as a souvenir of parting. Not long ago, I had the fortune to make a pilgrimage to the hometown of Pablo Neruda, himself an intimate friend of Ai Qing, and Ai Qing, as you know, China's most famous lyrical bard in the 20th century, incidentally Ai Qing is my mentor. Neruda is one of the greatest poets in modern times, a widely travelled man, but he chose to get laid to rest in a place close to the Chilean Straits. I paid my homage to his home and his graveyard. The trip also led me to visit a place called Patagonia in the north of Chile, where an Indian tribe used to call it home. Somehow by a quirk of misfortune, the Kaweskar Indians had all deceased except one old lady, dubbed " Grandmother Rossa" who lived to 98 of age. But the time I went to pay her my visit, she also died, symbolizing the tragic and inexorable ending of a whole Indian tribe. I composed the swan song dedicated to the memory of Grandmother Rossa and her people.

Grandmother Rossa

Dedicated to the last Indian of the kaweskar tribe in the Patagonia region of Chile.She lived to the age of 98 and was known as grandmother Rossa

You were a final rose

Withered in the wind

你的离去
曾让这个世界在瞬间
进入全部的黑暗
你在时间的尽头回望死去的亲人
就像在那浩瀚的星空里
倾听母亲发自摇篮的歌声
悼念你,玫瑰祖母
我就如同悼念一棵老树
在这无限的宇宙空间
你多么像一粒沙漠中的尘埃
谁知道明天的风
会把它吹向哪里?
我们为一个生命的消失而伤心
那是因为这个生命的基因
已经从大地的子宫中永远地死去
尽管这样,在这个星球的极地
我们依然会想起
杀戮、迫害、流亡、苦难
这些人类最古老的名词
玫瑰祖母,你的死是人类的灾难
因为对于我们而言
从今以后我们再也找不到一位
名字叫卡尔斯卡尔的印第安人
再也找不到你的族群
通往生命之乡的那条小路

我今天就讲到这里,谢谢大家!

204

Your departure plunged the world
Into an instant of total darkness
At the end of time's corridor
You gazed back upon dead relatives
As if you listened to a lullaby
Amid the starry heavens
I mourn you, Grandmother Rossa
As I would an old tree
In these limitless cosmic reaches
How like grain of desert sand you are
No one knows where tomorrow's wind
May carry you
We are saddened by a life's cessation
Because its genes are forever departed
From the uterus of the good earth
For my part, at the far end of this planet
I cannot help but think
Of slaughter, destruction, banishment, calamity
These words as ancient as mankind
Grandmother Rossa
Your death is a human disaster
Because we who remain
Will never again find and Indian
Who bears the name Kaweskar
Never again can we find your tribe
And its little road leading to the land of life

大美青海:梦想世界与现实世界的影像

2009年在成都举行的四川金熊猫国际电视节上的演讲

2009年10月3日

尊敬的女士们、先生们,朋友们:

今天,我们满怀愉快、赞美和感激的心情,相聚在美丽的天府之国成都。我们因为置身于这生机勃勃的城市而愉快,因为置身于这其乐融融的氛围而赞美,因为置身于这亲如一家的支持而感激。首先,请允许我代表青海550多万各族人民,向出席今天开幕式的各位来宾、各位朋友,表示最热烈的欢迎!向你所有长期以来关心、支持青海经济社会发展的四川各界人士和各族人民,表示最衷心的感谢!

虽然已经进入立冬季节,成都平原的气候仍然如金秋一般高洁清爽,天府之国的人们依旧如春天一样热情灿烂。不难想象,作为一个自然创造和人文创造的富庶之地,这片美丽而慷慨的土地为人类文明奉献了多少惊喜和骄傲。正因为如此,很久以前它就进入了高原民族的视野,在"尔来四万八千岁,不与秦塞通人烟"的古蜀国时代,一脉相承、源远流长的江河就已经把两地的先民联系在一起了。经历了2008年"5·12"特大自然灾害的考验和洗礼,这片宽厚的土地埋葬苦难之后,更加增添了不屈不挠的英雄主义色彩,令世界为之敬仰。

Qinghai Travel-A Movable Feast of Sights and Sensations Guranteed

An Address at the 2009 Chengdu Golden Panda Intl TV Festival
3rd, October, 2009

Distinguished ladies, gentlemen and friends:

Today, overjoyed, imbued with pent-up enthusiasm and full of gratitude, we are meeting here in Chengdu ,the capital city of this famed paradise land of Sichuan. We are overjoyed at setting our feet on the soil of this magnificent city of Chengdu and the hospitality of our hosts simply overwhelms us that we see fit and necessary this moment to speak out what we have felt and experienced. First and foremost on behalf of the 5.5 million populace of Qinghai Province, I would like to extend my warmest heartfelt welcome to all the distinguished guests and friends attending this opening ceremony. This I will never weary of repeating to all those present on this occasion: we are deeply grateful for the long standing caring and supporting of our social and economic cause rendered on our benefit from all walks of society from our beloved neighbor Sichuan.

Winter has already set in back our Plateau home, yet on this shore of hinterland China proper, autumnal sunshine still illuminates golden and clear. People who have dwelt here radiate their share of kindness and warmth of spring days. For a land fabled for its rich culture and fascinating and eventful history, what human work but of heroic character and what lay creativity but of divine inspiration have not been expected and anticipated? This city of unbelievable beauty and plenty evokes in us a very intimate vision of ancient Shu Kingdom, then as self-contained and inaccessible to the mainstream civilization of the Central Plains as the ancient Qinghai, but due to two of China's major waterways——the Yangtse and Yellow Rivers rising in Qinghai and flowing eastward through the Sichuan Basin, our ancestors bound our destiny and sympathy together. We still retain alive the painful memory of The May 12th earthquake that struck this glorious land, devastated its innocent residents and left about 87,000 dead or missing one year ago. The tragedy, if anything, adds glory and glamour to Sichuan people and endear you substantially to a world spellbound, wide-eyed at the heroism and courage displayed by a people undetered and unfraid when confronting the ultimate terror of Nature.

成都是一座具有丰富的历史传承和开放创新精神的文化名城,借助这个城市的活力,借助四川金熊猫国际电视节这个成功的传播平台,现在,我们带着青海历史的嘱托、青海今天的自信和青海未来的期待,把一个"大美青海"展示在朋友们面前。

我要感谢朋友们对青海的关注,同时我将承诺,所有对青海的浓厚兴趣都会获得她慷慨的回报,那就是你能够用生命体验的快乐和惊喜、能够用心灵经历的感动与热爱。

首先请允许我对青海的基本特点做一个简单介绍。

如果我说,青海是一座孕育着文化梦想的高原;青海是一方洋溢着万物和谐的乐土;青海是一种启示着生存意义的境界;青海是一幅隐藏着造化之谜的画卷——用这样的话语描述青海显得过分吗?我相信一点也不会。

青海的确具有一些与众不同之处,呈现出迥然不同的地理风貌和文化个性,这些特点很容易使她同中国其他省份区别出来。也许我可以这样描述她的形象——

青藏高原创造了她的骨骼

青海省地处中国西部腹地,是世界屋脊青藏高原的主体部分之一。全省平均海拔3000米以上,面积72万多平方千米,总人口550多万。青海省因境内中国最大的湖泊青海湖而得名。

以高原为主体,青海省的地理构成呈现出十分壮观的多样性。包括辽阔草原、高大山脉、盆地、戈壁、江河、湖泊,尤其以纵贯的东昆仑山和发源境内的黄河、长江、澜沧江而被称为山宗水源之地。被誉为中国"第一神山"的昆仑山,是我国神话传说的摇篮和道教的发源地。千百年来,昆仑山孕育了博大精深的道教文化,留下了无数美

Chengdu has ranked beyond doubt among the most cultured, historical and innovative cities. However, this metropolis in the southwest of China has also been known as the home of the Giant Panda-China's No 1 animal which entitles Chengdu to play host to the Golden Panda Intl TV Festival since 2000.Entrusted by 5.5 million Qinghai people, I have embarked upon this trip of tourism promotion, determined to showcase Qinghai as your next ideal destination of long distance travel.

Words cannot express my gratitude at the quality and spirit of our friends who have shown their long standing interest in our geography and here's my promise that we will never let you down, and armed with the rich stock of tourism highlights and attractions ,old and new, coupled with a stable economic growth and increasingly improved social facilities, which is all to your advantage, we will see to it that your Qinghai tour will surely turn into a movable feast of sights and sensations.

Let me continue by sharing with you some of the more obvious rationales. For God's sake , my friends, awaken in your wisdom. Hear me for my cause so you may the better believe. I assert with full assurance that Qinghai, as a result of its strategic position on the Qinghai-Tibet Plateau has been increasingly seen as a new wonderland, a great place for both exotic landscape and cultural biodiversity which stands to unveil some of the most profound mysteries of life. Am I exaggerating things for effect? No, I am stating facts.

On the other hand, the same qualities have made Qinghai an attractive target for entrepreneurs and dream seekers of more spiritual bent. For this fascinating combination of cultural potential and economic prospects, Qinghai distinguishes itself easily from the rest of China, offering not only enchanting sights but also a setting that allows dramatic cultural events to take place on its forbidding snow-capped mount ranges, across its sprawling epic grassland and in the awe inspiring Buddhist shrines. You see, my friends, I simply cannot help recounting its story in terms other than poetic which is more yielding to the spirit.

Marvels Done by Nature's Hand

Lying in the interior innermost of the west of China, Qinghai forms partially the backbone of the The Tibetan Plateau, the world's highest and most extensive landform. With an average altitude of 3000 meters (10,000 feet), it has a territory of 720,000km 2 and a population of 5.5 million. The region derives its name after the largest saline lake 200 kilometers west of Xining ,ie, Qinghai Lake.

Many of the world's highest mountains are found in Qinghai, and two China's and even Asia's major rivers originate in the Plateau-Yellow and Yangtze, and the Mekong of Southeast Asia ——the last one eventually flowing throughout much of Asia and providing sustenance for a considerably large proportion of the continent's population downstream. Due to its alpine geography Qinghai for centuries lay self-contained and inaccessible between the high wall of the Himalayan mountain range to the south and forbidding deserts on the north. Kunlun Mountain,

丽的传说和难解之谜。

可以说，在中国，没有哪个地方像青海这样拥有如此众多，并且在中国地理、中国文化和中国人心理上都占有重要地位的名山大川。正因如此，青海高原才被誉为圣山之故乡、母亲河之摇篮。在这里，你看到的是一种由青海高原特殊地理环境和气候条件造就的美。这种出乎意料的"大美"，就蕴含着自然造化的神奇创意，它带给你视觉的冲击和心灵的震撼。

古羌文明孕育了她的血脉

考古学家证实，在距今三万年左右，青海高原已经有人类活动。诞生于四千多年前的舞蹈纹彩陶盆和柳湾氏族墓地出土的一万多件各式彩陶器，无论从艺术水平、技术手段还是内容表现，都被公认为人类彩陶文明的辉煌。青海是古代羌人部落集团的核心活动区，他们对中国的民族构成和西部民族文化产生了深远影响。

唐朝文成公主入藏，开辟了唐蕃通道，从此把整个青藏高原同中国内地联系起来，使青海成为农业文明与牧业文明融合的核心地区。青海高原的古代文化不仅丰富，而且具有鲜明的地域特点和精神内涵，体现了人们崇拜自然、热爱生命的思想伦理。

多彩生活构成了她的灵魂

青海的山川草原曾经是西部民族交融演化的大舞台。现在世居民族有汉族、藏族、回族、土族、撒拉族和蒙古族。在青海总人口中，汉族之外的民族占46%，其中藏族120多万，回族近100万，土族和撒拉族是青海独有的民族。各民族在不同领域中保持着既有鲜明个性又有现实适用性的历史文化、传统习俗和生产生活方式。

长期以来，青海就是多种宗教信仰并存和多种宗教文化共荣之地，藏传佛教、伊斯兰教、汉传佛教、道教、基督教等多种宗教在青海均有不同程度的传播，创造了一种神秘文化的氛围。不同民族创造形成了丰富的节日、歌舞、音乐、绘画、雕塑、建筑、表演、服饰、文学等艺术形式，这些是享誉中外的优秀文化遗产，又有极高的学术研究价值和旅游观赏价值。民间传统文化和宗教文化的传承，成为人们日常生活与精神生活的重要内容。

今年10月初，联合国教科文组织把中国的一项传统民间艺术列入了《人类非物

China's No.1 sacred mountain, a veritable cradle of cultural myths and Taoist folklores.

It could be safely assumed that no other place in China like Qinghai boasts such an array of awesome mesmerizing mountain ranges that occupy so lofty a place in the hearts of the Chinese race as a whole. So many marvels done by Nature's hand are bound to engender an alien beauty tinged with a pristine magnificence that shocks and captivates.

Earliest Settlers of Qinghai-the Qiang Ethnicity

Archaeologists testify that the first group of human beings intruded upon the region and disturbed its primordial quietude as early as 30,000 years ago. The famous painted pottery unearthed in the Liuwan Burial Ground in proximity to the present day Ledu County dates back to almost 4,000 years ago. In terms of its technology and its themes, Liuwan Pottery counts one of the more matured and accomplished varieties. The point is that Qinghai used to be the hub of the ancient Qiang civilization and the Qiang culture has exerted a profound influence upon the races that came after them that made Qinghai their homeland.

Another landmark artifact is arguably the Tang Tubo Ancient Road blazed by the Tang Princess Wenchen as she journeyed westward to Tibet in a marriage of convenience .Knowingly or unwittingly, for the first time she helped connect the agricultural Middle Kingdom with the pastoralist Qinghai Tibet Plateau.

A Melting Pot of Various Ethnic Groups and Various Spiritual Traditions

Qinghai's massive land mass serves a natural platform where a number of minority groups interact and integrate with one another including Han, Hui, Tu/Monguor and Tibetan. The local traditions and customs are influenced by these distinctive nationalities, in particular the Tibetan, Salar and Tu. The Han accounts for 54% of the total population of its 5.5 million among which the Tibetans number 1.2 million, and Muslims, close to 1 million .The Tu and Salar are rather native to the soil upon which we walk and stand.

Lifestyles aside, various belief systems thrive in Qinghai as Tibetan Buddhism, Islam, Taoism and Christianity have all identified the proper soil to take root in ,hence a special ethos imbuing the whole region for the uninitiated. In such a huge democracy of racial and religious diversity, one witnesses daily the symphony and drama of different festivals, dances, songs, paintings, sculpture, performing art, costume and literature each of which has a need of an entrenched place, a voice of power. These cultural legacies, whose triumphs over matter, over the wilderness, over racial enmities and distances, remain to be both rich food for academia and strong pull for tourists.

It thus came as no surprise to us that in the early October this year that Rekong Art, the pride of local art was added to the list of the Intangible Matrimony of Mankind by UNESCO. Essentially Buddhist in character, Rekong Thangka(scroll painting) prospers here as it meets the intrinsic need of the local people to visualize their potential of the enlightened nature that they see the necessity for the development of an art form which matches their aspirations In the religious

质文化遗产代表作名录》，这项民族智慧的结晶就是青海的"热贡艺术"。青海的热土培育的各类非物质文化遗产是青海各族人民奉献给世界文化的璀璨奇葩，蕴含着富足的文化底蕴和精神资源，是青海和世界对话的人文基础，因此保护好这些弥足珍贵的非物质文化遗产，就是在保护青海走向世界的权利，保护青海人民和世界对话的权利。

历史赋予她光荣的使命

由柴达木盆地被誉为"中国聚宝盆"这个美称，就足以想象青海自然资源的丰富。但是站在新的历史起点，青海省又显示了她另一方面的特殊优势。青海是生态大省，"三江源国家自然保护区"占全省面积的一半，又有"中华水塔"之称，关乎全局的生态地位十分显著。

青海不仅是中国生物物种形成和演化的中心之一，也是世界气候变化的气象哨，拥有世界上最大面积的高寒湿地、高寒草原、灌丛和森林等生态系统，被联合国教科文组织誉为世界四大无公害超净区之一。这里独特的生态系统，不但对中国、对东亚甚至对北半球的大气环流都有极其重要的影响，而且直接影响着我国的天气、气候的形成和演变。

我们提出"生态立省"战略，就是要以保护和建设生态环境为前提，以发展生态经济为核心，以培育生态文化为灵魂，坚持在综合循环利用资源中谋求又好又快发展，在保护建设生态中促进人与自然和谐，走出一条经济发展与环境保护双赢的可持续发展之路。尤其是自2005年国家实施总投资75亿元的三江源生态保护和建设工程以来，局部地区生态环境有所好转。我们相信，在国家的大力支持和全社会的共

arts of the world's many and diverse cultures, the artistic expression of the Rekong artists have reached considerable heights of inspiration unrivalled elsewhere beyond. We are proud to present this artistic jewelry to the world as we deem it not only in terms of its value as a variety of non material asset but also a basis upon which we engage a dialogue with other cultures and other peoples on the planet. In cherishing this artistic heritage, we reserve firm and resolute our right to speak to and with the world.

Our Historical Mission

The very mention of the Qaidam Basin evokes an image of China's Treasure House. When entering 21 st century, Qinghai demonstrates another soft power unique of her own, ie,Qinghai holds an important place in the overall green agenda of China from the macroscopic perspective. The inauguration of the Three Rivers Nature Reserve ,funded and sponsored by the central government, has brought half of the region's territory into protection. This fact alone speaks volumes about our determination to maintain well the last remaining Pure Land of the earth in the very belief that to us, Qinghai-Tibet Plateau, with its wealth of resources represents more than a valuable treasure house. We owe not only all the people living down the Roof of the World but also our children's children when it comes to the use of natural bounty.

Central to the formation and evolution of a host of Sinica biospecies, and deemed the watch tower of global climatic trends, Qinghai is endowed with an ecosystem composed of the largest alpine wetland, grassland, bushes and woodland, acclaimed by United Nations as one of the four pollution free super clean areas. Spread across the isolated tableland, much of it frozen for months, are deposits of dozens of valuable minerals; oil, coal and natural gas reserves; thousands of plant species; and a variety of native wildlife, much of which exists nowhere. In addition, as most of the Plateau river runoff flows downstream to much of China proper and the rest of Asia, Qinghai serves as both China's and even Asian watershed, it is also an "airshed" for much of the continent to the south and east. Already Yellow and Yangtze, China's two major waterways are diagnosed among the most heavily silted in the world. Deforestation and subsequent soil erosion in Qinghai exacerbate this situation, contributing to downstream flooding. Atmospheric scientists have theorized that the degradation of the Qinghai-Tibetan Plateau may have crucial transnational impacts on weather phenomena, like the Indian monsoon, endangering the livelihoods of millions of farmers in Asia who depend on these rains.

Drawing on the latest theorizing in the scientific community, we have devised our own green agenda featuring eco friendly, recyclable, sustainable and resource-conserving solutions and striving to strike a balance between construction and protection. Initial signs and evidence of progress are many and very promising since the 7.5 billion worth Three River Nature Reserve Project was implemented in 2005.Such costly projects testify to our moral commitment and remitting effort in marching in the direction of an eco province ,the exemplary, cultural and ethical, that the whole world awaits and wishes for, given the fact we also owe an obligation to

同努力下,再造"中华水塔"大美山川的梦想能够早日实现。

"大美青海"理念的提出

我想,"大美青海"最显著的特点,在于它原始壮丽的自然之中蕴含的人类文明与文化,这种文化就像它生存的环境一样,具有某种神秘性,或者说具有某种虽然古老却又不失新鲜和活力的特殊性,它丰厚博大的人性内涵对现代人是一个不可忽略的启示。这种自然和文化正以它特殊的魅力引起世人越来越多的兴趣和探讨。在此自然环境中诞生与发展起来的人类文明和种种文化现象,对重新评判现代文明的得失、揭示人与自然的关系,具有深刻的意义。

所以,青海并不因为地处高原而远离世界,相反,我们可以凭借位居地球之巅的优势而放眼世界,更加清晰地认识我们自身条件的优劣,从而有效地取长补短、扬长避短,走向世界。

近年来,我们在对自身特性和当代社会环境充分认识的前提下,以较大力度进行了一系列文化创意,并且拥有了成功的范例。主要包括以诗意话语书写青海的青海湖国际诗歌节,以文化记忆再现青海的国际唐卡艺术与文化遗产博览会,以交响音画传播青海的国际水与生命音乐之旅——世界防治荒漠化和干旱日主题音乐会,以影像青海融入世界的三江源国际摄影节和世界山地纪录片节以及"大美青海"展示推介活动。还有环青海湖国际公路自行车赛、青海高原世界杯攀岩赛、国际抢渡黄河极限挑战赛三个体育品牌。这些既有青海自然人文内涵,又具独特创新视角的文

support well the regional civil society on the materialist plane ,because ultimately reaching our goals depends on high levels of economic growth with reference to a win-win green blueprint.

The Concept of Qinghai-as an Exotic World, a Land of Pristine Preeminence

In light of the above considerations, when urged to produce a neat characterization of Qinghai,I have proposed to center our promotion on The Concept of Qinghai-an Exotic World ,a Land of Pristine Preeminence as we believe Qinghai's claim to distinction lies in its special topography, racial harmony and religious diversity. The combination of its religious shrines, scenic spots and natural resources original to the Plateau forms the core of its charm, all irreplaceable sources of life and inspiration. They constitute an important part in the tapestry of China's history and also represents significant economic and cultural potential for the future. While mapping the special cultural history unique to the Plateau, we need to amass the details, capture the events, identify the heroes and icons, the artifacts and art works of them and present them to China's and the world's tourist population as we believe with the tourism industry in ascendency, people are more and more weary of the over industrialized ways of life and more and more hungry for the exotic, the pristine and the wild. We as decision makers of local tourism industry, must respond to this yearning by unveiling, unlocking and enriching this hitherto best kept but ill-articulated cultural heritage of Qinghai.

People are naturally drawn to things genuinely exotic, delicate and precious to the heart and they marvel at what they have discovered where they least expect-Qinghai, a land of stark contrast, of supreme spiritual plenty and relative economic poverty, a land where some of the most enchanting sights, with such an intensity of alienness and beauty, still remain locked in the forbidding landscape and to be explored in the wildness. Our task is to present and articulate properly so that when tourists flock to Qinghai they will be able to better understand the cultural background of these worthy destinations they visit and appreciate the emotional ,the physical and spiritual aspects of the Plateau. In my opinion, moreover, various cultural phenomena, artifacts and art works born of such special wild context have critical implications in our reappraisal of modern urban centered civilization and human relationship with Nature.

Therefore distance becomes a merit, plus. We see from our Plateau vantage point better and more clearly where we humans came and where we are heading.

Fully aware of our strength and limitation, we have in recent years come out with a scenarios of culture oriented promotional projects to market Qinghai as an ideal destination of long distance travel to the world, with a considerable measure of success. For example, The International Poetry Festival of Qinghai Lake, inaugurated in August 2007,(first session) through an energetic and massive poetic action, The Festival's theme reflects the universal nature of poetry as a bridge between cultures, fostering global unity and concern for maintaining well the last remaining Pure Land in China and the world as a whole .Ventures of similar character include the International Exhibition of Thangka Art and Cultural Heritages, Intl Musical Journey of Water

化旅游体育品牌,已经成为我们进行文化创意的代表作。

通过近些年来的对外开放和对外交流,我们认为,关于青海的评价,至少有几点已经得到国内外的共识:对于发现生命、捕捉人与自然之美、把瞬间化作永恒的摄影艺术来说,青海是摄影家梦寐以求的天堂;对于探索生存、感知文化,把时空流逝化作记忆的影视艺术来说,青海是纪录片创作取之不尽的富矿;同样,对那些执着于特殊环境与人性秘密的解读者、对那些迷恋着神奇生活和情感故事的讲述者来说,青海是西部片拍摄的最佳基地;对世界各地的旅游者来说,青海是一个在远方寻找自我、在他乡回归家园的旅途。

"中国(青海)三江源国际摄影节暨世界山地纪录片节",正是依托了这种自然造化之奇和人文智慧之美的双重优势而举办的国际盛会。我一再强调,青海是昆仑山的故乡,是黄河、长江、澜沧江的发源地,而这山宗水源是一个具有独特地理标志的文化概念,也是我们重点创意的国际品牌。它的目的在于,以文化的内涵,以艺术的形式,构建一条从高原通向世界的大路,通过这条道路扩大开放、传播信息、增进交流、推动发展,让青海与世界并肩而行。

2006年到2008年,我们连续三年成功举办三江源国际摄影节,借助于世界对青藏高原的关注。2008年,我们同时策划并举办了世界山地纪录片节,成功打造了又一个使世界不同国家、不同地域、不同种族的影视艺术家们创作、研讨和交流对话的国际性平台。世界山地纪录片节旨在以影视的形式、艺术的视角、人文的思考,致力探

and Life by means of symphonic and visual works, Concerts featuring call to action to fight aridity and desertification worldwide, The Three River Nature Reserve Areas Intl Photographing Festival, World Mountain Documentary Festival of Qinghai China. On top of these heavyweight campaigns, we have also launched three new sports brands-the Tour de Qinghai Lake International Extreme Challenge of Crossing the Yellow River Qinghai China, World Cliff Climbing Tournament. These efforts, among others, have been crystallization of our relentless searching for more appropriate ways to discover the inner beauty of our Plateau home, to capture fleeting moments of sanctity and excellence of our physical and cultural environment, weave in considerable strands of history and lore, and communicate them to the world in a manner that is both original and effective.

The result is that Qinghai is now increasingly seen as a wonderland of pioneering spirited photographers, a veritable goldmine for documentary artists who find a worthy story to narrate in a wild world reminiscent of America's West. For tourists home and abroad, Qinghai means a journey home, a journey to reconnect with their SELF lost somewhere at a point in history but restored at a remote lovely place called Qinghai.

The Three River Nature Reserve Areas Intl Photographing Festival &World Mountain Documentary Festival of Qinghai merits one more word of eulogy as it is launched to present Qinghai in its most favorable light-the natural and the spiritual. Let me reiterate again: Qinghai is home to Kunlun Mountain which comprises the DNA code of the cultural traditions specific to the Chinese race. Qinghai also serves the fountainhead of the Yellow ,Yangtze and Lancang Rivers. These two essential facts prompt us to have an inkling of the enormous challenges lying ahead .For the story to be fashioned must be archetypal in scale ,having a cosmic ,if rough somewhat, visual appeal, presented with care and tact to lure more and more people and tourists to see them and understand their true meaning. Evidently our success will be judged by the extent to which we have constructed an expressway, both virtual and real, that admits and allows the free traffic of information and personnel, to and fro, linking this Plateau province with the world. This must happen if Qinghai is to keep abreast of the rest of mankind.

Today in the presence of distinguished friends here, with buoyancy and pride ,I would like to announce that many years of our arduous endeavor has paid off in the successful hosting of the Intl Photographing Festival of Three River Nature Reserve in a row from 2006 to 2008. Plus the organizing of the World Documentary Festival (2008,the first session).These two festivals supply a mega venue where artists and documentary makers of different races exchange ideas, showcase their talent, publicize their research and swap experience about each's renowned trade. The latter event especially is praiseworthy as the stories told are both credible and fresh, using real people and highlighting true location, aided by the state of art technology, to explore the relationship of the ethnic people with their environment and reflect upon the common destiny of mankind in large to expand public awareness of cultural diversity. These undertakings involve artists in action recording and presenting areas rarely accessible to urban dwellers, culture forms otherwise

索一种特殊的地域环境和文化背景下人与自然的关系，讲述万物生存的故事，并以此反省社会的发展和人的共同命运，为实现人类多元文化的共享与传承而努力。同时通过交流艺术、传播文化，充分展示大美青海的无限魅力，推动青海走向世界。

青海自然和人文的博大丰厚，感召我们以艺术的目光发现她的魅力，以充满想象力的话语讲述它的故事。

大美青海正等待着你的到来。

deemed arcane and esoteric as well as the heartfelt values upheld by humans like us, no matter where they are located and what kind of lifestyles they exhibit.

To conclude, Let me extend an invitation to everyone who is one way or another drawn to Qinghai which beckons tourists far and wide to listen to its story narrated with rich imaginative power and taste its primordial qualities with their own eyes and ears.

青海最后净土的入口与现实中的文化创意及其品牌
——一个诗人副省长亲身经历并讲述的文化事件

广州讲坛主题演讲

2009年9月

有机会到广州来跟大家见面,我觉得这是一种缘分。了解中国宗教文化的人,特别是了解中国历史背景的人都知道,青海是中国很重要的文化发祥地之一,尤其是我们的昆仑神话。昆仑神话可以说是中国文化最重要的根脉之一,大量的文化遗迹和遗址就在青海。人类进入了21世纪之后很多国家和民族都在重新诠释自己的神话。重新诠释神话我想不是偶然的,当离出发点越来越远的时候,人类往往在回望自己的过去、回望自己的童年,特别是在重塑自己的文化神话的时候,要找到一些最根本的东西,也就是人类的文化根基。

青海可以说是中国昆仑神话的重要遗址留存地,也可以说是中国昆仑神话最重要的发祥地之一。从这个角度来说,青海是一个烧高香的地方,非常讲究缘分,今天这么多的朋友相聚在广州,相聚在这么有特殊意义的讲坛,我认为也是一种缘分。按照藏传佛教的说法,我们擦肩而过是五十年修成的,如果我们成为朋友,像今天这样近距离地交流,这是一百年的修为,我们一百年前已经有了缘分,所以我非常高兴今天能够在这个地方跟大家见面。

我首先要感谢朋友们对青海的关注,同时我特别希望对青海感兴趣的朋友,如果听了我的演讲能够到青海去,看看这个地方壮美的自然风光、人文历史和民族风情,我认为这是给我最大最好的回报。另外我也相信,大家到青海去会体验到一种从

Qinghai the Entrance into the Last Pure Land
A Poet-Politician Talks about Himself at the Nucleus of the Burgeoning Provincial Creativity Industry Agendas
September, 2009

I must call this opportunity to be able to address an audience in Canton the karma coming down all right. To the initiated and knowledgeable, Qinghai has been lately proven to be a major cultural sphere of Chinese civilization. For one thing, Mt.Kunlun, running parallel to the Himalaya range, the highest of its kind-further north and through the land mass of Qinghai is where several China's great rivers take origin, fed with cold water from its melting glaciers. Mt Kunlun is also associated with the creation of the most important body of cosmogony myth of the Chinese race, testified by the Pre-historical excavation sites scattered across the province. Entering the 21th century, many countries and peoples tend to reinterpret their own mythological systems, a trend I personally believe to be of no accidental nature. We all know ,myths, as a basic constituent of human culture, a self-image of people in a given world, occur in the history of all human traditions and communities. The primacy of myths stands out most clearly at momentous moments when a living mythology has to come to terms with the world in which it is transmitted and inevitably goes through processes of historical transformation.

Geologically speaking, China's most important stock of cultural myths, ie, the Kunlun Mythology, is found in Qinghai. In other words, Qinghai is the birth place of the Kunlun myth, the repository of China's racial memory. In Buddhist terms, Qinghai is the No 1 sacred shrine for pilgrims. I repeat, I really deem this encounter in Canton the law of karma at work. A Tibetan Buddhist lama advises that, even rubbing shoulder with someone, takes 50 years of good deeds accumulated in one's previous life. What happens under our very noses, I mean, we are at this moment sitting face to face and talk as good friends with friends, should be the result of a century of good will and meritorious deeds. This piece of Buddhist wisdom concerns our prenatal existence and its implication is we should cherish this meeting because we met one another 100 years ago.

I must first of all applaud your concern with Qinghai and I shall deem this trip to Canton mostly rewarding if, some of the audience today ,inspired and moved by what they hear from me , pack their things and make a field tour of Qinghai tasting and savoring the majesty and beauty of

未有过的快乐。

现在人类在经历工业化和后工业化时代，特别是像珠三角这样的地方，作为中国改革开放的前沿，应该说是发展非常快的。整个世界如果按照海洋经济分布的话，中国沿海的经济发展与世界其他海洋经济相比，也是发展很快的地区之一。越是在这种时候，我认为人类恐怕更得寻找一些差异性的东西，我们都在和我们过去的文化，和我们走过的历史进行不断地比较。所以越是在这种时候，我越是希望大家有机会到青海去，去感受这个地方特殊的高原地理、特殊的自然风光和这个地方民族的文化生态。

青海的基本情况

我想简单介绍一下青海的情况，希望大家有一个概括的了解。

过去很多人问我青海有什么标志性的建筑，或者说你去了这么多年能不能给我们介绍一下青海的宗教或者地理人文资源。我跟这些朋友谈的时候，往往会问他们几个问题。首先，长江、黄河和澜沧江的源头在哪里？一般人回答说长江的源头在西藏，黄河的源头在甘肃这一带。这是很多不太熟悉中国地理的人的回答。甚至一些学者在一些学术著作里面也会发生一些误差，前不久有一本书《西藏之水救中国》，这本书在谈到长江、黄河、澜沧江的源头时发生了一个很严重的地理错误。

我在这里并不是说西藏的水对中国不重要，它是非常重要的。西藏是中国的一块宝地，特别是雅鲁藏布江的水，不光对于中国，甚至对于整个亚太地区都是非常重要的。实际上，长江、黄河和澜沧江都发源于青海。现在黄河水的49%是从青海流下来的，长江水的26%一开始是从青海流出去的，澜沧江作为一条国际性的河流流入中国，在中国境内要占46%的水源。从这个意义上来说，长江、黄河、澜沧江这三条养育了东方文明的伟大江河都是从青海流出去的。

大家知道河流对于文明来说是非常重要的，世界上最重要的文明，长江文明、黄河文明、埃及文明、尼罗河文明，都和河流有关。人类最早的生活区域必须选择水源非常充足的地方，这些河流的两岸往往都是最容易、最好发展农耕文明的地方。我们向人类的伟大文明致敬都要向这些河流致敬，因为它们养育了人类的历史和文明。

Qinghai. I certainly can guarantee one thing: you will come back home a happier man.

Most people feel our planet, caught in an era of industrialization and even post-industrialization, is spinning too dizzily fast. As the vanguard of China's opening up drive, Canton has undergone a breathless transformation in the past few decades. Even by world standards, among the coastal economies, the Pearl River Delta is one of the top frontrunners. This fact explains we I exhort you to retrace your way to the less developed areas to place things and events in perspective. The allure is all the more tempting because culture tends to show most authentically where the human trace is the least. Although modernization and change are inevitable, Qinghai is still alpine and wild enough few other places can be. For either in terms of Cultural and Natural Heritage, come prepared and compensated by seeing some of the most authentic and distinctive manifestations and expressions.

Some Facts about Qinghai at Your Fingertips

Allow me only to present the essentials by way of information.

Now with several years of life and work behind in this plateau province, At times I have been accosted by questions put to me such as "What is the landmark building there?" or "Could you please tell us something about its religious/humanistic traditions." A very convenient way to start such a conversation concerns the fountainheads of China's great rivers such as the Yangtze, the Yellow River and the Lancang. Regrettably some slips of tongue or memory do ensue as one ascribes the origin of the Yangtze to Tibet and another, that of the Yellow River, to Gansu. Well, such misconceptions, if ridiculous and annoying, matter little, but if they appear in academic monographs, they warrant a correction. Such is the case with a book entitled *The Water Of Tibet Saves China.* recently released in which the author erroneously identify Tibet as the birth place of these great rivers.

Don't get me wrong here .I am not saying the water of Tibet matters little to China. Far from that. Tibet is crucial to China and even the Southeast of Asia, we know the Yalutsampo courses its way south into India to become the Ganges, India's mother river. This common sense should be taught correctly in the primary schools as the three grand waterways all have their source in Qinghai.49% of the water of the Yellow River and 26% of the water of the Yangtze are supplied by the glaciers of the two mountain ranges, is, the Geladandong and the Kunlun. Even the lancing River runs through China with 46% of the volume of water before emptying into the Non-China segment which is the Mekong. In this sense, the water of Qinghai nurtures and nourishes the Oriental civilization.

Rivers, of course, are vital to civilization. Several pivotal civilizations, the Indian, the Egyptian, and the Chinese, all evolve along the riverbeds of great waterways such as the Ganges, the Nile and the Yangtze. If the first light of civilization dawned on the African savanna scorched by the sun, it was nourished by two great rivers, the Tigris and Euphrates. Similar things happened in the other centers of civilization, the Indus valley, the Nile delta, the Yellow River

长江和黄河对于中华民族尤为重要，这两条江河都是我们的母亲河。我们讨论中华文明时讨论得最多的是中原文明，现在历史学家和大量考古学家发现文明是多源头的。不管怎样，这两条河流，同样包括澜沧江，对中华民族来说都是非常重要的，它们的源头都来自青海。

还有一些朋友问我，青藏线主要在西藏还是在青海？我告诉大家一个比较准确的数字，整个青藏线总长1958公里，但是有1400公里在青海。很多人问我有没有去过可可西里，西藏那里有很多的人文资源，但是可可西里在青海，很多人过去不了解可可西里。藏羚羊是北京奥运会的五个吉祥物中的一个，这是青海省政府和青海的老百姓共同申报的。藏羚羊主要生活在青海的可可西里，当然它也横跨西藏，有一部分到了西藏，不断地迁徙，但其主要生活区域仍然是在青海。

我过去长期在北京工作，全国的31个省、直辖市、自治区我基本上全部跑完了，香港、澳门我也去过，但是很长时间根本就没有去过青海。什么原因呢？有几个原因，第一个原因是，藏族的文化代表是西藏，所以无论是从地理还是文化的角度，去了西藏不一定去青海。说到伊斯兰教的文化，人们会想到宁夏或者是新疆。青海虽然生活着很多信仰伊斯兰教的民族，但是人们恐怕觉得它的代表性不是太强。说到整个西北的文化和高原性的文化，除了考虑西藏代表性的高原文化之外，往往考虑到黄土文化的代表，陕西、甘肃这样的地方。所以说从地缘上来说，很长一段时间，不光是很多普通的老百姓，还包括一些不是专门研究中国民族学和地理学的学者，恐怕都容易犯这个错误，对青海不了解。

实际上，在文化的多元性以及别的很多方面，青海是不可替代的，是具有唯一性和特殊价值的省份。青海有藏族、回族、土族、撒拉族、蒙古族六个民族，自汉代以来，大量民族不断迁徙和融会。这个地方的文化充分体现了中国文化多元的特征，你中有我，我中有你，不断进行交融，相互依存。所以从某种意义说，青海的民族文化也是中华民族文化的一个缩影。

另外，中国特别是西部的很多少数民族在寻根的时候都会寻到青海去，大量西南的少数民族都有从北向南迁徙的历史。他们最早的祭祀活动，从人类学和民族学的角度来说很多的符号都和青海有着很重要的关系。羌族的后裔大部分形成了西南

valley when some communities of agriculturalists developed techniques for cultivating either arid wasteland or alluvial soil and successfully effected the shift from Neolithic tribalism to civilization. It is certainly no accident that the evolution of several civilizations, despite their distinctive characteristics, shared a common general pattern. So in celebrating major civilized cultures, we must acknowledge our huge debt to the existence of these great rivers. When it comes to the genesis of Chinese civilization, despite the controversy among archaeologists and historians about the multi origins of world civilization, that the Yellow River and the Yangtze River rising in Qinghai gave birth to the Chinese race is crystal clear and beyond any doubt.

Still, some friends approach me, even ignorant of where the Qinghai-Tibet railway line lies, more in Qinghai or less in Tibet? The date given is not approximation, but pinpointed for the sake of both convenience and research: 1958 kilometers, of which 1400 kilometers is found in Qinghai. One more interesting question concerns the exact locale of the fabled Koh Xil nature reserve. Well, while Tibet boasts of an impressive array of humanistic riches, the Koh Xil is not found in Tibet, but in Qinghai. Tibetan antelopes, one of the five mascots of the 2008 Beijing Olympic Games, are indigenous to the third largest "no man" zones in the world. Tibetan antelopes follow a traditional migration route to Tibet for some time of the year, yet their habitat is again found in Qinghai.

In a sense, Qinghai remains for a long time the Koh Xil in the nation's map of culture, lying at the edges of the Chinese consciousness. Take my ignorance as an example. I used to be based in Beijing and had plenty of opportunities to tour almost the whole 31 provinces and municipalities, and Hongkong, Macao. Yet, before I was transferred to work for the Provincial Government, I had never set my foot on the soil of Qinghai. Two reasons, I surmise, are behind this compulsory claustrophobia. First, people tend to associate Tibet with Tibetan Buddhism. That means a trip to Tibet suffices if one wants to dip into the esoteric charms of Tibetan Buddhism. Qinghai travel is not a must. Second, among the two classical options of the Plateau culture and the Loess Uplands culture, while Tibet is the more representative of the former, Gansu, Ningxia and Shanxi definitely are the most typical specimen. Even with the pull of Islamic culture, Xinjiang is indisputably the citadel of Islamic learning and culture. The implication: Qinghai is always relegated to the back seat. So from a geo-cultural point of view, the misconception of Qinghai being a cultural backwater is widespread not only among the populace, but also among the experts and seasoned travelers like me.

In sum, there is a good case for the assumption that Qinghai, occupying a gigantic expanse of glaciered mountains, waterless basins, and of course, epic grassland for herding, and river valley suitable for farming inhabited successively by an amazingly eclectic blend of peoples and cultures, among other things, could be deemed another heartland of Chinese culture at large. Six nationalities have emerged the select out of the long ordeal of intertribal warfare and dynasties rivalries -Han, Tibetan, Hui Tu, Salar and Mongol. The local traditions and customs are influenced by these distinctive nationalities, in particular the Tibetan, Salar and Tu. The Han accounts for

的少数民族，还有很多并入中原融入汉族。所以说青海的多元的民族关系也是一个中华民族关系的特殊的缩影，我们由此也可以看到中华民族史的一个发展过程。

青海还有很多特殊地域，很多人并不了解。青海是以青海湖而得名的，每一次中国，或者是国际上重要的地理杂志，或者旅游机构评选中国最美的湖泊，不管是五大湖泊还是十大湖泊都离不开青海湖。很多人问，你们去青海湖有东西值得看？我告诉他们，青海湖面积4500多平方公里，一个青海湖里面可以放四个香港、七个新加坡，你想它的面积有多大。我们有的时候开车去检查工作，围着青海湖转一圈，不停地开车，你转一圈要开多长距离呢？360公里。青海湖的自然地貌和文化有很多东西在中国都是唯一的。最近报纸上报道在青海发现了可燃冰，这是中国经济发展最重要的战略储备。据初步探测估计，青海有很多重要的战略性资源，对未来的中国很重要。

青海虽然不是一个民族自治区，而是一个多民族的省，但是少数民族的人口比例在全国占了第三，超过了很多的自治区。青海现有人口540万，其中藏族120万、回族80万、土族20万、撒拉族10万、蒙古族8万，这些少数民族占了青海总人口的46%。不同民族丰富的歌舞、音乐、绘画、雕塑、表演等多种文学艺术形式都有着自己的独特文化传统，而这些民族文化的形式对于我们今天保护非物质文化和口头文化的遗产是非常重要的，其价值是非常高的。

青海在历史上就是一个多民族共生共融的地方，不同的民族文化在这个地方共存，在这个地方相互影响，而同时又保留着自身的特点，一直发展到今天。青海作为国家和民族的一块宝地，它是青藏高原和黄土高原的一个连接点，无论是从地缘政治方面看，还是对于我们国家政权的稳固，或者作为我们资源的储存，这个地方都是非常重要的。如果从文化美学和历史人文来说，这个地方都有着灿烂的文化和不可替代的重要地理资源和文化资源。

谈青海的文化创意和重要文化品牌，离不开对青海的人文历史和地理状况的介绍。青海的人文地理是这些重要的文化事件产生的基础，如果没有这样的地理资源、人文资源，甚至是宗教资源，我们也无从谈起对这些文化创意和文化品牌进行新的创造，或者是根据它的地理资源、文化资源、宗教资源这些特殊的优势来创立我们的文化品牌。

54% of the total population of its 5.5 million among which the Tibetans number 1.2 million, and Muslims, close to 1 million .The Tu and Salar are rather native to the soil upon which we walk and stand. Suffices it to say over centuries, the tendency is towards a greater homogeneity-racially, culturally if not necessarily linguistically. Eventually,

The resident races are one side of the coin. Ethnologists believe many other ethnic groupings now inhabiting the southwestern China could trace their ancestral beginnings to Qinghai. The reason behind such epic migrations is to be found in Qinghai's topography. Anthropologists identify a "Han-Tibetan Corridor" between 95 C to 105 C east longitude and there has been a hypothesis long prevalent among ethnologists that the majority of minority nationalities living in present day Yunnan and even Burma- were descendants of ancient Qiang, that is, the earliest ethnic groups identified to have roamed and settled down in Neolithic Qinghai.

Indeed, Qinghai remains a wonderland to be discovered. It derives its name after the namesake lake within its territory. In several "beauty pageantries" sponsored by geographical journals or tourism operators at the national of international level Qinghai Lake came off triumphant ,touted with unanimity as one of the most beautiful lakes .Remember this is a huge alpine saline lake covering 4500 square kilometers , the five times' size of Hongkong and seven times' of Singapore. Once we were driving to check out the real circumference of the lake and it turned to be 360 kilometers to come full circle. Even in terms of economic utility, the province contains quite a few natural resources of strategic importance for China's sustainable development in the years to come. Recently the area is reported to hold the deposits of flammable ice, a genuine discovery of one of the most important reserves of fuels other than the fossil type.

Though not an autonomous region, Qinghai is peopled by several ethnic groups amounting to 46% of the total 5.4 million population, of which are 1.2 million Tibetans, 80000 Muslims, 200,000 Tu,100,000 Sala as well as 80,000 Mongols. Such an unimaginable mix of cultural diversity is bound to generate various forms of literature, dancing, music, painting and performing art, all potential and objects and candidates for our campaign for preserving the intangible cultural matrimony with varying degree of cultural value to be assessed and sifted.

As both potpourri to multi-racial and multi-ethnic presence and geo-political watershed between the loess uplands and the Tibetan Qinghai Plateau, Qinghai serves multiple purposes-a veritable goldmine of cultural diversity, a treasure house of natural resources as well as geopolitical beachhead. Again, my official charge inclines me to be more susceptible to its cultural potential from the perspectives of cultural aesthetics and historicity.

To forge cultural brands and foster regional creativity industry presupposes a deep understanding of the regional history and its humanistic legacy-a legitimate basis from which we set to work .Fortunately, Qinghai's topography and history combined makes it one of the favored regions that generated the material and themes essential for a burgeoning creativity business. To me, by instinct as a poet, Qinghai evinces a vision of the plateau cultural dream works and

青海是一座文化梦想的高原,是一方洋溢着万物和谐的乐土,这是我作为一个诗人对青海直觉的认识。青海与众不同的地理和特殊的文化,呈现着迥然不同的地理风貌和文化个性。中国其他的省份很难像青海这样,在中国文化、中国心理上有着重要的名山大川,正因为如此青海高原才被誉为"深山的故乡"。

喜马拉雅山是我们中国的一个高原,从古文化来说昆仑山是中华民族的文化高原,昆仑神话是我们中国最古老的神话,中国最古老的神话昆仑神话,从某种意义上来说是中国神话的奠基性的文化。昆仑山最高峰在青海,存留着大量的文化遗迹和大量的昆仑神话传说的遗迹。对于我们中国人来说,要遵循我们的民族文化,要在世界文化进行对话和沟通的过程中占一席之地,我们不可能忘记我们最古老民族的、最根基的文化。现在全世界都在重新诠释自己的神话,古罗马的神话、古希腊的神话,多少伟大的诗人、电影导演、文化学者都用不同的方式诠释他们的神话,最重要的一点就是在世界上表明这些古老的民族他们的文化都具有深厚的历史,有久远的文化传统,这一点来说是非常重要的。

青藏高原的地理结构构成了它这种伟岸的身躯。青海的面积非常大,达72万平方公里,青海的平均海拔差不多在4000米左右。国际上谈论和研究青藏高原的时候,离不开西藏同时也离不开青海。青海和西藏共同构成了地球的第三极,除了南极和北极之外的第三极,现在全世界非常关注这第三极。我说青海是最后净土的入口,因为在青藏高原和黄土高原的节点中,从青海开始我们迈向青藏高原大地阶梯的第一位。如果把青藏高原比喻成大地的阶梯,从蒙古高原开始海拔在1700—1900米,从青海开始我们踏上了青藏高原的第一个阶梯,它最高的地方海拔在5000米到8000米,这个高度上青海和西藏是连接在一起的。

我过去在北京工作的时候去过五次西藏,并且去的地方很多,但从地貌的角度了解青藏高原,其地理变化最大的就在青海。有一个学者说因为你在青海工作,所以你说青海这个地方好看。我说绝不是,我过去从未去过青海。青海的海拔从1700米一直到8000米,不同的海拔高度往上走就像人在爬楼梯。大家知道,气候、地理环境包括生物,都随海拔而变化,所以生物的多样性和文化的多样性随着海拔的不断提升,会发生很大的变化。

paradise of natural solidarity. For one thing, no other place in China like Qinghai boasts such an array of awesome mesmerizing mountain ranges that occupy so lofty a place in the hearts of the Chinese race as a whole. So many marvels done by Nature's hand are bound to engender an alien beauty tinged with a pristine magnificence that shocks and captivates, styled by many as Home to Mountains.

In essence, myths, as specific accounts concerning gods or superhuman beings and extraordinary events at the core of the cultural identity of a nation, is one kind of symbolic communication. People in almost every culture have developed their own stock of myths in addition to other forms of literature .Modern studies of various mythologies are frankly an means to an end, whether it is the efficient administration or the cultural renewal. It is noteworthy as the Himalaya range dominates all other mountainous systems, the Kunlun mythology is definitely the foundation laying project for the Chinese race. The highest peak of the might Kunlun is found in Qinghai together with a spate of cultural relics and sites associated with the Kunlun myths. It must be borne in mind that a great variety of myths, such as the Greco-Roman and our Kunlun myths, stand undisputed for answering almost all the crucial problems in man's existence. Distinguished poets, directors, and folklorists never tire of reinterpreting them in the light of the present, indicative of one dimension of such sustainable interest in myths as a source of inexhaustible inspiration and cultural confidence.

Geography, like character, is destiny. Qinghai's primary point of interest is its size (1.5 time's of France or 3.5 time's of England) and its height (average 4000m elevation up on the Tibet Qinghai Plateau). Qinghai and Tibet are habitually contracted into one lump because the two regions comprise the third terrace of the earth, together with the Arctic and Antarctic Circle .The concept of the third terrace has been of much interest worldwide lately. My way of styling Qinghai as the entrance into the Last Pure Land makes sense because Qinghai links the Mongolian Highland (average height:1700—1900m) and the Tibet-Qinghai Plateau(highest between 5000m to 8000m).Entering Qinghai, you climb up the first staircase and continually ascend to meet Tibet at the top of the land ladder.

Before I was transferred to Qinghai, I took five trips to Tibet touring widely. Yet, geo-morphologically speaking, Qinghai presents the most kaleidoscopic configurations. I stand justified because someone might counter argue mine is one case of blowing my own trumpet. I demur. Say, Qinghai runs from its lowest point of 1700m elevation to its peak point which 8000m. Now we know with the sea level rising, there is bound to be a most exhilarating scenario of configurations of climatic pattern, fauna and flora, hence the constantly changing realignment of various social and natural forces set into play, ie, cultural diversity and biodiversity.

For example, the Yellow River, rising in Qinghai, as it passes through the Central Chinese loess plateau, fills up with the yellow earth that has suggested the river's name. Yet, along the Qinghai stretch, the Yellow River looks clean and blue, like the blue Danube. In historical terms,

在青海你可以看到蓝色的黄河谷,别的什么地方有蓝色的黄河?黄河不是黄的吗?不是叫黄河吗?这是过去的概念。黄河作为中国的母亲河,在我们民族的文化意念中象征一个坚韧不屈历经沧桑的母亲。而黄河有着她最美丽的少女时代,这个少女时代就在青海。所以你看到黄河的少女时代,要找黄河母亲最漂亮的时候就到青海去,一看到蓝色的黄河、黄河的少女时代,你就会想到我们的母亲,想到中华民族走过来的这种沧桑的历史。当然,今天我们的母亲历经了沧桑和5000多年的风雨,从河流来说她的历史更长,她依然很美,但是如果要追寻我们文化的根的话,还是要看她少女时代的形象,她的美完全来自特殊的自然。

从青海这种不同的地理高度再往上走你可以看到草原、湿地,你可以看到戈壁、沙漠,可以看到永久的冻土层、雪山,可以看到盐湖。其地理资源丰富,在全世界也很少能找到这样特殊的高原地貌。它也是高原野生动物的天堂,在这里有高原独有的动物野牦牛、藏羚羊、雪豹。特别是可可西里,这是一个动植物的王国。有一些摄影家把青海称为摄影家的天堂,这绝对不是溢美之词。青海的九寨沟是一个高海拔地区,它的这种美我们只能够在两个地方看见。一是在梦中,好多的景观都是超现实主义的东西。二是在超现实主义的图画里,像美国拍的很多大片,背景是电脑制作的,其实在青海就有这样的环境地貌。

中国有一个著名的摄影家林森,他带了一批中外的摄影家到离九寨沟不远的地方。在玉树他们看见了山上的一块巨石,一群超现实主义的景观,很多摄影家泪流满面。在这种天地自然伟大的造化面前,人是充满敬意的,是渺小的。我看到这种特殊的自然景观觉得非常特别,我全世界跑了几十个国家,尤其是美洲南美经常去,因为我喜欢搞文化比较,特别是原生态的文化丰富的地方我就越愿意去,在那个地方感受人类最初的生活状态。特别是在世界同质化的状态下文化差异性越大的地方,我越愿意去感受。青海这种地貌它生成的生物的多样性和文化的多样性是不可多得的,地理资源、宗教资源和文化资源的唯一性是不可复制的。

以高原为主体,青海省的地理结构构成了十分的多样性。草原、山脉、盆地、戈壁、江河、湖泊,尤其是横贯昆仑山发祥地的黄河、长江和澜沧江,对于青海非常重要,对于中国非常重要。如果用一个准确的名词概括西藏的话是"天上的西藏",从某

the Yellow River is undoubtedly the most important river in China, chiefly because its irrigated area was the earliest center of Chinese civilization. Hence, it is the icon of Chinese culture. Given to radical shifts in its course and frequent flooding (a result of early deforestation and heavy silt deposits) the Yellow River has been through the centuries a source of anxiety to generations living by the river. Some tend to compare the river to a strong, indomitable mother. Yet the Mother has a most flowering maidenhood .If you really want to see the Mother in her prime, you have to travel to Qinghai to see the blue Yellow River.

So on a single land ladder, rather vertical and steep, which is Qinghai, one will capture, in a single sweep of the eye, all the spectacular scenery Mother nature has to offer-grassland, wetland, Gobi wasteland, and desert, perennial frozen strata, snow-capped mountains and salt lake. Similar alpine situations are hard to come by anywhere as it is home to alpine fauna, wild yak, Tibetan antelope, and snow leopard. Koh Xil, now billed as a national park, is literally the animals' kingdom, enraptured by photographers, professional and amateur alike. The counterpart of Qinghai's Jiuzhaigou Nature Reserve is a natural alpine wonderland of stunning beauty, abounding with scenes surrealistic in character which one often sees in Hollywood's blockbusters. The difference: what Hollywood artists achieve in computers are rather mundane sights in Qinghai.

Qinghai's natural wonderland-Jiuzhaigou is found in Yushu Prefecture, 500 kilometers south of Xining. Yang Seng, one of China's top photographers, once took a band of talented peers, home and abroad for a filming tour. On the way, they spotted a boulder, so peculiar in shape, that beguiled everybody to tears. In the company of such surrealistic scenes and top attractions which pose for photographers and painters, Nature demands total humility and deference. I have been a seasoned traveler, touring altogether 40 odd countries and Latin America has a perennial hold on my imagination because it retains more of the indigenous cultures than elsewhere and it is the gap between homogeneity and heterogeneity that titillates me. Qinghai, as luck would have it, boasts an unusual combination of biodiversity and cultural diversity ,unique of her own and irreplaceable, and has been a replica of Latin America on my own soil.

Aside biodiversity and cultural diversity, Qinghai features also geographical diversity, composed of large swathe of grassland, mountain ranges, Gobi wasteland, rivers, lakes, especially the three super waterways, ie, the Yellow River, the Lancang River and the Yangtze River that rise here and flow through China's land mass. Some cultural experts dub Tibet "Tibet on High" in terms of Tibet's deep-seated Buddhist traditions. We in Qinghai propose the concept of "Greater Beauty Qinghai" .Unlike Tibet, whose charm is of a more other worldly nature, Qinghai's focus of beauty is wild, pristine and breath-taking, unlike anything of what other provinces have to offer in terms of both natural endowment and cultural distinction. I do hope serious cultural experts and adventure-minded tourists make the trip and seeing is believing.

At this point I must dwell upon the topic of the Qiang's role in the making of the Chinese

种意义上来说，从它的海拔和宗教文化的属性来概括它可能更准确。"大美青海"这个概念的形成也不是青海人自己提出来的，这是青海的人文地理和历史文化所决定的。它的这种壮美、这种大美是我们国家自然风光、历史和民族文化非常重要的组成部分。作为中国人，我想我们一定要在祖国的名山大川、在不同的差异性的文化中畅想，我们可以到这些地方去感悟和感思，认识中国古老的昆仑文化和认识青藏高原文化的多样性，了解我们民族的这种丰富性。我认为在有生之年，我们特别是有很多喜欢文化的学者和喜欢旅游的朋友都应该到青藏高原看一看，特别是到青海看一看。

我在这里想介绍一下，古羌文化所孕育的丰沛的血脉为什么对中华民族的文明非常重要。考古学家证实，距今三万年左右，青藏高原就有人类活着。诞生于四千多年前的五人舞蹈彩盆和一万多件各式各样的彩陶出土，青海有一个柳湾彩陶博物馆，彩陶的出现是农耕文明非常重要的标志。青海发现的距今四五千年的彩陶量非常巨大，现在已经发掘的量可以说是中国的彩陶之最，现在我们推测还有几十万件埋在地下没有动。要用彩陶文化了解中国的古文明，特别是黄河上游、长江上游的文明，青海已经提出了一个很重要的佐证。有些东西不光对中国重要，对于世界来说也是很重要的。彩陶最早的跳舞的纹饰在青海而不是在埃及被发现，四五千年前就已被记录在我们的古文物上，这些资料对于深入研究中国舞蹈史和世界的舞蹈史有十分重要的价值。

意大利说面条是意大利人发明的，实际上在青海的考古中已经发现了，全世界第一碗面条就诞生在青海而不是在别的地方。青海发掘出来的四五千年前的古文物里发现了用竹子做的刀叉，跟现在西方人用的刀叉一样。中国的道教文明、中原文化历史上很早就在青藏高原这个地方进行传播，伊斯兰的文明、藏传佛教的文明、西方的文明和印度文明在这个地方不断地交汇融合，可以说这个地方是多元文化交流并存的地方。它的古文化已经形成了一个非常好的历史传承的作用，一直传承到今天，而这个文化传统从来没有被中断过，就像中国五千年的文明没有被中断过一样。对于研究我们民族的历史，特别是面向未来的时候，弥足珍贵。

随着青藏线的开通，人们对青海的认识发生了很大的变化。原来有很多人不知道柴达木盆地在什么地方，以为是在新疆，实际上是在青海。现在国内98%的钾肥都

nation. Archeologists tell us 30000 years back certain human communities made the Plateau home. Liuwan Painted Pottery Museum in Ledu, 68 kilometers east of Xining, houses the largest display of painted pottery in China. Of its 10000 items on show, a bowl bearing the pattern of five girls dancing is the most noteworthy. Painted pottery counts the typical artifact of the Neolithic village life and the amount of the pottery articles unearthed so far is the largest in China and experts further infer hundreds of thousands more still lie intact underground. Regional archeologists have advanced solid evidence to the revolutionary hypothesis about the existence of the original center of civilizations upstream of the Yellow River and the Yangtze River, although much still remains conjecture. Painted pottery bearing dancing girls was first excavated by Egyptians in the Nile river valley. For there is an established view that 3500.B.C is accepted as the approximate date for the emergence of civilization in Mesopotamia, then corresponding approximations may be given for the other centers of civilizations. in Egypt, about 3000 B.C, in the Indus Valley, about 2500.B.C.;in the Yellow River valley of China, about 1500 B.C, and in the Mesoamerica and Peru, about 500 B.C. The idea is simple: since similar cultural relics were unearthed and identified as early as 5000 years ago, does this mean Qinghai promises to be a cradle of civilization even of bigger antiquity than that of the Yellow River?

What follows about the origin of noodles is by no means conjecture. Italians claim they are the inventors of noodles. The first bowl of noodles, it so happens, was dug up in Qinghai, not in Italy. Other cultural relics dug up include fork made of bamboo, shaped exactly like those used by contemporary Westerners. Like Middle East, ancient Qinghai was a crossroad where major religions spread and encountered: Taoism, Islam, Tibetan Buddhism and Hinduism all took root here and identified their own group of followers, a tradition never disrupted until today, enjoying a historical continuity identical to the Chinese. Such a harmonious mix of cultural and religious traditions is immensely valuable in its own right.

The railway from Qinghai to Tibet, opened to regular service in 2009, has benefitted economically both Tibet and Qinghai by spurring curiosity about Qinghai's rich and unique culture. Before 2009, many people in the interior provinces even had no idea of where the Qaidam Basin is located .Fewer knew 98% of domestic potassic fertilizer is manufactured in Qinghai. Potassic fertilizer's raw material is potash, mined from salt lakes. Salt is Qinghai's No 1 commodity and natural resource, in such abundant deposits that even a highway is totally paved with salt. Much of the Qaidam Basin is actually encrusted in salt.

China's extraordinary economic growth and heavy reliance on increasingly expensive foreign oil, mineral ores ,periodic power shortages all have impressed upon Beijing that alternative source of fossil oil(renewable energy like water power) and non-ferrous mineral deposits must be identified to sustain China's economy in the new millennium if China is to both complete its economic transformation and achieve "energy security". Over 120 mineral reserves have been proven of which 20 ranking 9th and 10 ranking the first place in China. The inauguration of the

是青海生产的,青海的盐湖资源中国人光是吃盐用几百年没有问题,甚至那个盐多到什么程度呢？有一条公路都是用盐铺的,你在全世界找不到这样用盐铺的公路。柴达木盆地中间有很大一块积层是盐的积层。

　　青海资源非常丰富,可以说是中国的一个聚宝盆,现在已勘探的资源有120多种矿产,差不多有近20种在全国排前9位,差不多有10种在全国矿产资源排列全国第1位方,这些矿产对于未来的战略储备和物质储备是非常重要的。青海有三江源自然保护区,同时青海被称为"中华水塔",其生态地位不光在中国,在世界上都是非常重要的。青海省提出"生态立省",这也是很多朋友所关注的,这到底是一个政治口号还是一个形象宣传？都不是。"生态立省"是我们在青海省落实科学发展观一个重要的手段。青海在全国第一个提出来,像在三江源这样的地区我们不考虑GDP,我们就要保护好生态。青海人保护好生态和环境不仅仅为青海540万人,更是为中华民族,甚至是为人类。长江、黄河、澜沧江所有重要的源头都是从青海上去的,如果上游发展高耗能的产业,我们的资源很丰富、矿产很丰富,水能很丰富,黄河上游的水电全国都是很有名的,但中下游就会发生灾难性的问题。

　　对于我们民族来说,河流和水的重要可以说是超过了历史上的任何时候。有人预计,未来引起战争可能最重要的原因是水资源。现在以色列为什么占领格兰高地,因为它控制了水源,在中东尤其是以色列、巴勒斯坦、约旦这一块,水控制了命脉。中国着手开发利用雅鲁藏布江,印度马上就很紧张。为什么呢？水资源。但我们是在自己的地域上合理地利用我们的资源,这是合乎国际准则的。苏丹上面就是埃及,所以尼罗河的水资源,很多国家都是很敏感的。但是对于我们来说,青海承担着一个很重要的保护环境和生态的任务,我们一定要把这个水资源保护好。所以青海面临着一个怎么能够保护好我们生态环境的问题。从这个意义上来说,保护生态环境是以发展生态经济为核心,以培育生态文化为龙头的,我们坚持在综合循环利用的基础上谋取又快又好的发展,促进人与自然的和谐,我们也希望这种观念和理念在具体的工作实践中能够得到很好的实践和运用。

　　这几年很多国际性的组织非常关注青海,他们非常关注我们的发展方式,说你们到底怎么发展青海这个地方的,长江中下游的省份对青海同样也是很关注的。青

Three Rivers Nature Reserve, funded and sponsored by the central government, has brought half of the region's territory into protection. This fact alone speaks volumes about our determination to maintain well the last remaining Pure Land of the earth in the very belief that to us, Qinghai-Tibet Plateau, with its wealth of resources represents more than a valuable treasure house. We owe not only all the people living down the Roof of the World but also our children's children when it comes to the use of natural bounty. The Provincial Government comes out with its No 1 development strategy, literally meaning "putting ecology at command". There arises some suspicion as to the sincerity of the statement. All said, to be ecologically friendly does not mean we sit idle to be professional takers of alms giving. In fact outside the natural preserve (accounting 25% of the region's territory)there are still other businesses to be pursued, such as hydro power, recyclable industry, etc.. But within the territory prescribed, industrial activities basically come to a halt for ethical and ecological reasons

Water is a vital element for human life, and any human activity relates somehow to water. Moreover, political scientists project future wars in the Middle East or elsewhere are more likely to be fought over water than over oil,. Access to key resources, mainly water, has caused external tension between sovereign states. In 1958 Israel reinstated the National Water Carrier Project. The Arab states responded by damming the tributaries of the Jordan and Yarmouk Rivers. As part of the joint Syria-Jordan Headwater Diversion Plan, the two Arab states began building additional dams to divert the flow of the Banias and Dan headwaters of the Jordan River. Israeli attacked the Arab state water works projects in March, May, and August 1965. These tensions directly contributed to the war in 1967, which culminated in the Israeli takeover of the Golan Heights in 1967.The Brahmaputra flows from Tibet, tracing the border between China and India before flowing south through India. The development of the Yalutsampo River has been a genuine headache for Indians downstream. In similar vein, access to key resources, mainly water, can also be a source of internal conflict within a nations. The development of the headwater area, which is Qinghai, has been a matter of great concern to the whole country.

In recent years, Qinghai, especially the region's mode of growth has drawn acute attention from international bodies and organization as well as to those provinces downstream of the Yellow River and the Yangtze River. The bone of contention is the ecological dimension. We know, in other parts of China or even the world, most of the developed areas have industrialized with little regard for the environment, with consequences that are now beginning to seriously jeopardize human life. Qinghai, in a way, is in a quandary. For, with 5.4 million populace to be fed and clad, it too has to eradicate the backwardness and poverty from which we suffer. In the meanwhile, where its resources are tantalizing for exploitation, its share of responsibility are disproportionally huge. The options are difficult ,yet we choose to sacrifice some of the interests and play the exemplary game. We are trying to restructure our industrial sep-up and seek new modes of growth and new areas of GDP growth. Recyclable industry featuring low diffusion of heat trapping carbon dioxide

海承担着很重要的环保任务,在这个方面青海的老百姓是作出了巨大的牺牲的。但是另外一个方面,这对于我们调整产业结构,寻找新的 GDP 增长点,寻找新的发展方式提供了一个新的契机同时也是压力。我们现在非常重视发展低碳利用青海的生物资源发展循环经济,中国为数不多的循环经济区柴达木循环经济区就在青海。

同时,我们发展高端和特别的产业,也就是文化创意产业。发展经济和保护环境,适应时代的要求,这两者是相互依存的。青海原始壮丽的自然环境所孕育的这种文化,就像它生存的环境一样具有某种神秘性,它虽然古老,但又不失其新鲜和活力,它丰富博大的人性内涵对于现代人来说是一个很大的启示,这种文化的特殊魅力已引起世人越来越多的探讨。我们今天建设青海的文化品牌和文化创意,我们要给 540 万的老百姓提供财政支持,所以我们必须要发展经济。

但我们到底发展什么样的经济?一是发展高科技的经济,特别是对于矿产资源的一些产品,怎么能在循环经济的要求下不断地加大我们的产业链,提高科技含量,既在环保上提高门槛,同时也增加附加值。二是要发展高端的、特种的经济。青海的旅游虽然在作宣传,比如说可可西里旅游,有一些深度旅游不是谁都让你去的,你不具备环保意识,不具备一定的旅游条件,你说背一个包拿几个馒头到哪里逛一圈,垃圾到处扔也不是可能的事情,有些地方也去不了。我们要具备生态旅游的意识,达到这种条件。

青海规划了很多不同的旅游带,有大众的旅游带,有特众的旅游带,有生态的旅游带,要保护我们的地域。有的旅游地点人多了不见得是好事,我们要求去的人有这种旅游意识、生态的意识。我们的旅游基础设施必备的条件一定要达到,这样才能够很好地发展旅游业。我们的文化产业和文化创意产业怎么样能够很好地发展,利用民族的文化资源、地理资源和宗教资源发展新兴文化产业,带动老百姓的经济收入,为大家增收致富提供一个手段,这就是我们一切工作的出发点。

过去一直有一个观点,经济滞后的地方一般创意也滞后。大家知道,创意经济在英国、日本、美国等国家,是和整个经济发展的基础有直接关系的,包括人才、资讯等是发展文化创意产业不可或缺的基础。青海人口面积很大,地理资源、宗教资源、民俗资源都很丰富,我们怎么样能够走出这样一个悖论,就是在一个经济比较滞后、人

is prized and as you know, the Qaidam Basin is targeted to be one of the few State-level Demonstration Recyclable Development Zones.

Beyond compulsory decrease in GDP for the sake of the nationwide ecological effort and experimenting with new modes of growth such as low carbon industry, we have naturally turned our attention to develop the creativity industry, absolutely environmental clean and friendly. As I have reiterated ,Qinghai has a potential of cultural diversity and other forms of cultural legacy, mysterious, exotic ,aging but fresh, full of vitality and humanistic pull to modern people, out of which brand new creativity industry can be forged and fostered. This rich past has bequeathed a generous crop of spectacular sights and cultural resources, full of interest and atmosphere. Honestly, our cultural enterprise is largely driven by economical considerations. The pressure is there to accommodate a growing population out of the tiniest GDP base.

Top regional decision makers and administrators come out with a scenario of development strategy focusing on high-tech and cultural enterprises. With high-tech, two requirements must be met: high-tech products (mainly mineral products deep processed) must be able to fetch a super price and added value in the market and they must be super clean. With the latter, there is a built-in brake on both entry and expansion. For example, local tourism operators do promote touring the Koh Xil Nature Reserve, but with significant reservations: one has to be part of an approved tour group ,highly ecologically conscious, littering nothing, in fact, the Koh Xil admits but of the few elite connoisseurs of the pristine beauty in the wilderness. Independent trekking is not feasible even if you are prepared to be self-sufficient in food, fuel and shelter.

Local tourism operators have devised a somewhat "divide and tour" policy based mainly upon ecological and sustainable reasons. Certain destinations are open to all, group or individual. And some, only to approved tour groups with special permit. Legions of men are not all blessings. We preach an ecological ethic for all tourists. In the meanwhile, we must keep improving the infrastructure for a sustainable future. Hand in hand with the thriving tourism business, our cultural enterprise get under way with the twin considerations of ecology and economics uppermost in our consciousness.

One opinion prevails the economic backwaters must necessarily want creative ideas and cultural inspiration. In a sense this is true , evidenced by the boom in the creativity industry in the developed countries such as Great Britain, Japan and USA, as their opulence presupposes a rich supply of talent and material resources essential for the cultural enterprise. In this connection, I must say Qinghai is both land of plenty and scarcity. Plenty of cultural resources, geological, religious and folklorist barely sustained by small local economy which is a fraction of the national economy. The struggle between the rapid development and the preservation of the past can be distilled down into the question of pioneering a new path of effecting both an economic and cultural take-off without compromising the ecological quality. We are swimming against the stream. The intent of this economic revamping is nothing less than to make Qinghai both an

口市场不大的地方能够走出一条欠发达地区文化创意的成功之路,这对于我们来说是一个考验。经济欠发达地区往往又是文化旅游资源很富集的地区。

青海是西部旅游的一个重要省份,过去很长时间我们把矿产资源、农业资源、畜牧业资源作为资源,却没有把文化资源、地理资源甚至包括宗教资源作为重要的资源。我们怎么样进行很好的文化创意?无论从政府工作的层面,还是从文化产业发展的角度来看,这都是摆在我们面前的一个必须回答的问题。越是交通不便、贫困的地区,越保存着古老丰富的原生态文化,如果把文化产业的发展和贫困地区的脱贫致富连接在一起,既可以使我们的文化传承得到回报,又使其他的产业包括旅游发展具有更大的想象空间和发展的空间。发展文化产业是西部地区实现经济社会发展跨越式发展、缩小与东部地区发展距离的方式,是欠发达地区突破封闭实现发展的光明大道。

地处西部高原、经济发展水平较低的青海,除了那些我们必须谨慎对待、科学有序开发的自然资源,还有什么优势呢?我们有丰富的地理文化资源,但在浩瀚博大的中国文化的盛宴里有哪些可以塑造青海文化的独特形象呢?我们认为,以藏文化为特征的多民族文化共存的民族文化,和以三江源为代表的民族文化,为我们创立符合青海历史地理民族标准的现代文化品牌奠定了坚实的基础。我们必须要在这个基础上进行文化创意,我们必须在文化创意上跨越式发展。

我们不能跟珠三角比,也不能跟长三角比,我们这个地方经济的差异、差距可以说不是一步两步,而是很大。广州的 GDP 是 8000 多亿,青海省的 GDP 才接近 800 多亿。北京、上海、广州、深圳、成都、西安这样的一些很重要的、人口很多的文化城市,人才资源也比较多,有利于发展文化创意产业。如果我们在文化创意上不采取一个跨越式的方式,不寻求我们对民族文化、地理文化、宗教文化这种特殊的理解,我们就不可能创立这些文化品牌。我们不寻找一种在创意上的跨越式的思路,也不可能使我们的文化品牌变成受国际影响的品牌,这是相互依存的。

要突破这个发展悖论应该从哪些方面入手呢?首先要重新认识资源,认识到有些资源具有唯一性和不可复制性。有的人到了青海,说,为什么要去塔尔寺?很多人对青海的藏传佛教的文化感到很神秘,非常想了解,而塔尔寺是黄教创始人宗哈巴

inhabitable center and of cultural interest.

Qinghai has in recent years emerged as a major player in tourism industry, marking a shift from previous bias in favor of tangible assets (mineral deposits, agricultural and livestock resources) to the neglect of managing the intangible assets (cultural, religious and geological).To begin with, how can one proceed to develop the cultural enterprise? This is the crucial issue confronting top government administrators .It is to be noted the indigenous cultural resources usually reside where infrastructure and economics are in a deplorable state. The more backward the area, the more indigenous the resource. There is the moment of enlightenment. Why not shake off poverty by growing the cultural business? While the impoverished masses make money and reap the harvest of their own handicraft and wisdom, the government gets what it wants-tourism expanded and infrastructure improved. Concerns over global ecology and disparity between affluent east and underdeveloped west are thus addressed in a rather smart manner.

Remote from China's industrial heartland, an economic backwater, endowed with rich resources to be exploited at a discretion, Qinghai is left with one good option, nevertheless, or rather, with a generous crop of natural sights and cultural legacy. Culturally speaking, the supreme attraction would be the vibrant religious life of Tibetan Buddhism. In historical terms, the headwaters of the three great rivers, shorn of any human trace, would set the tone and pace for regional campaign to combat the environmental decadence on the third terrace of our planet. These are epic themes out of which we forge our cultural brands and get our creativity industry off to ground.

It is self- defeating for us, from the mountain fastness of Qinghai, to try to emulate the Pearl River Delta, one of the countries' wealthiest and most forward looking coastlines. When Deng chose the area for the spearhead of his reform and opening up initiative, the rising star of opulent Canton seems set to put even Hongkong in the shade. Canton's GDP alone reaches 800 billion RMB, and Qinghai's GDP, less than 80 billion RMB, roughly one tenth of the former's. A number of metropolises like Beijing, Shanghai, Canton, Shenzhen, Chengdu and Xian, with their high living standard, pulsating nightlife and cosmopolitan air, have a natural concentration of talent and material wealth to develop the creativity industry. The insightful and wise elite government administrators must realize and acknowledge necessarily Qinghai is Qinghai.

It follows we must break out the bottleneck or the vicious circle of ugly, reckless industrialization by brainstorming us top decision makers. The only way out seems to boil down to the ability to see the cultural value of wilderness and the added value of cultural value. Certain relics of the past are unique which defy duplication. For example, for most of the people the main point of attraction in Qinghai is Ta'er Si, Lying about 25km southeast from Xining, which attracts droves of pilgrims from Tibet, Qinghai and Mongolia all the year round. . Both as the birthplace of Tsongkhapa, the founder of the Yellow Hat Sect, and the former home of the current Dalai Lama, the monastery is one of the most important outside Tibet, a very good introduction to Tibetan

大师的诞生地。宗喀巴大师有两个弟子，一个是达赖，一个是班禅。达赖和班禅都是一个称谓，历史上出现过若干世的达赖和班禅。现在很多人喜欢收藏唐卡，唐卡是青海的好还是西藏的好？都好，但是我要告诉你，真正的唐卡最好的地区在整个藏区是青海的热贡，热贡的藏语是"金色的土地"，历史上是藏文化、藏族艺术的中心之一。9世纪到13世纪是藏传佛教的一个重要的时期，当初灭佛的时候很多高僧在坎布拉这个地方修行和布教。20世纪初，还有很多高僧大德在青海。这些资源都是需要我们去认识的。

  人类进入21世纪之后，很多问题需要我们人类共同解决，比如现在全球变暖、雪线上升，南极、北极的冰川在融化，现在全世界都在讨论二氧化碳的排放量的问题，都在讨论低碳经济的问题。我们要保护我们的生存环境，保护我们人类赖以生存的这些土地、我们生存的空间，一方面要按照国际的标准，对国际社会负责；另一方面还要结合我们国家的实际，为我们的子孙后代考虑。

  为什么人类现在特别重视文化遗产？过去的一二十年人类对人类文化的遗产，不管是物质文化遗产还是非物质文化遗产的保护，超过了历史上任何一个时期，因为人类发展到今天才发现这些文化遗产的重要性。人类的存在最终是文化的存在，特别是一个民族与另外一个民族的差异主要是文化的差异，如果这个差异都搞成一种缺少他民族文化的特色，全世界搞成一样是不行的。生活的多样性和文化的多样性是同等重要的，联合国很多准则定下来对生活的多样性要进行保护，文化的多样性也是同样的。现在世界进入21世纪，人类有很多共同的责任，我们才发现这些资源对于未来而言，特别是对于今后发展我们的创意经济、创意产业而言是多么重要。

  对于我们来说这是一个启示，除了改变我们的观念之外，我们过去对资源缺少认识，我们才发现原来我们在世界的第三极，是一个最后的禁地，在这些地方进行文化的多样性和生活的多样性非常重要，这些地理的资源、宗教的资源可能对于发展我们的创意经济是一个重要的动力和基础。另外，我们要克服缺少人才的困难题，提出"青海不为我所有，但是为我所用"。广东创意方面好的人才可以请到青海来帮我们做一个项目，北京有一个这方面的人才我们可以把他请到青海去，上海还有一个

Buddhism. The Thangka, or scroll painting, a special art of Tibetan Buddhism has come into fashion. I have been approached to assess the merits of Thangka made in Qinghai and Tibet. I answer them all Thangka are good, but the best Thangka are to be found in Rebgong district, Tongren county, Qinghai. Tongren is the seat of the Huangnan Tibetan Autonomous Prefecture in Qinghai, located at the junction of the Qinghai-Tibet Plateau and the loess Plateau. Most Tibetans here are nomads. Called "Rebkong" (golden valley) in Tibetan, Tongren is famous for the Tibetan Buddhist art. A big majority of frescoes, embroideries, and statues in the monasteries in the Tibetan world are made by the artisans from Tongren. The 400 odd years spanning from the 9th to 13th centuries was a critical period for Tibetan Buddhism. The earliest well-documented influence of Buddhism in Tibet dates from the reign of King Songtsn Gampo, who died in 650. In the 8th century, King Trisong Detsen (755—797) established Buddhism as the official religion of the state. But Buddhism almost disappeared after 842 when the infamous Langdarma came to the throne, having assassinated his brother. A fervent supporter of Bon, he set about annihilating the Buddhist faith. Temples and monasteries were destroyed, monks forced to flee and the previously unified Tibet broke up into a number of small principalities. Many high profile lamas fled to Qinghai to continue the spiritual tradition which gave rise to the art of Thangka that depict Tibetan gods and other religious iconography. The artists here practice the Rebkong style of Thangka painting that has flourished since the 17th century.

Entering the 21th century, a cross-section of global problems requires joint action, such as global warming, the rising of the snow line, the retreating of the glaciers in the Arctic and Antarctic circles. Global concerns over ecology centers on the curtailing of emission of carbon dioxide and the developing of low carbon economy, which are, of course, two names for one problem. Zest about either issue demands a long term view of conservation and a historical perspective. We must protect the land on which our people subsist in line with international criteria. On the other hand, we must pioneer new mode of development other than emulating the historical experience of the more affluent ones through ugly, dirty getting-rich-quick modernization for posterity and sustainable potential.

Why has the international community recently become so conscious of Intangible cultural heritage (ICH) that ICH needs and deserves international safeguarding? By common assent, Intangible cultural heritage (ICH) refers to all immaterial manifestations of culture, represents the variety of living heritage of humanity as well as the most important vehicle of cultural diversity. The essence of this holistic view of cultural heritage, which is composed not only of tangible properties, but also and especially of all immaterial elements that are considered by a given community as essential components of its intrinsic identity as well as of its uniqueness and distinctiveness in comparison with all other human groups, is at the very heart of its distinctive idiosyncrasy, hence the importance of safeguarding of cultural diversity. At present, we are aware on a daily basis of the definitive loss, throughout the world, of languages, knowledge, knowhow,

我们也可以把他请到青海去。他可能去三四天,也可以待一两个月。我们不可能储备这么多的文化创意人才,但是这方面的重点是要合理利用好人才。

我们做这些文化创意的时候,起点必须要高,要把它做成国际水平甚至世界一流水平。我们要塑造我们的文化形象,提升对外文化的影响力,有的品牌不光是为青海做,甚至是为中国做,这样才能提升我们的文化品牌。这些是我们在文化创意方面所做的一些非常重要的基础性工作。

在21世纪国际关系和世界秩序的重建过程里,文化的影响已经从旧时代的从属地位上升到绝对的主导地位。历史学家认为,这种影响使政治、经济、军事更加强大,文化作为一种源于人类世界与创造的生产,它是提升整个社会经济发展水平的巨大动力。当前我国正处在重要的经济转型期,对文化和济发展有了更新的认识和更高的要求,我们需要进一步解放思想,在青海这样的地方尤其需要。

我们国家甚至全世界都把文化作为综合国力的一个很重要的组成部分。美国除了有强大的经济和军事之外,还向全世界输出它的价值观的输出,而价值观的输出主要是靠文化为载体。美国这么多的大片,你看哪个最终塑造的英雄人物不是美国的,它并没有说这是美国的代言人,但绝对是正义战胜邪恶,都是按照美国价值观的标准制作出来的。美国价值观的输出还包括美国的信息产业,包括在世界上占非常大比重的软件。文化的力量是无穷的,我们现在越来越感觉到中华民族在矗立于世界民族之林的时候,必须使我们的文化占有重要的一席之地。

现在西班牙的塞万提斯学院、德国的歌德学院在很多国家都建立了分院,法国、意大利虽然没有这样做,但是它们在宣扬其文化价值方面是做得非常扎实的。现在中国正在国际上建孔子学院。一个国家、民族的文化塑造、文化遗产是这个国家、民族的重要标志。你用军事短暂地占领一个地方是没有用的,你不可能长期在那儿占领,你的部队一撤走,你的影响就消失了。但是,文化的消失是没有那么简单的。我们去土耳其伊斯坦布尔,在遗迹里你可以看到不同的民族之间、不同的文化之间在历史、战争的交流过程中留下来的遗产。再比如以色列耶路撒冷,世界上最重要的几大宗教都诞生在那儿,你可以看到文化的影响力是多么重要。

对一个欠发达地区来说,走出文化创意成功之路的关键是我们必须要面向世

customs, and ideas, leading to the progressive impoverishment of human society. Such global bemoaning highlights the necessity of the creativity industry in place of or concomitant to the traditional economic set-up geared mainly to the production of tangible properties at the expense of the degrading biota.

Such global awakening has dissolved on our part into a self-discovery, alarmist in nature, that Qinghai is situated on the third terrace of the earth, the last Pure Land as well as the last Forbidden Land in terms of reckless modernization. When we use words like "global awakening", we admit at the outset the thing badly in need must grow from within, that is , we must realize and make the new mode of growth as the engine for fostering sufficient income. If creativity industry fails to achieve this higher aspiration, then what else is the line of human effort for? Enlightenment aside, here again we encounter the classical bottleneck of lack of talent as creativity business refers to a range of economic activities which are concerned with the generation or exploitation of knowledge and information. They may variously also be referred to as the cultural industries (especially in Europe or the creative economy. Howkins' creative economy comprises advertising, architecture, art, crafts, design, fashion, film, music, performing arts, publishing, R&D, software, toys and games, TV and radio, and video games.Our policy is to the skirt the traditional possessive mentality by inviting talent in the rest of China to work on special project temporarily for a few weeks or two months. The duration of their sojourn depends upon the length of the project. They do not have to move their families together with permanent residential permit and arrangement. This has saved huge paperwork process and logistic problem. Over the years we develop our talent tank at our disposal.

Thanks to our forward thinking, the creative industry, which features a combination of the human brain, culture and technology, has quickly grown from an emerging "fledgling" industry to an important pillar industry of the province, a new engine for its economic development. Our secret is we aim high from the very beginning. Creative industries not only are designed to account for higher than average growth and job creation, they are also vehicles of cultural identity that play an important role in fostering cultural diversity. We have recognized this fact and started to develop specific policies to promote its growth.

The advent of the 21th century has ushered in a process of rebuilding of world order in the context of which the cultural archetypes and interests of dominant societies globalize, to the prejudice of minority cultures, leading to cultural hegemony and uniformity at the local, national, regional, and international level. While the world is the theater, the main player is the culture, superseding even the combination of politics, economics and military prowess. Culture is at the core of human origin and human activity and as such the new locomotive for economic evolution. To sum up, western styled industrialization once dominated the human scene and shaped our society. It still yields us economic benefits and destroys part of our nature. Reaping the harvest by modern cultural enterprise not only yields GDP but also more eco-friendly and a higher existential

界,当然我们首先要认识到我们的资源。青海是原生态文化和旅游资源的富饶地,我们过去长期形成的对社会的认识,不能适应当今社会发展的态势,这种认识有意无意还是存在于人的思维常态之中。我们对于发展经济已经达成共识,但怎样发展我们的文化产业,特别是文化创意产业,还需要我们在知识和认识领域不断地解放思想。我们必须有足够的知识储备,才可能进行一系列的文化创意。

比尔·盖茨说过一句话,"创意具有裂变的效应,一盎司的创意能够带来难以计数的商业利益"。在青海,我们应该怎样利用我们民族和地域、宗教的资源,怎么样使之具有当代的意识,怎么样能够和世界的文化发展和经济发展结合在一起,来完成我们的创意品牌?我们并不是先知先觉到了那儿马上就那么做,实际上,青海很多干部一直在做这方面的思考,只不过我们在最近三年做的工作比较多。我们对前面很多的事物进行不断的认识,完成了现在国内外很关注的一些重要的文化品牌和体育品牌的创立。

下面,我把青海文化创意的几个品牌,包括品牌的形成作一个简单的介绍。我们放眼世界来看待我们的优势,更加认识到我们的优势从而有效地扬长避短,真正意义上地走向世界。近年来,在充分认识我们资源的特殊性和当代社会环境的前提下,我们以较大的力度进行了一系列的文化创意开发并且有了成功的范例,主要包括青海国际诗歌节、青海国际唐卡艺术与文化艺术博览会、青海艺术生命之旅、中国青海世界山地纪录片节和三江源文化节,还有环青海湖国际公路自行车赛、青海高原世界杯攀岩赛、国际黄河极限挑战赛,这些具有青海的内涵又具有独特创意视角的文化体育品牌作为我们的文化创意的代表作,给青海带来很多荣誉包括一些国际上的荣誉,引起了广泛的关注。很多人说,没有想到你们青海会做出这么有国际性的品牌。刚才我说的一系列的话题都是我们的创意和文化品牌的很重要的基础性工作,也是我们完成对这些资源进行再认识和改变观念的过程,这些前提对我们来说是非常重要的。

青海国际诗歌节

我首先给大家介绍的是青海国际诗歌节。中国是一个诗歌的国度,古代诞生了屈原、杜甫、李白、苏东坡,近代诞生了郭沫若、艾青等众多伟大诗人,但是中国没有

dimension rarely evoked by circumstance.

The 21th century is frequently dubbed of globalization. As we have mentioned above, to globalize in the modern context means more often than not dominant societies globalize their own cultural norms and value judgment to the detriment of the authenticity and integrity of those associated with the weak cultures and indigenous traditions by means of cultural products. For instance, export of American core values are in two forms, blockbusters tailored to the American classical recipe and ingredients of poetic justice and information industry. The inundation of software in world market. American success epitomizes the supreme worth and power of culture and highlight the importance of the ICH for us Chinese to enhance and promote and proclaim our spaces or forms of cultural expression.

As is pointed out above, cultural heritage includes all immaterial elements that are considered by a given community as essential components of its intrinsic identity as well as of its uniqueness and distinctiveness in comparison with all other human groups. Several European countries have learned to promote their cultural and racial uniqueness and distinctiveness. For instance Spain has opened its franchise of Don Quixote Institute and state-sponsored Von Goethe Institute also branches out in many parts of the world. Though France and Italy might have refrained from following the suit, they have evolved other means of cultural expression equally effective and efficient. China is now emulating Spain and Germany, bringing our own chain of Confucius Institute in dozens of countries. Ultimately, the pen is mightier than the sword. To resort to military occupation makes no sense. The moment your troops are gone, your influence is nil. Yet cultural effect proves to be enduring. I once travelled to Istanbul and saw a plethora of cultural relics, ruins and sites, all living testimony to the interactions of a multiplicity of races and peoples and cultures either in wars or in other forms of contact in history. Take a tour of the city of Jerusalem, claimed by Israel as its capital at the beginning of the 1970s, remains a symbol and inspiration of the three great monotheistic religions of Judaism, Christianity and Islam, a living proof of cultural potential.

In terms of historical background, as we know, creativity industry arose from the context of post-industrial and knowledge economies to create wealth and increase employment rate so as to promote social development and the welfare of people. Our point of departure, however, is a status quo of a typical pre-industrial society locked on the most ecological sensitive third terrace of the earth. Such a challenge also holds a promise. An economic backwater can contain the most authentic and distinctive resources for tourism operators. Such alpine tourism destinations can turn out to be very lucrative. The global trend, in which the rise in demand for cultural products and the growing search for identity, are pushing culture and business increasingly interlocked, is out there to be capitalized to our advantage. We need to educate ourselves first before we can lead our people to blaze a new path of getting rich without neutralizing our environment which is at its most fragile at the altitude we are.

一个真正意义上的诗歌节。我曾经多次出席世界上几个重要的国际诗歌节,全世界最重要的国际诗歌节有六个,其中有五个在欧洲,分别在德国柏林、意大利圣马力诺、马其顿斯特鲁加、波兰华沙、荷兰鹿特丹,一个在美洲哥伦比亚麦德林。我过去在中国作协工作时,在陈至立同志的支持下和文化部的支持下,中国作协做了一个中国诗歌节但不是国际诗歌节,仅仅是中国诗歌界参加的,每两年举办一次。

中国是一个产生了《诗经》、唐诗、宋词、元曲的伟大国度,又是一个代表东方文明的古国,却没有一个真正意义上的国际诗歌节,这和中国的国际形象是不相称的。一般意义上,国际诗歌节应该在上海、北京或者某一个经济很发达的地区来做。中国没有这样的一个国际诗歌节,这给我们留下了一个很大的想象空间。

既然欧洲已经有了这么多的国际诗歌节,亚洲的国家应该搞,而日本和韩国的诗歌节规模不是很大。所以2007年我们正式创立了青海湖国际诗歌节,我们有一个理念,要吸引国际上重要的人士到青海。现在全世界都在关注环保、关注生态、关注人类的生存环境。人类正处在工业化和后工业化时代,处在一个商业主义和物质主义的时代,人类又在寻求自己的精神走向,人类一直在试图回答一个问题"我们从哪里来?我们要到哪里去"。我们的经济和科技高度地发展,但是环境遭到了很大的破坏,资源被过度地消耗甚至是掠夺性地消耗。这是人类发展的一个悖论,一方面要迅速地发展,但是环境和生态、生存空间所带来的这种破坏给人类已经亮了红灯,已经提出了一种挑战。

我们在青藏高原举办一个国际诗歌节,就是要重新让人回归自然,让我们的心灵和灵魂能找到一个可以放松的地方,用诗歌来抚慰我们的心灵,在这片净土之中寻求人类不同文明的对话和沟通,在这个沟通过程之中来表达我们东方和中国人的一种哲学思想。中华民族是一个热爱和平的民族,中国是一个热爱和平的国家。我们通过国际性的诗歌节为整个东方的哲学思想、东方的文明建立一个重要的平台。从某种意义来说,高层的诗人之间的交流,其重要性不比高层的政治家之间的交流差,因为这些诗人都是代表他们民族的精神文化,他们是本民族的象征,他们都是大家而不是一般的诗人,他们来进行沟通就是不同文明和文化之间的最高层次的沟通。如果不从政治层面讲而是从文化层面讲就是这样的,因为无论从东方还是西方的观

Bill Gates is quoted as saying that a creative idea can trigger a fission effect. And an ounce of good ideas is simply a cash cow. It would appear Nature and history have bequeathed an unusual combination of pristine wilderness and humanistic-religious traditions as raw materials or products to be further deep processed. Now a sparkle of originality would create their own economic satisfactions and cultural harvest with little attrition or degeneration of land or life.. All said, there is a point of intellectual humility. We are not omniscient beings .We are not hitting upon the idea over night. In fact, local people at different levels have groped for years all the way, experimenting with various approaches while we emerge ,the conditions are rather ripe and what we have achieved should be deemed the crystallization and the accumulative evolution of protracted striving to keep the area usable and beautifully wild for human well being and wildlife in the meanwhile.

Prior to this point is a lengthy account of the background and intellectual incubation of the regional creativity business. Now let me give you a brief introduction to each cultural product we have come out in recent years. The forging of several cultural brands (cultural products) awaits such latest thinking and the corresponding growth of perception of world trends. Placed in perspective, these are successful cases of creativity industry, having their repercussions felt across China and the world for enhancing local tourism expansion, generating cash flow and adding value to our unspoiled wilderness. The list includes:Qinghai Lake International Poetry Festival, International Thangka Exhibition and Fair, Qinghai Concert in Celebration of Water by the Side of the Yellow River, Qinghai World Mountain Documentary Films Festival, The Headwaters of the Three Great Rivers Cultural Festival, Tour of Qinghai Lake International Cycling Contest, International Yellow River Swimming Contest.

Qinghai Lake International Poetry Festival

We all know China is one of the earliest civilizations that flowered in Asia, persisting with an unequalled record of continuity from the Shang to modern times. Part of that record points to a prestigious lineage of poetic legacy and poets of lasting worth such as Chu Yuan, Du Fu, Li Bai, Su Dongpo and Guo Mojo and Ai Qing, the latter two being moderns. Given a culture prizing poetry as the finest gem, China had been never a host to an international poetry festival. I have been attending all the six distinguished poetry festivals, with five in Europe(Germany, Saint Mario of Italy, Struga of Macedonia, Warsaw of Poland, Amsterdam of Holland) and the sixth in Medellin of Columbia in Latin America. When I was working in Beijing prior to 2007, I took the initiative to organize a national poetry festival, twice a year, but it is national in character, with no foreign poets participating it.

You see, something is not right. This is a country that boasts a most glorious poetic tradition dating back 3000 years. The rich veins of poetic writing composed of brilliant Book of Songs, Songs of the South, Tang poetry, Song Ci and Yuan ballads stand supreme in the entire human heritage among the headwaters of all known literary expression. Such negligence in the cultural

念看,诗人是他们民族精神文化中和哲学家一样站在塔尖上的人。

　　这并不是说我看不起小说家,小说家低一个层次。在欧洲你看诗人的地位是很崇高的,他可能一贫如洗,但他的精神是富裕的。他的精神崇高是真正的崇高,你别看有的人兜里很有钱,但是精神不崇高。这些人代表了他们民族的精神文化,他们到这个地方来我们给他们提供了这样的平台。2007年8月9日,我们举办第一届青海湖国际诗歌节,发表《青海湖诗歌宣言》,来自34个国家的200多位世界级的诗人到青海来,这可以说是世界诗坛的一次盛会、国际诗歌界的一次盛会。这是很难得的,很不容易的。第一次举办就形成了一个很重要的文化品牌。首届青海湖诗歌节已经以它独特的地理诱惑和人文魅力,给这个有着伟大诗歌传统和多元文化共存的世界送来了惊喜,给离太阳最近的第三极、被称为"人类最后净土"的青藏高原带来了一次从未有过的文化震撼。著名诗人、波兰国家作协主席马雷克·瓦夫凯维奇说,"这是东方的一个创举",意味着世界上第七大诗歌节的诞生。青海湖国际诗歌节是被全世界共同承认的,已经进入全世界第七大诗歌节了,这既是青海的光荣,也是中国文化的光荣。

　　诗歌是最古老的一种艺术,同时也是最年轻的一种艺术。说它是最古老的艺术,是因为从人类诞生以来,诗和歌就伴随着人类,诗歌将会永远存在下去。有人问过我,说你认为诗歌今后还会不断地延续吗？我说其他我不敢肯定,我只能说只要人类存在,还有人活在这个世界上,那么诗歌就存在,因为诗歌作为一种古老的艺术形式,它从未失去过抚慰人的心灵、激励人类斗志,给人类心灵带来美好的愉悦的功能,它的形式会不断地进行改变,但是它的本质和精神不会改变。说它是最年轻的艺术,可能我们相隔几千年甚至几百年,诗歌都已经存在了,但是现在还有诗人不断地写作出新的诗篇,见证我们人类不断发展的过程。

　　作为一个诗人,我从不否认我对诗歌有着特殊的热爱和敬仰。青海湖诗歌节的创立有其深厚的背景,如果没有第三极的地理概念,如果没有青藏高原这一片最后的净土,如果没有这个地方多元深厚的民族文化,如果没有中国悠久的5000年的文

sphere, which constituted the most compelling justification, prompted me into a mood of brainstorming. This being taken for granted, I moved to find a proper venue or locale to anchor the forthcoming pageant. Normally one would anchor it either in the glitzy Bund of Shanghai or by the immense and spectacular Forbidden City. But I thought otherwise then.

The prime location, to me, is Qinghai .In 2007, the only biennial festival dedicated to poetic art in China, and the only cultural event kicked off by the shores of Lake Koknor, the brightest jewelry in the crown of the Qinghai -Tibet Plateau. QLIPF's job is to bring to highland the best of poets, and practitioners in related art forms worldwide. The successful inception in 2007 behind (240 poets from 35 countries and regions), QLIPF will continue to feature a strong list of leading poets from China and all over the world seeking to eulogize the last remaining Pure Land on this troubled planet and direct the world's attention to the conservation of the earth's third pole. We are living in an age of industrialization and post-industrialization, an age swept by commercialism and materialism. That has been, and is, the meaning of this poetic gathering, as attempt to return to our human rootage and to sound an alarm to the disoriented world community over indulgent in the gratification of material desires and sensuality. The quick depletion of natural resources and deterioration of our environment may well lead us to a blind alley.

QLIPF is taking root in the Last Pure Land, offering solace to over-urbanized people from rich coastal cities or car plagued metropolis. For here on the plateau one captures a glimpse of the amazingly sprawling grassland, bright green with many wild flowers and wildlife mixed in with snow capped mountains in the distance as well as a platform on which different cultures and religions collide into a civilized dialogue. We are peace loving people .And China is a country that habitually shuns war and other forms of hostilities. In a sense, that the established poets meet contributes no less than the politicians to world peace. Each delegate is the representative of their distinctive culture, the embodiment of their national spirit. One traditional line of thinking, both in the east and the west, puts poets and philosophers on the same pedestal ,both outstanding achievers in the venerable cultural domain.

I am not insinuating disparagement into your minds as if novelists are of a lower caste. In Europe, people still accord poets an honorable place in society. Poor he may be, he is held in esteem for his rich spirituality and vibrant humanity. Deservedly so. Our society is full of nouvaux riches. They are despised for leading a mean and materialistic life, with scant interest in things of the mind. We retain our age-old yearnings for the solar spirit of poetry as well as those who embody these spiritual qualities. The successful inception in 2007 drew over 200 poets of world class from 35 countries and regions and we are truly turning this festival an extravaganza without precedent. A fantastic start as QLIPF intends to grow to be recognized as the major poetry event in China, ranking proudly among the most prestigious international counterparts. Our repute hinges by and large upon a special motif or a special raison d'etre for which we come into being and into our own. That special motif is we appeal, down from the Roof of the World, on the tertiary pole of

明传统和我们的中国诗歌传人，如果没有数以千万计的中国最重要的诗人在不同的历史时期写出重要的诗歌篇章作为我们民族伟大的文化积累，我们也不可能创立这个诗歌节，这是前人的积聚，我们后人只不过在这个基础上在面对这个时代的时候找到一个历史性的机遇，是中国古老的文化传统把这个机遇给了青海，也是中国数以几千年的诗歌传统和诗歌文明把这个机会给了青海，同时也是我们今天在发展创意经济的过程中重新认识我们的资源、民族文化、宗教文化带来的机遇。所以我认为这些是最重要的，当然，也离不开我们在做这些工作的人对诗歌的热爱。

青海湖诗歌节每两年一届，它确实为我们提供了一个很重要的进行国际文化交流的平台。2009年8月，我们成功举办了第二届青海湖国际诗歌节。与第一届相比，这一届增加了很多新的队伍，规模更大了，有近50个国家的200多位诗人参加，来的诗人都是他们国家具有代表性的诗人。本届诗歌节除了举办一些很好的国际论坛之外，还设立了"金藏羚羊国际诗歌奖"，专门授予在诗歌创作方面成就斐然且具有较大国际影响的中外当代诗人，每届只授予一位健在的中外诗人。

本届评委由全世界不同地域的重要诗评家组成，评选了10位候选人，经过投票，决定把这个奖项授予阿根廷当代重要诗人、拉丁美洲最重要的伟大诗人之一胡安·赫尔曼。我们除了有一个很好的高峰论坛外，还在青海湖专门修了国际诗歌墙，有29位全世界最杰出的伟大诗人的名字被刻在诗歌墙上。这是全世界第一面国际诗歌墙，受到国际社会的高度关注。我们不是搞一个简单的碑，而是做了国际诗歌墙，采用了藏族的文化元素石经墙的形式。

作为一个刚刚创立就被普遍认同的文化品牌，青海国际诗歌节以它新颖的创意和深厚的诗歌文化内涵，已经成为国际上六大诗歌节之后的第七大诗歌节。我们要不断地做下去，这对介绍中国的当代文化，介绍中国的古老文明是一个重要的窗口。我们不断提出新的主题，第一届诗歌节的主题是"人与自然——多元文化的共享与传承"，第二届我们就"现实和物质的超越——诗歌与人类精神世界的重构"这一主题进行了很广泛的对话，取得了非常重要的国际性的学术成果，有些成果出版了很

the earth, in closest proximity to the sun, to mankind's latent ecological conscience that of all the causes that rivet the attention of contemporary people, the plight of nature might be truly a last call. A cultural shock experience dealt by the Last Pure Land, Malek Wawkavich, Polish poet and chairman of Polish Writers Union characterized the event as a piece of "Oriental pioneering undertaking."

Poetry is both the oldest and the youngest form of art. Oldest in that it has been in the companionship of mankind from literarily geological beginnings and hopefully till the end of the world. Some doomsayers worry about the fate of poetry. I tell them, in spite of all the cynicism, poetry will continue to grow in our lives, charged with the office of administering the much thirsted vitamin and dewdrops to nourish the parched and hungry souls. The letter and form may vary, but the spirit will remain to sustain us in extolling the virtues of endurance and strength in the struggle of life. Youngest in the sense that poetry was born thousands of years ago yet to this day up-coming poets continue to practice this art to attest to the fact human beings endure and will endure.

A poet myself, I have never lost my ardor and awe in poetry. As I have asserted, the successful launching of QLIPF is made possible by a number of favorable conditions, such as the concept of the third terrace of the earth, the presence of the Last Pure Land, the stock of multi cultural diversity that makes Qinghai it is, the rich veins of poetic legacy spanning 5000 years and lastly, the accumulative growth of poetic writing left by successive generations of poets. I must confess, as I stand humbled here, to a huge blessing bestowed upon me and Qinghai to avail this momentous opportunity to pass on our deeply entrenched poetic tradition. I feel doubly blessed because with this festival staged, we get our creativity industry under way and on the right track. For this reason, I owe all those with whom I work to realize our common dream, an emotional and intellectual debt. For they too, identify deeply as I, with poetic art and the spreading of poetic joy of life.

QLIPF is an bi-annual cultural event, organized by the Qinghai Province government and The Poetry Institute of China, the festival features a cultural summit forum, a night of poetry on Qinghai Lake, and a concert entitled "Poetic Qinghai and Harmonious World." In August, 2009, the second edition of QLIPF was held as scheduled, featuring a even stronger cast of characters as over 200 poets from nearly 50 countries and regions were invited. Add to the previous agenda was the establishment of Golden Tibetan Antelope Award to honor a living poet, each edition, for his excellent contribution to poetic art either in China or across the world.

The panel of judges is made of critics from different continents. Finally they voted out of ten candidates on Juan Hermann, one of the greatest living poets in the Hispanic world, to be the first recipient of the award. Aside the summit forum, we have erected lakeside a poetry wall on which the names of 29 world poets are inscribed, the first of its kind which made headlines over the world. It is not a bare monument .Our intent is more nuanced as the wall is erected inspired by

多书，在读者里面产生了非常广泛的影响。有的在国际上出版之后，国际文坛反应非常强烈。

在青海湖发表青海国际诗歌节的宣言，这本身就是一个创意性的举动，在国际上反响巨大，被评为世界十大重大文化创意之一，我们在"名人所创立的重要文化"上进行了专门的讲演。青海国际诗歌节期间，中外诗人面对青藏高原创作了大量的诗歌，这是第一次全世界众多的诗人以诗意的目光共同关注青藏高原这片最后的净土，无论他们使用什么样的语言，具有什么样的审美情趣，立足什么样的文化根基，我们相信诗人们履行了他们在青海湖的神圣承诺。我们将以诗的名义把敬畏还给自然，把自由还给生命，把尊严还给人类，把爱还给生活。青海湖国际诗歌节还将继续创办下去，继续地发扬光大。

青海国际唐卡艺术与文化遗产博览会

青海国际唐卡艺术与文化遗产博览会是打开记忆之门的一个重要的文化创意。2009年10月初，联合国教科文组织把热贡艺术列入了人类非物质文化遗产目录。热贡艺术是中国的一项传统民间艺术，这一项民族智慧的结晶包括唐卡、雕刻等艺术形式，享誉中外的唐卡卷轴画就是唐卡艺术的代表。在全球化的过程当中，"地球村"的概念现在已经逐步形成了，人类历史上从未有过像今天这么强大的资讯、网络，现在全世界任何一个地方出现一个突发性的事件，我们通过网络马上就知道了。过去的几百年可能是现在的几年，过去的几十年可能是现在的几个月甚至是几天，这个空间和时间都发生了很大的变化。在文化多样性的视域中，每个民族创作的文化有不同的特点，具有不可替代性。

1998年联合国第22号决议指出，不同文化构成的遗产是全世界文明的源泉。青海的热土培育的非物质文化遗产是青海人民奉献给世界文化的奇葩，它所蕴含的丰富文化是青海的文化资源。因此，保护好这些弥足珍贵的非物质遗产就是保护青海走向世界的权利，保护青海人民和世界的对话权。我们要跟世界对话，靠什么？就靠文化资源。中国作为一个文明国度和全世界对话因为它代表了一个文明，伊拉克代

Tibetan Buddhist sutra walls, an icon of religious devoutness and spiritual humility exhibited by local masses of Buddhist believers.

A bi-annual cultural brand instantly gaining recognition, QLIPF counts the 7th international poetry festivals for its inventiveness and cultural value, being a window on China and a channel through which we promote Chinese culture. For each edition, we set a new theme for the summit forum. For example, the theme for the second edition is "Transcendence Over Reality and Materialism-Re-forging Man's Spiritual World". Centering upon this topic, poets and critics engaged in wide-ranging dialogues and generated significant academic fruits, and when published, exerted profound influence upon the reading public, home and abroad.

The whole event climaxed in a highly emotional and symbolic ceremony of all the poets and writers present lining lakeside to proclaim a poetic manifesto .In one word, the simple aim of QLIPF was to celebrate poetry and nature together. This collective signing of a poetic manifesto is significantly creative to arouse global focus, touted by experts to be one of the 10 world class creative ideas. One of the highlights was a group tour of the lake areas calling forth and collecting poems done in praise of the scenic and holy Lake Koknor and the pristine Last Pure Land. All the poets were given a chance to refine one of the oldest humanistic endeavors and to pray for a world more eco-friendly and dedicated to the dignity of mankind.

Qinghai International Thangka and Cultural Heritage Exhibition Fair

Qinghai International Thangka and Cultural Heritage Exhibition Fair ranks one of the most forward looking creative ideas, a door opened to the historical memory. In October, 2009, Retkong art (Appliqué embroidery, sculpture, and mainly scroll painting called Thangka in Tibetan) was added to the Intangible Cultural Heritage list by UNESCO. Thangka is a Buddhist painting on a banner which can be hung or rolled up, sometimes called "scroll-painting". It often depicts images or stories of Buddha, great lamas or other deities and Bodhisattva. The Thangka, or scroll painting, is a typical specimen of regional Intangible culture heritage , the mainstay of culture diversity and human creativity. The process of globalization and social transformation have given rise to the concept of the global village. So powerful and pervasive is the force of the internet and digitalization that any local event will be instantly perceived elsewhere in the world. While it might take hundreds of years in the past, it is at present a matter of few years .While it might take dozens of years previously, it is at present a matter of few months and even a few days. Across the spectrum of cultural diversity, each race will display its art form with authenticity and distinctiveness which defies duplication.

UN pointed out in a statement in 1998 the fountain of human civilization is the accumulation of diverse cultural heritages. Rebgong art, nurtured in the soil of Qinghai's land mass, is a bouquet of beautiful flowers dedicated to the world community by local people. To safeguard this heritage is to safeguard our passport to the world forum in which we can engage dialogues with people representing various cultural traditions. By what are we empowered on

表了巴比伦的文明,伊朗是波斯的文明,埃及是古埃及的文明,这些文明都是了不起的文明。有着自己悠久历史的国家是一个幸运的国家。美国建国的时间很短,200年前是印第安人在那里生活,但是印第安是一个移民的国家。

谈到历史就要提到埃及、伊朗、中国、印度,包括古罗马、古希腊这些国家,他们的文化历史非常悠久。基于这样的思考,我们在青海正式创办了一个博览会,它以促进民族文化发展,特别是文化产业发展,保护物质文化遗产和非物质文化遗产为目的。这几年我们通过对非物质文化遗产的保护,把这些民族文化艺术推到前台来,一方面我们把这种传承好的艺术,把这个民族符号、文化链不断地延续;另一方面我们要建立我们的文化市场特别是文化艺术市场。怎么样能够利用这个市场,另外使它真正形成一个产业链,这是我们最根本的目的。全世界正处于一个同质化的过程当中,你影响我,我影响你,有的民族文化已经失去了它的个性、特点了。

在这个世界上每天都有几个物种,甚至是几十个物种在消失,非常可怕。物质是形成链条的,是相互依存的,生物链的破坏对未来人类的发展空间和人类的生存会造成很大的危害的,这是从生活层面来讲。如果从文化层面来讲,据社会学家和人类学家的考察,现在全世界每天也有一两种语言在消失,这也非常可怕,任何生活在地球上的有良知的人都应该感觉到很痛心。思维和语言是联系在一起的,一个古老的语言消失的时候,就相当于人类一个古老的物种消失,它所承载的文化消失,对于整个人类来说是一种悲哀,非常可惜。我们要站在这个角度来看文化,我们保护好每一个民族的文化,保护好我们每一个民族的历史,传承好我们在世界上不同的文化符号和文化链条,才会使这个世界形成一个多元文化并存的格局,这种格局会形成文化之间的相互影响、相互对话,从而在保持不同文化的同时又发展我们自身的文化。但是今天我们在做非物质文化保护的时候,不能说是你的地方你的唐卡,就像我们每个省每个地域有一些工艺美术、民间艺术。怎么才能把它做成国际性的品牌呢?文化和宗教都是全世界很关注的,我们只能利用我们的文化延续的重要性,在一个方面把它不断地推向市场,使它形成一个文化的产业。

equal terms with other people? Cultural heritage of course. China is the center of an early civilization, as modern Iraq emerges from the ruins of the Babylonian counterpart, Iran, from that of the Persian civilization, and Egypt, rightly descended from ancient Egyptian variety. The above mentioned are all great cultures. Blessed, indeed, are those countries that boast long histories. USA is a young country, built on an ancient land whose indigenous inhabitants were Indians, not of the Caucasoid stock.

A historical survey reminds us of the antiquity of a number of major spheres of cultural influences. In the light of the above thinking, we have decided to sponsor an exhibition fair to safeguard the intangible cultural heritage and to promote the development of the cultural effort. Awareness of the significance of intangible cultural heritage (ICH) has recently grown, due to the promotional efforts of UNESCO and its Convention for the Safeguarding of the Intangible Cultural Heritage (2003). However, the increased recognition of intangible heritage has brought to light its undervalued status in the market sector, and raised questions about the financing of the safeguarding work. The idea is to incubate a market to generate an unending flow of cash much needed to support the inheritors and bearers as well as employment opportunities. One of the most negative outgrowths is the rich cultural variety of humanity is progressively and dangerously tending towards uniformity.

At present, we are aware on a daily basis of the frightening loss throughout the world of several even dozens of species. The biotic community is shaped like a pyramid and all the species are interdependent .One link missing will eventually cause the chain to collapse. A deformed biotic chain, viewed on the existential plane, will ultimately put human beings, a link in the chain of life after all, in jeopardy. Culturally speaking, the loss of one or two languages daily in the world abodes absolutely ill for mankind. In Whorfian terms, languages encode cultural and cognitive categories which will in turn affect the way people think, so that speakers of different languages will tend to think and behave differently depending on the language they use. An old language dies out, so does an old race, because the culture encoded in that language disappears. As such, it entails in essence a human loss. Accordingly we must safeguard our own culture, our own history and conserve cultural icons and chains different from ours in the belief that conceived as the totality of perceptible manifestations of the different human groups and communities, all the human cultural traditions as they stand, are essential for the survival and development of all cultures. So our safeguarding effort must cover any form of intangible cultural products, of whatever origin, of whatever market estimate at the present. We venture to push Thangka to the market in the hope that its market value exponentially increased and discovered will in turn finance and sustain the safeguarding effort.

A seasoned traveler, I put Rebgong on your table, your next destination to tour and savoir the Thangka, one the important genres of Tibetan Buddhist art nestled in the golden valley (Rebgong). In the 14th and 15th century, the Tibetan Buddhism spread the Tongren area in the

你们有机会去青海,一定要到热贡去,就是到我们的"金色的土地"上去看看唐卡艺术。那个地方每一家都是画室,人人是画家,都画唐卡,还做其他的艺术和雕塑,技艺非常精湛。现在一个好的唐卡10万、20万是少的,特别是一个技艺好的大师的作品是几十万的,都是矿物质的颜料可以保存几百年不变色的。我们在规范市场,有一些其他材料画的都要严格规范,要对它进行认证。大家可以去看看这个地方,在青藏高原,特别是以藏文化为中心的文化形态的延续过程中,热贡从某种意义上是以藏族为主的一个文艺复兴的中心。在青藏高原,历史上最好的唐卡、泥塑、雕塑都出在热贡。现在你去藏区,去看看他们的庙宇,都是非常精美,里面的雕刻都是非常精湛的,都是一些大师的作品。他们通过这个可以获得很好的经济收入,这也是农牧民一个致富的办法。

但是我们为什么要把它做成一个国际性的文化品牌呢?现在全世界都在关注唐卡,特别是关注青藏高原藏传佛教的藏区的艺术。在这个过程当中,我们搞国际唐卡艺术是想提升一个品牌,在进行文化对话的时候我们来提升这个地方的文化影响,提升它对外国文化的影响,这是我们的真正目的。所以我们举办每一届国际唐卡艺术文化博览会,都会举办一些高水平的文化论坛,进行国际性的对话和交流。中国从中央到地方政府历来重视保护各民族的文化,政府对少数民族的保护是投了巨资的,这是历史的事实,我们要让世界看一下,我们用事实回应西方世界对我们进行的攻击。另外,我们要让大家看一下,我们在一个很自然的过程中为文化延续提供了一些很好的空间,我们并没有像西方所攻击的那样在搞文化灭绝,这些不是事实。所以说,这有双重的意义。

另外,打造国际品牌很重要的一点,是我们要让大家在更深层次上了解青藏高原灿烂的物质文化遗产的文明和非物质文化遗产的文明都是同样悠久和古老。比如说藏族的格萨尔王史诗,也是最早的史诗之一,世界上还有很多的史诗,蒙古的、中亚的、阿拉伯的,包括世界上有名的古希腊、古罗马的一些史诗,比如奥德赛史诗。但是格萨尔王史诗是一个活态史诗,现在还在不断地被整理。在青海撰写格萨尔王的

south of Qinghai. Gradually people there or nearby villages were engaged in Tibetan Buddhist art, including Thangka, sculpture, architectural painting, appliqué embroidery, murals, etc. Till the middle of 17th century, these villages in the golden valley (Rebgong) achieved fame with its distinctively brighter colors and finer lines and Thangkas from Rebgong were commissioned by monasteries across the Plateau. And this tradition has been handed down from generation to generation. Even today nearly every Rebgong man or woman is an artisan .In recent years, Skilled Thangka and mural painters are valued and individual collectors from Chinese cities and foreign countries have driven up the prices. A good Thangka can fetch from 100000 RMB, 200000RMB to half a million, it depends. Good pigments and other materials (non-transparent minerals and plants such as malachite and cinnabar, mixed with animal glue and ox bile to make the polish stay) ensure the luster last for a few hundred years. We are intervening to certify the supply of the raw materials vital for the art. The art tradition here suffered a break back in the 1960s and 1970s, but it has witnessed a revival. Most people agree the masterpieces, either of scroll painting or clay sculpture, are the work of Rebgong artists. The architectural style of the temples and monasteries is impressive indeed, frequently an art gallery that depict Tibetan gods and other religious iconography. The commercialization of Thangka has been much of a reality, a win-win situation at its best as it sustains the tradition and assists in the reduction of poverty substantially.

Now you may wonder what is the motive behind our striving to make Thangka an international cultural brand? Simply put, Thangka is the emblem of the intangible cultural heritage of Qinghai-Tibet Plateau, thus deemed by the international community and promoted by UNESCO. In promoting Thangka by hosting high profile forums and sponsoring international exhibitions, we are cashing in on a number of things, such as upgrading of the art tradition, economical alleviation of a considerable amount of local people, silencing of some of the rumors against the government being hostile to Tibetan art. We have consistently built roads, schools, railways, and a budding tourism industry. We must give the lie to the implication, advertent or inadvertent, that there is such a thing as "cultural genocide". We are continuously expanding and extending the spaces of ethnic expressions.

Another consideration to promote Thangka, no less important than the previously stated, is to remind the outside world of the distinguished antiquity of the alpine cultural heritage, both tangible and intangible. One more example is the Gesar epic, the central epic poem of Tibet, prized as one of the few living epics in contrast to the rest of world epic systems such as Greco-Roman epics. Living in the sense there is still no one definitive compilation plus an army of surviving ballad singers continuously to perform and chant, The epic, believed to be approximately 1000 years old, concerns the fearless king Gesar, who ruled the legendary Kingdom of GLing, considered the longest literary work in the world and one of the hottest topics engaging both regional and worldwide academic research. By way of leaven, let me tell you two anecdotes. A devout mother pleaded his son to fulfill her wish by prostrating himself around Qinghai Lake 99

史诗是最多的,格萨尔王史诗是一个传承的史诗,由老人传给年轻人,年轻人再传给后代,一代代传下来。这是一般史诗的规律,青海很多人在研究这个史诗,全世界很多人也在研究它。格萨尔王史诗有很多传说,有一个母亲跟他儿子说你围着青海湖去磕长头99圈,就能够完成我的愿望,这个磕完了很不容易的,他磕完了以后在一个寺庙里睡着了,一醒来可以口吐格萨尔王诗史,可以背十几万行。有一个人生了重病,格萨尔王的故事藏区到处能够传说,但是这个地区找不到一个人能够背几万行,他和外界的人没有多少的接触,他突然能够背十几万行,这很神奇。有的是托梦,梦里有人把格萨尔王的史诗口述给他,他醒来就会了。对于我们来说,对这些东西都要进行很好的研究。

我们搞国际唐卡艺术和国际文化的交流就是要传承我们的文化,把这个文化很好地延续。我们历来反对"经济搭台、文化唱戏"这一类的说法,这是轻视文化小看文化。我们就是让文化做主角,我们做就是做文化,做文化产业,把提升高品质的文化内涵作为我们的根本因素,而不是简单地践踏文化,把文化当成一个"托儿",当成一个可以利用的东西。我们不是这样的,我们都是以文化为中心的。

国际唐卡艺术与文化遗产博览会就是要把这些非物质的文化遗产传承下去。中国西部的少数民族中间有很多非物质文化遗产,需要我们很好地去研究。中华民族的文化是56个民族的文化的融合,各民族色彩斑斓的历史文化构成了我们中华民族的历史文化。在国际唐卡精品艺术展区内,我们有一次要展出西藏、四川、云南等地区的一些唐卡以及印度、不丹、尼泊尔等外国的唐卡,有些是过去从历史上流失出去的,有的是一些学者和其他地区做的一些物质文化和非物质文化的积累,让他们进行学习。

作为人类非物质文化遗产的热贡唐卡,被喻为火一样的唐卡,因其色调艳丽、造型优美、构图精致而广受欢迎。几个世纪以来,在青海热贡河两岸聚集了很多的村寨,那里已经成为很重要的唐卡艺术的故乡。这些作品已经走向世界的艺术殿堂,不但不断地延伸进入祖国各地的广袤地区,而且在藏传佛教地区尼泊尔和印度广为传

times. So the dutiful son undertook the arduous circumambulating, an impossible mission for any living soul. One day he finished the day's quota and fell into sleep in a temple. When he woke up next morning, he emerged a Gesar storyteller, recounting a few hundred thousand lines in a continuous flow. We know the geographical isolation of Tibet makes both internal and outside contact difficult. Another man, seldom seeing outsiders in his life, was stricken seriously sick. When he came to, he became a professional Gesar bard. Some attributed this feat to a case of the ghost of one's kith and kin, that is, some super being appears in his dreams and passes the art to him. Such anecdotes defy scientific reasoning.

Qinghai International Thangka and Cultural Heritage Exhibition Fair is launched in line with UNESCO's concern with safeguarding and propagating the intangible cultural heritage. I dismiss as puerile and nauseating the prevalent notion and practice of so called "economics as theater and culture as actors" because some shallow-minded administrators are treating cultural enterprise as a handmaiden to economic growth. For them, economics is always the deciding factor. Sponsoring cultural activity solely is a mission of mercy. To these devoid of imagination, a desert on the map is totally useless unless otherwise irrigated or forested. Cultural products, like things wild and free, have no intrinsic value unless harnessed in the modernization frenzy. Such mentality and action are a far cry from the spirit of UNESCO's convention. Cultural enterprise to me is not a job of subsidizing the needy artisans or sponsoring an exhibition fair to showcase their talent and hawk their goods, but of educating the public of the indispensableness of these traditional artifacts as a basic ingredient of humanness.

Thangka is merely an exercise of this higher order of human intellect regarding the conservation of intangible cultural heritage (ICH), made up of all immaterial manifestations of culture as the variety of living heritage of humanity as well as the most important vehicle of cultural diversity. The Chinese as a race, consists of 56 ethnic groups. And the Chinese cultural heritage necessarily is the accumulation and crystallization of 56 distinctive and authentic cultural traditions. Our exhibition reserves a section to Thangka samplings from Tibet, Sichuan and Yunnan and even from the Greater Himalaya area like India, Nepal and Bhutan as we believe in Thangka's transnational character, an art form evolved as a result of several art traditions interacting and drawing from one another across the whole Himalaya region. For instance historians note Thangka is a Nepalese art form exported to Tibet after Princess Bhrikuti of Nepal, daughter of King Lichchavi, married Songts?n Gampo, the ruler of Tibet. Tibetan and Chinese influence in Nepalese paintings, in turn, is quite evident in Paubhas (Thangkas).Mandela is a central icon both in Buddhism and Hinduism.

Rebgong Thangkas are widely appreciated valued for their distinctively brighter colors and finer lines, a prominent feature that some call "explosions of color." Rebkong , or a cluster of small villages, sits in a valley at 2500 m elevation. In Rebkong and in several of the small villages nearby, you can see the Tibetan artist's carefully painting Thangkas in great detail. Art students

承,逐步走向世界,成为世界人民所喜爱的中国民族艺术品和艺术收藏品的珍品。对于青海省而言,这些丰富的遗产代表了整体的民族风貌和风格品格,成为青海走向世界、走向全国、走向愿意认识青海的那些地域的一个最重要的载体。我想,对于我们进行文化创意,特别是对于打造国际唐卡艺术与文化博览会这一民族文化品牌而言,这些都是很重要的财富。

青海国际水与生命音乐会

我们正致力于从源头上治理荒漠化和干旱化的工作。水对于中国来说非常重要,如果离开了水我们的文明不可诞生,我们的历史不可延续,我们的生命不可存在。欧洲有一个重要的森林音乐会,在欧洲非常有名,但是全世界以水为主题的音乐会还没有。青海是长江、黄河、澜沧江的源头,所以我们想在青海打造一个国际性的音乐品牌,因此做了青海国际水与生命音乐会。

青海国际水与生命音乐会的主题必须全部是水。第一届的地点放在贵德,贵德在黄河的旁边,你到了贵德,到了青海,黄河全部是蓝色的,尤其是高空拍摄青海蓝色的黄河,你看到下面是一块块的宝石,长条带的都是江,全部是蓝色的,非常漂亮。青海有这么重要的地域资源,我们为什么不创立世界的品牌呢?第一届的7个篇章全部是关于水的,像《水的序曲》《水的梦幻》《水的诗篇》《三江源的故事》《水与生命的礼赞》等,都是世界级的作曲家来写水,然后由香港中乐乐团进行演奏。中乐乐团是连接东方文明和西方文明的节点。

第一届音乐会大家非常关注,很多国际上重要的作曲家参与了这个活动。尤其是这个活动在青藏高原举办,大家的眼睛更加关注,这个地方是不是又搞什么开发了,是不是对生态有什么影响,开发的延续过程当中是不是对环境进行了破坏?我们这个水与生命的音乐之旅,就是要表明中国是关注生态、关注环境、关注人类的生存空间的。我们自己的土地为什么不关注呢?全世界包括中国人都在关注。我们是爱国者,但是对人类的生存环境也是充满着忧虑的,这两者是不矛盾的。第一届音乐节得到了非常广泛的反响,影响力非常大。

青海"国际水与生命音乐之旅"已经成为我们一个非常重要的音乐品牌,我们刚

from Amdo (formerly the south and west of Qinghai) and beyond come here to study under skilled artists until they become master painters themselves. Thangkas from Rebkong can be found in homes and monasteries all across the Plateau and become items hotly pursued by collectors home and abroad. In a sense, among the knowledgeable high brows in the interiors of China, Thangka is often associated with Qinghai, deservedly so as home to the artistic tradition. We certainly deem this association a credit to be earned by striving harder to forge a cultural brand of substantial international renown.

Qinghai International Water and Life Concert

Drought and desertification are major environmental and socio-economic problems with negative effects on the livelihood of populations in many countries. We in Qinghai, placed on the tertiary terrace of the earth and at the fountainheads of the three great rivers, are literally in the frontline of combating drought and desertification. Water is cardinal for the growing and perpetuating of a civilization. We are trying to find a means of focusing attention on the importance of freshwater and advocating for the sustainable development. Again, drought and the scarcity of water are two names for one problem. The fundamental challenge of our time is to end extreme poverty and significantly narrow the global gap between rich and poor, without ruining the environmental basis for our survival. We know Europeans hold a forest concert each year and we finally hit upon the idea of a concert under the theme of water highlighting the increasing significance of water scarcity worldwide and the need for increased integration and cooperation to ensure sustainable, efficient and equitable management of scarce water resources, both at international and local levels.

Qinghai International Water and Life Concert's organization and logistics revolve around the theme of water. The premiere was held in a venue by the Yellow River, Guide County. Aerial overview of the Yellow River, as it flows along the Guide stretch, reminds one of the sweetest melodies of Blue Danube. We came across this super idea of holding a concert on the headwater of the Yellow River and proceeded to turn it into a cultural brand. The premiere consisted of seven movements, for example, Prelude to Water, Fantasy of Water, Poems of Water, the Genesis of the Sanjiangyuan (headwaters of the three great rivers) and Paean to Water ,all were composed by renowned composers, performed by Hongkong Philharmonic Orchestra. Hongkong is a symbolic bridge mediating between Oriental and Occidental civilizations.

The premiere made international headlines as it drew a legion of world class musicians to Qinghai-Tibet Plateau. Some even worried whether there was some big project kicked off with serious hazards to the environment. It turned to be a concert geared towards raising eco-friendly consciousness and environmental conscience. With dire warnings likely to surpass the worst fears about the effects of global warming, we have lent our support to the world community to address the twin challenge of curbing climate change while sustaining economic growth and to safeguard the world from runaway climate change. We are both patriots and world citizens. Our premiere

刚完成了第二届。这次请了全世界最重要的几大河流的歌唱家，包括印度最杰出的歌唱家唱恒河，俄罗斯的歌唱家唱伏尔加河，埃及的歌唱家唱尼罗河，巴西的歌唱家唱亚马孙河，中国最重要的歌唱家唱长江、黄河和澜沧江。把全世界最重要的歌唱家集中在一个生态最敏感的区域来赞颂水和河流，这是全世界第一次。我们做这些项目都是按照全世界第一来做，我们连续做下来了。

"水与生命"，这是世界关注的主题，超越意识形态，法国人可以来，德国人可以来，不管什么宗教信仰都可以来，但你必须是世界级的水平。令我们特别高兴的是这次请来了世界三大男高音之一的何塞·卡雷拉斯，他演唱的是《在那遥远的地方》，是我认为唱得最好的一位。他不懂中文，把它标成国际音标用中文来唱。你在现场听他的声音完全是天籁，我很多朋友说不相信是他发出来的。今后这个音乐会举办的时候，欢迎大家到现场去听一下，非常有意思。他还有一首是《我深情地呼唤》，主要是表现对水的赞颂、对生命的赞颂，抚摸地球的伤痕，关注人类的生存。

现在我们正在商议2010年请一些重要的演出机构，计划在海拔4000多米的地方选一个点，背景就是昆仑山，后面全部是雪山和冰川，我们把贝多芬的《第九交响曲》压缩到20分钟，《欢乐颂》5分钟，我们请世界级的华人作曲家写一个20分钟的《昆仑颂》，在一个具有象征意义的地方来完成一个东方和西方最重要的音乐创举。我们将请一个世界级的交响乐团到那个地方和中国的交响乐团共同完成，到时候我们要向全世界直播，以提升中华民族文化的影响力。我们将继续选定在黄河岸边，不仅由于这是人与自然的地方，还由于这是我们的母亲河不断流淌的地方。我们要把这个音乐节一直做下去，这是一个非常重要的国际文化交流平台。

面对世界的干旱和荒漠化，我们以音乐的形式来表达对人类的生存环境的关注。举办"青海水与生命音乐之旅"活动，传递了我们对和谐世界、生态文明、和平幸福的人类生存环境持有的乐观态度和精神，呼吁人们重视水资源、重视生态环境。我们立足于世界屋脊的青藏高原策划史诗美感的活动，激发世人对青藏高原和整个大自然的敬畏之情和感恩之情，让国内外更多的人关注水与生命，以理性的心态对待水与生命，对人类的社会活动进行思考和探讨，检讨人类的各种缺陷，从而真正迈步

turned out a spectacular success as dreamed and as scheduled.

The second edition has been brought to a satisfactory close lately, featuring a dream-like cast of world class tenors from great river civilizations, each singing out a hymn to his mother river, for instance, Indian tenor eulogizing the Ganges, Russian tenor, the Volga, Egyptian tenor, the Nile ,the Brazilian, the Amazon. Of course, Chinese singers in praise of the Yellow River, the Yangtze River as well as the Lancang River. What an idea to bring together renowned tenors to extol the virtues and benefits water and rivers bestowed upon humanity in Qinghai, one of the most environmentally fragile regions in the world!

Water and Life are the core global concerns. Tenors and singers, of whatever religious faith, of whatever racial background, are elcome provided you stand by a world distinction. We were really honored to have Jose Carreras, of the famous triumvirates along with Luciano Pavarotti, Placido Domingo, to sing In A Far Away Land, a popular love theme by Wang Luobing, considered the father of Chinese folk songs who actually wrote the incomparably lyric inspired by his love of a local Tibetan girl called Zhuoma in 1930s.Carailas knew no Chinese and ended up by matching each Chinese word with International phonetic transcriptions. Still, his performance brought down the house and many of my friends present simply could not believe their ears! One of the songs sung by Carreras that night is called I Plead With Affection, in tribute to water and life as well as expressing his anxiety about the earth and mankind in jeopardy.

Inspired by the successful start, we are now negotiating with some performing troupes to stage a most mind boggling concert at a venue 4000m elevation foregrounding Mt Kunlun, with glaciers and snow-capped peaks as backdrop. It will be a pioneering project as we will have a shortened Beethoven's No Symphony (20 minutes) Ode An die Freude (five minutes) plus a hymn to Mt Kunlun commissioned by oversea Chinese composer of world standing. To crown it all, in such a venue highly symbolic, we will invite two top established philharmonic orchestras, one from abroad, one from China to team up to complete the mission. To our plan, the concert will be broadcast alive to the whole world and the venue will be the riverside of the Yellow River, China's mother river.

Drought and desertification greatly affect agricultural productivity and environmental sustainability worldwide. Qinghai suffers due to vast expanse of desert/dry land or farming land eroded and degraded through use of unsustainable practices and technologies. It is a source of social and political frictions and conflicts in some communities and countries of the world. Desertification has other adverse impacts on non-dry lands as well. In addition to dust storms, biophysical impacts include downstream flooding, impairment of global carbon sequestration capacity, and global climate change. We hold a concert under the theme of Water and Life to dramatize the dilemmas of mankind to raise consciousness, build international and regional determination to natural hazards, accord high priority to water security in national agendas and promote water use efficiency, to mobilize action to curb the inroads of deserts, to arrest land

建设生态文明。如果我们人类不关注水和生存的环境,未来人类的生命是可怕的。所以我们呼唤人类在这种环境中苏醒过来,探索不同的发展道路。我相信,未来中国在这方面会做得更好。

世界山地纪录片节

人类的土地有近1/2都是高原,高原既是摄影家的天堂又是拍摄纪录片的好地方。怎么利用呢? 我们提出,山地既是一个地理概念又是一个文化的概念,它是生物多样性的自然保护,也是人类多元文化的诞生地和传承地。在高度工业化、信息化、城市化的今天,山地为人类保存了古老的和长期的物质生活和精神生活的家园,它是不能失去并且不能不被我们所关注的。我们举办世界山地纪录片节的宗旨,就是以影视的形式、艺术的视角、人文的思考致力于一种探索、一种特殊的地理环境与人文环境的对比,讲述外部的生存故事,以此反省人类的发展,实现人类的多元文化共享和传承。我们发现,世界上很多的古老民族特别是原生民族进入了21世纪以后还生活在山地。那个地区过去生活比较封闭,保留了大量的山地文化,为研究人类的未来提供了很多历史记忆,是人类的宝贵遗产。

广州有一个国际纪录片大会,它是以不同的主题进行展览。四川有一个国际熊猫节,它是做电视、电视剧等方面的交易,纪录片只是其中极小的一个部分。上海有一个白玉兰纪录片电视节,它做的这一部分也是范围比较广。2008年我们策划举办了中国(青海)世界山地纪录片节,这在全世界是第一次,以前没有人提出以山地概念做纪录片节的。山地纪录片节引起了广泛的关注,我们成功地打造了又一个使世界不同国家、不同地域、不同种族的影视艺术家进行创作、研讨、对话的国际化的艺术品牌。

我们把山地纪录片节定义为"生活与故事的对话",青海有很多的纪录片包括可可西里的和喜马拉雅山的,还包括其他一些重要的,比如青藏高原三江源的纪录片,还有一些关于人文历史方面的纪录片,国际上都有过,题材选的都是青藏高原。有些地方不是山地国家,比如法国,但是他们拍摄埃塞俄比亚和其他地区的一些原生态古老文化的片子,从人类学、社会学、民俗的角度去记录,非常有价值。

degradation and emphasize the need to invest in measures such as rehabilitation of degraded lands. Incidentally it is our pledge to the people living downstream of the three great rivers we will without fail bear the responsibility to serve the ecological Great Wall to ensure the national renaissance.

China(Qinghai)World Mountains Documentary Festival

While 50% of the land area of Earth is upland or plateau, mountains are paradise for photographers and documentary artists. There is the growing appeal of mountains because the concept of mountain has two dimensions, physical and cultural. Mountains hold an enormous potential of biodiversity to contribute to economic growth and poverty reduction. The unique species of plants and animals as well as ecosystems constitute the natural wealth. Conserving and promoting sustainable use of biodiversity is one of the challenges confronting all the civilized countries. On the other hand, mountains are birthplace and home to cultural diversity. In this age of post-industrialization, digitalization, and urbanization, mountains prove to be the last repository of historical memory. However, this spiritual legacy is undervalued and is being diluted at alarming rates. Preeminent of the reasons behind our intent to hold documentary filming festival point to of course Qinghai's extreme alpine topography and remote mountainous terrain as famed Roof of the World, which supports a diversity of bio-species of irreplaceable value. No less important is the region as potpourri of multi-religions, multi-races and multi-cultures. Much lies in store for enterprising artists to explore, examine and document while there is still time. Qinghai does dream of using art to bring to the world's attention the elemental processes of and human cultures attached to the mountainous terrain, to enact dialogues between various cultures to enhance the harmonious relationship between man and nature and assist the public to understand the implications of the environmental cataclysms that might jeopardize the alpine eco-system in the wake of the sweeping reckless modernization.

You all know Canton also hosts an international documentary conference operating under a different theme. Sichuan has an international TV festival which is essentially a hive of market activity selling and buying basically soap series. Then Shanghai's Magnolia Documentary Festival covers almost all the categories. In 2008, our mountain documentary filming festival took off. We focus only on documentaries. Art becomes a banner fluttering high calling global attention to the wilderness and cultural diversity in the mountains and uplands. This means we desire to enact dialogues between various cultures and help the world community gain awareness of the ultimate importance of man and nature in harmony. In the meanwhile, another cultural brand was born.

Our definition of mountain documentaries is "dialogue between life and story". Qinghai has a relatively rich body of Mountain documentaries shoot about the Koh Xil Nature Reserve, the Himalaya and the Sanjiangyuan Nature Reserve (the headwaters of the three great rivers) .There are still some touching upon the humanistic and historical by domestic and foreign makers in the Himalaya region. France is not a typical mountainous country, but French documentary artists

世界上已经诞生了大量以山地为讲述对象、不同风格、不同类别的纪录片,它们如同山地的自然、文化和生活一样丰富多彩。我们应该为世界山地纪录片节提供一个交流的窗口和平台。正因为世界山地纪录片节是世界首创,它得到了世界自然电影电视组织的关注。世界自然电影电视组织已经成立35年了,总部设在印度。2008年9月该组织授予我"胜象奖",认为我们的山地纪录片节为人类古老记忆的复活、为推动纪录片在各个国家的发展做出了很重要的贡献。我们希望借助这个平台,能够促使山地纪录片不断地做下去,这是我们举办山地纪录片节的初衷之一。

首届山地纪录片节包括了高峰论坛、纪录片展播和评奖活动,来自美国、日本、俄罗斯等22个国家和地区的343个纪录片参与了展播和评奖的活动,我们专门设立了"玉昆仑奖",包括最佳自然纪录片奖、最短纪录片奖、最佳的导演奖等25个奖项,这个奖得到了国际纪录片界的关注。

三江源国际摄影节

照片可以把瞬间变成永恒,因为它可以把这一瞬间记录下来成为一个永久的历史记忆。从2006年到2008年,我们已连续三年成功举办三届三江源国际摄影节。这个摄影节是中国目前最大的国际摄影节,也可以说是世界上现在最大的摄影节之一。国内的国际摄影节还有山西的平遥国际摄影节,它与我们的摄影节规模相当,但是我们的摄影节参加人数和参展作品更多,规格更高。

我们每年展出的作品达到4000幅至5000幅,最多的时候甚至到8000幅;参加每届三江源国际摄影节的中外摄影家都有300人到500人,他们分别来自全世界五大洲的近30多个国家和地区,很多国际性的摄影家都是我们摄影节的参与者。过去我们是一年举办一届,从2009年开始确定为双年节。国际诗歌节、世界山地纪录片节和三江源国际摄影节都是作为双年节,今年做青海湖国际诗歌节,明年就是三江源国际摄影节和世界山地纪录片节,但是我们的"国际水与生命音乐之旅"每年做,唐卡艺术节也是每年做,这是五大品牌不同的时间不同的安排。

摄影艺术是一种超越国家、种族、文化背景的国际通用语言,我们希望国内外的朋友能够通过摄影的桥梁,以艺术为纽带展示才华、增进交流,我们希望他们把青海

shoot some of the best pictures documenting the indigenous tribal societies in Ethiopia and other countries which prove to be ethnographically, anthropologically, sociologically and folklorically significant.

Not only in Qinghai. There is already a considerable collection of mountain documentaries in the widest range and spectrum of style, theme and focal point in the world, but there is a deplorable lack of an exhibition fair international in scope to facilitate the cross-fertilization of the minds and wisdom for documentary artists and critics. So the festival we have launched is without precedent and has received the attention of World Nature Movies and TV Organization (WNMTVO).WNMTVO, headquartered in India and with 30 years after its inception, is an international body dedicated to promote the development of nature documentaries, awarded us "Victorious Elephant" cup , crediting us render a useful public service by renewing the historical memory and elevating the human consciousness of mountain civilizations.

2008 marked the kick-off of the first edition of China (Qinghai) World Mountains Documentary Festival. we decide on a number of programs including a summit forum, field tour of local mountains for filming, exhibition display and showing of documentary films and finally, the "Jade Kunlun" awards falling into 25 categories, a prize increasingly valued and acknowledged in the milieu.

Sanjiangyuan International Photographing Festival(SIPF)

Photography is the art, science, and practice of creating durable images from fleeting second. From 2006 to 2008, we have successively staged three editions of the SIPF, the largest of its kind in China, and Arguably one of the largest in the world. We know domestically a similar photo festival resides in Pingyao, Shanxi, yet our SIPF is known to be more professional in character and attended by a larger amount of participants and entries.

Each year our entries amount to 4000 to 5000, peaking at 8000 ,with a population of photographers up to 300 or 500 from over 30 odd countries across five continents, of which a considerable proportion being professionals of world statue. We used to hold SIPF once a year but switch it to twice a year. Being owner and operator of five cultural brands, we devise a calendar alternating between even year as the season for poetry, mountain documentary and photograph and each year(both odd and even) in celebration of water and Thangka.

Photograph is a Franca lingua for artists. Again we intend to make it a window on Qinghai as well as a channel of free expression. Qinghai's alpine terrain, wilderness ,remoteness and mysteriousness ,long hidden from the rest of the world, makes a very good excuse for those intent on imaging something really pristine. For Qinghai-Tibet Plateau is not just a good cause. It is also a state of mind, a distant place onto which urbanized people have long projected their fantasies, especially in the face of the erosion of the traditional culture and the diminished state of human spirituality. We have consulted and teamed up with top photographing institutions such as National Geographic, which yielded some fantastic photos.

作为一个摄影家的天堂,大量地拍摄青海。我们一方面把摄影作为建设青海、宣传青海的一个窗口;另一方面我们加强与一些国际上的重要摄影机构的合作,比如,我们与美国《国家地理》杂志合作,取得了一些很重要的摄影成果。

我们组织世界一流的摄影机构来到青海,潜心进行专题性的创作而不是浮光掠影地拍一些东西,我们要求作品里面必须要有文化的内涵。另外作为一个国际性的摄影节,我们还要把大量国际上重要摄影展的作品带到青海,作为一个重要的参照,给中国的摄影展提供一个了解全世界别的摄影展他们现在关注什么题材,比如说城市题材,比如说妇女题材、儿童题材,比如关于战争的,比如关于贫困的,比如关于资源短缺的。

随着我们这几年在文化创意上的活动,三江源国际摄影节已经成为我们联系世界的最重要的桥梁之一。我们通过很多著名的摄影大师与众多的摄影爱好者包括旅游者,包括一些其他的机构进行互动,形成他们对青海、对青藏高原的深度了解。我们通过他们宣传中国多民族的文化和和谐的民族关系,让他们深层次地了解青藏高原的历史文化和我们现实的生存状况。

这五大文化品牌,我们创意的过程当中始终是和市场联系在一起的。我们不断寻求一些最重要的原生态的内涵共同完成这些创意,我们希望它们不光是青海的文化,更是塑造中国文化的当代形象。我们做的这些活动之所以能够引起国际的关注,最重要的一点是因为这些活动具有当代意识,其主题和内容都是国际社会现在普遍关注的。

除开五大文化品牌,青海还有三大国际体育品牌,简单介绍一下。

环青海湖国际公路自行车赛这是我们很重要的赛事,现在已经是世界四大自行车赛之一。其他三大自行车赛分别是环法、环意大利、环西班牙自行车赛。日本在做环日本海,新加坡在做环新加坡海自行车赛,中国的海南岛也在做环海南岛,但是亚洲的洲际赛就是青海湖国际公路自行车赛,它现在是2.1级。无论是每一次的参赛选手的规模,还是运动员的水平,这个自行车赛都可以说是最高的。每一次都有来自五大洲的20多支运动队、100多名世界上杰出的赛手到青海。它是青海与国家体育总局和世界自行车联盟共同举办的,它不光是青海的,还是中国的一个世界品牌,得到了世界各界广泛的关注和认可。

国际自行车赛的主席曾经说,环湖赛对亚洲自行车赛发展做出的贡献非常大,它已经成为一个世界性的重要自行车赛事,它的身影已经走向世界了。近几年我们

The ongoing project of bringing top photographers here cannot afford to be merely nostalgic about past culture or scenic vistas. We hope the occasion will develop a rich and substantial appreciation of the social transformation and recognize and act on the autonomous strength and character of things wild and natural in the Plateau. On the other hand, we hope to introduce important works gaining world recognition to streamline and enrich our photographing art. There is always a natural desire to get to know where the wind is blowing, for example, what themes are more trendy now? Women? Children ? War ? Or poverty? Or the scarcity of resources?

What emerges from our SIPF creativity effort is one more bridge linking us with the larger world. Many famous photographers and amateurs have evolved rather in-depth knowledge of this plateau province and of its rich potential of creativity industry. Their outstanding works reveal much of the fast changing alpine society but also of the constancy and profundity of mankind's relation to nature.

All the above five cultural brands are, in essence, creativity as commercial fantasies masquerading to satisfy mass desires for commercial gain. But In forging them, from the very onset, we take a genuine spiritual pleasure in nature and we have built-in brake on the minimum use of tangible resources while, the market in view, rely on the maximizing the most authentic and distinctive elements of the intangible cultural heritage. Indeed, what we have achieved is not only to project a positive image of Qinghai, but also of China to the world scene. We aim our cultural effort invariably at the international level, with themes gaining instant global recognition.

Three Sports Brands

Beside Tour de France, the Giro d'Italia the Vuelta a Espana, the Tour De Qinghai Lake , now recognized of the four major tours, is an annual bicycle race over areas around the remarkable natural wonder Qinghai Lake, the largest inland saltwater lake in China. Hence the name of the race. Japanese , Singaporeans and China's Hainanese all host tour de island races of their own, but in Asia, Tour de Qinghai Lake, now ranking 2.1 HC-category, co-organized by State Sports Authorities, Qinghai Sports Authorities and World Cycling Association, is a top race attracting a total of 100 riders from 20 odd teams that form a typical line-up for each edition.

The Chairman of World Cycling Association thought highly of Tour De Qinghai Lake, lauding it a landmark event in the history of Asian cycling. Attempt to bring market into play has yielded initial results as a lottery has been approved and issued to pool funds for further development. I am told the lottery sells well in Canton and I owe a word of gratitude to sports fans in Canton. The owner of the lottery, State Sports Authorities finances the event by allocating a handsome sum of earnings to Qinghai each year.

Why, again , a road cycling race in Qinghai? Well, this is another flash of mind. Normally, cycling in lowland and island is a comfortable exercise taxing little in the way of oxygen diminution. Tour de France was intended to boost circulation of L'Auto, so Emilio Camillo Costamagna, the editor of La Gazzetta dello Sport newspaper, aimed to increase his circulation.

不断地加强运作,现在我们已经发行了环湖赛自行车彩票,据说广东不少的彩迷买了我们的彩票,我们对他们表示感谢,每年由国家体彩中心发行的彩票返还几千万都是用在自行车比赛,我们不断地发展出高原自行车赛的一条路。

我们为什么要在这个地方做自行车赛?这和我们的创意也有关系。要骑自行车海南岛多好啊,海拔又低,氧又多。法国有一个环岛了,环法的海多漂亮啊,古老的法兰西文化,走过大量的文化古迹和文化遗迹,环日本海不用说了,环意大利海、环西班牙海都是环海,意大利的地中海风光是世界一绝。为什么我们做这个环湖赛呢?也是延续我们的概念,很多的自行车运动员有探索自身身体极限的冒险精神,愿意到地球的第三极来实现"更快、更高、更强"的体育梦想。

作为国际自行车运动组织来说,也希望在地球第三极完成。地球第三极有西藏有青海,但青海有青海湖,西藏没有这么大的湖。围绕青海湖是360度,每一次自行车赛设计的公路是1400公里,有9个赛点,有的是11个赛点,海拔在2000米左右,一般自行车运动掌握在2000米到3000米,落差在1500米全世界这样地方很难找,更何况围绕着神湖骑自行车。

外国的自行车运动就是一个文化运动,除了比赛、技术水平、组织水平要达到国际标准外,它对地理高度和环境的高度都有很高的要求。环湖赛之所以不断地提升,除了我们不断地举办好自行车赛、搞好组织工作之外,最重要的是我们不断地在挖掘我们的文化内涵,把我们的差异性的地理高度和宗教文化资源注入这个赛事里面。你要到西藏去骑也有很多地方,但是能够找到一个面积4700平方公里大的神湖吗?没有,这是上天对青海的恩赐。

现在每年到青海进行自行车赛的运动员水平是很高的,运动员排名要积分,你全年的排名到什么名次。比如说他参加海南岛的自行车赛,但是它不积分,因为它没有到那个级别。世界上的自行车运动员每年有一个排名的积分,这是世界对青藏高原的关注。这个赛事现在已经是世界四大自行车赛事之一了,可能朋友们在电视上经常能够看到,因为每一届自行车赛都是直播的。

青藏高原世界攀岩赛

我们连续做了三届,我们就是要把它做成国际品牌。我们2009年搞世界锦标赛,把国际攀岩第十届锦标赛请到青海。世界的攀岩赛前九届全部是在欧洲举办的,是在意大利、法国、比利时、德国这些国家举办的。

最后介绍一下中国青海国际抢渡黄河极限挑战赛,这是一个户外运动,在含氧

What a poetic route map Tour de France features! The rider cycles into the most scenic sea beaches and living museums of French cultural legacy and ruins of historical interest. The Giro d'Italia and the Vuelta a Espana circulate around the fabled Mediterranean. Again, Tour de Qinghai Lake was opening its door to anyone passionate pushing his sportsmanship to the limit on the third terrace of the earth, aspiring to realizing his dream of "Higher, Faster, Stronger" in the name of two wheels.

Tour de Qinghai Lake appealed from the start not just for the distance and its demands but because it played to a wish for World Cycling Association to stage the highest road race in Qinghai-Tibet Plateau. Tibet was of course good enough but not ideal devoid of a alpine lake like Qinghai Lake .Initially the race was made up of 1 prologue and 9 or 10 stages, covering a total distance of 1400 kilometers at 2000m elevation. What makes Tour De Qinghai Lake so special is the 1500m drop in elevation in such a road race while the blessed procession basically runs around the perimeter of a holy lake in the popular consciousness of Tibetan Buddhism.

The Tour is culturally important for Qinghai. It puts rigorous demands on organization, logistics, terrain, elevation and environment. Like the initiator of Tour de France, Desgrange, whose's drive was to educate and improve the population and that inspired the French to know more of their country, our intent is nothing less than to enhance the world awareness of the authenticity and distinctiveness of our cultural heritage, ie, the mix of the alpine height and the vibrant Buddhism. Again Tibet is a good choice save that they'd find it really difficult to locate a lake of 4700 square kilometers, a blessing bestowed by the merciful Avalokitesvara .

High entry requirements are made to sift out the top cyclists for the race. Currently, there has evolved a very complex classification of points.2.1 HTC category demands points earned only in Tour de France, the Giro d'Italia the Vuelta a Espana.Points collected in the above is essential for qualifying the Tour de Qinghai Lake. That means an entrant in Tour De Hainan Island may not meet our entry threshold even with his points rewarded for a high finishing position .Currently, Tour De Qinghai Lake is broadcast live by CCTV.

Qinghai–Tibet Rock Climbing Contest

We have succeeded in hosting three editions, including the 10th edition of World Rock Climbing Contest(the previous 9 editions were held in a European venue, such as Italy, France, Belgium and Germany), another initiative on our part aiming to invest in the workings of this event and eventually turn it into a sports brand internationally prestigious.

Lastly, a word for Qinghai International Yellow River Swimming Contest, an outdoor game held on the Yellow River, low oxygen level and frozen water temperature. We play host to the event, co-sponsored by several provincial TV stations, which has achieved popularity among outdoor sports fans. As you can see, several sports meets, sprouting from the alpine soil, have quickly grown from their humble beginnings, into major sports brands at the national and international levels. We are even harboring a very audacious plan to start an amateur car race

量最低、气温最低的黄河上游进行,由我们与中央电视台和若干省的地方电视台共同举办,现在已经成为很多户外运动爱好者的一个重要品牌。这是一个高海拔的国际性赛事,已经举办若干届了,每一届参赛者非常多。我们有一系列的高原体育运动的品牌,应该说在青海有的已完全形成,有的正在完成过程当中,有的还是雏形。非职业汽车穿越柴达木盆地,今后也会进行,我们正在请西班牙人设计路线。

　　青海之所以这几年建立一系列文化创意和体育品牌,很重要的一点就是我们得益于思想观念的更新,对过去的这些不被认知的地域资源、文化资源、宗教资源进行再认识、再利用。同时也因为我们现在的开放的国家和开放的社会,给我们很多在做地方工作的文化官员——我个人就是一个诗人走向政府工作岗位的,提供了难得的文化平台,给我们提供了实现自己文化梦想的一个很重要的平台,使我们能够把这些活动一个个变成现实。当然还得益于中央对青海发展的支持,得益于全国各地包括广东广州很多朋友,特别是喜欢旅游、喜欢户外运动、关注差异性文化、关注民族文化的朋友们的支持。

　　感谢大家百忙之中来听我演讲,我觉得这不仅仅是对我个人的尊重,更是对青海古老民族的文化和历史、对青海这一片高地的尊重和理解。再次感谢,希望大家有机会到青海看一看!

across the famous Qaidam Basin. We are consulting some Spanish professionals on the mapping of territory.

To sum up, what is so revolutionary about the ongoing building up of a number of cultural and sports brands in a Plateau situation, of which I am at the core both as initiator and designer lies in our raising awareness of the importance of creativity and innovation for personal, social and economic development. Even in an economic backwater, creativity industry has unequalled opportunities. The most important reason for our intense exposure to world media is that creativity industry operators require a deep understanding of the formations of the most significant, productive realities that shape the modern society that it is, capable of being manipulated for public good. A poet turned top administrator in charge of educational and cultural affairs, I deem myself very lucky placed in a position to make things happen in the firm belief the essence of cultural enterprise boils down to the maximizing the potential of individual creativity, skill and talent and the most authentic and distinctive elements of the intangible cultural heritage. Last but not the least, I would like to extend special recognition to the financial assistance accorded us by the central government. I am also deeply grateful to the great concern you have showered upon us. By you here I mean many of my good Canton friends, those passionate about outdoor adventurous activity and authentic cultural traditions.

I reserve my greatest gratitude to all those present at today's forum. I take it a token of respect, not only for me, but also, to a larger extent, for the alpine province called Qinghai where I come from. I thank you again with an invitation extended to come to my place at a time convenient to your schedule.

当代世界文学语境下的中国诗人写作

在北京师范大学举办的当代世界文学与中国国际学术研讨会上的演讲

2008年10月20日

我尊敬的各位同行，各位朋友：

非常高兴能出席北京师范大学举办的"当代世界文学与中国"国际学术研讨会，非常高兴能在北京师范大学这样一所著名的学府见到我尊敬的同行。各位远道而来的文朋诗友，尽管想尽量避免因客套而带来的所谓礼节，不要让它影响我们之间，从一见面开始就已经感受到了的那种亲切，以及只有在作家诗人之间才会有的某种来自心灵世界的感应，当然这无疑是人与人敞开了各自的心怀之后，才能获得的一种最为美好的，同时也是最为直接的思想与感情的交流通道。

但是这样，我还是要以一个中国诗人的名义，向今天到会的各位同行，特别是向远涉重洋而来的各位文朋诗友致以最崇高的敬意！我相信因为你们的到来这个具有特殊意义的关于"当代世界文学与中国"的学术论坛，一定会取得圆满成功！下面请允许我就"当代世界文学语境下的中国诗人写作"谈几点意见。

我想说明的是"当代世界文学语境下的中国诗人写作"是很宽泛的一个题目，它所包含的内容是极为丰富的。就这个题目和它所包含的内容而言，完全可以写一本关于此方面的专著。但是为了说明今天的中国诗人与世界文学关系，我还是固执地选择了这个似乎太大的题目。另外，作为一个个体的诗人我想我的看法和见解，也不能完全代表文学气质有着很大差异的中国不同民族的诗人。

不过在这里，有一点是可以肯定的，那就是今天几乎所有的中国诗人，都在一种更为开放的状态下写作，特别是随着中国文学翻译界近三十年的卓有成效的工作，

Chinese Poetic Writing in the Context of World Literature
Speech Given at an International Workshop Entitled Contemporary World Literature and China
20th, October, 2008

It is wonderful to be here attending this workshop. I thank you for your invitation. Beijing Normal University is one of the leading educational institutions in the world. The honor is peculiarly mine to meet so many esteemed peer poets, and fellow writers and experts who have journeyed all the way from four corners of the globe to assemble here ,share some thoughts and open new vista of perspective on such an exciting topic as we address today. Although we try our best to cut the red tap as befits this occasion, the worry that such ritualized formalities might bar more direct and intimate communion quickly gives away to a magic affinity that animates the encounter, an affinity that comes only natural to the spiritual union of poets and writers.

All said, I must avail this opportunity to express my highest regard to all the guests and friends. It is my privilege to address such an outstanding international conference on Contemporary World Literature and China, a conference graced by your arrival which promises a most propitious progression. Now let me begin by sharing with you some observations.

The topic of Contemporary World Literature and China is my whimsical option, seemingly too general and open-ended and luxuriant, a topic capable of being addressed from a number of angles, and a topic, which deserves academic treatment of the most rigorous kind, say, in a monograph form. Yet I stubbornly cling to it as I believe it might shed some light on the more difficult issue chosen by the organizers of this conference. A word of warning at this point that my view to be presented tends to be of a very personal nature and in no way do I intend it as the voice and the mind of China's republic of poets and writers distinguished by so varied thought patterns and literary temperament exhibited.

One thing that can be safely generalized about contemporary Chinese writing is the present relaxed cultural environment. The purely negative character of the two or three decades prior to the adoption of the reform and open up policies in the late 1970s had been able to stop the growth

可以说当代世界不同地域、不同种族、不同国度的大部分代表性诗人的作品也都在近几年里被大量翻译成中文出版，许多当代中国诗人在写作中，无疑都受到了当代国际诗坛创作思潮的影响，特别是在当代诗歌的实验写作方面，不少外国重要诗歌流派以及重要诗人的作品，可以说对中国大部分当代诗人在创作上的影响都是十分明显的，对有的诗人的影响就更为深刻，他们所受的影响不仅体现在写作技巧上，有的甚至在写作风格和文体上，也留下明显的外来文学的影响的痕迹。

当然在这里我需要说明的是，中国文学传统，特别是中国诗歌的美学传统，依然是中国诗人在文学传承上所受影响的主要来源，因为中国现代诗人，从20世纪20年代到今天，走过了一条中国新诗歌不断探索，甚至是历险的道路，其中有抛开中国语言自身的特性，尤其是割裂中国古典诗歌美学传统的根脉，而一味全盘模仿外来诗歌的沉痛教训，同时也存在过完全在形式上和写作方法上沿袭中国古典诗歌，在整个创作思想上反对创新的问题。

特别是就创造新的诗歌艺术形式毫不宽容的主张和现象，这似乎从另一个角度，也给我们留下了需要去正视的失误。

但最为可喜的是，虽然存在着这样或那样的一些问题，但中国现当代诗歌的发展，其主流还是健康的，在近一百年的中国诗歌发展过程中，应该说有一些重要的诗人和作品，就是今天我们把他们放在当时不同国家和民族的代表性诗人中间，如果把他们以及他们创作的作品进行比较，应该说他们都是毫不逊色的。特别是这些诗人和作品中所体现出的东方文化精神，尤其是诗歌中的哲学和美学意境，客观地讲，在当时所谓的世界文学这个大格局中均具有不可替代的价值。

简单地回顾这些历史过程，我试图阐释一个问题，就是想说明无论是过去的那一个世纪，还是今天在当代世界文学的语境下，中国诗人的写作或者说中国大多数是人的写作，都在进行某一种所谓的"纵的继承"和"横的移植"，其实简言之，"纵的继承"就是对中国数千年来所形成的伟大文学传统或者说诗歌传统的继承，而"横的移植"就是对世界各国、各民族优秀文学作品，当然，包括经典诗歌作品的学习和借鉴，在今天尤其是要对当代世界各国各民族的优秀作家诗人的作品进行学习和借鉴，这正好印证了中国一句古话"他山之石，可以攻玉"的道理。

of a spontaneous, brilliant, and flourishing literature, but it has now taken on a new lease of life. All the poets, so to speak, are left to their own devices on their creative work. Thanks to the enthusiasm of the mass of translators who are always on the look-out for new isms in the past three decades, there has been a steady supply of foreign literary works featuring almost every region, country, race, style or school. Great imaginative poets, without exception, find their way into the purview of the Chinese reading public to the extent that many Chinese poets subscribe, consciously or inadvertently, to their influence. They are of various persuasions and they are too many for the experimental gropers to take advantage of their variegated sources. For some, foreign tendencies are cultivated more ardently in terms of both technique and style.

Of course, I must emphasize, the domestic tradition, especially the aesthetics of the New Poetry still constitutes the main source of inspiration. New Poetry has grown up through the years full of vicissitudes and detours, the result of constant change, of constant forces working from outside and inside on the texture of the civilization. For a time, Chinese poets have cut themselves adrift from the past, but the past is always returning as antidote to the slavish emulation of western models.

On the other hand, the campaign started by Hu Shi for introducing the vernacular came at the right moment when Chinese classical versification was suffering excessive allusion and formulism. The absorption of western examples was combined with a tortuous search for a vernacular style free from the stiffness and formality of the Classical tradition. There might be important lessons to be gained here.

What most deserves elation is the contemporary poetic writing has zigzagged all the way to the right track now. After long imitation of western models and tenuous adaption of the classical poetry, it has achieved mature individuality and identity. The last century has produced important poets and works that command world-wide respect. In terms of the Oriental cultural spirit and aesthetic ethos manifested, Chinese poetry has earned for Chinese letters an irreplaceable place in world literature.

The above survey leads me to a tentative thesis: contemporary poetic writing in China is really the outcome of "vertical transplanting" and "longitudinal inheritance" operating during the first phase of the disoriented New Poetry against the large backdrop of world culture. The 20th century has been one a period of considerable experiment and innovation. "Longitudinal inheritance" applies to all the classical versification mellowed in the Tang dynasty spanning two millennia."Vertical transplanting" refers to an assiduous study of all the best having been written, metaphorically and allegorically, by outstanding poets and writers of all ethnic origins else where in the world. Such deference is picturesquely captured in a Chinese saying to the effect there are stones in other hills that are good for working our jade.

其实说到这里，我还想说的是，中国文化本身具有一种极大的包容性，也可以说在学习和借鉴外来文化方面有着悠久的传统。据有关学术机构统计，近几十年中国翻译出版的外国人文类著作达到十万种以上，而世界各国所翻译出版的中国人文类著作却与这个数字相差甚远。这也说明了进一步开展好文化交流的重要性。其实我们今天这个论坛的交流就是一个好的开端，因为它让许多不同种族、不同国家、不同宗教信仰、不同文化背景用不同语言、文字写作的作家和诗人坐在了一起。

第二，我想讲的问题是在当代世界文学语境下，中国诗人的写作，到底受到了哪些具体的影响，而这些影响又是如何产生的？当然这同样也是一个很大的题目，用一两句话是很难说清楚的。就是让不同的中国诗人来阐述这个问题，我想也会有很大的差异，因为每一个诗人都会从自己不同的角度来谈自己所受到的外国作家和诗人的影响，这是一个很自然的事情。所以说在这里我想谈一些更具有共性的、有关当代中国诗人在写作中学习和借鉴当代外国文学的问题。

同样在以下的举例中，我会随意谈到一些当代外国诗人，他们以及他们的作品被介绍到中国之后所产生的影响。我想从上一个世纪五十年代的一些重要外国诗人谈起。俄罗斯及苏联诗人的作品对当代中国诗歌创作的影响是巨大的，除了革命诗人马雅可夫斯基之外，著名的俄罗斯乡土诗人叶赛宁，诗人曼德斯尔塔姆，著名女诗人阿赫玛托娃、茨维塔耶娃，诺贝尔文学奖获奖诗人帕斯捷尔纳克等等，他们诗歌中的人道主义精神以及俄罗斯文学所特有的悲悯情怀，可以说从灵魂和心灵世界中深刻地影响过几代中国诗人，就是到今天，这些天才的俄罗斯诗人作品仍然在影响着当代中国诗人的写作。特别是他们所特有的那种高贵的道德勇气和力量，对中国当代年轻诗人的思想和精神所产生的影响同样是巨大的。

这可能是一个文学现象，俄罗斯诗歌似乎在中国诗人中一直有着崇高的地位，前不久，许多年轻的中国诗人就俄罗斯楚瓦什共和国杰出的诗人格拉基·艾基的作品又展开了广泛的讨论，作为当代俄罗斯特殊的先锋派诗人，他的作品深刻地记录了人类存在的真实以及诗歌所描述的大自然的本质，他的创作真正继承了俄罗斯诗歌中有关热爱自由、不屈服专制、同情弱者、歌颂生命尊严的优秀传统。

盎格鲁-撒克逊民族及英语国家的当代世界文学同样对中国诗人的写作有着

My point here is really about the great resilience and vigor of the Chinese cultural spirit which displays a readiness to influences from outside. To cite one of the authoritative figures that translations in the humanities and social sciences effected in the past few decades amount to 100, 000 in kind. The circuitous translations of Chinese works in similar fields are by no means of such bulky size. These figures point to the potential of reciprocal exchanges. The present workshop is a perfect platform as it allows writers and poets of various cultural, racial, religious, literary backgrounds to congregate for a most exhilarating session of brainstorming on an interesting topic.

Second, the first question of Chinese poetry as major beneficiary of foreign influences being answered, its corollary is: what kind of influences do Chinese poets subscribe to from outside? Where do they originate specifically? This, again, is too big a question to warrant a convenient reply. Furthermore, I bet Chinese poets other than me will be predisposed to phrase the question quite differently. Given literary temperament and idiosyncrasies of each poet, I will try to place things in perspective and come out with observations more typical of the coterie of Chinese poets.

In what is to follow I will make a random mention of the foreign poets and writers as well as the influences they have exerted attendant upon their works having been translated into Chinese. I will begin with some very good poets that emerged in the 1950s of the 20th century. Preeminently no single movement or tendency seems to have established so complete a dominance upon the Chinese reading public than the mass of Russian and former Soviet Union geniuses, such as revolutionary futurist Mayakhovsky, folk poet Yeseinin ,Mantastalm, poetess Akhmatova, poetess Tzevetayeva, Nobel prize winner Pasternak. Their work is characterized by an intense humanitarianism and the powerful atmosphere of sadness and gloom which pervades Russian writers. These tormented souls have exerted the fatal pull over several generations of Chinese poets and writers and elevated their literature to a level unrivalled in world literature. Even to this day, the nobility and moral strength with which they keep singing paeans of human dignity and the suffering of the innocent in defying the most unimaginable horrors is still a source of inspiration and courage.

It is an amazing phenomenon that Russian literature always means something vastly different to us from what it might do to any poets elsewhere in the world .Recently there has arisen a heated debate upon the works of Gennadiy Aigi from Chuvash republic of Russia. Though distinctly modernist in tone, his poetry shows the influences of the classical novelists. He is able to contain in poetry even the harshest aspects of reality, making him the true heir of a great literary tradition critical of tyranny, warm-hearted to the injured and the insulted, thirsting for freedom and trumpeting for human dignity. His genuine fondness for nature has been sustained by the deft employment of some Avant Garde devices of a mind extremely sensitive to the sensuousness of sound and the peculiar power of rhymes.

Modern Chinese writing also derives its inspiration from the writers and poets of

重要的影响。远的不用说,从上一个世纪后半叶开始,美国诗人艾兹拉·庞德的印象派诗歌被陆续翻译成中文,诗人艾略特的杰作《荒原》就有多个版本在中国翻译出版,美国杰出的民族诗人佛洛斯特、肯明斯,美国垮掉派诗人代表人物金斯堡,美国自白派天才女诗人西尔维亚·普拉斯以及英国诗人塔·休斯等众多英语语系的诗人被大量翻译介绍到中国。现在从中国现当代诗歌的发展轨迹中可以看出,英语现代诗同样深刻地影响了许多中国当代诗人的创作。在诗歌意象的运用上,在诗歌深层次表现人类世俗生活以及用诗歌语言探索人类心灵世界方面,都为中国现代诗的创作注入了一种异样的活力。

　　在谈到当代外国诗歌对中国诗人影响的时候,我们不能不谈到西班牙语系的诗人,他们是西班牙诗人洛尔迦、智利诗人巴勃罗·聂鲁达、秘鲁诗人巴列霍、阿根廷诗人博尔赫斯、古巴诗人尼古拉斯·纪廉、墨西哥诗人奥克塔维奥·帕斯等等,他们就像夜晚天空中的群星,各自闪耀着迷人的光芒。在这里我不可能一一列出他们全部的名字,但是他们杰出的诗歌,已经像鲜红的血液一样,流进了许多中国诗人的血管,是拉丁美洲诗人教会了我们应该怎样尊重自己的本土文化,应该怎样通过自己的创作去复活我们民族深层的历史记忆和文化记忆。

　　需要说明的是,中国是个多民族的国家,中国的文学也是个多民族国家的文学,在当代世界文学大格局中黑人文学、犹太人文学等民族或者说区域的文学,也同样对当代中国不同民族的作家、诗人产生过不可忽视的影响,在这方面美国黑人诗人兰斯顿·休斯、犹太民族诗人萨克斯、意大利犹太诗人萨巴、以色列犹太民族诗人耶夫达·阿米亥,阿拉伯巴勒斯坦民族诗人达尔维什、波兰民族诗人米沃什、波兰女诗人申博尔什卡、捷克民族诗人塞弗尔特、塞内加尔黑人诗人桑戈尔、圣卢西亚民族诗人沃尔科特等等,他们对当代中国诗人的影响是多方面的,特别是对中国许多少数民族诗人的影响尤为深刻。这些伟大的民族诗人,他们既是民族文化和精神的代言人,同时他们也代表了一个民族或者说一个时代的良心,他们的全部创作成果既是他们民族的文化遗产,同样毫无疑问也是全人类的文化遗产。他们给中国诗人带来的影响,我相信随着时间的推移将会越来越深远。

　　尽管以上我都在进行选择性地举例,来证明当代世界文学对中国诗人写作的深

Anglo-Saxon stock and those operating in the English-speaking world in general. The most influential figures are without exception associated with modernism. Back in the 1950s of the 20th century, Ezra Pound the imagist was translated into Chinese. T.S.Eliot's *Wasteland*, Nobel Prize winner, has appeared in Chinese in version more than one. Indeed, a host of major Anglophone poets ,such as Frost, Cummings, Allen Ginsberg, Sylvia Plath, and Ted Hughes have been introduced by means of translations. It has been agreed that the most conspicuous influences of the Anglophone poets upon the Chinese poets is to be found in their stylistic preoccupations and their concern with craft. The imagists seem to have given the best they had to give, ie, instilling vitality and vigor into Chinese experimental poetry by gaining effects in "imaging" things and exploring new means of expression to delineate both the mundane and the inner modern life in the psychological vein.

When it comes to the foreign influences, mention must be absolutely made of the Spanish speaking world. A host of outstanding poets are adored by Chinese poets, Spanish poet Garcia Lorca, Chilean poet Pablo Neruda, Peru poet Vallejo, Argentinean poet Borges, Cubean poet Guillien and Mexican poet Octavio Paz, to name but a few of the most eminent, like stars in the starry heavens, radiating lasting brilliance. Their best verse has entered into the veins of Chinese poets. In a sense, it is the Latin American poets who have taught me how to value the riches of my Yi culture and all the poetic devices of revitalizing our cultural and historic memory lying dormant for long.

It must be pointed out, at this juncture, that China is another melting pot, composed of over 55 minority nationalities. In world literature today, ethnic writing figures prominently as Yiddish literature, Black writing and other regionalist varieties are bound to make an indelible mark on contemporary Chinese poetry. Again, we have a whole galaxy of the most glorious poets to thank for their talent, melody, and wisdom-USA black poet Langston Hughes, Jewish poet Nelly Sachs , Italian Jewish poet Sabah, Israeli poet Yehuda Amichai, Arabian Palestinian poet Mahmoud Darwish, Polish poet Milowosz, Polish poetess Borska, Czech poet Serfeit, Senegalese poet Senghor and Saint Lucia poet Walcott. Their influence in China is permanent, especially to writers and poets of ethnic origin. Both the tangible expression of their own ethnic genius as well as the conscience of their people or age, they have left "whole treasures of wisdom, bright gems of thought and golden veins of language", the inheritance to their own people, the common property of the whole world. Their work, shot through by flashes of love, penetrating social criticism and a strong undertone of moral encouragement, insures them a lasting niche in world literature and to whose memory the Chinese posterity will always be grateful.

I have tried my best, to identify a highly selective list of writers and poets in world literature

刻影响，但是我仍然感到很遗憾，有许多重要国家和民族的诗人未被整体地提及，在这里为表达对他们的敬意，请允许我列出这些诗人的名字，我知道这仍然是一个充满遗憾的办法，因为同样我不可能列出所有诗人的名字，他们是印度诗人泰戈尔、法国诗人圣琼·佩斯、法国诗人米肖、意大利诗人夸西莫多、意大利诗人蒙塔纳、意大利翁加尼雷蒂、瑞典诗人朗姆斯特罗姆、希腊诗人塞弗利斯、希腊诗人埃利蒂斯、土耳其诗人希克梅特等等，我深信这里还有许多我没有提及的杰出的外国诗人，他们所有被翻译成中国文字的作品，已经毫无例外地成为中国诗人和中国读者学习和阅读的精神食粮，他们的作品已经在另一个民族古老的语言文字中获得了新的生命。凡是阅读过他们作品的中国诗人和读者，将永远会记住他们的名字。

　　第三，我想简单地谈一谈在当代世界文学语境下的中国诗人写作，应该持什么样的写作立场的问题，或者说我们应该用什么样的写作姿态来面对这个世界。在今天全球化的背景下，一个诗人的文化自觉就尤为重要，当然，诗人的创作永远是个体的创作，无论他是面对这个纷繁复杂的外部世界，还是面对他的灵魂和内心世界，真诚和诚实，正直而富有良知仍然是今天诗人所应该具备的条件和要求，只有这样，我们这个时代的诗人才可能承担起历史赋予我们的责任和使命。当前，我们希望有更多的诗人来关注人类的命运，来共同关注人类的前途，来共同思考在全世界现代化过程中，人类所取得的进步以及人类所遭遇到的前所未有的异化和灾难。

　　另外，作为人类精神世界的代言人，不同种族、不同国家、不同地域、不同文化背景的诗人们，还应该为今天人类精神生活的重构发挥我们应有的作用。我想这恐怕是我们这个时代任何一个有着责任和良知的中国诗人应持的写作立场和写作态度，同时，也是我们这个时代所有的诗人应该共同努力的目标。保护生物的多样性是这个世界已经被认同的普遍原则，那么保护文化的多样性同样是这个世界应该被认同的普遍原则。今天的中国诗人，应该为中国古老语言和文字进行新的诗意创造做出贡献，应该在自己的诗歌中充分展示中国古老文字的魅力，应该在中国文字神秘的音乐性中创造出更具民族性和东方精神的现代诗。我相信，随着这个世界不同文明、不同文化之间对话的加深，必将进一步地推动世界不同国家间、不同民族间文学的交流。我相信，这种对话和交流最终将从更高的层面上为促进世界和平和全人类进

and pinpoint their salutary influence upon Chinese poets and writers. This list is, indeed highly selective as it passes too many illustrious names unnoticed. A perfunctory mention of them, as the space allows, at least, excuses me from a lapse of sense of guilt. They are: Indian poet Tagore, French poet Saint-John Perse, French poet Henri Michaux, Italian poet Salvatore Quasimodo, Italian poet Montale Eugenio, Italian poet Giuseppe Ungaretti, Swedish poet Tomas Transtromer, Greek poet George Seferis, Greek poet Odysseus Elytis, Turkish poet Nazim Hikmett. Still more remains to be called upon, I must acknowledge. Their work, having been translated into one of the most ancient languages in the world, has gained a second life being read and browsed in, affording mental food for the Chinese reading public who will forever cherish their renown.

Thirdly, let me touch upon the issue of social purpose of a Chinese poet in the context of world literature. By social purpose I mean the proper attitude we should strike when we set to pen vis-a-vis our world in transition. I trust a sense of culture is essential for a poet to begin with. That is to say a poet should be a cultured man. Of course, there is the eternal ethic of individual responsibility as a poet is always left to his own devices vis-a-vis both an external world and an internal world of his soul. Nobility of mind, obvious sincerity, unsullied goodness, moral courage are some of the most redeeming features in his character. Only so can we undertake the time-honored mission to write for the sake of mankind. For awareness of the complexity of the human condition and vulnerability of the human race underlies the intrinsic poetic need in the increasingly congested world of the 21th century, a world of "perfection of means and confusion of goals."

Ultimately the civic voice of mankind, poets, irrespective of whatever race he might belong to, whatever ethnic origin he might be of, whatever cultural background he might identify with, have a role thrust upon his shoulders to play in reinstating of the wholeness of life. This is rightly what I mean by striking an ethic attitude towards writing, a common goal all poets should aspire to. Since the conservation of bio-diversity has been a universally acknowledged tenet, so is the conservation of cultural diversity. The mind of man glorifies in nothing more than in struggling successfully with difficulty, and nothing certainly excites our interest and admiration more than the view of our poetry enriched, our mother tongue revitalized and purified to new heights. All the musical and sensuous qualities should be developed with the greatest sensitivity. I, for one, trust today's forum is a perfect opportunity for deepening understanding and spreading of the finest literary fruits across the world. And on a higher plane, it will contribute to world peace and human progress in its own indispensable way.

步事业做出不可替代的重要贡献。

我的演讲就到这里,不妥之处请各位尊敬的同行予以指正。谢谢大家!

The above are some of my ruminations on the workshop subject. I feel both honored and humbled in the presence of such a distinguished audience. I thank you again for your attention.

我们向大山呼唤,并倾听它的回声

在世界山地纪录片节高峰论坛上的演讲

2008年8月4日

女士们、先生们:

下午好!

和许多场合一样,我一直在想:对于这么多翻山越岭甚至远涉重洋而来的宾客和艺术家,我应该用怎样的词句表示欢迎与感谢呢?最终我决定,还是放弃那种虽然出自真诚,却难以消除距离感的热情或者彬彬有礼。因为我深信,至少有三个原因让我们聚集在这里:一、对纪录片的热爱与交流;二、对山地自然和山地文明的关注与思考;三、对世界屋脊青藏高原神秘召唤的呼应。那么基于这样的理由,无论我们曾经相识还是从未谋面,这个节日都是一次志同道合的朋友之间的聚会,我们每个人都是这个聚会的主人。

我们都注意到,这些年来,在众多思想者和艺术家对山地的关注与行动中,世界上诞生了大量以山地为讲述对象的不同风格、不同内容的纪录片,它们如同山地的自然、文化和生活一样丰富多彩,在当代世界纪录片之林,以其枝繁叶茂而占有显要的位置。然而据我们了解,目前世界上还没有一个较大规模的针对这一主题而搭建的国际性展示与交流的平台。那么,地处世界屋脊、群山之巅的中国青海,有责任,有义务,也有自信的理由,承担起这一时代的需求和历史的重托。

这就是我们决定举办世界山地纪录片节的初衷。

这个世界山地纪录片节,目的是要借助并且充分发挥青海高原得天独厚的自然

Mountains Are Beckoning Us to Lend Them an Ear
A Speech Given at the Summit Forum on World Documentary Filming
4th, August, 2008

Ladies and Gentlemen:

As the like occasions prompt me into thinking: what kind of courtesy on my part to be displayed as befits greeting this huge band of talented documentary film artists who have journeyed across the vast oceans from distant lands? I fumble and grope all the way into illumination the best policy for me is to dispense with the formalities, though honest but still tinged with a grain of stiffness , usually associated with hosting a similar grand event. I trust there are three considerations we play host to a cultural event like this. First is our fascination with documentary filming. Secondly, our awakened ecological conscience about the fate of the civilizations in the wilderness and mountains encroached by the modernization frenzy. Thirdly, our response to the call from the Realm of the Tibet-Qinghai Plateau-the symbol of the pristine soul and the icon of eternal life. Given the above rationales, I believe the atmosphere is greatly leavened by the sense of kinship with men of like mind to such an extent each of us is a host instead of a guest, no matter most of us are by far only nodding acquaintances.

As we have noted, there has been a remarkable resurgence of interest among thinkers and artists in documentaries, a trend which spawns an upsurge of documentary films which may vary in style , outlook and focal points but all sharing a common social concern . As a consequence of these ambitions, the audience may well find the usage of the medium is diverse and rich, embracing the different facets of the mountains in its wilderness and cultural connotations. This richness points to the reasons why documentary filming is such a promising cultural enterprise, for it invokes the extension and realization of the medium's hidden potential. To our dismay, there has been a flagrant absence of forum or platform across the world that puts together documentary makers to swap experience, compare notes and showcase their talent for public screening or cashing in on their good deeds and effort oriented towards natural solidarity. Our major altruistic consideration in filling this vacuum largely arises from this noticeable negligence in the cultural sphere.

存在、人文积淀和人类生活延续的资源优势,以众人之手树起一面具有号召意义的旗帜,进一步增进当今世界对山地自然和山地文明的关注,促进人与自然的和谐共荣和多样性文化之间的对话沟通;以影视的形式、艺术的视角、人文的思考,致力于探索在一种特殊的地域环境和文化背景下人类历史的发展、人与自然的关系,讲述万物生存的故事,并由此反省人类的共同命运和人类社会发展的得失。所以,我们把本届世界山地纪录片节的主题定为"山地世界、人与自然,多元文化的共享与传承"。

那么,山地给了我们什么,以致我们不得不对它投以格外关注的目光?换句话说,在当代以都市、工业和信息为主导的文明背景中,山地之于我们的生存、生活和思想还具有不可或缺的价值与意义吗?

回答当然是肯定的。

我出生在大山之中,生长于群山的怀抱,这使我对山地有一种特殊的眷恋和至深的敬意。实际上,即使生长于都市、祖祖辈辈生活在平原的人,谁又不曾对遥远而神秘的群山魂牵梦萦呢?谁又不曾面对崇山峻岭在敬畏中沉思默想或者在惊奇中欣喜若狂呢?说到底,我们明白,在这个地球上,山地既是一个特殊的地理概念,又是一个文明载体,也是一种心灵寄托。也就是说,从自然的角度看,山地是这个地球上生物多样性和物质丰富性的资源宝库;从文化的角度看,山地是人类多元化、多元生活的诞生地和传播地;从精神的角度看,山地是生命的肇始、记忆的故乡和灵魂的神秘归宿。

山地是万物的乐园。因为它是一个多姿多彩、张扬着生命的欢乐和自由的世界,这是其他地域环境所不能相比的。群山之中,茂盛的植物、美丽的动物按照造物主的意愿生长繁衍,连岩石、流水和风雪云雾都充满灵性,它们形成各自独立又相互依存的有机秩序,堪称和谐存在的典范。没有山地,我们不能想象大自然的奇妙。

山地是人类的摇篮。人类学和考古学家目前普遍相信,东非高原的山岭峡谷是人类始祖的诞生地;中国的巫山人、元谋人以及山顶洞人,都是山的儿女。世界上还有许多学者相信曾经存在这样一段往事:数百万年前的青藏高原,群山连绵,气候温

We in Qinghai deem this absence both a mission and an opportunity. Preeminent is of course Qinghai's extreme alpine topography and remote mountainous terrain as famed Roof of the World, which supports a diversity of bio-species of irreplaceable value. No less important is the region as potpourri of multi-religions, multi-races and multi-cultures. Much lies in store for enterprising artists to explore, examine and document while there is still time. Qinghai does dream of placing itself at the forefront of China's campaign for eco-system balance and conservation of cultural diversity by using art to bring to the world's attention the elemental processes of and human cultures attached to the mountainous terrain, to enact dialogues between various cultures to enhance the harmonious relationship between man and nature and assist the public to understand the implications of the environmental cataclysms that might jeopardize the alpine eco-system in the wake of the sweeping reckless modernization. That is why we set the keynote tone for this festival to the effect "Man and Nature in the Mountains-Co-sharing and Inheriting of Diverse Cultural Legacy."

Then, one might ask:"Why turn our gaze at mountains?" In other words, in our present age of globalization, seething with stubborn problems arising mainly from urbanization and digitalization, and crying out for remedies, what good is there for us to draw from the alternate ways of thinking and doing associated with the mountainous terrain?

Personally, my tribal village lies perched in the Daliangshan Highlands, adjacent to peaks close to 3000m meters above sea level, mountains are invariably the object of my keen and constant attachment. Yet ,despite of origin, rural or urban, whatever we think mountains are-a treasure house containing bio-diversity DNA (a naturalist's perspective),a birth place and diffuser of diversified human cultures,(a humanist's point of view),a homeland of historical memory and a mysterious abode from where life sets sail and to which our spirits eventually return (a case of Jung's psychoanalysis),we begin the process of truth and give wording to a lifelong deep-seated fantasy, or the need for "things wide and free" in the lofty and "pristine places, places substantially unaltered by man .Even If we don't visit them, they matter to us." We need to know though we are surrounded by forests of concrete and cement, there are vast places where the world goes on as it always has.

Mountains are paradise of all creatures, untrammeled and untamed, free of human artifact, full of color and motion, beyond compare with any other type of terrain. All forms of life, vegetations, fauna and flora, grow and flourish heedless of nothing but God's will. Rocks, running brooks, winds, snowfall, clouds and fogs form a mysterious biotic community, just as fresh, untrammeled but interdependent as at the dawn of geological beginnings eons ago. Devoid of mountains, where lies the goodness and wondrousness of Nature?

Mountains are the proven cradle of mankind. Anthropologists and archaeologists both credit the eastern African savannas to be ideal for the order of the primates (tree shrews, lemurs, apes monkeys, tarsiers),to which man's earliest ancestors Homo Sapiens belonged, at that level of

和温润,动植物的生长一派兴旺,人类的祖先古猿是其中的智者;随着高原持续隆起、气候变迁,古猿开始走出大山,走下高原,走向世界各地,从而诞生了今天的人类。学者们相信,有朝一日,青藏古猿会从万年冰雪和岩石中现身,向我们讲述那个伟大时空中的故事。也许往事过于苍茫,而今天生活在世界各地山地高原上的民族,不是依然如此鲜活生动地向我们展示着生、爱与死的意义吗?没有山地 我们不能想象人类生命的尊严。

山地是我们的灵魂的故土,茫茫昆仑、雄伟的阿尔卑斯、绵延的安第斯、高耸的乞力马扎罗以及冰雪下的喜马拉雅让我们看到,山地之于我们生存的意义不仅仅是衣食和呼吸,它还是诸神的领地,人类精神的象征和我们想象力与创造力的殿堂。从古老的神话传说、创世史诗到歌舞、绘画,直到我们今天的纪录片,都与山地血脉相连,密不可分。因为有山的呵护、山的包容、山的启示,我们懂得创造艺术,从而人类不仅仅拥有了充满活力的血肉之躯,更拥有了高贵的灵魂以及灵魂存在的方式。没有山地,我们不能想象艺术的永恒。

然而,不能让我们乐观的是,在当今后工业化、信息化和城市的大趋势中,山地的自然和谐正在被打破,山地的文化传承正在流失,山地的文化共性和文化个性开始变得模糊而抽象。山地民族、山地居住者,作为山地自然文化的保持者、继承者,变得比以往任何时候都更加脆弱和孤单。但是,山地的自然构成,山地民族的艺术、思维、宗教、历史和生活方式,是不能失去和不可取代的。这是自然的悲剧、文化的悲哀和人类的悲伤。一个由山地高原为我们保存的物质生活和心灵的家园正在哭泣,就像山脚下身穿染花布衣裳的美丽的少女,因为迷路而愈显孤独无助。所以,它比任何时候都需要我们倾情关注。

我知道,有许多人和我一样,并不懂得纪录片的创作,但是这丝毫不影响我们对纪录片的热爱甚至迷恋。因为影视艺术家们并不是在向我们炫耀技术或者技巧,而是向我们呈现事实、讲述故事、传达思想,让我们产生共鸣。在中国乃至全世界,我们无法知道每年有多少纪录片诞生,它们涉及各个领域、地域,不同题材和风格。这些

evolution, as the climate was warm enough to make the lack of clothing bearable, and the open grasslands, in contrast to dense forests and deserts, afforded both water and animal foods. Several anthropological regional varieties, such as Wushan Man (Homo erectus wushanenis),Yuanmou Man (Homo erectus yuanmouensis) and Peking Man (Homo erectus pekinensis), were all mountain citizens. The story of man begins with his dispersal throughout the globe in the wake of continuous uplift of the earth surface caused by tectonic or deformational forces or by accumulation of volcanic rocks. Some scientists entertain the wildest leap of human fancy that one day that the hominid Homo erectus (man's immediate ancestor) would emerge from the perennially frozen rocks of the Himalaya and recount the most exhilarating story of Genesis in the dim past. Who knows? Yet ,without mountains, where lies the intrinsic dignity worthy of man?

Mountains are our spiritual home. When the logic of history hungers for bread, all the existing mountains, Mt.Kunlun, the Alps, the Andes, the Himalayas and the Kilimanjaro handle out without fail. Other than economic utility, that the mountains yield a cultural and esthetic harvest is a fact long known, but latterly often forgotten. Mountains are the enclave of the deities and the immortals and the continuous source of the knowledge needed for cultural renewal. All the human authored cultural products, from cosmogony mythologies and epics of antiquity, to modern dance, painting and documentaries, are more or less inspired by the presence of mountains. Indeed, we owe mountain a huge debt, literally our body and soul. For mountains banished and pillaged, where lies the eternal charm of art?

Yet, to our astonishment, our society, so obsessed with the larger trend of post-industrialization, digitalization and urbanization, may have crossed the threshold to topple the harmony between man and nature in the mountains and to dilute and blur the cultural identity unique of the cultural products associated with the alpine background. The basic forces of mountains, once beyond man's reach due to its remoteness and inaccessibleness, fall a prey to man's greed and rapacity. Mountain indigenous residents and advocates of mountain cultures find themselves increasingly encroached and submerged. This shameful condition is definitely the tragedy of nature, the sorrow of culture as well as the woe of humanity. We bewail of our spiritual home under siege, as helpless as a girl at a loss, at the foot of a hill, for a proper way out. We plea for a mountain ethic which is even more urgent and timely now.

I, for one, am ignorant of the technicalities of the documentary filming. But this does not in the least affect my passion and even infatuation with the art. We know most of the documentary makers are as much as us imbued with an ecological conscience. They come here not to show off their talent or brag about their skills. They are here to reveal a truth, tell an interesting tale, impart a message and render a public service. Each year, in China or across the whole world, there has been a countless output of documentaries made or in the making, varying in style, theme, focal point but all sharing the same social concern for preserving "thing wild and free". These tales and footages excite us, delight us, disquiet us and bring us into lapse of a more reflective mood. At

故事和画面让我们感动,让我们喜悦,让我们平静,或者让我们沉思,有时它们甚至毫不怜悯地让我们震惊、畏惧、愤怒或者羞愧。这就是纪录片的伟大。这是艺术家用心灵、思想和智慧在我们对生活和文化的关注之间架设的桥梁。我们的共鸣证明我们每个人都与这个世界的每个角落、每个层面息息相关。

我们欣喜地看到:纪录片正在走向国际重大影视节的领奖台。一部纪录片可以引起万人空巷影院爆满,一部纪录片讲述的故事能够改变我们的观念和生活态度,能够对社会的纵深层面产生影响。我相信,人类文化中一个纪录片的时代正在向我们走来。而纪录片的繁荣,标志着人类社会和人类文明开始进入一个新的成熟期,标志着人类的目光开始从关注生活的物质表象向关注生存的价值取向转变。纪录片已经成为当今世界衡量一个国家、地区和民族的文明程度、文化品位、人口素质的新型标准之一。

我认为,纪录片对人类文明的贡献,首先在于它以目前人类最为先进的手段生动直观地记录了这个瞬息万变的世界上不可复制、不可再生、不可忽视的瞬间。然而它的价值远不仅限于此。因为这个记录迫使我们回望那转眼成为过去的事物,迫使我们停下喧嚣的思绪审视我们曾经的话语和行为,迫使我们调整当前的身姿和步履面对前方的路程。纪录片记录的是过去,警示的是现在,它指向未来。纪录片作为人类的记忆库而拓展着我们思考与生存的空间。

关于这个话题,我相信影视专家和大师们能够给我们奉献许多精彩的见解和智慧的结晶,这也正是我和大家共同期待的。

对于山地的概念,我知道从地理或者地质学的角度有着规范准确的界定。但是我更愿意把山地和高原视为同事物的不同层面。我觉得,如果高耸的山脉是手臂或者头颅,高原更像是宏伟的胸膛。我们的地球只有三分之一是陆地,而陆地的主体构成又是山地高原。中国地形图显示,占国土面积近四分之三的第二和第三阶梯几乎都处在山地高原的范畴之内。如果没有山地高原承载万物和人类生活,我们无法想象有限的平原和江南水乡会是怎样的境况。当然这不是事实,也不可能成为事实。

times, they simply shock us or turn us ashamed of being humans and aghast at the dirt doings of mankind in general towards nature. Isn't it this the much needed and distinct service documentary artists rendered for our society? By awakening the ecological conscience of human community to the biotic community, by bringing to the world's attention the plight of nature, they help us understand "why theraw wilderness gives definition and meaning to the human enterprise."

To our jubilee, documentaries makers are frequently seen mount the podiums of the major film festivals. A tool for a social change, a single documentary often packs the cinema to full house and exerts profound influence, indicative of the maturing of our society and our civilization. The vogue of documentary films constitutes a major human leap from fixation upon the surface of things to probing into the values of existence as well as one of the current standards by which the quality of demographics, cultural taste and national/regional/ethnic civilization are measured and graded.

The essential point is that where words struggle to convey reality, and paintings could not catch the fleeting moment, documentary films come to achieve both, presenting in a flow of dramatic images instant history to be stored for immediate projection or future retrieval. Beyond technical flair, they are not just more than that as good film makers always believe in the dual functions of the documentary films to interpret history and to promote human understanding.

The documentary films for this festival, I am sure, carry more weight and authority than mine of individual artists who address the vital issue of preserving the cultural legacy associated with the mountainous terrain with eloquence and a sense of urgency required by the disturbing status quo.

From a geological point of view, mountains and uplands are rigorously defined as a tract of land rising considerably above the surrounding surface, in opposition to sea and plain. My temperament and upbringing incline me to picture peaks as head or arms of the earth, uplands or plateaus as chest. In the one third of the land of which the earth makes up, mountains and uplands dominate. If you look at the map of China, you will see topography falls into three geological terraces and about three fourth of the country's territory including the first and second terraces is mountainous, hilly or high plateau. Although the third terrace is formed by plains and lowlands, it is generally on the lower reaches of the larger rivers rising in the Tibet-Qinghai plateau and supports the majority of the Chinese population. Literarily we might say it is the mountains in the west of China that sustain the agricultural and industrial heartland along China's vital coastal stretch.

My argument is crystal clear: in historical terms, all the existing mountain ranges and great river systems, such as the Tibet-Qinghai Plateau, the Yunan-Guizhou Plateau, the varied loess uplands, the Inner-Mongolian Tableland, the Tianshan Mountain Ranges, all the upland that fall into the prospective geographical divisions of Hunan, Sichuan, Shanxi, the Yangtze, the Pearl River, all bear witness to the grand genesis story of the Chinese nation and the region, in

我想说的是，青藏高原、云贵高原、黄土高原、内蒙古高原和苗岭、十万大山、天山或者巴山秦岭等等，它们与黄河、长江、珠江、松嫩平原一样，创造并见证了不朽的中华文明，并且它们对这个文明有着独特的、不可取代的贡献。

青藏高原平均海拔在4000米以上。作为当前公认的世界四大超洁净地区之一，它的物种的原生态价值可想而知；作为黄河、长江、澜沧江、雅鲁藏布江等著名江河的发源地，它对亿万人的生存环境和对东方文明诞生与发展的影响可想而知；作为多民族共生、多宗教共存、多元文化交流融合的舞台，它对保持人类文化多样性和生活多样性的意义可想而知。那么这样一片充满神性的山水，这样一些深受神灵保佑的生灵，这样一种在神奇中延续的生活，对山地纪录片创作的价值和诱惑当然也可想而知。

青海的山水环境创造了这片土地上特有的生命现象和生存秩序，而在这个秩序中，人类创造了让自然接纳的历史、宗教、艺术观念和生活方式。这是一个深邃广阔的秘境。而我们对它的认识、记录和讲述远远不是万一。

庄子说："天地有大美而不言，四时有明法而不议，万物有成理而不说。"青海就是一座在大美中沉默的宝库，它期待艺术家们犹如说出"芝麻开门"一样说出你的咒语，来开启这宝库之门。

世界山地纪录片节，作为青海省人民政府和国家有关部门共同主办、国际与国内众多影视机构和艺术家共同参与打造的一个个性化文化品牌，今后每隔一年举办一届。我们相信它将成为世界不同国家、不同地域、不同种族的纪录片艺术家们创作、研讨、和交流的极好的平台之一。

我们为本届纪录片节设立了玉昆仑奖，分别授予参加展播评选的优秀纪录片和创作人员。当然任何评奖都不是完美无缺的，我倒是愿意把它看作对纪录片本身的一种赞扬，是对一种执着和探索精神的褒奖，而这种精神存在于每位艺术家心中，展现在每一部纪录片之内。

中国古籍中记载说："玉出昆仑。"昆仑山是美玉的故乡。北京第28届奥运会奖

particular, around the confluence of the Yellow River formed the cradle of the Chinese civilization.

This terraced structure is the outcome of massive tectonic movements beneath the Chinese land mass. The highest terrace is the Tibet-Qinghai Plateau under discussion, which rises 4000 meters above sea level and comprises mainly Qinghai and Tibet. Touted by UN as one of the four super clean regions in the world, the Plateau contains a plethora of priceless biodiversity DNA. The fact that all the major rivers of China and Southeast Asia originate in here, flow east, south and southwest, coursing their way through and irrigating the major swathes of the Chinese land and some of China's southwestern neighbors speaks volumes about the strategic significance of the Plateau. Furthermore, as potpourri of a multiplicity of ethnic races, religions, and cultures, the Plateau exhibits one more pivotal dimension as the hub of cultural diversity and existential diversity. That is why I assert the blessed Plateau is a veritable treasure chest for documentary artists. Once opened, its riches will surely glitter and dazzle.

The unspoiled Qinghai land mass exhibits the beauty and order of an earlier time prior to man's invasion. Being remote, subject to extremes of weather, thinly populated, and literarily beyond the pale of the so called civilization, the region boasts an awesomely array of ways of life, conception of history, idea of art, all closer to the spirit of nature. Lack of visualizing resources of such a mysterious and celestial realm simply belies our ignorance, our narrowed visual threshold and aphasia.

In salutation to Qinghai, Taoist Sage Chuangzi's adage gains a poignant pertinence herein when he asserts "Heaven and Earth evince a beauty that endures, because Heaven and earth seldom boast of it. The pageant of four seasons is an ending and thrilling drama following a wordless script. An inner but supreme law governs the life and death of all creatures."Qinghai, to me, looks like a unique world of all powerful sorcerers and ubiquitous jinn, of fabulous wealth and exotic beauty, awaiting the artists who know the code of "Open Sesame!"to crack open the cave.

Thanks to the co-organizing work of both the Provincial Government of Qinghai and the relevant agencies of the Central Government, and thanks to the kindness and professionalism of artists and experts in the field of documentary filming, we have been able to host this festival twice a year in the hope it will continually provide a platform on which top documentary makers showcase their talent and mirror the hidden beauty and undiscovered splendor of various mountain regions and uplands across the world.

An honor dubbed "kunlun Award" is established to encourage the entries and documentary makers who come off victorious, deeply aware any award is not without its drawback. I prefer to deem the award as a celebration of the medium itself, as an incentive to the adventurous spirit with which the heart of each artist throbs.

A word should be in place put for the Kunlun jade of which the award takes its name. In the ancient Chinese literature pertaining to jade, Mt.Kunlun commands very good commendation. Since the 28th Olympics wherein the jade was chosen as the materials for medals, Kunlun jade

牌镶嵌昆仑玉之后,它的物质价值和文化价值得到极大提升,这也正是我们用昆仑玉制作纪录片奖杯的原因之一;中国玉文化源远流长,它象征高贵、纯洁和矢志不渝的气节,而产生于东方圣山昆仑山的美玉更是山之精华、大自然的造化。这也正是山地纪录片节的精髓所在——高贵美丽,天然质朴。

正如我开始说的那样,我不需要对大家光临说一些溢美之词,以免破坏我们之间的亲切交往和心灵的默契。但是我们仍然十分珍惜在青海高原的相聚,珍惜各位艺术家奉献的作品、思想和才智。

几天以后,我们各奔东西,又将重新相隔千山万水,但是我们不再陌生,友谊使我们心灵相通。也许在一个又一个繁忙的白天,在热闹或者紧张的工作室,你无暇想到这短暂的聚会,但是我相信,一定会在某个夜晚,在明月清风的梦里,在流水一样的思绪里,一种清凉芬芳的感觉会突然升起,你睁开眼睛,穿越茫茫时空,看到了你在世界最高的一片土地上留下的身影。你一定会带着你的朋友再来! 谢谢大家!

trinkets and ornaments are in vogue. Traditionally, jade in China is embodiment of integrity of character, nobility and loyalty. Jade mined from Mt. Kunlun is certainly the paragon of natural beauty. The Kunlun jade award contains the qualities of plainness and nobility which I hope all the entries will illustrate.

Again I try my best to curb the impulse of resorting to superlatives to eulogize our situation and all those present, lest the courtesy and formalities keep us from a more free-hearted communion. I only want to say this that I deeply appreciate your arrival and cherish the ardor and zest each brings to the art of the documentary filming.

In a few day's time, we will part hands. But art brings us together and makes us friends. Meanwhile, I surmise this encounter, brief as it may be, whatever tongue you might speak, wherever you might make home, together with all the footages and possibly your own films on the air, will ignite your perennial sense of wonder for the hidden natures and over one of the sleepless nights, you might decide to take wings and drift back amongst these forgotten uplands with your friends!

太阳的使者，大地的祭司——诗人艾青
在"光明的歌者"艾青百年诞辰纪念诗歌朗诵会上的演讲

2008年8月4日

数千年前，当先民们以敬畏的姿态仰视长空、眺望大地的时候，其中的智者就创造了人类原始的诗篇——神话。那些光明和生命的使者，记述了正在觉醒的人类精神的最初渴望：关于万物存在，关于生与死，关于未来。

我一直有一个感觉，那些以神话方式崇拜太阳的灵魂从来都没有消失，他们在光明中延续，在大地上生生不息。于是，一百年前，艾青诞生了——一个必然要以手持火炬的形象行走在东方大地上的诗人。

诗人艾青诞生的时代，是动荡与巨变的时期，是阴暗与严寒笼罩的岁月，所以他将注定成为新纪元的盗火者。对这片土地和古老文明的热爱，使他的眼睛饱含泪水、他的心灵燃烧着火焰、他的口中充满光明；对太阳的歌颂、对真理的敬仰、对生活的热情、对黑暗和丑恶的鞭挞，是艾青贯穿终生的诗歌创作主题。读着艾青不朽的诗句，我们意识到他从来没有离开过我们。

因为人类社会依然处在一个动荡与变革的时代，人类生活进入了一个物质主义的时代，人类文明进入一个技术与信息爆炸的时代，人类心灵生活面临前所未有的考验，诗和诗意的高贵与纯洁面临前所未有的挑战，人类精神世界由于物质的挤压变得渺小而脆弱，我们需要从文化的精髓中获得营养以完成自我的精神救赎，需要重建诗人的信仰以确立生命、灵魂、真理、责任和爱的价值。当我们的心灵被光明照耀的时候，艾青已经回到我们中间。

艾青是20世纪诞生并且具有广泛国际影响的中国诗人，他对诗歌的贡献是杰出的，同时也是多方面的。作为一个担当使命的诗人，渴求光明、追求真理、礼赞自由、思考人生的主题贯穿他创作的始终，他的思想同诗句一样表现得激越、深沉而凝

Herald of Apollo and the Shaman of the Earth
A Speech Given at the Poetic Reading in Celebration of the 100 Anniversary of Ai Qing, China's Greatest Bard of the 20th Century
4th, August, 2008

Suppose one draws back in time, say, ten millennia in a primal society, in the company of shamans with their reverent gaze into the celestial vaults or the horizon lost to view, listening to voices of the gods speak from the wind and thunder, standing watch over the holy spirit flow in every tributary brook, and the whole earth blooms as a sacred place-then and there myth comes into being. Or rather the first poem in the mythical mode cut off from the umbilical cords of Mother's womb. The first breed of poets in the guise of priests and shamans, messengers of light and life, are at that moment participating in one of the greatest jumps of the awakening human soul to a knowledge about creation, life and death and future.

There arises at times a mental picture before my eyes those mythical souls making the sun their idol have never departed. They have been reincarnated in light, exulting in an exuberant life of the Immortals.

Then came forth the poet Ai Qing, possibly the incarnate of these Immortals, a torch in hand, to the country of his birth and to the people of his blood in their hour of need.It was a most perilous and tremendous moment when disasters one after another struck down China, a land just off the yoke of the Qing dynastic tyranny, but rent again with civil feuds and foreign invasion. Under the severity of that inclement season, Ai Qing the poet, fearless, eloquent, large of mind but chaste in heart, came forth, destined to be Prometheus of a new era, preoccupied with the burning thought of the salvation of his beloved country. Patriotism, pathos, praise of the sun, respect for truth, passion for life, loathing of darkness and evil-all the worthy time-honored poetic themes are there, thus ensuring the survival value of the poet among us.

The age in which we live throngs with turmoil and turbulence, explosion in information and technology. On the other hand, it is also a time for trying man's soul and heart, judged to be given too much to materialism, incapable of new literary greatness. Our spiritual world finds itself increasingly diminished and squeezed between some alien forces, some of our own making, and some beyond comprehension and control. There is a critical need for catharsis and spiritual

重。他这样唱道:"为什么我的眼里常含泪水?/因为我对这土地爱得深沉……"作为一个富有才华的诗人,他的诗篇充满多彩的想象和智慧的灵动,在独特的象征和意象中饱含哲理,如同他用"太阳的话"说:"让我进去,让我进去,/……让我把花束,把香气,把亮光,/温暖和露水撒满你们心的空间。"

作为一个自觉而自信的诗人,他具有鲜明的诗歌美学理想,并且以成功的个性化创作实践,达到了他所追求的"朴素、单纯、集中、明快"的艺术境界,他淳朴的诗歌语言超越了华丽而臻于高贵。由此在中国新诗的历史上,艾青已经成为划时代的旗帜和领袖,他不朽的诗篇已经成为民族文化的宝贵遗产。

人类最为高尚的品质,莫过于对光明和爱的追求。艾青诗歌创作的主题及其杰出的艺术成就,注定使他成为世界的诗人、人民的诗人。在他生前身后,他的作品不断被翻译成许多国家的文字,受到国际诗坛的重视与好评,也深受不同人们的喜爱和敬佩,艾青已经作为影响广泛的中国诗人而享誉世界。

艾青生前曾经同世界许多著名诗人交往密切,与他们结下了深厚的友谊,包括智利诗人巴勃罗·聂鲁达、西班牙诗人拉斐尔·阿尔贝蒂、古巴诗人尼古拉斯·纪廉、巴西作家亚马多、苏联作家爱伦堡等等。由于艾青的广泛影响,西方世界把他同智利诗人巴勃罗·聂鲁达和土耳其诗人纳齐姆-希克梅特,并称为"20世纪三大人民诗人"。

在那个时代,艾青以捍卫真理、追求光明的诗人形象和明快、优雅的诗歌语言讲述中国,在精神与文化层面同世界沟通交流,从而增进了世界对中国人民的理解,传播了中国的文化和思想,也成功地树立了现代中国的文化形象,这是极其难得的成就。

艾青是一位具有社会责任感的现实主义诗人,同时也是一位具有文化使命感的浪漫主义诗人。他的诗歌立足于社会生活而获得一种精神的象征之美,如同茉莉花盛开在山坡上,散发着凝练了天地精华的芬芳,这使得他和他的诗篇,都成为我们的典范。我认为,今天我们有许多诗人恰恰缺少这样一种感悟、一种境界,或者说缺少一种作为诗人的宿命意识。一些人往往为写诗而创作,或偏执于象牙塔里的遣词造句,或沉湎于技术形式的矫揉造作,或者干脆以极端的态度追逐"非诗"的标新立异,从而无意甚至有意地失去了对文化、社会、生存和人性的观照。我知道,我们今天的确处于一个文化多元的时代,但是文化的精髓并没有遗失,艾青所追求的境界将永远是诗的终极价值。

regeneration before we can successfully draw on our cultural legacy of the past century. There is a critical need to reaffirm the olden verities and virtues of life, soul, truth, love and duty. And there is a critical need we return to Ai Qing the poet whose inspired songs will leave us enlightened again.

Ai Qing remains one of the most distinguished poets of the 20th century China to have achieved international reputation in terms of output and lyrical excellence. His success as a poet lies in his willingness to be used by a purpose bigger than himself, the poet with a mission, which is, to transmute into poetry his passion for truth, light, freedom and life. More than any other poets he attaches importance to patriotism, but voiced with refined lyrical quality:

Why tears always glisten in my eyes?/This land fills me with special affection. He has produced some of the finest poems in our language, of rare artistic skill, soaring imagination, rich in ingenious imagery and philosophical import. Thus Speaks the Sun is such a superb performance:

Let me in./ let me in./ Let me sprinkle your heart with flowers, fragrance, light ,warmth and dewdrops.

Ai Qing is a highly artistically conscious poet. In fact, one of his ambitions is to incorporate his 4-element aesthetics of poetic creation into his exquisite songs, ie, simplicity, concentration, innocence and lucidity. His simple art has a brilliance and nobility to it, unsurpassed in the history of New Poetry in China, making him the natural leader, the model to his contemporaries. He is bound to have permanent influence on us, for with his translucent spirit and patriotic sentiment, his high place in the history of our literature is once and for all secured.

True devotee of light and sweetness, Ai Qing has a profoundly moral nature, capable of genuine indignation, sympathy and passion .His songs go straight to the heart and he is the poet of common men, not only of China, but also of the world. Alive and dead, Ai Qing has been widely translated into many languages. His lyrical poems have found their way into the bosoms of world peoples, because they speak for themselves.

Ai Qing is a widely travelled poet. His acquaintances with poetic giants with Pablo Neruda from Chile, Raphael Alberti from Spain, Nicolas Guillien from Cuba, Amado Jorge from Brazil, Ehrenburg from former Soviet Union spawned salon topics and forged legendary friendship. One critical estimate in vogue in the west is rank him with Pablo Neruda and Nazim Hikmet to form a "triumvirate of the 20th century commoners".

It should be remembered Ai Qing's mature years coincided with some of the most tumultuous years in recent history. It should be deemed a boon for China to have a devotee of light and sweetness to act as the cultural ambassador of New China, isolated and secluded from Cold War shaped globe. In this office he attempted the far more difficult task of communicating in China's favor with the outside world in the fields of high culture. His technical virtuosity and graceful language has served his purpose admirably.

我爱戴并且由衷地敬仰艾青。从踏上诗歌的道路，我就一直是艾青的追随者，犹如在混沌中跟随一支火炬前进。在我诗歌的学习和创作生活里，我有幸得到他的教诲，得到他的鼓励和支持，他身上体现出来的是长者的慈爱、温和以及在诗歌圣殿前的平等与坦诚。我从他的心智中，不仅学到了诗艺，更学到了人品，这使我终生受用。

被聂鲁达称为"中国诗坛泰斗"的艾青和他的诗，代表着向往光明、捍卫自由、敬仰生命、抗争黑暗的东方民族精神，这也正是人类诗歌的灵魂。他是一个昭示。只要艾青的诗还在，人类历史中那些伟大诗人的英灵还在，我们就能够获得力量，得到启迪，在民族文化的广阔时空里拓展天地、创造奇迹；我们就能够豪迈地高举火炬，向太阳！

那么我坚信不疑：我们今天这个聚会，并不仅仅是追忆和纪念，不是对过去的感慨与叹息，而是一个庄严的迎接仪式——迎接艾青归来，迎接一个伟大的灵魂从诗歌的时空向现实世界凯旋！最后，请允许我用献给艾青一百周年诞辰的诗歌《等待你的归来》结束我的讲话：

　　我们迎接你的归来
　　依然选择在你热爱的黎明
　　当夜色渐渐退去
　　你赞颂过的土地、村庄以及人民
　　都会在你的呼唤中醒来
　　那是黎明的通知
　　它从一双含着泪水的眼睛出发
　　把最深沉的语言和诗句
　　都奉献给了曾经灾难深重的祖国
　　你伟大的心灵时钟
　　就如同海浪中的礁石
　　每时每刻都响彻着
　　对一切被压迫者的同情和呐喊
　　你是火焰
　　你是光明的使者
　　你是亘古不变的太阳的儿子

Ai Qing is both a realist on account of his joy of life, his robust faith, his profound patriotism and a romanticist imbued with a strong sense of mission. Such an extraordinary juxtaposition of two traits blended in one constitutes the surprise and delight of reading Ai Qing. His field is the troubled vigorous civic life, but his poems usually suggest a deeper symbolic meaning other than their verbal relevance, like jasmines in full bloom on the grassy slopes, giving out a supernatural fragrance. Ai Qing is no ivory tower poet. He shows himself capable, at times, if not always, unless hampered by his age, of writing directly, melodiously and with simple elegance and gracefulness while others, or some of us, are found to lack profoundness and play with artificial emotions, ivory tower poetic dictions, technical verbosities or simply un-poetic originalities to the neglect of caring for the society, culture, human condition. We are indeed, living in a world some call by the name of cultural diversity. But Ai Qing's poems contain some pertaining insights for us that ultimately the proper subject matter is still the man in society.

I feel so honored to have my name linked with Ai Qing as disciple. The first reading of him made him my mentor, a torch lighting my pathway out of chaos. His influence upon my writing is benign and tremendous. His strength, his patronizing in time of ill luck, his encouragement in moments of hesitation and self doubt, has entered into me, making me a different poet and a better man.

Ai Qing deserves the title of "Homer of Chinese Poetry", because, of all the modern poets in our literature, no other is so completely, so consciously ,so magnificently embodying the essence of poetry. He poignantly feels his mission of faith and courage in an age of turmoil and timidity, a road sign to remind us it is devotees of light and sweetness like Ai Qing who have filled history with their deeds and the earth, with their renown.

I, for one, rest fully assured we are gathered here today not simply to pay our tribute of respect to a literary giant of the past century. Rather, this grand occasion must be symbolically taken as a welcoming ceremony in honor of the triumphant shadowy returning spirit of Ai Qing.

To conclude, I take great pleasure in citing my tribute prepared for the event of the honored dead's 100 anniversary:

I am Waiting for Your Return.
We are on tiptoes for your return
At dawn you used to celebrate
When night recedes
The land, villages and people in your tribute
Awaken to your call/ The notice issued by Dawn
sets off from eyes glistening tearfully
Dedicating his hymn /to his country once raging with wars and disasters
You, the Clock of Soul/ like the rocks beaten by waves
Sonorously striking to the cries of the oppressed

在你有限的生命岁月中
你曾历经沧桑和苦难
在你的背后黑暗从未消失过
但当你提起笔，写下每一句
泪滴般晶莹的诗句时
我知道,你把不幸和悲哀都埋在了心里
却把自由、尊严和希望
又还给了所有祈求得到它的人们
你的诗章和生命
从未离开过火焰、光明和太阳
那是因为你要战胜黑暗
给这个世界带来些许的温暖
艾青,艾青,艾青
现在是黎明的时刻
现在是诗歌的时刻
现在是生命的时刻
现在绝不是死亡的时刻
我们在山冈上,我们在大海边
已经列好了欢迎你的队伍
等待你的归来！
等待你的归来！

You are a torch fire/messenger of Light
son of the eternal Phoebus
 In a brief span
You were cruelly tested
with your back against the shadow of Darkness
When you resumed writing/Each line at the tip of your pen, glittering with tears
I know you buried your personal sorrow and grief deep in your heart
but dispensing freedom, dignity and hope
among those for which they prayed
Your verse and your life
are forever in the presence of Fire, Light and the Sun
Because you desire nothing but to conquer the darkness
And bring this world some warmth much needed/Oh!
 Ai Qing! Oh! Ai Qing!
Now is dawn at last
The moment for poetry
Now is the time for life
Instead of death
We are uphill and we are at the port
In procession for your return
In procession for your glorious return!

青海湖国际诗歌节:通向世界的门扉

在首届青海湖国际诗歌节新闻发布会上的讲话

2007年4月16日

今天在这里我要高兴地告诉大家,具有悠久的伟大诗歌传统的中国,将在地处人类"第三极"的青藏高原的青海,创立一个具有国际影响的诗歌节——青海湖国际诗歌节。不言而喻,这个具有特殊意义的诗歌节,从她诞生之日起,就将作为一个重要的文化事件,被载入中国当代文化史和诗歌史。

我相信,由于这个诗歌节所承载的特殊文化元素以及她将要显现的卓越的文化影响,她必将与世界其他国度的重要诗歌节相媲美。在这里请允许我怀着敬畏的心情,提及这些诗歌节的名字:波兰华沙之秋国际诗歌节、马其顿斯特鲁加国际诗歌节、荷兰鹿特丹国际诗歌节、德国柏林诗歌节、意大利圣马力诺国际诗歌节、哥伦比亚麦德林国际诗歌节。同时我也深信,因为青海湖国际诗歌节的诞生,她必将为这个世界文化的多样性,为不同文明的对话和沟通,为不同种族和文化背景相异的人们进行心灵的交流,提供一种更为坚实的可能。同样,青海湖国际诗歌节,将把弘扬中国诗歌传统、表现东方文化精神、传播构建和谐世界的理念作为我们神圣的使命。我们相信,今年8月在青海如期举行的青海湖国际诗歌节,将给这个世界一切向往美好生活的人带来一个惊喜!

在这里,作为一个诗人,我只能用诗的语言来向你们介绍青海。你到过青海吗?如果你没有到过青海,你一定曾经在种种亦真亦幻的传说中对青海高原产生过强烈的向往。也许其中包含了较多的猜想与梦幻,至少说明这个向往本身就是一种诱惑。当你来到高原时,你一定会发现,你所体验和感受的一切,都将成为你最难忘的人生

Qinghai Lake International Poetry Festival-A Door Opened to the World
A Speech Given at the Press Release Conference
16th, April, 2007

This is indeed a momentous day as we will solemnly proclaim the inauguration of a new international poetry festival—Qinghai Lake International Poetry Festival (QLIPF), in the Qinghai-Tibet Plateau of China—the great and ancient nation that has given the world the richest veins of poetic legacy of such unparalleled antiquity. It goes without saying that the Chinese people's celebrating poetry in a time of global deterioration of nature under the inexorable march of globalization in the forefront of combating ecosystem collapse on the tertiary pole of the globe, is surely a cultural event of enormous repercussions that will echo down in the histories of contemporary Chinese culture and poetry.

I trust, due to the specific cultural values inherent in the event and the extraordinary influence it is intended to exert, Qinghai Lake International Poetry Festival is bound to, in a certain way, put the Qinghai-Tibet Plateau in the world map of culture and match some of its most prestigious counterparts, to name but a few, Warsaw Autumn of Poetry, Struga Poetry Evenings in Macedonia, Amsterdam International Poetry Festival, Berlin International Poetry Festival, San Marino International Poetry Festival, International Poetry Festival of Medellin. I restfully assured, in the meanwhile, the festival will supply an ideal concourse where dialogues between different civilizations and communications involving people of various ethnic origins and racial identities will take place in the conviction that poetry must and has to play a fundamental role in the process of renewing the Chinese poetic tradition and exemplifying the Oriental spirit. It also has the certainty that arts and poetry will contribute decisively to the emerging of a new humanity, a new human society.

A poet myself and the mastermind of this festival, I cannot get around the fact that a good part of the inspiration of the Festival is due to the keen and constant sense of attachment I have

经历——在青海高原,天地时空的博大给你带来悠远的思绪,雪山草原的壮丽为你增添豪迈的情怀,江河大湖的奔放激发你无限的灵感,古刹梵钟的庄严赋予你深沉的超越,田园牧歌的静美升华你身心的和谐。

正如青海是黄河、长江、澜沧江的发源地一样,她还是诗与歌的摇篮。在这里,三万年前先民们敲打石器的铿锵之声依稀可闻,四千年前黄河儿女舞蹈于彩陶之上的优美韵律历历在目,一千多年来代代相继的宏伟英雄史诗《格萨尔》仍在传唱,盛行于各民族民间的诗歌如草原上的花朵随手可撷。这里是一片积淀着爱与美的土地,是一片盛装着礼赞与感恩的土地,是一片充满着欢乐与梦想的土地。

难怪有哲人说:这是世界最后的净土。

为了让更多的人了解诗歌节的主要内容和活动安排,以下我将做较为详细的介绍:

今年8月在青海举办的首届青海湖国际诗歌节,是为了进一步展示青海得天独厚的自然、人文、历史资源,发挥青海丰厚的历史文化和独具特色的民族文化资源优势,通过诗歌节的形式赋予青海更多的文化内涵,打造特色文化品牌,展示青海的新形象,进一步促进世界不同文化之间的交流,从而推动世界和平和人类的进步事业。

本届诗歌节将充分贯彻和体现胡锦涛同志构建和谐社会以及和谐世界的重要思想,以"人与自然,和谐世界"为主题,以诗歌艺术的形式,表现中华民族奋发图强的时代精神,诠释中国多民族的丰富文化积淀和灿烂历史,展示世界多元文化的精髓,使广大人民群众接受诗歌艺术的陶冶和熏陶,丰富精神文化生活。

本届诗歌节由青海省人民政府、中国诗歌学会主办,青海省文化厅、青海省人民政府新闻办公室、青海省广播电视局、青海省新闻出版局、青海省文联承办,青海西部矿业有限责任公司、北京中坤投资集团有限公司、中国长城艺术文化中心协办。

本届诗歌节定于2007年8月7日—10日在青海省省会西宁市举行,同时在海南州、海北州、黄南州设分会场。诗歌节期间将邀请130位左右国内外著名诗人参加这一诗的盛会,预计将有近百位来自中国内地和中国台湾、香港、澳门以及其他华语世界的诗人到会,同时,还有来自德国、法国、意大利、美国、波兰、西班牙、委内瑞拉、日本、韩国、埃及、爱尔兰、英国、葡萄牙、希腊等国家和地区的近30位著名诗人

evolved to the majesty and beauty of the highland. In an age of globalization a mere visit to the fabled Roof of the World, isolated and impenetrable beyond the world's highest mountains, must still remain one of the fondest dreams of anybody who retains a passion for adventure, both physical and spiritual. The mystery and allure are there, though tinged with a great deal of fancy and wishful thinking. Once you truly set your feet on the tertiary pole, after you have had your fill of epic flyovers in Beijing or Shanghai, prepare for a steep learning curve for what comes into view is enough to instill a sense of wonder. The extreme altitude makes the azure blue sky sparkle with luminosity. The epic grassland and the snow- capped mountains seem to belong to another world. Three world-famous mega waterways roll on unrestrainedly while the gloomy temples, housing a host of exotic deities lit dimly by yak butter lamps, are believed by locals to hold both the wheel of life and the key to the afterworld.

Just as the Yellow River, the Yangtze and the Lancang are proven to originate in Qinghai, archeologists believe this area should be the cradle of Chinese lyrics and songs. Dating back 30,000 years, our Paleolithic ancestors began making stone tools here. Unearthed painted pottery, believed to be 3000 years old, bears beautiful and vivid images of Neolithic dancing girls. For over one thousand years, the chanting of Gesar's heroic exploits resonates across the highland. And local variety of folk songs called Huaer (literally meaning "flowers") are out there prime for plucking, on the tip of the mouth of indigenous inhabitants. This is indeed a land of unsurpassed beauty and variety, an imaginative mix of the landscapes with songs of love and joy of life, benediction of the deities on the other shores and thanksgiving of the mundane pleasures on earth. No wonder a certain sage dubs this area the "Last Pure Land."

For the benefit of the public, let me now give an outline of the major activities of which the August QLIPF consists.

The idea of the forthcoming QLIPF is simply to forge a cultural brand and put the Qinghai-Tibet Plateau in the world map of culture by availing of the natural, humanistic and historic resources, unique of the highland. Incidentally we hope the QLIPF can and should contribute to the construction of world peace, the progressive cause of mankind, as well as the restoration of dialogue between various cultures.

The motto of the QLIPF is "A Harmonious World of Man and Nature". One of the things that really makes our poetry festival special is precisely this: poetic art makes China's and indeed the whole world's civilized past shine out with new haloes. It awakens people's awareness to beauty and enable them to inhabit the world poetically.

QLIPF will be held between the forthcoming 7th to 10th August in Xining, capital city of

参加。

本届诗歌节设有诗歌论坛、诗人采风、"青海湖诗歌宣言"签名仪式、青海湖诗歌之夜以及"诗意青海·和谐世界"大型诗歌音乐演唱会等活动。

本届诗歌节有以下主题活动：

1.举办诗歌高峰论坛。8月7日，在西宁市青海会议中心举办以"人与自然·和谐世界"——21世纪诗歌的责任与使命为主题的诗歌高峰论坛。论坛将与青海湖国际诗歌节开幕式有机结合，有中共青海省委、省人民政府领导同志和嘉宾出席会议，组委会负责人将作《21世纪诗歌的责任与使命》论坛主旨报告，中外著名诗人代表发言。

2.举办诗歌宣言签名活动。在诗歌节期间，将在举世闻名的青海湖畔举行"青海湖诗歌宣言"的签名仪式，诗歌宣言的内容将体现文化的多样性、诗歌的责任与使命、不同文明的对话与交流、对人类生存环境的关注以及对世界和平和人类进步事业的赞颂。

3.举办创作采风活动。为激发诗人的创作精神，首届青海湖国际诗歌节期间将组织中外诗人，以环青海湖地区为重点，分赴海南州、海北州、黄南州等地，进行"同一首诗咏青海——中外著名诗人聚焦青海"采风创作活动。国内外每位诗人将以青海为主题，以青海人文历史、自然景观为线索，创作50行以上的诗歌作品，用诗的语言表现青海的历史变迁和日新月异的发展风貌，届时有关报刊和媒体将及时推出诗歌作品专版。活动结束后将出版《同一首诗咏青海——青海湖国际诗歌节中外著名诗人聚焦青海》作品专集。

4. 举办青海湖诗歌之夜。中外著名诗人将用自己的母语朗诵自己的诗歌代表作，将这一具有特殊意义的诗歌交流活动办成诗歌节多元文化交流活动中的真正亮点。届时，《文艺报》和青海纵横文化有限公司将举办这一活动，多家媒体将全方位报道诗歌之夜的花絮和诗人们的精彩朗诵。

5.举办诗歌音乐演唱会活动。8月10日在西宁举办"诗意青海·和谐世界"大型诗歌音乐演唱会，届时将邀请众多国内著名的朗诵艺术家、歌唱家，与青海省内文艺工作者联袂奉献一台高质量的诗歌音乐演唱会。演唱会上将朗诵中外著名诗人的优

Qinghai Province and three cultural venues in the vicinity of the capital city. 130 established poets, home and abroad, will populate the spiritual atmosphere of the highland with their poetic expression. Around 100 Chinese poets from China and overseas will be attending the event. About 30 foreign poets of world standing will be present from Germany, France, Italy, USA, Poland, Spain, Venezuela, Japan, ROK, Egypt, Ireland, England, Portugal and Greece. Major activities include a poetic forum, a lake area tour, signing ceremony of the Manifesto of QLIPF, poetic readings called Qinghai Lake Evening as well as a concert to crown it all.

Major programs are as follows:

Firstly, a summit poetic forum entitled "A Harmonious World of Man and Nature—Responsibility and Mission of Poetry in the 21st Century" will be inaugurated on 7th August in the Qinghai Conference Center. The chairman of QLIPF will deliver the keynote speech.

Secondly, there will be a signing ceremony of the Manifesto by the shore of the Qinghai Lake, a highly symbolic gesture reaffirming the importance of cultural diversity, clarifying the responsibility and mission of poetic art in the new century, heaping praise upon the dialogue between various cultures, demonstrating concern for the balance and sanity of the ecosystem as well as showing support for the promotion of world peace and the progressive cause of mankind.

Thirdly, a lakeside tour will be organized both to entertain and to spur inspiration involving all the participating poets. The idea is to show poets around into three places within the territories of prefectures in proximity to the Qinghai Lake with one compulsory homework in view, that is, each poet is supposed to compose one poem of no less than 50 lines in celebration of local scenery and customs as they excite their fancy. A book project containing these odes and lyrics for the sake of the hosting province will be in place.

Fourthly, poetic readings called Qinghai Lake Evening will be the highlight. Any poet who ever craves an audience in the open air surrounded by grassland, out and beyond, in the cool of the highland evening, by the famous Qinghai Lake, will be satisfied.

Last but not the least, we desire to bring the first session of QLIPF to a most exhilarating fruition by staging a concert on 10th August. Basically this is a singing and chanting pageantry involving famous singers reciting classical lyrics and poems of established poets.

To conclude, let me extend to you, dear friends present at this press release, an invitation to attend the forthcoming QLIPF. At the chosen locale and date, trust me, I will await your arrival by the sacred and beautiful Qinghai Lake with Tibetan barley wine and auspicious khata. Finally, let me crown this occasion with the reciting of a few lines of my verse:

秀经典诗歌。演唱会将由中央电视台文艺部、青海电视台、中国长城艺术文化中心、全国青联文化艺术界委员会共同主办。届时由青海卫视直播,中央电视台将录播。

在这里,我代表青海省人民政府向在座的朋友们发出盛情邀请,欢迎大家届时到青海来,我们将在圣洁美丽的女神湖——青海湖畔为你献上青稞美酒和洁白的哈达!最后,请允许我引用我的一段诗来结束今天我在新闻发布会上的讲话:"是大地赐予了我们生命/让人类的子孙/在它永恒的摇篮中繁衍生息/是大地给了我们语言/让我们的诗歌/传遍了这个古老而又年轻的世界"。

The land gives us life

May our children and children's children

Enjoy fully the pleasures of life in her eternal cradle The land gives us languages

And let our poetic art

Spread throughout this ancient but young world

青海湖国际诗歌节宣言

2007年8月7日

　　青海是人类诗和歌的较早摇篮之一,在长江、黄河和澜沧江的发源地,在苍茫的雪域高原,诗的圣灵之光,召唤我们来自中国和世界其他各国的诗人,会聚于中国美丽的青海湖畔,在这里见证一个事实,那就是以诗人的良知和诗歌的神圣,庄严发布"青海湖诗歌"宣言。

　　首先,我们确信,自远古至今,人类最伟大的精神创造就是拥有了诗歌。诗歌诞生于古代先民中的智者同神灵的对话和与自我的交流,因而诗歌是引导人类走出混沌世界的火把。诗歌是人类话语领域最古老的艺术形式,因而也是最具有生命力和感染力的艺术。无论过去还是现在,诗歌都是不可或缺的。它是滋润生命的雨露和照耀人性的光芒,只有它能用纯粹的语言,把一切所及之物升华为美。诗歌站在人类精神世界的前沿并且永远与人类精神生活中一切永恒的主题紧密相连。

　　回顾刚刚过去的一百年,人类为自己创造了太多的光荣,也酿制了太多的屈辱;经受了沉重的痛苦和灾难,也激发了一次又一次的历史变革和思想奋进!工具理性的飞速发展,充分开发了人类潜在的智能,把科学技术和物质文明推向了前所未有的高峰,人类在开发生存环境和开发自我的过程中,获得了前所未有的自由;同时我们的精神世界也变得浮躁和窒息,对机器与技术的过分依赖,正在使我们的生命丧失主体性和原创力。

Manifesto of Qinghai Lake International Poetry Festival
7th, August, 2007

One of the earliest cradles of human songs, the fountain head of three China's mega waterways, Qinghai boasts a topographical position in the world's highest plateau, standing in pristine magnificence and hemmed in with poetic halo, luring and beckoning poets ,thither and hither, far and wide, to gather by the shores of the holy Lake Koknore, bearing witness to a major cultural event. Today, we--this small migratory compact community of 220 poets from 23 counties, are lining lakeside to solemnly proclaim a manifesto, firmly affirmative of our poetic conscience as well as sanctity of poetic art.

First and foremost, we are convinced, since time immemorial, the most beautiful thing that happened to us humans is we are possessed of and by poetry, And thanks to the first generation of troubadours and ballad singers, man came out of chaos, striking out from the Jurassic jungle of the survival of the fittest into the dawn of civilization. Poetry took its origin from our ancient sages', prophets' and poets' dialogue with the deities, in their communion with themselves. Invariably the oldest art form within the compass of varied human discourse, poetry has proved to be the most vital and influential. It is inconceivable that man could have survived all the odds thrown his way without an inner prop like Illiad, Gesar or Book of Songs. Poetry is the raindrop that nurtures life, the sunshine that soothes melancholy, the ultimate divine force that purifies and uplifts human nature. A few inspired lines of Homer Li Bo and Shakespeare refine things around us and turn a stark coarse environment into a fairy land. Ever standing vigil in the forefront of human activity, poetry has been closely interwoven with all the cultural themes that make our spiritual life possible.

Looking back, the past century has seen an overflowing of human glory as well as of disgrace of his own making. There is too much undeserved suffering. There is also an abundance of divine-inspired redemption. Challenge is turned into opportunity, and crisis, into new impetus. The fermentation of Instrumental Rationality has led to a flourishing science and technology by tapping the huge potential latent in the inner recesses of the human psyche. In his efforts to

既然诗歌是民族文化的精粹和人类智慧的结晶，诗就应该是人类良知的眼睛，为此我们只有携起手来，弘扬诗歌精神，才能营造出人类精神家园的幸福与和谐。世界各国的诗人，虽然有着不同的宗教信仰和文化背景，却有一颗同样圣洁的诗心。现在，我们站在离太阳最近的地方，向全世界的诗人们呼唤：

在当今全球语境下，我们将致力于恢复自然伦理的完整性，我们将致力于达成文化的沟通和理解，我们将致力于维护对生活的希望和信念，我们将致力于推进人类之间的关爱和尊重，我们将致力于创建语言的纯洁和崇高。我们将以诗的名义反对暴力和战争，扼制灾难和死亡。

缔造人类多样化的和谐共存，从而维护人的尊严。我们将致力于构建人与自然、人与社会、人与文化、人与人之间的诗意和谐。这无疑是诗的责任，同样也是诗的使命。

我们永远也不会停止对诗歌女神的呼唤，我们在这里，面对圣洁的青海湖承诺：我们将以诗的名义，把敬畏还给自然，把自由还给生命，把尊严还给文明，让诗歌重返人类生活。

harness and exploit nature, man has achieved the fullest measure of freedom which hangs heavy in his daring all hands. On the other hand, overdependence upon machine and computer has taken its toll, spawning a spiritual debasement and a choking of personality en mass, as well as a drastic decline in creativity in its wake.

But there is still hope and hope there is again found in poetry, the essence of human intellect and the eye of human conscience. For poets, regardless of origin or religion, are all endowed by the Creator with a pure poetic heart, throbbing and burning with a zest for Truth, Good and Beauty. At this moment, from where in closest proximity to the Sun, we appeal to all our counterparts and all those wishing to be enlightened afresh to lend us an ear for the proclamation of our manifesto.

We proclaim solemnly we will commit ourselves to restoring the integrity of a natural ethics governing human contact with nature, bridging of communication and understanding between cultures, upholding of the torch of the ancient hope of and faith in life and pushing for a globe where mutual respect ,caring and love prevails.

We proclaim in deadly earnest that we shall undertake to purify language and exemplify poetic art in the name of which we oppose peace to war, evil to justice and with the means we excel, we will endeavor to deter suffering and death

Last but not the least, we will go all out to bring harmony to fruition, one that is essentially poetic by all accounts, cosmic in scope, deserving of human dignity, in refashioning a healthy and loving relationship involving all the sentient beings on earth. There lies, we believe, the very responsibility of poets as well as the mission of poetry in large.

For the sake of our responsibility, for the mission of this vital human art, we will keep up our warm entreaties with the Muses relentlessly. Never forsake us. Give us inspiration and render us vulnerable to your charm so that here and now, in face of the holy Lake Koknore, we resolve and pray:

Let Mother Nature be deeply revered.

Let life in all shapes loose and free.

Let civilization be held in genuine sanctity.

And finally let poetry retake root in human hearts.

一个彝人的梦想
——漫谈我的文学观与阅读生活
在清华大学人文学院的演讲
2005年11月9日

今天非常高兴有机会和在座的朋友们见面。这对于我来说是一件非常荣幸的事情，因为清华大学是中国最高学府之一。这个地方，无论是传播科学精神还是传播人文精神都是很重要的阵地，现在有机会和大家交流，我非常珍惜。在物质主义、消费主义很盛行的这个时代，清华的一些同志对诗，尤其是对人的精神生活还是比较关注的。

因为现在，关注诗的人，严格意义上不是很多。大家知道，目前整个诗歌创作的情况还是不错的。在座的很多同学可能过去也读过很多诗。我们当年也是这样。可能每个人都有一个季节、一个年龄段，都在做着当诗人的梦。我个人有很多成长经历跟你们相似。

我的故乡在四川凉山彝族自治州。那个地方文化历史比较悠久，是个很独特的地方。我在那里读小学、初中、高中，然后在西南民族大学读书，经历跟在座的同学可能差不多。我为什么想说这个呢？现在有的热心读者非常关注中国现代诗歌创作，尤其是朦胧诗之后，包括后朦胧诗，当然也包括现在的诗歌创作。

我想通过我对目前一些诗的理解，谈一下我的一些感受。就像我刚才说的，现在说起来，在中国关注诗的人不是很多，这恐怕也是一个客观事实。因为在人类进入一个数字化时代、一个传媒时代之后，人的精神生活是比较多元的。我们所了解到的很多情况，无论数字传媒还是图像，抑或是其他的出版物，是多种多样的。加上阅读范围的广泛，阅读者实际上被分散了。你要让很多人来关注诗，严格意义上是不可能

A Yi Poet's Dream
By Way of a Personal Testimony to Contemporary Chinese Poetry
A Talk at Institute of Liberal Arts of Tsinghua University
9th, November, 2005

I consider it a distinct honor for me to be in the presence of so distinguished audience as found in Tsinghua University which boasts so eminent and illustrious tradition of teaching, learning and research in the highest echelon, either in pure science, polytechnics and the humanities nationwide. In an age swept by commercialism and materialism, there is still interest in the things of the mind, and right here, isn't this a big consolation?

All said, it must be added that the interest of the majority people in poetry is faint and perfunctory.

I assume most of the students tonight have been exposed to poetic reading as I was in adolescent days. It looks like we are all gripped, at a certain point of our life, or at the most emotionally charged periods of life, by some daydreaming to be a poet. There is the elusive enchantment that defies definition.

My hometown is in the outlying Daliangshan Highlands, west of Sichuan Province where the Yi are clustered. I was brought up there and picked up my step up the scholastic ladder from primary to secondary before enrolled in Northwest Minority Nationalities University. Nothing really special in my life so far. I take occasion to mention this again for the benefit of those who take an interest, perhaps some fancy in the poetic situation in China, Fuzzy Poetry, for instance and my poetry as well.

To draw a global picture of Chinese poetry is out of my reach. I only content myself with some reminiscences and comment of personal nature. As I say just now, Interest in poetry is rather scant in China. Although there is a high level of performance in poetic creation, its importance in society is declining. This is true in the days of TV, but the effect is increased by internet and laptop computers. Further, the conditions of modern life have told against reading. Varied channels (multi media and screened images available at the click of a mouse) give vent to spiritual pursuit and satisfaction. Poetry reading can develop only as a minority activity. Love of poetry as a central feature is a thing of the past even in the west.

的。现在在欧洲,如法国、意大利、英国,乃至美国,真正关注诗或者阅读诗的人不是太多。

关注诗或者阅读诗的这部分人,一是喜欢诗,二是对诗的精神生活有很大需求。实际上,有几个数字是可以提供给大家的,我们通过《诗刊》和中国诗歌学会了解到,在中国进行新诗创作的人,大概有一百多万。这个数字当然对我们十三亿人口来说,好像比例不是很大。但是全世界有一百多万人在写诗的国家是很少的。据不完全统计,中国现在写旧体诗词的人大概有四百多万人,可见旧体诗现在正在复苏。全国从各个省市,到很多县市,乃至到乡镇,都有很多人参加诗词学会,这一部分人大都写旧体诗。这方面的刊物也是很多的。可以说中国现在是诗歌刊物最多的国家。中国作为一个具有悠久的诗歌传统的国度,诗歌在民族的精神生活中占有很重要的位置。但是诗现在到底是什么状况?作为我个人,一个诗人来说,我只想结合自身的创作来谈一点体会。

我开始写诗的时候,是朦胧诗兴起的时代。那时候像北岛、舒婷、顾城等,年纪都比我们大一些。那时候他们大多数人在北京,除了舒婷在福建,他们都有一些非常重要的作品。从一定意义上说,那是一个诗的时代。

为什么这样说呢?那时候刚粉碎"四人帮",在整个大环境下,人能阅读到的作品、能看到的出版物是很少的。那时候如果哪个作家写出一本小说,大概相当于现在某个明星在中央电视台春节联欢晚会露两次面,全国人民都知道。比如说刘心武先生写出《班主任》,在座的同学们年龄还很小,有的可能不知道。他当时写的就是在"文革"过后的特定环境中一部分学生和老师的心灵世界,包括精神世界被扭曲的东西。那时候一部小说让人可以一夜成名。当时《人民文学》的发行量可以达到150万份,《诗刊》的发行量可以到120万份,现在看起来是天文数字。

一些欧美作家到中国来,我们说到《人民文学》曾经有过的发行量的时候,他们认为根本不可能。那时候《诗刊》登了一首很重要的诗,就是雷抒雁先生写的《小草在歌唱》,是写张志新烈士的。那首诗发在当时的《诗刊》上,那期刊物可以说是被抢购一空,听说后来又加印了很多,同样也销售一空。现在时代已经发生了很大变化,无论是从时间还是从空间上来说。

This minority, who still subscribe to the pull of Homer and Li Po, must be necessarily inveterate and partisan in terms of reading penchant.Let me quote some authoritative statistics by way of information to illustrate my point, courtesy of the national journal of Poetry and China's Society of Poetry. We learn from the above two sources roughly poetic writing population is at one million, delusively large but substantially small for a country of 1.3 billion. All in all, one million poets across the globe is an impressive force. Added to this is another 4 million classical poetry practitioners, registered with the official Society of Poetry and facilitated by a multiplicity of publishing accesses, widely scattered even down to township level, a sure sign that classical poetry is still in vogue. One thing is clear now: The Chinese people, who used to regard poetry as the flower of their culture, still accord it a high place in their spiritual life. As I have said, an attempt at a survey of the entirety of modern Chinese poetry is above me. In light of my limited experience, I will offer,however, some personal observations.

My apprenticeship coincided with the rise of Fuzzy Poetry. Famous practitioners included Bei Dao, Shu Ting, Gu Cheng and other lesser poets, all my seniors based in Beijing except Shu Ting, a Fujian native. Fuzzy poets, true to their plan and ambition, produced worthy works. In a sense, theirs was age of poetry.

The post -Mao reform and opening up brought a flowering of poetic production. Decades of leftist policies left a spiritual void to be filled. What few novels or poems written made their authors instant celebrities, to be devoured with hunger and fervor. One novelette entitled Class Teacher, written by an author by the name of Liu Xinwu, became a legend in portraying a few tormented souls in a school context during the chaotic Great Cultural Revolution. Liu Xinwu rose to fame over night. To offer another figure by way of information: the subscription of People Literature reached 1.5 million and the Journal of Poetry,1.2 million, astronomical in scope, isn't it? Too good for belief.

Sounded outrageous to a number of writers touring China when I told them. One more piece of anecdote: a veteran poet Lei Shuyan came out with a poem in the Journal Of Poetry, a hymn in tribute to a woman martyr crucified for independent thinking, created a sensation as all the current issues, plus the reissued editions, had been all sold out.

At a literary seminar held in Zhengzhou, not long ago, Comrade Wang Meng (writer and former Minister of Culture)and I were attending to discuss the ultimate end of novels as narrative literature. Literary seminars are infested with apocalypticians gloating about possible phasing out of other forms of literature, including poetry everywhere, not only in China. They reflect a universal tendency of poets, novelist and poets becoming more and more self-questioning. The vital topic engages cultural experts, critics and researchers of poetry to a tentative conclusion: in the foreseeable future, at least, poetry, or other genres of imaginative works, is yet to outlive its utility, despite doubts about the economics of publishing fiction and poetry, and the deeper aesthetic suspicion about the viability of their form.

上次在河南郑州,我和王蒙同志出席一个小小说会议的时候,有很多人提出来一些问题,问关于"小说作为叙事文学的终结"的问题,问小说可不可能继续延续下去,同样也问诗歌可不可能继续延续下去。其实这些问题不光是中国在讨论,世界其他许多国家也在讨论。但是最后无论是文化学家、文学理论家还是诗歌研究学者都认为,从中国乃至世界的情况来看,诗歌不可能消亡。

因为它作为人类记录精神生活的独特方式,有不可替代的价值,这种独特方式对于人类认识世界和掌握世界是非常重要的。从某种意义上说,我们每个人都是诗人。因为我们都经历过这个阶段,愿意把自己精神世界的东西记下来。而记下来的东西只要在形式上接近于诗,有诗的意味,就是诗。我们不少人甚至在形式上还可以进行更新更多的创造,那么我们每个人都是诗人,或者都经历了诗的创作过程。只不过这种作品是否发表,那是另一个问题。从这个意义上说,只要人类存在,诗歌就将继续存在。

对于中国诗坛的现状,大家也是非常关注的。继北岛他们之后,后来的这些后朦胧诗人(姑且这样称呼吧),包括后来的更年轻的诗人,他们创作的作品使得目前中国诗坛呈现出一种多元的状态。我认为目前中国诗歌状态是历史上最好的。这不能简单地看,比如说刊物发行量没有过去那么大啦,有的诗人写一首诗发表在《诗刊》上,就能让全国人民都知道的历史也已经一去不复返啦。

我觉得很重要的一点就是,中国目前的精神文化生活,尤其是很宽松的文化氛围,形成目前中国诗歌的良好的多元的状态,这是非常重要的。所以我认为目前中国诗歌状态非常好。

另外,也有很多问题。在21世纪的消费主义、物质主义的时代,人的精神困境也加剧了,历史进入一个悖论阶段。这个悖论是随着经济的快速发展而出现的。

我们回顾20世纪的时候,发现20世纪就是一个充满悖论的世纪。20世纪的两次世界大战给人类带来无穷的灾难,但是20世纪同样有很多伟大的思想、很多伟大的科技成就,包括人类上月球、信息革命,可以说都是20世纪的重大事件,它们甚至已经影响了人类在21世纪的生活。但是现在人类也面临着前所未有的困境,这是不可否认的,因为我们今天面临的精神困境已经超过了历史上任何时期。前不久我带

For the ultimate reason: literature is the unique medium for man to document and chronicle his spiritual life as it provides important clues to the exploration and understanding of both our inner and outer world. In a sense, we are all poets. At a certain point of our life, we all have some fancy to follow and there is a spontaneous flow of feeling and emotion, a flash of mind , worth of note and jotting down. What gets written down on paper, when composed to conform to some rhythmical and acoustic standard, is poetry or something approaching it. Some of us might be willing to try more innovation in form. Whether meant for publication or not matters little. The bottom line is what gets on the printed page, sifted by time, provides satisfactions that are more permanent, not of transitory interest.

Let me get back from my digressional comments. Following Bei Dao and other Fuzzy poets, poetry has been in a vigorous condition, contrasting with the stagnation of pre-Cultural Revolution years and the technical clumsiness of Fuzzy poets. There has been a large body of highly talented post-fuzzy poets, for want of a better appellation, are moving in all directions and writing excellent poetry. They show a greater linguistic vigor and achieve a degree of artistic perfection surpassing much of the previous poetry. I reckon this possibly the Gold Age for poetry, which cannot be measured by publication statistics, of course.

It should be noted- the days are gone forever when a poet becomes the center of a cult, thanks to one poem printed in the Journal of Poetry. One good thing conducive to such benign development is the relative laxity of the macro cultural environment of literary expression in which poets now operate.

Problems, of course, do exist. The last three decades of the 20th century is a period of fast GDP growth and affluence brought up by the reform and opening up of China, the great monuments being more of the material than the spiritual, or of the triumph of commercialism and consumerism over high culture. Growing economic prosperity has been the single most important shift of Chinese society. While material prosperity is at its apogee, man's inner world dwindles and shrinks.

Cultural historians all agree the 20th century worldwide is a century of paradoxes, one of scarcity and plenty, the best of times which has seen advances, intellectual and technological, such as manned spaceship landing on the moon, information revolution, and the worst of times which has borne witness to the outbreak of two world wars and their attendant damages and human tolls we all know of. The massive changes and upheavals wrought even make their repercussions felt in the new century of the 21rst century. The whole world is in a plight undeniably in that the spiritual crisis that agonizes and torments us is also unprecedented in magnitude. Not long ago, I led a delegation of writers and poets to attend a meeting in Belgrade. The same spectre of the deepening human predicament hovers over our heads at every turn.

My reasons for an optimistic assessment of Chinese poetry are threefold. The first concerns a relaxed cultural atmosphere pervading the whole poetic scene. Poets enjoy the fullest scope of

了个中国作家代表团到贝尔格莱德出席第四十二届国际作家会议，它讨论的一个主题是怎么消除人类日益加剧的精神困境，这恐怕是一个世界性的主题。

我认为中国诗歌的状况比较好，理由有三个方面。一是刚才说的整个文化环境的宽松，无论怎么写、怎么表达精神愿望，都是非常自由的。你们也许已经注意到，现在《诗刊》的上半月刊基本上是发中老年人的作品，比较传统的作品，下半月刊基本上是发年轻人的作品，更多地给广大年轻诗人提供了一个广阔的自由创作的平台。第二是由于现在创作思想上的自由。现在创作的自由度是很大的。在今天世界上出现任何一个问题，第一时间都能在网上知道。这在过去根本是不可能的。实际上，网络已经很深刻地改变了人类的思维方式。对我们诗歌创作来说，也提供了无限的可能，特别是对想象力解放的可能。第三是无论你用哪一种诗的方法、哪一种艺术方式进行写作，谁也不会认为你不好。

现在形成了一个对诗歌创作的好的艺术环境，彼此尊重的艺术空间。根据这几点来看，我认为现在中国诗歌状况是历史上最好的。但是这个最好不等于说马上就有很好的作品出现，最后还是要看结果，要看是否有好作品。

比如20世纪40年代艾青先生写出了《吹号者》《手推车》《我爱这土地》《北方》，还有50年代一些重要诗人写出了一些重要作品，包括朦胧派诗人们写出了一些重要作品。现在文化环境特别好，非常有利于诗歌创作，但是我们仍然缺少更多的关注人类命运的作品、关注他人命运的作品。我认为这是相当重要的。

新诗的发展一直在经历着纵向的继承和横向的移植。我们现在了解到一个数字，就是从20世纪50年代以来，我们现当代文学翻译成西方文字的（我指的不是学术著作，主要是作家的作品）也就几千种。而我们翻译的西方的文学作品，在十万种以上。这个比例是很不相称的。当然有翻译的原因，也有文化交流中不对等的原因。但是从另一种角度来看，这对我们也是有好处的，就是中华民族毕竟还是一个开放的民族。在了解西方文化、借鉴西方的重要创作这方面，我们的开放度是很大的。几代翻译家为把西方的杰出文学作品、诗人的作品翻译成汉语，付出了巨大的心血。五四以来的文学发展，特别是新中国成立以来的文学发展，都得益于这一点。虽然有很长一段时间，我们的政治生活不正常，以阶级斗争为纲，但是在文化开放的几个时期

literary expression. They can follow whatever fancy that overtakes them. You might note a major shift in the editorial policy of the Journal of Poetry, now a bi-monthly, with the first half devoted to writings by senior poets and the second to the young poets. The second reason is associated with the ideological aspect of the freedom of literary expression. Again, the straightjacket is gone, with no political insistence on purges and authorial reform and there is no inhibition of whatever persuasion that might be induced by or ascribed to leftist ideology in the past.

Another factor that contributes to the erosion of ideology is the internet. In fact, one can hardly overestimate the role of the cyber space in reshaping the human thinking. For poets, PC suggests an infinity of poetic possibilities and the scope of the liberating of the human spirit. Thirdly, there is a free, open-mindedness to methods and skills to be pursued almost whimsically. Leftist influences, the bane of poetic impulse, churned out stereotyped heroes and uniformity of plots on the note of propagandistic socialist realism.

Nowadays no official judges parroting leaders' directives sit in judgment on either character or author. Follow your own fancy and adopt whatever method-that is your choice and nobody will mind your business. In sum, there is the environment most beneficial for literary zeal. But good cultural environment and good even patronizing policies do not lead automatically to a cultural renaissance. Initiative and creativity are of the essence for serious writing.

For example, Ai Qing, a committed, impressive talent, wrote some of the finest poems in the 1940s, war time years. Even in leftist 1950s,a typical milieu totally hostile to works of genuine merits, many of his poems stood-and they still stand today- as examples of poetic intelligence and skill. The same observation applies to many fuzzy poets. Paradoxically, in spite of the best intentions, the current literary product has been generally deplored void of depth and intensity, devoid of the outspoken and truly indignant, the mark of genius. Too many practice the art with ingenuity and artistry without substantially adding to its form and range. What they really lack is the sincerity and courage of Ai Qing's or Bei Dao's art; they fail to portray life with lyrical warmth and dignity.

New poetry moves in two directions-there is the classical tradition to be grafted, albeit restrictive and constricting for some and there is, hand in hand, the borrowing from peer poets abroad by dint of translation. A rough estimate of foreign contemporary literary works is put at several thousands, of classical and modern totaled, at 10 thousand. Such a large inventory proves both a necessity and a boon, A necessity in that civilization like China grows in isolation from the west. Millennia of self-sufficiency tend to breed a dormant state of mind, a tyranny in guise of tradition which hampers creativity and innovation. A boon because human history is full of examples of rich periods when translation spurred domestic cultures. Chinese politics in the interim between 1950s to the end of the 1970s were by any measure sick and abnormal. Foreign literary works have been crucial to bring about s state of cultural thaw and the flowering of Chinese literature we witnessed in post 1970s years.

都可以看到西方的一些经典作品被翻译成中文,这对我们了解西方文学与推动我们的文学创作是非常有利的。

就我个人来说,我开始写诗也跟在座的同志现在的年龄差不多。当时的阅读条件很差,我的出生地在凉山彝族自治州,当时"文化大革命"刚要结束,要找到一些很好的诗来读几乎是不可能的。那时候我读到的第一个外国诗人的作品就是普希金的诗。很偶然得到这样一本诗集,诗集被很多人传看过,别人都拿去抄,传到我手上已经没有封皮了。当时读普希金的诗,我大概只有十六岁,读后非常震惊。他所表达的对自由、对爱情、对伟大的自然的赞颂,完全引起了我心灵的共鸣。可以这样说,是读普希金的诗集改变了我一生的命运,因为从那一天开始我就立志当一个诗人。对于我来说,诗是实现我梦想的很重要的途径。从这个意义上说,一个诗人走上写作道路可能都有诱发点。

但是我觉得很遗憾的是,那个时候我们的阅读面非常窄,因为可以看到的东西非常少。后来考上大学,随着国家的日益开放,很多经典文学作品才开始再版。由此我想说,我走上文学创作的道路是因为普希金,是普希金的作品点燃了我的心灵。看了普希金的作品,我认为它有一些普遍的人类价值。比如说他写的《致大海》《致西伯利亚的囚徒》,比如说他写的关于十二月党人的诗,比如说他写《茨冈》,俄罗斯的一个少数民族,也就是吉卜赛,写他们独特的生活。他表达的文化愿望,对自由的憧憬,对人类的友爱,对世界前途和人类命运的关注,反对专制,向往人类生活的和平,很多东西都充满着人类意识。

我在写诗的过程中,当时考虑得最多的就是怎么用全人类的优秀的文化来武装自己。我受的文化影响来自三个方面:一方面是自身民族的文化影响。彝族是很古老的民族,在西南,彝族是文化历史极其悠久的民族之一。彝族现在的人口有八百多万,彝族历史上的神话创世史诗就有十余部,在全世界来说恐怕也是创世史诗非常多的民族之一。藏族的《格萨尔王》是现在世界上最长的史诗,其次恐怕才是希腊的《伊利亚特》和《奥德赛》。彝族还有许多抒情长诗、叙事长诗,其数量也非常惊人。比如说《阿诗玛》就是彝族一个支系的一首抒情长诗。完全可以说彝族是一个诗的民族。

Personally, my poetic career, or rather, my apprenticeship coincided with your college years. My reading was limited due to a paucity of books in the library. As I have said, my hometown is a backwater in the Dalaingshan Highlands, a place both culturally and economically dispossessed. Good works were hard to come by. The first foreign poet I chanced upon was fortunately Pushkin, a household name in China. The first book of translation of Pushkin that I was able to lay my hand at was without a cover, due to excessive thumbing through. It was both a shocking and liberating experience for a boy of 16 years of age. His robust faith in freedom, joy of life and love ,regard for humanity, overwhelmed me. I can assert with the fullest assurance that the first sight of Pushkin made me a poet. I instantly succumbed to the temptation of being a poet. I guess the same thing does happen to many other poets, I mean a chance encounter with a real genius wrought a miracle in his spiritual universe.

The only regret for a would-be poet then was lack of books to read. Destiny extracts a price for rustication. Then the downfall of the radically leftist Gang of Four and the comeback of Deng Xiaoping upon the political scene. Almost over night, things took a decisive turn. I was enrolled in the Northwest Minority Nationalities University. Bookstores were inundated with translations of Gone Are With the Wind, thousands of other works and even best sellers, in reprinted editions mostly. Fed upon them, I served my apprenticeship assiduously, aspiring to fame like the one enjoyed by Pushkin, the incalculably beneficial influence upon my creative work ,the beacon light upon my rough road to success. To the Sea, To the Prisoners of Siberia and poems in honor of Decemberist heroes, reaffirms the universal verities he espouses with tenacity, about love, sympathy for the maimed people, distain for tyranny, longing for peace. One of his Oriental tales The Gypsies is the blossoming of his warm nature for the downtrodden. There is a great strength of feeling in his verses.

Being plunged into the arts and enlightenment of the cultured west and the world, I was struggling with my writing. Three influences proved to be seminal for me. The first should be my closeness to my Yi culture upon the sacredness and benignity of natural life. I would bring to the Chinese poetry a sense of the primacy of nature and a romantic evocation of the tribal life. My people, known in Chinese as the Yi, and in English as the Lolo, comprise one of the most numerous and ancient minority nationalities in China, about 8 million people. The Yi have a rich and varied cultural heritage, having evolved the most complex system of creation myth, up to 10 canons, making the Yi one of the top owners among other races .

The Yi are also known to boast one of the largest body of poems, lyrics and epics. The popular Ashima is one of the longest lyrical narratives, contrasting with Gesar in Tibetan as the longest epic in the world, with Illiad and Odyssey sagas far behind in length.

Besides, the Yi people are credited with initiating one of the three brands of indigenous scripts in China, ie, the Chinese, the Yi and the Dongba for the Naxi people, dating from two millennia, as ancient as the Chinese. I pride myself in being firmly grounded in my own culture in

彝族是在中国创造原生文字的三个民族之一。这三种原生文字，一个是汉文，一个是彝文，另一个是纳西族的东巴文。彝文的创造时间非常早，已经有一两千年的历史了。彝文的使用时间与汉文的使用时间一样悠久。东巴文是一种象形文字，它的使用面不像汉文、彝文这么广泛。我个人深受彝族原生文化的影响，特别是彝族的创世史诗和古老民歌。诗人需要从原始文化之中汲取营养，这对诗人来说很重要；同时，还要汲取大自然的养分，并从中获得想象力和创造力。

第二是来自用汉文创作的文学经典。这个范围很广，包括《诗经》、楚辞、唐诗宋词元曲到五四以来的所有的用汉文写出的优秀作品。尤其是闻一多、艾青等人的作品，对我影响非常大。

第三个是外国文学。外国文学对于改变我的整个诗歌观，起到了决定性的作用。我的创作一直受到非洲、拉丁美洲文学的影响。在20世纪80年代初我就这样思考：说起来这个世界非常大，实际上从地球村的概念来说，这个世界并不大，为什么在世界上有很多民族人口并不多，甚至在所谓主流文化的边缘，而他们的民族会养育出世界性的作家？当时就此问题，我和一些同时代的少数民族作家进行了文化上的反思。

苏联有个少数民族作家艾特马托夫，他的故乡是吉尔吉斯共和国，现在已经独立了，在当时是一个加盟共和国，人口并不多，只有四百多万，但是出了这样一个很了不起的作家。艾特马托夫在苏联基本上是继肖洛霍夫之后与拉斯普京、阿斯塔菲耶夫及哈萨克作家艾玛埃佐夫等齐名的大作家。可以说他是苏联极有代表性的作家之一。在他不到四十岁的时候，作品已经被翻译成了全世界七十几个国家的文字。对于苏联一个很小的加盟共和国的一个区域性作家，我认为这是一个很了不起的成就。他的作品影响了中国很多作家，比如说张贤亮、张承志，张承志的《黑骏马》就是受他的小说《查米莉娅》的影响。

我认为这个影响是正常的。据说《查米莉娅》发表以后，被法国现代派作家阿拉贡看到，他有一个很高的评价，认为这部作品是20世纪或者说那个时代，所有重要作家能写出来的极好的描写爱情的中篇小说之一。这个评价是非常高的。他亲自把这个小说从俄语翻译成法语，后来这部小说在全世界产生了广泛的影响。

two aspects, crucial for my later growth, ie, the Yi animism and the Yi's terrestrial connection with Nature. The Yi arts and traditions have revived in recent years partly because of the realization of the desirability of preserving Yi culture and partly because of the patronage the Yi have received from the government.

My second intellectual equipment consists of the canonical works written both in Wenyen and the vernacular, ranging from Book of Songs, Poetry of the South, poetry of the Tang, Song, Yuan, Ming and Qing dynasties to modern free verse by masters like Ai Qing and Wen Yiduo. Since I basically compose in the standard Chinese, the one enjoying the widest national currency, familiarity with Chinese classics and facility in using Chinese, technically speaking, is a matter of life and death. So there is a mixture of the psychology of the Yi and the culture and language of China in me.

Foreign literature, the third in my arsenal, has remade me as a poet, in a sense. To be more specific, I have drawn inspiration heavily from poets and writers from Africa and the Hispanic world. One finds unmistakable affinity at work between their creative work and mine. Back in the 1980s, this matter of back-fire affinity was upmost in my mind: our world is both large and small. Why some authors from a very small country break into world literature and turn into literary nurses for authors from major world powers? I even took up the issue with some ethnic poets on occasion.

For example, Chingiz Aitmatov, from Kirghizia in Central Asia, one of the 14 republics that made up former Soviet Union, with slightly 4 million people. Aitmatov is a convenient success story, because coming from Kirghizia and writing in Russia, he represents a minority writer who hits the top by world standard, together with Sholokhov, Lasputin, Astafeyev and Amaaizova from Kazakhstan. Before he was forty, his well-crafted fictions set in the Kirghiz mountains won him state prizes and world recognition, translated into over 70 languages. One of his novels *Jamila* circulated in China and he exerted an influence upon mainly writers of ethnic origin. One hearsay goes that Zhang Xiangliang's *Black Horse* was inspired by his Jamila.

The above example shows affinity works in all sorts of ways, one not restricted to any one period, but can cut across divergent cultures, languages and traditions. It is said Jamila appealed to French modernist Aragon when he came across it. Aragon even bothered to translate it from Russian into French, hailing it as one of the finest love novelettes in the 20th century.

Such success stories prompted me to ponder a number of questions vital for my creative work. Why has he become a writer of world status? What books does he read? What problems is he preoccupied with? How can I one day, neither political nor traditionalist in spirit, transcend racial and national problems? I dream one day luck will bless me to dramatize in my own idiom, the more universal themes of love, justice, the dilemma of language and man's alienation with nature.

Of all the poets I admire Pablo Neruda the most because he has greatly influenced me. A

这样的作家是我当时进行重点研究的作家。为什么他能成为世界性的作家？他的阅读范围是什么？他平时在思考什么问题？我怎么不能写出既具有民族的特点，又具有人道主义精神的作品？怎样真正写出人类的命运，使自己的作品具有普遍的人类价值？这些问题都是我最初走上文学道路就开始思考的具有本质意义的重要问题。

当时还有一位诗人对我的影响是巨大的，他就是巴波罗·聂鲁达，智利的一个大诗人，可以说是20世纪非常伟大的现代主义诗人之一，是诺贝尔文学奖获得者。这个诗人为什么能成为世界性诗人？这对我来说也是一个很重要的启示。秘鲁诗人巴列霍、西班牙诗人洛尔迦，对我的启示也很大。洛尔迦是把他的民族的很多民歌和现代派诗歌进行融合，他的诗是非常有节奏的，旋律感很好。他作为一个区域性的诗人，将他民族的民歌和现代派手法融合在一起，创造了新型的西班牙语诗歌，这种诗歌在全世界风靡一时，是非常了不起的。他在活着的时候就已经是一个世界性的大诗人了。他为什么能取得这么大的成就？这也是我当时研究的一个重要的文学现象。

包括美国的一些重要诗人。美国的黑人文学，长时间处于美国主流文学的边缘，除了当时的小说《根》之外，黑人文学根本进入不了美国的所谓主流文化圈，进入不了正规高校的教材。但《根》之后有几个重要作家的出现改变了这一现状。一个是黑人诗人兰斯顿·休斯，一个是小说《看不见的人》的作者埃里森，另一个就是诺贝尔文学奖获得者托妮·莫里森。美国黑人作家通过一百多年的努力，终于使他们的文学进入了美国的主流文学范畴。

犹太文学也是这样。诺贝尔文学奖获得者辛格、索尔·贝娄，改变了移民文学的现状。他们的作品也进入了美国的主流文学范畴。《麦田守望者》的作者塞林格也是犹太人。还有一大批犹太作家通过他们的创作，极大地丰富了美国的现当代文学，从真正意义上改变了美国文学的种族和文化结构。

这种现象对我们来说也是进行文化反思的对象。那时候最令人感动的是拉丁美洲文学的复兴。马尔克斯的《百年孤独》是一个标志，《百年孤独》的出版和成功给我们生活在边缘地带的少数民族作家和诗人树立了很大的信心。当时《马尔克斯中短篇小说集》在中国出版之后并没有引起很多人的注意，销路不好，有的书店甚至将其

notable Chilean, he belongs to a mild aspect of modernism (surrealism),but his "intuitive capturing and crystallizing of the spirit of the individual Latin American nations through their landscape and history was unanimously praised", winning him the Nobel prize. I am also in the debt of Vallejo from Peru and Garcia Lorca from Spain. Lorca charmed me because of his folk element. His writing has color, verve, and rhythm. His diction is simple and striking as in the ballads. His catching melodies and dramatic effects are all rooted In the Andalucian tradition, making the name of Lorca circle the earth. Why has he come out so surprisingly almost in every language?

For reasons not hard to reason, literary treatment of black life in the USA, especially by major black writers, who were very slow to enter into the mainstream of American culture, has been a matter of great curiosity for me. *Roots* by Alex Hailey, a tale of black's search for their identities, created both a sensation in the States and China. Following in his footsteps, three black writers and poets, Langston Hughs, Ellison (*the Invisible Man*) and Tony Morrison (Nobel prize winner) are milestones in American literary history .

The same case is with Immigrant literature, exemplified in the writings of Singer, Saul Bellow, both Jewish immigrants from eastern Europe, and Salinger with his the Catcher in the Rye, also a Jew by birth and faith. The rise of Yiddish writing has revolutionized American literature in ways more than one.

All these critical breakthroughs doubly girded and spurred me into more relentless effort.

One of the most exhilarating literary developments in the 20th is found in the Andes world associated with a school by the overworked critical term of magical realism .The fact that Latin American literature has grown into a universal and cosmopolitan literature, is attributable to masters such as Marquez and Borges. It is written mainly in a language, peculiarly expressive and beautiful, if not superior, at least equaling to the best the Occidental world can offer. The influence of *The Solitude of a Hundred Years* quickly reached me and ethnic writers and poets operating on the margin of the mainstream literary traditions. Yet, the publication of The Selected Novelettes and Short Stories of Marquez in China met with popular indifference and critical apathy, to the extent many bookstores even consigned copies unsold to the paper mills.

Almost by instinct, I turned to these writers for model and my faith was reinforced in sharing the same views with Tibetan novelist Zhaxi Dawa. Latin American literature has an extraordinary characteristics as it is at once based upon the previous achievements of the west, and at the same time deeply rooted in the native soil of the Andes life. A non Hispanic who feels in the great Latin American writers all those intimate memories and cherished symbols belonging to the mainstream of European culture, is apt to be all the more awed by the discovery of other features which are wholly unlike anything European.

Again, to the enormously important question, "What, of all that has been written, is one to read?"My reply has been, by explicit exhortation from Mathew Arnold: all that is the best in

作为废纸变卖。那时候,北京、上海、广州等文化中心的作家和读者,很少人提及马尔克斯并阅读他的小说。那时候我们完全是凭着一种直觉,开始关注马尔克斯等拉美作家的作品。

记得藏族著名作家扎西达瓦与我,那个时候就经常在一起交谈拉丁美洲文学给我们带来的新鲜感受。我们一致这样认为,拉美作家超越了地域和他们的文化带,他们的作品所表达的人类精神,已经达到了很高的水平,是我们学习的榜样。那个时候我们就有这样一个认识:一定要把自己的文学标杆的确定放在整个世界而不仅仅是在中国。马尔克斯引起中国文化界最为广泛的关注,还是在他的作品《百年孤独》1982年获得诺贝尔文学奖之后,而我们对他的关注和热爱要远远早于这个时间。

那时候我们阅读和涉猎的作家是非常广泛的。比如非洲的塞内加尔前总统桑戈尔,是一个伟大的诗人。他曾在法国留学,获得过法兰西文学博士学位。他是法兰西文学院唯一的黑人院士。他在法国留学时,提出了著名的黑人性问题,这无疑是非洲文化崛起的一个标志。他的诗歌创作吸收大量的现代派手法,他把从欧洲现代诗人那里汲取来的营养与本民族的生活进行了神奇的嫁接,创作出了一系列表现非洲故土生活的诗篇,获得了全世界不同种族的千千万万读者的尊重和热爱。我的写作就是从阅读这些大师的作品并深受他们的影响开始的。在写作时,我更多的是想通过表现我的民族的生活,去表达我们对自身赖以生存的自然和文化的热爱。

我坚信所有的人都是一个生命过程,不管你生活在哪个地方,是哪个民族,有很多有普遍价值的东西是人类必须共同遵从的。比如说,阅读普希金的作品会让我们感动,那完全是因为普希金的作品中具有这种人类普遍的价值。普希金离开我们已经近一百七十年了,为什么我们现在读他的作品还会心潮起伏、感慨万千呢?那是因为普希金的诗歌能抚慰我们的灵魂,给予我们生活的勇气,能给人带来温暖和希望。我想,优秀的诗歌之所以能成为永恒,恐怕还是因为这些东西是诗歌的真正本质。

我很幸运的是,我开始写诗的时候就在用一种全新的方式进行写作,是普希金教会了我应该如何认识自己的民族,是艾青的诗歌道路,让我明白了一个诗人必须把自己的命运与自己的民族和祖国的命运联系在一起。我的创作曾经得到过许多前辈诗人的鼓励和帮助,我的第一本诗集就获得了第三届国家诗歌奖。北岛当时也是

former and contemporary writers. Senghor, Senegalese poet, philosopher, Africa's most respected writer, the only African admitted into the Academie Francaise, came into my reading purview, who was later to become president of Senegal. Out of the group of Presence Africanne, a review founded by several eminent black intellectuals, emerged the concept of negritude, a concept which marked the emergence of negro self awareness and the first phase of black cultural revolt against the western hegemony. Cesaire and Senghor co-authored the definition of negritude as "the sum total of all the cultural values of Africa". As such, negritude became the name of a new literary movement for black writers to claim for themselves the right and obligation to express his cultural specificity as manifested in his culture and temperament. In technique, he drew heavily on modernism, which he learned in European universities ,but there is the miraculous juxtaposition. By invoking ancestors and protecting spirits, the poet "attempts to recover his African identity and richness and innocence of Africa itself."Senghor wrote some of the most charming love poems, personal in tone and subject, but his major poems are fiery, passionate and declamatory statements concerning negritude. Senghor has taught me a great deal as how to identify with and to translate faithfully the realities of Chinese life.

I firmly believe human beings, wherever they happen to be ,irrespective of origin or race, share some universally valid values which reflect our human greatness and include such social ideals as freedom, brotherhood and justice. They teach us also an intuitive and emotional process of acquiring knowledge, without which one simply is bewildered at the warmth and wondrous beauty pervading Pushkin's verse. Pushkin has left us for almost 170 years, but his poems still excite us and uplift us, an invariable fountain of solace, zest, mystic knowledge, poetic inspiration, embodying the universal cultural values in such an adorable way that they should be taken as ultimate comment on the nature of poetry and the poetic process.

I deem myself very lucky to have grown into an intimate acquaintance with them when embarking upon a poetic career as I was provided with completely fresh models to follow beyond the orthodox writing that is too much silly, wooden, dull, hackneyed and crudely slogan riddled. Pushkin has shown me how to empathize with my own Yi culture. It is Ai Qing, China's most gifted and versatile lyrical poet, a French-returned student at the heyday of modernism, but extraordinarily unaffected with the modernist obscurities and symbolist oddities, who has taught me as how to identify my own fate with that of our country. In war times when others searched fastidiously for imagery, he broke away from lingering academic traditions and foreign influences to a crude style of peasants and soldiers to have attained a high level of simplicity and passion. As luck would have it, thanks to the patronage and kindness from several seniors and predecessors, my first book of verse came off with a national award much coveted by would-be poets. As I remember, the godfather of Fuzzy Poet Bei Dao were mounting on the same podium on that occasion. This honor brought me immediate fame and elation, really something for a beginner.

I have tried to summarize my recipe of success, if any, I deem it an award in recognition of

获奖者。这对一个诗人来说是很重要的,因为你创作的东西得到了肯定。当然我们不是为了得奖而创作,我想说的是诗人在创作作品的时候,必须具有一种人类意识和广阔的文化眼光。

我相信如果没有拉丁美洲古老的印第安人的原生文化,没有伟大的拉丁美洲文学传统,就不可能有奥克塔维亚·帕斯这样伟大的墨西哥诗人。他是1990年诺贝尔文学奖获得者。

据我所知,他的阅读面是非常广泛的,像中国的古典诗词,其中包括李白、杜甫、王维、李商隐等诗人的诗歌都是他非常喜欢的。当然,他读的都是翻译本。美国诗人埃兹拉·庞德,据说他的许多意象诗歌的创作就受到了中国古典诗词的深刻影响,尤其是山水诗的影响。是这些伟大的诗人从一开始就教会了我应该如何进行广泛的阅读和合理的借鉴。一个诗人要真正成长起来,就必须接受多种文化的影响和养育。我的思维方式常常徘徊在汉语与彝语之间,我的精神游移在两种甚至多种文化的兼容与冲突之间。我想,也正因为这样,才给人类很多优秀文化的创新开拓了无限空间。

我在写作时,一直强调要写出我们民族生活中的人性光辉和美好的心灵世界。对太阳、土地、河流、森林、原野、群山等等这些养育了人类原生文化的母体的赞颂,从来就是我诗歌的主题。因为,这些对我们民族来说赖以生存的一切,就像血肉一样成了我们生命中不可分割的部分。一个诗人最重要的,是能不能从他的生存环境和自身所处的环境中捕捉到人类心灵中最值得感动的、一碰即碎的、最柔软的部分。我认为这才是诗。我认为对一个诗人来说,忠实于你的内心世界,从某种角度而言,比忠实于这个喧嚣的外部世界更为重要。诗人需要良知,诗人是这个世界道德法庭上的最高法官。

有人问我,如果我们要写东西,怎么才能更好地表现自己民族的生活呢?就这个问题我可以谈一点感想。非洲有一位著名作家叫钦努阿·阿契贝,他是尼日利亚一位杰出的当代作家,据说也是多年诺贝尔文学奖候选人。大家知道尼日利亚作家索因卡曾经在1986年获得诺贝尔文学奖,但是就文学影响和在非洲的文学地位而言,索因卡是远远不如阿契贝的。索因卡本人也说过这样的话:阿契贝不仅是尼日利亚,而且是非洲文学之父。我想举他的例子来说明,我们怎么才能更好地去描述自己民族

my sense of humanity and my wide vision of world culture. We know that currently Spanish-American literature has been growing , because of the admittedly high reach of its great intrinsic value It is known widely enough to be considered one of the major bodies of world literature. And we know behind the emergence of the Mexico Paz, Nobel prize winner in 1990,two powerful traditions are at work: the deep-seated indigenous stress which stresses the primacy of nature and a most impressive galaxy of several generations of noted novelists and leading poets. These include several generations who have attempted to first imitate their European models before raising them to the level achieved by European teachers.

Paz to my knowledge, is also a widely read man. His reading list consists of Chinese classical poetry, including works by Li Po, Du Fu, Wang Wei and li Shangying. Of course, he came to know Chinese poets through the translations of Ezra Pound. According to one account, he derived much of his inspirations from Tang and Song Poetry, the genre of landscape in particular. Great poets have taught me two things: be a wider reader and a smart adapter. The coming-of-age of a true poet is necessarily fed and nurtured on a diversity of traditions. A Yi poet writing in Chinese, I tend to transcend or fuse my sometimes relatively narrow realistic or romantic approaches into one that is wider, more universal in nature and more sophisticated in style.

In my writing, there is one salutary leitmotif that proves to be discernibly prominent; it is devoted primarily to native themes (regard for the sacredness of natural life and innocence of Indigenous folks ,joy of nature ,hymns of the motherhood of sun, land, rivers, forests, wildness, mountains. Together with writers and poets, from the continents of Africa and Spanish America in particular,I am preoccupied by some universal issues: alienated and divided society, evil, despoiled eco-systems, the decline of traditional values.I want to express myself in an ever purer, more personalized idiom, one divorced from overblown rhetoric, nevertheless, rich in aesthetic and lyrical intensity, in order to provide some solace for these widely experienced afflictions, which is the true definition of poetry. For an emerging cultivator of this time-honored art, poetic integrity consists in being true to the inner necessities of his deeply personal creativity. In his Defense of the Poetry, Shelly enjoins poets (unacknowledged legislator of the world)to tell the truth and be morally exemplary.

One of my readers once threw a question to me:"How can a poet better communicate to others the special way of life of his people?" Here I attempt to offer some observations as a Yi poet. We all know contemporary African literature is full of master figures. Nigeria has produced many prolific writers winning accolades for their work, including, Chinua Achebe, Wole Soyinka. For example, Soyinka was awarded the Nobel Prize in 1986.And still another Nigerian, of more notable merits, Achebe has been a powerful contender for the prize for many years .Even Soyinka ranks Achebe above himself, calling the latter " the father of Modern African Writing." It is Achebe that I often turn to for counsels and inspiration because of his faithful chronicling of the tragic ending of tribal life, a job he did with a prophetic vigor.

的生活,这一定是具有典型意义的。

阿契贝的小说不是一般意义上的简单叙事,他的作品具有非常深刻的思想内容。他的小说《崩溃》《神箭》和《人民公仆》,是黑非洲文学具有史诗品格的三部曲。

尤其令我震惊的是,他在写《崩溃》和《神箭》时,在朴实平静的叙述中,把一个非洲部落在外来文化的冲击下从兴盛到衰亡,最后到消失的过程表现得淋漓尽致,充满着悲剧色彩。这个小说像一则寓言,既古老而又现代,其中还包含着某种宿命的东西。在一种强势文化的压迫下,如果弱势文化不能与强势文化进行平等交流,那么弱势文化必然会走向衰亡,甚至毁灭。我说这个小说,同时还具有预言的作用,其实已经被今天的现实所证实。

今天,就有不少弱势的文化和传统需要人类去拯救,因为它们的消失是全人类的损失。阿契贝的小说对我们来说是光辉的典范,他真实地写出了一个部落的命运,其实这就是人类的命运。我希望,每一个有才华和责任感的民族作家都应该向阿契贝学习,写出你那个民族心灵的史诗。

有人还问我,要写出什么样的作品才能感动别人呢? 在这里我就举一个我们身边的例子。舒婷的诗曾经感动过很多人,那是因为她的诗表现了我们对人类美好生活的向往。这些诗都是她心灵世界的真实写照。特别是在"文革"之后,她的诗充满着人道情怀,她的诗歌如同一掬甘泉,给我们的心灵世界带来久盼的甘露,所以我们才会被深深地打动。我写诗也是这样,一直力图写出一些更为关注人类命运的诗篇。

今年意大利翻译了我的一本名叫《天涯海角》的诗集,是意大利著名汉学家薇尔玛翻译的。最近罗马大学来信邀请我去讲我的诗歌,我还不知道能否成行。据悉,罗马大学很多学汉学的学生看了那部作品很受感动,特别是我写的那些关于土地的诗篇。我曾经写过一首叫《土地》的诗,我比较感性地描述了我们民族和土地的关系。土地就像彝人的父亲,在我们最痛苦和悲哀的时候,只有土地这个伟大的摇篮,才会把我们的身躯和灵魂轻轻地摇晃,并让我们的身心获得永远的幸福和安宁。

我还写过群山,因为我的部族就生活在海拔近三千米的群山之中,群山已经是一种精神的象征。在那里要看一个遥远的地方,你必须找一个支撑点,那个支撑点必然是群山,因为,当你遥望远方的时候,除了有一两只雄鹰偶然出现之外,剩下的就

In the hands of Achebe, a novel is not merely a narrative written to entertain. His African Trilogy,ie, *Things Fall Apart, No Longer at Ease, Arrow of God*;are epic-ranging and morally committed. Achebe's novels focus on the traditions of Igbo society, the effect of Christian influences, and the clash of Western and traditional African values during and after the colonial era.

Achebe brings to his novels a sense of tragic pessimism and it is the stoic restraint with which he evinces that strikes me as cool. They are parables with a moral that failure on the part of weak cultures to negotiate on an equal par with powerful cultures are doomed. Achebe's works, to me, belong more to the prophetic order than the aesthetic as the meanings of his parables are borne out everywhere.

Achebe has been revered for his depiction of Ibo life that the plot and characters are little more than symbols representing a way of life lost irrevocably and inexorably to western influence. The fate of Ibo society awaits us. Achebe basically raises cries of protest and warning emphasizing the importance and vulnerability of cultural traditions. He has set a good example for all ethnic poets and writers, up-and-coming ,morally committed and aesthetically aspiring, that a traditional community in its death throes makes the perfect theme.

One more question put to me is this "what kind of literary works are soul-stirring?"One example stand-by will be Miss Shu Ting, my friend and colleague, a woman of uncommon lyrical and sensual talent. Much of her verse deals with love, personal grief, nostalgia, friendship, longing for better life. She has been among the most celebrated of women poets in our time despite her occasional lapses of sentimentality and didacticism.

This year, thanks to the translating effort of Miss Wilma, a famous Italian sinologist, my poems entitled The Ends of the World were published in Italy. I have been recently invited by prestigious University of Rome to lecture on my writing. I am told the book meets with a good response, from students majoring in Chinese. Furthermore, one poem entitled Land portrays our Yi's terrestrial connection with Nature, in lyrical warmth and passion. The poem likens the land to fathers and later to a cradle. In moments of spiritual agony and torment, our body and soul will be pacified and stroked into assurance and tranquility.

Since my tribal village lies perched in the Daliangshan Highlands, adjacent to peaks close to 3000m meters above sea level, mountains are invariably a symbol of my racial identity, an icon of my cultural heritage, and incidentally the few rich elemental materials from which I draw my subjects. A mountain resident, you turn your gaze into the horizon at every turn and the only thing that comes into sight is chain upon chain of mountain ranges sprawling in every direction. The scene has remained unchanged for eons. Into the scene of tranquil beauty, overhead, are one or two eagles circling in a cloudless sky of azure blue.

You see, this rugged terrain to us indigenous inhabitants are animate, teeming with life forms, visible and invisible. Here, each part of nature, every grove, every hilltop, every running

是绵延不断的群山。

群山是一个永远的背景。在那样一个群山护卫的山地中,如果你看久了群山,会有一种莫名的触动,双眼会不知不觉地含满了泪水。这就是彝族人生活的地方,这样的地方不可能不产生诗,不可能不养育出这个民族的诗人。我写过土墙,就像犹太诗人写石头一样。看土墙的时候,土墙会给我带来一种莫名的伤感。

诗人的第一感觉和直觉是最重要的,真正的诗,离人类生命的本原是非常近的,有的其实就蕴藏在人类生命的本原之中。诺贝尔文学奖获得者帕斯写得最好的作品《太阳石》就是一个证明。他本人有印第安人血统。《太阳石》是对古代印第安文明特别是玛雅文化的赞颂。如果帕斯没有对印第安文化的深刻的理解和热爱,他绝不可能写出这样的诗。这首诗充满着哲理,有不少段落甚至就如印第安巫师的呓语,可以这样说,这首诗是诗性的印第安人哲学。

西班牙诗人洛尔迦写得最好的一首诗是献给一个斗牛士的。他不断重复和描述斗牛士在死的一瞬间,这个客观世界和主观世界所发生的一切。他用这种方式来告诉我们什么是生命,什么又是死亡。我每次读这首诗都会产生新的感受,我认为这首诗是人类所创作的极其好的诗篇之一。

我写过一首诗叫《彝人谈火》,我想通过写火来表达我们彝族人的生命观和死亡观。在我们彝族的历史典籍中,有很多写火的东西。在西方哲学里,火是一种有创造性的力量。历史上很多民族都对火有一种崇拜,其中包含着很多形而上的东西。诗是很奇怪的一种东西,它很多时候是在"是"与"不是"之间,如果把一首诗写得一览无余,这肯定不是好诗。我还写过一首诗叫《骑手》,我想写的不是骑手在他动的时候的感觉,而是写他在静的时候的感觉。骑手在寂静的时候,血管里一定会有马蹄的声音在响。我就是想写出这种反差性,这不就是诗吗?

我的创作一直受到很多优秀的外国诗人的影响。以色列诗人耶夫达·阿米亥,这个诗人来过中国,我非常喜欢他的诗,但我非常遗憾,他大前年离开了这个世界。捷克诗人塞费尔特对我的影响也是至关重要的。他教会了我怎么把复杂的事物,用最简单的方法表述出来。当然,这不是一般意义上的简单,这是复杂之后的简单,需要多年的积累和修养,不是一件容易办到的事情。1984年他获得了诺贝尔文学奖,这一

brook, every singing skylark, is sacred in the estimation of my people. They hold us in awe and we worship them. Even a long gaze at the mountains serves as stimulus to which we respond in tears, as a poetic moment into which we fall unrestrainedly. The Yi people are born poets. I write of muddy walls of our traditional abodes, the way Jewish poets of the Dome of the Rock, both a living proof of tradition and age-old cravings which trigger a flow of nostalgia and poetic feeling.

The first requisite for a poet is to possess his poetic sensibility, or poetic intuition. There is nothing mystic about this as good verse comes straight from the heart and goes straight to the heart. Octavio Paz ,often referred to as the dean of Mexican letters, Nobel laureate for Literature in 1990, with Pablo Neruda and Vallejo, is one of the several Latin American poets whose work has had wide international impact. Octavio Paz was born in Mexico City to a family of Spanish and native Mexican descent. His long poem *Piedra del sol/Sun Stone* (1957), a tribute to his own cultural heritage (Aztec and Maya civilization), centers on the Aztec Calendar Stone that symbolizes the loneliness of individuals and their search for union with others. Paz's success can be partly accounted for by his Indian blood and his deep love and understanding of his own culture. With passages saturated with philosophical musings and even Indian exorcism, the poem is considered one of the most penetrating studies of Indian character and thought. Paz illustrated the magical experience of poetry ,upholding fine quality and great human values.

One of Spanish poet Garcia Lorca's most meritorious poems addresses a bull fighter. In a repeated flashbacking of the last moment of the bull fighter, Lorca sets into a visionary interplay between subjective and objective world, in a conscious but very contrived way to crack the riddle of death and life. The poem is one of my favorites.

Fire is also an elemental theme in my poems, a convenient icon I manipulate to set forth my somber view of life and death because there were innumerable references to it in the Yi canonical works. In the Greek philosophy, fire was one of the four cardinal elements of which the earth consisted. Throughout history, worship of fire was widespread among many aboriginal races. My understanding of fire acquires a metaphysical dimension. We all know Paz's writing often deals with opposites, passion and reason, society and the individual, word and meaning. In the same vein, I see fire as inherently dual, something between "is" and "is not". Total clarity is not a critical virtue. One of my poems is about a horse rider. It is not the motion(his galloping) that titillates my imagination. The stasis does. I surmise the boisterous and earthshaking sound of hoofs must bubble in his veins when the rider and his horse are standing still. "The poetic image is an embrace of opposite realities" Paz wrote. What a brilliant point he has scored for my benefit!

My writing is the result of diverse influences. I must confess I also owe a great deal to Yehuda Amichai, a renowned Israeli poet who died in 2000. Amichai makes me aware again that great lyrical poetry is capable of translating the deepest emotions into poetic language available to the ordinary people of the streets. Jaroslav Seifert, another vital nourishment, has taught me to produce simple hymns to this life "full of paradoxical disappointments and exhilarating passion."

定不是一个偶然,他通过隐喻来展现他的生活。读他的作品,你才知道什么是真正意义上的朴实无华。他太了不起了。他的作品中文翻译得不多,漓江出版社给他出过一个翻译诗集。在他获奖之后,全世界才有很多人开始了解这位杰出的诗人。塞费尔特有这么一首诗,我认为凭着这首诗他就可以进入世界伟大作家之列。他写他老年的时光,写布拉格这座城市曾经给他带来的苦难和他所经历的沧桑。他在诗中对布拉格说:对你我什么都可以原谅,甚至是所有的不幸和悲伤,但有一点我不能原谅你,就是在你林立的高楼背后冒着黑烟的烟囱上,没有为小鸟留下一点栖息之地。我想这首短诗的震撼力,要超过那些几千行的无病呻吟之作。

有一个现象,在这里我想说一说,就是自20世纪80年代以来,瑞典的诺贝尔文学奖和英国的布克文学奖开始关注区域性作家和文学,特别是对那些亚文化圈的作家给予了更多的关注。捷克诗人塞费尔特是一个,圣卢西亚诗人沃尔科特是一个,尼日利亚诗人、戏剧家索因卡是一个,墨西哥诗人帕斯是一个,爱尔兰诗人希尼是一个,前几年刚获奖的波兰诗人申·博尔斯卡是一个。我认为申·博尔斯卡是当今活着的最伟大的女诗人。最近,中国翻译出版了她的诗集。据说,她从创作诗歌作品到现在,所发表的诗歌不足一百五十首,可见,诗歌的质量是多么重要。

前不久,诺贝尔文学奖评奖委员会有三个评委应邀到中国参加《斯特林堡文集》首发式和研讨会。在会议期间,我与其中一位评委进行了交流,他对申·博尔斯卡的诗歌作品评价极高。申·博尔斯卡也是一个诗歌语言的大师,就像塞费尔特一样,他们都能把最复杂的东西,用最简洁的办法表现出来。其实,中国的艾青与这两位诗人也有许多相同的地方。艾青20世纪40年代的时候,写"雪落在中国的土地上,寒冷在封锁着中国",就是这样看上去非常普通的句子,却隐含着无穷的诗意。在那个年代,艾青能把口语写得那么纯净,无疑为汉语诗歌的纯洁性做出了不可磨灭的贡献。

在这里,我想谈谈诺贝尔文学奖的问题。有好几位听众递上来的条子涉及这方面的问题。首先我要说,诺贝尔文学奖是北欧瑞典一个国家设立的国际性文学奖,它肯定不能囊括这个世界所有民族的文学,当然,它也不是评价作家成就的唯一的最高的标准。比如说,俄罗斯作家列夫·托尔斯泰、瑞典本国作家斯特林堡、奥地利作家

Anything but simple indeed! It takes years and decades of self-disciplined apprenticeship and reading. Serfeit's poems are easy on the surface and yet profound, charged with metaphor and yet remarkably concrete. He is not well translated in China except a small selection of his poems published by Lijiang Publishing House. To showcase his genius, I cite one of his poems in which he addresses to Prague as an indictment of modern ecological crisis here and I believe this one alone assures his standing among literary giants of all ages.

Prague,I forgive you for every wrong done to me,
Even for all the agony and grief.
Yet you should plead guilty;
In the forest of chimneys churning out black smokes,
You have failed to reserve a nesting corner for birds that pass you for ages.

There is so much wisdom in these lines and one can forget about volumes of poetry written by thousands devoid of genuine poetic sensibility.

Let me digress a little bit about an emerging critical trend from the panel of judges either of Novel Prize committee or of the Book Award. And that trend is that more attention has been now shifted to writers of non-main stream traditions. There is a long list of recent recipients including Serfeit the poet from Czech, Derek Walcott from Saint Lucia, Soyinka the dramatist from Nigeria, Octavio Paz from Mexico, Seamus Heaney from Ireland as well as the latest laureate Wislawa Szymborska from Poland. Personally I believe Borska is the greatest living poetess in the world and the translation of her poems was made accessible rather lately to Chinese readers. One hearsay is that she is such a perfectionist that her published poems amount to less than one hundred and fifty.

Not long ago, three judges from the Novel Prize committee were invited to attend the premier ceremony of Selected Works of Strindberg and a seminar on the famed Norwegian. I was able to chat with one of the judges and he saw eye to eye with me on the lasting qualities of Borska. Like Serfeit, the Polish poetess speaks in the most accessible idiom, and her poems are one specimen of linguistic beauty and loaded message, making hers one of the most intimate, wise, and durable poetic voices of this century. My mentor Ai Qing followed the same "simple but profound" formula back in the 1940s war years when he wrote: "Snow falls on the ground of China, whereas freeze blockades her." Lines disarmingly and delusively simple, but rich in allusion and significance. Back in those years when modern Chinese was in the making, Ai Qing learned to achieve a highly condensed style in guise of bare, direct and unadorned diction, a symbol of the power of the emerging Chinese writing.

Until now, let me slip in a word about the Novel Prize for literature. My stance resembles that of Achebe when he was asked by a reporter for Quality Weekly In 1988 how he felt about never winning a Nobel Prize; he replied: "My position is that the Nobel Prize is important. But it is a European prize. It's not an African prize...Literature is not a heavyweight championship.

卡夫卡、苏联文学之父高尔基、中国作家鲁迅等，这些世界级的大作家都未获得过此奖，有的甚至被长时间排除在评奖范围之外。这已经说明这个奖的局限性是存在的。当然，同时我们也应该看到，诺贝尔文学奖是当今这个世界影响最为广泛的一项文学奖，它的存在是不可被忽视的。有人说，沈从文先生、艾青先生，他们所取得的成就是具有国际性的，为什么一直没有得到诺贝尔文学奖的青睐，我想这个问题非常复杂。

文化背景是一个方面，另外，翻译也是一个非常重要的原因。不可否认，意识形态的差异也是一个不可忽视的因素。汉语是一个独立的体系，它和拉丁语系派生出来的其他语种，在语言学上有很大的差距。要把汉语的经典文学翻译成西方语言文学，是一件很难的事情。

北岛的诗在欧美有不少译本，据我所知，非常重要的一个原因是，一个美国诗人给他翻译了一本非常好的英文版诗歌。但听说，这个美国诗人并不懂汉语，他是通过懂汉语的翻译家对北岛的诗歌进行转述，然后进行二度创作。不难想象，这是一个很好的译本。因为经验告诉我们，诗歌的翻译最终必须由诗人来完成。北岛的诗歌在欧美的许多译本，大部分都是从这本英文诗集转译的，可见，在拉丁语系大的范围内，翻译文学作品特别是诗歌，要比把汉语翻译成这些语种要较为容易一些。

意大利汉学家安娜·布亚蒂、玛希、魏尔玛都是非常重要的翻译家，她们翻译过鲁迅、郭沫若、艾青、王蒙、邓友梅、张洁等老一辈中国作家、诗人的作品，也翻译过年轻一代中国作家，比如余华、苏童等人的作品。但这样高水平的翻译家太少，她们都早已进入古稀之年。诗歌的翻译是所有翻译中最困难的，对许多翻译家都是一个考验。

有一次我和邓友梅一起接待外国作家，邓友梅是写北京世俗生活，尤其是市井生活小说的，可以说是继老舍之后最有名的京味小说家。有个外国作家对他的身世很感兴趣，当时就给他提了几个问题。外国作家问他："你文章中写你戴了右派分子帽子之后，二十多年没有写作，为什么要戴这个帽子呢？谁给你戴的？这个帽子很漂亮吗？为什么戴上这个帽子就没法写作了呢？"他还说："你为了写作，为什么不把这个帽子摘下来呢？"当时，邓友梅先生一脸无奈，只好说，这个事情一两句话说不清

Nigerians may think, you know, this man has been knocked out. It's nothing to do with that". Nor is it the sole criteria of literary excellence. Masters like Leo Tolstoy, Kafka, Gorky, Lu Xun and even Strindberg, himself a Norwegian, all have been shunned for various reasons. Judges, eminent and wise as they may be, are humans and can make mistakes, let alone sometimes ideological or political or intellectual factors might be at work. Who knows? All said, I believe it remains the most authoritative prize in honor of the human imagination of the highest order. Still some apologists of leading Chinese writers, such as Mr Shen Congwen and Ai Qing, keep pestering to the effect that since its impact is global, why does the Nobel Prize Committee fail to cast a reverent glance upon them?

Again, I sense aside other than non-literary considerations, translation is a big headache and poses many difficulties. The marked and typological differences between the Chinese and the Indo-European family and the rest of the linguistic systems are well discussed in that linguists agree the Chinese is simply a lingua franca in its own right. Monosyllabism, the complete lack of inflection, or grammatical endings, the use of 4 tones to convey semantic differences between words otherwise similarly pronounced, among others, are some of the most nettlesome stumbling stones. Compounding the problem of "untranslatability "is a literary tradition and its attendant "initial norms" evolved in total isolation which is bound to induce a more insidious form of "violence" (interference).Given the above minuses, there has been no end of decrying of the infidelity incurred in the process of translating between Chinese and European languages, despite the undeniably high quality of many recent translations.

Bei Dao is the most celebrated and translated Chinese poet in North America and Europe. So far as I know, all European translations are essentially adaptations based on the first rendering, provided by an American ignorant of Chinese, albeit a very brilliant version, which happens to be also an adaptation. Intuitively I know one has to be really good to withstand or attract so many adaptations, but it does show within the family of the Romances languages the relative ease with which translators set to work on an interesting non-European writer.

Among the sinologists from Italy I have come to know, Anna Bujatti, Machi and Wilma Constantini all produced solid translations of contemporary distinguished Chinese writers and poets, such as Lu Xun, Kuo Mojo, Ai Qing, Wang Meng, Deng Youmei and Zhang Jie. The emerging writers Yu Hua and Su Tong also attract their notice. It is a pity this first-rate performance is only seen once in a blue moon. Besides, veteran translators, who spend decades of training to attain to such status beyond all possible dispute, age as a matter of course. By far, poetic translation tries most both the hand and soul of a translator.

Let me pause here to tell you a funny story by way of leaven. Once Deng Youmei and I played host to a delegation of writers overseas. Mr Deng's stories, are in a sense, comedies of manner (Beijing manners),best remembered for its vivid characterization, graceful handling of the Beijing dialect and racy dialogue and a good natured sense of humor, running through his stories.

楚。可见外国人要进入中国的文化背景是很难的。如果把这个内容翻译成别的文字，我看就是注释也要写很长一段。不过我相信，随着中国文化的影响在世界上的不断提高，会有很多优秀的中国作家和诗人的作品走向世界。我们必须要用一种正常的心态来对待诺贝尔文学奖，其实说到底，它就是北欧瑞典皇家文学院十八个评委评的奖。

上次诺贝尔文学奖三个评委到北京后，其中有一位谈了一件非常有趣的事。诺贝尔文学奖十八个评委，现在有两个不上班了，据说是因为英籍作家拉什迪《撒旦的诗篇》。《撒旦的诗篇》出版后，霍梅尼颁布了追杀令，号召全世界的穆斯林在任何地方，都可以以真主的名义，杀死拉什迪。这个事件发生后，英国等西方国家提出，这是干涉作家的创作自由，这是违背人权的。但是霍梅尼认为，此书是对伊斯兰教的亵渎。据悉，在拉什迪能否获奖的问题上，评委会发生了激烈的争论，最终在该年度颁发的诺贝尔文学奖的获奖人不是拉什迪。也因此，有两位评奖委员会委员不再上班。再加上去年，不知什么原因，又有一位评委提出不上班了，现在诺贝尔文学奖评奖委员会真正上班的评委就只有十五位。当然，严格按照规定而言，诺贝尔文学奖评奖委员会还是十八个评委，因为只有评委离世才能进行新的替补，所以那三位不上班的评委仍然是正式的评委。

在这里，我还想通过自己的写作经验，谈一谈作家的良知，特别是作家为什么要忠实于自己的心灵。这是很重要的。诗人、作家最怕违心地去写东西。巴金先生说"讲真话"，但有的人却攻击巴金先生，说"讲真话不等于讲真理"，我认为这种攻击是很荒唐的。一个人如果连讲真话都做不到，怎么可能去讲真理呢？作家和诗人是社会的良心，我们必须时时刻刻关注人的生存状况和人民的命运。我们不仅要关心我们身边发生的一切，还要关注这个世界每天发生的一切。

我非常关注巴勒斯坦阿拉伯人和以色列犹太人的问题，我还非常关注科索沃的问题，非常关注卢旺达的种族屠杀问题。前不久，我写了一首诗《在希望与绝望之间》，这首诗是为韩国今年举办的"为世界和平祈祷"的活动而写的。这首诗是我献给巴勒斯坦人和犹太人的。

因为对外文化交流的关系，这两年，我与不少阿拉伯诗人和以色列诗人都有所

Some critics rank him with Lao She, not without reason. One of the foreign colleagues posed him a few questions. One of them concerned a passage in Deng's biography to the effect Deng explained he was barred from writing for over 20 years after he was branded a rightist in a nationwide purge back in the late 1950s.The picturesque Chinese way of saying "being purged "is donning a "rightist cap". Our foreign colleague, in the dark, came out upon the humorist with a barrage of humorless questions" With a cap donned, you stop writing for 20 years? What kind of magic cap it is? Is it beautiful? How come one is silenced by a cap? Since the cap is a hindrance to writing, why not take it off to resume your beloved pastime?"I remember my friend's reaction then was one of total despair and dumb-confoundedness. The anecdote illustrates the difficulty in carrying your message across the cultural barrier. Of course, globalization and China's rise are oiling the wheels. Even then, we must take it easy when it comes to the annual verdicts from the Nobel Prize committee composed of 18 arbiters of Northern Germanic stock.

One more anecdote pertaining to the panel, told by the three judges at the Strindberg seminar. We know the panel, as a rule, consists of 18 judges, but nowadays only 16 officiate as stipulated. This absenteeism was associated with Satanic Verses controversy, also known as the Rushdie Affair, the heated and frequently violent reaction of some Muslims to the publication of Salman Rushdie's novel *The Satanic Verses*, which was first published in the United Kingdom in 1988. Many Muslims accused Rushdie of blasphemy or unbelief and in 1989 Ayatollah Ruhollah Khomeini of Iran issued a fatwā ordering Muslims to kill Rushdie. Numerous killings, attempted killings, and bombings resulted from Muslim anger over the novel. The same year, the issue of Rushdie's being contender was brought up and controversy ensued among the judges. Angered at Rushdie being out, two judges boycotted the committee from then. In fact, due to some reason unclear, one more member ceases from functioning and the panel now shrinks to 15.Of course, three absentees are life members and the addition of alternate judges has to wait until boycotting members demise naturally.

I now turn to the topic of the conscience of a poet. I absolutely hold it divine for a poet to be true to himself and abstain from telling lies against his better knowledge. Veteran novelist Pan Jin enjoins people to speak from their own hearts. Some cynics play paronomasia with his sincere advocacy, jibing to the effect speaking from your own hearts does not guarantee everything you say is truth, even from the bottom of your heart. What a piece of sophistry! How can we expect a person to tell the truth before he speaks from his own heart? A poet's works should be the expression of his conscience. A poet should be the civic voice of the people. He should make the human condition and the fate of the people his two burning preoccupations. He should speak out against oppression and injustice anywhere in the world, masquerading in whatever guise.

I am deeply agonized over what has happened in the Middle East, Kosovo and Rwanda, despairing at times of the deadlock that afflicts both the Palestinians and the Jews, the military pestilence that ravages Kosovo people and the Rwanda holocaust that is raging while UN and

接触。在同他们的接触和交谈中，我才发现，这两个民族的关系是如此复杂，从人类学的角度来说，阿拉伯人和犹太人是同父异母的兄弟。我曾经问过一个以色列诗人这样的话："你们两个民族不断以暴易暴，当我们无数次地对巴勒斯坦和以色列的和平计划燃起希望之后，事实又让我们再一次地陷入了绝望。这种周而复始的以暴易暴不知还要轮回多久。"

他跟我说："我们和阿拉伯人是什么关系呢？我给你讲一个故事就能说明这个问题。我的先辈和巴勒斯坦人生活在一起已经有很多年。但是忽然有一天阿拉伯人把我祖父和祖母从生活的村庄赶了出来，把我们的家园夷为平地。从我懂事开始，在我幼小的心灵中，我就知道我们这两个民族水火不容。但是你知道吗？我母亲在弥留之际突然开始说话，我的兄弟姐妹都听不懂她在说什么，这似乎是一种陌生的语言。但是我母亲的妹妹听懂了，她告诉我们她说的全是巴勒斯坦人的方言。这非常令我们吃惊。我想，你问我，我们和阿拉伯人之间是什么关系，这个真实的故事就能说明一切。"听到这个故事之后，我一直在想，这个以色列诗人从来不知道母亲会说巴勒斯坦话，但他母亲在要离开这个世界的时候，说起了巴勒斯坦话。这说明这两个民族的关系是多么复杂、微妙！那种血液、眼泪、憎恨、情感是外人很难理解的。

无独有偶，南斯拉夫的事情也很复杂。我认识一个黑山的汉学家，南斯拉夫的科索沃发生了种族清洗。她也说，她母亲是黑山人，后来到了德国，平时讲的都是德语，但她母亲在病重和弥留之际，说的却是塞尔维亚语。这两个发生在不同地域和不同民族的真实故事，竟然完全一样，不能不引起我们对人类现实世界的深层思考。说了这么多，在多元文化共存的世界，我们多么希望不同宗教、不同信仰、不同国籍、不同种族的人们都能和平共处。我在写作中，一直把表现和张扬人道主义精神，作为自己神圣的职责。这对于一个诗人来说是必须具备的。这也是我二十多年写作生活所追求的一个方向。

我想谈谈对语言的学习问题。文学创作非常重要的是对语言的运用。作为一个少数民族诗人，我是用汉语进行创作，要创作出优秀的并具有汉语特殊魅力的作品，就必须要求我在语言上进行严格的训练，并真正能从很高的层面把握汉语的真谛。

我的思维常常在彝语与汉语之间交汇，就像两条河流，时刻在穿越我的思想。我

other world bodies are sitting idle with their hands out stretched and motionless. Not long ago, I penned a poem entitled Between Hope and Despair for the forthcoming conference to be held in Seoul in pray for a turn of event for the better between Israeli and Palestinians.

In recent years I have been participating in a number of cross cultural exchanges and some of these events involve meeting with both Jewish and Palestinian poets. Extensive contacts and deliberate talks prove to be enlightening. I once challenged a Jewish poet: Ethnologists all testify you are cousins. Yet you two people are simply locked into this vicious circle of eye for eye violence game, without fatigue, without end. Some good guys suggest a road map occasionally. You take the olive only to resume the old trick of surprise attack and reprisal!

My Jewish colleague told me a story to educate me on the matter. "our ancestors ,in days long past, rubbed shoulder against shoulder and lived in the same place. One day ,we were driven out of our homes by Arabs and our homes were ravaged and leveled down. That is the origin of this feud that endures for thousands of years. As my Mother lay dying, she broke silence and talked in a language oblique now for my brothers and sisters, yet intelligible to my sisters on the paternal side. My Mother explained she was simply speaking in the dialect of the Palestinians, to our shock. Now, dear Chinese friend, you want to find out the quirk, the real relationship between us and this parable speaks volumes."The story has deepened my understanding of the subtlety and complexity of the racial enmity between Israel and Palestine. How can an outsider take any clue of this Gordian knot since everything, love, hate, suffering, tears, are in the blood?

The same case is with the unhappy happenings in the Balkan Peninsula.I came to know something about the" racial cleansing"(holocaust by dominant Serbians against other lesser ethnic groups)through a sinologist from Montenegro. She said her mother was a black mountain native and later emigrated to Germany.Her mother kept talking to her in German until one day she lay dying she suddenly shifted to Serbian. Two true stories yet with the same plot. Despite the stubborn, gruesome and desperate realities, as a poet, I have considered it a duty incumbent upon me to advocate humanitarianism and fraternity. This might be a dream, some contend, but man is a dream animal. Poets should move towards the ultimate solution by dramatizing this shameful condition and by quickening the feeling of brotherhood lying dormant in the minds of the people.

Last but not the least, I will dwell a little bit about the importance of language to a poet. Proficiency in a language presupposes a poetic process. Yet, for ethnic poets, a different problem beset me. Nigerian Achebe chose to write in English despite opposition from other black writers who had moral neurosis about using colonizers language but who had no canonical resources to fall upon. I don't have this syndrome for two things: we Yi people don't experience trauma of being flagrantly brutalized (the process of China's racial integration and acculturation took centuries to complete, and in a relatively mild manner).Besides, Chinese and its literary traditions are well established and very prestigious. To excel in this honored tradition, one must take pains and make assiduous effort to get the real feel of the language, "the one central language enjoying

非常庆幸的是,如果说我的诗歌是一条小船,这两种伟大的语言,都为这条小船带来过无穷的乐趣和避风的港湾。作为诗人,我要感谢这两种伟大的语言。正是它们,给我提供了这无限的创造的空间。

我长期坚持阅读川籍小说家李劼人的小说,是他的作品让我懂得了汉语的从容和幽默。我长期坚持阅读苗族乡土作家沈从文的小说,是他让我真正体会到了汉语的细腻和韵味。我还长期坚持阅读"白洋淀派"作家孙犁的作品,是他让我真正体会到了汉语淡雅和不同凡响的朴实。我还经常阅读艾青和穆旦的诗篇,是他们的作品让我深知中国诗歌的语言是这个世界上为数不多的极其美丽的语言之一。阅读对于一个作家和诗人将是他一生都要去完成的课题,而只有捍卫我们民族语言的纯洁性,同时还要为这个古老的语言进行新的创造,才是我们义不容辞的光荣职责。

语言和阅读有着密切的关系。刚才在谈语言的时候,实际上已经涉及了阅读。阅读对我们今天来说很重要。现在有很多作家几乎在一个水平线上。一个诗人、作家,对除了文学之外的作品,比如哲学、人类学乃至心理学作品的阅读是很有必要的。作家创作水平距离的拉开,除了创造力的差距之外,很大程度上和作家综合性的修养有极大关系。阅读是作家增加综合性文学修养的一个重要方式。

现在,我们研究国外一些重要作家,比如说意大利作家莫拉维亚,以及意大利后现代作家卡尔维诺,他们的阅读都是非常广泛的。还有阿根廷作家博尔赫斯,可以说没有广泛的阅读就不会创造博尔赫斯。难怪西方有人把博尔赫斯称为"作家中的作家""图书馆中的作家"。

阅读面一定要广,这对我们来说是一个启示。今天的现实告诉我们,阅读对我们来说比什么都重要,这看来似乎是很浅显的道理,但是这个道理并不是所有的人都明白。阅读要有方法和重点,如果你不是研究肖洛霍夫的,你就不可能也没有必要把肖洛霍夫的《静静的顿河》这么厚的四部书拿来看无数遍;如果你不是专门研究托尔斯泰的,你也不可能也不需要把托尔斯泰的全集阅读无数遍。所以我说,阅读要有重点,同时要有方法。人类历史留下的文学财富是非常丰富的。人的生命时间同样是有限的,在阅读中进行选择,使阅读更加有效,这就要讲究方法。

我从十六岁开始写作,阅读一直是我生活中的一个重要组成部分,就是在我行

nationwide currency" and to allow my books to be read by the largest readership ever.

For a Yi adept at writing in Chinese is not without its joys. I often find myself moving between two languages, caught in a salutary situation that I would liken them to two rivers flowing through my mind, and my poetry, to a boat floating down leisurely. I feel myself blessed with a facility with both after a strict, rigorous and extended self-disciplined apprenticeship.

I have kept reading novels by a Sichuan native Li Jieren, written in a supple and humorous tone. Another protracted reading habit is with Sun Li whose works exude an unadorned simplicity and grace. Regional writer Shen Congwen has a lesson on the delicacy and flavor to teach about the language. To crown all, Ai Qing and Mu Dan have held in their hands "Open Sesame" to the cave of the Chinese poetry, one studded with fabulous riches and fantastic treasures. The greatest enlightenment in my life is the realization Chinese is one of the most refined, aesthetic and resourceful languages any would be poet can thirst to be blessed with. All my life I will try and contain what I want to say within the limits of conventional Chinese and meanwhile expand and extend the frontiers of Chinese so as to accommodate Chinese thought-patterns .A mastery of Chinese, willingly and consciously, not out of innocence ,is a lifelong task .

Let me reiterate the importance of reading. I must say one can almost tell how far a writer or a poet can go by the size of his library and the quality of his spiritual companionship. Modern writing is necessarily cultured and complex, the result of varied influences. Granted one's creativity is partially innate or divinely sparked, it is ultimately sustained by an intensified sensibility fed and nurtured by systematic and extensive reading.

There is a modern tendency that leading writers of world renown, are without exception, great readers. Moravia and Calvino are exemplary. Borges is called "the writer of writers" or "the writer of the library". All excellent writers and remarkable prose stylists, they have written prolifically, showing an ever-deepening intelligence and complexity as they research the intersection of philosophy, religion, art, politics, and the nature of time and role of the individual. By doing so, they evince a level of originality and erudition unrivaled and baffling to the uninitiated and unlettered.

Be an extensive reader! Thus they exhort us. Modern realities necessitate the width and breadth of reading. This is almost common sense ,but unfortunately we have too many innocents home and abroad who ignore the exhortation. Moreover, if you are a conscious reader, you are beset by two problems-what to read and how to read. Personally I believe, in an age of Internet, unless you are students and experts of Tolstoy or Sholokhov, you are not supposed to thumb through each page of Silently Flows the Don River or War and Peace. Life is short and there is no end of books already written ,being written and to be written. We must make a choice to make reading more profitable and more rewarding.

At the age of 16, I started to learn to write and all the while writing and reading go hand in hand like twins. An increase in administrative responsibilities proves to be no deterrent to my

政工作非常忙的时候,我也从未放弃过阅读。我们是世界文明的儿子,我们只有用全人类的优秀文化来养育自己,才能使自己的思想变得广博而深远。

学者需要阅读,作家也同样需要阅读,阅读是我们吸收新思想、新知识的重要来源。我前不久到南斯拉夫去访问,专门抽时间会见了《哈扎尔辞典》的作者帕维奇。大家知道,前几年中国文坛上出现了一场很大的争论,就是关于韩少功的《马桥词典》到底是不是受了《哈扎尔辞典》的影响,是不是在形式上模仿了《哈扎尔辞典》。我个人认为这场争论没有多大意义。中国作家受外国作家影响,或者外国作家受中国作家影响,我想都是很正常的事情。我与帕维奇有一个多小时的对话,这个对话涉及他的创作生活,涉及他的艺术观点,很重要的还涉及他的阅读。我发现,他是一个知识非常广博的作家,难怪他的每一部作品在形式上都会有新的创造。

说实话,我们现在很多作家,包括20世纪50年代成长起来的作家,如果和20世纪30年代的鲁迅、郭沫若、郁达夫等作家比较起来,有一个很大的差别,就是鲁迅、郭沫若、郁达夫他们都是学贯中西的。他们的外语都非常好,同样他们中国的旧学功底也非常扎实。他们除了创作之外,还翻译了大量的外国文学作品,为中国的新文化启蒙做出了重要的贡献。

我们现在的很多作家由于成长经历的关系,外语都不好,可以说成长阶段在营养上都是先天不足的。现在更年轻的一代作家,他们的教育环境有了很大的改变,但同样,他们也有许多不足,那就是对中国传统文化缺少了解。人的时间非常有限,选择优秀的经典作品进行阅读,选择更适合自己的好作品阅读,这一点非常重要。有许多作家,他们的禀赋和天才的素质都非常高,我们只能通过阅读来提高自己的思想深度,才能站在更高的文化制高点上,去观照和回望自己民族的生活,去审视自己民族的历史。

简单地说,只有我们的思想武装起来了,我们才能用我们的笔去触摸事物的本质。人类今天正在经历现代化的过程,现代化未必就是进步,现代化过程中也会丢失很多东西。我们对"幸福"的理解也不一样,人类相互之间有很大的文化差异,你认为他不幸福,实际上他过得很幸福。从哲学的层面进行分析,什么是得,什么是失,这是一个很复杂的问题。今天我们读叶芝的诗,依然会被他的诗深深地感动,甚至会潸然

inveterate hobby. We are sons and daughters of world culture and our survival hinges upon the fusing "of a plurality of possibilities for harmony and truth, outside the limited range of our inherited dogmas."

Modern writers are Renaissance men again, and vice versa. Reading opens us to new trends and new intellectual advances. I toured Yugoslavia not long ago and made a point to see in person Milorad Pavic , *Dictionary of the Khazars*: A Lexicon Novel . There arose a few years ago a heated debate whether *Dictionary of Maqiao* by novelist Han Shaogong was modeled on Pavic's work, or at least in form. To me, this debate made no sense. Cross cultural influences are legitimate. I conducted an interview with Pavic over one hour, touching upon his life, his creative process, his view on artistic creation. His reading scope was of interest to me in particular. I find, to my joy and expectation, sitting face to face, is a man of wide and huge learning .No wonder innovation and adaptation occur to him almost in every book he is writing, as naturally as he breathes.

To tell the truth, there is a marked difference in terms of Intellectual equipment and breadth of learning, between the generation of writers emerging in the 1950s and those distinguished in the 1930s, say, Lu Xun, Ko Mojo and Yu Dafu. The latter group brought to their creative work two added gifts of an intellectual superiority both in the Western learning and Chinese studies and a facility in foreign languages. These old guards also acted as translators and did much in the drive for cultural revival.

The contemporary generation, flawed by an incomplete education, lacking in foreign languages' plus, nourished literarily or poetically by some circumstantial factors, turn out to be circumstantial writers. They drop out half way, intellectually drained and emotively depleted. Serious writers must make the crucial choice of a lasting companionship of books. For talented aspirants to literary fame, sophistication in style and complexity in thought will only take place as a result of conscious delving into the Chinese history and meditation and evocation of the enduring dilemmas of the spiritual life of our own people.

Simply put, unless we are adequately cultured, we are not in position to get down to the essence of things. We are living in an age of modernization. There is a widespread, but puerile and fallacious, tendency to identify progress with modernization.This is not necessarily so. Modernization entails its share of tolls in its wake. No other buzz word than happiness divides men in such a way that they seem unable to approach even a semblance of agreement. Looks like happiness belongs to the category of words culturally loaded than semantically defined.

You believe some one leads a happy life, whereas in fact he is in a plight. Raise this question gain- or- loss to the metaphysical level and one is ensnared in the labyrinth of paraphasia. Yeats draws metaphors from mythology, picturing olden days, traditional Ireland, rural and medieval, at the zenith of civilization. To read him, with his idealized pastoral scenes, plunges me into tearful emotion and melancholic spleen. Empathetically, in my reflective moments I will assert modernization is not all bliss, let alone post-modernization. Not long ago, I finish a poem entitled

泪下,他写的东西完全是对农耕文明的歌颂,是对爱尔兰那种古老美好生活的回忆。这些东西对我们来说是久远的怀念。我不认为现代化所体现的都是进步,我们对工业化和后工业化所带来的一切,都要进行反思。前不久我写了一首诗叫《时间》。这首诗表达了我对时间和生命的理解。时间本身似乎是很抽象的,然而对于我们的现实它又非常具体。借此机会,我把这首诗念给大家听。

"在我的故乡/我无法见证/一道土墙的全部历史/那是因为在一个瞬间/我无法亲历/一粒尘埃/从诞生到死亡的过程/哦,时间!/是谁用无形的剪刀/在距离和速度的平台/把你剪成了碎片/其实我们/不用问时间的起源/因为它从来/就没有所谓的开始/同样,我们也不用问它的归宿在哪里/因为在浩瀚的宇宙/它等同于无限/时间是黑暗中的心脏/它的每一次跳动/都如同一道闪电/它是过去、现在和未来的桥梁/请相信,这并非上帝的意旨/仿佛是绝对的真理/当时间离开了我们/它永远不再回头//所有的生命、思想和遗产/都栖居在时间的圣殿/哦,时间!/最为公平的法官/它审判谎言/同时它也伸张正义/是它在最终的时刻/改变了一切精神和物质的/存在形式/它永远在死亡中诞生/又永远在诞生中死亡/它包含了一切/它又在一切之外/如果说在这个世界上/有什么东西真正地不朽/我敢肯定地说/那就是时间!"

我写这首诗,主要是想表达人类自身对时间的认识。最近我写了很多诗,主要是关于人类的思想,人类对生命、死亡这些终极命题的思考,包括对个体生命的理解。我历来相信,诗歌过去是,现在是,将来依然是人类精神世界中最美丽的花朵,只要人类存在,诗歌就会去抚慰一代又一代人的心灵。诗歌作为人类精神财富中永远不可分割的重要部分,它将永远与人类的思想和情感联系在一起。诗歌永远不会死亡!对我个人来说,创作诗歌是我对这个世界最深情的倾诉。作为一个彝族诗人,写诗是我一生必须坚持的事业。

Time, by far the most philosophical utterance on the nature of time and life.

In my tribal village/I did not witness/what happened when the muddy wall was erected/The same case as at a critical moment/I was absent from witnessing/ a single grain of dust/from birth to death/Oh! Time!/Who performed the magic cutting/on the platform of Time and Speed/of you into shreds?/In fact, we/are justified refraining from asking/when Time starts ticking/There is simply no such thing as a beginning/The same reason we remain ignorant of its ending/As ,in the vastness of space/Time means Infinity/Time is the heart of Darkness /Each pulse/like lightning/forms a bridge of Past, Now and Future/Trust me: this occurs as no divine message/like one of the Super Truths/when Time departs/It will never return/Oh! Time!/All life forms, thinking and heritage/residents of the Hall of Time/Oh! Time!/Respected Justices/Sitting in judgment on liars/Giving the righteous their due reward/At the last moment/it will transform all entities/reincarnated In death/And dying in the incarnation/It contains everything/It resides beyond everything/If, there is truly something Immortal/In this world of ours/I will speak out for Time!/

Time represents my latest probing into the recalcitrant issue of Time. My recent output is large and most of them demonstrate a widened perspective and deepened sophistication in style as well as meditation on the ultimate themes about thinking and death, existential anguish of individuals in a time devoid of certainties of any sort. My poetic tenet remains apodeictic, desperate and indelible that poetry, the flowering of human spirituality, the eternal solace of agonized souls, has formed the essential and integral part of human cultural heritage, interwoven inextricably with the duration of some of the most basic human experiences that require and bring forth our constant endorsement and strongest affirmations. Poetry dies really hard. For a Yi poet, it is invariably my profound entreaties of love with the world in which I live as well as my powerful plea for a better cosmos.

为消除人类所面临的精神困境而共同努力
在第 42 届贝尔格莱德国际作家会议开幕式上的讲话
2005 年 9 月 17 日

  与历史上的任何一个时代相比较,今天的世界肯定是一个物质主义盛行和消费欲望空前膨胀的时代。也可以说,在经济全球化的背景下,人类虽然在物质文明和科学技术方面取得了过去从未有过的进步,但在全世界普遍性地存在着这样一个事实,那就是人类的精神缺失已经到了令人吃惊的地步,人类在所谓现代文明的泥沼中,精神的困境日益加剧,许多民族伟大的文化传统遭到冷落和无端轻视,特别是不少民族的原生文化,在后工业化和所谓现代化的过程中,开始经受多重的严峻考验。

  正因为此,人类心灵的日趋荒漠化,已经让全世界许多对人类的前途心怀担忧、充满着责任感的有识之士开始行动起来,大家以超越国界、种族、区域、意识形态和宗教的全球眼光,达成了这样一种共识,那就是要在地球上任何一个生活着族群的地方,为消除今天人类所面临的精神困境而共同努力。

  作为生活在今天这个时代的诗人和作家,在这里我还必须郑重声明,在我们今天身处的物质主义世界,我们的文学应该发挥怎样的作用呢?其实真正意义上的文学,从来就是人类精神世界中不可分割的组成部分,它为净化人类的灵魂,为构建人类崇高的精神生活,发挥着最为积极的重要作用。文学的真实性和作家、诗人所应该具备的人道主义良知,必然要求我们今天的作家和诗人,更多地关注人类的命运,关注今天人类所遭遇的生存危机。

  作家、诗人在面对并描写自己的内心冲突的时候,无论从道德伦理的角度,还是从哲学思想的层面,都应该时刻把关注他人的命运和人民大众的命运放在第一位。

Striving to Reverse the Global Trend of Spiritual Decline

A Speech Given at the Opening Ceremony of 42nd International Writers Conference at Belgrade
17th, September, 2005

In one sense we can utter some grand pronouncements with confidence that the age we are living in is one given with abandon to materialism and consumerism. In other words, poetic concern about the human condition has grown largely as a reaction to the manifestly global sweep of contemporary events, with appalling "overstimulation of material desires and sensual gratification" dwarfing the interest in the poetic side of things. Mankind is mired in the creature comforts. The change for worse is in the air we breathe to the extent many illustrious traditions and cultures are thrust forth to scorn, especially many aboriginal cultures are landed on the Procrustean bed of modernization frenzy.

The trend towards spiritual desertification must be arrested. Caring people, awakened to the perilous condition of man, united by beliefs, which transcend tribal, national, racial and religious loyalties, embark upon a massive crusade to counter the spiritual decline that afflicts and plagues human races and people wherever they happen to be.

I solemnly declare, as poets in this age of uninhibited materialism, what we are up to is to harness our words in the service of human cause to defend the earth from its myriad indignities. Great literature, with vitality and reality, has been an integral part of our common cultural heritage. Poetic creation envisages a nourishing pasture in the soul where dreams of infinity and a sovereign aspiration of light are born. The two cardinal virtues a poet is supposed to possess and cultivate, integrity of character and humanitarianism, necessitate him to be in the vanguard of this crusade against all the blind forces held accountable for the present mess we are stranded in. To arrive at the Truth by following the paths of poetry is to drop all other mundane concerns and place the fate of others and of the people in general above anything else.

因为只有这样,我们作为作家和诗人才能为继承、纯洁和再构建人类伟大的精神生活传统,选择一条正确的道路。为了呼吁更多的作家和诗人,来参加消除今天人类所面临的精神困境这一具有特殊意义的活动,我们必须更加尊重世界各民族文化的多样性,这个地球上多元文化的共存、不同民族文化的平等原则,已经为世界上大多数国家和一切追求正义的人们所接受并赞同!政治文明的建设、物质文明的建设以及精神文明的建设,是当今世界上许多国家在不同社会制度框架里所追求的目标和内容。但是如何消除今天人类所面临的精神困境,无疑将是我们生活在不同社会制度、不同国家、不同地域、不同种族的作家和诗人们共同的、最为光荣而艰巨的任务。

Only so are we poets the worthy heirs of the great spiritual traditions that distinguish humans from all other species on earth. In order to rally for more people to be part of this symbolic act of reinstating the wholeness of life, we must pay homage to the cultural diversity of each race, fully cognizant of the consensus reached among all justice-thirsting people of the dual sacred principles of the co- existence of multi-plural cultures and the equality of multi-plural cultures.

For our poets, living under various social systems, of various ethnic origin, from various geographical dimensions, word is our common arsenal, the herald of the Truth, with which we march into the most glorious battle of combating the global debasement of the human scene and building a spirit strengthened by the beauty, light and fire of poetry in these tragic times.

鲁迅与我们这个时代

在意大利马切拉大学的演讲

2004年11月4日

　　时间已经进入了21世纪,我想这无论是对于鲁迅,还是对于所有与这个伟大人物有关的人和事,都将引发我们更多的思考。可以这样说,在中国20世纪最为杰出的作家中,鲁迅无疑是一个奇异的生命现象。不管是在他活着的时候,还是在他死了以后,他都是在中国思想文化史上,一个被争论得最多的,同时也是最为复杂的生命个体。多少年来,鲁迅的追随者层出不穷,从未间断过。他的思想作为一份不朽的精神遗产,深刻地影响着中国的现实和人民的精神生活。当然鲁迅的敌人也同样从未消失过,他们和鲁迅的追随者就如同一对孪生兄弟。

　　正因为鲁迅对黑暗的揭露真实而尖锐,他的全部作品都体现了一种不可妥协的立场,他始终如一揭示的就是这个时代的真相。也正由于此,鲁迅遭到的攻击是最多的。在这里我还想说明这样一个基本事实:鲁迅作为一个天生敏感、激烈,甚至有些怪异的天才作家,其作品渗透在文字背后的深刻思想,被别人误读的概率,要远远超过俄罗斯作家陀思妥耶夫斯基和奥地利作家卡夫卡。

　　1881年是鲁迅出生的年份,他的故乡绍兴是中国一个古老的小镇,可能是因为地处中国沿海,那里也是新思想和外来文化最早的传播地。就在一个传统的中国封

Lu Xun and Our Age
A Speech Delivered at Macerata University, Italy
4th, November, 2004

This young 21st century, in which we live, forebodes no diminution of ancient literary feuds over the status and worth of Lu Xun, arguably the most controversial figure in modern Chinese history. One aspect of his enduring strength lies in his scathing indictment of traditional ways of Chinese life being cruel and hypocritical and his creation of the famous hero Ah Q as the embodiment of national disease. The recognition of "spiritual victory" as the predominant trait in the Chinese character, whereby manifest defeat is rationalized into moral superiority, constitutes his true contribution to rousing the conscience of the nation as it gives a hilarious but piercing commentary on China's pathetic stance when repeatedly humiliated and defeated by bullying world powers. Alive and dead, Lu Xun has been a source of vehement intellectual debate and the range and sophistication of his legacy both exasperate and fascinate. There is no dearth of followers and disciples in his camping. And there is no doubt of his artistic influence extraordinarily valuable and ineradicably established.

Of course, intellectual cynicism against him dies hard. The anti-tradition is as old as the adulation, like twins hand in hand. The butt of the most virulent invective, vicious diatribe and flimsy calumniation, Lu Xun evinces fully his satiric intelligence and moral courage to probe into the tragic national vices by presenting nothing but the unadorned truth about his age. What Lu Xun appears to have meant in this connection is that China has become so feeble-minded and diminutive that it cannot contain so sensitive, even perversely sardonic, erratic and indigestible a character as Lu Xun. His argument, couched in language richly allusive, scathing, terse, is so serious that it lends itself paradoxically to distortion and misunderstanding, with an inherent vulnerability that bedevils sardonically disruptive thinkers like Dostoyevsky and Kafka in the similar vein.

Lu Xun was born in 1881 in Shaoxing, Zhejiang in the east of China. Proximity to the coastal cities made his hometown easily accessible to foreign influence and intellectual trend. A study of

建社会结构被打破的时候,鲁迅的创作从一开始就包含一种宿命的色彩,其中最主要的是为了捍卫人的权利和生存所要承担的痛苦。写到这里,我在思考这样一个问题:鲁迅对我们今天这个时代,还会产生更直接和更巨大的影响吗?回答是肯定的。

首先,鲁迅见证了中国封建专制主义的黑暗,他希望在现代化的进程中,促进专制政治向民主政治的转型。他的小说所创造的世界,主要是在揭露封建专制主义对人的轻视和蔑视。他对小说中的人物给予深刻同情,特别是那些灾难深重的中国农村妇女,是他倾其一生关注的对象。从这个意义上讲,鲁迅是一个伟大的人道主义者,他对人的生存权和发展权的尊重,对于我们今天这个尤其需要公正和正义的世界,其现实意义和历史意义都将是深远的。

就人而言,鲁迅还是一种独立的存在。作为中国知识分子的杰出代表和良心。鲁迅对社会和现实生活的介入,从来就是以一种批判的姿态。用独立的人格立身,来面对和剖析这个世界的所谓真实性。从这个角度讲,鲁迅的反叛精神是终其一生的。鲁迅清醒地意识到,一个作家只有从自己的心灵和独立的立场出发,他才可能具备自由的意志。有人说鲁迅属于一个阶级,有人说鲁迅属于一个集体,甚至还有人说鲁迅属于一种正统的意识形态。其实鲁迅所有的作品已经回答了这样一个问题。可以断言,鲁迅永远是这个世界黑暗的目击者,他给我们提供的真实,从某种意义而言,也将是唯一的真实。

另外,鲁迅作品的预言性早已被无数的鲁迅研究专家所证实。今天我们阅读鲁迅,会重新思考鲁迅作品的真正价值。鲁迅作品中所表现出的多义性和独特的象征,对于我们打开人类未来历史和秩序的真实之门,无疑是一把宝贵的钥匙。特别是当人类面对自身的生存境遇和种种困难,我们就会坚信,鲁迅的精神思想,作为人类精神殿堂中一束永恒的烛光是不会熄灭的。

his life and works is at the same time a study of the social and political affairs of China as she was ready to throw off the feudalist rule and become a modern republic. His early works are inevitably informed with a strain of fatalism demanding that, if his writing is to be incisive and enlightening, the writer himself must act in the capacity of a martyr hero and visionary like Prometheus. My problem is, has his legend outlived its function, and moreover, does his teaching even carry with itself a larger message for human beings? The answer, I believe, is in the affirmative.

At the turn of the century, Lu Xun, a returned student from Japan, shocked at and "despaired of the sloth, hypocrisy, superstition and cruelty of the rural and town people, repudiated his hometown and symbolically the traditional way of Chinese life." He bore witness to the collapse of the tyrannical rule and even hastened its end by awakening in the people an ardent desire for better society and better life. His works in the finer creative tradition of the Literature Revolution gave impetus to transform traditional dynastic politics into democratic politics. He brings his attack upon the inexorable sway of autocracy with its attendant moral decadence, cruelty and distain for human rights to its logical conclusion. His realistic exposé of the callousness of traditional mores, as exemplified in his rural scenes in which the plight of those less favored in life, the poorest farmers and women in particular, is explored, informed with understanding and lyrical warmth, constitutes some of the flagrant imaginative heights in modern Chinese literary history. One example is Xianglin Sao in "New Year Sacrifice," the tragic tale of an unlettered peasant woman hounded to death by superstition and feudalism, exhibiting the author's moral seriousness and humanitarian impulse. A great humanist like Lu Xun, who cares about the lot of underdogs and champions their human rights of subsistence and development, certainly has relevance to our world in transition, a world blighted by an unequal distribution of wealth and justice.

Second, Lu Xun still charms us because of his impressiveness as a personality. Lu Xun's brand spirit of defiance, when roused and challenged by powerful evil forces in society, earns him the laurel crown as the conscience of the nation. Such critical stance has universal significance in an age of increasingly intellectual uniformity. Capable of true insightful indignation, he dares to probe into the dark sides of the world. The truth, only the unembellished truth, remains his lifelong passion. He never hopes against his better knowledge that a writer will never possess independent will until he speaks directly from his heart. Some class-conscious people claim him as mentor. Some allocate a special interest group for him to identify with. Still some believe Lu Xun operates within the bounds of a certain ideology. To see the perversion of truth in this manner, one needs only to take up his works to be informed afresh of the fact that Lu Xun stands revealed as an eternal witness and muckraker of the evil that plagues this world. The stark truth, which he presents and dramatizes in his "The True Story of Ah Q", is the only truth worth knowing.

One more difficult aspect in Lu Xun to grasp is the man as visionary as a prophet, a topic that, fortunately, has been well discussed by researchers home and abroad. There are few creative

特别让我感慨的是,今天在美丽、古老而又现代的意大利,我们来共同研讨鲁迅,这本身就说明了鲁迅作为一个伟大的小说家,不仅属于中国,也属于世界。我们这个时代不能没有鲁迅!

pieces in modern Chinese literature that readers can return with such assurance of reading pleasure and revelatory value. One marvels at the complex structure of meanings and the peculiar inventiveness of imagery attempted to furnish us with an array of possible avenues to the forging of new social orders in the future. This is particularly true when modern crisis situations that crop up as if from nowhere compel us to be open-minded to clues and solutions that emerge in quarters unimagined. As a prophet, and a liberator of the human spirit, Lu Xun is of first importance and his critical legacy, like a beacon light, will shed lasting honor upon the face of our globe.

It is solace enough to think that I am so honored to be invited here in Italy, so cultured and civilized, where modern and ancient blend, to speak to you about China's top writer, a genius wholly individual who belongs both to China and the world, simply because one cannot understand China without coming to terms with Lu Xun.

在全球化语境下超越国界的各民族文学的共同性

在汉城热爱自然文学之家的演讲

2002年6月12日

  我非常高兴能出席中国、韩国、土耳其三国作家的这个对话会,这是一次令人难忘的聚会,为此我要感谢汉城市政府和汉城热爱自然文学之家的盛情邀请,正是你们这个特殊的友好举动,使我们最终能在这个充满诗意的季节来到汉城。在这里请允许我,以"在全球化语境下超越国界的各民族文学的共同性"为题,作以下的发言。

  如果说20世纪是一个从真正意义上完成了工业革命,而科学技术的发展无论就其速度,还是就其规模,都大大超过了过去所经历的几百年的世纪,那么就是在今天,还无须我们等到将来,就可以断言,两个世纪的确是一个令人难忘、创造了无数精神和物质奇迹的世纪。诚然,同样在这一个世纪,人类经历了难以言说的痛苦和极为残酷的战争。我们不会忘记,就在20世纪向人类告别的时候,有多少政治家、思想家和哲人在预言着21世纪,有无数的诗人还为此写下了泪水和梦想编织的诗章。

  尽管这样,当我们真的生活在21世纪的现实中,当我们再一次发现,人类并没有因为进入了一个新的世纪,而改变了过去的一切不幸时,我们的心情虽然是沉重的,但我们从未丧失对人类未来的信心。21世纪,是一个更为快捷的信息和数字化的时代,人类生活方式所发生的重大变化,必然会带来思维方式和其他行为方式的改变。特别是经济高速发展,经济全球化日趋加快,国家间的联系、不同文化背景的各民族文化间的交流,也大大超过了过去任何一个时代。可以这样说,由于资本的跨国流动,各国在经济中所形成的紧密关系,客观上也带来了不同特质的文化间的对话

Commonality in the Literature of Various Nationalities in the Context of Globalization
A Speech Given at the Love of Nature and Literature Society of Seoul
12th, June, 2002

It is such a great honor to be attending this high profile literary dialogue between writers from Korea, Turkey and China. I deeply appreciate the kindness of the invitation extended to me by the Seoul Municipal Government and the Love of Nature and Literature Society of Seoul, a most beautiful gesture in celebration of the literary enterprise and the charming season of spring. Now let me, as scheduled, address the meeting. The topic of my speech is Commonality in the Literature of Various Nationalities in the Context of Globalization.

In one way we will remember the 20th century as having truly seen the crystallization of the Industrial Revolution, a term widely accepted as denoting the change-over from Neolithic styled subsistence farming to mass machine productions in factories. The Industrial Revolution brought with it not only greatly increased productivity but also manifold problems with factory systems and urbanization. Today, with computer, internet, digitalization, space science, the tempo of scientific technological advances is accelerating and what man has achieved in one century far surpasses what he had done in the previous several centuries prior to the last one. We don't have to waiver until another day to assert the 20th century will go down in history as a time when man has worked wonders both materially and spiritually. Of course, it can also be insisted in superlatives as the worst in history because of the destruction of two world wars with a human toll of more 71 million people killed than in all previous wars in the annals of civilization. We will never forget on the eve of the 21th century while politicians, thinkers and philosophers rack their brains mapping the territory and charting the courses for mankind to take, countless poets dwell on the glories and miseries of the past century, looked back to with nostalgia.

It may be argued that this young century is one of great crisis and great promises, of great hazard and great potential. While our hearts are drooping at the vast residuals of problems, we take consolation in the fact that such a see-sawing has been characteristic of all the great ages of the past. For major transformations in lifestyles require major revising of traditional intellectual make-up. With acceleration of economic growth, with a widened process of economic globalization in full swing, interactions on various levels between countries and under various auspices ,societies everywhere are affected to a greater or lesser degree by this inexorable march of

与互动。当然这是一种极为复杂的关系，其中有相互的学习和兼容，同样也存在着一定层面上的矛盾与冲突。

让这个世界上所有民族的文化都能发展和延续下去，并真正做到多元文化共存，我想这恐怕也是进步人类早已形成的共识。但是我们无法回避也不应该回避的事实是，今天强势文化对弱势文化的包围和消解，已经到了非常严重的地步。任何一个有良知和灵魂的人，无论你生活在这个世界的哪一个地方，都不应该对这一现象表现出熟视无睹，甚至漠不关心。人类不能没有道德的力量。对正义和真理的追寻，是人类不断走向公正、自由和更加民主的力量源泉。

据我所知，人类对自然界物种的消失，已经有了足够的警惕，并且开始在全球范围内，对其进行最大限度的保存，以维护生物的多样性。但是就文化而言，人类所实施的保护，无论广度还是力度都是远远不够的。在这个世界上，每年都有无数种语言在消失，有不少民族的文化也面临着难以传承下去的危险。当然，文化的继承、发展和融合是一个非常复杂的问题。但是面对这个多元文化并存的世界，作为人类精神文化代言人的作家和诗人，我们必须表明自己的严正立场，并身体力行地捍卫人类各民族文化的多样性。我想，正因为人类不同文明共存，人类不同民族文化共存，这个世界才会是丰富的，这个世界的全面发展也才是合乎人道的。

讲到这里，我要请大家原谅，因为你们一定会说，你不是在谈全球化语境下超越国界的各民族文学的共同性吗？是的，正是因为我要讲这种超越国界的各民族文学的共同性，我才有必要把这种超越国界的各民族的文化（包括文学）理应存在的前提讲清楚，因为只有这样，我们才不会忽视各民族的文化和文学存在的特殊价值，也只有这样，我们才会从内心深处尊重世界上任何一个民族的文化，并对这个文化所养育的伟大作家和天才的诗人们致以最为美好的兄弟般的敬意。正是这些不同国家、不同地域、不同民族的作家和诗人的创造性劳动，才使人类的文学宝库不断得到丰富和补充。这些闪耀着人类智慧光芒的文学经典，真正超越了国界和民族，被翻译成世界上众多的语言文字，被大家所热爱和阅读，事实上这些经典作家和作品，已经成为人类精神生活中极其重要的一个组成部分。

globalization. It might be concluded the mobility of capital and the attendant interlocking of all the economies facilitate cultural exchanges and dialogues between heterogeneous cultures. This assumption, to a greater or lesser extent, must be calibrated, as such interactions and dialogues presuppose a willingness to give credit to the virtues of an alien culture; it presupposes wisdom in order to understand the Other on its own terms while not jeopardizing the wholeness of our own cultures.

I believe in the ancient maxim of "live and let live". That is, the diversity and peaceful co-existence of diverse races on earth, has been a consensus among all the enlightened races. Yet one fact, albeit very inconvenient, remains: weak cultures find themselves now in the throes of modernization, a process dominated by powerful cultures of Western origins. Today it is customary to talk about two modes of life, the "progressive one of the modern industrialized west and the "traditional one of the underdeveloped non-agrarian west. The onslaught of modernization has everywhere eroded the cohesion and legitimacy of the traditional societies. Anybody with a conscience and soul is in his own right to ask this question:"Whoever is authorized to make modernization and progress a pair of synonyms?" I believe any progressive movement, if it wants to be worthy of the epithet, must be driven by a higher purpose and a moral commitment to the diversity and peaceful co-existence of diverse races on earth, which is part and parcel of the 2th century ethic code and quest for justice and truth as well as the source of strength and inspiration that will allow us to move towards a more just, free and democratic world.

To the best of my knowledge, there has existed a global awareness ,in the civic society, of the menaced species in the wilderness, and man has achieved a great measure of success in the conservation campaigns. Yet, we do not seem to understand that cultural diversity deserve perhaps more sustainable and greater caring efforts. I am told with each passing year numerous languages die out and many aboriginal cultures find it difficult to be preserved and passed on. Of course, in a multi-cultural and multi-racial world, there is a very complicated inner logic at work when it comes to cultural interaction. We poets, as spokesmen of each ethnic group, must speak out our minds and demonstrate our determination in the drive for protecting cultural diversity. The world has much to gain , becoming enriched and more human in the drive for the co-existence of a multiplicity of cultural traditions.

I pause for a while, for I seem to owe everyone here an apology ,as someone might counter saying this:"You must be off the mark, since the topic for today suggests a summarizing of the common features governing world literature and overriding national and racial loyalties." Friend, I am not off the mark. On the contrary, the commonality governing world literature necessarily is predicated upon the particularity of various national literature. For only so will we retain enough respect for the specific values of each regional variety that specific ethnic groups claim as theirs. Only so will we hold in awe all the established poets and literary geniuses nurtured on the cultural traditions of their own nationalities. As we look back over the several millennia of world literature,

现在我想就超越国界的各民族文学的共同性再谈一点意见。首先,我想重申的是,今天的人类,无论政治上、经济上还是文化上,都面临着许多共同的问题。我们怎样建设一个更加和平而富有人道精神的、有利于人的全面发展的 21 世纪,文学应该起到什么作用,对于生活在这个时代的作家和诗人而言,都是必须严肃对待的问题。我不想把这个时代,简单归结为一个被核原子威胁的时代,但是冷战结束后的形势已经真实地告诉我们,人类并没有因为东西方两大阵营对垒的消失,而从此变得天下太平。

区域性的战争从未停止过,种族和宗教间的,常常以数以千万计的生命和流血代价。我们都曾祈盼中东能降临和平的曙光,但我们最后得到的却是更大的失望。震惊世界的美国 9·11 事件,对国际关系和地缘政治的改变,对新的世界格局的形成,都将产生极为重大的影响。世界多极化和经济全球化产生的新的矛盾,不同的意识形态、宗教和价值观差异,等等,总而言之,我们的地球是失衡的。生态的严重恶化、人口的暴涨、资源的日渐匮乏、人的生存权利在许多地方遭到侵犯,都给生活在今天的有责任心和良知的作家和诗人们提出了要求。我们只有真实地反映出这个时代的精神,把人民的意愿客观地反映在自己的创作生活中,我们才会真正体现出一个作家和诗人应有的人类意识。

虽然和平与发展仍然是今天人类世界的两大主题,但人类的心灵世界和精神生活的巨变,其深刻性和复杂性,是过去任何一个时代都无法比拟的。但同时我还想说的是,可怕的物质主义已把人类变得越来越缺少信仰,人的异化也到了非常严重的程度。人类似乎永远在回答这样的问题。那就是我们从哪里来?还要到哪里去?一句话,作家和诗人,只有关注人类的命运,才能写出真正意义上的具有人类意识的作品。

另外我想讲的是,我们应该为"世界文学"这个大的概念做出自己的贡献。如果我没有记错的话,"世界文学"这个概念,最早是由德国伟大的思想家、作家、诗人歌德提出来的。历史已经证明,人类的文化,当然包括文学,从来就不是在孤立和封闭中发展的。我们不可想象,在中国文学史上如果没有《诗经》、楚辞和唐宋诗词,中国

we have ample reason to be thankful to the republic of all the poets and writers the world has ever produced, of whatever ethnic origin, from whatever region, for the rich veins of poetic works and immortal creations through the means of translation left us, for they truly command the regard of posterity because of their "inheritance not of empty names and sounding actions, but whole treasures of wisdom, bright gems of thought, and golden veins of language".

Now let me get to the core of this topic. First of all, I must reiterate no matter how many thorny issues confront us, politically, economically and culturally, the ultimate question we are faced with is this: can we make the present a century of peace, one that is more humanitarian and exemplary? Much has indeed been achieved, and it is only natural much will continue to be expected from us. And as poets and writers, how can we put our creative work in the service of this grand goal? I don't want to merely say we still in dread of a thermal nuclear holocaust, but what has happened in post-Cold War years has proved that full-fledged optimism was a bit hasty.

The onset of the 21th century has not ushered in one of peace, contrary to what most good-intentioned people desire. Regional hostilities at times flare out, under either the cover of racial feud or the auspice of religious bickering, often with a toll of countless thousands decimated. We used to pray for the dawn of lasting peace in the Middle East, but our lulling faith was repeatedly betrayed. The September 11 attacks ,orchestrated by Bin Laden, turns out to be the single event whose impact extends beyond geopolitics into society and culture in general. Witness a global imbalance deplored with the headlong advance of economic globalization, geopolitical multi-polarization, the resulting dislocations ,disruption of traditional habits of life and social tensions arising from massive rural exodus .Poets and writers feel compelled to raise fundamental questions about the ecosystem under threat, demographic spiraling, increasingly depleted natural resources and subsistence rights belittled in so many a place. We must combine our extensive knowledge of the human condition with our firm convictions, channeling them into a life of commitment and solidarity by creating work identified with the social and moral aspirations of the people.

Peace and development remain two overriding concerns of the 21rst century. Although modernization produces more abundant supply and permits wider distribution of material goods, it has manifestly degraded the human spirit. There is a serious perhaps, undreamed of, problem of alienation or of ennui in the face of a uncertain and unpredictable future to the extent man is forever rendered speechless when challenged with the ultimate key question:"Whence do you come?"True poets or writers cannot fail to reflect on these grim realities while seeking both to entertain and enlighten.

This brings me to the concept of world literature and if my memory serves me right, it should be Von Goethe, one of the greatest German thinkers, poets and writers who initiated it. History has proven time and again, human culture, including literary traditions, has never evolved in a vacuum or isolation. Rather it is often the outcome of constant forces working from outside

文学史还会像今天这样辉煌吗？我们不可想象，在韩国文学史上如果没有诗人李圭报的杰作《东明王篇》，世界文学能像今天这样丰富多彩吗？我们同样不可想象，如果希腊文学史上没有《伊利亚特》和《奥德赛》这样宏大的史诗，它还会得到世界广大读者的长久尊崇吗？回答只有一个，那就是这些伟大作家、诗人和他们的伟大作品，已经不折不扣地成为全人类所共有的文化财富。

特别是在东西方文化的交流史上，老庄的思想，古希腊和古罗马的哲学，佛经、《圣经》以及《古兰经》，等等，都对人类精神思想产生了重大的影响。由此，我们在谈到俄罗斯文学时，不能不谈到伟大的天才诗人普希金；我们在谈到中国文学时，不能不谈到中国新文化的旗手、现实主义的小说巨匠鲁迅；我们在谈到美国文学时，不能不谈到20世纪最杰出的乡土小说家威廉·福克纳；我们在谈到韩国文学时，不能不谈到崔志远那些充满了灵性的诗歌；我们在谈到拉丁美洲文学时，不能不谈到加西亚·马尔克斯；同样，我们在谈到非洲文学时，不能不谈到尼日利亚杰出的黑人作家阿却贝。我想，由于翻译家们的卓越贡献，超越国界的各民族文学，已经越过了文字的局限，成为歌德所倡导的那种真正意义上的"世界文学"。

尊敬的各位朋友，我还要说的是，因为这种超越国界的各民族文学的共同性，再一次肯定了一个事实，这就是作家的责任心和使命感。无可讳言，我们所强调的文学共性，从来就是包含在各民族的文学个性之中。我们只有成为一个民族和时代的见证人，才能真正担当起这个民族和时代精神的诠释者。最后，请允许我借用1992年诺贝尔文学奖获得者、圣卢西亚诗人德瑞克·沃尔科特的一句话来结束我的讲话："要么我谁也不是，要么我就是一个民族。"

and inside on the texture of the civilization. It is common sense that two most well known foreign influences upon Chinese poetry in ancient times were the songs of the South of the state of Chu, which almost altered the shape of the poetry and the five-and-seven-syllable lines introduced from the barbarian tribes in the Han dynasty, two typical verse forms in vogue in the Tang poetry. And we all look to Li Guibao, the distinguished Korean poet, with the same affection. We look up to him as a shining example of poetic wisdom that has greatly contributed to world literature. Then we have the truly brilliant, most revered Homer, of all poets, "an Olympian", from his unattainable height, he casts a glance on our petty worldly affairs with indulgent, but detached approval. Our answer is unanimous: their creative work has formed mankind's splendid civilized past.

Indeed, throughout the history of intellectual endeavors, the cross-fertilization of minds involved almost all the spiritual traditions pivotal to representative civilizations, such as Zhuang Zi's and Lao Zi's Taoism, Greek and Roman philosophies, Buddhist sutras, the Koran as well as the Bible, the veritable source of doctrine, law, poetic inspiration, solace, zeal ,mystic experience. Just as we cannot talk of modern Chinese literature without invoking Lu Xun, master novelist and the drummer of China's new Culture, it makes little sense to leave out the name of Faulkner at the mention of American literature, of Cui Zhiyuan, of Korean poetry, of Marwuez, of Latin American literature, of Achebe, of African writing. Good deeds credited to translators have made world culture a most apparent reality.

Dear and distinguished friends, here is my essential point and let me summarize to the effect: we have two cardinal qualities overriding geographical divisions, ie, awareness of literary responsibility in the poet and the sense of mission that makes him seriously care for the fate of mankind. This is what makes world literature not an empty name. Needless to say, the literary commonality under discussion here, is revealed and illustrated in the specific literary works of individual poets and writers. In these critical times we poets must explore the paradoxes and complexities of our age. We must bear witness to the excellent resilience and the wondrous human power to endure one ghastly episode after another without being spiritually exhausted and nihilistic. To quote a saying by Derek Walcott, Nobel Prize winner in 1992, "Either I am nothing or I am the whole race".

永远的普希金

——献给普希金二百周年诞辰

在纪念普希金二百周年诞辰大会上的演讲

1999年3月9日

我们说普希金是永远的普希金,那是因为如果我们要深入了解俄罗斯,要伸出手去真正抚摸到俄罗斯的灵魂,有一种最好的办法,那就是虔诚地走进亚历山大·谢尔盖耶维奇·普希金的心灵。恐怕在这个世界上,还没有一个诗人和智者,能像普希金那样神圣地、完整地、纯粹地,把一个古老民族的语言和文学,在如此短的时间里推到了极致。每当我们想到俄罗斯文学的黄金时代,我们就不会忘记这位伟大的天才诗人所给予我们的一切。从这个意义上讲,作为诗人的普希金,无论他的肉体是否还存在,他的精神所代表的永远是俄罗斯的灵魂和良心,代表的是俄罗斯伟大的文学传统,代表的是人类的自由、正义与公正。

对于伟大的俄罗斯民族而言,他们可以没有沙皇,没有叶卡捷琳娜二世,但不能没有普希金。是普希金照亮了俄罗斯民族的心灵,是普希金把那些行将逝去的最美好的事物变成了永恒。普希金是属于俄罗斯的,但他同时也属于全人类。虽说普希金离开我们已经很长时间了,但对于今天的世界和人类,他依然那么重要。他的全部精神财富,把爱、怜悯、同情、善良、真诚、忍耐、自由等等都包括在了其中。

我们说普希金是永远的普希金,那是因为当我们回溯俄罗斯诗歌的历史,我们不能不对普希金表示出最崇高的敬意。是他使俄语变得更加朴素和纯洁,使诗歌的界限及其深不可测具有深远的意义。普希金是那样一类诗人,那就是他还在活着的时候,他的不少脍炙人口的诗篇就已经进入了俄罗斯文学经典的行列。普希金的每

The Eternal Alexander Sergeyevich Pushkin
A Speech Dedicated to the 200th Anniversary of Alexander Pushkin
9th, March, 1999

If there be any single word in the wealth of the Chinese language which best characterizes us Chinese poets' admiration of Pushkin, that word is eternal. For the simple reason, 200 years after Pushkin was born, the eternal key to come close to the Russian mind still lies in returning to the collected works bearing the sonorous name: Alexander Sergeyevich Pushkin. Eternally Russian's greatest poet and sage, like Shakespeare with English, Pushkin succeeds in fashioning an integrated Russian style and language within such a brief span of time. The very mention of the Golden Age of Russian literature (in post-Decembrist years) calls attention to the fact that not only writers and poets of Russia owe something to him, but men of letters throughout the world are in his debt. In this sense, we might say his influence is seminal, general, pervasive and eternal. Eternally the most representative poet of Russia, Pushkin has become a synonym for the soul and conscience, unusually outspoken, contemptuous of autocracy, championing freedom, justice and fraternity unflinchingly in the teeth of repeated censorship and exile.

Pushkin has become indispensable for Russian literature and a proof of this fact is that Russian history can be written even absent the chapters on the tsars, and Catherine the Great, but not Pushkin, for the latter, being a bright light, has eternally shone upon the agonized Russian soul and his brilliant poems, like magic, have turned the momentary and ephemeral into the eternal. Pushkin's claim to fame is global in character. A Pushkin in the corporeal sense, whether alive or no more, makes no difference, but the spiritual legacy left to us, his disdain for tyranny, his singing of cardinal human virtues and sentiments such as compassion, honesty, patience as well as his fiery passion for freedom, makes a world of difference to his contemporaries as to us.

While we use epithets like eternal to speak of Pushkin, it is our sole way to register our profound gratitude to the extent of his poetic art. He has refined Russian and pushed the poetic frontier to the utmost limits by tapping all possible resources of the language, sifting them carefully, giving them exactly the right weight and shades of meaning, and then using them with perfect precision. After a very brief apprenticeship, Pushkin has made the then Russian reading

一次创造，都给俄语注入了生命和活力。难怪诗人约瑟夫·布鲁斯基被迫离开苏联时，曾致信给戈尔巴乔夫，说明自己无论身在何处，都不会忘记伟大的俄罗斯语言，因为这个语言曾养育过普希金，也曾被普希金所创造。

由此我们还会想到，俄罗斯文学白银时代的梅列日科夫斯基、索诺维约夫、勃留索夫、勃洛克、阿赫玛托娃、古米廖夫、帕斯捷尔纳克、茨维塔耶娃、别雷、伊万诺夫、霍达谢维奇和曼德尔斯塔姆等人，因为普希金的哺育和滋养，使他们都成了普希金和俄罗斯最纯洁诗歌语言的继承者和把这古老语言发扬光大的后来人。历史已经证明，这些俄罗斯的精英，他们都无愧于普希金，无愧于悠久、古老、厚重而历尽了沧桑的伟大的俄罗斯文学传统。

我们说普希金是永远的普希金，那是因为我们仍然面临着核原子的威胁，面临着世界某些地方还存在着的专制、独裁、不公平以及对弱势群体的杀戮和迫害。在这样严酷的现实面前，普希金对于我们来说就显得尤为可贵。因为就是这位俄罗斯诗人，曾在他的诗中反复歌唱过神圣的自由，他把自由视为生命，甚至超过自己的生命。普希金为了追求自由、平等和友爱，用承受苦难来证明自己那美好的梦想的真实性。普希金式的人道主义精神，无疑是人类社会中极其宝贵的思想财富。很显然，对于大多数读者来说，普希金不仅是一流的俄国诗人，同时也是某种亲密无间的、最为珍贵的东西。

这里，我们不会忘记俄罗斯的苦难，不会忘记俄罗斯历史上所经历过的一个又一个极其令人绝望的时刻。但是往往就在这样的时候，普希金给人们的都是献身自由的信心和勇气，是对美好未来的期盼和希望。正如俄罗斯诗人曼德尔斯塔姆1917年所写的诗句："亚历山大的太阳停在/ 一百年前/ 始终在闪耀……"或许正因为普希金作为一种象征和精神，每当俄罗斯社会和文化面临转折的关头，人们便会到他那里去寻找慰藉和力量。普希金还是一个启示，他告诉我们人是热爱自由的，而维护自由和崇尚自由，将是人类社会一个应该受到普遍尊重的准则。

我们说普希金是永远的普希金，那是因为今天生活的时代，是一个多民族多元文化并存的时代。普希金的巨大存在，还说明了一个最为朴素，但极其深刻的真理，

public aware that a fresh vital force is bursting into the Russian literature at a time when its divorce from real life becomes scandalous. And as this genius arises, Russian is miraculously revitalized to new heights. No wonder when dissident poet Joseph Brodsky was forced to emigrate, he sent a letter to Gorbachev explaining what anguished him most was not the fear of oblivion in USA, but the gloomy prospect of alienating from his mother tongue—Russian, the language that nourished Pushkin and was remade by the same man.

This anecdote brings me to the remembrance of a roaster of literary geniuses associated with the Silver Age: Merezhkovsky, Solovyov, Bryusov, Blok, Akhma- tova, Gumilyov, Pasternak, Tsvetaeva, Andrei Bely, Ivanov, Khodasevich and Mandelstam. These and other lesser artists have survived charmingly because they have carried on and vigorously developed Pushkin's tradition. Their creative work, equally thoughtful, austere and intellectually suggestive, charged with the characteristic grain of sadness over the innocence of the injured and the insulted, serves the sacred duty to tell the truth, stir the sleeping conscience of many, and awaken in the people the feeling of human dignity.

While we speak of an eternal Pushkin, we realize the horror of a nuclear holocaust still hovers over us. In this new global order ushered in by the end of the Cold War, it remains a matter of great concern that the lives of a considerable segment of human beings in the world are still embittered by the fetters of criminal tyrannical governments. Atrocities are still committed against the culturally and economically disadvantaged groups. Such grim and grisly realities underscore the defiant spirit of a bold Pushkin in the wake of the savage crushing of the Decembrist Movement. Forced confinement dampened the bright wit of early years and left in its place spleen. In the darkest hour of Russian history, Pushkin refused to be tamed and keep silent. The pro-freedom rhythms continued to flow from his pen, the heroic grandeur of which equaling that of his mentor Byron at his best. Humanitarianism mattered to him more than anything else and he lavished his poetic wealth in the service of man's aspiring to freedom and justice. This shows Pushkin endears himself mostly not as aesthete or literary dandy. He was, first and foremost, a fearless fighter.

We honor the memory of Pushkin today because both China and Russia share a long history of being brutalized under the duress of tyrants. Dynastic cycles in the Chinese annals match repeated Decembrist periods in magnitude and extent. Such dark hours call forth warrior-poets like Pushkin who stands in relation to the cause of human dignity like Prometheus to ancient Greeks, just as Mandelstam aptly wrote in 1917:

"The Alexander's sun, motionless and still,

Immobilized wherein 100 years ago,

Shines as ever."

Pushkin, indeed, has personified a universal craving for freedom and justice and at each critical juncture, he is one of the few prophets that Russians return to with certainty of solace and

那就是各民族的文化应该相互尊重，取长补短。普希金代表的是俄罗斯的历史和文化，代表的是俄罗斯这块诞生过无数天才的土地。普希金和他的同胞列夫·托尔斯泰、陀思妥耶夫斯基、莱蒙托夫、列宾、叶赛宁、柴可夫斯基等等，都是组成俄罗斯文化链条的缺一不可的重要环节。在世界文化的大格局中，普希金和他所代表的俄罗斯文化，无疑有着举足轻重的地位。

普希金的诗篇，是把民族性和人类性结合得最为完美的典范，他所表达出的俄罗斯人最真实的内心情感，是对人性的最为深刻的揭示和理解。为此我们没有理由不相信，诗人和作家永远是一种精神文化和生命的代言人。其实普希金从诞生之日起，就是一个标准的精神文化和生命的守望者。他的不朽诗篇《茨冈》便充分证明了这一点。是普希金教会了我们要敬畏和热爱这个地球上的一切生命，而生活在这个地球上的每一个民族都是平等的。

我们说普希金是永远的普希金，那是因为普希金已经进入了人类的文明史，已经成为人类记忆中最美好的那个部分。他那无与伦比的美妙诗句，多少年来就曾以不同的方式温暖着人类受伤的心灵，他给今天的人们提供的，不仅是诗所包含的美学价值以及阅读时带来的愉悦，从更深层的意义上讲，普希金就是一部心灵的《圣经》，人类越是向前发展，就越会感到普希金的宝贵和不可替代性。当今的世界是个物化的世界，人类的精神生活似乎正在逐渐走向萎缩。毋庸讳言，今天的人类已经到了在精神和信仰必须给予拯救的时候了。

亚历山大·谢尔盖耶维奇·普希金，我最后想对你说的一句话，那就是你从未离开过我们，我们也从未离开过你。正如你在诗中所写的那样，你的灵魂存在于你的诗歌当中，将比你的骨灰活得更久长，而你也将属于不朽。

zeal. Among other things, Pushkin unravels one more secret of the heart that human beings are prone to freedom by nature and it is incumbent upon any decent government to operate by the rule of the law and upholding freedom for all at whatever cost.

We gather here to pay our eternal tribute to Pushkin in an age of globalization, one that is characterized by co-existence of a diversity of cultures and races. Pushkin's monumental presence speaks volumes of the truthfulness and profoundness of a simple truth: we must learn to be respectful of others, no matter how alien or other he might seem, and cash in on our humility and courtesies. Pushkin is undoubtedly a lionized poet giving Russian literature the present shape and range. The generation that followed, Leo Tolstoy, Dostoyevsky, Lermontov, Ilya Yefimovich Repin, Yesenin and Tchaikovsky, who had grown up in his shadow, all full-fledged devotees of light and sweetness producing works deserving of Pushkin's name, have set the tone and mood of much of the best of Russian literature, known to the rest of the world.

Crystallized specimen of Russianness and universal human qualities, Pushkin's poems have been deemed the best anatomy of the Russian mind and the human heart at one swoop. This has led to an unarguable conclusion: poets and writers are essentially spokesmen of the spirit of a certain race and barometer of a mental life. Pushkin was, in actuality, at the forefront of Russian spirituality. He achieved immortality when he executed his famous ode The Gypsies. It is Pushkin who has taught us to be reverent of all the sentient beings on earth and all the races, irrespective of religion, origin, color of skin, language, stand equal side by side.

We are talking of Pushkin ad infinitum not only because of his lyrical gifts being styled the quintessence of the Russian genius, but also because they have become the common property of mankind due to their intrinsic qualities and seminal influence. His poems, haunting tales agreeably versified, human passion for freedom forcibly expressed, everyday sorrows and joys tenderly ornamented, an eternal balm for the agonized heart, have furnished our minds lasting reading pleasure. In a deep sense, Pushkin's songs are a Bible in the lyrical mode and one marvels at its inexhaustible beauty and truth living in an age given increasingly to commercialism and materialism.

Alexander Pushkin, my dear mentor, you should take comfort in the thought that you have held in your hand a crucial remedy for our age's woes and ills. It is your aesthetic activity on behalf of mankind that earns you our eternal respect. We never see the last of you as you have never departed from the human scene. To paraphrase one of your lyrical lines, since your soul lives in your poems that will outlive your bones, you remain eternal to human memory.

莱奥帕尔迪和他的诗将属于不朽

在纪念意大利诗人莱奥帕尔迪二百周年诞辰研讨会上的讲话

1998年9月19日

今年是意大利杰出的民族诗人莱奥帕尔迪诞生二百周年，我想无论对他的祖国意大利，还是对整个世界而言，莱奥帕尔迪和他的诗，都将是永恒的和不朽的。

我们大家都知道，18世纪末和19世纪初，在这个世界上曾产生过许多伟大的诗人，他们的作品深刻地表达了各自民族的精神世界以及人类的良知。每当回想起那个黄金般的年代，我们常常还会激动不已。因为就在那个两个世纪相交的五十年间，在德国出现了伟大的诗人和思想家约翰沃尔夫冈·歌德、伟大的诗人和思想家弗里德里希·席勒，以及稍后出现的杰出诗人海因里希·海涅；在俄罗斯出现了伟大的诗人亚历山大·谢·普希金；在英国出现了伟大的诗人乔治·拜伦；在法国出现了伟大的诗人和作家维克多·雨果；在波兰出现了伟大的诗人亚当·密茨凯维奇；在美国出现了伟大的诗人亨利·朗费罗和伟大的诗人埃德加·爱伦·坡。当然，同时我们也不会忘记，在那个天才涌现的时代，意大利有一位伟大的民族诗人，他凭借他天才的充满着人性和悲悯的诗篇，同样站在了那个时代诗的精神高地。这个人不是别人，他就是我们所崇敬和景仰的莱奥帕尔迪。

莱奥帕尔迪是丰富的，他的诗具有极大的包容性，无论是对人性深刻的理解，还是对生命和大自然的哲学思考，他所为我们提供的一切，从来就不是单一的。作为意大利伟大的民族诗人，莱奥帕尔迪无疑是优秀的，是当之无愧的。1818年，莱奥帕尔迪写下了两首极为著名的颂诗：《致意大利》和《但丁纪念碑》。诗人在诗中追忆了祖国意大利曾经有过的光荣和梦想，哀悼她现在所遭受的屈辱和不幸。他把意大利比

The Fatal Charm of Giacomo Leopardi as a Poet
A Speech Given at the 200th Anniversary of Giacomo Leopardi
19th, September, 1998

The year of 1998 marks the 200th anniversary of Giacomo Leopardi's birth, the 19th century Italian poet. Molte grazie for the hunchback genius that a dreary provincial town of Italy has ever produced, fated to contribute to the power, prestige and cultural greatness of his native land, the land of culture, art and ideas. We all know the turn of the fin-de-siè cle of the 18th century into the dawn of the 19th century, so full of hope and promise, was a moment teeming with an awesome array of noble-gifted souls and heavyweight reflecting spirits who have been deemed the impersonations of each nation's ideal or average human character magnified. We cannot help but being exulting in the irresistible charm these figures have exerted.

To the student of literature, the western European literary tradition of the first half 19th century looks at first like something of a miracle. In about half a century's time, all of a sudden one great figure after another begins to emerge as if from nowhere, and as if sprung fully grown from the banks of the Danube to the steppes of the Urals. First Johann Wolfgang von Goethe, then Johann Christoph Friedrich von Schiller and Heinrich Heine, all first-rate lyrical poets and thinkers, and after that George Byron and Victor Hugo across the Dover Strait, Adam Mickiewicz in Poland, and in the meanwhile, Henry Longfellow and Edgar Allan Poe in New England, and what an unbroken line of great names! Last but not the least is our Giacomo Leopardi, certainly the culmination of such an awe-inspiring lineage, who has forever charmed us with his songs sung in tender but plaintive tones.

Leopardi is a man of varied talents as lyrist and philosopher, endowed with insights into the riddles of the human heart and Mother Nature. A patriot, he has given inflammatory publicity to the liberating ideals of his countrymen involved in the grim battle to break loose from the yoke of tyranny. In two tour-de-force hymns, i.e. "All'Italia" and "Sopra il monumento di Dante che si preparava in Firenze", he compares Italy to a scarred bewailing woman, deeply tormented with the tragedy of Italy being dominated by hated foes. Filled with anguished cries, Leopardi saw "ruins and mementoes of past glories about him but not the laurel crowns of heroes and the steel

喻成一个遍体鳞伤、掩面哭泣的妇女,对祖国和人民所遭受的灾难和痛苦表示出极大的悲愤,字里行间都洋溢着爱国主义的激情。

特别是在《但丁纪念碑》里,莱奥帕尔迪以伟大爱国者、争取自由的战士但丁的形象激励同代人,要重新追回意大利人在历史上创造过的辉煌和荣耀,并以此作为拯救祖国意大利的精神武器。我想也只有那种深爱着自己祖国和人民的诗人,才会写出这样悲哀和深情的诗句:"她双手戴着镣铐／一头秀发蓬乱,没有面纱／衣着褴褛,失望地坐在地上／双手掩住面孔,嘤嘤啼泣／你有理由悲伤,我的意大利／人生来就是为着胜利／无论是一帆风顺还是身处逆境的时刻／"。单从这个意义上讲,莱奥帕尔迪所完整地表现出的意大利人的民族精神,就足以让我们对他表示崇高的敬意。

也正因为有这些充满着深情的爱国主义的诗篇,莱奥帕尔迪才能称得上伟大,也才能属于永恒和不朽。任何一个诗人,都离不开养育他的土地、人民和祖国。莱奥帕尔迪也一样,他的诗代表着意大利的文化,体现了意大利文艺复兴抒情诗的传统。作为一个伟大的民族诗人,莱奥帕尔迪无疑首先属于他那梦幻般的故乡雷康那蒂,属于诞生过但丁、彼德拉克和米开朗琪罗的意大利,当然,同时也属于这个多元文化并存的世界。

另外,我还想谈及的是,莱奥帕尔迪诗的人道主义精神。众所周知,人道主义精神从来就贯穿在古希腊和意大利的文艺传统中。对人的关怀和对人类命运的关注,是莱奥帕尔迪诗的一个重要主题。他对自身和他人都是怜悯的,他在诗中常常呼吁人类相亲相爱,发扬团结互助的精神。尤其是那首优美动人的抒情诗《致席尔维娅》,表达出了一种刻骨铭心的对生命的珍惜和对美的赞颂。从莱奥帕尔迪身上,再一次向我们证明了这样一个事实,那就是属于人类精神现象的诗是永远也不会消亡的,诗人抚慰的永远是人类不安的灵魂和受伤的心灵。

我们热爱莱奥帕尔迪和他的诗,我想只有一个最简单的原因,那就是我们在朗诵和阅读《致月亮》《节日的傍晚》《亚细亚流浪牧人的夜歌》《暴风雨后的宁静》等诗篇时,被深深地感动过。我想无论是东方的诗人,还是西方的诗人,无论是东方的读

weapons which were to make the country free."

Especially in the hymn in praise of Dante, Leopardi exhorts his people to emulate the great patriot and warrior of freedom and reclaim "past glories" forged by their eminent and worthy ancestors. Leopardi bitterly railed foreign conquerors across the Alps and vehemently wept in the "fatal gift of beauty" which attracted foreigners' appetite. The following lines serve as the battle cry:

> Che lividor, che sangue! oh qual ti veggio,
> Formosissima donna! Io chiedo al cielo
> E al mondo: dite dite;
> Chi la ridusse a tale? E questo è peggio,
> Che di catene ha carche ambe le braccia;
> Sì che sparte le chiome e senza velo
> Siede in terra negletta e sconsolata,
> Nascondendo la faccia
> Tra le ginocchia, e piange.
> Piangi, che ben hai donde, Italia mia,
> Le genti a vincer nata
> E nella fausta sorte e nella ria

Poems imbued with such burning patriotism and optimism of a possible national regeneration have won the poet our sincere grazie and adulation.

Chinese readers, with similar painful memories of centuries of being dominated by foreign enemies, find a combination of wonder and satisfaction in Loepardi's patriotic canti, highly polished and mellifluous, perhaps, along with Dante, he best represents the idea of the Italian hero, dreaming of a "new state" in which peace, law and virtue would prevail, of desiring to avenge his people's ruin and humiliation and of awakening his people to a sense of their new mission. Leopardi is typically a native son of the town of Recanati and Italy in that one easily discerns him quick to sympathize with misery, given to admire virtue and above all, a great lyricist of love well steeped in the Renaissance tradition. No doubt he and his equally illustrious country men, Dante, Petrarch and Michelangelo, come close as to deserving the title of a universal genius as any man who has ever lived.

One buzz word accounts for why Leopardi, a product of his own time, still appeals to us and that word is humanism, which sums up the most common and basic Renaissance intellectual ideals. The normal (not technical sense referring to a program of studies replacing the arid medieval scholastic learning with the revived humanities with practical applications)sense of humanism has at its core a stress on the nobility and possibilities of the human race. Although his central thought is profoundly pessimistic: love, knowledge, and all that man seeks is essentially illusion, he still urges his readers to cultivate the classical virtues of love and sympathy, which,

者,还是西方的读者,我们都不会忘记莱奥帕尔迪的短诗《无限》,这首写于1819年的诗作,至今已被译成27种文字,有近120种翻译文本。法国文艺批评家圣伯夫、奥地利诗人里尔克、俄罗斯诗人阿赫玛托娃、西班牙诗人阿尔维蒂分别将它译成法文、德文、俄文、西班牙文。

几个世纪以来,不知有多少伟大的诗人和哲人在思考着宇宙的无限与永恒,在思考着人类的现实与未来,在思考着时间的存在与虚元。但我们每一次阅读莱奥帕尔迪这首最著名的短诗时,我们的心都会被它所震撼,同样我们的思绪也会像他那样,在那无穷无尽的天宇中沉没,充满着从未有过的幸福和甜蜜。最后请允许我借用我的朋友、我国著名意大利文学翻译家吕同六先生翻译的莱奥帕尔迪的这首伟大诗篇,来结束这个简短的讲话:

  这荒僻的山冈
  对于我总是那么亲切,
  篱笆遮住我的目光
  使我难以望尽遥远的地平线。
  我安坐在山冈
  从篱笆上眺望无限的空间,
  坠落超脱尘世的寂静
  与无比深沉的安宁;
  在这里,我的心不用担心受怕。
  倾听草木间轻风喁喁细诉,
  幽微的风声衬托无限的寂静;
  我于是想起了永恒,
  同那逝去的季节,
  生气盎然的岁月,它的乐音。
  我的思绪就这样
  沉落在这无穷无尽的天宇;

though unable to improve the human lot, can make it bearable. A Silvia is the expression of a profound and tragic love of life itself, which Leopardi, despite all the suffering, the psychological torments and the negative philosophizing, could not suppress in his spirit. This poem demonstrates why Leopardi's so-called "nihilism" does not run deep enough to touch the well-spring of his poetry: his love of man, of nature, and of beauty.

I, for one, keep returning to Leopardi because the more I read him, the more I am awed by the vigor of his soaring imagination, the subtle complexity of his emotions. A La Luna,Silvia Tramonto della Luna , Canto notturno di un pastore errante dell'Asia . La quiete dopo la tempesta are some of my favorites aside my pillow. Above all, one of his loveliest of lyrics L'infinito, written in 1819, even when assuming the exotic garment and distant music, still breathes a freshness with increasing years and has now survived the usual violence incurred in the process of translation, demonstrating inexplicable translatability in 27 languages and 120 versions all told. This pure "thing of beauty" compelled the attention of writers and poets of statue, Saint Beuve, Rilke , Akhmatova and Alverti and their transmutations into leading world languages, ie, French, German, Russian and Spain, are testimony to the miraculous timelessness achieved by Leopardi.

Fascinated by what lies beyond the boundaries of the human experience, men and women have throughout history irresistibly been drawn to ponder the riddle of time and the infinite, being and nothingness. Each time I take the Selected Poems of Leopardi from the shelf, I feel both humbled and enlightened, exulting in the reverie of an evanescent lurking surreality, packed away behind the nebulosity of the light and sweetness of the human mind, the meaning of which even eludes the reflecting spirits of the highest order. To conclude, I take liberty in citing the translation of Mr Lü Tongliu, top translator of Italian literature, and my good friend:

L' Infinite
Sempre caro mi fu quest'ermo colle,
e questa siepe, che da tanta parte
dell'ultimo orizzonte il guardo esclude.
Ma sedendo e mirando, interminati
spazi di là da quella, e sovrumani
silenzi, e profondissima quete
io nel pensier mi fingo, ove per poco
il cor non si spaura. E come il vento
odo stormir tra queste piante, io quello
infinito silenzio a questa voce
vo comparando: e mi sovvien l'eterno,
e le morte stagioni, e la presente
e viva, e il suon di lei. Così tra questa

在这无限的海洋中沉没

该是多么甜蜜。

immensità s'annega il pensier mio:
e il naufragar m'è dolce in questo mare.

我的诗歌，来自我所熟悉的那个文化

在全国青年文学创作会议上的发言

1986年12月10日

　　我从我生活的故土——遥远的大凉山来到北京参加这样的盛会，心情是非常激动的。然而我坐在这里，却又害着一种相思之苦。特别是在此时此刻，我想问候大凉山每一条孤独的河流、每一块沉默的岩石，我想问候大凉山每一片寂静的森林、每一棵仁慈的树林。我祝福我的亲人们，以及那些山羊，因为在那个地方，现在同样还是寒冷的冬天。

　　我问候那一片彝语叫古洪木底的土地，不言而喻它是我文学的根。能跻身在这里，同各民族的青年作家一起聚会，我感到非常高兴。这充分说明了我们社会主义多民族的文学正在蓬勃发展，我们文学的未来充满了希望。我们生活在这个世界上，我们渴望的是人类的友爱。彝人的祭师毕摩想为我们寻找另一个世界，其实那永远是一个令人望而生畏的谜。我们在探索生命的意义，我们在渴望同自然有一种真正的交流，这种神圣的交流当然是来自心灵而不是来自表面。

　　多少年来，我们一直想同自己古老的历史对话，可是我们常常成了哑巴。

　　我写诗，是为了表达自己真实的感情和心灵的感受。在那绵延的大山里，无论是在清晨，还是在黄昏，都会有一种神秘的力量在感召着每一个人。我想通过我的诗，揭示人和自己生存环境的那种依恋关系，而不是一种什么固有的敌对。我写诗，就希望它具有彝人的感情和色彩。一个民族的诗人，如果没有进入他的民族感情世界的

My Poetic Inspiration Rooted in the Daliangshan ,My Quantock Hills
Hints for Up-and-coming Ethnic Writers and Poets
10th,December,1986

My presence here today amongst you is both a cause for pride and nostalgia. My thoughts are instantly drawn to each sluggish streamlet and each recalcitrant rock of the rugged Daliangshan Highlands where my ancestral tribe sits. Please join me in greeting my physical and spiritual home district-the Daliangshan , ie, my Quantock Hills. I love each silent grove, each merciful tree, my tribal Nuosu women sitting in small groups in front of their houses, weaving strips of cloth on waist looms, those little imps frolicking and milling about, and goats contently feeding themselves on the grassy hills. This moment it is bitterly cold, the now and there, in this winter season.

This sudden descent into remembrance points to my mental connection to a land called Guhongmudi in the Yi language, my source of poetic inspiration. My joyous presence here amongst a new breed of writers and poets of indigenous origin gives the heart reason to flutter for the promising outbursts of literary glory in China. No matter who we are, we crave the life of the spirit and in our questing for brotherhood, our tribal shaman figures, the Bimos seek a supernatural realm, murky and oblique for us ,an act of cracking the No 1 awesome human riddle "Why am I here?" Such riddle embodies our inner longing for a genuine communion with Mother Nature.

For reasons not hard to guess, our attempt more often than not lands us in a state of speechlessness.

I turn to poetry as a remedy to cure my speechlessness. It is noteworthy that all strong emotions, when expressed naturally, tend to lend themselves to poetry. As a tribal boy living far away from city lights, I have somewhat innate faculty of exploring my emotions with vividness and simplicity so that they will not only satisfy my inner desires but also appeal to others'. Incidentally I want to impart this message to people that my terrestrial connection is global in character, one of loyalty and attachment ,not one of hostility. My poems are as near as I come to appreciate Mother Nature for its own sake. Since they signify first and foremost, the special emotions and feelings of

中心，他永远不会成为一个真正的诗人。我生活在大凉山，作为一个诗人，应该说我天生就有一种使命感，可是我从来没有为这一点而感到过不幸。对人类的理解不是一句空洞无物的话，它需要我们去拥抱和爱。人类性和普遍性不是抽象的，对人的命运的关注，哪怕是对一个小小的部落作深刻的理解，也是会具有人类性的。对此，我深信无疑。

在这里，我不想引用彝人的《宇宙人文论》来说明我们民族文化的古老和悠久。但是一提到彝人的"十月太阳历"，我就会马上联想到美洲的印第安人，因为在历史上他们都曾创造过灿烂的文化。人类居住在这个不断发生着变化的大地上，人类面对万物和自身，时时刻刻都在寻找其本质和规律。每个民族都有自己的文化，民族的作家有权利和责任，在自己的文学中体现出鲜明的民族文化特性。纵观今天的世界文学，成功者的经验告诉我们，放弃自己的文化，摆脱自己的根基，将只会一事无成。

我们生活在大山里，我们的传统正在消失。当然其中有的是完全应该消失的，有的却还应该保存下来，它体现了一个民族的美德。在现代文明同古老传统的矛盾中，我们灵魂中的阵痛是任何一个所谓文明人永远无法体会得到的。我们的父辈们也常常隐入一种从未有过的迷惘。是的，这种冲突永远持续下去，虽然我们因此也感到忧虑和悲哀，但是我们知道这是人类在发展中必须经历的。现在我们需要把这种冲突真实地表现在自己的文学中。

作为一个民族的文学工作者，在很多时候都在经历着痛苦的选择，这种选择说穿了，就是在寻找自己的位置。没有一个恰当的位置，在艺术上不会有鲜明的个性，同时也不能体察和把握好本民族的特质。

各民族文化的背景和走向，存在着各自的特点，各民族都具有自己独特的审美意识、心理结构和思维定式。我们只有运用自己所特有的感知世界的方式和角度，才

my Yi compatriots ,I have become the poet of the Yi nationality. At this point, I must confess that back in my boyhood years I did discover a sense of mission awakened in me that I must compose and speak for my Nuosuo folks. Unabashedly I will acknowledge to this vanity in the belief a poet's attachment to his native village necessarily suggests the poetic possibilities that might otherwise pass unnoticed under feet.

In this connection, I feel tempted to cite our Yi Classic Mankind on the Globe to prove the antiquity of our Yi origin. But, nevertheless, the availability of canonical works together with other cultural artifacts such as "ten-month solar calendaric system" ,the Mesoamerican replica for the ancient Yi, are the very achievements by which olden civilizations are distinguished. They are testament to our ancestors', not confined to our Yi forefathers' courage and determination to respond to the opportunities presented by the surroundings, explore the mystery of life and adapt to the environment they were thrown in over the millennia .A plethora of traditional societies have evolved their own type of culture and it behooves us, writers and poets of each ethnic group, to stand up as spokesmen of our own people. Poets who renounce their roots, as experience shows, have seldom gone far, in literature if not in society.

We are mountain people bewailing the eroding of our traditions inexorably. Certain portions of them, of course, must go but certain portions should stay intact. Even in this cyber world, it is in the best interests of mankind that modern and ancient blend. Admittedly facing the increasing encroachment of modernization, the impact of progress mainly falls on the aborigines, those people who until recently placidly remained within their own boarders, usually in the periphery of the mainstream civilizations, are suddenly thrust into the vortex of frenzied GDP mania. Such intense changes, as registered throughout China, within such brief intervals of time, is bound to occasion drastic psychological dislocation. This is not grief of personal nature. Rather, it is the necessary rite of passage we have to undergo before reaching adulthood in an age of globalization. It reflects universal fear sustained by all people, one deserving refined aesthetic expression .

Poets and writers of ethnic origin, we are ,at times thrown upon our own resources, bearing the brunt of the anguish and travail of our race. We are pushed to the forefront of wrestling with" the problems of the heart in conflict with itself." which alone can make good writing. It goes without saying that subject matters other than these will lead us nowhere.

Setting themselves off from the rest of the metropolitan and mercantile societies, the diverse ethnic cultures scattered throughout China, and indeed, the world, share in a number of features ranging from modes of production to patterns of evolution. Naturally they also follow a number of customs, mental processes and aesthetic perceptions quite dissimilar in degree, if not in kind. This curious, even catholic conception of culture is necessarily a matter of creed and even the very essence of literature. Only by an Intense familiarity with our own cultures and by taking root firmly in the soil of our native villages can we produce songs of nature and of emotions of lasting value. We should follow no man's lead and obey no voice but that which we hear in our souls, with

能建立一个属于我们的文学世界。我们只有熟悉本民族的生活,扎根在自己的土地上,才能真正把握到本民族的精神实质。同时,我们还要强化自我民族意识,用全方位的眼光去观照我们的现实生活。任何文学,都属于它的时代;而任何时代的文学,无不打上时代的烙印。新的生活,给我们提出了新的问题,它需要我们去思考和回答。

对传统文化应该继承,可是对传统文化全盘地端来,只会阻碍我们的发展和提高,使我们无法完成自我审美个性的再造。横向的借鉴与比较,特别是和具有心理同构(相对而言)的地域文化(文学)的比较,今天对于我们来说还是非常重要的。彝人文化的本质在彝人的史诗和许多民间抒情长诗中已经表现得很清楚,它的忧郁色彩是一个内向深沉民族的灵魂显像。这个民族的痛苦在心灵的最深处,他从很早的时候就相信,万物都有灵魂,人死了安息在土地和天空之间。

我从未想到过我的创作今后会怎样,我也从未想到过今天我会到这里来发言。我是大凉山古候部落吉狄支的后代。根据我们的送魂路线和历史记载,我们的祖先生活在这块土地上,已经有很长的时间了。中华人民共和国成立前我们那里还处于全封闭的奴隶社会。整个大小凉山生活着一百多万彝人。我诗歌的源泉来自那里的每一间瓦板屋,来自彝人自古以来代代相传的口头文学,来自那里的每一支充满忧郁的歌谣。我的诗歌所创造的那个世界,来自我熟悉的那个文化。无论是在形式,还是在诗的内在节奏上,它都给了我许多不可缺少的东西。

我的第一首诗发表在《星星》诗刊上,当时我是西南民族学院中文系的学生,这对于我后来进行诗歌创作是非常关键的。我对这个刊物至今怀有深厚的感情。我的第一本诗集是四川民族出版社出版的。在这里我向那些在我的成长道路上,关心过我和鼓励过我的前辈和朋友,表示深深的敬意。

a sharp eye on the daily life thronging with new problems that cry for both a remedy and an answer.

Of all the key words for prospective ethnic writers, tradition is beyond dispute a double edge sword. Indeed, one of the greatest keys to success lies in a proper and balanced approach to it. Wholesale inheritance is absolutely out of the question as it will mar rather than assist in the growth of our poetic impulse, but I believe we must learn, among other things, from the creative models, of ethnic origin in particular, that illustrate similar psychological traits and mental processes. For example, the Yi mind has been traditionally endowed with an inherent pathos that has colored almost all the previous writings, the Yi epics and longer poems. One can hardly read a page of our traditional bards without finding this "natural juxtaposition of smiles and tears".Our ancestors had visions of the deities" majestic but luminous" and trusted them implicitly. To them, nature was a huge spiritual symbolism ,wherein they saw elves, fairies, devils, demons, all looking at them in friendship or in enmity through the eyes of flowers and stars and trees and rocks. All the sentient beings had souls like us and they buried the dead between the sky and the earth.

It has never occurred to me where my poems will lead me since embarking upon a poet's career. Certainly it has never dawned upon me one day I will step upon the platform to speak to you. A descendant of the Jidi branch of the Guhou Tribe on the Daliangshan Highlands, I have studied written records left and retraced the time -honored soul-farewells route (exemplified in a funeral procession). I have learned the Yi had been farmers for thousands of years preceding the establishment of PRC. And In pre-PRC times, serfdom prevailed in the rather isolated Yi societies wherein the Yi population amounted to one million. An economic backwater, the Daliangshan featured an economy based upon slash and burn agronomy, far from being self-sufficient from the most remote antiquity. Most of my Yi tribe men were the excellent type of the Yi farmers, poor, honest, deity-fearing, who toiled from dawn till dark to wrest a living for their families from the stubborn land. I used to live among my rustic compeers and their careworn and hunted look furnished the initial flicker of my poetic inspiration .And from the oral traditions handed down by word of mouth, and from the plaintive songs of traditional Yi bards learned and memorized, I started to chant the melodies that fired my young heart to enthusiasm. An acknowledgment is due to the traditional Yi ways which have taught me much both in terms of prosodic forms and in inner cadence.

When 21 years of age, a student majoring in Chinese in Southwest Minority Nationalities College, I attracted literary attention by getting my first poem published in a literary journal Stars. This unexpected triumph meant much as it almost instantly catapulted me into the orbit of a lifelong literary passion for which I am deeply in debt today to the editors of Stars. My fondness for poems bore further fruit in seeing my first book to light by Sichuan Minority Nationality Press. Indeed, along the rough roads of my poetic sprouting, I have had a sizable roaster of cheerleaders, ie, veteran poets, pen friends, poet colleagues, critics to thank, for their kindness and thousands of

我是大凉山的儿子,我深深地爱着我的民族。文学这条道路,对于我来说,还十分漫长,还十分艰难,但是请相信,我会执着地写下去。谢谢!

petty courtesies which make my journeying more endurable and enjoyable.

I am a native son of the Daliangshan Highlands, my spiritual Quntock to which I keep returning in dreams. My keen attachment to the ancestral ceremonial center has been my primary poetic theme. Whatever station of life I might find myself, whatever may lie ahead of my literary adventure, I will trudge on with my literary pursuit until the day approaches .

总有人因为诗歌而幸福

在剑桥大学国王学院徐志摩诗歌节"银柳叶诗歌终身成就奖"颁奖仪式上的致答辞

2017年7月29日

各位女士、先生们，朋友们：

感谢你们把本届诗歌节"银柳叶诗歌终身成就奖"颁发给我，我以为这是你们对我所属的那个山地民族诗歌传统的一种肯定，因为这个民族所有的表达方式都与诗歌有着密切的关系。诗歌作为一种最古老的艺术，在过去很长一段时间里，我们的先辈几乎都是用它来书写自己的历史和哲学。这种现象虽然在世界许多民族中并不少见，但在我们民族所保存遗留下来的大多数文字经典中，其最主要的书写方式就是诗歌，甚至我们的口头文学大多也是以诗歌的形式被世代传诵的。哪怕在我们的日常生活中，诗歌中通常使用的比兴和象征也随处可见。特别是在我们的聚会、丧葬、婚礼以及各类祭祀活动中，用诗歌的形式所表达的不同内容，在本质上都蕴含着诗性的光辉。可以说，我们彝族人对诗歌的尊崇和热爱是与生俱来的，在我们古老的谚语中把诗歌朴素地称为"语言中的盐巴"，由此可见，数千年来诗歌在我们的精神世界和现实生活中扮演了何等重要的角色。我以为，我们民族数千年来从未改变，并坚持至今的就是对英雄祖先的崇拜以及对语言所构筑的诗歌圣殿的敬畏。特别是在当下这个物质主义的时代，如何让诗歌在我们的精神生活中发挥它应有的作用，我想这对于每一个诗人而言都不仅仅是一种写作的需要，而必须站在道德和正义的高度，去勇敢地承担起一个有良知的诗人所应当承担的责任和使命。其实在我们民族伟大的诗歌经典中，这一传统就从未有过中断。

朋友们，我们民族繁衍生活的地方，就在中国西南部广袤绵延的群山之中，我的

Some Are Numbered among the Blessed, Because of Poetry

Acceptance Speech for "Silver Willow Lifetime Achievement Award" at Xu Zhimo Poetry Festival, King's College Cambridge
29th, July, 2017

Ladies, gentlemen and friends:

Thank you for giving me this year's "Silver Willow Lifetime Achievement Award." For me this affirms the poetic tradition of the mountain people I belong to, because our means of expression has always been tightly linked to poetry. As one of the most ancient arts, poetry has long been the medium used by my forebears to inscribe their history and philosophy. This phenomenon is observable in other peoples, but almost all the classics preserved by my ethnic group were written in poetic lines, and this holds true of our oral literature passed down through generations as well. Even in our daily lives, one regularly encounters the kind of resonant images and symbols used in poetry, especially at social gatherings, funerals, weddings and various ritual offerings. Many messages are conveyed in verse: in essence they are all illuminated by poetic feeling. One could say that Yi people are born with reverence and fondness for poetry. In the plainspoken words of an ancient proverb, we say that poetry is "the salt of language." From this you can see what an important role poetry has played in our spiritual world and in the reality of our lives. In my view, my people have unbendingly adhered to two things over thousands of years: our worship of heroic ancestors and our awe of a sacred realm constituted by poetic language. As for how poetry is to exert its rightful effect in our spiritual lives, especially during the current materialistic era, I think this needs to be addressed by each poet not just in terms of writing, but also from an elevated standpoint of morality and justice, as a mission and responsibility to be undertaken boldly by every poet of conscience. In fact, in the great poetic classics of my people, this kind of tradition has never been interrupted.

My friends, the place where my people live and thrive is a far-stretching expanse of mountains in southwest China. In the Yi language of my region we call it "Nipmu Liangshan," which is the largest concentrated dwelling place of the Yi people. In terms of spirit and culture, one could also say it is also the sacred ground of my people. Today we can still find the holy mountains, pastures, gorges and rivers that are praised in epics. Using legends as a guide, we can

故乡彝语名称为"尼木凉山",它是中国最大的彝族聚居区,也可以说是我们民族精神和文化的圣地,今天在那里我们还能随处找到史诗中赞颂过的神山、牧场、峡谷以及河流,还能根据真实的传说去寻找到我们的祖先在这片土地上留下的英雄业绩。这片20世纪中叶以前还与外界缺少来往的神秘地域,毋庸置疑,它已经成为了我们每一个彝族诗人终其一生都会为之书写的精神故土。在这片土地上有一条奔腾不息的大河,在彝语中被称为"阿合诺依",它的意思是黑色幽深的河流,在汉语里它的名字叫金沙江。这条伟大的河流,它蜿蜒流淌在高山峡谷之间,就像我们民族英勇不屈的灵魂,它发出的经久不息的声音,其实就是这片土地上所有生命凝聚而成的合唱。朋友们,我的诗歌只不过是这一动人的合唱中一个小小的音符,我作为一个诗人,也只是这个合唱团中一个真挚的歌手。谢谢大家!

still find sites where our ancestors did heroic deeds. That little-known realm, lacking contact with the outside world until the mid-20th century, is none-other than the spiritual homeland written about in poems by each Yi poet. Across that land races a great, restless river which we call "Axhuo Nuoyy" in the Yi language, meaning a black, deep-set river. In the Chinese language we call it Jinsha River. In its winding course through deep gorges, amid high mountains, that great river resembles the indomitable soul of my people. The lasting, unceasing sound it makes is actually a chorus compounded from all living things on that stretch of ground. My friends, as for my own poems, they are only a small note within that chorus. As a poet, I am only an earnest singer within that choir.

    Thank you, everyone!

Translated by Denis Mair (USA)

个人身份·群体声音·人类意识
在剑桥大学国王学院徐志摩诗歌艺术节论坛上的演讲
2017 年 7 月 29 日

十分高兴能来到这里与诸位交流，这对于我来说是一件十分荣幸的事。虽然当下这个世界被称为全球化的世界，网络基本上覆盖了整个地球，资本的流动也到了几乎每一个国家，就是今天看来十分偏僻的地方，也很难不受到外界最直接的影响，尽管这样我们就能简单地下一个结论，认为人类之间的沟通和交流就比历史上的其他时候都更好吗？很显然，在这里我说的是一种更为整体的和谐与境况，而沟通和交流的实质是要让不同种族、不同宗教、不同阶层、不同价值观的群体以及个人，能通过某种方式来解决共同面临的问题，但目前的情况与我们的愿望和期待形成了令人不安的差距。进入 21 世纪后的人类社会，科技和技术革命取得了一个又一个重大的胜利，但与此同时出现的就是极端宗教势力的形成，以及在全世界许多地方都能看见的民族主义的盛行，各种带有很强排他性的狭隘思想和主张被传播，恐怖事件发生的频率也越来越高。就是英国这样一个倡导尊重不同信仰的多元文化国家，也不能幸免地遭到恐怖袭击，2017 年以来已经发生了四起袭击，虽然这一年还没有过去，但已经是遭到恐怖袭击最多的一年。正因为这些新情况的出现，我才认为必须就人类不同种族、不同宗教、不同阶层、不同价值观群体的对话与磋商建立更为有效的渠道和机制，毫无疑问，这是一项艰巨而十分棘手的工作，这不仅仅是政治家们的任务，它同样也是当下人类社会任何一个有良知和有责任感的人应该去做的。是的，你们一定会问，我们作为诗人在今天的现实面前应当发挥什么作用呢？这也正是我想告诉诸位的。很长一段时间有人怀疑过诗歌这一人类最古老的艺术形式，是否还能

Personal Identity·Group Voice·Human Awareness

Speech given at the Xu Zhimo Poetry and Art Festival, Cambridge University

29th, July, 2018

I feel honored to gather here for an exchange of ideas with all of you. We are told that our current world is a globalized world, that Internet coverage basically extends over the whole planet, and that the flow of capital crosses boundaries of almost every nation. Even in apparently remote places, it is hard to escape direct influence from the outside world. Even so, can we conclude from this that human communication and exchange are better now than in any past era? Clearly we are talking here about something that facilitates overall harmony. In substance, communication and exchange are supposedlymeans to solve problems faced in common by people of different religions, different classes, and different value systems. Yet the present situation is unsettling because it falls so far short of our wishes and expectations. As the twenty-first century unfolds, the technological revolution has proceeded from victory to victory, but for humanity this has been accompanied by the emergence of extremist religious forces and a resurgence of nationalism in many areas of the globe. We have seen the dissemination of narrow-minded, exclusionist views and positions, and terrorist incidents are happening with increasing frequency. Even a country like England that upholds respect for different beliefs has not managed to elude terrorist attacks. Four attacks have happened already in 2017: the year is not over, but this is already the highest number of attacks in one year. Precisely because of such developments, I think there is a need to establish more effective channels and mechanisms for dialogue and consultation between different races, different classes and different value systems. This is doubtless an arduous and thorny job. This is not just a task for politicians; it is something that any person of conscience should take upon himself or herself. You may ask what function we as poets can fulfill in the face of current reality. This is what I want to talk with you all about.

For quite some time some people have been questioning whether poetry——this most ancient of arts——can go on existing. Well, facts have demonstrated that such doubts are completely superfluous. Why? Because those who raise such questions are thinking in terms of technology and logic. They believe that all old things will inevitably be replaced by new things.

存在并延续下去，事实已经证明这种怀疑完全是多余的，因为持这种观点的人大都是技术逻辑的思维，他们只相信凡是新的东西就必然替代老的东西，而从根本上忽视了人类心灵世界对那些具有恒久性质并能带来精神需求的艺术的依赖，不容置疑诗歌就在其中。无须讳言，今天的资本世界和技术逻辑对人类精神空间的占领可以说无孔不入，诗歌很多时候处于社会生活的边缘地带，可是任何事物的发展总有其两面性，所谓物极必反讲的就是这个道理。令人欣慰的是，正当人类在许多方面出现对抗，或者说出现潜在对抗的时候，诗歌却奇迹般地成为人类精神和心灵间进行沟通的最隐秘的方式，诗歌不负无数美好善良心灵的期望，跨越不同的语言和国度进入了另一个本不属于自己的空间，在那个空间里无论是东方的诗人还是西方的诗人，无论是犹太教诗人还是穆斯林诗人，总能在诗歌所构建的人类精神和理想的世界中找到知音和共鸣。

　　创办于2007年的中国青海湖国际诗歌节，在近十年的过程中给我们提供了许多弥足珍贵的经验和启示，有近千名的各国诗人到过那里，大家就许多共同关心的话题展开了自由的讨论。在那样一种祥和真诚的氛围中，我们深切体会到了诗歌本身所具有的强大力量。特别是我有幸应邀出席过哥伦比亚麦德林国际诗歌节，我在那里看到了诗歌在公众生活和严重对立的社会中所起到的重要作用。在长达半个多世纪的哥伦比亚内战中，有几十万人死于战火，无数的村镇生灵涂炭，只有诗歌寸步也没有离弃过他们。如果你看见数千人不畏惧暴力和恐怖，在广场上静静地聆听诗人们的朗诵，尤其是当你知道他们中的一些人，徒步几十里来到这里就是因为热爱诗歌，难道作为一个诗人，在这样的时刻，你不会为诗歌依然在为人类迈向明天提供信心和勇气而自豪吗？回答当然是肯定的。诸位，我这样说绝没有试图去拔高诗歌的作用，从世俗和功利的角度来看，诗歌的作用更是极为有限的，它不能直接解决人类面临的饥饿和物质匮乏，比如肯尼亚现在就面临着这样的问题，同样它也不能立竿见影让交战的双方停止战争，今天叙利亚悲惨的境地就是一个例证。但是无论我们怎样看待诗歌，它并不是在今天才成为我们生命中不可分割的部分，它已经伴随我们走过了人类有精神创造以来全部的历史。

　　诗歌虽然具有其自身的特点和属性，但写作者不可能离开滋养他的文化对他的

They fundamentally ignore the reliance of human inner life on art that possesses enduring qualities and meet a spiritual need. Poetry is unquestionably one such art form. There is no denying that, in today's world, human spiritual space is pervasively occupied by capital and technical logic. There are many times when poetry is situated at the margins of social life. Yet there are two sides to the development of any entity, which is the basis for the saying——"extreme things tend to swing the other way." I take solace in one thing: when many aspects of human affairs stand in overt or latent opposition, poetry miraculously becomes a hidden means for bridging the inner worlds and spiritual realities of human beings. Poetry does not let down the collective hopes of kind-hearted, beauty-loving people. Spanning different languages and nationalities, it takes one into a space that was not originally one's own. Within that space, it makes no difference whether you are Oriental or Western, Muslim or Jewish: you can still find a receptive heart that resonates with yours in mankind's realm of spiritual ideals.

The Qinghai Lake International Poetry Festival, founded in 2007, has provided precious experience and insights over the ten-year course of its operation. Nearly 1000 poets from various countries have made the journey there, where they engaged in free discussion on topics of mutual concern. In that ambience of felicity and earnestness, we could deeply sense the inherent power in poetry. What is more, it was my good fortune to be invited to attend the Medellin Poetry Festival in Columbia. There I saw the important effect of poetry on public life in a strife-torn society. Hundreds of thousands of people have died violent deaths in Columbia's civil conflicts lasting over half a century, and thousands of villages have been reduced to rubble. Only poetry has stood up for the sufferers and never spurned them. So thousands of people braved the risk of violence and terror to listen raptly to readings by poets in Medellin; many of them had walked dozens of kilometers to reach that Square. If you had seen how they made their way there, out of enthusiasm for poetry, wouldn't you as a poet be proud that our art still helps to provide faith and courage for human beings as they stride toward tomorrow? The answer will surely be affirmative. My friends, in saying this I am not trying artificially to elevate the effects of poetry. From a mundane, utilitarian angle, the effects of poetry are inherently limited. It cannot directly solve the hunger and material shortages that humans face. Right now, for instance, Kenya is facing such problems. Likewise, poetry does not automatically take effect to defuse the kind of civil war that Syria is mired in. Yet however we figure things, poetry became an integral part of our inner being long before yesterday. It has kept company with humans for as long as we have been producing creations of the spirit.

Although poetry has its own qualities and attributes, one who writes it cannot separate himself from the culture that nurtured him, especially against a backdrop of globalism as its trend toward uniformity becomes overwhelming. In all honesty, we must admit that the ingredients of poetry are by no means uniform: this is all the more true on a metaphysical, philosophical level, where poetry's ultimate telos and creative resources of language offer limitless possibilities. Thus

影响,特别是在这样一个全球化的背景下,同质化成为一种不可抗拒的趋势,诚然诗歌本身所包含的因素并不单一,甚至在形而上的哲学层面上,诗歌更被看重的还应该是它最终抵达的核心以及语言创造给我们所提供的无限可能,因此诗歌的价值就在于它所达到的精神高度,就在于它在象征和隐喻的背后传递给我们的最为神秘的气息,真正的诗歌要在内容和修辞等诸方面都成为无懈可击的典范。撇开这些前提和要素,诗人的文化身份以及对身份本身的认同,就许多诗人而言,似乎已经成了外部世界对他们的认证,因为没有一个诗人是抽象意义上的诗人,哪怕保罗·策兰那样的诗人,尽管他的一生都主要是用德语写作,但他在精神归属上还是把自己划入了犹太文化传统的范畴。当然任何一个卓越诗人的在场写作,都不可能将这一切图解成概念进入诗中。作为一个有着古老文化传统的彝族的诗人,从我开始认识这个世界,我的民族独特的生活方式以及精神文化就无处不在地深刻影响着我。彝族不仅在中国是极古老的民族之一,就是放在世界民族之林中,可以肯定也是一个极为古老的民族,我们有明确记载的两千多年的文字史,彝文的稳定性同样在世界文字史上令人瞩目,直到今天这一古老的文字还在被传承使用。我们的先人曾创造过光辉灿烂的历法"十月太阳历",对火和太阳神的崇拜,让我们这个生活在中国西南部群山之中的民族,除了具有火一般的热情之外,其内心的深沉也如同山中静默的岩石。我们还是这个人类大家庭中保留创世史诗极多的民族之一,《勒俄特依》《阿细的先基》《梅葛》《查姆》等等,抒情长诗《我的幺表妹》《呷玛阿妞》等等,可以说就是放在世界诗歌史上也堪称艺术经典,浩如烟海的民间诗歌,将我们每一个族人都养育成了与生俱来的说唱人。毫无疑问,一个诗人能承接如此丰厚的思想和艺术遗产,其幸运是可想而知的。彝族是一个相信万物有灵的民族,对祖先和英雄的崇拜,让知道他的历史和原有社会结构的人能不由自主地联想到荷马时代的古希腊,或者说斯巴达克时代的生活情形,近一二百年彝族社会的特殊形态,一直奇迹般地保存着希腊贵族社会的遗风,这一情形直到20世纪50年代才发生了改变。诗人的写作是否背靠着一种强大的文化传统,在他的背后是否耸立着一种更为广阔的精神背景,我以为对他的写作将起到至关重要的作用,正因为此,所有真正从事写作的人都明白一个道理:诗人不是普通的匠人,他们所继承的并不是一般意义上的技艺,而是一种只有从

the value of poetry lies in the spiritual height it attains, and in the breath of mystery imparted by its symbols and metaphors. Genuine poetry can serve as a model in terms of both content and rhetoric. Putting aside such assumptions and inherent qualities, seeing the cultural identity of "poet" affirmed seems to offer confirmation from the outside world to many poets. That is, there is no such thing as a poet in an abstract sense. Even for a poet like Paul Celan, despite his lifetime of writing in German, his sense of spiritual allegiance belonged to paradigms of the Jewish cultural tradition. Of course no outstanding poet, when actually sitting down to write, would diagrammatically reduce all this to concepts to be included in his poems. As a poet of the Yi people, which possesses an ancient cultural tradition, I was pervasively and deeply influenced by our unique way of life and our spiritual culture, right from the time I was aware of the world. Not only are the Yi people one of China's most ancient minorities, we hold a place in the grove of the world's most ancient peoples. We have records in writing that clearly date back 2000 years. The stability of the Yi writing system is noteworthy even in the context of the world's writing systems, and our ancient writing system is still being used and handed down today. Our forebears created the illustrious "Ten Month Calendar." Worship of fire and sun have instilled fiery passions in my people, but aside from that our mountainous dwelling place has given us gravitas like a silent boulder on a slope. Within the extended family of humankind, we are one of the few ethnicities that has preserved an impressive number of creation epics: Hnewo teyy, Asei-po seiji, Meige, Chamu. We also have long lyrical poems like My Youngest Cousin and GamoAnyo: when placed in the history of world poetry, they deserve to be called classics. An ocean of folk poems has instilled the knack for verse storytelling in minds of all my compatriots. Without a doubt, it is a blessing for a poet to inherit such a rich intellectual, artistic heritage. The Yi people embrace pantheistic beliefs and worship ancestral heroes, causing those who know the history and previous social structure of the Yi to associate them withancient Greeks of the Homeric era, or perhaps with ways of life in Sparta. Our Nuosu society of the past two centuries miraculously preserved features that harken back tothe ancient Greek aristocracy: this phase persisted right down to the 1950s. I think that the question of whether there is a powerful cultural tradition behind one's writing has essential importance: that is, is there an intangible background of great breadth looming behind a poet? For this reason, those who are genuinely engaged in writing poetry all understand one truth, namely that we are not ordinary artisans, and what we inherit is not a craft in the general sense. Rather, it is something marvelous that can only be obtained at a spiritual fountainhead. In traditional society of the Yi people, there was no worship of a monotheistic god. Instead, we firmly believed that all things in Nature have souls. The bimo-priest of the Yi people was the medium between people and the world of divine beings. The bimo is like a shaman in Shamanism. Even today there are bimos who undertake the duty of making offerings and exorcising ghosts. What needs to be explained here is that our Yi society has undergone huge changes. In our social consciousness and in a spiritual context, many things from outside coexist with what was handed down. Like many

精神源头才能获取的更为神奇的东西。在彝族的传统社会中并不存在对单一神的崇拜，而是执着地坚信万物都有灵魂。彝族的毕摩是连接人和神灵世界的媒介，毕摩相当于萨满教中的萨满，就是直到今天他们依然承担着祭祀驱鬼的任务。需要说明的是，当下的彝族社会已经发生了很大的变化，在其社会意识以及精神领域中，许多外来的东西和固有的东西一并存在着，彝族也像这个世界上许多古老的民族一样，正在经历一个前所未有的现代化的过程，其中所隐含的博弈和冲突，特别是如何坚守自身的文化传统以及生活方式，已经成了一个十分紧迫而必须要面对的问题。我说这些你们就会知道，为什么文化身份对一些诗人是如此重要，如果说不同的诗人承担着不同的任务和使命，有时候并非他们自身的选择。我并不是一个文化决定论者，但文化和传统对有的诗人的影响的确是具有决定意义的，在中外诗歌史上这样的诗人不胜枚举，20世纪爱尔兰伟大诗人威廉·巴特勒·叶芝、被誉为"巴勒斯坦骄子"的伟大诗人马哈茂德·达尔维什等人，他们的全部写作以及作为诗人的形象，很大程度上已经成为一个民族的精神标识和符号，如果从更深远的文化意义上来看，他们的存在和写作整体呈现的更是一个民族幽深厚重的心灵史。诚然，这样一些杰出的天才诗人，他们最为可贵的，是他们从来就不是为某种事先预设的所谓社会意义而写作，他们的作品所彰显的现实性完全是作品自身诗性品质的自然流露。作为一个正在经历急剧变革的民族的诗人，我一直把威廉·巴特勒·叶芝、巴勃罗·聂鲁达、塞萨尔·巴列霍、马哈茂德·达尔维什等人视为我的楷模和榜样。在诗人这样一个特殊的家族中，每一个诗人都是独立的个体存在，但这些诗人中间总有几个是比较接近的，当然这仅仅是从类型的角度而言，因为从本质上讲每一个诗人个体就是他自己，谁也无法代替他人，每一个诗人的写作其实都是他个人生命体验和精神历程的结晶。

　　在中国，彝族是一个有近900万人口的世居民族，我们的先人数千年来就迁徙游牧在中国西南部广袤的群山之中，那里山峦绵延，江河纵横密布，这片土地上的自然遗产和精神文化遗产，是构筑这个民族独特价值体系的基础，我承认我的诗歌写作的精神坐标，都建立在我所熟悉的这个文化之上。成为这个民族的诗人也许是某种宿命的选择，但我更把它视为一种崇高的责任和使命。作为诗人个体发出的声音，应该永远是个人性的，它必须始终保持独立而鲜明的立场，但是一个置身于时代并

ancient peoples of the world, The Yi ethnic group is undergoing an unprecedented process of modernization. As we face an interplay of clashing forces, how to maintain our cultural tradition and way of life is a question that we urgently need to face. When I speak of these things, you will realize why cultural identity is so important for a poet. If we say that different poets undertake different duties and missions, then there are times when this may not be by their own choice. I am not a cultural determinist, but the influence of cultural tradition on some poets may be decisive. The history of poetry in China and elsewhere holds numerous examples of such poets. Two examples from the twentieth century come to mind: William B. Yeats and Mahmoud Darwish, who has been called the pride of Palestine. In both cases, poetic oeuvre plus public persona can be taken as spiritual emblems of their people. In terms of deeper cultural significance, through their existence and their writing, they manifest the deep-seated, long-accumulated inner history of their people. In truth, these highly talented poets deserve esteem because they did not write to convey a certain predetermined social message. The reality manifested through their works flowed naturally from the inherent poetic qualities of the poems. As a poet of an ethnic group that is going through intense transformation, I have taken these figures as exemplars and models: William Butler Yeats, Pablo Neruda, Cesar Vallejo, and Mahmoud Darwish. In our special family made up of poets, each of us is an independent being, but one is drawn more closely to a certain few. Of course, this is a matter of affinity by types, but in essence each poet can only be himself, and no one can replace anyone else. Each poet's writing is a crystallization of his life encounters and his spiritual journey.

The Yi people in China are a long-standing, stationary minority with a population of over nine million. Our forebears came in waves of nomadic migrants, over thousands of years, to the vast mountain ranges of southwest China. That is a land of far-stretching successive ridges, densely interlaced with rivers. This natural patrimony and our intangible cultural heritage underlie the unique value system of my people. I admit that the intangible coordinates of my writing are established based on the culture I am familiar with. To become a poet of this people was perhaps my predestined choice, but more than that I view it as an exalted responsibility and calling. One's voice as a person who writes poetry should forever be that of an individual, and it should reflect one's independent, distinct stance. Yet a poet who finds himself in this particular era and who dares to launch his life into its turbulent currents cannot help but concern himself with human fate and with living conditions of the majority of people. Behind his voice we should be able to hear reverberations of a choir of voices. I feel that only in this way can an individual voice be rich with charisma; only then will it carry value with which The Other can identify. We need not speak of distant eras. In comparison with many great poets of the mid-twentieth century, today's poets seem to be declining in terms of spiritual scope and of witnessing life in our era. Part of the reason for this lies with the poets themselves, and another cause is the fragmentation of our social environment. Among poets today there is a lack of what Holderlin could do at a metaphysical

敢于搏击生活激流的诗人,不能不关注人类的命运和大多数人的生存状况,从他发出的个体声音的背后,我们应该听到的是群体和声的回响,我以为只有这样,诗人个体的声音才会更富有魅力,才会更有让他者所认同的价值。远的不用说,与20世纪中叶许多伟大的诗人相比较,今天的诗人无论是在精神格局,还是在见证时代生活方面,都显得日趋式微,其中有诗人自身的原因,也有社会生存环境被解构而更加碎片化的因素,当下的诗人最缺少的还是荷尔德林式的对形而上的精神星空的叩问和烛照。是否具有深刻的人类意识,一直是评价一个诗人是否具有道德高度的重要标尺。

　　朋友们,我是第一次踏上英国的土地,也是第一次来到闻名于世的剑桥大学,但是从我能开始阅读到今天,珀西·比希·雪莱、乔治·戈登·拜伦、威廉·莎士比亚、伊丽莎白·芭蕾特·布朗宁、弗吉尼亚·伍尔芙、狄兰·托马斯、威斯坦·休·奥登、谢默斯·希尼等等,都成了我阅读精神史上不可分割并永远感怀的部分。最后请允许我借此机会向伟大的英语世界的文学源头致敬,因为这一语言所形成的悠久的文学传统,毫无疑问已经成为这个世界文学格局中最让人着迷的一个部分。谢谢大家。

level, which is to interrogate and illuminate the starry reaches of the spirit. Whether or not a poet is deeply conscious of humanity has always been an important measure of his or her moral dimension.

My friends, this is the first time I've set foot on English soil, and it is my first visit to Cambridge University. Even so, from my early efforts at reading until today, I have been grateful to British writers and poets for being an essential part of my growth through reading. The ones who come to mind are Percy Byshe Shelley, George Gordon Lord Byron, William Shakespeare, Elizabeth Barrett Browning, Virginia Woolf, Dylan Thomas, Wystan Hugh Auden and Seamus Heaney. Finally, let me seize this chance to give thanks to the literary fountainhead of the English speaking world, from which a time-honored tradition has emerged, because no other portion of the world literary edifice has been quite so captivating.

Translated by Denis Mair(USA)

向河流致敬，就是向诗歌致敬

在 2017 年度波兰雅尼茨基文学奖颁奖仪式上的致辞

2017 年 6 月 20 日

尊敬的雅尼茨基文学奖的各位评委，尊敬的各位女士、各位先生、各位朋友：

今天我们大家从四面八方来到了这里，现在就置身于中国非常古老的人工运河之一——京杭大运河的岸边，共同来见证这样一个对我而言十分重要的时刻。不知道为什么，当看见身旁这条已经流淌了一千多年的河流，我突然想到了中国人经常说的一句话"山不转水转，水不转人转"。其实，眼前的现实就已经不折不扣地证明了这句话的正确，正是因为诸位从不同的地方，甚至从十分遥远的地方来到这里，才让我们的相见和邂逅充满了某种不可预知的感觉。尤其是这条河流的影子通过阳光，被再次反射到我们眼里的时候，我们不能不相信人类的诗歌与河流从来就是一对孪生姐妹，它们旺盛蓬勃的生命都来自共同的自然和精神的源头，难怪在中国哲学中有"上善若水"的表述，其实诗歌和水所隐含的形而上的精神意蕴，就完全代表了人类至真至善至美的境界。我们不能想象，在人类能够繁衍生息的任何一个地方，如果没有河流和洁净的水，人类的思想、哲学和诗歌还能在漫长的时间中被滋养和孕育吗？也正因为此，从某种意义而言，我们向河流致敬，其实就是向诗歌致敬，我们向水致敬，其实就是向一切伟大哲学致敬。朋友们，为此，我要由衷地感谢京杭大运河国际诗歌大会为我提供了一个特殊的颁奖地，当然我更要感谢波兰克莱门斯·雅尼茨基文学奖的诸位评委，你们从遥远的地方给我带来了一份如此厚重的礼物，除了让我感到激动和幸福之外，我的内心也有某种不安，作为一个诗人，面对你们赠予的荣誉，我确实无以为报。因为我知道，这个奖项是以 16 世纪波兰文艺复兴时期的人文

A Salute to Rivers Is a Salute to Poetry
Acceptance Speech for Poland's Janicki Prize, 2017
20th,June,2017

Respected judges of the Janicki Literary Prize, respected ladies and gentlemen, friends in the audience:

Having gathered here today from all corners of China and the world, we find ourselves on the bank of an ancient waterway, the Peking-Hangzhou Canal. We are here to witness an occasion that is tremendously important for me. I'm not sure why, but looking at this waterway that has flowed for over a thousand years makes me think of an adage we often hear from the mouths of Chinese people: "The mountains do not revolve, but water does; water does not revolve, but people do." Indeed, the reality before our eyes inarguably proves the correctness of this saying. Precisely because we have come from so many places, some of them quite remote, our encounter here is like a collision with the unknown. Especially as dappled sunlight is reflected from the river into our eyes, we cannot help believing that poetry and rivers are like two sisters, born as fraternal twins. Both surge with a vigorous life-force that comes from common spiritual and natural wellsprings. No wonder we find this adage in Chinese philosophy: "the highest good is like water." In fact the metaphysical purport of both poetry and water represent the highest plane of human truth and goodness. We cannot imagine, in any place where people were able to flourish, that human thought and poetry could have been incubated over long periods without the pristine water brought by rivers. Precisely for this reason, our salute to rivers is, in some respects, a salute to poetry. When we offer salutations to water, we are really offering salutations to great philosophical thinking. And so, my friends, I want to express heartfelt gratitude to the Peking-Hangzhou Canal International Poetry Gathering for providing this wonderful site for receiving a prize. Of course I want to thank the judges of Poland's Klemens Janicki Literary Prize for bringing me such a precious gift. Aside from feeling deeply stirred and blessed, I feel a tinge of unease within my heart, because as a poet I have no way make recompense for this honor you are bestowing on me. As you know, this prize is named after Klemens Janicki, a humanist in Poland's 16th century Renaissance who was an outstanding Latin poet known as Ianicius. After its founding in the

主义者、最杰出的拉丁语诗人克莱门斯·雅尼茨基的名字命名的，它创立于20世纪90年代初，这个奖项已经颁发了二十多年，波兰有许多重要的作家、诗人和艺术家获得过此项奖励，近两年此项文学奖开始面向国际颁发，十分荣幸的是因为评委会的慷慨和选择，我的名字已经和这个奖项永远联系在一起了。朋友们，不知你们是否真的理解，我为什么如此看重这份荣誉。那是因为作为诗人，我对波兰这个产生伟大诗人的国度充满着敬仰，对这片土地所承受过的苦难、悲痛和不幸，有着切肤的理解和同情。我曾经告诉过一些朋友，如果把现代波兰诗歌，放在20世纪以来的世界诗歌的天平上，波兰诗人和诗歌所创造的辉煌，都是令人赞叹和瞩目的，这些诗歌就像粗粝的含金矿石，将毫无悬念地将天平压倒在他们的一边。今天的这个世界并不太平，人类并没有消除核武器的威胁，同时不安全的其他因素也还在上升，如何进一步增进不同文明和文化的对话与交流，仍然是我们今天不同民族和国家的诗人的神圣责任。我相信，越是在一个需要包容、沟通和相互尊重的时代，诗歌的作用就越会显现出来，朋友们，难道不是吗？今天正是因为诗歌，我们才相聚到了这里，这就是诗歌不可被替代的作用。谢谢大家！

1990s, the prize has been awarded for over twenty years, and its recipients include many of Poland's most famous writers, poets and artists. Only in the past year or two has this prize broadened its scope to international recipients. I am greatly honored that, due to the generous decision of the judging committee, my name will forever be linked with this prize. My friends, I don't know if you truly grasp why I value this prize so highly. As a poet I am filled with admiration for Poland—a country which has produced so many great poets. I have visceral awareness and sympathy for the terrible adversity and suffering which have been visited upon Polish soil. I used to tell my friends that if you place modern Polish poetry on the scale of world poetry since the 20th century, the brilliance of what was created in Poland will cause people to gasp in amazement. Their works are like coarse but rich gold-bearing ore, with weight that inevitably tips the scales in their favor.

Our world today is by no means peaceful, and humankind has not managed to phase out the threat of nuclear weapons. At the same time, other factors of insecurity are on the rise. The task of enhancing dialogue and exchange between different civilizations is more than ever a sacred duty for poets of different peoples and nations. I believe that the more an era needs tolerance and respectful communication, the more poetry's function will manifest itself. Don't you think so, my dear friends? It is precisely because of poetry that we are gathered here today. In this we see poetry's irreplaceable function. Thank you, everyone.

Translated by Denis Mair(USA)

附录 1

重读《献给土著民族的颂歌》

海南大学　李鸿然

中国著名彝族诗人吉狄马加20世纪80年代初期步入诗坛，至今已走过三十年的创作历程。他三十年间大约出版20部诗集，其中不少诗分别在十几个国家以英、法、德、朝、波、意、西语出版，在国内外产生了广泛的影响。这些诗大致分两类：一类是民族元素的诗歌，常从民族写到人类，既有强烈的民族色彩，又有普遍的世界意义；另一类是关注现实社会问题，特别是关注当下国际社会问题的诗歌。后一类诗因为大多写国内外读者共同关注的问题，又表现了深刻的思想和精湛的诗艺，所以也像前一类作品一样，受到国内外读者的共同喜爱。

值得注意的是，吉狄马加从步入诗坛之日起，就非常重视对世界土著民族的书写，他1985年出版的第一部诗集，即获国家级诗歌大奖的《初恋的歌》，就有直接或间接书写世界土著民族的作品，有的现在已成为国内外普遍认可的名篇。自那时到现在，吉狄马加的土著书写一以贯之，新世纪以来涉及土著民族的创作数量倍增，艺术质量也节节攀升。这中间，有许多是当下国内外读者耳熟能详的佳作，不少篇什有可能进入世界土著文学经典的行列。总的看来，在近三十年来的中国诗坛，吉狄马加对世界土著民族的书写数量最多，质量最高，在国内外诗坛影响最大。而作为今日中国顶级的土著诗人，他的书写堪与当今世界大师级土著诗人媲美，其成就将成为世界土著文学史上的新篇章，进入人类的永久性记忆。笔者认为，只有在这样的背景下和高度上，才可能对吉狄马加《献给土著民族的颂歌》做出较为准确与深入的解读。

《献给土著民族的颂歌》写于1993年，副题是《为联合国世界土著人年而作》。

Appendix 1

Jidi Majia's An Eulogy of World Indigenous People Revisited
Li Hongran, University of Hainan

It is already thirty years since Jidi Majia, China's most renowned Yi poet, set upon his poetic career in the 1980s,with about 20 books of verse published to his credit in a span of 30 years, of which a considerable proportions having been made available in English, French, German, Korean, Polish, Italian, Spanish etc. Indeed, this Yi poet has understood the great things in the literature of our time and all time, the poems of Pushkin, Li Bai, Neruda, Paz, the novels of Juan Gelman, Principau d'Asturies, Sholohov, thus establishing his popularity with readers home and abroad. Jidi's prodigious poetic output centers around the ethnic elements, ranging from his Yi identity to humanity. A major variant concerns the social issues in present day China and the world, both practiced with intelligence and skill, earning him a lasting niche with passing years.

What is more pertinent to our topic today is Jidi's preoccupation with the fate of world indigenous people, a focus that is his trademark since his poetic debut, attested by the ethnic themes running through his first award winning book of verse My First Love ,many poems of which have been since canonized. Since the 1980s,Jidi has continued to produce poems in similar vein with a craftsmanship increasingly refined and matured, which ultimately conspires to push him to the peak of his poetic career as the top ethnic poet in China in terms of output, dexterity and renown. It must be conceded his poetic supremacy compares no less admirably to his distinguished peers outside of China, to the extent he is on the threshold of having his name carved on a stone in the Hall of Fame of world poets.

This topic brings me to a critical reappraisal of his opus An Eulogy of World Indigenous People Published in 1993,sub-titled dedicated to the 1993 International Year for the World Indigenous People. UN and other world bodies have always attached great importance to the problems confronted by indigenous people. The 1993 International Year for the World's Indigenous People was proclaimed by the United Nations General Assembly "to strengthen international cooperation for the solution of problems faced by indigenous communities in areas such as human rights, the environment, development, education and health". "The Year was

国际社会一贯重视世界土著人问题。20世纪90年代初,联合国宣布1993年是联合国世界土著人年,当年联合国土著居民工作组通过了《关于土著人权利的联合国宣言草案》,同年9月"土著人问题国际会议"在莫斯科召开,11月吉隆坡举行了"土著人民前进之路"国际研讨会。这一年土著人代表要求通过有效的行政和立法手段承认和保障土著人民的权利,并要求联合国宣布1995年至2004年为"联合国土著人十年"。《献给土著民族的颂歌》在这样的世界情境中问世,充分体现了吉狄马加的世界公民意识和历史担当精神。作品所蕴含的观念、情愫和内在精神,是与世界土著人的诉求和全世界人民的共同愿望完全一致的。全诗五节二十四行:

歌颂你/就是歌颂土地/就是歌颂土地上的河流/以及那些数不清的属于人类的居所

理解你/就是理解生命/就是理解生殖和繁衍的缘由/谁知道有多少不知名的种族/曾在这个大地上生活

怜悯你/就是怜悯我们自己/怜悯我们共同的痛苦和悲伤/有人看见我们骑着马/最后消失在所谓文明的城市中

抚摸你/就是抚摸人类的良心/就是抚摸人类美好和罪恶的天平/多少个世纪以来,历史已经证明/土著民族所遭受的迫害是最为残暴的

祝福你/就是祝福玉米,祝福荞麦,祝福土豆/就是祝福那些世界上最古老的粮食/为此我们没有理由不把母亲所给予的生命和梦想/毫无保留地献给人类的和平、自由与公正

诗的第一、二节,关键词是"歌颂土地"和"理解生命"。"土地"和"生命",不论在实际生活中还是诗歌里,都是吉狄马加最关注的问题。他去年出版的一本访谈随笔

requested by indigenous organizations and is the result of their efforts to secure their cultural integrity and status into the twenty-first century. It aims above all to encourage a new relationship between States and indigenous peoples, and between the international community and indigenous peoples-a new partnership based on mutual respect and understanding". In the same year, an international forum was called in Moscow followed by another convened at the end of the that year in Kuala Lumpur urging the UN to proclaim ten years from 1995 to 2004 dedicated for indigenous people in succession. Jidi's Eulogy appeared to match the new attitude and activism in favor of the cultural values of the indigenous people rediscovered.

> In praise of you, Is to praise the land, the rivers overflowing the land,
> The innumerable human habitations.
>
> To understand you is to understand life
> The reasons for progeny and propagation,
> Who knows how many races, of unknown names, inhabit the earth?
>
> To take a pity upon you is for our own sake,
> For the common lot befalling us.
> Some witness our people ride a horse through the streets of the civilized cities,
> But lost mysteriously.
>
> To stroke you is to stroke the human conscience
> The price of human suffering and cultural displacement in the balance.
> History stands witness to the most unspeakable decimation and slaughtering,
> Ever committed against the indigenous people.
>
> To bless you is to bless corn, potatoes, buckwheat, To bless the world's most ancient staple foods.
> In no way should we be justified in not leaving life and dream to our children
> For the sake of world peace, justice and liberty.

The two key words of the first stanza of the poem are land and life, a twin preoccupation with Jidi both in real life and his poems. A book of interviews and essays he published last year took the title of For the Land and the Life. In fact, eulogizing the land and the life are two red threads cut across the world ethnic literature. Invariably the arch metaphors for all indigenous people, the connotations of the land differ to varying degrees from race to race, but basically in the literature of the most marginalized ethnic groups, the metaphors have received the most

集,书名就是《为土地和生命而写作》。世界不同种族和民族的文学,都歌颂或曾经歌颂土地,而且经常把土地作为隐喻或象征。然而,不同种族和民族的土地隐喻,其喻义和喻用的差别,也普遍存在。在我的阅读印象中,把土地隐喻使用得最深刻最有力的文学,是弱势民族的文学与土著民族的文学。读吉狄马加的"歌颂你/就是歌颂土地",让人立刻联想到两篇现已名满天下的印第安人口述文学经典,即《西雅图宣言》和《黑麋鹿这样说》。

1854年美国总统皮尔斯要求"购买"夸美什部落的土地,部落酋长西雅图有理有据地予以回绝,于是有了流传至今的《西雅图宣言》。"大地母亲""生命之网"等笼罩天地万物的超级意象,"我们是大地的一部分,大地也是我们的一部分"等现在被频繁称引的至理名言,在今日的物化世界形成了巨大的思想冲击波,给人们很多启示。《黑麋鹿这样说》是奥格拉拉苏族人"黑麋鹿"的回忆录,由美国诗人奈哈特转述,被推崇为印第安人的《圣经》,讲述的不是一个人的故事,而是大地上"所有生命神圣而美好的故事"。"难道苍天不是父亲,大地不是母亲,所有长腿的或带翅的或生根的生命不都是他俩的孩子吗?"这一感天动地的设问,道出了一个绝对真理式的宇宙秘密,是我们考察人与自然、人与人、人与社会关系的黄金通道。

从这样的土著文学经典中,我们进一步加深了对土著民族和土地关系的认识,深感吉狄马加的许多观念与它们血脉相通,也懂得了吉狄马加"歌颂你/就是歌颂土地"和"理解你/就是理解生命"所包含的诗性逻辑和深层意义。吉狄马加关于土著民族的诗歌中,有大量关于土地和生命的篇什,几乎都可以作为上述诗行的注脚。如吉狄马加大约三十年前创作的《古老的土地》,诗人在歌颂"埋下祖先头颅"的凉山土地时,很自然地联想到印第安人"在南美草原上追逐鹿群",黑人兄弟"踏响非洲鼓一般的土地",还有埃塞俄比亚大地上"远古金黄的光"、顿河岸边哥萨克人在"黄昏举行婚礼",诗人写道:"到处是这样古老的土地/婴儿在这土地上降生/老人在这土地上死去……"诗中歌颂了世界各地土著民族的生命活力、创造精神和历史贡献,而诗人对"生命"的理解,也没有局限于个体生命的生存与死亡,他特意暗示了土著民族生命系统从远古到现在的无限延展,即《献给土著民族的颂歌》中说的"理解生殖和繁衍"。这种蕴藉深邃悠远、极具艺术张力的话语,对读者思索世界土著民族的生命价

exuberant poetic expression. The beginning line "to praise you is to praise the land" instantly reminds us of the two Indian masterpieces "the Alternate Statement" of chief Seattle and "Thus Black Elk Speaks."

The story dates from In 1854,when American president Pierce offered to purchase the land of the Suquamish tribe. Seattle, chief of the Suquamish and other Indian tribes around Washington's Puget Sound, delivered what is considered to be "one of the most beautiful and profound environmental statements ever made" in reply to Pierce's pleadings.The city of Seattle is named for the chief. Two super metaphors "Mother Land" and "the Net of Life" have since found their way into modern idiom of various peoples around the world,. Black Elk Speaks, hailed as "a religious classic, a North American bible of all tribes ,one of the best spiritual books of the modern era and the bestselling book of all time by an American Indian," is a 1932 book by John G. Neihardt, an American poet and writer, who relates the story and spirituality of Black Elk, an Oglala Sioux medicine man or shaman. Black Elk Speaks however is more than the epic story of a super Indian, it is famed as a spiritual classic because of John Neihardt's sensitivity to Black Elk's resounding vision of the wholeness of earth, her creatures, and all of humanity. "Isn't it the sky is not Mother, the Land is not Father, all the creatures with legs, their descendants?". A striking rhetorical question like this paves the way to illumination and enlightenment.

Such ethnic classics speak to us with lyrical and compelling language about the tenacious clinging of indigenous people to the land encourages us to emphasize with their age-old view of the land's indispensability to their inner and outer being. Indigenous peoples are descendants of the original inhabitants of many lands, strikingly varied in their cultures, religions and patterns of social and economic organization. At present at least 5,000 indigenous groups can be distinguished by linguistic and cultural differences and by geographical separation. Some are hunters and gatherers, while others live in cities and participate fully in the culture of their national society. But all indigenous peoples retain a strong sense of their distinct cultures, the most salient feature of which is a special relationship to the land. Jidi Majia alerts us to this vital aspect of human experience to make us much more informed of the inner logic and rhetoric underlying his poetic outburst: "To praise you is to praise the land" "To understand you is to understand life." In all his ethnic output, poems extolling the virtues of the land are in plenty, easily identified as the footnotes to the above manifesto-like slogan. His Age-old Land ,composed 30 years ago, is frankly a paean in celebration of his home district, The Daliangshan in the west of Sichuan, his ancestral land, reminiscent of the North Americans hunting deer and buffaloes, the dark continent where black brothers dance to the rhythmical beats of sonorous African drums and the mighty Don river banks where the fiercely brave Cossacks briskly reveling in the middle of a wedding ceremony. The poet sings out:

"Here is the age-old land,

Babies are born while old man in their death throes."

值和生存意义,以及他们世世代代编结的生命生存长线对人类历史发展的贡献,都有启示作用。

法国著名诗人雅克·拉达斯的文章《在吉狄马加的"神奇土地"上》写道:"我们这些欧洲人,早已把古老的土地抛到一边,但在我们面前,我们惊异地看到了吉狄马加——一位把祖先的自然话语和当下的现实洞察成功地融为一体的榜样诗人。"这段话对我们解读吉狄马加《献给土著民族的颂歌》,特别是以上两节诗,颇有参考价值。

诗的第三节表达对所有土著人痛苦和悲伤的"怜悯",以及对土著人"最后消失"的焦虑。第四节"抚摸人类的良心",诉说土著民族在漫长历史中遭受的"最为残暴的"迫害。两节有一个共同的思想指向,即歌唱人道主义精神。诗人的情思徘徊在历史剧痛和现实焦虑之间,其悲悯横跨几大洲,纵贯几世纪,令人想到那些大师级诗人的"世界太息"和"世纪太息"。"有人看见我们骑着马/最后消失在所谓文明的城市中",是20世纪汉语世界极好的文学意象之一;而20世纪中国文学中有关土著消失的意象,无出其右者。可以说,现代文明对传统文明的吞噬,强势族群对弱势族群的挤压,确保土著文明在现代社会中生存与发展的重要性和紧迫性,维护人类文化多样性对人类自身的救赎性意义,即庞德讲的"各种不同的观念的联合",都在这个视觉的、如画的和动态的意象中呈现,真与幻、虚与实、意与象在这里达到了完美的交汇融合。

这一意象,让人想到1915年在美国旧金山世界博览会上荣获金奖的关于印第安人的雕塑——詹姆斯·E.弗雷泽的名作《路尽头》。《路尽头》刻画一个无名印第安人身陷在一匹累垮战马的脚镫上,以隐喻暗示印第安人受殖民者压迫走投无路而濒临灭亡。应当说,吉狄马加关于土著文明在现代城市文明中"最后消失"的意象,与弗雷泽的雕塑异曲同工。从人类社会生活层面看,世界土著文化和土著民族的消失,是近几个世纪世界各地一直发生的历史事实。当今世界,不仅动植物种群面临灭绝,许多土著民族也面临灭绝。

据联合国不久前统计,1900年巴西亚马孙河流域有270个土著族群,可现在不到180个,已经消失90多个。事实告诉我们,吉狄马加所营造的这一意象,有充分的

He sings the praises of the vigor, vitality, creativity and historical contribution of indigenous people. Death in his dictionary necessarily encompasses the individual mortality and the infinite collective continuity, enriching our understanding of cross-cultural interrelatedness and the inter-connection of us human beings with all creatures.

Jacque Ladas, French poet, wrote in one of his reviews of Jid iMajia(In the Miraculous Land of Jidi Majia):"We Europeans have long dumped our age-old land as worthless, yet jidi Majia, has amazed us by performing a feat, in front of us, in that he is an exemplary poet practiced in the language of his ancestors to probe beyond the immediate reality."

Coming to the third stanza of the eulogy, we learn to empathize with the poet's indignation at the suffering and pathos borne by all the indigenous people and the anxiety he expresses at the" lost way of life".

In the fourth stanza, the poet urges us to awaken in our conscience, "to stroke our conscience" in his words, for the sadness and injustice of the atrocities sustained by indigenous people. Both stanzas, of powerful humanitarian import, point to the greater truth of compassion as the poet's great sadness at the cosmic historical injustice and the immense anxieties in the immediacy are movingly conveyed, Here we come upon the epic metaphor, arguably the best metaphor about the indigenous cultures in decline in the 20th century Chinese literature.

"Some witness our people ride a horse through the streets of the civilized cities,

But lost mysteriously."

Under the march of modernization, the spread of non-indigenous religions and the relentless encroachment of GDP mania, indigenous groups have seen their traditions eroded . More generally, indigenous peoples who are integrated into a national society face discrimination and exploitation in housing, education and in matters having to do with language and religion. But the growing awareness about human rights in the post-war era of the past 60 years or so has delivered impetus to campaigns for enhancing the rights of indigenous groups and given rise to an new activism ,charged with a sense of utmost urgency, to conserve the cultural diversity as an act of self redemption. Jidi's originality at coining this fantastic metaphor is best understood in a world enthusiased with this new ethos .

An arch imagery like this also calls to mind the doleful "End of the Trail" , James Earle Fraser's most prized Gold Medal sculpture produced for the Panama-Pacific International Exposition held in San Francisco in 1915. This lone figure on his weary horse is one of the most recognized icons of the American West. By many it is viewed as a moving elegy to mourn the passing of a great and valiant people cornered to the point of defeat and subjugation. It must be conceded Jidi Majia's imagery of "indigenous riders lost in the city" exerts a similar powerful emotional impact as Frazer's doleful Indian knight did. It is no exaggeration to say that some indigenous peoples live under the threat of extinction encroached by the menaces of mainstream civilization and lifestyles everywhere together with the perishing of many rare fauna and flora. As

历史和现实依据,不是凭空臆造的。正因为这样,它才有那么强大的思想冲击力和灵魂震撼力。第四节"多少个世纪以来……土著民族所遭受的迫害是最为残暴的"与第三节诗意相接,指的是几百年来世界各地土著民族惨遭杀戮、被迫迁徙、面对歧视、濒临灭绝的历史境遇。"抚摸你/就是抚摸人类的良心/就是抚摸人类美好和罪恶的天平",是诗人灵魂深处的话语,字里行间,流溢着真挚的人情、善良的人性、美好的人类友爱,当然也涌动着对当年殖民主义者滔天罪行的义愤。不过我们也可以感受到,吉狄马加的诗行里拥有一般诗人缺乏的深度的历史意识和高度的道德理性。美国诗人、翻译家梅丹理说吉狄马加是"中国西南部少数民族的伟大灵魂","在他的一些描述现代社会危机的诗作里……对于暴力进行了强烈抨击,但他从不提倡'以暴易暴'的做法或观念"。这一评价是合乎实际的。在第四节中,即使控诉当年"最为残暴"的罪恶行径,也没有"以暴易暴"意味,却有当今少见的节制和理性,诗句最能打动我们心灵的,正是这种高尚而又成熟的人道主义精神。

最后一节诗的开头"祝福你/就是祝福玉米,祝福荞麦,祝福土豆",乍读让人纳闷,怎么把人的日常食品作祝福辞,还把这些最普通的食品与土著民族等同起来？然而读了第三句"就是祝福那些世界上最古老的粮食",我们逐渐明白了,因为这三句话组合一起,给读者提供了一个广阔的思维空间。诗人以语言点金术点亮了前两句,又机智地停止言说,让读者自己思索许多历史学、人类学、民族学和文化学问题,与他一道完成作品的文本建构。

我们从英国伟大历史学家汤因比的名著《人类与大地母亲》中知道,美洲土著居民大约在公元前3000年开始驯化玉米,后来玉米成了他们的主要粮食,"美洲文化也发展为一种与旧大陆不相上下的文明"。再后来,欧洲人把玉米运回欧洲,玉米也成为欧洲的粮食。我们还从印第安人神话和文学作品中知道,玉米是印第安人的谷物母神,被称为"玉米妈妈"。1967年获诺贝尔文学奖的印第安人作家阿斯图里亚斯的一部重要代表作就取名"玉米人"。"玉米人即玛雅人","神用玉米创造了人类",就是书中引用的印第安人经典话语。知道这些以后,吉狄马加为什么"祝福玉米",我们就一清二楚了。土豆也是很早以前由美洲土著居民驯化栽培,后来被欧洲和其他大洲引进,成为人类主要粮食的。在全球性饥荒时期,土豆曾拯救过世界,当然也包括

the indigenous people are on the frontlines of environmental degradation, they have the largest interest at stake when it comes to sustainable land management and land-use in the areas in which they live.

The world's estimated 300 million indigenous people are spread across the world in more than 70 countries. Among them, One recent UN census indicates, 90 indigenous tribes out of 270 who lived in the Amazon forests in 1900 now vanish. These alarming facts are behind Jidi's impulse to create his heartbreaking image. In the two lines that follow, ie,

"History stands witness to the most unspeakable decimation and slaughtering,

Ever committed against the indigenous people."

The poet speaks in vehement denunciation of all the atrocities committed by mainstream human communities in the name of civilization against the aboriginal societies by various agencies, for example, the spread of non-indigenous religions and the secular ideologies, the reckless trumpeting of development and industrialization. The result: indigenous people have fallen a helpless prey with their cultures maimed and marginalized, their landholdings confiscated or signed away as part of the economic coercion to which they were subjected. Such legacy has been accountable for the deplorable fact that everywhere, indigenous peoples emerge invariably the most disadvantaged groups on Earth. This historical sense, combined with the profound reason as one perceives in his poems, brings American poet ,Denis Mair, to declare: "Jidi Majia has never stopped being what he always was: a great soul who emerged from among an indigenous group in southwestern China and undertook to bridge his people's ethos with realities of the outside world." "Jidi Majia accepts suffering as part of the human condition: it is the underlying melancholy color on which the hopeful patterns of creative expression appear by contrast. In his poems about crises of the modern world, he denounces violence but does not seek to attach blame or exact retribution." Hereby I believes Denis Mair scores a very important point about the high moral tone in Jidi's poems.

The last stanza begins with:

"To bless you is to bless corn, potatoes, buckwheat and tomatoes,

To bless the world's most ancient staple foods.

Some readers might be baffled about this point: why use solemn blessings for a so mundane daily kitchen situation? The enumeration of such an array of staple food mixed with so lofty a topic as cultural diversity in decline? We are illuminated eventually at the sentence: "To bless the world's most ancient staple foods", a piece of common sense in cultural anthropology.

In his masterpiece Mankind and Mother Nature, British historian Arnold Toynbee tells us the unforgettable story of how Indians in America first cultivated corn about 5000 years ago and corn became their staple food ever since. After Columbus discovered the New World, corn was taken back to Europe to become Europeans' staple food accordingly. From other literary and mythical sources we are told corn for Indians represents more than something to keep them alive

欧洲。史载，17世纪末彼得大帝从西欧带土豆回俄罗斯，到19世纪中期土豆已是俄罗斯的重要食品。不久前中国取代俄罗斯成为世界土豆生产第一大国，美洲先民培育的土豆对我国经济发展、社会稳定和保障人民生活的作用相当重要。想到此处，我们也要和吉狄马加一道"祝福土豆"了。饶有趣味的是，吉狄马加"祝福土豆"是1993年，十五年之后，即2008年，土豆竟成为联合国国际土豆年的主角，是全人类的焦点热点话题。难道诗人吉狄马加也是彝族的毕摩，有先知先觉的特异功能吗？关于荞麦，吉狄马加早有《苦荞麦》诗，赞美她是"大地的容器""高原滚动不安的太阳"，还说"我们歌唱你就如同歌唱母亲一样"。其深沉和真挚，与《献给土著民族的颂歌》相同。

这一节的结语，"为此我们没有理由不把母亲所给予的生命和梦想／毫无保留地献给人类的和平、自由和公正"，也是全诗的结语。"母亲"指地球母亲，"我们"指所有生活在地球村的人。诗人希望所有人都为保护地球母亲及人类的和平、自由、公正而献身。吉狄马加这里表现的使命感和担当精神非常感人，当今诗坛非常需要具有这种精神的诗人。

重读吉狄马加《献给土著民族的颂歌》，感触很深。到明年，这首诗就已发表二十年，但它的意义没有消减，反在增添。前面说到诗人"祝福玉米，祝福荞麦，祝福土豆"，不是赞美他"先知先觉"，而是说他的诗具有持续的意义生成性和持久的艺术生命力。1993年歌颂土著民族和大地母亲，十九年后重读，仍能感到新颖、鲜活、丰富、博大，还有流沙河赞扬《初恋的歌》所说的那种"灵魂的深邃"。这是为什么？中国诗歌大师绿原说："吉狄马加不仅属于彝族，也属于中华民族，还属于世界。可以说，他是用汉语写诗的人类代言人之一，他是一位真正的诗人。"波兰当代著名诗人、波兰文学家协会主席玛莱克·瓦夫凯维支也说："吉狄马加在自己的诗歌里证实了他是世界公民，这不只是他到过许多国家，认识了当地人民……他没有在那些地方刻意寻找差异，而是寻觅到能够使人们更加亲近的因素，因为他是一位人道主义者。"（均见2012年版《吉狄马加的诗》）深广的世界意识，愿做人类的代言人，表达高尚的人道主义精神，正是吉狄马加的诗歌博大深邃，具有持续的意义生成性和持久的艺术生命力的最重要的原因。《献给土著民族的颂歌》，就是有力的证明。

与此同时，为了使自己的诗歌更具思想底蕴和艺术独创性，吉狄马加三十年来

daily. Corn is their farming Goddess, alias Mother Corn. Principau d'Asturies, the Nobel prize winning novelist from Repú blica de Guatemala, even titled one of his novels Coremen."The deities created man out of corn" is a famous lead at the beginning of many an Indian canonical works. Besides, potatoes were again domesticated by Indians. A knowledge of cultural anthology helps us in the decoding of Jidi Majia's playful congratulation upon these most ancient staple foods tamed by Indians which in several major famines that stalked the globe saved millions upon millions of human lives on all the main continents. In the latter part of the 17th century, Peter the Great introduced potatoes to Russia and by the middle of the 19th century, potatoes became the lifeblood of Russians. Readers might be intrigued to know just recently China has replaced Russia to become the largest producer of potatoes in the world. Potatoes's significance in safeguarding China's food security being realized, Jidi's readers will happily join him in celebrating corns. One more digression: while Jidi blessed corn in 1993, corn was billed as the host for 2008 as the Year for Potatoes.

The eulogy concludes by these two lines:

"In no way should we be justified in not leaving life and dream to our children left by Mother
For the sake of world peace, justice and liberty.

Mother refers to Earth , whereas we, obviously us human beings inhabiting it .The ardent poet urges us to take charge and shoulder our responsibility for our Mother earth, deadly serious in the furtherance of his causes.

A rereading of Jidi's Eulogy affords a soul searching moment. 2013 will mark its 20th anniversary. While it is difficult to gain any just perspective in estimating a great , and still a contemporary figure, and despite the vagaries of literary taste, we feel quite assured of the increasing immortality of this poem. Its dazzling freshness and enduring spiritual message have not been lost to me when I come back to it 19 years later. There is a "depth of soul" in it which has insured its survival value. Lu Yuan, a major veteran, tries to decode this Yi poet's success: "Jidi Majia is a poet whose name and fame both the Yi and the Han claim .He belongs to the world also. His is the example of an ethnic poet writing in Chinese ended up lending strength to both the Yi and the Chinese languages . "Only a great-souled poet could have succeeded in the project that Langston Hughes attempted: to revive a people's identity, from the roots up, in a modern setting of cultural dislocation and anomie." Writes Denis Mair in his preface to Jidi Majia's book of poems in English edition done by him. The combination of wide social enthusiasms, profound sense of global cultural identity, temperament to speak to the world and for the world, plus a genuine artistic gift for form, helps to forge a poetic legend China's republic of poets long awaits.

In the meanwhile, Jidi has never stopped in his pursuit of constructing his own poetics. To my view, Jidi's own aesthetic system took shape initially in the early years of the 1990s. Following in his footsteps, researchers will discern two shifts in his poetics in the expanse of 30 years. He is impatient of clumsy workmanship in poetry .To compare his early writings with those of his latest

一直在努力建构属于自己的诗学体系。笔者以为,"吉狄马加诗学"已经于20世纪90年代初期基本成熟,可是近二十年来他从未间断相关探索与建构。进行追踪研究,可以看到"吉狄马加诗学"的升级与完善。他对世界土著民族的书写,三十年来有两次转型,又如前面说的,同时具有一以贯之的基质。他作诗历来注重探索与创新,几乎每写一首新诗,都会在内容和形式上出现新元素。《献给土著民族的颂歌》也是这样。这首诗不但注意感性和理性的结合,而且注意知性因素的融入。诗中"祝福玉米""祝福荞麦""祝福土豆"等,把感性、理性、知性、诗性统一起来,使诗、思、史、智合为一体,是一种难能可贵的探索和创新。法国诗人拉达斯对吉狄马加在诗中讲故事很感兴趣,举了许多例证,说吉狄马加"是一位伟大的讲故事的人",这是很有见地的评论,道出了他说的"吉狄马加诗歌的独特性"。让人感到奇妙的是,吉狄马加在《献给土著民族的颂歌》中,还引而不发,用不讲故事的话语组合为召唤结构,引导接受者联想许许多多故事。对于世界土著民族来说,玉米、荞麦、土豆的"故事"实在太多太重要了。这些"故事"连接着世界土著民族千万年的生死存亡、世世代代的酸甜苦辣,是他们对世界对人类发展做出伟大贡献的见证。吉狄马加以它们来引导相关的故事,可见其诗思的丰厚和诗艺的圆熟。

最后想说吉狄马加诗歌的语言艺术问题。关于吉狄马加诗歌的语言艺术,可谓好评如潮。当今拉丁美洲非常伟大的诗人之一、阿根廷著名诗人胡安·赫尔曼还专门写诗,盛赞吉狄马加诗歌的语言:"吉狄马加,/生活在赤裸的语言之家里,/为了让燃烧继续,/每每将话语向火中抛去。"不过,中国也有几位评论家对吉狄马加的诗爱用"大词"提出过批评。对"大词"的批评,是当今西方诗坛不时可见的一种倾向,中国诗坛现在甚至有人对"大词"完全否定。笔者很敬重上面说的几位中国评论家,但对他们的批评不很赞同。吉狄马加诗中的确常有"人民""国家""世界""人类"这类"大词"。《献给土著民族的颂歌》里,"大词"也不少,但是用得很好。因此我觉得不应该笼统地否定"大词",而要看"大词"该不该用,用得怎么样。我们称赞吉狄马加有世界意识,关心人类命运,写了不少涉及世界和人类的大诗和好诗,却又让他不用"世界""人类"之类的"大词",这不是自相矛盾吗?而且,古今中外,哪一位大诗人不用"大词"?歌德、雨果、普希金、惠特曼、李白、杜甫等等,谁不喜欢用"大词"?以最后一位而

poems is to realize at once his advance in construction and the management of his verbal art. The Eulogy under discussion is a perfect specimen of his more matured writing, a blend of sensuality and intellectuality ,too many things, ie, poetic enthusiasm, metaphysical insight, intellectual argument and lyrical narrative all crowding up for admission into his Eulogy. One of his originalities lies in his knack at storytelling ,so impressive that the French poet Ladas credits him as "a great storyteller", a comment that is peculiarly to the point. For in the Eulogy, he has developed this trait with great boldness in language, and more important, with a capacity for revealing highly complicated thoughts in verse. It is a miraculous feat he performs in the Eulogy that he would allow the mundane staple food such as corn and buckwheat to hint at and call forth implicitly a string of stories as these staple food has long sustained the world peoples, the importance of which could have never been overly estimated. He has succeeded in making an intricate mosaic of his favorite Hispanic writers and poets, particularly those who affect the grand and mythical manner.

Lastly, a word for his verbal art. Jidi started as a lyric poet ,remains so and draws the critical attention for it, with an ear as keen as Aiqing's (his patron and mentor, the late most reputed lyrical bard of modern China)for what is subtle in Chinese. Juan Herman, One of the most prestigious contemporary poets in the Hispanic world, rates him highly for his verbal facility:

"Jidi Majia, residing in the stark house of language,

To keep the flames

Hurling words into the stove."

This tendency to use big words in poems has understandably invited criticism from some quarters, indeed, a phenomenon, disparaged widely in various parts of the world as a weakness. Excellent though his poems, they have been sometimes found by a few critics as too ornate, too high sounding, arguably a penalty exacted by his crusade against cultural and economical deprivation for his indigenous fellow human beings. I, for one, take leave to agree to disagree. Big words like "people" "country" "world" "humanity" do crop up occasionally in his poems, but there is a matter of necessity and appropriateness to be pondered, to begin with. While we deem his interest in the common fate of mankind and his social attack at the declining cultural diversity and his wide moral enthusiasms as a definite plus, indeed, one of his major inspirations, how could we reconcile our disparaging comments on big words with our lauding of his lofty themes? These poems, I believe, will remain the most durable element in his achievement. It seems an invariable rule that big poets tend to use big words. Delete all the big words in Pushkin, Goethe, Hugo, Du Fu, Whitman and how much is left of the best poetic legacy of world literature? In case of Du Fu, his anthology throngs with big words like "sky and earth" "universe" "ancient and modern" "ten thousand miles" "a hundred years". Do a surgery on them and Du Fu is dead on the spot. My argument is simple: Jidi Majia is one of the rarest cases in which he has erected such a poetic monument on a pedestal made of his poetic exuberance and profound sense of cultural

论,他的诗中经常有"天地""宇宙""乾坤""古今""万里""百年"等等,人们都很佩服,古人舒章甚至说:"'大'字是工部家畜。"试问,倘若"工部"不用"大词",他还是杜甫吗?所以我认为,在吉狄马加用"大词"的问题上,我们应当再思量,不能把长处看成短处。要不,我们可能难以读到《献给土著民族的颂歌》这种好诗大诗,看不到吉狄马加抛话语让火焰"继续燃烧"了。

interrelatedness with all creatures, his poems should be best read with the majestic themes and uplifting purpose for a redeemed world for all the people in mind. Let us keep cheering him up for a new surge of his poetic brilliance and grandeur.

全球化语境下土著民族诗人的语言策略
——以吉狄马加为例

首都师范大学　吴思敬

诗歌创作的核心因素是语言。诗人与世界的关系,体现在诗人和语言的关系中。海德格尔说:"诗是一种创建,这种创建通过词语并在词语中实现。"他还指出:"诗乃是一个历史性民族的原语言。"可见诗歌正是源于一个民族的历史深处,而一个民族诗人的心灵,也正是在该民族语言的滋润与培育之下,才逐渐丰富与完美起来的。

民族的语言对一个诗人的成长及其作品的面貌起着决定性的作用。民族的血缘,是奇妙的,在诗人出生之际就已铭刻在诗人的基因之中,此后在漫长的创作生涯中,它又时时在召唤着诗人。黑格尔指出:"艺术和它的一定的创造方式是与某一民族的民族性密切相关的。"对于一个民族群体来说,共同的自然条件和社会生活,使他们在世代繁衍过程中,能够自觉地根据有利于群体生存发展的原则来行动,形成在观察处理问题时的特殊的视点、思路和心理定式,表现出共同的心理素质。这种共同的心理素质通过一代一代的实践积淀于心理结构之中,又会作用于民族成员的一切活动,包括诗歌创作活动。

一个国家或地区的主流民族诗人与土著民族诗人,都是在本民族语言的环境下成长起来的,也都面临着运用哪种语言写作的问题。对于主流民族诗人来说,问题比较简单,只要按照自己从小习得的并在后来的创作实践中得心应手的语言去写就是了。土著民族诗人的情况要复杂一些。有些诗人从小生活于土著民族地区,精熟本民族的语言,他们终生都用本民族的语言写作。随着全球化的进展、各民族地域经济的快速发展、各民族文化的交流与融合,完全使用土著民族语言写作的诗人越来越少,

The Linguistic Strategy of Adopted by an Indigenous Poet in the Context of Globalization

Wu Sijing, Capital Normal University

The core factor of poetic expression is language. What a given poet to his world is exemplified in the way a poet manipulates his language. Heidegger writes: "Poetry is creation, one attained through the medium of words." He further points out: "Poetry is the primordial language of a historical nationality." This German philosopher is trying to drive home a point that poetry is embedded in the earth's core in the history of a nation. A major poet of any nation, to flourish and prosper, must be fed with the nectars of his language.

Language is central to the spiritual growth of any poet who attempts to emerge from among his indigenous people. The mysterious blood of a nation, usually pre-sculptured into his genes before his birth, will exert a lasting influence on all his mature output. That's why Hegel says: " Art and its mode of production is closely bound to the national characteristics." For the members of a given nation, common natural circumstances and collective communal existence, necessitate them, in the protracted process of self propagation, to act for common good, to form special perspective and viewpoints, and demonstrate some mentalistic qualities unique of all the members of the same group. These mental qualities will surely precipitate in the deep recesses of the psyche of the nation which will in turn make their subtle influence in the way the member of the same group act , behave, and compose poems.

Poets, mainstream or indigenous, growing and emerging from their own linguistic milieu, are confronted with the same fundamental dilemma: which language am I using for poetic creation? For mainstream national poets, the question is simple: set to pen in the language acquired at birth, and continually refine it to the point of perfection. For an indigenous poet like

而采用当地主流民族语言写作的土著民族诗人则越来越多。这是由于在全球化的今天,一成不变地维持传统的生产方式与生活方式的土著民族越来越少,在一个开放的社会当中,土著民族已融入现代化的浪潮之中,现代化的生产方式与生活内容,使土著民族诗人的写作不再同于他们的前辈,而呈现了开放性。这种开放,一方面表现为在全球化背景下土著民族诗人所涉及的题材、所选取的意象、所表现的情感,与不同种族、不同肤色的人们所共同关切的问题的贴近;另一方面则表现在他们的语言策略上,那就是相当多的土著民族诗人不再坚持用土著民族的语言写作,而采用主流民族的语言写作。

土著民族诗人使用主流民族的语言写作,并不意味着其民族特点的丧失。一个土著民族诗人的民族性,主要表现在长期的民族生产方式和生活方式下形成的观察世界、处理问题的特殊的心理定式和思维方式,那种烙印在心灵深处的民族潜意识,那种融合在血液中的民族根性,并不会因说话方式的不同而改变。相反,借助主流民族语言的宽阔的平台,土著民族的特殊的民族心理和民族性格反而能得到更充分的表现。在这方面取得成功的土著民族诗人很多,吉狄马加就是一个杰出的范例。

吉狄马加是一位彝族诗人,他熟悉本民族的语言,但是在诗歌创作中采用了中国的主流民族语言——汉语。这是一个彝人的后代在世界进入全球化时代,在彝人社会已随着整个中国现代化的步伐而发生了重大变化的今天,所做出的重要的选择。

作为用汉语写作的彝族诗人,吉狄马加既不同于用汉语写作的汉族诗人,又不同于用彝语写作的彝族诗人。作为彝族诗人,要用并非自己母语的汉语写作,平添了写作的难度,他承受的语言痛苦,要远远大于一般汉族诗人承受的语言痛苦,然而诗歌创作带给诗人的快感之一,就是在征服语言痛苦中诗情的迸发与诗思的精进。吉狄马加对于少数民族诗人采用汉语写作,是有着自己的深切理解的。他认为阅读少数民族诗人用汉语写作的诗歌,"使人置身于一种相互交织的语境之中。少数民族作家的作品不能只在现代主义的修辞风格框架内解读。因为他们既置身于汉语写作的场域,又显然植根于本民族经书、神话、民间故事的地方传统。这似乎是一种考验,因为他既要在很高的层面上把握汉语的真谛,又要驾驭两种语言、两种思维方式的碰

Jidi Majia, his fate is a bit more difficult and challenging. Some indigenous poets, acculturated in their own language and their own way of life, stick to them all the way through. Yet the forces of industrialization and globalization in particular, are at cross purposes, pressurizing them to shift to or alternate between their mother tongue and the mainstream language. Indigenous people, as a rule, are increasingly drawn into the grand project of modernization. In its wake, new mode of existence inclines new generation of aboriginal poets to display a large degree of openness in their writing. Such openness involves ,in a globalized context, the choosing of theme, leitmotif, plot, imagery, emotional response, easily accessible to many regardless of color and race. On the other hand, in terms of linguistic means of poetic creation, some ethnic poets simply forgo their mother tongue in favor of the mainstream language.

The downright shifting to the mainstream language in the hands of an ethnic poet does not necessarily entail the erosion of his national characteristics. An ethnic poet's nationality, which is reflected in his mentality, viewpoint, formed in the long process of particularist mode of communal existence and production, in his national root already melted down in his veins, will not alter as his mode of speech varies. On the contrary, what he loses he makes up on a more grander and broad plane of the mainstream linguistic means by which his communal characteristics and mental processes are revealed into sharper relief. Jidi Majia is one of the exemplary examples among many who develop dexterity in and craftsmanship with the language of the Chinese.

A yi poet, Jidi Majia is quite familiar with his mother tongue. Yet in his major poetic work, he opts the Chinese, a vital option he takes in the present day context of globalization, and more pertinently, his Nuoso societies are basically incorporated into China's drive for modernization.

A Yi poet, Jidi Majia, alternates between the Chinese and the marginalized Yi language, caught in the cross fire understandably, a fate compounded exponentially. The linguistic pains he suffers is definitely greater than that of a mainstream poet. Yet ,as Emerson says, "Nature, when she adds difficulties, adds brain." In battling with a natural paucity of the mainstream linguistic resources, syntactical, verbal or rhetoric in nature, Jidi Majia prevails and flourishes with both refinement of the Chinese and an usual outburst of poetic genius. Jidi Majia has this to say, with full assurance and justice, for a poet in his position: " thrust into an intertextual context, the works of an ethnic writer cannot be approached simply within the framework of modernist rhetoric.

撞和交融"。

当然,运用非母语写作,虽然增大了写作难度,增添了诗人的语言痛苦,但是给诗人运用语言开辟了新的天地。把彝人的体貌、性格、心理用汉语传达出来,为当代诗歌带来新的场域、新的气息,这是一个方面;另一方面,吉狄马加用汉语写作,又直接激发了他对汉语的深层次的学习与把握。吉狄马加说:"我的思维常常在彝语与汉语之间交汇,就像两条河流,时刻在穿越我的思想。我非常庆幸的是,如果说我的诗歌是一条小船,这两种伟大的语言,都为这条小船带来过无穷的乐趣和避风的港湾。作为诗人,我要感谢这两种伟大的语言。是因为它们,才给我提供这无限的创造的空间。"

吉狄马加是语言天赋很强的诗人。彝语与汉语这两种各有其独特的文化内涵与不同的语言构造的语言,竟能在他的头脑中自由地融汇在一起,互相渗透,互相交融。当然,由于吉狄马加最后是用汉语把诗写出来的,我们不太可能窥见他头脑中两种语言方式的冲撞与融合,但是就他的作品而言,尽管是汉语写出的,但其格调、韵味又不同于一般的汉语,而是彝人化的汉语。这是他笔下的岩石:

> 它们有着彝族人的脸形
> 生活在群山最孤独的地域
> 这些似乎没有生命的物体
> 黝黑的前额爬满了鹰爪的痕迹

这不只是孤独的群山中的岩石,更是彝人的民族精神的写照。尽管是用汉语写出来,但透露出的生命气息绝对是彝人的。如果对比一下艾青的名篇《礁石》,两个民族的优秀诗人的不同胸怀与境界立刻就显示出来了。此外,在《往事》《彝人梦见的颜色——关于一个民族最常使用的三种颜色的印象》《故乡的火葬地》《史诗和人》《告别大凉山》《色素》等诗作中,均能发现在汉语写作后面的一位彝族诗人的民族性与独特的灵魂。

吉狄马加是彝人的优秀的儿子,但不是仅仅龟缩于古老的彝族文化传统中的守

Placed both in a field of the Chinese writing and an alien tradition embedded in a different communal existence, set of canonical works, myths, storytelling, folklore is definitely a moment to try one's soul. I must strike the balance between a true grasp of the ropes of using the Chinese admirably and managing the impact borne as two languages and two cultures collide beautifully."

Of course, handling a language other than the one acquired at birth adds difficulties and opens new possibilities. To display Yi's mentality and personality in Chinese brings new field of discourse and ethos to contemporary poetry. Further crops harvested include a Yi poet inspired to new dimensions and heights of comprehending the Chinese and the Chinese culture. Jidi Majia writes: "My thinking often converges at the crossing of the Chinese and the Yi, just like two rivers, to rush through my thought. I congratulate myself my small boat of poetry, made of these two great languages, glide through many storms to be always anchored in the safe harbor. Thanks to the Chinese and my mother tongue, I begin to evince increasingly greater possibilities in poetry."

Obviously a promising poet, Jidi Majia evinces the prospect of one with two opposed languages in syntax and cultural connotation merged in his soul. We read him in his Chinese poems, though in a language not his mother tongue, its ethos, spirit, tone, set them apart from other Chinese poetry, a mark of genius and success. He writes about rocks:

These rocks are featured like Yi faces,

Living amongst the most solitary peaks.

These objects, seemingly without being given life,

Dark foreheads filled with traces of eagles' talons.

These are not certainly common rocks in the solitary mountains, but a personification of the Yi spirituality. Written in the Chinese, the ethos and the spirit are unmistakably Yi's.Jidi Majia's rocks compare supremely to Ai Qing's rocks in his Reef, both masterpieces in praise of perseverance and hardiness of both nationalities two major poets belong to respectively. In Jidi Majia's famous poems like Recollections of the Past, The Colors A Yi Dreamd,A Cemetry of My Home District, Adieu to Daliangshan, Pigment, one reads the soul and unique genius behind his brilliant writing.

A worthy son of the Yi, Jidi Majia is not confined to the time-honored Yi traditions. Fully

成者,他意识到,每一种文化都是一条河流,它们可以平行,也可以交汇。因此他在自觉地开掘民族文化传统的同时,又敞开胸怀,去学习与吸收汉族文化,拥抱世界文化,从而为他创建的诗国投射进几缕明丽的阳光,更显得雄奇瑰丽。

aware every culture is a river which runs either parallel to another or converge to become a mightier one, he takes the initiative to plunge into his own heritage and embrace Chinese culture and world cultures unflinchingly which lends to his own poetic experience some rays of alien sunshine ,making him the pride of his Yi people and of the mainstream Chinese poetry.

附录 2

拥抱一切的诗歌[1]

[俄罗斯]叶夫图申科

"人有三死,而非其命也。"——孔子[2]

只有一位非凡的作家方能写得如此明晰和朴实[3]。

甚或,只有一位背靠汉语格言警句之长城的中国作家方能如此写作,这道城墙并未使汉语格言警句与人类的其他区域相隔绝,反而将中国哲学与整个世界的哲学峰峦完满地连接为一个整体。我为之作序的这些格言警句的作者,就是无所畏惧的吉狄马加。孔子在《论语》中所说的一句话完全适用于他:"温故而知新,可以为师矣。"

他的诗歌将世界历史的所有时代,将世界诗歌的各种语言连接为一个整体,犹如一道人类智慧的彩虹。吉卜林说过一句名言:"东方即东方,西方即西方,它们都无法挪动地方。"可是,这句话对于马加来说却是陈腐之词。俄国与中国已完全恢复兄弟般的关系,我因此对中国充满感激。中国有许多可供学习之处,其中就包括其政治克制。中国的经济比许多欧洲中等国家都更文明、更强大。美国负债于中国。一切都在相互交替,一切都在相互交结。阿拉伯国家的大量移民拥入欧洲,这使得之前的所有预言皆成虚妄,他们完全不愿心悦诚服地被欧化,反而对好客的接纳者展开恐怖活动……圣诞节期间,650辆法国汽车被焚毁,一位突尼斯裔司机驾驶大卡车碾压那些给了他工作机会的法国人。是世界末日?一切归根结底都取决于我们自身的随机

---

[1] 此文为俄罗斯著名诗人叶夫盖尼·叶夫图申科(Евгений Евтушенко)为吉狄马加俄文诗集《从雪豹到马雅可夫斯基》(От снежного барса к Маяковскому)所作序言,写作时间为 2017 年 2 月。

[2] 孔子此语之俄译与原文有出入,俄译为"每一种死亡皆为投向生活的谴责"。

[3] "明晰和朴实"是俄国人对普希金诗歌风格的著名归纳。

Appendix 2

The All-Embracing Poesy
[Russia]Yevgeny Yevtushenko

"EACH DEATH, IT'S AN ACCUSATION AGAINST LIFE." CONFUCIUS

Only a very complicated writer could write so clearly and simply.

It could even perhaps be only a specifically Chinese writer, behind whom stands a grand wall of adages, one that is not separating them from the rest of humanity but holistically connecting their Chinese philosophy with the high peaks of philosophy of the entire world. The author of the aphorism in the title of my foreword to his poems, Jidi Majia, is an intrepid human being. To him a maxim by Confucius from Lun Yu (The Analects of Confucius) fully applies:

He who perceives the new, while cherishing the old,

He can be a teacher.

His poetry connects all the ages of world history, and all the different-tongued poetries, as a rainbow of human wisdom. The Kipling aphorism: "Yes the West is the West. The East is the East, and they won't be moved from their places", forMajia, is an anachronism. I am grateful to China for the fact that Russia and China have fully reestablished their fraternal relationship. And one can learn from China, in particular, political self-restraint. Chinese economy is more civilized and more potent than the economies of many central European countries. The U.S.A. is now a debtor country to China. Everything has shifted; everything became intermingled. Mass emigration from Arabic countries into Europe has menacingly jumbled all predictions and not the least bit wishes to quietly Europeanize, terrorizing the hospitable place that invited them in... 650 French cars torched in France at Christmas, a truck with a Tunisian driver crushing the very French people who gave him employment. The apocalypse? In the end, everything depends upon our personal ability to find solutions. Confucius made fun of people who keep only clutching their heads and moan, "What should one to do?" "How to be?" One ought to... just be. Be yourselves, and try being even better. Recall the American philosopher Emerson's adage that has often rescued me, "Any wall is a door." He was once quoted by the great Algerian, Camus, in the foreword to a French edition, at a time when what is happening today one couldn't have imagined even in a most

应变。孔子曾嘲笑那些只会因为"怎么办"而伤透脑筋的人,他认为重要的是去做。去做自己,则更好。请你们想一想美国哲学家艾默生,他有一句格言常能让我步出困境:"每一堵墙都是门。"伟大的阿尔及利亚人加缪①在为一部法文著作作序时引用过这句话,当时,即便在最可怕的噩梦中也很难预见如今的局面。

　　出路总是有的。应当将世上的所有智慧融为一体,所有的宗教无论如何都不该相互争吵,所有的"主义"也当如此。应当淡忘所有的相互猜疑,以拯救人类。在马加看来,世界哲学的所有峰峦上均留有先人遗迹的神奇一环,那些人的确视人类为一个大家庭,他们在这个家庭中寻求共同出路,那里有他们留给我们的召唤的遗迹,以使我们大家不再无动于衷,共同加入这样的追寻。马加是一位实践的理想主义者,当下需要这类理想主义者。我与马加仅有过一个晚上的交往,但他令人难忘。他身上充盈着对人类的爱,足够与我们大家分享。这是一位中国的惠特曼。他的身材并不魁梧,他的手也不算大,可他的身与手却足以使他拥抱整个地球。他的诗歌也是这样,是拥抱一切的。马加呼应着当年还相当年轻的叶夫图申科:

　　　　我喜爱一切都相互交替,
　　　　一切都在我身上相互交结,
　　　　从西方到东方,
　　　　从嫉妒到喜悦。
　　　　边界妨碍我……我会不好意思,
　　　　如果不知布宜诺斯艾利斯和纽约……②

又如:

　　　　当边界尚在,我们只是史前人。
　　　　历史开始时,便再无边界。③

————————

①法国作家加缪生于阿尔及利亚的蒙多维,成长于阿尔及利亚贝尔库的平民区,后在阿尔及尔读中学和大学,当过阿尔及利亚竞技大学队足球队门将,曾在阿尔及尔大学攻读哲学和古典文学。
②这是叶夫图申科《序言》(1955年)一诗中的诗句。
③这是叶夫图申科的长诗《禁忌》(1963—1985)中的诗句。

horrifying dream.

A way out always exists. All the world's wisdoms just need to be submerged into one; all religions mustn't quarrel under any circumstances, and all the "isms" should do the same. It is the time for rescuing humanity itself, forgoing our customary distrust of each other. According toMajia, on all the summits of philosophy there is a fairylike chain of tracks left by people seriously apprehensive about humankind's being one single family, and searching a common solution within this communality. And there are there also his own beckoning tracks that urge us not to remain indifferent and join these searches. Majia is one of the practical idealists, who are so sorely needed now. I have spent just one evening with him but this man is unforgettable. There is so much within him of sheer love toward humanity; it is ample enough to cover for all of us. In his own way, this is a Chinese Walt Whitman. He is not at all a giant in terms of his physical height, and he has diminutive hands, but they are large enough for him to embrace the entire earthly globe. Such is his poetry, too, it is all-embracing. Majia echoes with a once youthful Yevtushenko:

I love, hence all is entwined
And so much of all's tangled up in me
From the West to the East
From envy to delight.
Borders are bothering me... I feel awkward
To know not Buenos-Aires or New York...

Or,

Until there'll be borders, we'll beprehistorical.
Real history starts when borders will be no more.

A mind and heart such as those thatMajia has feel tight within any boundaries, since for him borders are simply the scars from wars that have wounded our Mother Earth. True boundaries separate not countries but people.

The poetry ofJidi Majia is a mosaic from so many of the world's best poets, that amalgamates the Hungarian singer of freedom Attila Joseph; the Russian futurist chieftain Mayakovsky; the antifascist Spaniard Garcia Lorca; the Turk Nazim Hikmet; the Chilean Pablo Neruda; and includes the Georgian poet Titian Tabidze, who was trampled into the earth while still alive, by Stalin's executioners. He comprises all of them, together.

He even consists of death, but of death that grants immortality.

Not everyone will have the courage to take death for a collaborator, in order to accuse life of criminal depravity in its treatment of people. Not if it permits the murder of those who are still

马加拥有的这种智慧和胸怀，在任何一种边界之内都会令人感觉逼仄，因为对他而言，这些边界只是战争在我们地球母亲身上划出的道道伤痕。真正的边界实际上不存在于国与国之间，而存在于人与人之间。

马加的诗歌是一幅由世界上许多优秀诗人的创作构成的镶嵌画，这里有匈牙利的自由歌手尤诺夫，有俄国未来派首领马雅可夫斯基，有西班牙反法西斯主义者洛尔迦，有土耳其诗人希克梅特，有智利人聂鲁达，有被苏联时期的刽子手活埋的格鲁吉亚诗人塔比泽。马加是由所有这些诗人构成的。

他甚至是由那种注定能使人不朽的死亡构成的。

并非每个人都敢于与死亡结盟，以便谴责生活对于人所持的犯罪性的无人性态度，当生活允许人们在童年时，甚至婴儿时就被战争、疾病、经常性的营养不良和饥饿所戕害，他们无论如何也不该遭受这些不幸。我记得，很多人曾感觉萨哈罗夫院士很天真，当他作为氢弹的发明人试图征集签名，认为一切战争均属非法，因为战争的大多数牺牲者都是无辜的时候。他和许多核物理学家一样成了和平主义者，因为他们最早意识到在核战争中没有赢家，尽管直到如今，他们仍无法说服世界上的当权者宣布一切战争非法，因为若停止一切武器生产和武器改进，数百万人便会失去工作。

不应忘记，同样不愿看到又一次世界大战爆发的许多美国人在其潜意识中既无关于美国境内战争的深刻记忆，也不像欧洲人那样对外国占领者建立的集中营刻骨铭心，可他们记得，正是世界大战和军事工业的发展帮助他们走出了经济大萧条。因此，"战争"一词对于他们而言并不像对于欧洲人那样令人恐怖。于是，一种悖论便持续下来，即被送上法庭的只有被抓获的个人杀人犯，而参与大规模屠杀即战争的罪犯却不承担任何责任，甚至还不时获奖受勋。在战后的美国曾涌现出一批经历战争的杰出的反法西斯作家与和平主义者，如海明威、冯内古特、斯泰伦、金斯堡、鲍勃·迪伦等，他们勇敢地谴责越战。这些作家中的许多人都成了我的生活导师，他们长眠在如今对我而言已不陌生的美国土地。谢天谢地，如今许多美国人前往越南和广岛旅游，他们会在留言簿上写道："永不再战！"

可遗憾的是，在电影课上观看我那部描述我这一代人在二战期间经历的影片《幼儿园》之后，一位可爱的美国农场主之女却在作业中写道："尽管俄国在二战期间曾与希特勒狼狈为奸，我仍对叶夫图申科先生充满感激，因为他向我们展示，某些俄国人也很善良可爱。"呜呼，某些美国中小学教师正是这样教授历史的，他们甚至不会提及，如果俄国人没有在斯大林格勒打败希特勒，我们的美国盟友就无法于1944

young, and sometimes even while infants, at wars, and through illnesses, and by means of constant undernourishment or simply by starvation which they did not earn by virtue of some, or any, sin. I remember how the academician Sakharov seemed to many a native person when he, the inventor of hydrogen bomb, attempted to collect signatures concerning the criminality of any war, since the majority of a war's victims are innocent. He was transformed into a pacifist, as were many other nuclear scientists, because they were the first to grasp that a nuclear war will not have any winners. Yet despite this, so far even they didn't succeed in convincing the powers that be to render any war illegal, because stopping the production and development of weapons would leave millions of people without jobs.

One mustn't forget that in the subconscious of many Americans, who of course likewise do not desire a new world war, there is no deep memory of either bombing of their territory or of concentration camps as in Europe, built by foreign invaders. Instead, there is a call to mind that it is precisely the world war and the development of weapon industry that once aided them in ending the Great Depression. Because of that, the word "war" lacks for them such a sinister meaning, as it does for many Europeans. Thus, the paradox continues: only individual murderers are prosecuted, if of course they can be found, yet those who take part in mass murders, known as wars, somehow end up not being responsible and even at times receive medals. After the Second World War, there was in the United States a magnificent array of writers, antifascists and pacifists who lived through wars, Ernest Hemingway, Kurt Vonnegut, William Styron, Allen Ginsberg and Bob Dylan: they found within themselves the mature strength to oppose the war in Vietnam. Many of these writers became for me the teachers of life, and they are buried in America, a land that is no longer alien but became kindred to me. Thank God that many Americans now go as tourists to Vietnam, and to Hiroshima, leaving their comments there in books of commiserations: "Never again!"

Sadly, after watching, in a film class that I've taught, my own film "Kindergarten", about the role of our generation it the Second World War, one farm girl wrote in her student assignment: "Notwithstanding that in the Second World War Russia fought on the side of Hitler, I am grateful to Mr. Yevtushenko that he demonstrated that some Russian people were very kind and goodpeople." Alas, this is how some teachers of schools in the US teach history, without even mentioning that had the Russians failed to crush Hitler at Stalingrad, our American allies would not have been able to land in 1944 in Normandy. I am delighted that Chinese students have Jidi Majia as their teacher, for he absorbed the experience of history of the entire planet, with many of its best people. From among the politicians he chose one of the people closest to me, Nelson Mandela a person whose one incendiary word would have been enough, after his long years of incarceration, for the black majority of South Africa to annihilate, in blood, its white minority. Instead, he spoke the unequivocal "no"! to the racism-in-reverse, and extended his hand to his white opponent, Clark. Everyone has leaped on him, with gratitude; the most beautiful shirts of

年在诺曼底登陆。我感到幸运的是，中国的大学生们拥有吉狄马加这样的老师，他汲取了整个地球及其众多杰出人物的历史经验。在政治家中间，他选中了我最亲近的人之一——纳尔逊·曼德拉，这个坐牢近30年的人只需一声召唤，便可让占南非人口大多数的黑人消灭占人口少数的白人，可他却对反向的种族主义坚定地说"不"，并向他的白人政敌德克勒克伸出手去。众人心怀感激地拥向他，全世界最好看的衬衫拥抱着他，因为他有一颗诗人的心灵。曼德拉在阅读孔子和甘地的著作之后，以他不愿为旧怨而复仇的胸襟，把一个没有人性的种族主义国家变成了人道的国度，用这位中国先哲的比喻来说就是："子曰：里仁为美。择不处仁，焉得知？"

1972年，我应美国27所大学邀请为大学生读诗，也在麦迪逊花园为人数甚多的听众朗诵。在此之后，美国总统尼克松邀我前往他位于白宫的椭圆形办公室，说他想了解我的看法，即他如果为修复中美关系而先去北京，俄国人是否会感到不悦。遗憾的是，当时中苏之间爆发了珍宝岛冲突，但我回答说，这对于国际局势而言将非常有益，如果之后能对中苏关系产生正面影响则更加有益。结果果然如此，我也因此而十分高兴。顺便提一句，当时我写过一首关于珍宝岛冲突的诗，"文革"结束后不久我访问了中国，我很快意识到我那首诗是错误的，置身于那些冲突，最正确的事情就是避免作出单方面的结论。在这之后，我曾在越南见到一位中国水兵，他正在船舷旁洗涤海魂衫。他知道我是俄国人，他有些担心地环顾四周，见无一人，便兄弟般地冲我挤了挤眼，我也冲他挤了挤眼。于是，我写下这样一首诗：

> 谢谢你，瘦小的水兵，
> 谢你提心吊胆的挤眼，
> 谢你用睫毛抛弃谎言，
> 即便有些担心，即便一瞬之间。
> 无人能消灭人民。
> 人民终将醒来，
> 只要有人依然能够
> 富有人情味地挤眼。

1985年，我作为威尼斯电影节的评委在威尼斯与当时担任主席的一位中国著名女影星结下友谊，她允诺完成一项友谊的使命，即把我的一首新诗转交给中国的翻译家们，该诗就是献给他们的，尽管红卫兵们试图禁止他们工作，禁止他们将全世

the world hugging him, for he had the soul of a poet. A country of inhumanity, of racism, Mandela, reading Confucius and Gandhi, has transformed South Africa into a region of humanness, thanks to his unvengefulness vis-à-vis former offenses; it was in accordance with the metaphor of a Chinese philosopher: The teacher said, "It's wonderful there, where there is humanness. How can a smart person, having a choice, not settle in such a land?"

In 1972 I was invited by 27 American universities to read my poetry for their students, and also at Madison Square Garden, an immense auditorium. After that the U.S. president, Nixon, invited me to the Oval Office at the White House, saying that he would like to know my opinion on whether the Russian people would be offended if he went to Beijing first, to mend the relationship with China. At that time, unfortunately, we had a conflict over Damansky Island and I responded that this would be very good for the international situation, especially if then this might positively affect the relationship of China with the U.S.S.R. And that's how it indeed has turned out, and I am delighted about it. By the way, I wrote just then some poems about this conflict, and when I came to China right after the Cultural Revolution I realized that these poems were misguided in such conflicts the right thing to do is to steer clear of one-sided conclusions. After that, seeing once in Vietnam a Chinese sailor washing his shirt aboard his little vessel and who, a little apprehensively, glanced at me, but realizing that I was a Russian and that no one was around, he winked to me in a brotherly way, and I did the same to him. The poem ended as follows:

Thank you, skinny little sailor,
For your timid wink
For throwing away lies with your eyebrow
Even if anxiously even if for a twinkling of an eye.
A whole people no one can annihilate.
It'll wake up some day
As long as there is someone who can wink,
Wink, as a human being can.

And in 1985, being in Venice as a member of the panel of judges at the Venetian Film Festival, I befriended its then-chairperson, a famous Chinese film star. She agreed to perform a mission of friendship to forward to Chinese translators my new poem, dedicated to them for their courage in translating the literature of the world into Chinese, in spite the Red Guards' attempt to boycott their work. Later I found out that this poem was translated by a Chinese authority on Russia, my friend Liu Wenfei.

I nurture a hope that my foresight will come into existence and there will be erected in Beijing a monument to the Unknown Chinese Translator, perhaps accompanied by my words in

界的一切非中文文学译成中文。后来我得知，我的这首诗由中国俄语学者刘文飞译成汉语，我和译者也因此成了朋友。

我一直存有一个希望，希望我的预见能够实现，即北京将建造一座中国无名翻译家纪念碑，它的基座上或可刻上我诗句的译文：

> 伟大的译文就像是预言。
> 被翻译的细语也会成为喊声。
> 要为中国无名翻译家立一座纪念碑，
> 可敬的基座就用译著垒成！

这些勇敢的人在最为艰难的处境中翻译我的诗句，我也成了第一个获得中国文学奖的俄国人，我因此而充满感激，我希望我能完成在全中国的诗歌朗诵之旅。

吉狄马加教导我们：不要忘记，人类就是一个大家庭，该为全世界诗歌的共同荣光树立一座座共同的纪念碑了。

(刘文飞　译)

(叶·亚·叶夫图申科，1933—2017，俄罗斯诗人。他是苏联20世纪50年代末、60年代初"大声疾呼"派诗人的代表人物，也是20世纪极具影响力的诗人之一。他的诗题材广泛，以政论性和抒情性著称，既写国内现实生活，也干预国际政治，以"大胆"触及"尖锐"的社会问题而闻名。)

translation:

> Grand translations may be likened to prophecies.
> A translated whisper is able to rouse as a scream.
> Arise, Memorial of Glory to the Unknown Chinese Translator
> Upon a pedestal of utmost honesty-of translated books!

I am grateful both for the fact that my poems were translated by these heroic individuals under the most difficult circumstances of deportations, and that I was the first Russian poet to receive a Chinese literary prize. My hope is that I'll travel someday across entire China with readings of my poetry.

Jidi Majia teaches us not to forget that humankind is one family-and it is high time for creating combined monuments of collective glory to all of the world's poesy.

Yevgeny Aleksandrovich Yevtushenko

(18 July 1933—1 April 2017) was a Soviet and Russian poet. He was also a novelist, essayist, dramatist, screenwriter, publisher, actor, editor and director of several films.

Translation from the Russian by JacobKohav

吉狄马加——"黑色河流"上的传奇诗人

[美国] 杰克·赫希曼

　　这本书里收录的是杰出的中国当代诗人吉狄马加的一些重要的诗作和部分他在不同场合所作的有关诗歌和文学的演讲或致辞，这些作品充满了吉狄马加对人类和人类文化的敬意。

　　如果你想深刻地理解《从雪豹到马雅可夫斯基》这本书的内蕴并到诗人的内心世界做一番冒险之旅的话，那么首先请你记住：吉狄马加是一位彻底的国际主义者。

　　吉狄马加的这些诗是他用汉语写成的，由美国著名诗人、汉学家梅丹里翻译成英语，无论原作还是译文无疑都是十分精彩的。

　　吉狄马加是中国五十五个少数民族之一的彝族的一员，是这个有着近900万人口的少数民族的灵魂人物之一。吉狄马加现任中国作家协会副主席，不仅在彝族而且在全中国当下的文学界特别是诗界，他都是当之无愧的领军人物。作为一个彝族的子孙，吉狄马加为自己的民族和部落感到自豪，他的很多诗歌都是在这种民族和部落的精神维度上写出来的，譬如，本书中所收录的两首长诗之一的《我，雪豹》，其意象组合里充满了诗人的中国心和中国魂，更盈溢着作者对居住在中国西南部的彝族同胞的情和爱。

　　彝族有很多支系，吉狄马加属于彝族中的诺苏，又称诺苏彝族（诺苏在彝语中意思是黑色的民族）。吉狄马加的诗歌之河就源自中国西南地区的"这条黑色河流"，他是带着"这条黑色河流"走上诗坛的。

　　固然黑彝在这里并不意味着种族色彩，但一个看似矛盾其实颇有关联的事实我

Jidi Majia-Nuosu Bard of the "Black River"
[USA]Jack Hirschman

This book is really an anthology of some major poems of the great Chinese poet, Jidi Majia, as well as texts of some of the cultural manifestoes and speeches he has given upon receiving awards himself, or paying homage to others in the realm of planetary culture.

To better understand the adventure you are undertaking in reading From the Snow, Leopard To Mayakovsky, it's important to know that:

Jidi Majia is an internationalist to the core.

His poems here are written in Chinese and brilliantly translated by the American poet Denis Mair; but Jidi Majia is also a member and leading figure in one of 56 minorities in China, the Yi people, which numbers 8 million. It's very important to keep that ethnic fact in mind because Majia, though a deputy in the high office of the All China Writers Association, is also the cultural director of the 55 minority peoples within the ethnic dynamic of China. He is devotedly proud of his own origin as a child of the Yi people, so much so that their particular dimensionality figures deeply in many of the poems here.

Indeed, in the I, Snow Leopard poem——one of two major long poems in this book——the images are imbued with the spirit and heart of all of China and particularly the southwest mountainous territory of the Yi people.

Its important also to know that the Yi people have many diverse strands. Majia belongs to the Nuoso or Black strain (Nuo means Black in the Yi language) and Majia's River poem is a deeply evoked homage to that Deep Black River in the southwest of China from which he emerged as a poet as a young man.

And though Black here is not meant as a racial color, the paradoxical fact is also true that, from a youthful time——under the influence of Maoist anti-colonial cultural politics as well as his own avid reading of African and Caribbean poets——Africa came to have a powerful meaning in Majia's heart, so much so that he spells that meaning out in his essay, "The African Complex of a Chinese Poet", which is included here; and his empathetic attachment to Africa is so profound, he

不得不予以提及——吉狄马加在青少年时代受到了毛泽东的反殖民主义文化政策的影响，加之他自身渴望读非洲和加勒比诗人的诗，在他的心里，非洲有着非同寻常的意义，在他的随笔《一个中国诗人的非洲情结》里可见一斑；此外，他对非洲的情感是如此之深，以至于他在一首悼念纳尔逊·曼德拉的诗里，采取移情方式，将纳尔逊·曼德拉称颂为"我们的父亲"。

吉狄马加用诗赞美南非的传奇式人物曼德拉是因为曼德拉的胸怀之宽广到了能够原谅那些囚禁他多年的人的境界。此外，在这本诗选里，受到吉狄马加赞美的人物还有匈牙利诗人阿提拉·约瑟夫、西班牙诗人费德里戈·加西亚·洛尔卡、德国著名摄影师安德里亚·古尔斯基等。

这本诗选里的另一首长诗是《写给弗拉基米尔·马雅可夫斯基》，经过跨越世纪的等待，这首具有划时代意义的诗作终于横空问世。

当绝大多数的美国人、欧洲人、非洲人还有亚洲人提及中国的时候，一个亚洲人的影子就会即刻浮现，这也是我从诗人和文化工作者、官员和彝族的双重维度来写吉狄马加的缘由之所在。

毫无疑问，在中国，五十五个少数民族并不是微小的，他们都有成千上万的人，构成了中国社会的多样性。这点，凡是访问过中国的人都会明显地感受到。彝族都会说汉语，同时也说彝族的语言；他们有自己的历史和史诗，他们亲近自然、敬畏自然，这些，在吉狄马加的这本诗选里都有呈现。正如我们一直用狭隘的民族维度看待中国的少数民族一样，我们对当下中国的现代诗歌的看法也是近视的。

这些日子一直萦绕在我脑海的是"中国"式的中国诗歌写作。中文——这是中国诗歌的方式，它看起来像这像那，听起来如何如何，而吉狄马加的诗歌在这方面与之有很大的不同，他的抒情感觉根植于自然的东西：河流和山脉。这些自然对象是他认定人类生存环境和英雄存在的核心条件。他的诗在中国诗歌传统的叙事风格的基础上融入了西方诗歌的国际主义维度，在吉狄马加诗歌里出现的这些现象源于如下两个主要理由：

一方面，诗歌统治着吉狄马加的生命，共产主义和宇宙意识同时存在于他的思想意识中，构成了他的世界观。他的诗歌、演讲、散文以及有关诗歌的宣言或主张扎

entitles his great ode to Nelson Mandela Our Father.

That wondrous South African whom Majia apostrophizes because Mandela was able to arrive at a level of consciousness wherein he could forgive even those who imprisoned him, is not the only figure that receives Jidi's honors: the great Hungarian poet, Joszef Attila, Spain's Federico Garcia Lorca, Germany's photographer Andrea Guersky——all are homaged in poems in this volume.

And of course the other long poem in this book, the epochal For Vladimir Mayakovsky, is a poem that two generations of contemporary poetry have been waiting to be written. Now, with a grand lo-and-behold, it's finally, miraculously here!

For most Americans, and Europeans and Africans and Asians too, when China is mentioned, an image of an Asian people emerges all of a piece. That's why I've written about Jidi Majia's twofold dimension as a poet and cultural worker, as a man both within the government of China, and as a member of the Yi people.

There's no contradiction here. 55 minorities aren't a piddling. They constitute millions upon millions of people, and they contribute to the overwhelming diversity of Chinese society, which becomes evident to anyone who visits China for more than a quickstop.

The Yi people all speak Chinese but they also speak the Yi language and indeed a lot of Yi history and its proximity to nature is evoked in poems in this book.

And just as we've been narrow-minded when it comes to the ethnic dimensions of contemporary China, so too do we have a myopic view of Chinese poetry.

For example, imbedded in most minds these days is that there is a "Chinese" way of writing Chinese poetry. It looks like such and such, sounds like this and that, ie., it's Chinese: that's the way Chinese poetry is. Jidi Majia's poetry is very different in that respect. His lyrical feelings, as translated by Mair, come with roots in the naming of the things of nature, from rivers and mountains, and these natural objects are central to his affirmations of the human conditions and the heroes thereof. In an epical style which engages both traditional Chinese poetry but evokes as well an internationalist dimension of western poetry, there are two major reasons for these phenomena in Majia's work:

On the one hand, poetry is the ruler of Jidi Majia's life. It is the existential——yes, in the both communist and cosmic sense——root of his affirmations in both poetry and his ever solidaritous manifestoes and speeches in prose: trees are trees and mountains, mountains; but the naming of them in a poem with heartfeltness and imaginative spirit is in Jidi Majia's mind the apotheosis of spirit itself. And since the Yi people are noted, among other aspects, as being obsessed with the origin of everything in nature (expressed in their Book of Origins), just as are China's Lao-Tse and Meng-Tse, one should understand Majia's poetry as coming from the shamanic tradition of the Yi people, as well as from modern Chinese poetry, one of the great sophistications of this age.

根在自然中：山、树木和河流。吉狄马加崇尚自然，认为万物有灵，他借助山地、树木和河流这些自然之物抒发他的内心世界。他的这方面的一些诗作表现了他丰富的想象力和自然崇拜的思想意识，这也是彝族的精神本质。彝族，在很多方面是很优秀的，譬如他们有关自然和起源方面的探求（在他们的有关人类和彝族起源方面的史诗中可见一斑）甚至可以和老子和庄子相提并论。总之，吉狄马加的诗歌精神源自彝族的萨满教，也源于自朦胧诗以来中国当下的各种诗歌思潮。

另一方面，吉狄马加不仅是一位伟大的诗人，还是一位杰出的文化活动家——他发起并创建了青海湖国际诗歌节、西昌邛海丝绸之路国际诗歌周等。这本诗选收录了吉狄马加写的包括《青海湖诗歌宣言》在内的有关诗歌方面的宣言或主张的散文，这些文字曾被黄少政翻译成英文，被克劳迪娅·科特翻译成德语，被拉斐尔·帕迪诺翻译成西班牙语，被弗朗索瓦丝·罗伊翻译成法语，被罗莎·隆巴尔迪翻译成意大利语，这些都充分印证了吉狄马加是中国的一位具有国际主义观念的文化工作者。

这里，我想顺便提及一下费尔南多·任东，他是麦德林国际诗歌节的长期主舵者，也是一位杰出的哥伦比亚诗人，曾因为组织这个举世闻名、一年一度的国际诗歌节以及该诗歌节所引发的社会功能（如铲除泛滥于麦德林的毒品犯罪和在20世纪末结束长达五十年的内战等主题）在数年前被授予另类诺贝尔奖。

2011年的麦德林国际诗歌节期间，我有两件幸事：一是我有幸读了吉狄马加赞颂费尔南多·任东的文字（那届麦德林国际诗歌节，露天朗诵会那天，倾盆大雨下个不停，然而，包括观众在内的5000多位到场者，无一人因雨而中途退席）；二是我有幸和其他来自世界各地的35位诗人和文化工作者一起发起和组织了世界诗歌运动。自从世界诗歌运动发起及相关机构成立以来，在费尔南多·任东的主持下，我们的会员每三周在网络上举办一次有关诗歌和诗歌运动的对话，一直坚持至今。

2015年8月，我和妻子阿格妮塔·福尔克（一位在瑞典出生的诗人）一起应邀出席第五届青海湖国际诗歌节，这是吉狄马加和他的同志们在2007年创办的一个国际性诗歌活动。诗歌节期间，我和妻子以及其他几乎所有各国诗人朗诵了我们各自的诗作，进行了一些交流活动。让我感到最为惊讶的是，摆放在青海湖诗歌墙上的聂鲁达、兰斯顿·休斯、杜甫、内莉·萨克斯、惠特曼、保罗·策兰等几十位古今中外著名

The other reason is not only because Jidi Majia is a writing poet, and a great one at that. There are poets whose lives are dedicated not simply to writing poems but to actively organizing international poetry festivals——for example at Qinghai Lake or Chengdu, as well as in other places around China. Majia's Manifesto For the Qinghai Lake International Poetry Festival, which is here translated into English——as are all the prose works in English in this book——by Huang Shaozheng, also is translated into German by Claudia Kotte, into Spanish by Rafael Patiño Gō ez, into French by Françoise Roy and into Italian by Rose Lombardi as a brilliant multiple example of Majia's profoundly internationalist perspective as a cultural worker.

Indeed his speech in honor of the Colombian poet and fellow cultural worker, Fernando Rendon, the longtime organizer of one of the grandest Festivals in the world in Medellin, Colombia, who was awarded the alternative Nobel Prize in Sweden some years ago for having---with that Festival, an annual event——erased the stain of "drugs" re Medellin, as well as helping bring the 50 year civil war in that country to an end.

I was overjoyed to read Majia's luminous apostrophization of Rendon because I've read at the Medellin Festival (5,000 people in attendance and not a single one leaves, even if there is a downpour of rain). With Fernando and 35 other poet/cultural workers from around the world, I was among those who in 2011 founded the World Poetry Movement (WPM), whose members every three weeks or so have a planetary chat with each other on computers, with Fernando at the helm.

And I'm proud to say that, since we met at the Qinghai Lake Festival, which Jidi Majia and comrades organized a couple of years ago, at which I and my wife, the Swedish-born poet Agneta Falk, were asked to read our poetry, I became convinced, through the Great Wall of Poets (including images of the likes of Pablo Neruda, Langston Hughes, Tu Fu. Nelly Sachs, Paul Celan and many others, and the Field of 24 statues of the heroes or the authors of the greatest Epic poems of the world, including Gilgamesh, Beowolf, Roland, Dante Alighieri, Walt Whitman and others)——all convinced me that Jidi Majia was not only a wondrous poet but, as a cultural force for the transformation of the world through the infusions of the art of poetry, he was deserving of the Nobel Prize for Literature, if ever any writer was deserving of it. In all the countries I've visited to read my works, I've never seen a more radiant homage to Poetry than what China has manifested through the energy of Jidi Majia.

His poem for Vladimir Mayakovsky is the finest portrait of the first street poet of the 20th century and the first poet to wholeheartedly embrace the communist revolution a hundred years ago. It is a centennially redemptive and resurrective poem that I've been waiting to read for more than two generations, and it's here with a majesty of image, rhythm and breath that will I'm certain fill the reader's imagination with a great strength to continue resisting the fascism and corporatism that beset all truly human beings these days.

Majia brings Mayakovsky to life just when we need him. The Slava on the lips of Mayakovsky

诗人的雕刻在玛尼石块上的画像，现场还耸立着包括吉尔伽美什、贝奥武夫、但丁的《神曲》以及中国藏族的《格萨尔王》、彝族的《勒俄特依》等 24 部人类英雄史诗或创世史诗及史诗作者的铜塑雕像。诗歌墙和诗歌广场上的这些雕像以及诗歌节的一些文化活动让我确信：吉狄马加不仅是一位杰出而奇特的诗人，还是一位用诗歌为转型期的世界注入文化力量的社会活动家。在我所走过的国家中，中国是当今世界最具诗歌辐射力的国度，这与吉狄马加为诗歌所注入的能量密不可分。我认为，吉狄马加和他的诗是值得用诺贝尔文学奖来予以褒奖的。

吉狄马加的长诗《写给弗拉基米尔·马雅可夫斯基》为马雅可夫斯基这位一百多年前第一位竭诚接受共产主义革命思想的伟大诗人勾画了一幅完美的肖像。这首诗是对于马雅可夫斯基百年一回的纪念，让已经故去的马雅可夫斯基得以"复活"，而我们等了超过两代人的时间才读到这样的一首诗。我敢肯定：诗里面庄严的形象、节奏和气氛肯定会给读者带来无限的想象空间，并给人们一种伟大的力量，去继续抵抗困扰人类社会的法西斯主义和社团主义。

在我们需要马雅可夫斯基的时候，吉狄马加用诗给我们送来了马雅可夫斯基。无论马雅可夫斯基还是吉狄马加，他们都用诗给人类的未来注入了动力！

2017 年 1 月　于美国旧金山

（杨宗泽　译）

（杰克·赫希曼，美国当代杰出诗人，1933 年出生在纽约市，已出版诗集一百多本，其中多半被翻译成法语、西班牙语、意大利语等十几种语言在国内外出版，其主要著作《神秘》出版于 2006 年；他连续数年被评为旧金山市桂冠诗人。他是旧金山革命诗人旅的创始人，同时也是二十世纪五六十年代以来美国最具有代表性的诗人之一。）

is the Glory of Poetry and Revolution on the lips of Jidi Majia, giving us new lyric strength for the future!

——Jack Hirschman   San Francisco, 2017

Jack Hirschman(born December 13, 1933) is an American poet and social activist who has written more than 50 volumes of poetry and essays.Luareate poet for San Francisco for many years.

《敬畏群山》翻译后记

吉狄马加是中国当代著名的少数民族代表性诗人，同时也是一位具有罕见国际视野、人类意识和文化底蕴，产生广泛影响的国际性诗人。吉狄马加已在国内外出版诗集近42种，涉及20多种外国语言。其散文作品，一如其诗歌作品，具有"浓郁的抒情气质，深挚而柔美的语言"，以及毋庸置疑的审美价值。

本书精选吉狄马加激情澎湃、遐思飞扬的演讲40篇，译成英文，全面展示诗人的学术谱系、心路历程，以及其诗歌乃至为人为文主要成就（地域文化差异性，文化多元性，环保，普遍意义上的正义、真理、众生平等），将补足一个大诗人在英语平台上的文本资源，给域外同行和研究者提供方便。

笔者最早读到的吉狄马加的文字，是他为青海湖国际诗歌节撰写的青海湖诗歌节宣言，惊为至文，如饮醇醪；及至翻译大美青海成都行，群山的回忆流淌成河，则不仅为吉狄马加先生喜悦，更为中国知识界、诗歌界开始和国际同行同步行动而欣慰。吉狄马加一手打造的青海湖国际诗歌节，及其一系列文化活动（如国际山地纪录片节、世界少数民族诗人圆桌论坛、世界史诗与格萨尔论坛、昆仑神话国际研讨会），代表中国诗人和知识界开始发声，声援并介入在全世界蔚为壮观的诗歌介入现实的大行动，有力地捍卫人类的自然环境和资源的可持续性，及文化遗产的多元性，特别是保卫边缘种群少数民族文化生存的基本权利。

Translator's Notes

Jidi Majia, China's most renowned Yi poet, set upon his poetic career in the 1980s, with about 42 books of verse and prose published to his credit in a span of 30 years, of which a considerable proportions having been made available in English, French, German, Korean, Polish, Italian, Spanish etc. Jidi Majia's prodigious poetic output centers around the ethnic elements, ranging from his Yi identity to humanity. Major variants concern social issues and olden verities in present day China and the world, both practiced with intelligence and skill, earning him a lasting niche with passing years.

This translation is prepared for general and sophisticated English readers, native or non-native. The book contains 40 literary and cultural speeches given by Jidi Majia, hailed as China's most popular ethnic poet & visible public intellectual (several cultural movement initiator), on various occasions spanning over 25 years since his debut in the poetic scene. As Jidi Majia's poems have been rendered into over 18 foreign languages, translation of his prose work into English, the lingua franca of modern world, in which he has systematically elucidated his views on life and man, his elemental themes about conservation of our physical world and cultural diversity, the innocence and sacredness of indigenous cultures, his terrestrial connection to Land and Life, to which he has carried over his brand rich rhetoric, the flowing Latin sentences and his vibrant lyricism, has been long overdue.

On a fine afternoon 2008, I chanced upon his "Manifesto of Qinghai Lake Intl Poetry Festival " and instantly became his admirer and translator in recognizing it as a finished example of the genre of public speeches ,hearkening to the somber but fiery oratory of youthful Marx and Engles which possesses all the virtues of "The Communist Party Manifesto" in great intensity: deft, succinct characterization, evocative description , cool but logical analysis, resounding call to action, the keen awareness of the mission forced on him by various catastrophes to conserve human heritage, physical and cultural ,in his case. In retrospect, the inauguration of QLIPF, the first of its kind to be held in China, a harbinger of things to come, turned out to be a worldwide

诚如吉狄马加先生自述，他的知识谱系来自大凉山和神奇的南美大陆，精神则在普希金、李白、艾切布非等世界文学巨人的庇荫下茁壮成长。马尔克斯的《百年孤独》是这样开头的："多年以后，站在行刑队面前的时候，奥雷良诺·布恩迪亚上校想必会记起父亲领他去看冰块的那个遥远的下午。"这样繁复从属句式，曾被众多中国作家模仿。

如此铺陈华丽的句式，加上各种神话意象，关切人类博爱，全球化威逼之下家园的沦丧，呵护世界净土上的有限资源，在吉狄马加先生的演讲中比比皆是。收录本书的演讲看似题目众多，但其实"群山"一词足堪概括吉狄马加为人为文的核心。作为大凉山腹心地区吉狄部落的酋长的儿子，吉狄马加不仅把广义的山地视作文明的起源（包括两河流域初民也是从高地迁徙来到河谷地区的），同时，一如绍兴是鲁迅小说的灵感之源，山地文明也是他写作最重要的源泉，进而言之，他也把捍卫中国情景下的少数族群边缘团体文化遗产的持续传承和生态环境及资源的可持续性发展视为天降大任，为此奔走呼号，竭尽心力。这就使他的写作从内容到形式，呼应了国际知识界最新最重要的介入现实的脉流，从而自动具备"世界性"眼光。

对于一个独立翻译学者，没有什么比读到吉狄马加的纯净、灵动、从容、高雅、丰沛，给汉语增添光彩的文字更令人愉快的。我相信，我们手头这些演讲可堪视为现代汉语最精美的文本。和这样的作家相遇，翻译这样的文字，无疑是一场终生受用的"艳遇"。

出于职业自尊，笔者的翻译主张可以概括为：精确而精彩，非雅不翻译。任何译者，以达译雅既是对原作的亵渎，也是对目标读者的不敬。可叹，国内流行的汉译英生产——20世纪90年代初外专局专家爱泼斯坦称之为"用洋文出洋相"至今没有什么根本改观——主流翻译研究期刊上提供的范文多是基本上满足语法正确性，低劣恶俗的造句，导源于满足词典指称意义及单句结构的表面对应——美其名曰"忠实原文"的原教旨主义。其死译、硬译、欠译、伪译，其幼稚、恶俗、苍白的文体俗称为"中式英语"，从而造成大面积压倒优势的语用失败。

cataclysmic event, an integrative process, fostering a sense of shared ideals among poets from around the world. It was particularly a high point for Chinese poets who found themselves united together with their overseas peers by both prosodic and cultural causes.

For all its range and length, this book is satisfyingly cohesive where it might be sprawling. The key to this unity is the word Mountains ,the arch metaphor for Jidi Majia both as poet and cultural movement initiator, simply because as a descendant of a former chief of a Yi tribe in the heartland of the Daliangshan, mountains are his homeland and his principal source of inspiration, but also because his wide reading and identification with the black and Hispanic literary traditions make his speeches taut with a sense of menace encroaching upon the lofty terrain to be urgently diffused and alleviated . Hence the emergence of a mighty initiator of several cultural movements as mountains for him embody a life-renewing power and a worthy endeavor meriting the most exuberant poetic expression and materialist enterprise. Mark the opening sentence of One Hundred Years Solitude: "Many years later, as he faced the firing squad, Colonel Aureliano Buendí a was to remember that distant afternoon when his father took him to discover ice." Such potent indictment of brutal assaults on ethnic terrain and culture, vibrant lyricism and dense syntactic Latinism blend to form a wholly Jidi Majia style, rendering the causes he espouses peculiarly convincing ,leaving a rich, sweet and pungent aroma behind.

The beauty of Jidi Majia's advocacy is its authenticity and intimacy, but also its fervor and intensity. A sense of urgency pervades his speeches which often glides off into poetry, tense and dense, approaching prose poetry yet tempered with cool-headed intellectual analysis , a lesson he takes from his Mexican mentor Octavi Paz. The tone is at times prophetic and apocalyptic as an informed Western reader will easily detect distinct echoes from the book of Revelation, with expressions of increasing emotion conveyed by escalating exclamation revealing a powerful mind paradoxically nurtured in the Yi animistic beliefs.

To the translator, translation of these beautiful and important speeches into English is both a blessing but full of perils as Jidi Majia has carried over to his prose the same rich rhetoric, the flowing Latin sentence and dense lyricism to buttress his serious themes. For one thing, his spiritual affinity with Spanish tradition defies convenient rendering as English is notoriously neutral and less emotive than Romance utterances.

For another, the mainstream Chinese translation has been very hostile to work of similar emotional concentration and rhetorical sophistication. A look at the proliferation of translation from Chinese into English in the hands of Chinese translators over the last sixty years of the 20th century inclines one to the validity of Epstein's (a resident expert in the authoritative All China Foreign Experts Administration) curt dismissal "travesty of English in English". In large measure, this come as a result of misreading and under-reading of Yan Fu's translating career prizing the stylistic distinction of the originals and his famous tri-party criteria (fidelity ,smoothness and elegance) capable of being adapted and transformed in line with modern translation predicated

本书一反国内流行的汉译英仅仅满足于文通字顺(忠实通顺,自1949年以来一直为翻译管理当局规定,流行翻译教程尊奉)平庸低俗,肇始于对严复"信达雅"标准的阉割(保留信达)、下移(去雅就达)、错配(现代翻译基于文本分类,信息、工具类文本达意则可,渲染记录性文本非雅无信)。国内汉译英基本上就是以电饭煲说明书翻译策略应对所有文类及文本,以致多数汉译英译本其句法词法大大简化,口语笔语界限模糊,上焉者不过拼法正确,句子平稳,合乎英语用法,但通常欠缺神韵,无人爱读;下焉者则是勉强造句,佶屈聱牙,令人不忍卒读。这些不能目为标准英语,至多算作二语造句和习作。

本书译者主张回到晚清民初严复、林语堂、辜鸿铭开创的雅译传统,摈弃时下流行的所谓"忠实通顺"。非雅不文学,非雅不翻译。"雅"一字不变应万变,不仅以雅译雅,以雅易达,在充分满足现代英语高阶写作句法复杂性、词法复杂性及英文修辞诸项技术指标前提下,在和原作内在神韵高度契合时工而入逸,开启写作模式,最后产出为高端英语读者喜闻乐见的文本,为跨文化交际成功提供新的经验。同时,为打破国内汉译英半个多世纪"用洋文出洋相"的僵局开拓新路。严复"三字经"在新的历史条件下,一分为二,自动获得转换,信达应对信息工具类场景,信雅则专注文学文本的审美价值提升和创造。

国内汉译英的尴尬由来已久。其表象不外译品芜滥恶质化和译学研究教条化,旷日持久满足于对脱胎中古译经的晚清翻译标准"信达雅"走偏的浅表的语义转换(忠实通顺)。对其认识论基础的浅陋、落后的揭露,及方法论的无效、虚妄的批判,是汉译英走出困境的必由之路。西方译学研究已超越语文学及结构语言学阶段,进入多元化时代。20世纪80年代以来在西方蔚为壮观的功能主义,特别是德国基于文本类型分类而强调"语内连贯"的"目的论",对国内目前陷入停滞的汉译英研究有关键的救弊作用。因之,在追求职业尊严和重建自信方面,我们不仅需要取法前沿西学的智慧,也需要回归民国汉译英巨人林语堂和辜鸿铭的审美取向。

upon the textual typology (informative vs expressive, instrumental and documentary) and a bifurcated translation strategy with smoothness and intelligibility for informative texts and elegance for expressive/vocative texts.

In a way, this volume grows in revolt against the austere post 1949 Chinese translation castrating the famous Qing Scholar-Mandarin Yafu's tri-party criteria (fidelity, smoothness and elegance) into a Draconian duality of fidelity and smoothness. The result is the everyday fare of a much simplified and weak lexicon and syntax, awfully wooden ,banal, childish and stilted. Modern translation theory has been related to language functions informing a group of text types. Prevalent opinion is in favor of Buhlerian model (informative, expressive and vocative) with the aesthetic function, ie, to mainly please and delight the senses by literary devices as metaphor, sound effect and rhythm, believed to operate in literary texts. My challenge consists in endeavoring to preserve the letter and the spirit of the originals across the cultural and language barriers.

It seems essential therefore to make this English translation as readable as possible, though with some necessary abbreviation or editing, but on the whole, I have endeavored to preserve the letter and spirit of what he says as well as, across the language barrier, of how he says it so that the reader at the receiving end will be offered a fascinating spiritual record of a major Chinese poet in terms of his intellectual affinity with the African and Hispanic world literary giants and the lifelong causes he has engaged himself with dedication and commitment. The fascination of modern translation theory lies in its pertinence and, with its procedure and tenets, fulfils admirably its advocacy to grapple with the problems raised by a contemporary life, predominantly commercial, technical and intellectual in nature. But concern with nuances and subtleties of (target) language remains translator's basic challenge and appeal. Translating is writing in that invariably the reader only perceives an end product, no matter how many dilemmas and difficulties inhere in the decision process of a translator. What is finally available for scrutiny is always the version that counts, and the access or the pathways leading to the final result is not in the nature of things for the average reader to know.

I take solace in the rich humanity and sporadic outbursts of spontaneous wisdom of a great empiricist, the flowering of lifelong good sense and painstaking penetrations when Newmark puts the essence of the new orientation so admirably:"All translation problems finally resolve into problems of how to write well in the language". And another heavyweight translation scholar Gouedac as he advises good writing, like Yan Fu, is almost fit for all translation commissions and occasions, be it informative, or expressive or vocative. In his words:" Just like any other form of communication, the translation must be readable, coherent, logical and preferably well written."

So at last ,East meets West and we are all Yan Fuists, incurable ones.

吉狄马加主席与本书译者黄少政(左)在首届西昌诗歌周活动现场

黄少政，独立翻译学者，中国作协会员。毕业于上海外国语学院，从事疑难西方文本的翻译，疑难汉译英文本的翻译。2010 年以来，以策划、组织、口译、笔译及翻译协调人身份参与多届青海湖国际诗歌节、青海帐篷国际诗歌圆桌会议，及西昌、成都、泸州、遵义、自贡等地高端国际诗歌交流活动，包括中国作协主办的多届国际写作计划。主要代表作有：《先知》(英译汉)、《沙与沫》(英译汉)、《翻译的成色》(翻译研究)、《为土地和生命写作》(汉译英)、《圣经·新约》(英译汉)、《从雪豹到马雅可夫斯基》(汉译英)、《敬畏群山》(汉译英)。

Huang Shaozheng, He graduated from Shanghai Foreign languages Institute in the early 1980s.His lifelong passions are for translation of literary works ,either in Chinese or in English, which do not lend themselves to easy and normal rendering, either from Chinese into English, or the other way round. For example, Gibran's Prophet (2011), eminent Chinese Yi poet Jidi Majia (In the Name of Land and Life, 2013, From Snow Leopard to Mayakovsky, 2016), New Testament (2016).The upgraded and expanded Jidi Majia's literary and cultural speeches Mountains That Humble and Hold Us in Awe (forthcoming) is an audacious attempt to represent this Yi iconic figure as a matured thinker and refined speaker on literary and cultural issues, brimming with fertility of poetic imagination and an intellectual curiosity of wide scope combined with a clairvoyant vision of mankind befitting a foremost cultural leader of Chinese letters who champions the timely solidarity, courageous actions and united fight of world poets and writers conscious of their power to transform the world. Starting from 2010,he has attended a host of high level intl poetic events, including Intl Writing Residency organized by Lu Xun Academy of Literature ,orchestrated and initiated by Jidi Majia, as event manager, translation project coordinator, chief interpreter, chief translator, special editor etc.